Praise for *Legends of the Dragonrealm*

"It's always fun to go back and see where an author started—the raw work, full of energy and with hints of the good things to come. Such is the case with Richard Knaak's *Legends of the Dragonrealm*. All of the ingredients—great world building, memorable characters—that have marked Richard's long and successful career are there, and in reading it, it's easy to see why Richard has enjoyed so much success."

—R. A. Salvatore, *New York Times* bestselling author of
The DemonWars Saga, Forgotten Realms®, and more

"Richard's novels are well-written, adventure-filled, action-packed!"

—Margaret Weis, *New York Times* bestselling author of
Dragonlance Chronicles, Legends, and more

"Richard Knaak's fiction has the magic touch of making obviously fantastic characters and places come alive, seem real, and matter to the reader. That's the essential magic of all storytelling, and Richard does it deftly, making his stories always engaging and worth picking up and reading. And then re-reading."

—Ed Greenwood, creator of the *Forgotten Realms*®

"Endlessly inventive. Knaak's ideas just keep on coming!"

—Glen Cook, author of *Chronicles of the Black Company*

LEGENDS
OF THE
DRAGONREALM

RICHARD A. KNAAK

SAGA PRESS

LONDON SYDNEY **NEW YORK** TORONTO NEW DELHI

SAGA PRESS

AN IMPRINT OF SIMON & SCHUSTER, INC.

1230 AVENUE OF THE AMERICAS, NEW YORK, NEW YORK 10020

This Saga Press trade paperback edition December 2021

SAGA PRESS and colophon are trademarks of Simon & Schuster, Inc.

For information about special discounts for bulk purchases, please contact Simon & Schuster Special Sales at 1-866-506-1949 or business@simonandschuster.com.

The Simon & Schuster Speakers Bureau can bring authors to your live event. For more information or to book an event contact the Simon & Schuster Speakers Bureau at 1-866-248-3049 or visit our website at www.simonspeakers.com.

Designed by Renata Di Biase

Manufactured in the United States of America

1 3 5 7 9 10 8 6 4 2

Library of Congress Cataloging-in-Publication Data is available.

ISBN 978-1-9821-6662-5
ISBN 978-1-4391-5596-7 (eBook)

For my mother, my father, my siblings, and the rest of my family—and all those who have enjoyed this series over the years! This is how it all really got started!

Special thanks also to Pat McGilligan, Brian Thomsen, Barbara Puechner, and Margaret Weis! Some are no longer with us, but all played a part, whether they knew it or not, in the realization of the Dragonrealm. . . .

CONTENTS

N
W E
S

Sea of Andramacus

Land of the
Hill Dwarves

Gordag-Ai

Elven
Settlements

DAGORA
FOREST

ESEDI

ZUU

LAND OF
QUEL

Legar
Peninsula

THE BARREN

The Dragon Kings and Their Domains

Ice Dragon - The Northern Wastes
Red - The Hell Plains
Blue - Irillian by the Sea
Storm - Wenslis
Black - Lochivar
Crystal - Legar Peninsula
Green - Dagora Forest
Gold - Tyber Mountains

Brown - The Barren Lands
Iron - Unnamed area in the Northwest
    that includes the Hill Dwarves
Bronze - Region that includes Gordag-Ai
Silver - Land that exists below the Tyber Mountains
Talak is bound to Gold's Domain and is just
   south of the Tybers
Penacles is ruled by the Gryphon

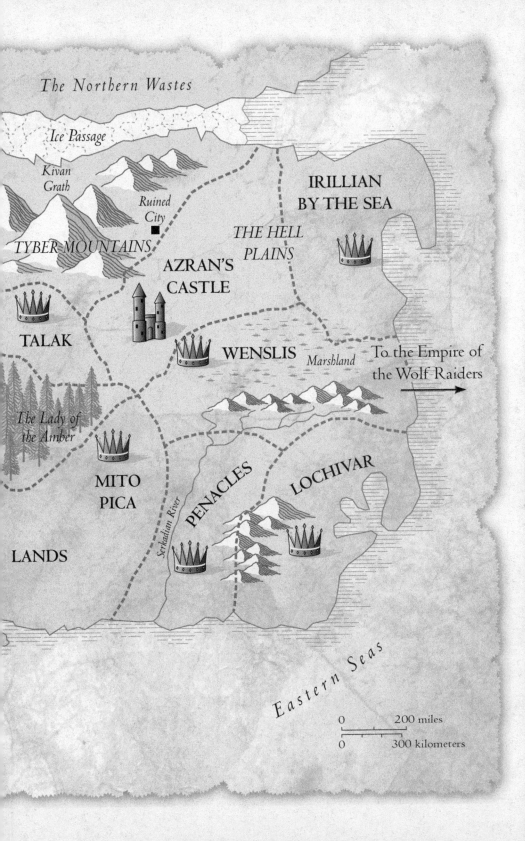

A JOURNEY AROUND
THE DRAGONREALM

THE DRAGONREALM IS a place of myriad domains and fantastic creatures, and a careful traveler should know much of the land if he wishes to travel it safely. Here, then, are some of the places that you will come across. . . .

The Legar Peninsula thrusts out of the southwest edge of the continent. This is where the burrowing Quel—once masters of the Dragonrealm—live. This mountainous domain is inundated with gleaming crystal formations. Here is the domain of the most reclusive of the Dragon Kings, the Crystal Dragon.

The Sea of Andramacus: The violent waters west of the Dragonrealm. Little is known of them, but legend has it that they were named for a demon. . . .

Land of the Hill Dwarves: There is no true name for this region, but the hill dwarves are said to live in the eastern part of the region and the ambitious Iron Dragon rules without mercy.

Esedi lies southwest of the Iron Dragon's realm. This is where the Bronze Dragon holds sway and the human kingdom of Gordag-Ai is situated.

The Kingdom of Zuu: This other human kingdom is located southwest of Esedi and deep in a valley that is bound to the edge of the vast, magical Dagora Forest, situated in the center of the continent. The people of Zuu are famed for their horses. . . .

The Dagora Forest: This far-stretching forest is where most elves are said to live and where the more benevolent Green Dragon rules.

Mito Pica: A human kingdom lying east of the Dagora Forest and at the edge of the Hell Plains, Mito Pica holds a secret that will change the history of the Dragonrealm. . . .

The Hell Plains: To the northeast lies the volcanic Hell Plains, ruled by the Red Dragon. Here, it is rumored, also lies the castle of the foul sorcerer Azran Bedlam. It is guarded by the Seekers, an avian race once masters, but now slaves.

The Silver Dragon rules the unnamed land to the north of the Dagora Forest. He serves also as confidant of the Dragon Emperor, but covets his position.

The Tyber Mountains are situated north of that and include the mountain citadel of the Gold Dragon, also known as the Dragon Emperor. The mountains are riddled with deep caverns.

The Kingdom of Talak lies at the base of the Tyber Mountains. Though somewhat independent, it is supposed to show fealty to the Gold Dragon. Its ruler is Rennek IV, but his son, Melicard, is already taking much of the reins.

The Northern Wastes may be found far north of the Tyber Mountains. They are home to many great burrowing creatures and are the domain of the Ice Dragon.

The Barren Lands lie south and southeast of the Dagora Forest. Once lush, they were destroyed in a magical upheaval during the Turning War. What remains is ruled by the bitter Brown Dragon.

The Kingdom of Penacles, east of the Barren Lands, is no longer ruled by a Dragon King. Instead, during the Turning War, it was liberated by forces led by the Gryphon, a unique creature who resembles the mythic beast. He now rules, but must constantly be on guard against the Dragon Kings. The Serkadian River runs north to south next to Penacles.

The mist-enshrouded land of Lochivar, east of Penacles, is ruled by the Black Dragon. It is said he has dealings with the Wolf Raiders, who come from a land across the eastern sea.

Wenslis is a rain-drenched kingdom under the rule of the Storm Dragon, whose domain is north of both Penacles and Lochivar. The most vain of the Dragon Kings, the Storm Dragon thinks himself a god.

Irillian by the Sea, ruled by the Blue Dragon, is northeast of the Storm Dragon's lands. An aquatic being, the Blue Dragon is not as benevolent as his counterpart in the Dagora Forest, but sees use in humans and has allowed them to be an almost-equal part of his kingdom. He has, of recent times, had dealings with the Gryphon, much to the frustration of many of his kind.

These are but some of the fantastic places a traveler will discover. The Dragonrealm is a place in flux, and new and ancient wonders are revealing themselves. . . .

FOREWORD

IN THE BEGINNING, there were dragons . . . or . . . maybe not. . . .

Every author starts out as a reader, generally a voracious one. I was no exception. The moment I learned the written word, I devoured one story after another. I read mysteries, science fiction, humor, and more, but what most fascinated me was epic fantasy . . . and what fascinated me most in epic fantasy was dragons.

It probably helped that I was heavily into dinosaurs, too—that's another story—but whatever the overall reasons, my initial story attempts had to include dragons . . . but not just big, lumbering, fire-breathing beasts. Oh, those were handy, but I liked my dragons a bit different. Yes, they were intelligent and yes, they were shapeshifters—things done in the past and that will continue to be done in the future—but I didn't just seek to make their society and hierarchy different. The truth is . . .

Well, that's, hopefully, for another volume.

Firedrake, the first novel, was also my first completed manuscript. I had come very close to sales on a couple of other partials, but *Firedrake* was the one I was determined to finish completely before sending it out. In it, we are introduced to many of the essential characters of the world: Cabe Bedlam, heir to a legacy both good and evil; Gwendolyn, the Lady of the Amber; the mythic Gryphon; the Dragon Kings; and, of course, the enigmatic Shade and the impossible Darkhorse. There were hints of the mysterious history of their land, hints of a succession of ruling races and, more current, tragedies to befall both heroes and villains.

Upon a suggestion, I took *Firedrake* to a publisher about an hour and a half away. Literally walking in off the street, I asked to speak with the editor (and no, you really can't do that these days). After some surprise, the editor came out, accepted my material, and said to contact him again in two weeks. I did so and was told that while he had enjoyed *Firedrake*, in truth, the company was publishing only their own series at this time. However, because of the strength of the manuscript . . . was I interested in submitting some material based on their series?

I was. I did . . . and for those of you interested, this became my first foray into Dragonlance, soon leading to my *New York Times* bestselling novel, *The Legend of Huma.*

Introduced to an agent by none other than Margaret Weis, I pushed on with *Firedrake.* We submitted it to Warner Books. I ran into the editor at a convention and he informed me that he was interested in picking up the novel and asked if I had a sequel in mind. I told him I did (I actually had three!) and he offered to pick one of them up as well.

That was *Ice Dragon*, the chilling follow-up in which Cabe and our other heroes continue to face the treacherous drake, Toma, and the fatalistic lord of the Northern Wastes. Both books were hits and I was quickly contracted for a third and fourth. The first of those, *Wolfhelm*, is contained in this omnibus and concludes a running "trilogy within the trilogy" concerning the Gryphon—part man, part creature—whose own origins lie across the eastern sea in a realm ruled by the Wolf Raiders and their god. It introduces a land at least as fantastic as that of the Dragonrealm, including some characters who would become significant as the world moved on.

I hope that you will enjoy my world, which continues to this day. Happily, the series has been published worldwide, with new readers discovering it and longtime fans returning to relive the saga. The Dragonrealm has many stories still to come and I look forward to sharing them with you. . . .

All the Best,
Richard A. Knaak

LEGENDS

OF THE

DRAGONREALM

FIREDRAKE

I

BELOW, TOWARD THE great Tyber Mountains, they came. Some in pairs, some alone. Fierce dragonhelms hid all but the eyes; eyes that, in most cases, burned bloodred in the coming darkness. Each was armored in scaled leather, but anyone testing that protection would find it stronger than the best of mail. Flowing cloaks, like wild specters of the night, made the riders appear as if they were flying and, in truth, any onlooker would have believed such were possible for these men.

If men they were.

Eleven they numbered, gradually coming together in one group. There were no words of acknowledgment or, for that matter, the simple nod of a head. They were known to each other, and they had traveled this way countless times for countless years. Sometimes their numbers were different, but the path had always been the same. Though each counted the others as his brethren, feuding was common among them. They thus rode silently for the entire journey, ahead of them the Tyber Mountains, stretching to the heavens, beckoning.

At long last, they reached the first of the mountains. Here appeared to be an end to their travels. No path wound through the mountains; rather, the road ended abruptly at the base of one of the largest of the leviathans. Nevertheless, the riders made no attempt to slow. They seemed intent on charging into the very earth itself. The mounts did not question their masters, but merely pursued their course as they had always done.

As if bowing to their defiance, the mountain seemed to melt and shift. The impregnable barrier of nature disappeared, and a vast path now led through. The riders, ignoring this fantastic act, continued on at their hellish pace. The horses snorted smoke as they passed the barrier, but showed no sign of fatigue. This journey was nothing to their kind.

Through twisting and turning road they moved. Icy trails and treacherous ravines did not slow the group. Again, though things not of man's world hid and watched, the riders were not hindered. Few creatures would be so foolish as to confront them, especially knowing the travelers' nature.

Quickly looming up was the great sentinel of the Tyber Mountains, Kivan Grath. Few humans had ever seen it up close, and fewer still had ever attempted to climb it. None had ever returned. Here the path led. Here the riders came. They slowed their animals as they neared the great Seeker of Gods, as its name translated. At its base, they stopped and dismounted. They had reached their goal.

Buried in the mountain was a great gate of bronze that seemed as ageless as the land. It towered over the onlookers, and on the face were carvings ancient and undescribable. One of the riders walked up to it. Beneath his helm were eyes like frost. What little of his face that was visible was also white. Grimly, he raised his left arm, fist clenched, and pointed it at the gate. With a groan, the huge, bronze door slowly opened. The pale warrior returned to his companions. The riders led their mounts inside.

Torches provided the only light inside the cave. Much of the cavern was natural, but the work in expanding it would have left even the hill dwarves overwhelmed. It made little difference to the riders; they had long stopped paying attention to their surroundings. Even the sentries, only shadows, but ever present, were ignored.

Something dark and scaled and only barely humanoid crawled up to the riders, its clawed, misshaped hand outstretched. Each of the cloaked travelers turned his horse over to the servant.

The riders entered the main cavern.

Like some resplendent but ancient temple, the citadel of their host gave forth a feeling of tremendous power. Effigies of human and inhuman form stood here and there. All were long dead, and even history had forgotten their kind. Here, at last, did the riders show some measure of respect. Each knelt, one at a time, before the great figure seated before them. When all had done so, they formed a half circle, with their host before them.

The serpentine neck arced. Gleaming eyes surveyed the group. A bloodred tongue lashed out momentarily in satisfaction, the tremendous, membraned wings stretching out in full glory. Despite the dim light, the gold sheen of the dragon's scaled body completed a picture of pure majesty, befitting the king of his kind. Yet there was just the slightest note of something akin to insecurity. Whether the others noted it or not was hidden in their own thoughts.

In a voice that was a hiss, yet caused the very room itself to vibrate slightly, the Gold Dragon spoke.

"Welcome, brethren! Welcome and make this home yours!"

Far spread apart, each of the riders became blurred, as if they had become nothing more than illusion. Yet they did not disappear. Rather, they grew; their bodies became like quicksilver, their shapes twisting. Wings and tails sprouted, and arms and legs became clawed, leathery appendages. The helms melted into the faces of their wearers until they had, in actuality, become the faces. Mouths spread back into maws, rows of long, sharp teeth glistening in the dim light. All traces of humanity disappeared in the space of a minute.

The Council of the Dragon Kings came to order.

The Gold Dragon nodded. As emperor, King of Kings, he was pleased to see that the others had followed his command so readily. He spoke again, and this time smoke issued out as he did.

"I am pleased that you could make it. I feared that some of you might have let emotions overrule you." He stared momentarily at the Black Dragon, monarch of the sinister and deadly Gray Mists.

The Black Dragon did not speak, but his eyes blazed.

The Emperor of the Dragon Kings turned his attention to the nearest of his brethren. The Blue Dragon, more sea serpent than land creature, bowed his head in respect.

"The council has been called due to the request of the master of Irillian by the Sea. He notes strange happenings and wishes to discover if such events exist in the lands of his brothers. Speak."

Sleeker than most of his kind, the Blue Dragon resembled a race animal, his movements fluid, as was appropriate for a being who spent much of his life in the seas of the east. The smell of salt and fish filled the room as he spoke. A dusty, tan dragon, Brown, wrinkled his nose. He did not share his brother's fondness for the sea.

"My liege. Brethren." He studied all around him, especially the Black Dragon. "In the years gone by, my domain has been very placid. The humans have remained quiet and my clans have had good hatchings."

This time there was a grunt from the Brown Dragon, who was lord of the Barren Lands in the southwest. Since the end of the wars with the Dragon Masters, he had seen his clans decrease. Most claimed it was the work of the self-styled Masters themselves, but no one was sure what sorcery the warlocks had used in their attempt to defeat the Kings. They had caused the Barren Lands, but whether they had caused the loss of fertility in the Brown clans was open to speculation in private. Brown was still the fiercest of fighters.

The master of Irillian by the Sea ignored the slight outburst and continued. "Recently, however, things have changed. There is unrest—no, that implies too much. There is . . . a feeling. That is all I can call it. Not just among the humans. It appears to affect others, even the wyverns and minor drakes."

"Ha!"

The remark was followed by a wave of bone-numbing cold. A slight frost settled wherever the Ice Dragon's breath had reached. The Gold Dragon stared disapprovingly at him. Gaunt to the point of being cadaverous, the king of the Northern Wastes laughed again. Of all the dragons, he was one of the least seen and the least loved.

"You are becoming an old dame, brother! Subjects always become unsettled. One merely places a restraining claw on a few and crushes such thoughts."

"Speaks the monarch of a land more empty than that of Brown."

"Speaks the monarch who knows how to rule!" A blizzard threatened to erupt from within the Ice Dragon.

"Silence!"

The thundering roar of the Gold Dragon overwhelmed all else. The Ice Dragon fell back, his snow-colored eyes averted from the brilliance of his emperor. When the King of Kings became angered, his body glowed.

"Such infighting nearly brought calamity on us once! Have you forgotten that so soon?"

All held their heads low, save for the Black Dragon. On his massive mouth was just the barest hint of pleasure. The Gold Dragon looked at him sharply but did not reprimand. In this instance, the king of the Gray Mists was justified.

Drawing himself to his full height, the Emperor of Dragons towered above the others. "For nearly five human years did we fight that war—and nearly faced defeat! Our brother Brown still feels the aftereffects as he watches his clans dwindle! His problem is the most evident; yet we all have scars from the Dragon Masters!"

"The Dragon Masters are dead! Nathan Bedlam was the last, and he has long since perished!" bellowed the Red Dragon, who ruled the volcanic lands called the Hell Plains.

"Taking the Purple King with him!" Black could restrain himself no more. His eyes became like beacons in the night.

The emperor nodded. "Yes, taking our brother with him. Bedlam was the last and deadliest of the Masters. With his final act, he crippled us. Penacles is the city of knowledge, and Purple was its master, he who planned our strategy." The last was said almost reluctantly, for Gold did not care to remind his brothers who had really led in those days.

"And now his lands have been usurped by the Gryphon! How much longer must we wait before we strike? Generations of man have since come and gone!" Black shook his head in anger.

"There is no successor. You know the covenant. Thirteen Kingdoms, thirteen kings. Five and twenty dukedoms, five and twenty dukes. No one must break the covenant . . ." For now, the emperor added to himself.

"While we wait for a successor, Lord Gryphon plots. Remember, he was known to the Masters."

"His time will come. Perhaps soon."

Black eyed his lord warily. "What does that mean?"

"As custom, I've taken Purple's dams as mine. The first hatchings produced only minor drakes, most of whom were put to death, of course. This hatching, however, looks more promising."

The other kings leaned forward. Hatchings were of the utmost importance. A few bad hatchings could threaten any of their clans with extinction.

"Only a handful of the clutch turned out to be minor drake eggs. The majority were firedrakes. However, four eggs contain the speckled band!"

"Four!" The single word was like a cry of exultation. The speckled band, this was the sign of Kings. Such eggs were to be guarded, for successors of Dragon Kings were extremely rare.

"It will be weeks before hatching takes place. The dam guards against unruly minor drakes, not to mention scavengers of all forms. If luck holds, they will all break free."

Black smiled, and a dragon's smile was something sinister. "Then will we crush this Lord Gryphon!"

"Mayhap."

All turned to he who would dampen their rejoicing. Once again, the master of Irillian by the Sea stared at them, his eyes challenging each of them to speak. When none would protest, he shook his maned head sadly.

"None of you will listen! Must I speak again? Do not misunderstand me. This news brings great happiness to me. Perhaps my fears are unjustified. Nevertheless, I must speak, or I will always have regrets."

"Then speak and be done with it! I grow weary of this prattling on!"

Ignoring Black, the king of the Eastern Seas continued. "I have felt such a stirring of uneasiness only once before. That last time, it foreshadowed the coming of the Dragon Masters."

There was a hiss of anger—and, perhaps, fear—from more than one of the great lords.

Black was now smiling. "In truth, brother Blue, I must apologize for myself. You have brought up the very point that I wished to discuss."

The emperor shook his head. "This land is old. The Dragon Kings have ruled for ages, but our reign is young compared to that of some of the earlier races. Even now, traces of ancient powers turn up. This stirring of our subjects' feelings may very well be magical in nature. Still," he paused and studied the cavern, "we have tried to weed out those who might possess some sort of attunement to those ancient ways. I know of few humans now living who are a threat."

"There is one that may threaten us." The words were quiet but firm. Without looking, all knew that Black had spoken out again.

"And who may that be?"

The Dweller of the Gray Mists spread his wings in confidence. The audience was his. "We know his family well. Very well. He is young, untrained, but his name is Cabe Bedlam."

As one, the Dragon Kings, even Gold, backed slightly, as if just bitten. "Bedlam!" was whispered by more than one voice.

The emperor fairly shrieked. "Why have we not known of this human? Where is this hatchling of a demon-warlock?"

"In the lands now held by the Gryphon. Nathan Bedlam placed the child, who is his grandson, in Mito Pica. Since the region is known for the spawning of warlocks and their like, I have sometimes sent spies forth. It was one of them who discovered the human."

Red growled. "You crossed two borders at least, brother! I wonder how many spies you have."

"We all have our ears and eyes. Besides, this human had to be watched!"

"Why did you not have him killed?" the Green Dragon asked. "This is most unlike you, Black. When have you become hesitant in pursuing your goals?"

Bowing his head subserviently to the emperor, Black replied, "I would not do so without permission from my lord."

Gold snorted. "There is a first for everything, apparently."

"Do I have your permission?"

"No."

There was silence.

"With the hatchings only a short time away, I will not permit a conflict that may draw the Gryphon in against us. He is cunning; he knows the importance we place on the speckled-band eggs. His agents could cause us harm in that respect. As long as the Bedlam whelp remains where he is and knows not his danger, we will leave him alone."

"If we wait much longer, this youngling could take up the mantle of his accursed ancestor!"

"Nevertheless, we must wait. When the hatchlings are strong enough, this last of the Bedlams will die."

He settled back. "This council is over."

The emperor leaned back and closed his eyes as if to sleep, pointedly ignoring his brethren from this point on. Wordlessly, the Dragon Kings spread themselves apart. Their bodies quivered and shrank. The great reptilian faces pulled away until they were once again dragonhelms covering near-inhuman faces. Wings shriveled and tails ceased to exist. Forelegs became arms while the hind ones straightened.

When all was done, the riders saluted their lord and departed from the chamber. Gold did not watch them leave.

The dark thing that had taken the reins of each horse waited as the travelers took their mounts, and then shambled back into the vast, eternal night of the caves.

Out of the bronze gate the Dragon Kings rode. Some in pairs, others single, all following the one path through the mountains. A wyvern, just waking, accidentally stuck its head out in their path, and sighting the riders, pulled itself to one side and cowered. It did not move again until they were long by.

At the end of the Tyber Mountains, the group split apart, each one going his separate way, knowing that mortal men would pay little attention to a single rider. Those who dared impede them would only be leaping into death.

A single rider, heading to the south, slowed as his fellows disappeared from sight. Ahead of him was a small grove of trees, and it was here he finally halted. Staring into the darkness, he settled down to wait.

His wait was short. Within minutes, he was joined by another of the Dragon Kings. Wordlessly, they acknowledged one another's presence. There was no friendship in their actions; they merely had a common goal and sought to accomplish it through the easiest means possible.

The newcomer pulled a great sword from its sheath and held it out, point first, to the other. His companion reached forward and placed a gauntleted hand on the tip. His eyes glowed brightly as power emanated from him. It flowed through his arm, through his hand, and finally into the weapon itself.

When they were finished, the sword glowed and pulsated. Slowly, the light dimmed, as if the power were being absorbed by the object itself. After a moment, the sword had returned to its former state, save for a slight vibrating. The other rider replaced it into the sheath.

The two stared at each other, communication taking place on a level far different from those of men. They nodded. What was to be done was necessary. Then the newcomer kicked his mount and rode off. He was not headed in the direction of his kingdom; rather, his destination appeared to be south.

The remaining rider watched until his comrade was out of sight. His gaze turned momentarily to the overwhelming mountain range and to Kivan Grath in particular. Then, turning away, he rode off in silence.

The floodgates had been opened.

II

"WHERE'S MY ALE?"

The Wyvern's Head Tavern was known for its diversity of customers, some human, many not. One such nonhuman was the ogre that now banged down his meaty fist, breaking off a good portion of a table. His demeanor matched his face—cruel and ugly.

His eyes sought a black-haired human in his twenties who even now was hurriedly filling a mug with ale and cursing the slowness with which it poured from the spigot. To the ogre, his features were as ugly and incomplete as any other human's, but by human standards, they were regular. His face was not the face of heroes, but the strong chin, slightly turned nose, and attentive eyes gave him a rough sort of handsomeness.

Customers standing nearby formed an unintentional barrier that hid him from the thirsty creature's sight, but the human knew it was only a matter of time before the ogre came searching for him.

Cabe rushed forward, nervous, but forced to confront the ogre because he was a serving man of the tavern. Quickly, he dropped the heavy mug on the table and almost blanched when a drop nearly hit the ogre in the face. He waited for his rather dull life to flash before him.

The creature eyed him murderously, but decided the ale was more important. Tossing a coin to Cabe, the ogre picked up the mug and drank with a gusto that would have outdone most men. Cabe made a quick retreat to the kitchen.

"Cabe! Brought Deidra a present, did you?" A deft, slender hand relieved him of the coin and a well-endowed form wrapped itself around his body. Deidra gave him a long, moist kiss and then artfully deposited the coin into her blouse, a piece of clothing that did very little to conceal her generous attributes.

She flung back dirty-blond hair and smiled as she saw him staring at her ample chest. "Like a view, do you? Maybe later." It was always later for Cabe, never now.

Deidra turned, wiggled her backside, and carried a tray out into the tavern. Cabe watched until she was out of sight and then remembered the coin he had lost. It might've been worth it—later on, anyway.

He knew that Deidra liked men with money, but she still seemed attracted to him—somewhat. Admittedly, he was not ugly, and while he was not the stuff of heroes, he was still capable of handling himself in a fight . . . providing that he stayed long enough. For some reason, Cabe almost always backed away if a fight seemed close. That was why he was working in a tavern and not making his way in the world, like his father, who was a huntsman for the King of Mito Pica. Although Cabe had been useless on the hunts, his father had never seemed too upset about it. He even seemed pleased when his son told him that he had managed to find work at a two-bit tavern and inn. Rather odd behavior for a warrior, but Cabe loved him.

He pushed back a lock of black hair, knowing that somewhere under his touch was a wisp of silver that he constantly kept covered or colored. Silver streaks were supposed to be the sign of warlocks and necromancers. Cabe did not want to be killed by a mob just because he had hair like a sorcerer. The trouble was, it appeared to be spreading.

"Cabe! Get yourself out here, basilisk dung!"

The summons by his employer was one that Cabe would have obeyed even if he had not been employed here. Cyrus was a mountain of a man, and beside him, even the ogre looked small.

He rushed out. "Yes, Cyrus?"

The owner, who looked more like a bear than a man, pointed to a table far away in a dark corner. "I think I saw a customer back there! See what he's up to and if he plans on buying something!"

Cabe made his way to the spot Cyrus had pointed out, slipping around the various tables and customers. It was strangely dim, but he could see that no one was there. What had Cyrus—

He blinked and looked again. There *was* someone there! How he had failed to see him the first time was beyond him. Hastily, he moved to the table.

A cloak. That was all the man, if it was a man, appeared to be. A hand, the left one, slipped into sight and placed a coin on the table, and from beneath the hood of the cloak, a strong but unreal voice spoke.

"An ale. No food."

Cabe stood for a moment and then realized that he should be getting the customer's order. With a mumbled apology, he made his way back toward the bar.

The ale was handed to him by Cyrus almost immediately, but as Cabe started back through the crowd, he was caught up by a large hand.

The ogre dragged him over and stuffed a coin into Cabe's hand. "When you're done there, bring me another ale! Keep it in the tankard this time!"

Reaching the table, he placed the ale down carefully. As he did so, the gloved hand reached out and grabbed him by the wrist.

"Sit, Cabe."

Cabe tried to loosen the grip, but it was as if the hand were stiffened in death and would never let go. Resignedly, he sat down on the opposite end of the table. As he did so, the hand released him.

He tried to look at the face under the hood. Either the light of the tavern had become dimmer or there was no face beneath the cowl. Cabe jerked back in fear. What sort of man had no face? Worse yet, what would such a creature want with someone as insignificant as he? As if amused, the stranger turned his head for better inspection.

But there was a face. It was slightly out of focus and always in half shadow. He caught a glimpse of silver hair amidst a field of brown.

Warlock!

"Who are you?" It was all he could get out.

"You may call me Simon. This time."

"This time?" The words made no sense to Cabe.

"You are very much in danger, Cabe Bedlam."

"Danger? What—Bedlam? I'm not—"

"Cabe Bedlam. Can you deny it?"

He started to speak, and then thought. Regardless of what he thought, Cabe could not make himself deny the bizarre accusations of this warlock. No one had ever called him by that name, nor had he ever thought of it. . . . But for some reason, it sounded right.

The face of the stranger sported a small smile. Maybe. It was so hard to tell. "You cannot deny it. Good."

"But my father—"

"—is your stepfather. He has served his purpose. He knew what had to be done."

"What do you want of me? I mean— Oh, no!" Cabe remembered what sort of tales surrounded the name. It was a name of legend . . . certainly not one suited for a serving man in a tavern. Cabe was not, did not want to be, a warlock. He shook his head frantically, trying to force the reality away in much the same way he tried to deny the silver streak in his hair.

"Yes, because your name is Bedlam."

Cabe wrenched himself away from the table. "But I'm not a warlock! Get away from me!" Quickly realizing his outburst, Cabe looked around the tavern. The customers were drinking as if nothing had happened. How could they have missed that shouting, even with the noise of the crowd? He turned back to the warlock—

—only to find that no one was there.

Frowning, he searched under the table, half expecting the shadowy form to be there. There was nothing . . . except a coin, perhaps left by the warlock. Cabe was uncertain about taking money from a necromancer, but finally decided that the coin appeared normal enough. Besides, he needed it.

With one final, uncertain glance, he hurried away. The crowd was barely noticeable to him. Only the words of the warlock demanded his attention. He was a Bedlam. He could not deny it, even though he had never known it before.

New thoughts issued forth. A warlock was a person of power. Why had his ability not manifested itself? Who was this stranger who called himself Simon—"this time"?

Cabe broke out of his reverie as someone grabbed him by the shirt. He found himself staring at the grotesque features of the ogre, its hot, fetid breath wrapping over his face in waves. Cabe felt like throwing up.

"Where's my ale?"

The ale. Cabe had taken the ogre's coin and had forgotten the drink.

"Try to run off with my coin, eh? Thought I'd be too drunk to notice, did you?" The creature held up his other meaty fist and prepared to swing. "You need a lesson!"

Cabe shut his eyes and prayed the blow would not break his jaw. He waited, expecting it to fall any second.

And waited.

And waited.

Opening one eye a slight crack—and then both wide—Cabe saw the crumpled body of his attacker. The ogre's companion, a heavyset thug, was trying to revive him by throwing water on his face.

Those in the crowd who had seen the incident appeared awed.

"Did you see?"

"I never saw a man move so fast!"

"One punch! Igrim never went down from just one punch!"

"Igrim never went down before!"

The thug helped a still-groggy ogre out the door. Cabe had a dark suspicion that he had not seen the last of the creature. Most likely, he and his friend would be waiting in some dark alley.

Some customers congratulated him while others merely watched warily. Cyrus, far in back, was nodding in what could only be described as confused satisfaction. Cabe wondered exactly what it was he had done. As far as he was concerned, he had been motionless.

Gradually, the crowd returned to normal. Cabe went about his duties, but his mind was on other things. Occasionally, he would turn his attention to the table in the shadows, and once or twice he thought he saw something, but when he looked again, the spot was empty. Oddly enough, none of the new customers chose to sit there.

Dark was falling, and with it came the first signs of storm. Most of the customers had disappeared for some reason or another.

He did not hear the rider enter, but he could feel his presence. So could those around him. The silence that came so suddenly spoke much for the power of this newcomer. Cabe dared a glance and immediately wished he hadn't, for that short glimpse revealed to him an armored figure whose very presence caused those customers near the door to scurry out in a hurry. Each step taken by the newcomer was arrogant, threatening in its precision. The warrior, whoever he was, scanned the interior of the inn as he walked toward the backmost booths, and every being who had not yet left secretly prayed that they were not what the silent visitor sought.

As the armored figure sat down, most of the remaining customers departed. The eyes of the armored figure watched each and every person leave and then began to study the various employees of the inn. Cabe tried to find other things to do, but knew he could not avoid the newcomer for long. Cyrus came over and whispered to him.

"Quickly, man! Serve him whatever he wishes, and don't, for Hirack's sake, ask for payment!" He gave him a shove in the general direction of the stranger. Cyrus only called upon Hirack, the local god of merchants, when he was extremely nervous.

What, Cabe wondered, had happened to the peaceful existence he'd once maintained? Slowly, he made his way through the now-empty tavern and finally stopped in front of the stranger's table.

The helmeted head turned to him. With a start, Cabe realized that the man's eyes were bright red. Little of his face was visible, and the skin seemed clay-brown and as dry as parchment.

"C-can I get you something, sir?"

The eyes appraised him. Cabe now noticed the sinister dragonhelm the traveler was wearing.

"I want none of your poor ale." The voice was nearly little more than a hiss.

"Food?"

The unblinking eyes continued to appraise him. Cabe shuddered, re-membering he had just asked if the stranger wanted food. He had not in-tended to offer himself in that respect.

"Your name is Cabe."

"Yes."

"So simple." The words were not intended for Cabe, but were merely a comment.

"I am going to leave now. When I leave, you will come with me. It is of the utmost importance."

"But I can't leave! My employer—"

The figure paid little attention to this. "He will not prevent you. Go and ask him. I will wait outside."

Cabe backed away as the other stood up. Even considering the elaborate dragonhelm, the stranger still towered over him. There was little doubt in Cabe's mind that this was one of the Dragon Kings. He shuddered. When a Dragon King summoned, even the highest of men obeyed.

The rider left without another word. Cabe hurried back to the others, most of whom had hidden in the kitchen.

"What happened? What does he want?" Cyrus no longer acted like the bear Cabe remembered. Fear covered him.

"He's waiting outside. He wants me."

More than one pair of eyes widened. Cyrus looked at him closely. Cabe might as well have been a leper. "You? What have you done to incur the wrath of the Dragon Kings? It has to be something horrible for one of their own to come amongst us!"

The others, including Deidra, backed away. Cyrus continued to rant and rave. "Go! Quickly! Go before he chooses to destroy my tavern! I'll not protect you!"

Cabe tried to defend himself. "I've done nothing! Someone! Tell Lord Gryphon's agent here!"

One of the cooks, with his arm around Deidra, picked up a cleaver and waved it in his direction. "We're too far away from Penacles for the lion-bird's protection! Get out before we throw you out!"

Reluctantly, Cabe backed out of the kitchen. The sound of thunder warned of the storm coming. He grabbed a cloak and reluctantly made his way to the front entrance. There was no chance of escape. If he attempted to hide or run away, the Dragon King would surely have him hunted down. Few would try to protect him.

It was raining outside. Cabe put the hood of his cloak up over his head.

A horse snorted. Cabe turned and found himself gazing up at the rider. The mount was a fiery, unnatural animal. Beside it, nervous, was a smaller, normal horse. It was the reins of this mount that were thrown to him.

"We ride! Hurry!"

Cabe climbed up. The Dragon King waited until he was settled and then started off. The serving man hurried after him, half wondering why he did so and knowing what might happen if he did not.

High above, the storm screamed unnaturally.

In the city of Penacles, in the midst of its bazaar, was the tent of Bhyram the fruit peddler. It was a stormy night, and Bhyram was cursing because he was having to put all of his merchandise in the tent by himself. With every sack, he cursed his assistant, a young man with great thirst.

An odd voice came to him from outside. "How much for two srevos?"

Srevos were sweet fruits that usually brought four coppers. Bhyram automatically said eight.

There was a clink of coins on the ground. The merchant turned around and rushed outside the tent. It was raining hard, but he could tell that none of his fruit had been stolen.

He could also tell that no one could have been nearby. Muttering an old saying to ward off sorcery, he cautiously picked up the eight coppers.

After all, he was still a businessman.

On and on they rode. The dark rider seemed untroubled by the storm, and Cabe had long since given up fighting it. Even when the rain ceased to fall, neither noticed it.

They were heading west, and in the deep recesses of his mind, Cabe vaguely recalled that these were the lands ruled by the Brown Dragon, the aptly named Barren Lands. Dry mud and occasional weeds made up most of the Barren Lands. It was not the most hospitable of places . . . and they were heading into the heart of it.

Reason told Cabe to run. Reason told Cabe that his end was surely in sight. Reason, however, could not overcome the fear that Cabe felt when he dared a glance at his unholy companion. Fear—and something else.

A duty for him to perform?

It seemed so muddled in his head. He frowned. His head had not felt straight ever since the . . . since the . . .

He could not think about that time. Something was blocking all such thoughts, protecting him.

Protecting him from the Dragon King.

They were now well into the Barren Lands. Despite the heavy rain, the ground beneath their mounts' hooves was dry and brittle. Such was the curse, for no matter how much water poured into the Barren Lands, none of it was absorbed. Instead, it just disappeared. Cabe knew that the Dragon Masters had been responsible for this.

They had seen. They had known. The firedrakes of Brown were the deadliest of fighters. Only because of this waste had their power been checked—but to no purpose. The Dragon Kings still ruled, and the warlocks and witches who had fought against them were no more.

Cabe looked up. The clouds above the Barren Lands were breaking up; yet the storm still raged elsewhere. Even the giver of rain dared not stay long. If there was a land cursed, it was this one.

"Stop."

The hissing voice of the Dragon King pierced through his mind. The helmed figure was staring at the ground as if searching for something. After a moment, he dismounted and ordered Cabe to do the same.

"Wait here."

The lord of firedrakes stalked off into the wastes. Cabe waited, knowing that flight was foolish. Perhaps, he thought, the Dragon King merely wished him to perform some task. Somehow, though, that did not ring true. The Kings had more than enough servants capable of handling anything Cabe could do.

It was not long before the other returned. His hands were empty. With great purpose, he walked up to Cabe and, with one sweeping motion, pushed him to the ground. The great sword that had hung in its scabbard was now out and pointing at the hapless human.

The Dragon King was a figure terrible to behold. The eyes burned— yes, burned—bright, fiery red. The dragonhelm seemed to smile the smile of a predator, and Cabe realized that he was seeing the true face behind the human form. In the pale light, the scales of the Dragon King's armor glistened brown. The sword, held in his left hand, did not shine. Rather, it seemed as black as an abyss.

The hiss that was not quite a voice reached Cabe's ears. "These were once my lands. They were not barren. Once, they were the most bountiful of grasslands and forests." He glared at the shivering human with total hate. "Until the time of the Dragon Masters!"

The point of the sword brushed back Cabe's hood. The eyes of the King widened. "A warlock! The final proof!"

The silver streak in his hair was evidently visible. Cabe wished that he really had all those powers that were supposed to be at the beck and call of a sorcerer. At least he would have stood a chance of escaping. Why had he come with him? All along, some part of him knew that the Dragon King meant to kill him.

The dark figure raised the sword as if to swing. "By the blood of fire-drakes killed with his own hand, Nathan Bedlam destroyed the life of my clans! By the blood of his own kin, I will bring that life back!" The edge of the sword came screaming down at Cabe.

The point of a gleaming shaft came through the front of the Dragon King's chest, the blade of his sword stopping short of Cabe's head.

Transfixed by the sight, the human could only watch as the reptilian monarch stared at the arrow that had pierced his body completely. A look of incomprehension passed over what little was visible of his face. He touched the point gingerly.

And fell forward.

Cabe only barely managed to roll out of the path of the Dragon King's body. The corpse hit the ground with a dull thud. The black blade slipped from the grasp of the limp left hand and clattered to one side.

Slowly, unbelievingly, Cabe stood up. No one came forth to claim the shaft. No one. He stared at his feet, and the enormity of the situation hit him for the first time. He was alone in the midst of the Barren Lands, and at his feet was the lord of those lands.

Dead.

A TRIO OF firedrake dams, in human forms, scratched and clawed at an emerald-colored piece of amber in which stood a human form. They had scratched and clawed at it in one form or another for several decades, but had never made so much as a single mark in it.

A FURRED HAND moved an ivory piece on a game board, and leaned back, looking for a comment from the opposing player whose mastery of the game made each move a lesson.

"Brown appears to be in a weak position," was all his companion had to say.

CABE GINGERLY PICKED up the dark blade and hung it in his belt. It made him feel only slightly better to be armed. He debated on what to do with the body. If he left it where it was, the dead Dragon King's subjects might consider this an act of disgrace and hunt him down. If he buried it, he might not give it the proper ceremonies. Again, the subjects might seek him out.

He left it where it was.

There was no sign of the Dragon King's mount. That had seemingly disappeared at some moment after its owner's death. Cabe's own mount was still where he had left it. He climbed on and considered his next action.

He could not return to his village. That would be suicidal. Where, then? The city of Zuu? No, Zuu was too well controlled by the Green Dragon and was too close to the Barren Lands. Though the master of the Dagora Forest rarely interfered, it was just too much of a chance to take.

Penacles? The Gryphon ruled there. He had taken over the City of Knowledge after the death of the Purple Dragon. Most claimed it was for the better. Everyone knew that the Gryphon was an enemy of the Dragon Kings.

That was it. It would mean several days extra, but it was the only safe place for him to travel. If he survived the journey.

He took one last look at the form on the ground. The strange, gleaming shaft protruded from the backside. Somewhere, there appeared to be an ally, but where? Nervously, he looked around and then rode off at full gallop.

HOURS PASSED.

Riders came. They were seemingly without substance, mere shadows of men. Yet they bore some semblance to the Dragon King who lay at their mounts' hooves. They paused, uncertain of what actions to take. Finally, one stepped down and touched the body. He noted the wound that went clear through, but saw no sign of the projectile. Gingerly, he turned the limp form over. At sight of the helmed face, there arose a muttering from the group, of which there were five.

Two more riders climbed down and helped the first. The body was placed with one of the mounted horsemen. When that was done, the others remounted their own animals.

The riders turned and headed off at full pace. They did not move toward the direction they had come from. Rather, they now faced north. There was fear in their movements. It was so rare in their kind that it became that much more noticeable.

Above them, the two moons traveled on, oblivious to the happenings of human and inhuman. Below them, however, at the site at which the Dragon King had fallen, a few small, daring blades of grass had shot up.

They were soon to be followed by others of their kind.

III

WITH THE BLACK blade clattering against his leg, Cabe rode through the wilderness. The Barren Lands had long ago given way to grassy plains, which had soon given way to woods. Nevertheless, he was not fooled by the beauty around him. Wyverns often made such trails their hunting grounds. Though the small dragons had only a minute amount of intelligence compared to the Kings, they were still more than cunning enough to fool a man.

The sun was bright overhead. By Cabe's estimate, he was nearly halfway to Penacles. That he had encountered no obstacles so far had sped up the trip, but he was sure his luck wouldn't hold.

The basilisk rose in front of him. Such creatures had an acute sense of hearing, because in order to make his presence unknown, a basilisk had to keep its eyes closed or else it would leave a large pile of statues wherever it went.

Cabe caught sight of the creature just before it tried to catch sight of him. The horse was not so fortunate; even as Cabe jumped, the basilisk saw it. The stone animal tipped over and fell to the ground, nearly catching its rider as it toppled.

Rolling into the woods around him, Cabe fought to pull out the sword. Somewhere off to the side, he could hear the basilisk moving slowly in his general direction. Giving up on the weapon momentarily, he picked up a piece of wood and threw it as far as he could in another direction. There was a pause and then the sound of the basilisk pushing through the brush toward the noise.

Pulling the sword free, Cabe made his way back toward the trail. Moving through the woods would alert the creature. The trail, while it would leave him in the open, promised him better speed and quieter steps.

He could hear the basilisk searching the area for him. With any luck, the monster would keep heading away. If it didn't . . .

Cabe did not care to complete such thoughts.

The trail was soft. That was good. Cabe padded along quietly, the sword ready. He doubted that he would stand much of a chance if he came face-to-face with the basilisk, but it still made him feel a little better. He stepped over the frozen form of the horse. That loss would make his journey three times as long.

A crashing noise erupted from the forest to his rear. Cabe tore off on a dead run. His only chance—and he knew it was a slim one—was to outrace the creature. Judging by the closer and closer sounds, even slim seemed to overrate his chances.

He stumbled. The blade nearly flew out of his grasp, but somehow he held on. The trampling of the basilisk was so loud that the monster had to be nearly on him. Completely in reflex, Cabe turned around to confront the lizard, not realizing how foolish that would have been for any other man.

The basilisk leaped out in front of him and stared.

Cabe's first reaction was his surprise at not being turned to stone. His surprise was mirrored by the basilisk; it had never failed to freeze a victim before. The beast stood rock still, almost as if it had been petrified like its countless victims.

Brandishing the dark blade, Cabe took advantage of his newfound immunity and stood up. The basilisk looked at the sword and shrank back. Cabe took a step forward, and the creature cowered. Putting on a grim face, the man waved his weapon only an arm's span from the monster and screamed.

The basilisk turned tail and fled.

Watching the beast run off, Cabe breathed a sigh of relief. Now that it was over, his body felt akin to a crushed piece of fruit. Fear, however, cautioned him not to stand around marveling at his luck; other, more daring beasts might come along.

Slowly, he trudged down the trail. It was always possible that he might come across a village on his route, but the odds of it were greatly against him. The lands around here were known to be fairly unpopulated, at least by humans.

He was still pondering the implications of his immunity to the basilisk when he saw the hooded figure. It was sitting near the side of the trail, a horse grazing next to it. The traveler appeared to have little fear concerning the creatures of the woods. Cabe recognized the figure and knew why.

The blurred face of the wizard smiled—or seemed to smile—at him. Cabe stopped, the sword pointed in the general direction of the shadowy form.

"Greetings, Cabe Bedlam."

"You're the one in the tavern, aren't you? The one who called himself Simon."

The necromancer nodded. "Yes. I see you've traveled since last we met."

"Traveled? I was nearly killed by one of the Dragon Kings, only someone killed him first!"

"So I've heard."

"He was going to use this!" Cabe held up the black sword.

Simon frowned. "A thrice-damned blade. If things were otherwise, I would tell you to throw it away and be rid of it. Unfortunately, it may be the only thing between you and death . . . that is, until your powers manifest themselves properly."

"Manifest properly?"

"As in the tavern. You remember your bout with the ogre."

Cabe's eyes widened. "That was me?"

The half-shadowed face may have smiled slightly. "You let yourself go. When the power is released like that, it can strike with potency."

The hood slid partly back. Cabe caught a glimpse of the great streak of silver in the other's hair. Unconsciously, he touched his own hair.

Simon nodded. "Yes, the silver has spread. My confrontation with you was the catalyst. Warlocks always react to other warlocks. Brown, the Dragon King who sought your death, also contributed, although by then your true nature was already very evident."

Cabe remembered the words of the reptilian monarch. Now there appeared to be no turning back. If everyone was determined to call him sorceror, Cabe was going to have to learn to use his power. As he came to this decision, he saw his companion nod again.

"It is the only path left for you. Without you, without your power, this land will remain under the dominion of the Dragon Kings."

"How could that be?" Such a prospect made Cabe shudder.

"There exists in you . . . power, for lack of a better word. Great potential. More than most men, even Nathan, have ever achieved—and you are untrained, which makes it all the more unusual. That power turned into skill is what we need. Since the Dragon Masters, the drakes have taken to seeking out humans with dangerous potential. You are one of the very few they have missed, which is why you are so valuable. Without you, we lack the power to withstand a concentrated struggle with the Dragon Kings."

"Then why have they never overwhelmed us? Why let us grow to be so dangerous?"

The hooded figure shrugged. "Two reasons, perhaps. We outnumber the major drakes, the intelligent ones, by a vast margin. Even in defeat, we stand a chance of turning them toward extinction. Their clans are too small. The second reason is related to the first. Their culture has become too intertwined with ours. We are too efficient a subject race. We do so much they no longer care to do, and we do it because we need to. Why disturb what worked so well?"

Cabe thought back to his own life. He could not say it had been too difficult. "Why do we need to fight, then? Don't we have everything? Can't we do everything?"

Though Simon's face was unreadable, the tone of his voice was not. "The illusion of freedom is always that, Cabe. An illusion. As long as the Dragon Kings rule, we will never rise further. We will stagnate and die with them."

An overwhelming sense of duty swelled within Cabe. His grandfather had given his life for this belief, and Cabe, understanding that belief at least a little, could at least help—especially with his own life at stake. "What should I do? Will you teach me?"

"Later, perhaps. For now, however, you should continue on your journey. The Lord Gryphon awaits your arrival."

"He awaits? How does he know about me?"

The warlock chuckled. "One does not kill a Dragon King without gaining a quick notoriety."

"But I didn't kill him! There was a glowing shaft! It pierced his body!"

The warlock's eyes became a deep crimson. The hands gestured in his direction. At first, Cabe believed that the shadowy figure was about to destroy him. He held up the sword, hoping it would protect him.

Simon lowered his hands. "You have nothing to fear, my friend. I was merely checking your story. It is true, what you have said. Brown, master of the Barren Lands, died by the power of a Sunlancer's shaft. These are strange times indeed."

Cabe lowered the sword. "What is a Sunlancer? I feel I know that title."

"You should. It is most likely a part of your power. Sunlancers were Dragon Master elites. Nathan was their leader. They could draw the light of Kylus and control it with their bows."

Slowly, Cabe looked up to the sun. If he could control a part of that! It was beyond belief. Yet something was not right. . . .

"The Dragon King died under the Twins. He had chosen that time for my death."

"Hmm. It is possible that the blood of one such as you would revitalize the dead lands. The meeting of the Twins is a time well known to those with the power. It increases the potency of any spell that involves sacrifice. Still, the Sunlancers required day. To create such a weapon at night, one would have to use the Twins, and they are not noted for their generosity. They demand payment. I must investigate. Perhaps, by the time you arrive in Penacles, I will have an answer for you."

"You're leaving me? But I'll never make it on foot!"

The blurred face may have actually revealed a fleeting glimpse of surprise. "On foot? No. You will ride this horse. I brought it the moment I realized your plight." Despite his gloves, the warlock snapped his fingers. His mount walked over to Cabe and nuzzled the startled wanderer.

Cabe stroked the horse, somewhat awed by the abilities of his companion. He had lost his mount only some minutes before.

"I thank you for the steed, but what will you do?"

"I have no need of it."

Frowning, Cabe gazed at the horse. It was strong. Stronger than his other. He turned his attention back to the warlock—

—only to discover that Simon was gone.

He did not question the disappearance. The cloaked and hooded form had helped him. It would be best to make use of that assistance. The sooner he arrived in the Penacles, the better.

Sheathing the dark sword, he mounted. A quick scan of the area revealed no other path than the one he was on. The woods were too dangerous. Not that the path had proven to be simple.

Keeping his grip on the hilt of the sword, he rode off again.

NIGHTFALL WAS COMING. To Cabe, it seemed as if the day had been shortened by half. He had hoped to reach the end of the forest before this, but the path twisted frequently. A small portion of his mind suggested that sorcery might be involved, for no human would have designed such a winding trail.

Something strayed into his path. Cabe glimpsed a very feminine form. A woman screamed. He pulled his horse to a stop, barely missing the body in front of him.

Recently developed reflexes caused him to reach for the sword.

"Good sir, stay your hand! We mean you no harm!"

Cabe jerked his head toward the voice and caught sight of two women. Not ordinary women. Of that he was sure. They were clad in thin but ornate gowns. All the color of the forest. In fact, even their skin—and much of it was visible—had a slight greenish tinge.

The tallest of the three stepped up to him. She could have been elfin, with her narrow face and wheat-colored eyes. Her smile dared to chase away the coming darkness. "Hail to you, oh gentleman!"

Gentleman! Cabe held back a laugh. She had certainly overrated his status. "Who are you?"

"I am Camilla. This is Magda." She indicated a smaller but more voluptuous woman who smiled shyly and curtsied. Her face was almost a copy of her sister's, for such they had to be. Cabe stammered out a greeting.

Camilla turned to the woman whom Cabe had nearly run over. "This one here is our younger sister, Tegan, who, it seems, must learn to watch her path more closely."

Tegan was barely into womanhood, but there was a grace about her that seemed to argue years of experience. Like Magda, she was also nearly a double of her eldest sister. As she curtsied, her long, golden hair fell from her shoulders.

"And what, may I ask, are three fair ladies doing out here? Surely, a land filled with hazards, such as the wyverns, is no place for the trio of you to live. Where are your men?"

The eldest became quiet. "Alas, my husband is dead. As for my sisters, they never had the chance to marry. We do not fear the creatures of the forest, however, for they stay away from our home. My late lord believed that it was possible that some enchantment protects the area."

Cabe nodded. He had heard of such places. Some were said to be the former homes of sorcerors. Others appeared to be the work of spirits, benign or otherwise. These women were fortunate; some areas meant instant death for those who trespassed. For every oasis, there was also a trap.

The youngest came up to his horse and tried to pet it. The animal shied back, as if bitten. Cabe saw that it was breathing fast.

Camilla eyed his mount. "Your horse is obviously tired. Perhaps you would allow us the pleasure of your company. It is high time we had a guest in our house again. Such a handsome one makes the idea seem even more pleasant."

Unaccustomed to compliments that didn't end in sarcasm, Cabe nearly reddened. "It would be an honor for me to accompany you."

"Then come. It is only a short distance off the path."

He motioned his mount to step off the trail, but the animal refused. A second and third attempt failed to make the horse do more than shift back and forth nervously. Realizing the futility of his situation, Cabe climbed off.

"It seems I must walk, but I have no place to keep my horse in the meantime."

Tegan stepped up and gently took the reins from his hands. Up close, she took on an air of seductiveness that Cabe had not noticed earlier. Her voice was like the call of a Siren.

"Go with my sisters, Cabe. I will attend to your animal's needs and return shortly. Have no fear, he will be safe in my hands."

Few, if any, men could resist a voice and face such as hers. He nodded and thanked her for her kindness. Camilla and Magda each took him by an arm.

"You shall escort us as my husband once did. Today, we are again ladies of the manor." Camilla smiled, and Cabe had a deep wish to lose himself in that smile.

They led him into the forest, the man lost in his dreams. Behind him, strangely unnoticed, were the sounds of a horse both enraged and worried.

A moment later, the hiss of a larger, more sinister creature joined in, but by then Cabe was out of earshot.

MUCH COULD BE said about the diversities of taste in the Dragonrealms. Both humans and inhumans differed greatly from their nearest brothers, and these tastes were greatly evident in the type of dwellings that each respective member of each respective race chose to live within.

Such was the case with the manor of the three ladies, Cabe decided.

Great stone walls intermingled with barriers cut out of the earth itself. Parts of the house were cut wood, but the right side appeared to be formed from a massive tree. Plants of fanciful and bizarre appearance filled the areas around it. High above, like the symbol of the manor, a fierce-looking avian prepared to swoop down on all comers. Despite its being formed from metal, Cabe had to stare at it twice before he allowed himself to be led inside.

The interior of the manor was even more unreal than the exterior. While the floor was polished marble, here and there were spots where trees grew. Some went through the ceiling and beyond. Vines traced their ways along the walls, pillars, stairway, and, of course, the trees. It was strange to think that anyone could live here. He wanted to question his enchanting hostesses about its history, but decided to wait until the moment seemed right.

Camilla released his arm, allowing Magda to lead him to an elaborate chair. Cabe sat down cautiously, for the chair seemed so ancient that it would most likely collapse. He was surprised to find that it was actually very sturdy and quite soft. Unused to such luxury, he allowed himself to sink in deeply. The two women exchanged glances, as if quite amused by his fascination with an everyday object.

Magda leaned down, giving Cabe a splendid view of her womanhood. She smiled, and the smile was so much like her sisters'. "Are you pleased?"

It took him a moment to realize that she meant the chair. Red-faced, he nodded. "It's been a long time since I've sat in anything so comfortable."

"Good! We want you to be happy. Would you like to remove your sword? It must be terribly uncomfortable to wear!"

Cabe, for no reason that he could think of, felt a great desire to keep the blade with him. He shook his head and turned the conversation to other things. "This is a most unusual place. Who built it?"

"My sister Camilla's husband. He was a . . . a man of the forests. He could not do without the presence of the lands. We have come to love it."

"I meant no discourtesy."

She leaned even closer. "None was taken."

"Magda!"

At the sound of Camilla's voice, the woman pulled away quickly. She looked at her sister with eyes of fire. The eldest met her with an equally fiery stare.

"What is it, my dear sister?"

Camilla pointed at the door. "See to Tegan. Make sure that she is all right."

Her sister laughed. "That one? No creature—"

"See to it now!"

The younger one frowned and departed. Cabe watched her leave and turned to Camilla. "If Tegan is in danger, then perhaps I should help."

The woman took a goblet from a tray that she had placed nearby. "Be not overly concerned, Sir Cabe. I only meant that she might possibly have had trouble with your steed. It was a strong and spirited steed." She handed him the goblet. "Enough of this! My sisters together will have more than enough skill to take care of your horse. In the meanwhile, I shall do what I can for you."

Cabe nearly choked on the wine. Never had he met such hot-blooded women! Perhaps it was because of their isolation from other people. It was difficult to resist their charms, and he wondered why he was doing so at all. Most likely, he was afraid of what the other two might do if he showed any favor to one. Beautiful they might be, but they acted like a pack of wild dogs, each trying to claim a kill.

It had not escaped his notice that his hostess was dressed differently. She was now in a gown that very definitely failed to do what most clothing was designed for—covering one's form. If Cabe concentrated . . .

He need not have bothered to try. Camilla, with surprising speed, sat down in his lap, nearly causing him to spill his wine. Her arms were around him, and she spoke only when her lips were less than a finger's width away from his own.

"My sisters will take some time. They know that it is my right, as eldest, to be first. Why not remove that sword and belt? Come, now, am I unattractive?"

He managed to choke out, "No, my lady."

She smiled like a predator about to sink her teeth into her prey. The gown made it easy for Cabe to feel the warmth of her body against his. In fact, it was hard to tell if he was sweating from her nearness or from the heat she seemed to emit. Hot-blooded indeed!

The front door burst open. Camilla pulled away from Cabe, rage making her face decidedly ugly. She stopped short as she saw Magda helping an injured Tegan in.

"What happened?"

The youngest was only half conscious. Cabe watched her and squinted. She appeared slightly out of focus. He looked at his wine and hastily put the goblet down.

Camilla was giving quick instructions. "Magda! Not here! Bring her to—to her room!"

"Darkhorse! Darkhorse . . ." Tegan mumbled incoherently after that.

"He comes!" The words were Magda's.

There was a thrashing from the woods nearest to the trail. Cabe reached for the sword.

"No!" Camilla stopped him before his hand had touched the hilt.

"There's something coming!"

"It cannot enter here! We are safe!"

The crashing continued. Whatever it was, it was coming closer and doing so with great speed. Cabe wondered how safe they really were. He did not put much stock in his ability with a sword.

The two sisters helped Tegan into another room. Cabe stood by the open door, shaking, and looked out. Something was out there, but it appeared to have stopped a short distance from sight. Cabe put his hand on the hilt and took a tentative step out.

Something shifted in the woods. He caught a quick glimpse of a shape like a horse but not quite real. Two strange urges pulled at him. One was to step out into the forest and confront the creature; the second was to call the creature to him. Neither seemed very sensible, so Cabe fought both ideas as best he could. The beast snorted in irritation.

"What are you doing?"

Cabe spun around, his hand still on the hilt of his sword. It was Camilla, but she appeared different. She was still beautiful, but that beauty had now taken on a somewhat reptilian aspect. Cabe's grip on the sword became much tighter.

She calmed herself and moved closer to him. She was still very much the enchantress. "Calm yourself, Cabe. The creature cannot enter. We may ignore it."

He did not relax. "What is that thing? Tegan mentioned 'Darkhorse.' That sounds familiar, but I can't—"

Camilla put a hand to his mouth. "Hush. My sister was distraught. You need not worry about her. She will be fine by morning."

The thing outside created more noise but sounded no closer.

The woman so near to him was becoming less and less human, though she apparently had not noticed any change. When the snout stretched forth from her face, Cabe was struck by sudden realization.

He pushed Camilla away with his free hand and pulled out the dark blade with the other.

"Firedrake!" he roared.

The whole demeanor of his hostess had changed. With an inhuman roar, she altered completely. Wings sprouted from her back. The beautiful face stretched out until much of it had became gaping jaws with great, sharp teeth. The slender arms and legs became scaled legs that tried to claw at the man.

Cabe had walked into a trap. He had heard tales from adventurers who told of firedrake dams who enchanted and then devoured unwary male travelers. They were more successful in their shapeshifting than the males. A male firedrake, even the Dragon Kings, could not make his form into a perfect copy of a man. That was why the males always appeared in the guise of armored warriors.

The females, however, could not only make themselves appear human, but could even improve on the image. Hence their ability to seduce unwary victims.

Somehow he had been freed from whatever spell had been laid on him.

Maybe it was the sword in his hand. It had come from a Dragon King. Perhaps, he thought, it had more advantages than he had believed.

All of this had gone through Cabe's mind in a fraction of a second. Fear can be a great motivator. With nowhere to go, save toward the creature in the forest, he held the point of the sword in the direction of the dragon and prayed.

The thing that had been Camilla, about to lunge, stopped abruptly. It seemed to shrink into itself. Heartened, Cabe took a step forward and pretended to attack. It had worked against the basilisk. The firedrake backed away, its tail between its legs.

The creature spoke. "Have mercy, man of the Horned Blade! I will not attack you!"

Cabe paused. "Do you swear to that?"

"By the emperor, the Horned Blade, and the Dragonrealms! Please!"

The dark sword, which now had a name—and an ominous one—throbbed in his hand. There was power there. Power to do anything! Power that could meld with his own! Give him mastery over beast and man!

There was the neighing of a great warhorse. Cabe blinked and realized that he had fallen under the influence of the blade. Small wonder that Simon had called it thrice-cursed!

The firedrake had nearly dug itself into the floor in its fear. Cabe found himself disgusted. "Change back, blast you! I'd rather you looked human!"

"As you wish!"

The form melted, and the entire process began to reverse itself. Soon he found himself watching the beautiful, but distraught, Camilla. It was something to note; the sword had allowed her to regain her human disguise.

"That's better. Call in your sisters!"

She did so. Magda came in, the injured Tegan leaning on her. They moved to their sister.

Camilla looked at them. "He knows. He also bears the Horned Blade."

Magda's eyes widened, and Tegan let out a small gasp. Despite its evil nature, Cabe knew that he had better keep his hand on the sword or risk an attack.

"What would you want of us?"

He snorted. "Not what you had in mind, that's for sure! You were playing with me like a cat with its dinner!"

"We needed food. Our duke was out of favor with the Green Dragon and is now dead. Even we cannot face the glare of the basilisk. That power is reserved for the Dragon Kings alone. That is why we have been reduced to this!"

Cabe did not feel inclined to mention his own encounter with the monster. Any secrets he kept from the dams would be to his advantage.

"The sword kept you away." He phrased the thought as a statement of fact, not a question. It would not do for them to know that he was working by guess.

"Yes. The Horned Blade was created by a sorceror. It is a bane to both our kind and yours. Beware, human, it is treacherous. It might very well bring about all of our deaths."

"Yours will be first if I think I see a trick."

She raised a hand. "I will do nothing."

Little things were starting to come back to him. "You called me Cabe, yet I never told you my name. How did you know?"

Camilla became silent.

"If you do not tell me, I'll use this. Or—or I'll make you go out and face that thing." Any creature that preyed on the firedrakes could not be all bad.

That broke her resolve. "The Lady of the Amber told us of your coming."

Lady of the Amber? Cabe felt a light touch in his memory. There was something about her. He did not know what it was, but he knew that he had to see her.

"Lead me to her."

"Will you release us when we have?" Even defeated, Camilla still sought to bargain.

"We shall see."

The thing in the woods bellowed and crashed about. Cabe still felt the urge to call or go to it, but he fought it down. Such an action would most likely end in his death.

The eldest sister took the lead. Cabe made the others follow after her. Despite their frail appearances, he did not want these women behind his back. They moved slowly, since Tegan still needed the assistance of her sister.

He knew, even as they stepped into the garden in the back, that the firedrakes had taken over this manor from someone else. Someone who had not been quite human, yet was much more so than any of the great reptiles could ever claim to be. In fact, Cabe could almost feel a kinship with the former tenant as he followed his captives.

The garden was similar to the manor in that plants intermingled with the structures. Vines wrapped around arches, and flowers sprouted out from areas in the floor. It should have looked like anarchy; instead, there was an order that was so subtle that one almost took it for granted that it should be that way.

"Behold, man, the Lady of the Amber!"

They were on it so abruptly that Cabe had at first thought it was part of the garden's design. The large honey-colored crystal rested on a platform of marble. Here and there, creepers had grown around it. It was transparent. Also, the longer one looked, the more noticeable it was that it was glowing slightly from within. A greenish glow.

In that glow, the center of the crystal, was a woman.

IV

THE COUNCIL OF the Dragon Kings had been called hastily. With the exception of Black, only the nearest of the emperor's brethren had been able to attend. Yet the rumors of why the Council had been called together was enough so that those who could not be there were nonetheless making preparations for possible battle.

Silver was there. Green and Red sat on opposite sides, eyeing one another suspiciously. Iron, great and massive, second in power only to the emperor, had made one of his rare appearances.

Gold scanned over them. Even Iron was forced back by the stare. When the emperor acted in such a manner, things were ill indeed.

"I am sorry that the rest have not arrived—especially Ice, who is so close—but this number will have to do."

He paused, as if awaiting some comment.

"Fate, master of the game, has dealt the card once again. The Dragon-realms threaten to escape our rule once more."

The flatness of the statement served only to emphasize its importance. Only once before had their power been challenged. That enemy had come close to defeating them.

As if speaking what was in the mind of all, Iron roared, "The Dragon Masters are dead! None can challenge us!"

"The Masters may be gone, but their legacy lives on."

Red spat in disgust. The stain burned its way into the earth. "This sounds too much like the last Council."

"It will continue to sound like the last Council."

The despot of the Hell Plains gave an almost human look of curiosity. "What do you mean, my lord?"

Instead of answering his brother, Gold lifted his massive head, spread his wings, and bellowed toward the shadows, "You may enter!"

They came slowly. Two of them. There was much in their appearances that told of the close relationship between all in the chamber. Dragon-helmed, they might have pretended to be Kings, but the others knew better. In accordance to custom, they kneeled, their heads down.

Iron blinked. "Whose dukes are these?"

"They are Brown's."

"He sends his underlings and does not deign to come himself? Sire, let me take my legions and teach our arrogant brother hisss place!"

"I fear a lesson now would do little good." Gold turned to the two. "Summon those who carry the body."

"Body?" The single word issued from more than one mouth. There was consternation. And fear.

The newcomers stood up, bowed, and left silently. A short time passed, as if those who must enter feared to do so. The Dragon Kings shifted impatiently.

At long last, five figures, including a third warrior of the Brown Dragon's clans and two of the Gold Dragon's own warriors, returned. On a platform borne by four lay a shrouded form. One of the reptilian monarchs hissed as he recognized what that form truly was.

"Brown! They bear Brown!"

Unaccustomed to the power that had gathered in that room, the dukes fell to their knees, still bearing the platform between them. Though powerful, they feared for their very lives. To their monarchs, though, they were invisible. The Dragon Kings were too concerned with the death of one of their own.

"Who has done this?"

"He wears his man-form!"

"Someone must have struck him down soon after he left us!"

Gold noticed that Black was strangely silent. He called for order and received it. "Brown is dead! There is a wound, going through his chest, but I see no weapon, and the servants of our brother claim none was to be found! Even in a human form, we are nearly invincible. How, then, was this crime done? Who is responsible?"

Even as he spoke, his eyes turned to the keeper of the Gray Mists. Black smiled, but it was a smile that Death might have painted on, so grim it was. "Well? You seem strangely pleased by this! What have you to say, brother?"

Black inclined his head. "Respected brother, it is as I said. The blood of the Masters still exists. I suspect that there are others, too. We could never be absolutely sure. It was, after all, Purple's strategy, and he died facing the last and greatest of our enemies."

"Then you blame this on the grandson of Nathan Bedlam. I had ordered that this one should be watched! Where are my spies!"

Something flitted out of the darkness of the upper level of the chamber. It had no mundane counterpart, and even the emperor knew little about the history of its kind. The spy served, and that was all that mattered in the long run.

Something had happened to their intended target. The dark servants of the emperor had arrived, only to discover that he had vanished. Ordered out by one of the Magnificent Ones, it claimed. Both had ridden off into the Barren Lands. The servants had returned here, to the Most Magnificent's dwelling, but had feared to tell him.

"So." Gold dismissed the spy. It flew back up to its black roost and disappeared. "Brown chose to disobey. He sought to kill the Bedlam-hatchling by himself! His disobedience cost him dearly."

Most of the others kept quiet. Gold was generally a calm and reasoning leader. His knowledge was almost as great as that of the late master of the City of Knowledge. Purple, however, had turned down the power of emperor. This fact had always surrounded Gold. To him, such blatant disobedience indicated a lack of faith in him as ruler. It was one of his few weak points. No one dared to mention it.

The emperor calmed slightly. "Our brother was found in one of the most desolate—if one can use the term without sounding very repetitious—parts of the Barren Lands. It is thought that he died under the eyes of the Twins."

The reaction he received at these words did not disappoint him. The Twins' hunger for sacrifice was well known. In return, they would do much to increase the strength of one's spell. Brown had obviously intended to use the human to bring back his lush fields. That he had died instead left much to speculation.

"We must prepare." Gold's voice was dead. This was to be a command that must be obeyed in full. "We must mass together our legions once more. If a second rising of men is imminent, we must locate it while it is still in its birth stages."

Though he paused, they knew to what he was leading. Black was smiling, but Gold did not reprimand him.

"We must take Penacles. We must return to our power the City of Knowledge."

Iron roared his approval. "Yesss! I will take my Beast hordes down and crush the Gryphon! Then I shall collect the—"

"No! I will take charge of the defeat and sacking of Penacles!"

The emperor's words silenced all. While Gold's legions were superior to all others, they seldom saw action such as this. The real reason for this sudden switch was evident enough: to the Dragon Kings, knowledge was power. The King of Kings had no intention of letting any of his brethren take control of that power, lest they become a threat to him.

"Sire! To do so might threaten the life of your august self!"

The others nodded agreement. Silver looked to his master with worry. The emperor frowned as best a dragon might. Silver was loyal to him, but unfortunately that meant that the lord of Mines was unconsciously taking the position of the other side. Gold sighed ever so slightly. A compromise would have to be made.

"Very well. Black, you will bring your forces together. Iron, I appoint you to gather up what remains of brother Brown's and add it to your own. You will strike from the west. The master of the Hell Plains and myself will stand in reserve and then strike. Toma will lead my Imperial legions."

There was agreement here. Toma, hatchling of Gold, but only a firedrake, was still a well-trained battle leader.

"I shall remain here, issuing such commands as are needed." And playing dam to a pile of eggs, he thought. Still, it would keep the others on guard. Toma could protect himself. Though lacking the genes that would have made him an Imperial successor, his mind was the equal, if not the superior, of many in this chamber.

Damn the fickleness of the egg patterns!

"All servants are to watch for the Bedlam whelp! If he can be dispatched, then they are to do so. If not, they are to report to you immediately."

"The battle, sire. Are the rest of us to sit idle?"

Gold looked at them. "You and the others must police your lands. We may have missed something. I will want to hear from all of you." He stretched himself out to his full height. "This Council is at an end. You have your duties. Perform them."

The corpse of the Brown Dragon King was carried away. After that, the Dragon Kings departed. They did not speak. Their duties had been explained, and it would be shame if they failed to carry out those duties.

Watching them go, the emperor was grim. We have changed considerably, he decided. More and more, our thoughts become like those of the humans. Some who leave tonight may shirk their duties before this situation is resolved . . . if it is resolved.

We are meant to rule, but to rule, we must be united. I will crush the Gryphon and then use the knowledge to make an end to my other . . . concerns.

Satisfied, Gold curled himself up and drifted off to sleep.

SHE WAS BEAUTIFUL, breathtaking. A thousand words could not describe her well enough to suit Cabe's tastes.

"Who was she?"

Camilla frowned. "We know not. It has been hazarded that she created this house. We do know that she is a powerful witch."

"You speak as if she is still alive."

"Look at her, manling! Can you not see that still she breathes? She is merely imprisoned!"

He looked closer. It was true! She did breathe. Cabe waved the black sword at the three firedrakes. "Release her!"

Tegan let out a very human squeal. "We did not imprison her! She was like this when we first came here!"

Camilla nodded quickly. "True! We have tried for countless seasons to remove her from her prison, but we cannot!"

Cabe glanced at the figure inside. Long, flowing tresses of a fiery red fought with the emerald green of her thin dress. A shock of silver added to a startling contrast. Her lips were nearly the color of the hair, while her eyes matched more with the clothing. Her face was perfect; Cabe found himself unable to think of any other description for it. A goddess of the Dragonrealms, he finally half decided.

He was at a loss, for these creatures before him, even with their formidable powers, had been unable to even scratch the surface of the stone. What could he possibly do?

As if mocking him, the thing lurking in the woods cried out. Cabe shuddered and wondered why he still felt a desire to call the thing to him. Thankfully, whatever it was, it could not overcome the spell that protected the manor and the grounds.

Camilla looked at him expectantly, interrupting his thoughts. "We have brought you to her. Will you leave us in peace now?"

Something in her words added menace where there should have been none. Cabe eyed the female reptiles. "I don't know what to do yet. Tell me what you've done to try to release her."

Disgruntled, they told of using claws, strength, and branches to shatter the casement. With the description of each of their failures, Cabe's spirits sank further. How could he succeed where all others had been defeated? He finally swung the dark blade at the crystal, though he had little hope it would even make a scratch.

It was like metal scraping against metal. Green sparks flashed about as the two artifacts made contact, and the screech caused by the blade as it sank deep into the crystalline prison made Cabe shiver. The progress of the blade came to an abrupt halt, though, and he lost his grip on the weapon as well as his balance. As he fell, the firedrake dams let out a triumphant yell and began to alter their forms. The sword remained buried in the crystal.

Tumbling, Cabe was able to survive the first attack. Camilla, only half human now, made a leap for him. Even as she landed where he had previously been, her last vestiges of humanity disappeared. He was now confronting a full-grown firedrake, and to make matters worse, the other two sisters had now finished transforming and were about to join the eldest for what appeared to be an easy victory.

There was no way that he could reach the sword. He dodged as the creature that had been Camilla tried to rip his chest open, barely missing and taking off most of his shirt.

The thing in the forest bellowed in such a strange tone that Cabe almost believed that it was pleading with him to allow it to enter.

All three of the firedrakes were on him now. Cabe got just a glimpse of the slowly melting prison. Not only would they kill him, but he'd given them access to the Lady.

The pleading from the forest increased tenfold. Cabe had no choice and gave in. The thing would probably make short work of him, but also might put an end to the firedrakes. The words slipped out of his mouth automatically, and he understood nothing of their meaning.

"Enter freely, child of the Void!"

A triumphant cry answered his command. The three dams stopped in their tracks. The one that had been Tegan turned and fled, while the other two paused, measuring their chances.

It tore through the manor, the sound of its hooves on the marble like a sword striking rock. It cleared the inside of the building in record time and crashed through the back. With another cry, it landed between Cabe and the monsters.

It was blacker than anything he had ever seen. Its general outline was that of a horse, but it was much, much more than that. It pawed the ground, digging small ditches where there should have been none, its eyes not crimson red, as one might think, but icy blue, and colder than one would think possible.

The cry turned to a mocking laugh as it stalked the two retreating firedrakes. Even more shocking were the words that issued from its mouth. Bold and echoing, masterful!

"Come, my darlings! Are you so afraid to embrace a loved one? Have you forgotten so soon that Darkhorse finds you always? Come! Will neither of you be first?"

Both reptiles realized that the creature called Darkhorse would catch them if they ran. In desperation, they lunged simultaneously, hoping one of them would make a mortal strike. Darkhorse jumped nimbly aside and even managed to kick one of the monsters as it landed. The firedrake fell hard, stunned by the blow.

The other rose to attack.

Darkhorse laughed again. "Now, that's more like it, darling! Show a little teeth and claw!"

Even as the firedrake slashed, its opponent reared up and kicked it soundly on the jaw. Something cracked. The dragon fell, its mouth bent strangely out of shape.

Darkhorse laughed.

Unseen, the other had come to its senses and had attempted to claw the underside of the steed. Huge and sharp, the claws merely slid off the skin. Darkhorse, still on his hind legs, came down hard on the head of the firedrake. This time, the cracking of bone was unmistakable. The dragon grunted and went lifeless.

Blood dripping from its broken jaw, the other tried to run, but Darkhorse moved so quickly that Cabe could not believe it. Almost immediately, it was in front of the reptile, which could not slow its momentum and dove straight into the horse . . . literally.

As Cabe watched, the hapless monster fell into the emptiness that was Darkhorse, and, with a scream, it kept falling, getting smaller and smaller. In moments, it had disappeared completely.

The steed cried out triumphantly. Then, with blinding speed, it tore off in pursuit of the third firedrake. Cabe made no attempt to call it back. If it went far away, that would suit him just fine. He did not know exactly what Darkhorse was, but he knew that the name was familiar to him. He also knew that, more often than not, the creature brought death.

The events finally caught up with him. Free from the threat of the fire-drakes, Cabe sank to the ground and lost consciousness.

From far off came the triumphant bellow of Darkhorse.

HIGH ABOVE THE Barren Lands, a large, predatory creature circled. It was not scaled, as most of the nearest inhabitants were, but was nevertheless related. An avian. A bird, yet like no bird that had ever been seen, for it was more manlike. Silently, it landed near a large patch of grass.

The Seeker folded its massive wings and bent down. One feathered hand touched the long green blades. Hawk eyes watched carefully as dust nearby turned to rich soil and then became populated with small shoots. In all di-rections, especially those leading into the deepest parts of the Barren Lands, the field spread. In death, Brown had succeeded beyond his wildest dreams.

A horse, yet not a horse, snorted. The Seeker pointed one of its sharp claws in the direction of the sound. A moment later, a single rider appeared. His dragonhelm proclaimed him a firedrake, one of the late King's liege-men.

The reptilian warrior rode directly to the other, but despite this, the avian did not move. It stared at the firedrake with what appeared to be only mild interest. The warrior, oblivious to the form in front of him, slowly turned to the right. He bypassed both field and Seeker as if they were no longer there.

When the firedrake had left, the Seeker once again put its hand to the grass. The pointed claws ran lightly along, learning all, and, when it was satisfied, the creature stood up once more, turned this way and that, and scanned the lands around it. Within days, everything in sight would be green with life.

The massive wings spread once more. Into the sky it rose. The Seeker circled once and then flew off.

Below it, the field continued to spread.

ANOTHER HAND, THIS one furred, although sometimes it was feathered, depending on mood, of course. The hand belonged to the Gryphon, or Lord Gryphon as he was often called, and was running slowly over a smooth piece of glass shaped like an egg.

If one knew how, one could see pictures. Many did not make sense. Some were of the past. Others, the future. The rest were unidentifiable.

The Gryphon was most interested in these.

"I see a dragon, larger than any, mottled in color. Every color. Do you know it?" The Gryphon's voice was the proud rumble of a lion, though his eaglelike face would never have made that fact evident.

The one who called himself Simon nodded slowly, his sluggish response possibly indicating some worry. "The Dragon of the Depths. They say he lived in the deepest part of the seas, where water and molten earth meet. It is believed he died long before the coming of men."

"Believed?"

"One never knows about legends."

"No. What of this?" The furred hand indicated a new picture, one that showed a shattered skull.

"I do not recognize it, though I feel I should."

With the wave of a hand, the picture was dismissed. Yet another took its place.

The Gryphon stroked the large crystalline ovoid, his eye into the past, present, and, most important, the future. "Yalak's Egg is showing off today."

Simon nodded. "As peril draws closer, the crystal becomes more attuned with the multiverse."

"I recognize this. It is the chamber of Gold, King of Kings, greatest of the Dragon Kings."

"He appears to sleep."

The Gryphon nodded, his mane fluttering slightly. "His features have softened. I suspect that most of the others are the same."

"They have dared to take the treacherous path leading to humanity. It is reflected in their forms and actions."

"For our sakes, let us hope not."

The warlock indicated the device known as Yalak's Egg. "Change the picture once more."

"Very well."

Once again, the Gryphon dissolved the image, but this time, however, instead of another picture, only fog could be seen. The Gryphon looked up at his companion.

"Are you interfering with the Egg?"

"Yes. I am attempting to focus on a particular person in the present."

"I had no idea that you could do this. You've not told me everything about yourself, after all."

"I do not know myself very well. You know that."

"Indeed. My apologies."

Simon ignored him. Something was happening. "I've done it. Look quickly."

"I see a jewel with some sort of figurine inside."

"That isn't a figurine. That is an actual person."

The Gryphon glanced up. "Her?"

"Yes. The amber. Does it look unusual?"

"It appears to be melting."

Something unusual infiltrated the warlock's voice. It appeared to be pleasure. "He's done it! He's freed her!"

The image faded.

He fell back. "I'm sorry. I couldn't hold the image any longer."

"Say nothing." And with that, the lord of Penacles snapped his fingers. A servitor, not quite human, appeared from nowhere. "Serve my guest some refreshment."

Within moments, Simon was presented with a goblet of wine. The warlock drank the contents with one gulp, his host eyeing him with amusement, for the sorceror was not known for his drinking abilities.

Simon put down the goblet and nodded thanks. "When I learned of this Cabe Bedlam, I came to believe that he might be able to release the Lady Gwen. My faith has been justified."

"And how, may I ask, did he come across her? That was not his original path."

The warlock may have smiled. "I engaged the services of . . . an old friend. He took a different path, though Bedlam did not realize it."

"This . . . friend. I don't think I'd care to meet him, if he is the one I believe he is."

"Few would. That is why he and I have become so close."

The Gryphon shuddered, something he did rarely. Few things frightened him. Darkhorse, being what it was, did. He chose a different subject. "The Lady. How long has she been trapped?"

"Since just before Nathan Bedlam's death."

"Then the power has been building all this time. She was strong, I believe."

"The only woman capable of enchanting the greatest of the Dragon Masters. That alone makes her formidable, and love conquers all, they say."

"You are getting away from my question. What about the release of power?"

Simon leaned forward. He appeared to be lost in thought. Finally, he answered. "It will be as formidable as the Lady."

"What might it do?"

A long pause. "It might very well destroy the entire area, including Cabe Bedlam."

It was terribly, terribly hot.

No. It was freezing cold.

A dog with hands was playing the flute.

The skull kept laughing.

Cabe woke up. He shuddered. The dreams had been so incredibly real. He stood up, brushing the stardust from his body. A tentacled bird landed on a branch nearby and howled. Cabe's mind cleared enough to tell him that the dreams were no dreams. Madness, perhaps, but not dreams.

Strange, gnarled plant-creatures hurried along, complaining about the drought. A bullfrog flew by, only to be snatched up by the perched octopoid-avian. Cabe realized that all the creatures were coming from the Lady. To be precise, they were issuing full-grown from the crack in her prison.

It took little imagination to realize that a tremendous amount of power was escaping. It also was obvious that the crack was spreading, and when it had spread far enough . . .

The dark blade was still caught in the amber. The wisest choice would be to flee . . . but could he run far enough?

A small piece of the outer shell crumbled. As larger chunks slowly cracked away, releasing greater amounts of power, Cabe was astonished that he had not been affected so far. Part of his heritage, or just luck? It was senseless to run, he realized. Power such as this would overwhelm him no matter how hard he ran.

A great series of cracks developed all over the crystal. Shards began to fly off. This was it. Cabe fell to the ground and found himself wondering just how large an area the power would flatten. Miles probably.

The shell collapsed.

Cabe ducked his head, and the world became chaos.

V

C ABE OPENED HIS eyes and, to his surprise, the world still existed.

"I've not had a day like this in an eternity, my friend! This promises to be interesting indeed!"

Cautiously, he raised his head and looked to the voice. Infinity, in the shape of a stallion, greeted him with the twinkle of an ice-blue eye. The creature called Darkhorse was standing between Cabe and the Lady, and the great flood of raw power had washed over it with little more effect than a summer sprinkle. The creature seemed in a very good mood, in fact, something that nonetheless did not lower Cabe's level of anxiety.

"Come, come! One of your ability shouldn't grovel in the dirt! Get up! I mean you no harm!" Darkhorse chuckled.

More out of fear than anything else, Cabe rose. Even at full height, he was still dwarfed by the creature.

"That's better!"

His eyes glancing here and there for the sword, Cabe asked, "Who are you?"

The cold eyes stared through his very being. "I am Darkhorse, of course!"

"Are you a demon?" Cabe found it difficult to look at Darkhorse for very long, for to do so made him feel a dizziness that threatened to pull him toward the endlessness of the steed's inner body.

The creature snorted. "To demons I may be a demon! To most others, I am he who brings an end to all time!"

That sounded suspiciously close to death, Cabe thought. Small wonder the firedrakes had had no chance, even with there being three of them. "I thank you for your help, Lord Darkhorse."

Laughter rocked the manor grounds. "Lord! Darkhorse a lord? You do me great honor, Master Bedlam! Darkhorse can never be lord, for such was not written into the multiverse!"

Cabe covered his ears. The other's voice threatened to shatter his eardrums. Accidentally, he glanced toward the broken prison. Lying on the ground, apparently unhurt, was the unconscious form of the Lady.

The gaze of Darkhorse followed his. "You'd best see to her, my friend! I fear she won't take too kindly to my interference, even if I mean her only good!"

Cautiously skirting his unreal companion, Cabe moved over and bent down to examine the woman in green. He was again struck by her beauty. He was almost afraid to touch her, as if that touch would taint the perfection of her form. Fortunately, reason took over and he lifted her up and placed her on softer ground.

She stirred.

Cabe found himself staring into eyes that pulled at him as emotionally as Darkhorse's infernal form pulled at him physically. When she whispered something too softly for him to hear, he put his ear closer.

"Nathan." She smiled and lapsed into unconsciousness once more.

Darkhorse trotted up for a better look. "She has not changed . . . which is all the more reason for me to leave you for a time! You and the Lady Gwen may have to find some sort of transportation to Penacles if I do not return in time!"

"I have a horse—"

"Master Bedlam! I was your noble steed! I had to play the part of the fearful mount so that the dams would allow you to enter. A demon I am not, but my nature is much like theirs, and so stronger barrier spells affect me as they would them! Without someone willing to summon me, I cannot enter areas that are well secured by such enchantments! Especially when the spell was cast by a power like the Lady herself!"

The creature wandered away and studied the lands of the manor. It seemed somewhat annoyed. "When I leave this area, you will have to give me permission to enter when I return! If that woman awakes before I come back, do it quietly. She will never allow me in willingly! Ha!"

With a sudden leap, Darkhorse disappeared into the forest. Cabe felt a pulling, as if something were resealing itself. When he looked around, he discovered that, for all practical purposes, he and the Lady were alone.

Alone? Something else seemed to tug for his attention. Cabe used one hand to shift what remained of the amber prison. Uncovering the hilt of a sword, he pulled his hand away. It would not do to touch that blade. Not now, anyway.

With little else to do, he tried to rest. The creature called Darkhorse seemed confident of the woman's ability to survive. Cabe had no training in healing and knew that it would be impossible to locate anyone in this area. For that matter, any stranger could very well turn out to be another firedrake or some other sinister terror.

Reluctantly, he allowed himself to drift off into sleep.

"WE SHOULD NOT be so close to the Tyber Mountains, Twann."

Twann, a burly, very ugly man with more scars on him than many an army veteran, grunted at his equally ugly companion. "It couldn't a been helped, Rolf. The city guards back in Talak had all the southern roads watched. I know! I scouted 'em while you went off on a drunk after we hit that merchant!"

Rolf scratched his balding head. "I suppose you're right. I just don't like riding close to this area. You know what's supposed to go on here."

"Pfah! Legends! What do the Dragon Kings care about us, anyway? We're just two hardworkin' fellows. Like bugs to them."

"Bugs get squashed."

Annoyed, Twann turned on his companion. "Perhaps you would rather try riding through the Dagora Forest? At least here, we can't be surprised. We can see for miles and miles. Anything coming from the mountains will be so high up that we'll easily reach cover."

The other said nothing. It was futile to argue with Twann, and Rolf had no better ideas.

They rode on, now and then discussing plans for the future. Mito Pica seemed the most likely spot to head for. It was a city large enough to hide them easily, and it was located in the general center of the Dragonrealm. All they needed to do was head east for a short time and then turn southward. If Mito Pica proved unsatisfactory, they would head east from there to Wenslis.

They traveled near the base of a particularly large mountain. Something seemed unreal about it. Rolf slowed his horse and squinted at it. It was almost as if the mountain was not quite there. He grabbed at Twann's filthy shirt and attracted his attention to the great leviathan.

"Look close. Somethin' looks funny!"

In the dim light of the moons, Twann's tired eyes could see nothing. "You're beat! We'll ride another hour and then stop."

"I'm tellin' you that the mountain ain't there! Take another look!"

Twann sighed and humored his companion. The sight chilled him. Wordlessly, he pointed a finger. Rolf smiled, satisfied that his fool of a partner had seen what he had. He turned his head toward the mountain.

The dragons came out in great numbers.

Most were minor drakes, barely intelligent animals useful to their brothers only as shock troops because of their great numbers. Most lacked the vestigial wings and therefore ran or crawled or hopped. Firedrakes, in their true forms, flew overhead, keeping the masses under control. Scaled abominations and things that could not be described by words followed. It had to be an advance party ordered out at the last moment by Gold's commander.

The two thugs were in their path.

Rolf's horse panicked, threw him, and ran off, ignoring the man's shouts. Rolf looked at the advancing monsters and turned to his partner for help.

Twann, quickly measuring the shrinking distance between the dragons and himself, shouted, "To hell with you!"

The other man watched him ride off, the horror dawning on him. He tried to run, but the first of the minor drakes was already upon him. It was more serpent than lizard, and it half slithered as it moved. Gaping jaws clamped on to him. A scream of surprise and pain, then silence.

Ahead, Twann could hear the scream. He had only momentary regrets and then concentrated on increasing the speed of his mount. He had little to worry about on that aspect; the animal was doing its best to save its own life. Nevertheless, the distance was still decreasing. Minor drakes were the steeds of the ruling class. When Dragon Kings and their liegemen traveled in the forms of humans, minor drakes were enchanted to appear as horses. This allowed the dragons to travel through the lands without attracting attention. Though they ruled over nearly all of the realm, the Dragon Kings and their relations were, for the most part, solitary and private creatures.

Even with only the dim light of the moons, Twann was able to notice the dark shadow that passed over him. He looked up in panic. A huge firedrake, eyes glowing, came swooping down. The thug pulled out his sword, knowing full well how futile that would be.

The great claws closed upon him.

The horde raced on. Talak was their first destination.

* * *

WHEN CABE AWOKE, darkness was all that met his eyes. He did not know if he had slept minutes, hours, or days. Darkhorse had not returned. He shuddered, and almost wished the fantastic being was here.

There was a slight fluttering. Cabe stood up abruptly. The trees blocked most of the light from the Twins. Styx was barely visible at all. Cabe was not sure whether all of the strange creations of released magic had vanished. He began to grope for the sword. Now he was willing to hold it.

Something fluttered nearby. Cabe recalled the barrier to Darkhorse. Suppose his bizarre ally had tried to come, but had been prevented. He may have finally given up and left. That would leave him all alone to face—what?

That the barrier did not prevent all creatures from entering was evidenced by the dams. They had lived here for countless seasons. What else might have found its way here?

The sword. It should have been near him, but he could not find it in the darkness. He began to dig frantically. It had to be here! For a brief second, he felt something like the pommel. His search, though, was interrupted by the sudden sound of great, beating wings coming from behind him. He whirled about.

Something landed in front of him. He could not make out much of its features, but it did not appear to be a firedrake. . . . No, it seemed more birdlike, or manlike, he thought as two clawed arms reached for him. He ducked away, barely avoiding its touch.

The avian moved after him with such accuracy that Cabe suspected it had night vision. There would be no rescue this time. Whatever happened would depend upon his actions.

In the darkness, he nearly stumbled over something. It was long and hard, possibly a branch. He quickly reached down and picked it up. It was not much, but it felt better than being totally unarmed. At any rate, the bird-creature had now become more cautious in its attack.

Desperation set in. Cabe swung the branch at his opponent. The wings flapped, lifting the avian away from the piece of wood. It landed a short distance away and waited for the man to make his next move. Cabe started toward it, remembered his precious burden, and backed up. He would defend the Lady at whatever cost.

The avian fluttered up into the air until it was up more than four times Cabe's height. It flew toward him, hovered out of reach, and then flew around him. Cabe spun around, ready for the attack, but the bird-creature merely continued circling him. Its pace had increased, and the man found it hard to keep his eyes on the thing without becoming too dizzy.

Around and around it flew, never within striking distance. Cabe threw the branch at it, but missed. It was a foolish act, but he was quickly becoming disoriented and needed to do something.

Cabe paused to clear his head. That was the moment the avian had been waiting for. Swooping down, it landed behind him. Clawed hands reached out and grabbed hold of his head. Cabe jerked as his mind suddenly left the present.

He found himself traveling backward. The Seeker—the name came to him, though he knew not how—had found what it had sought.

IT WAS DARK, but not the dark of night. Rather, it was the darkness of nothing. A void.

Something of importance was lacking.

Cabe came screaming into existence, but he was not himself. Unborn, he was older than his mother and father.

Pain.

Memory of pain.

A bright light, quickly coming; he had to get away. He had to. Had to.

THE ONE WHO called himself Simon was alone. The Lord Gryphon had had other things to attend to, and the warlock wished to be alone anyway, for only in privacy could he find any hope at all.

A great voice shattered his thoughts. "As morbid as always!"

The warlock lifted his head and may have blinked. "Darkhorse. I wasn't expecting you yet."

The creature of eternity laughed. "Rubbish! You expect everything! I know you too well!"

Simon nodded. "More than anyone else could."

Darkhorse trotted closer. Despite his form, not one object was knocked out of place. Darkhorse moved only what he wished to move. "I come to tell you that young Bedlam has succeeded in freeing the Lady, with the Horned Blade, as you predicted and no doubt knew already, of course."

"Was there trouble?"

"The dams? They will seduce no man ever again."

"I meant with the power buildup. The Lady has waited a long time."

The creature snorted. "I absorbed everything! Wild energy is of little concern to me! If it had not been controlled . . . Ha! Why imagine disasters that did not happen? Now, as for those two, the only thing they need to worry about is rest."

The warlock said nothing. Instead, he picked up the Egg and held it up to his unearthly companion. Darkhorse shook his head in irritation and fixed a cold blue eye on the warlock. Any other man would have shrunk back, but he who called himself Simon did not.

"Look into the Egg."

"You know that I cannot! The Egg is useless to me. All I see is mist!"

"Try."

Something in the warlock's voice made the creature obey. Few others could do such a thing, but Darkhorse knew who and what it was he faced. Simon was beyond his powers, his fate in the hands of another. That may have been why the creature could call him friend. Eternity had been lonely.

An almost human sigh. "I will try."

Darkhorse stared into Yalak's Egg. Simon may have watched the mist closely. It swirled, like a beast of Chaos tearing at its chains, the darkness becoming deeper and deeper. The mist vanished, leaving a void so vast that it threatened to pull even Darkhorse into it.

The great steed pulled his gaze away quickly. "No more! I will look no more!"

"What was it?" Though the warlock asked a question, his tone was that of someone seeking confirmation of a fact already known.

The eye fixed on him. "It is where we two may not go. It is where I have sent countless others. It is the place from which none may return."

The blurred features of Simon may have added a deeper frown. "Then what does it mean? I am not like the Gryphon. I believe that anything the Egg shows us must have meaning."

"Perhaps, but then again, you may be wrong."

"No. I feel that there is some significance as far as Cabe is concerned. If I could see it again . . ."

"I will not go through that again!"

The warlock shook his head. "I would not ask you to."

Darkhorse changed the subject abruptly. "The Lady will soon wake. I do not relish returning there and confronting her. Though she cannot kill me, she has the power to exile me for a long time."

"She will care for you even less when she learns that I am the one who summoned you."

The spectral horse nodded. "You, I think, would face worse than exile."

The face beneath the hood was unusually distinct. There was an impression of a young man with eyes that seemed as eternal as his companion. "I already do. I do not fear her hatred."

There was silence. Darkhorse felt strangely mortal. He shook off the feeling. "I will return to Bedlam and the Lady."

"Safe journey, my friend."

Darkhorse started to laugh, thought about it, and sobered. With a roar, he opened up The Path Which Men May Travel Only Once and disappeared. There were sounds in the wake of his going. Unreal sounds that his companion knew all too well. *Damned souls* was the closest description he could find.

Thoughtfully, he who called himself Simon sat stroking the Egg.

THE CONTACT WAS broken.

He was back at the manor. The avian flew from him, shrieking in anger. Though it was dark, a strange light illuminated the nearby area.

"Wake up! The Seeker will try again!"

Cabe blinked. What had happened to him? Why had all the details of his life become so realistic yet so sketchy?

There was another shriek. He looked up and immediately regretted that action. Above him, almost hovering, was the huge bird-creature. It had arms and legs similar to a man's, save that the knees were reversed, like a real bird's, and all four limbs ended in great, clawed digits. It was musty gray, and the hawklike features of its face gave every indication of a predator. And it was starting to swoop down on him again.

A great ball of light burst in front of it. The avian stopped in midair, blinking rapidly and flying slightly wobbly. When another flash burst, the creature took flight into the cover of night.

Now that the threat was gone, Cabe whirled around to see his savior.

The Lady faced him. Though she had saved him from the Seeker, she did not seem to trust him. Cabe couldn't blame her. It would be hard to trust anybody after being trapped for such a long time. He decided that the safest thing to do would be to let her make the first move, providing that she did not destroy him outright.

"Who are you?"

The voice had a musical quality to it, and Cabe would have found it quite wonderful at any other time. Now, however, he could hear the menace in it.

"My name's Cabe. I—I freed you."

The expression on her face indicated that she found his story more than a little difficult to believe. "How were you able to free me? The spell that formed the prison was one of the most powerful ever used. No ordinary man could break it!" She glanced at his hair and saw the silver. "Warlock! I was right! No ordinary man could break Azran's spell!"

Something fluttered in the shadows behind the Lady. Cabe squinted. With shocking speed, the avian attacked.

"Look out!"

The sorceress turned, but had no time to defend herself. One of the Seeker's clawed feet struck her, and she tumbled to the ground. Cabe's frustration grew; he longed for the power to lash out. The bird-creature shrieked and came for him. Involuntarily, he thrust both arms straight out, the tips of his fingers aimed at the Seeker.

A line of force burst from his hands. The avian, unsuspecting, felt the full brunt of the attack, and was thrown back by a force much stronger than that used by the Lady. It tumbled into the nearest trees, striking one awkwardly with an arm. There was a crack, and the Seeker shrieked, this time in pain.

Flapping very ungracefully, the avian flew off. This time, however, it was obvious the creature had no intention of coming back. Cabe watched it disappear into the dark and then sat down on the ground in relief. It took him a moment to remember his companion. When he turned to check her condition, he saw that she was staring at him closely.

"Your actions are unskilled, but your power is potent." Her hands were once again prepared for attack. "Who did you say you are?"

Cabe groaned inwardly. "Cabe—Cabe Bedlam, if I believe what's been said."

The Lady's eyes widened. There was shock and . . . some emotion that could not really be given a label. She studied his face for several moments and then, much to Cabe's relief, relaxed.

"I should have seen it in your face. Power that great comes along only now and then. The coincidence is too much. What"—she paused to wipe away a tear—"is your relation to Nathan?"

"I've been told I'm his grandson. I found out only recently. One of the Dragon Kings—"

"Dragon Kings!" The hatred in the Lady's voice was so fierce that Cabe shrank back. "I had forgotten those cursed lizards! They still rule!"

She slumped. For a moment, Cabe thought she had fainted, but she slowly looked up again. "Nathan—is he alive?"

He could not bring himself to say it. He shook his head.

"Nathan!" She looked up to the heavens. Suddenly, she was not the Lady, but merely a woman named Gwen. Cabe had forgotten the name, so awed was he by her earlier.

"Azran!" This time, it was the Lady speaking. The hatred was as intense as that for the Dragon Kings. "By his son betrayed!"

Cabe had lost track of what she was saying, but did not dare interrupt. The Lady Gwen finally looked at him again.

"I knew your grandfather well. Loved him. I was on my way to help him when Azran imprisoned me. I suppose Nathan died in the struggle against the Dragon Kings."

"He took the Purple Dragon with him. Everyone knows that."

That made her smile. "Nathan! Even in the end he did his part! Who now rules in Penacles?"

"The Gryphon."

"We must go to him. I must learn everything I can before I face those reptiles again. And Azran." The smile turned grim. "You'd best come with me."

"I was going there anyway." The trials of the last few days started spilling out. "If the body of the Dragon King is found, they're sure to—"

"Dead? Which one?"

"I think it was the Brown Dragon. We were in the Barren Lands."

She nodded. "That would be Brown. So . . . they know about you too. You are in great danger. Every firedrake will hunt you in the hopes of gaining glory from their masters."

"I have a sword that frightens them. I used it on a basilisk and the firedrakes. I think it's called the Horned Blade."

The Lady shivered. "An evil sword. It will save you from one enemy, but draw the other to you. Azran had it cast—when he believed he could conquer both Kings and Masters—but lost it. Lost it only after he had murdered several times! He will want it, and you. I know not which he will desire more."

"Who is Azran?"

She pursed her lips. "Azran is one of the most powerful warlocks alive. His power rivaled that of Nathan's. Not surprising, really." Gwen paused. "Azran was his son." She watched Cabe's expression turn to shock.

"Your father, Cabe Bedlam."

VI

AZRAN WAS FURIOUS.
The ancient seer paced the length of his dim abode. Things of the dark chittered around him, waiting for commands but receiving only silence. None had the power to re-create the skull of Yalak, master of foresight. That was what Azran wished.

He snorted. Foresight. It had not saved Yalak from dying nor had it prevented his skull from being ensorcelled by Azran. The warlock had used the skull many times since. Never had it spoken of its own will. Something was amiss.

A dark shadow fluttered outside. Azran stopped his pacing and moved with great determination to his balcony. His tired legs screamed out their annoyance at such abuse.

It was waiting for him. Though the Seeker would have easily torn him to pieces, it could not. It was his. They all were. More ancient than the Dragon Kings themselves, the avians were still no match for the warlock's power. His slaves, they were his eyes and ears in the outside world.

The Seeker knelt. Azran put one hand gently on its head. This was no sign of affection. The old necromancer cared for no one. Not his late wife, his deceased brother, his son, or—most of all—his father. No, there was no affection in his touch. The contact served only to relay information from the mind of the bird-creature to himself.

A picture formed, that of the Tyber Mountains. This, Azran realized, was the spy he had sent to watch the Dragon Kings. For a brief moment, he wondered what had happened to the other. He shook his head. His mind must be clear for contact. He forgot all else and concentrated on the images.

The words of the reptiles were heard as the Seeker had heard them. The warlock nodded. As he had suspected, the Kings were on the move.

Azran briefly remembered kicking the pieces of the shattered skull as they lay scattered over the floor. Everything in this business had to be so mystifying. Why couldn't someone just come out and say what they meant? Where was it written that the dark arts had to be mystifying? Complex, yes. Otherwise, any fool could lay waste to the Dragonrealm. Mystery, however, tended only to irritate him.

He realized that he had broken contact, but the Seeker apparently had already told him all he needed to know. Now the avian awaited his next command. Azran pondered his next move. It would have been easier if the other had returned, but he knew that the creature would not fly back until it had completed its mission. Therefore, he would have to plan without the knowledge it might carry.

Penacles seemed to be an important factor in the coming crisis. Azran had always meant to wrest the city from the Gryphon, but the thought that the lionbird might have the knowledge to destroy him had always prevented such an act. It was well known that the Purple Dragon had been the real power of the Dragon Kings. Gold was strong, but he had ruled only because his brother had had no desire.

Still, his father had destroyed the reptile. Azran had to acknowledge that fact. Without a weapon like the Horned Blade, too. The old warlock was no fool; in his younger days, he would have never gone up against a Dragon King unarmed. Cursing, he remembered the loss of his sword. Who would have suspected that one of the Kings would be nearby when Azran had slain Yalak? Brown, his lands dying rapidly from the Masters' spell, had needed a weapon. To him, the young warlock was only an annoyance. Azran was just completing his spell to control Yalak's skull when the Dragon King had ridden by and grabbed the dark blade.

A sword meant to kill dragons in the hands of one. It was almost funny. Almost.

Nevertheless, Azran had felt something recently. The Horned Blade was making its way toward Penacles. It had also tasted Dragon King blood. Only such could have reanimated the life force that existed in the sword. Someone else had the blade, and that someone had great power. It was too much of a coincidence. Azran would have to send a spy to the City of Knowledge.

He motioned for the Seeker to stand. It did so, never taking its predatory eyes off him. He wondered what it would do if he ever released it from his power. Probably would rend him to ribbons. It was no secret to him that the avians hated him. It didn't matter; they also feared him too much.

His orders to the creature were short and simple. It was to watch for a traveler carrying the black blade. Whether the sword was hidden would not matter; the Seeker would recognize its presence. In the meantime, the avian must listen for whatever information it could find concerning the Gryphon's movements. There was no doubt that the ruler of Penacles would already be preparing for conflict. To underestimate the Gryphon was to invite disaster, for he was almost as devious as Azran.

The Seeker squawked once to acknowledge its understanding and spread its wings. Azran stepped back as the great creature flew off. He hated sending it away without knowing more about who had the sword. He scratched his chin. There was something else. The path of the Horned Blade would take it near . . .

Azran whirled and stalked over to his charts of the Dragonrealm. Selecting the one that interested him, he studied what he assumed would be the most logical path. After a moment, he nodded. The manor was a bit out of the way, but he had a strong suspicion that it had been a stopping point regardless. There were firedrakes there, but anyone with even the slightest ability would be able to hold them off with the sword.

Yes, he thought, *she is free.*

He knew that he should have destroyed her, but envy had prevented him. The Lady had preferred his father. The ultimate insult. Well, he'd taught her, trapped her so no one else could have her, especially him. The trouble was, he had always been the type to lust, but not the type to do something about it. Besides, the Lady intimidated him.

A wizened hand scratched a bald and wrinkled head. There was a third reason. The necromancer's time had been taken up by something far more important. So important, in fact, that he had forgone even casting spells of youth. Soon, though, he would be young again. Soon his masterpiece would be finished. That thought held him like a drug did an addict.

He chuckled. Casting a minor spell, he opened the passage to his most private of workshops. Only he could step through the gate; anyone else trying would find themselves randomly teleported to one of a number of hellish locations. Azran would allow no disruptions where his prize was concerned.

This was his true inner sanctum. Let them tear apart his castle; they would find only minor spells in comparison. But should they dare to attempt invasion of this place, they would suffer the consequences.

It was simple, a principle applied to his masterpiece as well. Each time he entered, Azran would leave a small portion of his power. Each time, then, the enchantment would grow. It drained him for a time, but it was well worth it. Especially if one knew of the results.

A thing not of any true world crawled toward him. Azran dismissed it back to the unnameable regions. A second spell dismissed the horrendous odor it had left behind. The warlock's nose wrinkled; sometimes it was almost not worth dealing with the things. The least they could do is learn to be clean.

Slowly, almost reverently, he turned his attention to a long, black casket in the center of the laboratory. It might have been the final resting place of a serpent—if Azran had ever had any pets—for its length. The width of it was slightly longer than his hand, as was the height. He caressed the lid in a loving fashion, for what it contained was truly part of him. He had poured more of his power into the contents of the box than he had into a hundred other potent spells. He took off the lid cautiously. This would be his glory and his triumph. This would lay the Dragonrealm at his feet.

Carefully, majestically, he reached in and grasped the hilt of the Nameless.

TALAK WAS A city somewhat secluded. Its closest neighbor was Mito Pica, but that city was more than two weeks' journey to the southeast. Not that it really bothered the inhabitants too much, for they produced nearly everything they needed and their army was considered one of the best in the lands. Besides, they had always tried to maintain peace with the Dragon Kings. The ruins of a sister city, some miles to the east, was a great incentive.

Rennek IV was now ruler of Talak. He was well into his fifties, plump and gray-haired. Once, he had been a powerful warrior, but today, some whispered that it would be better if his son, Melicard, sat on the throne. No one, of course, said it too loudly, for Rennek still had occasional outbursts of ability, especially when angered.

He was angered now. Something was persisting in dragging him from his dreams. He tried in vain to ignore the din, but it seemed only to increase the more he covered his head. Swearing by his three earlier namesakes, the ruler of Talak lifted his form from the bed, put on one of the royal robes, and burst into the hallway screaming.

"Hazar! Where are you? Come to me quickly or I will have a new prime minister!"

He looked around. Even the guards were nowhere to be seen. Ignoring his rather unroyal appearance, Rennek marched through the castle in the hopes of finding someone to lash out at. He caught a frightened servant who was crouching in a corner and pulled the man to his feet. The servant was quivering.

"Basil! What is going on? What is that noise? Where is Hazar?"

"They—they're here, milord! At the gates!"

King Rennek shook the man. "Who, blast you? Who? Where's Hazar?"

"At the gate!"

Cursing, he released the servant. Before looking for Hazar, he would first get a glimpse of this army. The story did not quite ring true; if there was an army at the gates, then why was there no sound of a clash of arms? If there was no army, then why were his servants so frightened?

He located the nearest window opening to the front and leaned out. It was still dark, but he could make out several forms, none of which seemed human. The sounds that had awakened him were those of animals, not men at war. Unfortunately, the night would show him little else, and he could not wait for the approaching dawn. He would have to go down now.

With no servants to attend him, Rennek was forced to dress himself. He was only partially successful; the years of the crown had made him lazier. When he was finally satisfied, he hurried quickly through the castle, slowing only when frightened servants or guards spotted him. He must seem in control, he knew, even if he really was not.

Coming down the stairs, he heard what sounded like the voice of his prime minister, Hazar Aran. The high-pitched tones indicated that Hazar was doing his best to please someone. Another voice interrupted, and King Rennek shivered at the sound of it. It was almost like listening to a snake.

Snake?

He walked majestically into the main hall. Hazar was not his usual sly self. He appeared actually pleased to see his lord. Rennek immediately knew why, and suddenly he wished he had followed the wishes of his people and allowed his son to take over.

The dragonhelm turned to face him. Half hidden by the enclosing darkness of the helm were a pair of red, glowing eyes. The helm itself was only slightly ornate. This was not one of the Dragon Kings, but one of their dukes, a firedrake in human form. As Rennek watched the massive warrior stalk toward him, the king knew he would have to treat this duke as if he were one of the Kings themselves.

"You are King Rennek?" The words were breathed, not spoken.

"I am." The monarch tried to look impressive.

"I am Kyrg. My force has come from the Tyber Mountains."

The Tyber Mountains. These were some of the hellish forces of the emperor. The Gold Dragon. To disobey would mean instant retribution. To make even a small mistake would mean the same conclusion.

"What is it your august majesty wishes with my city? We will, of course, help you in any way we can." He hoped he sounded formal enough.

Kyrg laughed, and it was the laugh of a mass murderer sizing up his prey.

"Your city? You may rule the people here, but this city belongs to the King of Kings! You will assist us because you are commanded to!"

Rennek felt his reserve slip away. "Uh . . . yes. Of course."

The infernal duke nodded. "Good. Now, then, we have a great journey ahead of us. We require food for that journey."

The sweetness of the reptile's words served only to make him more frightening. Rennek had horrifying visions of what sort of food the duke might want for his inhuman army. It would not have been the first time; such tales had been spread through the generations.

Kyrg seemed to read his thoughts. "We will take only livestock this time. Should you ever seek to betray us or should you fail us in some capacity, then we will come for other meats, starting with the leadership of this city. Do you understand me?"

Both king and prime minister paled.

Rennek managed a nod.

"Excellent." The duke motioned to his aides. One of them disappeared through the open entrance of the castle. Kyrg pulled out a piece of parchment.

"Can you read?" The voice dripped of sarcasm and contempt.

"Of course! One of the first thi—"

"Numbers?"

The king shrugged. "Fairly well."

The shapeshifter handed him the parchment. Rennek unrolled it.

"This will tell you exactly how much we require. You will gather it in four hours." The duke held up one of his gloved hands to emphasize the time. There were only three fingers and a thumb. Humanoid the firedrakes might appear, but human they were not.

The king of Talak glanced down at the list. While the numbers themselves were a little difficult to comprehend, the enormousness of the task did not escape him. "It will take us at least a day."

"Fourrr hoursss." Kyrg's voice had lost almost all traces of humanity it might have possessed before. "If you do not complete the task in the time period specified, we will take what we need. Indiscriminately."

Rennek shoved the parchment into the hands of his prime minister. The thin man looked at it as if it would devour him. The king looked at his adviser nervously.

"Get on with it, man! Hurry!"

Hazar stumbled away quickly. Rennek glanced at his unholy guest and caught just a shadow of a smile beneath the sinister dragonhelm. "Will there be anything else?"

Kyrg glanced around the room. "Yesss. I have not eaten recently. Nor have my officers. While your people gather up the necessary food, we will dine in your hall. You will have your butchers prepare two of your finest animals for us. You will join us. I wish to learn what I can of the lands to the south."

"Of course. Just let me instruct my cooks as to your pref—"

"The butchers will be sufficient. We prefer our meat very rare. Raw, in fact."

The king felt his stomach turn. This time, he could definitely see the smile on the firedrake's half-hidden face. The duke bowed to him in mock respect.

"Lead the way, Your Majesty."

DAWN CAME TO the manor, and with it came the flood of memories. Cabe tried to keep his eyes shut, but the sound of another finally forced him up.

The couch was now surprisingly uncomfortable. Cabe had been too exhausted and had simply chosen the first soft place to fall down on. The Lady Gwen had been slightly more discerning; she had created a bed of air. Even the sight of a woman floating three feet above ground had not been enough to prevent Cabe from collapsing. The unusual was just not so unusual anymore.

Dangerous, yes; unusual, no.

The Lady was wandering around the manor, apparently reliving memories. To Cabe, she was more beautiful than when he had seen her last. There was, however, a sadness in her movements. A hand would gently touch an object and then quickly pull away. Eyes would stare off into realms of the past, only to immediately lower and return to the present.

Cabe remained quiet in the fear of disturbing her, but she finally turned her attention to him.

"We should be moving on. I wish to speak with the Gryphon as soon as possible. As it is, it will take days to reach him."

"Can't you teleport? I've known of sorcerors who do."

"To teleport, one must know one's destination. I've never been to Penacles. Besides, I really don't feel well enough. We'd best ride. You have a horse, don't you?"

It was a difficult question to answer, especially when Cabe remembered

Darkhorse's remarks concerning the Lady's enmity toward the creature. "Sort of."

The frown of her face did not detract from its beauty. "Sort of? What answer is that?"

Cabe's response was prevented by a crashing noise in the forest. Gwen turned at the sound and stared, as if trying to see through both manor and woods.

"What is that?"

"My . . . horse."

"Your horse? How unusual an animal it must be. I think I'd like to have a closer look at it." She waved her left hand and with it drew two circles, the latter reversed from the former. There was a slight shuddering in the air, and then the eerie form of Darkhorse leaped into sight.

"At last! I thought I'd never get someone's attention!"

"Darkhorse! Demon!" The Lady pointed both hands in the direction of the steed. A wave of force erupted, aimed straight for the center of the darkling creature.

Her target merely stood there, taking the power as one might take a drink of water. Darkhorse laughed. "Raw power is not the answer, Lady Gwen! It never was! Besides, I come in peace!"

The Lady's face was a mask of rage. "Knowing you and those you deal with, I find little to believe in your statements!"

Darkhorse sighed. "Call me Prince of Darkness, Lucifer, Thanatos, Death—if you wish! You know my nature, but not my mind! If I am different, it is because one must be so when eternal! Otherwise, madness would've taken me long ago!"

Cabe felt forced to intervene. "He helped, Lady Gwen. The firedrake dams would have taken me."

She looked at him with eyes that burned. He knew that she was capable of leaning either way. She could possibly cast out Darkhorse, but Cabe was a target that had no such immunity. He tried desperately to hide his nervousness.

Finally, though, she lowered her hands. Cabe breathed only slightly more easily; the hands were still tensed. A wrong word or movement could quickly change things.

The fire-tressed sorceress spoke slowly. "Very well. I will trust you for now, Mount of the Infinite Journey. However, even the slightest of false moves will win you a long exile. You know I have the power. Be thankful my head was still muddled or I would have never tried so futile an act as using brute force."

The chilling eyes stared into her. "I will not play false, Lady Gwen. These events concern me as well as you."

Cabe chose to change the subject. "We were going to try and reach Penacles. The Lady wishes to confer with the Lord Gryphon."

"And he with her. The Dragon Kings are stirring. Something has done this, and events can now only be stalled, not prevented." Darkhorse nodded his head to the sorceress, who did not bother to respond. "You will be needed. We must also assure that Cabe reaches the city as well. He may be our trump card. He may be our one hope."

A deep chill passed through Cabe. If the dark steed's words were true, he would most likely find himself in the center of the worst situations. It was not a comforting thought, to say the least. He did not, however, say as much to his companions. It might lower him in their eyes, especially the Lady Gwen's.

Darkhorse lifted his head to the sky, his great, black mane falling back as he did so. "I cannot travel so swiftly in the light, but even that would not be safe for the two of you. We would also find ourselves easy targets for the Dragon Kings or others. I do not relish exile—for any length of time—and the options for you two are even dimmer. We must travel as most mortals do. We will attract fewer eyes."

"We have already attracted more than enough." It was the Lady Gwen who was speaking. "During the night, a Seeker attacked. Fortunately, it sought information more than anything else."

"Then Azran will know, being master over those ancients. He will also feel the presence of the Horned Blade."

She nodded. "We must hurry."

"I daresay. Azran is the sort who might even dare to slay me, if that is at all possible."

Cabe, remembering that they now stood in the center of the manor, thought of food. It had been a long time since he had eaten. He mentioned the idea to Gwen.

"I heartily agree, Cabe. I haven't had a decent meal in . . . several generations, I guess."

"Will there be anything left? I'm not sure I want to touch any food left by the firedrakes."

"We'll see. I kept most of my food in a hidden cellar. The place is sealed with a preservation spell. If it still holds, there will be plenty for us to eat."

A quick check by the Lady revealed that the cellar was not only still intact, but the preservation spell was also still in place. With Cabe's assistance, she gathered up a large amount of exotic foods. The would-be warlock's eyes feasted on the sight. Most of the items were unknown to him, but everything looked delicious.

The emerald enchantress then formed a second pile of much more ordinary foods. These, she indicated, were their supplies for the journey. Cabe nodded, mentally reminding himself to eat as much as possible before they left.

The two humans ate with a passion. Darkhorse commented on the sin of gluttony, but was interrupted by Cabe, who tossed a large, juicy piece of fruit to him. The eternal ceased his remarks and absorbed the food slowly into his form. Although having no need for sustenance, he apparently enjoyed the tastes.

When the meal was over and various other activities had been taken care of, the great steed reassumed his earlier form of an actual horse and allowed the two to mount. Cabe offered his assistance to the Lady, who seemed unsure about whether to sit on the back of a creature she hated. Assuring himself that the Horned Blade was secure in its sheath, Cabe climbed on in front of his companion.

There were reins, but no saddle. Gwen held on to Cabe. Darkhorse turned his head as best he could.

"Are you ready?"

Cabe looked at the Lady. "What about the manor?"

She stared at it wistfully. "I've strengthened the spells. This time, nothing will get in unless I allow it."

He nodded and turned back to the horse. "We're ready."

"Hang on! I will push us as fast as a horse can possibly go!"

With a laugh, Darkhorse reared. Both riders held on tighter as he raced out of the manor and into the forest. With such transportation, they would have no trouble reaching Penacles.

Barring unexpected incidents, of course.

VII

THE GRYPHON ADMIRED his chess set.

"Things just aren't made the way they used to be, wouldn't you agree?"

The one who called himself Simon shrugged. "My memory is patchy, you know that."

The lord of Penacles picked up a single piece that was shaped like a dragon in flight. Its detail was striking. If anyone looked closely enough, they could see that even the smallest of the monster's scales had been carved in. While this was fascinating in itself, it was the Gryphon's opinion that this chess set was for more than just games. Then again, it may have been designed specifically for certain games—of godlike proportions.

The warlock interrupted his train of thought. "They are on their way."

"How soon?"

"Two days. Maybe three. Darkhorse must be cautious. He cannot die, I think, but he may be exiled for some time. Add to that that his passengers are still mortal."

The feathered hand placed the dragon back on the board. "And does she know that you will be here?"

"I thought it wise to have nothing said about my presence here."

"Just so long as the two of you do not destroy the city. I recall the stories about Sika. She may too."

Something that might have been a frown may have played across the other's face. "I have tried to make up for Sika. As I have for Detraq, Coona Falls, and a dozen other cities through the ages. Until I can put an end to myself, I will continue to try and make up for my sins."

"While you add new ones."

"Perhaps. I can only try, though."

The Gryphon walked over and put a clawed hand on Simon's shoulder. The warlock stiffened momentarily and then allowed himself to relax. It was obvious that the touch of the other disturbed him.

"Forgive me, my friend. I spoke without thinking."

The warlock shook his head. "You spoke the truth. I have lived long enough to know that. I am completely accountable for my actions."

"Let us change the subject. What news have we of the Dragon Kings?"

"Forces led by the firedrake known as Kyrg have stopped at Talak. There they demanded a vast quantity of meat."

"And received it, no doubt."

"Of course. They are now heading toward Mito Pica, and from there, the destination becomes obvious."

Nodding, the Gryphon walked thoughtfully over to his chess set. He picked up another piece, this time an armored knight, and fingered it as he spoke. "So. After all this time, the Dragon Kings move to regain the City of Knowledge. This time, though, there are no Masters to help us."

"We have the Lady. We also have Cabe. His powers alone could make the difference."

"Could. I would prefer something more concrete. If only we had Nathan himself."

For the briefest of moments, both were suddenly bathed in sharp, searing gusts of icy wind. The wind disappeared without trace and the room returned to normal. The two looked at each another.

"You felt that, warlock?"

Simon stood up and walked to a window. Only after he had scanned the surrounding areas did he speak. "An unusual breeze for this time of year."

The lionbird grunted. "Unusual for any time of year. It chilled more than the bones. I felt it in my mind. What was it?"

"Difficult to say. Perhaps the city has the answer."

"An interesting thought. I believe it might be best if we investigated at once."

Replacing the knight on his proper spot, the Gryphon moved over to a huge tapestry that covered one of the walls. On the tapestry was a representation of the City of Knowledge. Though the figurines had been very detailed, they paled in comparison to the picture now before him. Every building, every street, every wall; nothing was left out and nothing was incomplete. Even the eye could not have viewed a city so thoroughly.

The tapestry was the only sure way of locating the legendary libraries of Penacles. They moved, though no one knew how or why save their long-dead creators. Without the tapestry for guidance, one might seek libraries forever.

The warlock came over beside him. "Where is it this time?"

"There. See the small scroll design in the window of that house? The libraries will be under there." The Gryphon pointed to a small home on the outskirts. The scroll in the window was barely visible, and only a trained eye would have found it so quickly.

"Ready?"

Simon nodded. The Gryphon put one finger to the spot marked by the scroll and began to rub it gently. As he did so, the room around them blurred. Neither figure paid the change any attention. They had seen it several times before.

Slowly, the Gryphon's chamber vanished. The two of them were now standing in the middle of a strange sort of limbo, the only real object other than themselves being the tapestry. As the ruler of Penacles continued to rub, a new room began to take shape. At first it was as out of focus as the original, but gradually things became more distinct. Walls filled with books appeared around them, save for one long corridor.

A bright light with no discernible source illuminated the libraries. The floors were polished marble and the shelves were of some substance similar to but obviously not wood. The libraries were ancient; any wood would have rotted, crumbled, or petrified by now. Yet the shelves looked as if they had been set up only a few days before.

The shadowy face turned to him. "Where?"

"I have no idea. We shall require the uses of a librarian."

No sooner were the words spoken than a small, incredibly ancient figure stepped into sight. There was something not quite human about him, for his legs were much too short, the arms nearly touched the ground, and not one strand of hair could be seen on the egg-shaped head.

This was a gnome, one of the learned kind. There were very few of them; solitary, they cared more for their books than the companionship of other creatures. They ate very little and lived far longer than most other beings. They were, however, perfect librarians. In all the years the Gryphon had ruled, the gnomes had always been there.

"How may I help the present lord of Penacles and his companion this time?" The voice was cracked and seemed to emphasize the age of the gnome.

The Gryphon took no slight from the use of the word *present.* "We wish to know about winds. Cold, unusually numbing winds that appear out of nowhere and vanish almost instantly."

"A wind spell. Is that all?" The little librarian's disappointment was quite evident.

"It may be a wind spell. It may be something else. Whatever the case may be, I want to find out what I can about it."

The gnome, whose name no one knew, sighed and nodded. "Very well. Follow me. It isn't far."

It never was. Some had speculated that the libraries had an intelligence of their own and did what they could to speed up any search. Adding fuel to this speculation was the fact that the rows of books were not always the same color. Last time, for example, the countless volumes had all been blue. This particular visit, they were a bright orange. The Gryphon began to wonder if he was even talking to the same gnome or whether there were numerous little librarians hidden away in each area. It was something to ponder on in quieter times.

The gnome moved swiftly for a being of his type. He who called himself Simon had barely enough time to glance at some of the books as the three walked down the corridors. Oddly free of any dust, they might have contained the sum knowledge of the multiverse. Sadly, though, that was not the case. For all its information, Penacles lacked, so far as he knew, that which would release the warlock from his curse.

For some reason, the walk was taking longer than anticipated. The gnome muttered something and seemed almost worried. The Gryphon said nothing, but he could not recall ever having to walk this far to find the information he wanted.

"Ah!" The gnome pointed a bony finger at a new corridor. "This is the one. About time!"

With the little man leading, they turned. The librarian was the first to notice, and he screamed as if someone had torn his arms from their sockets. The Gryphon cursed, and his furred hands suddenly revealed long, sharp claws. The warlock merely nodded, as if he had suspected such earlier.

Before them, where the volumes they sought should have been, was a great, charred space.

IN THE FOG-SHROUDED land known as the Gray Mists, ghostly figures dressed in coal-black armor slowly marched their way west. There was a look in their eyes that would have caused most men to turn away.

From the dark city of Lochivar, in the land of the Black Dragon, they came.

AZRAN LAY ON his bed, as still as if he had died. The spell always took a tremendous toll on his system, and it would be hours before he was well enough to stand. Nevertheless, he was pleased. Very pleased. His crowning glory was nearly completed, for soon he would have the weapon that would break all others before it. Soon—

A great rush of wings alerted him to the presence of one of the Seekers. There was something odd about the sound of its landing. Azran suspected that the creature had run into trouble. Hard trouble, judging from its difficulties. He waited, knowing that the avian would come to him when it could.

When it appeared, it looked even worse than he had imagined. It had obviously been flash-burned, and that meant sorcery. One arm was twisted at an odd angle, and the ancient mage suspected it was useless. What, he wondered, had happened to his servant?

The Seeker stared down at him with its predatory eyes. Even as weak as the sorceror was, the creature could not attack him. Azran's spells had assured that. Wobbling, the Seeker kneeled at the foot of his bed and moved close enough so that his master could touch the crested head.

The images came again. First, there were the Barren Lands. Oddly, they were now not so barren. Azran's eyes widened as he saw the patch of grass that was spreading rapidly toward the center of the Brown Dragon's domain. Tremendous power would have been required for overcoming the curse laid down by the Dragon Masters. It was one of their most potent, designed to crush the strength of one of the more lethal of the Kings, and it had succeeded well. Brown's clans were now fewer than two dozen groups. Only a fraction of what they had once been.

That it had been performed under Styx and his pale sister was apparent. That the blood used was Dragon King blood was shocking. Azran almost lost contact as his hand jerked. So, that was the fate of Brown. Quite likely, the Dragon King had been intent on sacrificing someone else and had fallen prey to some attack. Yet two things bothered the warlock.

The Brown Dragon had possessed the Horned Blade.

To succeed with such a spell, the victim had to be a being of power. Who had Brown's intended victim been? The sword's present carrier, obviously, but that did not tell Azran names. There were very few people of Master status in the Dragonrealms; the Dragon Kings had seen to that. He knew of the Lady, the Gryphon, and the cursed, blurred warlock best called Shade, although his first names had been many. There were others, but none were worth calling a threat.

This new warlock was an enigma.

There was more to view, much more. Through the gleaming eyes of the Seeker, Azran viewed the passing of the firedrakes. There was no danger from such as these; other than the Kings, few of the reptiles could master more than the most minor of spells. He mentally ordered the avian to advance to the next memory.

The manor.

He had dreamed of mastering the woman who had lived there. Only dreamed, of course. That stung him more than anything else. Now it was too late. If he understood some of what had taken place, the Lady Gwen was undoubtedly itching to repay him for past indignities.

There was a slight jarring. The Seeker had passed through a spell of Shunning. Azran supposed that the spell had weakened somewhat since being placed on the Lady's dwelling. It was either that or the avian was stronger than it appeared.

The creature had quickly flown over the manor itself. As it reached the back, the crumbled ruins of the amber prison could easily be seen. That did not interest the old mage as much as the two figures near it. One was most definitely the Lady Gwen, apparently asleep or unconscious. But the other . . .

The Seeker was swooping in on the unsuspecting male. Azran had just a glimpse of a young, startled, and hauntingly familiar face before the image gave way to something else entirely.

It took him only a second to realize that the avian had pulled the stranger into a memory lock. Well versed in the Seeker's methods, Azran easily picked his way through the rambling thoughts, occasionally picking out bits and pieces that might be of importance to him. It was only when he started through the most recent memories that he called for more thorough play-through.

A large, blank spot greeted him at one point. Someone, of obviously powerful nature, had blocked all attempts by the creature to record a particular scene at young Cabe's—at least he had learned the name of his new enemy—place of employment. He contemplated kidnapping and questioning the owner, but shrugged it off. Whoever had cast the spell was no amateur; the inn's owner would probably also have a block, as well as anyone else who had happened to be there. Still, it did no more than delay, something the caster no doubt knew as well.

The scene that replaced the blankness proved more interesting. There was no doubt as to the identity of the demonic warrior seated at the table. It was indeed the Brown Dragon. Sheathed at his side was a presence all too familiar to Azran. The lord of the Barren Lands had carried the

Horned Blade with him on this journey. It was to be the tool by which the Dragon King would have sacrificed this new, unsuspecting warlock to the Twins.

He laughed slightly. Even the lizards were fools at times.

Azran skipped ahead to the moment of decision. Brown had unsheathed the Horned Blade, and the warlock was pleased to see that his first sword had not lost any of its power in the time since its theft. The Dragon King was saying something. The blade rose in the air—

The memory was cut short. Azran cursed by several of his more unsavory deities. He was back to the scene at the manor, and it was apparent that the Lady had just attacked. The Seeker's view became distorted as it turned its head this way and that. Frustration set in. The sorcerer still had no idea of what his adversary's face looked like and who he really was. There were bits and pieces that could be formed into assumptions, but . . .

Then, as he watched the fight, even to the point where the stranger unleashed his power, he could not believe it. He stared at the face again and again, knowing by the look and the feel that what he saw was true. He had never seen the child, never really known the mother, except as his servant. His father had seen to that.

My son, he thought bitterly. *My son is alive.*

He would have trained the boy carefully, making him strong but obedient. His father had been a fool where Azran's upbringing had been concerned, caring only for Dayn, the elder of the two. Leaving the teaching to amateurs was a mistake that had cost him. Azran had secretly turned to the more desirable forces of magic, the so-called dark powers. Once entranced, he had never wished to be free.

Releasing the Seeker from his touch, Azran ordered the creature away. The taint of Nathan was evident on Cabe; the boy might very well have to be destroyed. To allow him to train with the Lady or the Gryphon would be suicidal. He, Azran, would be the first target. Against Gwen or the Gryphon, he would be victor.

Cabe, however, was family. That made him more dangerous than the Dragon Kings.

Yes, his son must be captured, and there were only two who could do it. It would be difficult summoning them. Azran would have to rest another day. Though they were forced to obey, they still had the will to resist somewhat. They would do so, knowing that they would weaken him and possibly cause him to commit some fatal error.

The dead never made things easy.

DEEP BELOW THE Tyber Mountains, in the midst of the flow of magma, lay the eggs. Most were ordinary—wyverns, weak-minded beasts barely fit to be called dragons. A smaller group, glistening in the fiery light, were those that would hatch into firedrakes.

There remained two other groups. One consisted of only two eggs. The misfits. Mutants. Whether they hatched or not mattered little to the Dragon Kings. They were allowed to grow only so long as they did not harm the others. If they were unfit to live, they would be killed, as many of the smaller drakes would be.

The fourth and final group consisted of a handful of colorful, banded, and speckled eggs. They were much larger than the others and were carefully watched over by the strongest and wisest of the dams. These were to be the hope of the future. New Kings to replace those who had died or might soon.

The first of the eggs began to crack open.

RIDING HAD NEVER been so painful. It was not that they had been jostled; in fact, Darkhorse nearly flew across the land. The problem was in dealing with the speed and the length of time. The Lady was determined to reach Penacles as soon as possible and bade the steed to run as quickly as safety would permit. Cabe was under the impression that his idea of safe speeds greatly differed from his two companions.

It was Gwen, however, who was finally forced to call a halt. She was still unused to the needs of her system, and nearly fainted, almost causing both riders to fall off their mount. Only the eternal's maneuvering kept both humans on. Slowing to a trot, he gave Cabe the opportunity to assist the Lady. Her decision was made almost the moment she opened her eyes.

They were now on an open road, one of the few in the Dragonlands. Darkhorse turned off and trotted over to a small grove of oaks. Once down, the Lady opened up her pack and removed some food. Cabe grabbed one of the waterskins. The two of them sat down under one of the trees while their transportation pretended to graze nearby.

Gwen leaned back. "What a fool I am! Even a novice knows when their body can take only so much!"

Cabe nodded. "Every point on mine aches."

They divided the food. Cabe bit into a biscuit and discovered that, while lacking much in the way of taste, it filled him up and revived his tired muscles. He asked her what it was.

"It's elfin bread. Eat it enough and you might want to take on the Dragon Emperor's armies single-handed."

Cabe was tempted to spit out the piece in his mouth.

She laughed. A smile appeared momentarily. The Lady looked around at the grove.

"Nathan and I used to go on picnics now and then. It made us feel like ordinary people, not high-level sorcerors. Still, I wonder how many ordinary people could protect their picnics from dragons. Or ants, for that matter."

"What was my grandfather like?" He hesitated as he saw her face. "If you don't mind telling me, that is."

She smiled at him, and Cabe was once more in awe over her beauty. It dawned on him that this woman was old enough to be at least his grandmother, and almost had been.

"I met Nathan when I was only an apprentice. My teacher was an old wood witch. She and Nathan's wife, Lady Asrilla of Mito Pica, had been good friends. Tica, the witch, had even acted as midwife at Azran's birth." Her face clouded over. "He killed his mother with his birth. Nathan should have realized then that his second son was first in evil."

Cabe said nothing, but his thoughts were on this new family of his. It was not one in which loyalty played an important part. Father against son. Would this be repeated?

Gwen did not notice his faraway look. "I was awed by the power inherent in Nathan. The colors glowed more brightly than any I had ever seen. Colors, which I will teach you to see, are the true aspect of any magic-user's character. Until trained, they are generally bland. Whether one chooses the dark power or the light determines the final rainbow. Azran's became a bleak combination of blacks and grays."

Darkhorse let out a snort, but said nothing.

"Tica could teach me no more, but she knew I had tremendous potential. Therefore, she asked help from this great warlock. He was an imposing sight in his blue robes and hood, stern face staring at this young, gangling girl. I think I first started to love him then. His elder son, Dayn, was just finishing his apprenticeship, and his younger was being tutored elsewhere. Out of friendship, he accepted me. I did my best to live up to the standards

I thought he expected. I nearly killed myself doing it. Progress came rapidly, but it was at great cost."

The food was long forgotten. Cabe sat there, taking in everything.

"One day, while I was berating myself for fouling up a fairly simple spell, Nathan came to my room. There was a sadness in his face, and I thought that he was about to dismiss me from his home. Instead, he merely sat down in a chair and talked to me. Talked to me about his wife, his dreams, the Dragon Kings, and . . . my future. Before my eyes, he conjured up the image of a woman." She smiled. "At the time, I thought her the most beautiful woman I had ever seen. I told him this, expecting it to be the form of his late wife. It wasn't. Nathan said that he was showing me a picture of myself, once my powers were fully realized. I was shocked. Tica had never had this much power. My awe increased. It was at that point that he bent down and kissed me. That was all. Just kissed me. He said nothing else. I watched him walk out wordlessly."

The Lady looked deeply into Cabe's eyes. "Only later did I discover that he had just received the news that Azran had murdered his own brother."

Cabe was at a loss. "What—what did Nathan do?"

"What did he do? He tried to forgive him. Tried to bring him back into the light. Tried and failed. Azran had delved too deeply. He'd even made slaves out of his tutors. Worse yet, he sought out and found the Seekers. Found them and made them his slaves too."

"The Seekers. That bird-creature. You said it was a Seeker."

She nodded. "No one knows the history of the Seekers. They are said to be older than the Dragon Kings. Much older. They live in dark rookeries somewhere near the Hell Plains. Few men find the Seekers, and fewer still survive."

"What are they?"

"They once ruled this land. Now they search. Constantly. Always seeking information. No one knows why, even Azran, I suspect. He may have enslaved them, but he could not have dominated them completely. They are a tool that must be watched."

Remembering the stealth and strength of the creature, Cabe could only nod in agreement.

The Lady resumed her story. "I understood after that meeting that I had been pushing myself too hard. Nathan allowed me to ease things. Strangely, my lessons seemed to become simple. I followed his word to the letter, ignoring any mistakes. The mistakes became fewer and fewer. I soon came to realize that I was now as one with my powers. Instead of rushing out in spurts, it now flowed smoothly. Three years later, I was the image I had seen. It was then that Nathan told me how much he really loved me."

Her eyes stared absently as she remembered memories of what might have been yesterday. She had even forgotten the presence of Darkhorse. The infernal steed was still pretending to graze, though Cabe realized that the creature was very silent. After a minute, she blinked, wiped away a single tear, and pretended as if she had never stopped talking.

"The Masters were Nathan's idea. His and Yalak's. They were determined to destroy the Dragon Kings, who had ruled for as long as men could remember. This lot is the worst. They crushed all resistance and any advances men made beyond our present level. All servants were ordered to specifically seek out warlocks and such and to kill them. Fortunately, their servants often lacked the power. The Masters grew in strength and numbers until they were prepared to challenge. Thus, the Turning War began."

Turning War. Few people Cabe knew ever mentioned it by that name. Whole lands had been set into disarray; upheavals were everywhere. It was a stalemate. Lesser mages died, but scores of firedrakes did also. The war had finally turned to the City of Knowledge.

It was well known that much of the Dragon Kings' strategy came not from the emperor, but from the Purple Dragon, he who ruled Penacles. Knowing that, the Masters planned the final offensive. Yalak led a group to the Barren Lands, the site of the Masters' only true victory. He was to prevent the coming of Brown and his remaining clans. Lochivar, the city of the Gray Mists, would hold back the tide of Black. Nathan Bedlam would lead the rest on an all-out assault of the city.

"They were betrayed from the start. Lochivar, long in the Gray Mists, turned traitor. Instead of holding back the dragons, they led the march toward Penacles. If not for the Gryphon, they would have made it. We had never seen his like before, yet he met the betrayers with a small mercenary army and pushed them back. It was because of this that he became the new lord of Penacles."

More and more, Cabe longed to reach the city before anything else happened. As things stood, it was their only real hope for safety.

"Yalak was also betrayed. By Azran. That thing Nathan called a son struck him from behind with the Horned Blade. Yalak never even knew he was there. For once, his future-sight had failed him."

"How did the Dragon Kings gain control of the sword?"

Gwen smirked. "Even Azran is not all-knowing. Brown, seeing his enemies in confusion, sought to crush them. The lord of the Barren Lands had chosen to fight in his human form, but his weapon was broken. Seeing the Horned Blade and knowing it for what it was, he struck down Azran and stole the weapon. Would that he had killed him! It was at that point that I fled, seeking to join Nathan and secure the city before all was lost. Brown, though he finally defeated the Masters, could not give chase. His clans were perilously close to extinction."

The words of the Dragon King filled Cabe's mind. The hatred had been so overwhelming. Cabe could feel little compassion for the reptilian tyrant. Brown had created his own destruction.

The Lady was looking at him with amusement. "I'd heard there was a babe. Your mother was dead, and Nathan must've stolen you from your father rather than see you fall to the darkness. I—"

"Wait!" Something had finally dawned on Cabe. "You saw me?"

"Yes, but—"

The idea seemed impossible. "You have been asleep for years, decades!"

The insinuations were not lost on her. "Yes. I see what you mean, but I cannot explain it."

"I am only in the midst of my third ten-year! Yet your claim makes me an ancient!"

Darkhorse had stopped his grazing. Though he still wore the form of a real horse, the intelligence in the icy-blue eyes was unmistakable. The ears were at attention. He, too, realized the implications.

The sorceress began to cast a simple spell. Her fingers moved quickly as she spoke. "You remember only a normal life?"

"Only that. No one ever commented on my growth."

"Strange. I see that some spell has been cast over your form, but it is now so much a part of you that I cannot read it. I can tell, however, that it was beneficial to you, if anything."

"What do I do?"

She removed her spell. Cabe felt as if small tendrils had gently detached from his body. "I don't know." She turned to Darkhorse. "I am open to suggestions from you."

The dark steed snorted. "How magnanimous! For the lad, however, I can make only two suggestions! The first is that the spell was most likely the

work of Nathan Bedlam and may be the reason for Cabe's strange childhood. You said it appeared to be beneficial. The second suggestion is that
we put this problem aside until we reach Penacles. We may receive more
information there."

"Do you think that the libraries would know something of this?"

Darkhorse uncharacteristically pawed at the ground. "I was thinking of
another."

Her face darkened. "Who?"

Cabe, not realizing the change of mood, suddenly recalled. "Of course!
Simon!"

Gwen turned back to him. "Simon?"

He nodded. "He brought Darkhorse to me. He said he would be at
Penacles."

"Describe him." Her voice was cold.

"Tall. Wears a cloak and hood. I can't describe his face. It always seemed
a blur—"

"Shade!" The scream was akin to the one Gwen had emitted at knowing
of Darkhorse. "You accept help from one more cursed than Azran! Fool!"

"Lady Gwen, you know Shade's curse as well as I!" Darkhorse shouted
even more loudly than the Lady. Cabe was glad that the road was empty.

"I will kill him!"

"Ha! You would do more damage to this land! He has shifted the balance
once again, Lady Gwen!"

She calmed somewhat. "He works with the Gryphon?"

"Until his destruction! You know that!"

"If times continue the way they are, that may be soon."

At a loss, Cabe looked from one to the other. Their words were meaning-
less.

The Lady stood up. "We have wasted enough time. Now that I know
who else awaits us at the City of Knowledge, I am even more eager to be
there."

Not waiting for Cabe, she walked over to Darkhorse and mounted. Cabe
followed quickly, still wanting to know the reason for her behavior. She was
obviously an emotional woman.

As he positioned himself on the dark steed, he spoke to his companion.
"Who is Shade? How will he figure in all of this?"

She looked at him, and her words were both blunt and puzzling. "He is perhaps the only warlock comparable to Nathan. He is also the most hated. Before this is over, he may be both savior and destroyer of us all. It is part of his dual nature."

Darkhorse reared before starting anew his run. This time, there was no laughter.

VIII

THEY WERE NEARING Penacles. They knew that from the tides that passed them or moved with them. Many seemed agitated. Some groups, heading in opposite directions, argued with each other. Cabe could not make out their words, but he suspected he knew the cause.

Gwen was also watching the lines of humanity. "Some believe Penacles is the safest place to be since it's so well fortified. Others believe that nothing can stand the onslaught of the Dragon Kings."

"Is there war already?"

She shook her head. "I have increased my range of hearing. What I hear has been mentioned several times. Firedrakes, wyverns, and creatures so foul that they have no name. All move south of the Tyber Mountains, and each bears the mark of the Dragon Emperor himself. I have also learned that the Gray Mists have spread toward Penacles from the east."

He tried to see if the city was visible from this distance, but succeeded only in spotting more humanity. "Can the city hold out?"

"The Gryphon has the knowledge from the libraries as well as his own unique abilities. It may well be a long fight."

A column of riders rode past them, choosing to avoid the crowds by traveling well off to the side. They were all dressed in leather, and each one had the look that could only come from years of experience in the art of war. Their small, metal helms failed to cover unruly, blond locks. By their faces, Cabe would have been tempted to believe that they were all brothers.

"Soldiers from Zuu. The Gryphon must have been preparing for this and sent for reinforcements."

"Won't that leave their own city defenseless?"

She shrugged. "Probably not. The Barren Lands are to their south. To the north lies the Dagora Forest, where the Green Dragon rules quietly and seldom interferes with the other races. Even during the Turning War. That was one reason that we never attacked him." There was a strange tone to her voice, as if there was really more to say.

Suddenly, Darkhorse became agitated and signaled that he wished to turn off and converse with the two. Cabe made as if he were pulling the reins, but it was the mount that made the actual decision.

When they had ridden far enough from the road, Darkhorse halted. He waited a moment before speaking.

"I feel something. Large forms, perhaps firedrakes. They appear headed this way."

"Do you think they're coming for us?" Cabe nervously scanned the heavens.

Darkhorse laughed. "Would it matter? If anything happens, we will most definitely be in the middle of it anyway!"

The Lady looked at the beast with distaste. "I find your humor somewhat difficult to understand. How many would you say?"

"Two. Both swift."

She nodded. "Scouts. How soon?"

"I daresay that they will be in sight just after we return to the road. Providing that we go back now, that is."

Cabe was looking at something in the direction of the City of Knowledge. "Something is disrupting travel up ahead."

All three looked. Darkhorse focused one gleaming eye on the area that Cabe had mentioned. "My apologies! I have obviously miscalculated! Two drakes flying quickly down the road! They appear to be harassing travelers at random points along the way!"

The sorceress was grim. "Hurry! We must destroy them!"

That made Darkhorse laugh again. "You accuse me of being bloodthirsty!"

Before she could reply, they were on their way back to the road. The drakes were swooping down here and there, taking great pleasure in what they were doing. As yet, they had merely confined themselves to frightening the humans, but it would not be long before the dragons began to play more seriously.

Darkhorse was almost to the road. "I suggest you dismount. Otherwise, we present ourselves as an obvious target once the fighting begins!"

The drakes were becoming more daring. They were seldom allowed to roam far from their masters and were now reveling in their freedom. One spotted the two travelers and their horse and roared. It soared toward them.

Cabe was on the ground, the Horned Blade out. Gwen dismounted just before the dragon came into range. Darkhorse backed up.

As the monster drew nearer, Cabe turned quickly to the steed. "Can you take him as you did the dams?"

"No! The air is not my element! If you can get him to land—"

The Lady's fingers were moving in swift patterns. "I hardly think that he'll be very happy to oblige us!"

Her spell went off. The drake suddenly found itself bombarded by small bursts of energy. They were going off constantly. The creature tried to fly around them, but they merely moved with him.

"Fireworks, Lady Gwen? This is no holiday!"

The other drake joined its companion. Prepared for sorcery, it flew in an erratic pattern, confounding the Lady's spell-casting. As it moved closer, its great jaws opened wide. However, instead of fire, a strange mist shot forth. Gwen was just able to dissipate the mist before it reached them.

"What was that?" Cabe had never seen a dragon use such a defense.

"Airdrakes don't breathe out fire! They breathe out poisonous fumes!"

The first, totally disoriented by the continual blasts, fell to the ground with a thud. Its partner, though, flew in once again, this time to totally crush its opponents. It moved in toward Cabe, using the same sort of confusing pattern it had earlier. Cabe knew it would not come within striking distance. Oddly, he found he did not care.

Darkhorse moved to cover him. "I will try to absorb the mist if the Lady fails to stop it!"

"No!" Cabe felt strange, as if something was swelling up inside of him. "Both of you, stand away!"

The authority in his voice was such that neither argued. The bizarre but comforting feeling filled him. The drake roared, sensing victory. Cabe remained steadfast.

When it was little more than fifty yards away, the dragon seemed to shrink. The closer it flew, the smaller it became. It was no longer in control; they could see it struggling to alter its course. At twenty yards, it was no larger than a dog. At ten, a small bird.

Three feet from Cabe, the drake ceased to exist.

There was only silence from his two companions. Still filled with power, Cabe turned his attention to the other drake. The creature continued to struggle, albeit much more feebly, against the bursts of energy. The warlock's eyes glowed. The dragon disappeared.

It was the Lady Gwen who first spoke to him. "What did you do?"

"I sent the drake to Penacles. One of their holding cells for wild beasts." Cabe's voice sounded alien to him.

"I meant the other."

A smile played on his face, though he had nothing to do with it. The Lady—and even Darkhorse—seemed taken aback. "Its ego was too great; I merely reduced both to a more appropriate size."

She was shuddering. The single word she spoke was barely even a whisper. "Nathan."

Cabe's head felt funny. He put one hand to it and promptly fell to the ground. Gwen was by him immediately. He opened his eyes and found her staring at him with new wonder. The moment was extremely pleasant, but it was suddenly interrupted by the arrival of several men on horseback. The soldiers from Zuu, to be precise.

The leader, a longtime veteran with jagged scars all over his face, frowned as he looked around. "What happened to the airdrakes?"

Gwen answered. "Gone."

"We saw them attack you. They ignored us. Too much manpower for the lizards, especially since we all carry bows as well." Each of the soldiers had a longbow. It would have been folly for the drakes.

"You are from Zuu?"

"Aye, milady. We have come on the Lord Gryphon's request."

She nodded. "Then perhaps you could escort us to the city. The Lord Gryphon is expecting us as well."

The commander grinned, his mouth revealing a fairly bad set of teeth. "Oh? And who might you be?"

"I am Lady Gwen of the Green Manor. This is my companion, Cabe."

"The Lady of the Amber!" The man was visibly impressed. He stared at Cabe. "A warlock, too! So that's what happened to the drakes! The Gryphon is going all out!"

The manner of the entire group changed. The commander, Blane, promised to give them the best honor guard possible. He would personally escort them to the Gryphon's lair. It was obvious that the addition of sorcerors to the city's defense was a great boost in morale. Especially when one of them was the Lady Gwen.

They mounted Darkhorse. Blane, seeing the horse closely, stared at it with expert eyes. "I've seen many a fine animal, but I sure as damned wouldn't race any of 'em against that! What is it?"

Smiling, the Lady pretended to pat the head. "A rare breed. Very strong and swift, but lacking much in intelligence."

Darkhorse snorted and threatened to throw both of them off. Blane shook his head.

"Seems pretty smart to me. I wouldn't go insulting an animal like that. Might throw me good if I did."

The dark steed snorted in agreement. The commander turned his horse back in the direction of the city. Darkhorse brought his companions even with the soldier. They started off, the troops following close behind.

The tides of humanity continued to flow back and forth.

IN THE LANDS of the hill dwarves, where iron is mined and shaped for trade through the Dragonrealm, there was a stirring. The dwarves, busy at their tasks, paused. Many muttered to themselves, for they knew only one reason for such shaking.

From mines long played out, a scaly head appeared. It was the very color of the metal so precious to the hill dwarves. It roared, causing the little people to scurry to their caves. A long, sinewy neck, followed by a strong, muscular body, completed the form of one of the dragons of the Iron clans.

No sooner was the creature out than another appeared. The first watched the area as his fellow made his way to the open. When that dragon was done, yet a third revealed himself. The first two kept watch, one looking to and fro. The original looked to only one direction. It was not southeast, where the city of Penacles lay, but rather east.

The Tyber Mountains.

THE CITY OF Knowledge might easily have also been dubbed the City of Beauty. Barring Mito Pica, there was no other city like it. Great towers overwhelmed all other buildings. Pointed spires topped many. Below, more on a level with men, gardens dotted the city's streets. The original creators of Penacles did not fight nature to build their metropolis; they worked with it.

Thousands wandered the streets, especially those around and within the city's bazaar. The travelers, escorted by Blane's troops, easily moved through the crowds. Their movement was slow enough so that they could enjoy the sights. Cabe, never having seen a city so large, spent most of his time staring at the throngs with an open mouth. Gwen looked at him and laughed lightly.

"You'd best close that great gap before someone takes you for a dragon!

Besides, it ill befits a warlock to be seen looking like some young boy from the outlands."

Cabe held back from commenting that that was exactly the way he felt. He turned his attention back to the city, but found new thoughts reshaping his view of the inhabitants. The Lady had mentioned dragons. As this thought lodged itself, he saw the fear and wonder in the faces. Many people were muttering or glancing this way and that, and especially at the column and its two sorcerors. He saw more than one person point at him, marking the way the streak had extended itself through his hair. They would be expecting miracles from him, he knew, but he had none to give them. Merely bursts of power at one time or another.

He prayed that the Lord Gryphon would be better prepared.

At long last, they reached the palace, though palace was perhaps a colorful term for the building. It was, Cabe decided, definitely a fortress. The walls were all gray stone, and the only entrance was a large iron gate. No decorative columns, no statues—save one of a real gryphon in flight—no decorations of any kind.

Something else was missing. There were absolutely no reminders of the reign of the Purple Dragon. The Gryphon had cleansed the city—and especially the palace—of any signs of the creature. To show his feel for the common people, he had erected few of his own.

The immense iron gate opened as they neared. They were expected. Blane ordered his men to head to the barracks. He was to accompany the two travelers; the commander's orders had been to report directly to the lord of Penacles himself.

To Cabe, the hardest part of their journey up to this point had to be the steps which they had just begun to climb. He estimated that there had to be at least a hundred. Surely, this had to be some sort of defensive measure. No doubt a charging army would soon find itself lying exhausted some two-thirds of the way up, easy prey for defenders.

When they finally reached the top, he looked down. Darkhorse was gone. The guard at the base, one hand clutching the reins of the commander's horse, seemed oblivious to the fact that his other charge had disappeared. Cabe knew his unearthly companion would meet them later.

A servant led them in. The inside of the palace proved almost as spartan as the outside. Their host had little time for luxuries, it seemed. Here and there, some strange artifact hung on the wall or stood nearby, but all of these seemed to pulsate with a life of their own. Cabe glanced at Gwen, and she nodded. Blane was ignorant of anything out of the ordinary and merely looked straight ahead.

Eventually, they reached an elaborately decorated door guarded by two beings who were only somewhat human. Both stared with sightless eyes and had skins the color of iron. They did not move at first, causing the three to believe them only statues. That belief was shattered by the servant, a small, wiry man who walked up to the one on the left and spoke to it.

"I come with three visitors of importance to the Lord Gryphon."

To their shock, the head tilted to look at the servant. Each movement was accompanied by the sound of metal hinges in sore need of oil. It peered at the man for several seconds, never blinking, and then turned to look at the three.

"The commander from Zuu will enter first and alone." The mouth had not opened, almost causing them to believe someone else had spoken.

The voice was melodious and totally the opposite of what they would have suspected. Blane moved slowly toward the doorway, his hand on the hilt of his weapon. He was no coward, but like most ordinary men, he tolerated magic when it was with him and distrusted it when there was even the slightest chance it wasn't. The commander turned his head from one guard to the other until he was through the doorway. The door closed behind him.

The servant made his apologies and left Cabe and his companion alone. The guard on the left continued to stare at them with sightless eyes, and Cabe had an urge to find some hiding place, preferably outside the city.

Gwen whispered in his ear. "Iron golems! I'd thought the forming of such creatures had been lost to the ages!"

"I wish it had been. Does that thing have to keep looking at us like that?"

"He's not looking at us. He has no eyes as we know them. The only reason he acts like that is that he wears a human shape."

He glanced at the two guards. "I wouldn't exactly say 'human.' If he can't see, how does he know if something happens?"

"I didn't say he can't see; I said that he has no eyes, at least as we know them. He sees by other means. Unfortunately, I don't know how."

Her voice trailed off. Despite her knowledge, the iron golems still made her nervous, too. She knew little of their limits, attacks, and defenses. The fact that the Gryphon entrusted his life to them made them all the more dangerous. The monarch of Penacles rarely placed his faith in anything unless he knew it would not fail him.

After several minutes, the door opened and the commander from Zuu stepped out. He was pale and sweating, but there was a look of respect on his face. He nodded to them.

"The Lord Gryphon awaits you."

As he passed them, Cabe whispered quickly to his companion. "Have you met the Gryphon?"

She shook her head. "No. I'm sure we have something to look forward to, though."

They walked through the open doorway, Cabe watching the golems as he went. Neither moved. Any unsuspecting person would have taken them for statues.

"Welcome, my friends."

Cabe turned. He stopped, no more taken aback, though, than the Lady.

Tall and regal, the Lord Gryphon was every bit the monarch. The aura of power and wisdom was unmistakable. Yet it was not this that so astonished the pair. For the Gryphon was more than man. Though his form was near-human, his features were not.

His face was that of a bird of prey, a proud eagle with eyes that saw all. The Gryphon walked toward them, and the great, golden mane that trailed down past his shoulders shook as he did. He extended his hand, and they saw that it was covered with fur but had claws much more avian. Though they should have felt repulsed by this picture, they did not. Rather, they felt the urge to kneel before the grand majesty of this man-beast. The Dragon Kings reigned through terror. The Gryphon, however, reigned through intelligence and understanding.

Cabe took the offered hand, feeling extremely clumsy in every movement. The monarch of Penacles did not move so much as flow. Every action was precise.

"Greetings to you, Cabe Bedlam, grandson of Nathan. I am honored."

He turned to the Lady and took her hand. As he did, his face altered. The lionbird was gone. In its place was a man of hawklike visage who could have easily stolen many a woman's heart. Gwen smiled as he kissed her hand.

He straightened and looked at both. "The Lady is known to me by reputation. You, friend Cabe, are known to me only through a mutual acquaintance."

The Gryphon indicated a figure, unnoticed until now, seated on a couch behind him. The hood and cloak were enough to identify him, but the blurred face clinched the matter for all.

"Simon!"

"Shade!" Gwen's face was a sea of hatreds.

The warlock may have smiled sarcastically. "I am pleased to see you, too. Especially you, Amber Lady."

She swung around to face the Gryphon once more. "How can you deal with someone like him? Even if he claims to be on our side? His mixed past condemns him beyond all justification!"

The lord of the city frowned at her. The stern look was such that she was forced to back away. "Simon pays for his sins with every moment of life, Lady Gwen. He will do what he can for us."

"Until next time!"

Throughout this exchange, the hooded warlock kept silent. Cabe could not read his face, but there seemed to be a great sadness prevalent in his movements. Sadness—and guilt. Tremendous guilt.

The Gryphon finally calmed the lady down by offering her a look at the libraries. The thought of that knowledge thrilled her. Cabe was also invited, but he declined. Something inside urged him to talk to the shadowy sorceror.

When they were alone, Cabe walked over to the man who called himself Simon. The other looked at him expectantly; but before Cabe could speak, they were both interrupted by the sound of thundering hooves.

"Couldn't someone at least tell me when it's safe to come up here? I remained in hiding so I wouldn't spook that fine commander from Zuu!"

Shade chuckled, his depression momentarily lifting. "Fine commander? He must have complimented you, my friend."

"Merely gave me the respect that some are rather reluctant to give."

"I have only the greatest respect for you."

Darkhorse snorted. "I was referring to the woman! I assume you were treated in similar fashion!"

Almost as quickly as it had gone, Simon's depression returned. "The Lady does not forgive easily. . . . Nor should she have to. I take full responsibility for my curse."

The warlock stood up abruptly. "If you will excuse me, I have some preparations to make. Keep the lad company, old friend."

Shade vanished.

Cabe looked to the dark steed. "What did he do? Why does the Lady carry so much hatred for him?"

A sigh. "Sit down, friend Cabe. This will take some time."

He did as Darkhorse suggested. The phantom mount stood before him.

Cabe tried to imagine what it would be like if someone walked in and found him talking to a sleek black horse. Then again, it would only take a minute to realize that this creature was no true animal. The aura of eternity was quite evident to anyone who looked.

A cold eye was fixed on him. "Once there was a warlock of tremendous power. Shade. A man possessed with one goal. The greatest goal men have ever sought for." A pause. "That goal was immortality."

Immortality. The word alone seemed to breathe magic.

Cabe remembered stories of countless individuals who had sought for the treasure that was greater than gold. The mere possibility would be enough to send whole nations to war, either with one another or against themselves. It never mattered.

"Did—did he find it?"

Darkhorse ignored the question completely. "Shade was a man of two minds, both hotly contesting with one another for supremacy. He walked the thin, gray line between white and black. At times he would teeter in one direction or the other, but never was he completely ensnared. As the years passed, he gained tremendous knowledge of both powers, and it was this combination of knowledge that led him to what he believed was the solution." He snorted. "In such a way have men's egos and greed brought them to disasters unparalleled."

Cabe said nothing. It was an age-old story.

"Shade invoked powers from both sides, strong powers unknown to men today. He failed to consider one thing, however. Where light meets dark, there is always conflict. His very nature proved that. Shade found himself caught amidst the fury of the two sides. Lesser men would have died. Shade, being what he was, faced a far more terrible fate."

There was a sadness in the creature's voice. Darkhorse had few friends, and none more important to him than the shadowy warlock.

"In their collective fury, the powers overcame his protections. He who would have been immortal instead found himself a puppet at the mercy of several masters! He was twisted, changed, melted, torn. Each power strove to make him their tool. Each only partially succeeded, and when it was over, the forces returned to their planes of existence. Of the warlock Shade, there remained only a battered corpse."

Cabe uttered a gasp.

The demonic horse nodded. "A corpse, yes. For a week, it lay where it had fallen. No one, of course, entered a sorceror's lair if they could help it.

Besides, it was not uncommon for Shade to remain inside for weeks. On the eighth day, the body dissolved, leaving no trace of the warlock. At the same time, in the midst of the Hell Plains, a figure rose from the magma pits. It was unharmed by the elements and reeked of evil. Shade's dark side had apparently triumphed, for it was he."

"Then the Lady was right about him?" Cabe's eyes darted here and there, looking for someplace to hide.

"Have no fear! The story is far from over!"

Darkhorse watched the boy relax slightly. "That's better! Where was I? This Shade, who gave himself the name Belrac, soon created terror that rivaled that of the Dragon Kings. He was now confident of his immortality and made reckless attacks. By sheer audacity alone, he won many of his battles. Yet, for all his seeming invulnerability, Belrac found that he was far from perfect. First, he had lost much of his memory from his former life. It was as if he were actually a son and not the real warlock. The second and far more important point he discovered was that he could be killed. He found out the hard way, when Illian of the Birds drove an enchanted staff through his form. Belrac crumpled to the ground and watched his life fluids spill out. Illian had his body burned in order to prevent a reoccurrence of the nightmare, but it was not enough. Three days later, in the Dagora Forest, he stepped out from the trees. This time he named himself Jelrath."

"Why the names?"

"I'm coming to that. Jelrath remembered only small fragments of his past lives, but enough to know who he was. Filled with remorse for his evil deeds, he dedicated his life to righting his wrongs and helping the people. There was no evil in his system; he was a servant of the light. He knew then that immortality was his, but it was perverted. The two sides of his personality had been torn asunder. Both dark and light claimed him; both dark and light controlled him. He was cursed to live an infinity of lives, alternating between good and evil. With one hand, he healed; with the other, he crushed all in his path. Each death brought forth the opposing personality. The names? It may be to hide his past. If he kept the same name, someone would eventually hunt him down. Shade does not die easily, but he can suffer as much as any man. Another possibility is the one I believe. Though all the lives are Shade, they are only portions. Incomplete. In their desire to be whole individuals, choosing a name would be the first place to start." Darkhorse lowered his voice. "Sometimes I think that they all believe the curse ends with them."

"How—how long has this been going on?"

"Ha! I stopped trying to remember the names centuries ago! You want a list, check any legend! Odds are that many will be him. If you know what to look for, that is."

Cabe studied the walls. He could really think of nothing to say at this point. How does one comprehend the pain and sadness of a thousand lifetimes? The Lady had a good point; there was no telling when Shade might suddenly be their most dangerous enemy. Yet he was now one of their few real hopes.

Could they pass up such a chance?

Did they dare take the chance?

THE GRYPHON BROUGHT Lady Gwen to a room remarkably similar to the one they had left. Like the first room, this one was guarded by two iron golems. She asked about their creation.

He smiled. "No doubt you are wondering where the information came from."

"I would assume it was the libraries."

"True, but the actual spells and items listed are from the days of the Harkonens."

"The Harkonens? But that means—"

He nodded. "Yes, the libraries contain many surprises." The Gryphon frowned. "Too many. It took me twenty years to understand just that one spell."

They passed through the doorway. The lord of Penacles led her to a tapestry hanging on the far wall. Gwen inspected it.

"Transporter?"

"Yes. The libraries move randomly. By what means, I don't know. This allows us to reach them, and, as far as I know, there are no other entrances."

"How did the Purple Dragon build this?"

As he started to rub the picture, this time a small shop, he looked at her strangely. "The Purple Dragon didn't build this. This was here long before the Dragon Kings gained control."

She would have asked more, but the room had begun to fade. Gwen watched in fascination. This was a mode of teleportation that she had heard of but never experienced. Within moments, the two of them were standing in one of the corridors of the libraries. Row upon row of books lined the walls, and the sorceress noticed that they were all the same.

A small gnome, who may or may not have been one of many librarians, was waiting for them. The Gryphon had mentioned him earlier, but he still came as a surprise. The little man said nothing; he would not move until he received word from the present lord of the City of Knowledge.

Somewhere along the way, the Gryphon's features had reverted to the lionbird. Gwen also noticed that the hands were now feathered with claws akin to those of a large cat. She wondered exactly what the limits were to her host's shapeshifting. In many ways, it was even more versatile than that of the Dragon Kings.

The monarch of Penacles spoke. "Lead us to the same location as before."

The gnome blinked. After a moment, he nodded, turned around, and started to shuffle away. They followed him. While they traversed the corridors, the Gryphon began to explain.

"As I mentioned, I know of no other way to enter. The librarian will back me up. However, something has happened to make me wonder if the libraries, and therefore Penacles, are truly safe."

"What do you mean?"

They turned a corridor. "What do we know about the knowledge in these hallways?" He indicated the endless walls of books. "Much of it contains ideas and spells we might never even think of but would be willing to do anything for. With these libraries, one could potentially rule the Dragonrealm and beyond."

"Why not have scholars start reading the books?"

He laughed, and the sight made Gwen smile. "Even if it were possible to gather enough scholars—trustworthy ones, mind you—and set them to work, they wouldn't get very far. Look."

The Gryphon paused to pull one of the large, imposing, leather-bound tomes out. There was no dust on it. He handed the book to her. She opened it up to one of the first pages. Her eyes widened.

The pages were blank.

She thumbed through the book. Every page was blank. Gwen searched for some spell, but she felt nothing. Looking up, she saw that the Gryphon was smiling as best as his animal face would allow him.

"Every one of these books is the same. I know; I looked through more than a hundred in various spots and had others do the same. Nothing."

"What about him?" She pointed at the gnome. The small, bent man was standing nearby, patiently awaiting his charges.

"Apparently, he can only read what someone requests. He does know, however, where to find something when I ask for it. He feels its presence."

"How long has he been here?"

The Gryphon turned to the librarian. "How long have you been here?"

The gnome closed his eyes momentarily. When he opened them, his answer was quick and short. "I have always been here."

"You see?" The Gryphon shrugged. Replacing the book, he turned back to the gnome. "Lead on."

They turned down a final corridor. The squat librarian stood to one side. The Gryphon watched his guest. The Lady gasped.

"That shelf! The books have been destroyed!"

He nodded, a grim look on his face. "Yes. It was like that when Shade and I came to investigate the cause of the icy wind."

"What wind?"

"Only a small breeze, but one that chilled the soul as well as the body. We came here seeking an answer. Instead, we found this."

"Who—"

The master of Penacles slammed his fist against a shelf. "Does it matter? The libraries have been invaded! Damaged! Whether it was Azran, the Dragon Kings, or some other evil, our most secure area is in danger!"

The Lady stared at the burnt area. The Gryphon continued to speak.

"I fear we may have been beaten before we have even begun the struggle!"

IX

B RONZE AND IRON.
   Colors of war. Strength.

The drakes swarmed into the Tyber Mountains. A flash of iron. A swarm of bronze. They came with one purpose. They came with one cause.

They came for betrayal.

Great Iron, surveying his legions, nodded in satisfaction. He was atop one of the larger mountains, commanding his clans. Small drakes, his messengers, fluttered around him. They were his contact with his commanders. They were also his contact with his ally, Bronze. Between the two of them, they would crush the emperor while his legions marched to Penacles. Iron would lead, with Bronze as a strong addition to his power. The Dragon

Kings would regain their momentum. Gold was weak, and should never have been made emperor.

There were a few pockets of resistance. A number of wyverns and basilisks died as unidentified creatures of darkness attacked. The deaths did not disturb him. There were always too many of the lessers. Besides, the defenders had eventually been overrun and killed. Dragon blood flowed easily this night.

In the distance, the war cries of the Bronze clans rose to a triumphant high. His ally had broken through. Now was the time for the final push. Soon, Iron would put his jaws around his brother's neck and end his reign.

As his legions poured into the cavern that was Gold's home, Iron climbed down from the mountain. He would be there when the final defenses were crushed. It would prove his cause.

They met in the chamber where the Dragon Kings held council. Bronze was already there. He had ordered his commanders away and waited for his brother alone.

Iron surveyed the vast chamber. "Where is he? Where is our weakling brother?"

"I have searched high and low. He appears to have escaped to the underground. Perhaps the hatchery."

The Iron Dragon stepped toward a tunnel to the rear of the chamber. As he neared it, he altered his shape. Gone was the beast, in form but not in spirit. The helmed figure of the Dragon King stepped up to the entrance of the tunnel.

"He has gone this way. To do so, he must be in a like form. Change and follow me!"

Bronze was skeptical. "Are you sure this is wise?"

"He is alone, save for the dam who guards. She will not sacrifice the eggs. If we choose to kill the emperor, she will not intrude. Come!"

Two armored warriors, they stalked down the dark cavern. The lack of light had little effect on them; their eyes were still those of the great reptiles. Iron led the way; Bronze guarded their rear. They were not fools. Though beaten, their brother might still have defenses of some sort.

The heat generated in the hatchery spread toward them in wave after wave. They ignored it. A thing of the dark detached itself from the ceiling of the tunnel and flew to meet them. Iron killed it with one stroke of his blade. He laughed as he did, for he enjoyed the destruction of foes.

They came to the hatchery, and Iron stepped inside. The old dam, a creature of unbelievable size even for a dragon, watched him cautiously. So long as he did not touch her charges, she would leave him in peace. It did not matter whether he was a king or not; her decision would be based on his actions.

The other joined him. "Is he here?"

"Are you a fool? Does it look as if he is here? We have no business in the hatchery! He must be farther on!"

They departed from the hatchery, not without some relief, and climbed deeper into the depths of the mountain. Much time passed. These were unfamiliar areas to the two conquerors. They were now in Gold's private domain. Both moved closer to each other, and Bronze cursed inwardly for not bringing some of his legion with him.

"I dislike the closeness of this tunnel, Iron! We cannot shift out of these human shapes!"

"Neither can the emperor! He may know these caverns, but it will not save him."

"At least let me call forth some of my clans!" Bronze was one of the few Dragon Kings able to master any sort of telepathy. The only other two were Iron and the very emperor they sought to overthrow.

Iron growled impatiently. "Very well! They had best arrive soon, though! I hunger for death!"

His eyes blank, the other summoned his warriors. He blinked. Iron watched him curiously. Something was obviously amiss.

"Well?"

Bronze turned to him. "I receive no answer to my summons!"

"The walls—"

"No!" Bronze was surprised by his own anxiety. "I would know that! They—they don't answer! As if we are alone!"

Frowning, Iron sought to summon his own clans. He felt only a great void, as if all had ceased to exist. He stood straight.

"This bears investigating! We must return to the chamber!"

"What about—"

"If there is indeed trickery involved, our brother will be close by. In the chamber, we may revert to our full forms."

Sword in hand, Iron marched angrily away. Bronze paused only momentarily and then followed quickly behind.

Nothing obstructed their path. They ignored the hatchery, knowing that the guardian of the eggs would never permit sorcery near her charges. The walk seemed to be both quicker and slower, and with each step, Iron's anger increased.

They stepped back into the council chamber.

Once out, their human forms melted. They stretched their wings nervously and surveyed the area. Nothing had changed.

"I still receive no word from my clans," Bronze muttered.

Something shrieked in the night.

Dragons fear little. The Dragon Kings feared almost nothing. Until this moment. The scream chilled their very marrow, yet, shocked as they were, they were still fighters. Angrily, Iron roared his challenge, and Bronze joined him. What could defeat two of the mightiest of the Dragon Kings?

"I have awaited you." There was mockery in the tone. Both knew who spoke.

"Brother Gold! Show yourself!" Iron glanced here and there, waiting for a chance to strike.

"Here." Out of a small hole stepped the emperor. Bronze laughed. Their brother was in human form and made no attempt to shift. His death would be quick.

The thing shrieked from behind them.

Bronze turned his great head in dismay. Iron, knowing that they had been tricked, tried to wrap his jaws around the small form in front of him. Both burst into flames. Nothing else in the room was touched.

Gold watched their tattered remains burn away. The thing wobbled up to him and placed its leathery head near his feet. The Dragon Emperor petted it softly on the head. The thing crooned happily. Gold continued to stare at the burning, smelling masses. He knew with satisfaction that the same scene had been repeated countless times outside.

The smile that played across his half-hidden face was neither dragon nor man, but the worst of both.

"Good-bye."

AZRAN FACED THE pit that opened to the Plane of the Dead. The smell of decay and rotting flesh bothered him, even though he had cast his strongest spells to keep the odor away. Death was something that just could not be ignored, apparently.

The pit bubbled and oozed. Azran waited for something to emerge from the muck. It had taken him much longer to recover than expected.

There was little doubt in his mind that his son and that witch had arrived in Penacles. The Seeker had not returned yet. He was forced to go blindly again.

The hand shot out of the ooze. The old seer nodded in satisfaction. A guardian of the dead rose to meet him, ooze dripping from its putrid flesh. Like a mixture of every dead creature, it stood a foot taller than Azran. The stench it brought with it overwhelmed the earlier smells. The warlock nearly gagged, but managed to hold on to his composure and the contents of his stomach.

"Whom do you seek?" The voice was raspy. Now and then, it changed completely.

He stiffened. "They know who I seek! They are bound to me until I release them!"

"Or die."

Azran tried to hide his discomfort. "Send them to me at once!"

"They are coming." The guardian sank into the mire almost as soon as it spoke. When its head disappeared, Azran was greatly relieved.

He waited patiently now. Once commanded, the dead had to obey.

A form broke through the murky surface. Another joined it. Unlike the guardian, neither dripped of the slime out of which they had come. Both stared at him with the blank eyes of their kind.

"We are here, Azran." Despite its being dead, there were hints of hatred in the form's voice.

The ancient warlock had noticed it, too. He allowed himself a smile. "So I see. I also see that you have tremendous spirit for one who should not. How about you, Tyr? Do you also have this spirit?"

The other figure, clad in what was once a robe of dark blue, said nothing, but the hands curled into fists.

"I see. Good! That should help you put more effort in your work! Now, then, Basil and Tyr, are you ready for your orders?"

The same tones. Basil, armored and wearing a leather cloak. "We will listen."

"You still know where Penacles is?"

"Yes."

"Good! I was afraid your brain might have rotted in all this time. Anyway, I want you to kidnap someone there."

Basil gave a ghost of a smile. "For this you need us? It is your brain that must have rotted."

Azran glared. "I think not. Hmm. You two are pretty active for undead! Maybe I should leave this to others."

"Fine! Then we may return to our rest and—"

"You'll go nowhere! It would take too much time to summon others. Besides, despite your unusual animation, you are bound by the powers to obey me until I release you."

"Or die," the ghostly Basil added with great desire.

"It takes a lot to kill me. Now, then, as to the kidnapping. His name is Cabe; he is a warlock. Do not underestimate him. He is my son."

He watched with satisfaction the looks on the faces of the undead.

"This Cabe is a Bedlam?"

"Have your eardrums fallen into the space where your brain used to be? He is my son, stolen from me by my damned father! I want him here! If he proves impossible to take, kill him! In fact, kill anyone who gets in the way! That witch, the Lady Gwen, will be there. So will the Gryphon and possibly others."

Tyr spoke, and his voice was like a tomb opened after generations of decay. "Why not send us to do battle with the Three Lords of the Dead? We stand as much chance if so many powers are there."

"First of all, my decrepit friend, the boy is untrained. Second, the Lady's powers are least effective against the dead. She may banish you at best. Between the two of you, you should be able to handle this."

Tyr turned away. There was disgust in his voice. "Do not make us do this."

"Why not? Who better to strike against a new rising of Dragon Masters than the old ones themselves?" Azran laughed. "I give you full use of your powers for this mission! Listen and I will now explain in detail what you will do!"

He made them kneel, just for spite.

THE DARK OF night was upon them, but something disturbed them too much for sleep to come. Darkhorse had no use for sleep anyway, and no one had ever seen Shade even doze. The Gryphon was on a balcony and staring out at the heavens and the lands beyond.

"Do you sense something?"

The lord of Penacles turned to face Shade. "I not only sense something, I feel almost on the verge of being overwhelmed by them. Events are on the move this night. We must be prepared for anything."

"Such as stars that vanish?"

The Gryphon nodded uneasily. "You've noticed. The Gray Mists seek to enshroud us. I fear that Black has stirred up his traitorous fanatics. Judging by the close proximity of the fog, they can be no more than two days from us."

"Two days? How is that possible?"

A sigh. "When I met them in battle, I knew only a little about them. One thing that I did discover immediately was that they seldom rest. They will march day and night for weeks, fight a battle for days, and then march home again. All without sleep. They eat as they march. Some say it is because they live within the Gray Mists."

The left hand rested on a marble rail. He who called himself Simon noticed that there were now deep gouges in the marble. He said nothing to his friend.

"Something else. I have heard that the Dragon Kings war against themselves this night."

Shade nodded. "Both good and bad. It lessens our enemies, but makes the few bolder."

He suddenly took hold of the Gryphon's arm and started to lead him inside. "I have something to show you."

They stepped into the room. The Gryphon started to speak, but his companion hushed him. Shade said nothing until they were far from the balcony. When he did speak, it was a whisper.

"Something watches and listens from above!"

"What? I felt no one!"

"It cloaks itself well. Fortunately, it was not expecting one of my abilities."

"What is it?"

"I suspect it is one of Azran's spies. A Seeker."

The Gryphon started for the door, intending to summon his golems. Shade stopped him, still whispering. "Hold!"

"Why? If he's been here for more than a day, he knows of the danger to the libraries and the presence of Cabe and the Lady! The gods know what else!"

"The golems will not be able to catch him. The Seekers are of the oldest magic. Only one versed in such stands a chance of stealth. I will go."

There was little room for argument. The Gryphon knew the warlock was correct. Simon told him to behave as normal. After a few moments of waiting, he then bid the Gryphon a good night and left the room as if intending to return to his quarters. The monarch of Penacles stared at the doorway.

The Seeker would notice a spell of teleportation. Shade would be forced to climb the stairs and then pull himself up to the roof. He hoped the avian would be turned the other way. The old spell of Shunning that the warlock was using would most likely work, but Shade had never really faced one of the creatures before.

He also had little knowledge of the Seeker's limits. It could not kill him, he believed, but it might be strong enough to hurt him. He sought death, for a good cause, not pain. Pain had a way of lingering that death did not.

Shade had reached the end of the stairs. His only option now was to climb through the window and pray that the ancient roof edge would hold him. He began a memory check of all flight spells that could be used at very short notice. He also hoped he would be conscious if such a spell was needed.

Summoning the strength of several centuries, he pulled himself up to the roof. Nothing attempted to push him into empty space. The warlock crouched down and studied his surroundings.

The Seeker was there, its back to him, its powerful wings folded behind it. At present, it appeared to be concerned with whatever movements the Gryphon made. He knew, however, that the creature's duties might change at any moment. Shielding his presence as subtly as possible, Shade made his way toward the Seeker.

Magic would blank out any sounds he made, but it would not do so for the roof itself. Thus it was that a crumbling piece of the roof alerted the avian to its danger. The warlock was just short of effective range for the spell he was preparing to cast, when, with a silence more frightening than any cry, the Seeker launched itself at him.

What he had originally chosen to cast was now useless. Shade was forced to throw a bright burst of light in the hopes that it would blind the creature. The Seeker easily bypassed it, but the spell gave the warlock much-needed time. He rolled away and started a new offense. His birdlike opponent turned with amazing speed and came in for a second attack.

This time, he was ready. Bright red bands, two feet in diameter, formed around the avian. The creature whirled to escape them, but the bands merely became tighter. Unfortunately, the wings were not included in the trap. The Seeker reversed directions and then shot up into the night.

Shade sought for his adversary, the powers adding to his night vision. Despite this, the Seeker was nowhere to be seen. He became worried that the avian had flown off to its master. If that happened . . .

He was suddenly struck violently from behind. Unable to control himself or his thoughts, Shade nearly rolled off the roof. Only a last-minute hold saved him from going over. He cleared his senses just in time to see the avian speeding toward him, arms free and claws bared. It was going for the kill.

Wrapping his cloak around him, the warlock disappeared. The Seeker was momentarily at a loss, and that was all that Shade needed. Materializing behind his foe, he leaped on the back of the flying creature and tried to force it down. The avian hit the roof—

—and was immediately off again. Shade found himself clinging to the avian as it soared off into the night. It could not free itself from him, but it was assuring itself of the advantage. The warlock was having difficulty holding on. If he lost hold, the creature would not allow him the time to cast a spell of flight.

He received unexpected assistance from the Seeker. In trying to pry him from it, it succeeded only in pulling him higher. Now they were both locked together in a struggle where Shade found he had an advantage in skill, and so started the one spell that might destroy his opponent. Like the warlock, the Seekers could be injured, but they were very difficult to kill. Shade needed this one dead. No word could be allowed to reach Azran.

The spell was nearly complete when he discovered that his adversary was also casting.

For all practical purposes, both spells were the same. Each had recognized the danger the other represented. The Gryphon, watching the sky for some sign, was the only one who actually saw the burst. The others only heard the explosion.

One second, both were lit up. The next instant, the flash of light that ripped through the heavens caused many to believe daylight had come. Of the two combatants, nothing could be seen. It was as if they had ceased to exist.

ANGRILY, THE GRYPHON spun away from the balcony and summoned his commanders. There was hope, some hope, that they might find the necromancer alive. The lionbird tried hard not to think about how little chance there really was.

* * *

IT WAS THE flash, not the explosion, that woke Cabe. Not that he had been able to sleep well. There were so many questions running through his head. They were all forgotten the instant the light flooded his room. The blast itself nearly threw him from the bed.

He ran to a window and peered outside. There was nothing but darkness in the heavens. Cabe failed to notice the gathering mists as his gazing was suddenly interrupted by the many voices echoing his confusion. He looked for something to throw on, only to discover that he was wearing his clothes. Before retiring, he had definitely removed them.

Shrugging off the incident in the heat of the present situation, Cabe departed from his room. His first intention was to find the Lady or one of his other friends. That proved to be more difficult than he thought. With people running this way and that, it was hard to tell who was who. Fortunately, it was Gwen who found him.

"Cabe!" She was clad in a tight, emerald-green hunting outfit, short skirt and feathered cap completing the picture.

"What's going on?"

"I don't know, but I feel it has something to do with your friend, Shade."

Her tone indicated that she still did not trust the other warlock. Cabe felt the need to defend the man, but was not given the opportunity. Instead, he found himself being led by his companion to the main chamber of the Gryphon's palace.

The Gryphon was there when they arrived. He was issuing orders to commanders and scouts. They could not make out what was being said, but several of them seemed to revolve around the shadowy warlock. Gwen gave Cabe a look. He turned his eyes away, refusing to believe as she did.

Their host finally turned his attention to them. "I'm sorry I was unable to speak with you any sooner! Things have gone terribly, terribly bad!"

The Lady nodded. "I'm sure we all saw and heard the same thing. Was it Shade?"

"Partially. He was locked in struggle with one of Azran's Seekers. It was spying on us and had to be destroyed."

Cabe was elated that his faith in the sorceror was justified. The Lady seemed to ignore this and asked the Gryphon some questions. When he described the blast, she shook her head.

"Power overflow. Rare, but deadly."

Both looked at her blankly.

She continued. "They both tried to use the same spell at the same time. Oh, maybe there were slight variations in each, but to the powers, they were identical. Instead of two separate attacks, there was one general spell of four times the strength. Most likely, it destroyed them instantly."

The Gryphon agreed. "Nevertheless, I intend on having the grounds searched. Thoroughly, I might add."

He did not say what was now on everybody's mind. That the Simon personality of Shade was gone. If that was true, then a new threat had been unleashed.

Cabe had an idea. "Where's Darkhorse? He should know what's happened to Shade!"

"If that demon was anywhere near here, he's failed to appear! I have no time to go searching for him!"

A scout came in. Begging his lord's pardon, he started to report on new movements by the hordes from Lochivar. The Gryphon turned his attention to this matter completely. Lady Gwen and Cabe excused themselves. Once outside of the room, they began to talk.

"What happens to me now?" Cabe was not terribly thrilled with the thought of taking on Dragon Kings. Especially with two of their strongest allies missing, one presumed dead—and quite possibly soon to be a new threat.

"I don't know. First the library, now this. We're on the defensive. We should take the offensive before it's too late!"

"Simon—Shade took the offensive; look at what happened to him!"

"That worries me little compared to what we face should he have perished out there. The legends of his evil side would chill the soul of even the strongest of men!"

They both paused, pondering the unpleasant possibilities. It was at that point that Blane appeared. The commander was obviously anxious about something, but he paused to talk to them before heading on to the Gryphon.

"I see that this hellish night has everyone up! My father always told me to beware times when both Twins are full!"

Cabe studied the man's uniform. It was grimy and wet. Blane caught the look.

"I've been scouting near the Gray Mists since darkness. I always like to know what I'm up against."

"Isn't that dangerous? What would happen if you were captured or killed?"

He laughed. "I'd kill myself through sheer will if captured! We're trained for that. Studied under a Shizzaran priest. If killed, my men know which of them is to take over. Actually, any of them are capable, but don't let them hear that. I'll have myself an army of leaders!"

Gwen was far more interested in the Gray Mists. "What did you discover?"

Blane's face hardened. "It's expanding. They'll be here in no time. Ever seen one of those zombies? No? I have! So doped up from living in the mists that they're hardly human! Gaunt, skeletal men who fight even if they lose both arms and both legs!"

Frowning, Cabe asked, "What could they do then?"

"Bite you, man! Their teeth are sharpened to a point. They've been known to play dead and then get a soldier in the ankle as he passes. Don't know what they have for blood, but most people bitten die fast. Any soldier with smarts knows that he better steer clear or lop off the head."

And these horrors were marching toward Penacles, Cabe thought despairingly. I'm to blame for most of it. Men will die—

"Stop that!" Gwen was looking deep into his eyes. "I know what you're thinking! This would have happened whether you existed or not! The Black Dragon has always coveted the City of Knowledge. He merely waited for the chance!"

Logic has little to do with love. At that moment, Cabe was willing to believe anything the Lady said. He was even willing to lay down his life for her, should the occasion arise. She now owned him heart and soul, though she may not have realized it. It did not matter to him that she had once loved his grandfather.

Though the enchantress did not recognize the look, being herself too caught up in all matters at all times, Blane did. The soldier, a good, honest man, had left more than his share of broken hearts and had seen his own men turn soft at the sight of some woman. He decided to remove himself.

"Excuse me. The Lord Gryphon will want to know everything I've uncovered." With that, he was off.

"We've got to think this out," Gwen was saying. "We have to strike back! Waiting for disaster will only get us killed!"

"Whatever you say," Cabe replied absently.

She blinked. "Maybe we're just tired. Get some sleep. There's nothing we can do right now. I'll see you in the morning."

"Right."

The sorceress raised an eyebrow in mild curiosity and then departed. Cabe watched her leave, amazed at the wonders nature could produce. So amazed was he that he failed to notice powers coming into play.

A bright light formed behind him. In that light, a golden bow, gleaming like the sun, floated purposely. A single shaft, aimed toward the ceiling, was ready to be fired. Cabe ignored all and, in fact, seemed almost asleep.

The arrow was released. Silent but swift, the gold shaft flew to the ceiling, finding its way to a dark corner. Its target had no time to utter a sound, if it were capable of doing so. With the shaft protruding through its neck, the creature of darkness fell to the ground.

Neither arrow nor victim touched the floor. Both vanished into nothing only halfway down. The bow and the light surrounding it dissipated.

Stirring, the young warlock stumbled off to bed, his thoughts focused on the fire-haired enchantress.

X

THREE RIDERS.

A dragon patrol.

The firedrakes dismounted from their lesser cousins. They were both awed and suspicious at the sight before them. The Barren Lands had produced many bizarre things, but this—this was not the work of the dying land.

Rather, the Barren Lands were giving way to a new, greater power. The small patch of grass had become a lush, green field that stretched as far as the eye could see. Trees of all kinds dotted the area. Birds, the first immigrants to this splendid wonder, had already started their nests.

One of the firedrakes cursed. He was young, and had never known the Lands to be other than what their name implied. This was wizard's work, the work of soft humans, warm-bloods. He pulled out a gleaming longsword, stalked over to the nearest green, and hacked away.

The first slices were made easily. The fourth was much more difficult; the grass seemed to swarm over and wrap around his weapon. He pulled it loose, ignoring the jibes of his comrades. They warned him to beware of his obviously dangerous foe. He could not pull his sword free.

New grass blades had sprouted under his feet. With stunning growth, they soon stood as tall as their fellows. The firedrake tried to step back, but his boots were entangled in the plants. It was almost as if they had grabbed hold of him. Unable to free his sword, he pulled out a small knife and tried to cut the trapping grass. Not only did his small blade fail, but both the knife and his hand were now caught as well. He was no longer angered; fear had taken root as strongly as the green around him.

The lesser drakes became nervous, one even emitting a very unhorselike hiss. One of the other firedrakes came forward to free his companion. He stopped abruptly; the grass was growing quickly toward him. He jumped back. The one trapped in the field was now half covered with strangling tendrils that threatened to pull him to the ground.

In desperation, the firedrake metamorphed. Gone was the warrior; in his place was a strong, tall dragon that rippled with muscle. A creature of power. A creature who still found itself unable to escape.

The other two had backed away from the tide that seemed intent on adding them to its collection. Since the entrapment of the first, the growth had sped up several factors. The two free warriors were forced to make a dash for their mounts, the grass close behind.

Fearful and enraged, the struggling firedrake let loose with a fierce rush of flame. The wave of fire and heat washed over the nearest of the greenery. For several moments, it seemed to burn uncontrollably; then, almost abruptly, it died out, revealing little more damage than a few singed tips.

His companions had reached their mounts. They were counting on their cousins' superior speed. One leaped up and kicked his agitated mount. Rider and animal rushed off.

The other was not so lucky. His mount, seeing his brother go and already panicked by the sinister growth, bolted. The dragon warrior fell to the ground and hit his head. It took only moments for his mind to clear, and his first thoughts were to take the lesser drake belonging to his hapless companion. He tried to rise, but found himself held fast. The mount he had intended on taking screeched nearby. He struggled to reach his sword, but the ever-present grass continued to envelop him. The tendrils wrapped around his throat. He succumbed to the lush field even while his companion still fought.

The young firedrake had exhausted himself. Failure to burn the field had sapped him of all hope. Even as the life went out of his mount, which had been trapped at the same time as the other warrior, he slipped. Plant life swarmed over the huge, dying form.

Moments later, there was nothing to indicate that anyone had passed this way.

The single rider pushed to the fastest pace possible. He received no objections from his mount. His destination was not the caves of his clan. Instead, he intended to reach the Dagora Forest and eventually make his way to the Tyber Mountains.

Small animals wandered into the field for the first time in its existence. A small burrower nibbled on a blade of grass. The birds above sang. The sea of greenery did nothing. Unlike the dragons, these creatures were welcome.

AT PENACLES, THERE was no sun.

The mists enshrouded the land almost as well as the night. Firewood had been quickly gathered, enough for two months. Soldiers watched warily from the walls of the city for some sign of the enemy. They could see little in the all-encompassing fog.

No one traveled the roads anymore. The Lord Gryphon had ordered all traffic halted. That kept people in. Why no wagons arrived at the city was anyone's guess. It was hoped that the mere sight of the mists would turn back the unwary travelers. If not . . .

Food would be no problem. The Gryphon, knowing his many enemies, had long ago ordered the storage of grain, water, and other food items. Workers were also trained to keep out rodents and other small pests. On the whole, they tended to succeed.

CABE STUDIED HIS reflection in the mirror. There was no doubt in his mind that what he saw was real; the silver streak in his hair now covered nearly half of his head. What that meant, he had no idea. It frightened him, though. It had something to do with his birthright. Coming from the family he did, it could only mean trouble.

Someone knocked on the door. Cabe walked over and opened it. It was the Lord Gryphon, standing patiently and without any fanfare. He nodded to the young warlock and then noticed the change in his hair. An expression passed over the inhuman face so quickly that Cabe was unsure exactly what it was.

"Excuse me for interrupting you, but I was wondering if you would step up to the nearest watchtower with me."

Curious, Cabe agreed. They left his room, the Gryphon leading the way. The ruler of Penacles was silent the entire time. Cabe thought of a hundred reasons for this walk, but discarded all of them. He would have to remain unsatisfied until his host told him.

They reached the top of the tower only after a breathtaking climb. Cabe paused, but the lionbird appeared not in the least winded. When he had regained his breath, he looked out to where the Gryphon was now pointing. At first, all that he saw was more mist; it was heady stuff, and Cabe longed to go back down into the palace proper. Then he noticed a dark movement far off in the distance. That did not seem right. What could make itself noticeable in such fog from that distance?

The answer came to him. His stomach wanted to curl.

"Yes, my friend, that is the army of Lochivar. Do you know why their darkness cuts through the mists itself? I do not. Normally, they should be invisible. The Gray Mists are their home; they know how to shape it to their will even as it has bent their minds. Why, then, does it betray them now?"

"Someone is interfering?"

The Gryphon looked at him sharply. "You are correct. I thought that perhaps Shade did not die. Or he did this before his death. Darkhorse! It might have been that creature! Or an enemy who brooks no interference from others."

"Azran?"

"Yes, it could be. He would covet the City of Knowledge. Good thinking."

Disturbed, Cabe watched the swelling mass. "How soon will they attack?"

"How soon? As soon as they can! Fortunately, we have been able to prepare a little surprise for them."

Even as the Gryphon spoke, the sounds of men rushing back and forth and moving large objects could be heard. Cabe wanted to ask for details, but it was obvious that his host wanted this to be a surprise for him as well as for the Lochivarites.

The Lady joined them. Cabe felt a wave of emotion wash over him, but he managed to hold it in check. After all, to this woman he was probably little more than a child. She smiled at him, looked back down the steps leading to the top, and faced the Gryphon.

"You two would be in the tallest tower. How goes it? I could sense the stench of those wyvern bastards even in my sleep!"

The Lord Gryphon chuckled, a strange action for one with a face like his. "I imagine so. You're just in time to see the opening shot. Come."

They stood and watched, Cabe and Gwen curious, the lionbird smiling grimly now. Below, most sounds of movement had stilled. The defenders of the city were ready and waiting for the word. The Gryphon stared at the swelling, dark mass for another minute and then dropped something over the edge. He turned to his two companions.

"They will spread out as soon as they are able to. Right now, though, they still think themselves safe enough. Their master does not realize the range of my new weapons."

As if on cue, a series of noises went off. To Cabe, they seemed akin to someone snapping a piece of wood in two. Large projectiles appeared briefly in the thick fog in front of them. Within seconds, they disappeared in the direction of the oncoming enemy.

"Catapults. Nothing new about them, save their range."

"Wait, my Lady. Watch."

The missiles took some time reaching their targets. When the first one did, though, the two humans backed away, shock all over their faces.

"By Havak!" the sorceress shouted. "What was that?"

A cold gleam was in the lionbird's eyes. "Final justice!"

Great bursts of green flame rushed out wherever the projectiles landed. A few missed, but most found some part of the enemy. The light from the fires caused the Gray Mists to take on a slightly different color for a change. There were obviously men on fire everywhere, but the dark shape of the army continued to advance with amazing speed.

Cabe watched in horrid fascination. "What was that?"

"Something I discovered in the libraries. Two potions, separated, placed in compartments of the missile. When the missile hits the ground, the violent action causes the inner containers to break and mixes the two liquids. That is the result. It is quite effective. One of the few items from the libraries that I've managed to make use of."

The Lady watched the advance of the legions. "Not good enough. They're still coming through. It seems like an endless line."

"I didn't expect this to stop them. It will, however, soften them up and lessen the odds. We shall deal with the survivors when we have to."

More projectiles flew up. It was obvious by their accuracy that the men had been training for this for some time. Cabe commented on this and received an approving nod from the Gryphon.

"Only a fool trusts the ghouls of Lochivar. We knew this day would come, and we estimated their most probable route."

"The Black Dragon would have thought of that. He must not care how many he loses."

"Unfortunately, he has many more warriors to lose than we do. He hopes to take us with sheer numbers. He may do it, especially if the forces of the Dragon Emperor join him." The Gryphon watched another volley. "Confidentially, I believe Black wants the city for his own. That is in our favor."

After the first few strikes, it was more than obvious to the invaders that their cover was gone. Quickly, efficiently, the armies of Lochivar spread themselves along the hills and fields. Successful shots became rare; only a few men would be hit, if any. The Gryphon called for a cease-fire.

Cabe grew uneasy. "What happens now?"

"That would depend on our visitors. I daresay they might return the favor we just gave them."

Sure enough, it was only moments before dark shapes began separating from the bulk of the forces. Larger than a man, they flew up into the air. That they were dragons of some kind was soon obvious. Whether they were airdrakes or firedrakes was uncertain. The lord of Penacles paced back and forth, waiting.

They neared the city in two formations. A hundred yards from the walls, they split up, one group going left, the other right. The Gryphon signaled his archers. The first of the dragons moved in to attack.

The front set of archers let loose. The sky was filled with arrows, but even as the shafts sought their targets, more dragons entered the battle. The second line fired. The drakes in front suffered heavy casualties, and a number fell to the ground in rapid succession. Still, the next group came closer. The Gryphon's third and final line of archers fired. More dragons died. The first set barely finished reloading before they were forced to fire. The strategy was obvious; Black was sacrificing numbers so that his airborne killers could get close enough for a deadly assault. Meanwhile, the Lochivarites moved ever nearer.

A drake flew swiftly over the battlements and unleashed a powerful smoke that turned the Gray Mists yellow. Those nearest to the smoke fell to the floor or over the wall. They screamed and tried to wipe the foul gas from their eyes. One killed himself rather than continue suffering. A few ran madly from the walls, only to plummet to their deaths in the city itself. The three onlookers watched in horror.

The Lady was the first to react. Cabe sensed rather than felt the first stirrings of the wind that formed around her. It was not strong enough to push the airdrake away, but it made his deadly weapon useless. In fact, the wind was carrying it in the direction of the advancing forces.

"I don't know whether I can keep it floating long enough, but that's not the point! Someone's got to stop the dragons!"

More drakes had made it past the archers. One set a catapult on fire, causing one of the chemical missiles to explode. The crew manning the catapult died instantly. Fires raged all over the area of the explosion. Two other war machines went up in flames before the men below could contain the fires.

The archers could not stem the tide of dragons. For every one shot down, two were making it into the city. If this were only a small portion of the enemy's strength, Penacles would stand little chance of survival.

The Gryphon had been silent for some time. Now he pulled something from an inner pocket. Cabe saw that it was a ring on which hung three small whistles. The ruler of the City of Knowledge chose one of the whistles. His face contorted as it assumed the more human appearance that was necessary for proper use of the instrument. The tiny metal pipe was placed to his lips and blown.

No sound came from the whistle, but something replied almost immediately. There was a challenging shriek, as if the intruding dragons had dared to enter into personal territories. From out of buildings, trees, and places invisible in the fog came a rushing of wings. Cries of a thousand different species formed into one. The deadly wave of lizards paused in confusion.

Birds covered the darkened skies.

The drakes, despite their speed, appeared almost motionless compared to the birds. From the tiniest of the plant feeders to the largest of the predators, countless feathered creatures clawed and bit at the invading reptiles. Hundreds died from flame and gas, but each helped cut the dragons' numbers down rapidly. The drakes snapped and grabbed for their adversaries, sometimes colliding with each other in the process. One firedrake thoroughly scorched his nearest neighbor, who happened to be an airdrake. The airdrake exploded, taking all within the immediate area with him.

The most surprising part of this bizarre battle in the sky was the way in which the birds herded the monsters out of the city before finishing them off. Few dragons actually died in Penacles itself. Those that did landed in the outskirts of the city proper. The loss of life was small compared to what it might have been.

At some point, retreat was called. Only a handful of the original force remained, and most of these were injured in some way. Even as they departed, more than one suddenly wobbled violently and fell to the ground. The birds continued to harass them until they were far away. When the last of the drakes had returned to the enemy lines, the feathered victors turned back to the city. Most never made it. Released from whatever spell had summoned them, the various birds returned to their normal ways of life, flying this way and that way. The few who reached the walls of Penacles merely continued on to their roosts.

It was as if they had never taken part in the war.

It had happened so quickly that none of the defenders could believe it was over. The entire battle had lasted only minutes. Calm now prevailed. The Lady ceased her spell, and then both she and Cabe waited for an explanation from their host.

The Gryphon's face had reverted to the one of legend. He held up the whistle to them. They could both see that it was rusting before their very eyes. Within seconds, it was dust.

Gwen smirked. "Another one of the surprises from your bag of tricks? What was that?"

"A gift to me from someone long dead. Call it part of my heritage and leave it at that."

"What about the other two whistles? What do they summon?"

The lionbird put the ring back into his pocket. "If the time comes, you will see."

He refused to say anything more on the subject.

The invaders had slowed down. Now that they knew some of the resistance they would encounter, the commanders would replot their strategy. For the moment, there was a lull. This was fine for the defenders. Enough men would be kept busy clearing away the wounded and dying, not to mention putting out the numerous fires that had been started by the dragons.

The Gryphon suggested they return to the main floor of the palace. The trip took them several minutes. When they reached the bottom, they were met by Blane and the general of the army of Penacles, a foxlike man by the name of Toos. The fiery-red hair on his head and face was almost a match for the Lady's, and there was also an ominous streak of silver that covered a good quarter of the right side.

When the general was introduced, Gwen commented on his appearance immediately. "I have seen many warlocks in battle, but I've known few who commanded armies personally."

The smile on the face of Toos served only to make him look even more like a fox. "My skills in sorcery are far too meager. They serve only to accentuate my ability to command and plan."

"What damage has been done?" the Gryphon asked, concerned about his subjects.

Blane's face grew dark. "The northeast wall was hit hardest. Thirty men dead there, most from the initial encounter with the airdrake. Gods! What man can fight the very air around him?"

The lord of Penacles nodded. "Yes, that is a problem. I shall have to consult the libraries soon. I'm sure there will be something—if I can understand it."

Cabe looked from one man to the other. "I don't understand. Shouldn't you be able to find what you need to win this war? I'd think that one long search in those libraries would tell you everything you wanted to know."

His host tugged at the fur below his beak as a man might tug on his beard. "You don't understand the libraries, Cabe. They give us what we need to know, with one exception. No page of any book is written straightforward. All are either riddles or verses. It is up to the reader to translate this into real information. In my own opinion, they were written by minds with a very warped sense of humor."

Toos cleared his throat. "There is something else you should know, sire. We estimate that the advance group of the Dragon Emperor is no more than three days away. The main bulk, under Toma, follows about a week—maybe ten days—behind. We will be hard-pressed to stave off both armies."

"Who of noteworthiness travels with the advance group?"

"A duke named Kyrg leads them. I have heard ill things about him—"

The Gryphon held up a hand. "You need not tell me of Duke Kyrg. I know the drake. A brilliant sadist. One I'd hoped was dead."

He looked from one person to another. The looks on their faces did not give much indication of confidence. Even the Lady, well known for her strength, appeared to be unsure of the days ahead. Only Cabe appeared to have anything remotely resembling hope. The others had seen too much destruction in the past. The Gryphon, therefore, fixed on the young warlock.

"You, young friend, are the key to this thing. In you is the blood of the greatest line of sorcerors. Nathan was the best—"

"—and Azran the worst!" Gwen interjected.

Ignoring her, the lord of Penacles continued. "The mark of the powers is the silver in the hair. Generally, the more silver, the greater the power.

There are exceptions. Toos has little in the way of practical power. Shade—
Shade was an enigma. The silver in his hair varied every time one looked."

The Gryphon turned to the Lady. "Train him. Train him quickly. I
suspect that everything we hold dear depends on his ability to harness the
powers properly and soon!"

IT WAS NEARLY finished.

With movements that would have left him gasping for breath only hours
earlier, Azran cleared away the various pieces of equipment from his room.
The Nameless required only one more burst of power, one very minor burst
of power. Already, it blazed with a fury. The box where it lay might as well
have been transparent; power from the sword cut through it like air.

He snapped his fingers. A spirit, one of those not-born that Azran had
summoned from the depths of the Other, flittered to him. He ordered a full
meal. Meat usually was bad for his system, but there was no need to worry
about that. Now he could eat and do as he wished. The spirit departed to
fulfill his command. Azran summoned another and ordered it to bring a
mirror. A full-sized one.

The mirror came first. He ordered the dark servant to place it against a
wall. When that was done, he straightened his clothes, freshly created for
this occasion, and stood in front of the mirror admiring himself.

It was good to be young again.

All those years of hard labor were about to pay off. He studied himself
critically in the mirror. The black of his outfit, more like a uniform than
anything else, was complemented by the navy blue band around his collar and his wrists. Azran paused and then added an emblem to his chest, a
dragon impaled on a sword. Good touch, he decided. Let them know he was
their master. The new Dragon Master!

His head was covered half by black and half by silver. Another indication of his power. The face resembled too much that of his father, but that
was also a plus in its own way. The Dragon Kings and their servants would
remember the past and tremble.

A beard. He hadn't worn a beard in decades. It would be the finishing
touch. A short, trim one. That would do it. He gestured, making the seconds turn into weeks.

Azran blinked. Like the hair on the top of his head, the beard was half
silver. It was a bizarre sight. Almost ominous.

He decided to keep it.

Boots, hip-length in the front, and gloves completed the picture. To an opponent, the clothing would appear as show. Try to cut it with a weapon and it would be revealed to be stronger than chain. Much lighter, though.

Smiling at his reflection, Azran walked out onto his balcony. No one would have ever suspected that he lived in the midst of the Hell Plains. It was far too close to the Tyber Mountains and was also ruled by the Red Dragon, one of the more bloodthirsty of the Kings. He laughed. His castle stood in the very center of the most naturally violent of lands. A volcano stood no more than two miles away. Yet nothing could harm this place. It was older than the Dragon Kings and invisible to the outside world. Azran had discovered it only by chance. He never did learn who had built it, and no longer cared. It was now his, and it served him well.

A shriek came from above. The Seekers were angry, perhaps frightened. The one sent to spy on Penacles had still not returned. The warlock suspected that it no longer existed. That was two attacks in the recent past. Events were rushing to a head. He had to ensure that he would control the flow.

His food was brought to him. It was a sumptuous feast. Azran planned on making up for years of corn mush and bread. Now, with new teeth, he would bite into all those delights he knew only from memory.

From within its casket, the Nameless pulsated. With each bite Azran took, the pulsating increased.

CABE AND THE Lady were walking to his room.

"We will begin your training with basics. I'll teach you some simple defensive spells first. Just in case. I—we don't want you dead before you have a chance to fight."

"Neither do I."

She smiled. "So much like Nathan. Still, even Nathan never had the head of silver. The Gryphon may be right. You could be more powerful than anyone."

They reached his room. Cabe opened the door for his companion, who stepped through. He followed immediately, closing the door as he entered. They were alone, he realized. Perhaps, he thought, he could tell her how he felt. Now, while no other living soul was around.

There were indeed no living souls around . . .

. . . But they were not alone.

The Lady was encased in a glow. The glow solidified, and, with a start,

Cabe recognized it as the same sort of prison that had held her captive for so many years. He pulled out the Horned Blade, feeling its power embrace him. He did not, however, have a chance to use it.

A hand touched him on the temple. Cabe felt his body quiver. Though he remained armed, the weapon was useless. His limbs were as solid as the marble columns of the palace. Frozen in time, he could only watch as the dark blade was wrenched from his grasp. His eyes widened at what he could only momentarily see.

"So simple." The voice was dry and curiously sad in tone.

The sword was tossed to the ground. He could hear footsteps behind him. Suddenly, he was floating. Gwen remained where she was, once more trapped in amber. They were after him, no one else. He drifted like a feather, randomly turning this way and that. During one of those turns, he caught sight of his captors.

The eyes that met his were eyes no more. Blank, upturned whites. Whites set in decaying, parchment skin.

He was a prisoner of the undead. One started to speak, then checked himself. His companion gestured. A great hole opened up in the middle of the room's reality. Cabe found himself floating into it. When he touched it, all conscious thought faded away.

Tyr turned to look at the Lady, trapped in the amber, and then at the Horned Blade. His companion put a hand on his shoulder.

"We must go."

They stepped into the portal. Undead and hole disappeared.

XI

THE EXPLOSION ROCKED the palace.

At first, the Gryphon feared some sort of attack by the Lochivarites. This fear was laid to rest by Blane, who reported that there had been no movement by the forces from the Gray Mists. The lionbird then thought of Azran and suddenly remembered where his guests were being quartered. Summoning his golems, he rushed to Cabe's room.

The door, what was left of it, lay in the hallway. Small fragments of some crystalline substance, vaguely familiar, dotted the area. The Gryphon ordered the two golems forward. They would form a shield for him. He hoped the two creatures would prove sufficient. He was unsure of their limits.

Nothing stirred in the room as the three entered. Dust obscured most of his vision, but he did see the Horned Blade lying on the floor nearby. He left it where it was; nothing would be gained by possessing the accursed sword at this time.

Someone moaned. The dust was settling, and the Gryphon could finally make out a form lying near the bed. He ordered the two golems to stay and investigated cautiously. It might have been a trap, but he doubted it.

The figure on the ground turned out to be the Lady Gwen. She was half conscious and strangely untouched by the dust that filled the room. In fact, whenever she moved, the dust that had settled around her shifted away so as not to be near. There were no marks on her body. Exhaustion seemed to be her worst problem. Assured that she would recover, the Gryphon had his two unliving bodyguards carry her to her room. They picked her up with a gentleness that was surprising for such strong creatures. As they carried her out, the Gryphon took one last look around the room.

Cabe Bedlam was nowhere to be seen. The Horned Blade, left behind, was the only indication that he had ever been there.

Dark thoughts racing through his mind, the lord of Penacles stalked out of the room. He hoped that the lady would be well enough to answer some questions. He already knew most of the answers, but there was always the hope that he might be mistaken.

The two golems flanked the door of her room. They were becoming surprisingly competent servants. Lady Gwen was lying on her bed, awake. She looked up as her host entered the room. The expression on her face said everything he feared it would, but he was determined to ask despite that.

"What happened?"

"We were struck from behind. Shadow people! Do you understand what I'm saying? Shadow people!"

He nodded grimly. Shadow people. The undead. Those who were forced to obey a master until granted release. They could not truly rest until then. He did not know whether to hate or pity the kidnappers.

"They almost caught me by surprise! It's fortunate that I've become somewhat paranoid. I swore I'd never be trapped like I was. Only that saved me from another amber prison!"

"They used the same spell?"

She nodded. "Yes. Weaker, though. Not that they didn't have the power. They were strong. I just don't think they really wanted to do it."

"How many were there?"

"Just two. This time I was able to keep consciousness. One struck me while the other froze Cabe in place. Gryphon, they took him! They took him from under my nose, and I couldn't do a thing to stop them!" Tears threatened to fall.

The Gryphon noted her tremendous anxiety but said nothing of it. This was not the time or the place. "How did they get in? Where did they go? I received no reports from my sentries."

"Blink hole. They needed it so that they could pass his body through." Her eyes regained a bit of their fire. "I might be able to trace it! Sometimes they leave afterimages. We could follow them to Azran's castle!"

"Where he will no doubt be waiting for us. I think not. Besides, would he be that foolish? Rest now. You've expended far too much energy to go charging into the hidden fortress of Azran."

"But Cabe—"

He stopped her. "You believe you failed Nathan and now you will fail his grandson. I tell you that this is unfounded. Nathan did what Nathan had to do. He would not have done any differently if you had been there. As for Cabe, he was kidnapped, not killed. That means that Azran wants him alive. I think he's curious about his son. Cabe will be all right."

She was only half listening, but that was as much as the Gryphon could have expected. She put her head down and closed her eyes. The lionbird quietly departed. Her concern for the young warlock was great, far greater than it would have been for any other person.

The Gryphon was also concerned, but he had different priorities. Penacles and its people came first. There would be no chance to rescue Cabe if the city fell. If they were to act against Azran, Penacles must be cared for in the meantime.

There were still no attacks. This in itself was unusual. It could mean only that control of the army was in the hands—or claws—of the Black Dragon's firedrakes. The Lochivarites never would have waited so long. They had little interest in saving their necks; death in battle was one of the few things important to those drug-filled fanatics.

He remembered the first time he had faced the hordes from the Gray Mists. No one knew their real loyalties then. It was assumed that they would fight for man just as most other cities would. There were always traitors, of course, but never on this scale.

Thousands of men had died that day. Many others would never be whole. The remnants of that Lochivarite army had drawn back into the shadowy lands from which they had come. Only a fraction of the original force had remained.

In taking control of the City of Knowledge, the Gryphon had been forced to recruit more mercenaries and outsiders. His original group had been almost totally wiped out. Building up to his former strength had taken several years and tremendous amounts of money. Yet the Lochivarites, with little in the way of enticements, somehow rebuilt their invasion force from scratch. Granted, generations had gone by, but even an increased birthrate could not account for the numbers.

Lochivarites, Dragon Kings, and Azrans.

There were always too many enemies.

He summoned Toos, Blane, and the rest of his commanders to him. Cabe was important; he could not ignore this fact. But he could not desert Penacles. The people were looking to him.

A chilling thought occurred to him. Would Azran be able to corrupt Cabe? The idea of a warlock of his potential being controlled by such a fiend shook him almost as much as the thought of possibly having to fight off Shade. Even the Dragon Kings would think twice.

His war council was complete. Grimly, the ruler of the City of Knowledge put on a mask of confidence and determination. Inside, he cursed himself almost constantly.

INTO THE DEN of the Beast.

He was no longer frozen. Not that it mattered. The bonds around his wrists, legs, and waist held him as securely as the spell. They were not, needless to say, normal restraints. Each glowed; each glowed brighter if he struggled to free himself. When they grew brighter, they burned him. Not outwardly, but in his very mind. That was why Cabe remained motionless. The first attempt had been sufficient to teach him.

His kidnappers had left him. That was fine with Cabe; the undead made very poor company. Especially these two. They had spent most of their time staring at him with the whites that were their eyes. To make matters more uncomfortable, they seemed sad and ashamed about something. He had the annoying feeling that it had something to do with him and who he was.

A shadow flittered. He blinked. This was not one of the nameless things that lurked in the shadows of the room. This was something much more physical, yet also more powerful. In the dim light of the room, he could make out only its outline, but that was enough to tell him he was being studied by one of the Seekers. Was this his captor? Probably not. More likely, it was just another one of the servants. Deep down, he already knew who was in charge. It could be none other than Azran, his father.

There was little he could do at the moment. He was the helpless prisoner of a madman. The Seeker, still watching him intently, let out a low squawk. It almost sounded sympathetic. The Seeker did not, however, make any move toward removing the bonds.

AZRAN FACED HIS two decaying slaves. The blank eyes glared at him, more so now that he was young once again. He did not have them kneel this time. He wished to look at them face-to-face, despite their odor of rot and their peeling skin. He wanted them to see his face, his hair of silver and black, to feel his vitality and life. To feel his power.

"I must commend you both," he said dryly. "I see you were able to carry out my plan in record time. Your fears were, of course, unfounded. The Lady never had a chance, and my son, strong though he may be, had no skill. Yes, overall, I am pleased."

"Are we free to return to our rest?" Basil's face revealed no emotion, but his voice was sullen. He was disgusted with his own actions.

"No, not quite yet. I may still need you. Besides, you and the boy haven't been formally introduced!" He laughed at that and laughed even harder when he saw Tyr's fists clench in rage that his face could no longer reveal.

Basil longed for the ability to spit in his tormentor's face. "You are black, Azran. Black as the darkest of the powers."

"Thank you. I try. Shall we go?"

Against their will, the two corpses shambled ahead of their master. Azran made Basil play butler, even nodding to him as he walked by. In what was left of his mind, the undead warlock cursed, but he was unable to break free of the servile position he had been forced to assume.

Cabe turned wide-eyed as the trio entered. The zombies he had seen before, and, though they still frightened him, they were dismissed from his mind at the first sight of the sinister figure with them. Even despite the two-toned hair covering the face, he could see the family resemblance. Father and son faced each other at last.

The dark mage turned his head momentarily to one of the windows. There had been—what? Nothing was at the window. Nothing. He turned his attention back to his son, who now looked only a few years younger than he did. The brilliant head of silver, covering more than three quarters, made him blink. By all rights, this Cabe would be a very powerful warlock. Even more than Azran himself.

The boy must be corrupted or die. Those were the only two choices.

He greeted Cabe affably. "So, you are my son!"

"Azran?"

"Of course! Who else could I be?"

"What do you want with me?" There was fear in Cabe's voice, but there was something else: defiance.

"You're my son! Every man likes to see his son once or twice. I thought you died at birth. You have no idea how much your life means to me, son!"

Cabe shuddered.

Azran's eyes narrowed, and the humor was gone from his voice. "I saw your small, limp form. Nathan tricked me! You were very much alive. He'd spirited you away in a futile attempt, no doubt, to raise you as a tool against me!"

The black warlock smiled. "Now, however, I have you back. I look forward to teaching you about the dark powers, my son. You have great potential. Nathan saw it. I will use it. Together, we will make the Dragonrealms ours!"

He broke off suddenly, his eyes focused on Cabe's side. Azran whirled around to face Basil. He said nothing, but the undead knew what was on his mind.

"He was not wearing the Horned Blade when we captured him. It was not in his room. There was little time to search for it. The Lord Gryphon is known for his promptness when danger arises."

"Damn you, Basil—"

"We are already damned."

"You were supposed to bring me the Horned Blade, too! You failed!"

Cabe looked from one to the other. He had carried the sword; one of the kidnappers had taken it and tossed it to the side. Why was this creature lying?

The other, Tyr, chose the outburst to look toward the captive. Cabe watched as the animated corpse waggled a finger in his direction. Cabe understood. Azran did not have the power over his servants that he believed he had. There was hope yet.

Calming himself, Azran turned back to his son. "Never trust the undead, my son. They are highly inept. Especially these two. Untrustworthy, also."

He waved his hand. His unearthly servants stepped forward. "An object lesson, Cabe. Before you, you see two shambling wrecks that were once full of life and in command of their own existences. This bear of a man was called Basil. Basil of the Eye. He could freeze a person solid in a prison of amber or merely paralyze with a touch. His friends called him Basil Basilisk. I borrowed his powers to take care of the Lady Gwen. Pity it didn't hold. His angry friend here was named Tyr. Just that. Don't let his priestly garments fool you. He was known to go into berserker rages that doubled his abilities. Both were Dragon Masters under my unlamented father, your grandfather, Nathan Bedlam. Both, despite their so-called prowess, fell easily at my hand."

Cabe choked.

"They didn't protect themselves too well. Overconfidence, Basil?"

The voice sounded of dirt and death. It was also filled with vast hatred. "Yesss!"

The dark sorceror smiled grandly. "Poor Dragon Masters! They are now forced to obey me until I release them."

"Or die!" Tyr's voice was just loud enough to be heard.

"Enough of that! You may return to your rest until summoned again. This time, come swiftly!"

The two decaying figures shambled out of the room. Cabe caught just a glimpse of Tyr's face as the ghastly warlock turned his head to look back at him. It was the face of the damned. Cabe swore then and there that he would find some way to release them.

Azran gestured. An elaborate chair, more a throne, appeared just behind him. With great satisfaction, he sat down. Another spell removed the bonds holding his captive.

"There! That should be more comfortable. I would, however, not recommend trying something foolish. The area around and including your seat has been set up as a sort of warning system. Do something disruptive, or even get up, and you will find yourself in for a big shock. Literally."

"What happens now?"

"Now? Now I give you your first lesson in how the world of magic really works. Especially where the powers come in."

Cabe could not hide his interest. His father smiled approvingly.

"To begin with, the titles warlock, sorceror, necromancer, enchanter, their female counterparts, and any term I've forgotten are used fairly interchangeably these days. Once, they each meant something specific. No more. Once the key to colors became obvious, anyone with the ability to control the powers could raise themselves to the levels of masters. This nonsense about good and evil powers is just that: nonsense! Some merely choose different colors of the spectrum. I found the darker shades much more efficient. Nathan could never understand that."

Understand? Cabe felt that his grandfather had understood very well. There was no doubt in his mind that choosing the dark side of the spectrum was the same as falling under the seduction of evil. Azran, being one who had succumbed, could no more see the truth than any addict.

Azran mistook his thoughtful expression as a sign that Cabe was being won over. He pushed on. "The Dragon Kings also have magic. Thus, most of their names are colors. Even their skins take on the color they have chosen to use." He paused. "You may think that Iron, Ice, Crystal, and Storm differ from their brethren, but they do not. Have you ever studied the appearance of iron, the metal? It has a color all its own. Not quite blue, not quite gray, not quite anything. Crystal diffuses the essences of the spectrum and, therefore, uses many fine fractions of each. Storm takes his power from lightning, and what is that but light itself? Ice posed an enigma; he seemed not to use the spectrum in any way. This was false. Ice is similar to Crystal; both diffuse the colors. Crystal takes the pure. Ice, the impure. By standards, this makes him more evil than his fellow Kings."

He smiled knowingly at Cabe, who shifted uneasily on the treacherous chair.

"Where have you been all these years?"

The change in direction totally disarmed Cabe. "What?"

"I am, perhaps, the only one who would've noticed the discrepancy immediately—if I hadn't assumed you were dead, that is. I know it takes a long time to grow up, but really . . ."

Cabe shook his head. "I don't know. I don't remember anything strange or unusual about my childhood."

"Well, we'll have to come back to that some other time. Are you hungry?"

Another abrupt change in direction. Azran was no doubt mad as well as evil. Cabe did not answer.

Azran appeared uncomfortable. "No? I am. I must say, ever since I rejuvenated myself, I've had an appetite like one of the Dragon Kings! Sure you won't join me? Roast vinbeast!"

Cabe shook his head numbly. Better to eat with the Gold Dragon himself!

"Then I shall leave you for a time. If you change your mind, speak out. One of my servants"—he indicated a thing flitting in and out of the darkness—"will tell me. Good-bye, Cabe."

With a flourish, chair and sorceror vanished. A faint smell of brimstone drifted near the hapless young warlock. He sneezed.

There was nothing else to do but sit. Sit and think. Not that the latter would probably do much good. Cabe was finding himself too dependent on others. He was supposed to have powers, but with no one to teach him properly, he was helpless.

Something fluttered near one of the windows. To no surprise, it was a Seeker. He was not sure if it was the same one and realized that it didn't matter. The creature swooped through the window and landed soundlessly on the stone floor.

Several shapes detached themselves from the dark corners of the room. They flew toward the Seeker. The avian waved a clawed hand in their direction. The servants stopped in midair, remained there a moment, and then returned to their nests—backward! It was as if time had been reversed for Azran's pets.

With incredible grace, the Seeker moved to Cabe, who was nearly tempted to test the power of his father's trap. Something, though, kept him where he was. It was not fear, he discovered, but the need to know. To know what it was that this servant who was not a servant wanted. It was not, obviously, Cabe's death. That could have been accomplished easily enough already.

The Seeker reached out for the top of the other's head. Cabe stiffened, but the touch was gentle. It was not the pulling that had been used the other time. Rather, the avian was communicating. Communicating in such a way so that Azran would not discover.

Words did not form as he had half expected. Rather, images appeared. The Hell Plains, a path leading southwest to Penacles, a sword, and then Azran. The intention was obvious: the Seeker wished to free Cabe. In return, Cabe would reclaim the Horned Blade and use it to kill his father. It did not bother him to fight Azran—the man was his parent only by nature; there was no love—but the odds were not very much in the young warlock's favor. Azran had years of experience. He had none. There had to be another way.

The avian shook itself, a gesture indicating its irritation. Withdrawing contact, it stared at the prisoner. The eyes were ancient and arrogant.

Humans were a lesser form to it. That Azran forced the Seekers to do his bidding was an insult beyond all, as far as the creature was concerned. All this was as evident as if the images had been shown to Cabe.

Returning to the window, the creature looked at the prisoner one more time. The head was cocked to one side, emphasizing the Seeker's nature. When Cabe made no sign of agreement, the winged enigma flew out the window. The would-be warlock was left to himself again, this time his hopes even dimmer. If there had been any hope of assistance by the Seekers, Cabe's lack of confidence had destroyed it.

SILVER, RED, AND Storm were the only ones summoned. They were the only ones trusted.

Ice cared only for himself. The Dragonrealms could sink into the seas for all he cared. Green allowed his humans too much freedom; soldiers from Zuu had added to the strength of the Gryphon's army. Crystal was an unknown and, therefore, not to be included. As for Black, the Dragon Emperor had suspicions concerning the master of the Gray Mists.

They did not meet in their natural forms. Instead, four armored warriors conferred in the great chamber. Though they dressed alike, it was simple to tell which ruled over his companions.

"Treachery! Bronze and Iron have paid for their folly! Let this be a lesson to those who would usurp my power! I shall be obeyed!"

Gold stood. The others, seated before him, nodded agreement. Each knew that a new distribution of the kingdoms was imminent; there were too many dead rulers, and the royal hatchlings would take far too long to grow to adulthood. Add to that the knowledge that Gold contemplated taking the lands of Blue and Green, and each of his servants who remained loyal would be rewarded well.

Red, most of all, awaited the change. Gold would no doubt split the kingdoms of Iron and Bronze between himself and Silver. That would leave Irillian by the Sea for Storm and, most important, the thick, lush Dagora Forest would belong to Red himself. It would make a welcome change from the Hell Plains. That such alterations in the ruling structure meant the downfall of his brothers did not bother him in the least.

There was a fifth figure in the chamber, hidden by both the shadows and his or hers or, quite possibly, its voluminous hood and robe. That it was not a firedrake was the only thing any of Gold's companions knew as fact. It was something that they could feel. The spectral visitor had spoken only to the emperor, and it was partially for this the three had been summoned.

Curiosity was not limited to the human race.

Through his helm, Gold studied those with him. He knew very well what thoughts were going on in their minds. They were his. They would serve him well. Greed was a perfect motivating tool.

"We find ourselves in a new war. The Gryphon seeks to re-create the Masters. Our own brethren have turned traitorous. The son of Nathan Bedlam comes out of hiding and dares to make noises of conquest!" He pounded his fist on the table. "For countless years, these lands have been ours! They shall remain ours!"

There were shouts of agreement.

"I have received information concerning the warlock Azran. He lives among us! He lives, yes, he lives in the domain of our brother Red!"

The lord of the Hell Plains started. His two companions eyed him suspiciously. He glared back at them.

Gold smiled. "Peace, Red! I accuse you of no treachery. The sorceror lives in a castle hidden from the sight of man, firedrake, or beast. Until now."

The emperor snapped his fingers. The dark figure stepped out, its face still hidden by the folds of its hood. From within the robe it drew out a large rolled parchment. This was placed on a table in the midst of the Dragon Kings. Unrolled, it proved to be an accurate map of the Dragonlands.

"There!" The Gold Dragon put a finger on a spot in the lower portion of the Hell Plains. The others studied it, Red most of all.

"There is nothing there! I and countless of my clans have been there often enough!" The crimson monarch fairly bristled. "It is merely volcanic land!"

"This is a castle of the old races."

The voice brought shivers to each of the Dragon Kings, even Gold. It was the sound of the grave, the touch of a wind from the underworld. No one kept their eyes on the stranger for more than a moment.

The emperor was first to recover. "This is Madrac. You need know no more save that he has little love for our enemies, as they would treat him no better than they would us. His studies unearthed the secret of the castle, and he urges us to hurry. You see, with one strike, we may rid ourselves of the last of the Bedlams!"

"Son and grandson are both within the castle walls?" Red bared his teeth in a very inhuman smile of satisfaction. Not only would honor be restored to him, his feats would be told for generations. All this could only give him the favor of his emperor. No doubt, the Dagora Forest would be his soon after.

The faceless Madrac spoke again. "You will need a sizable force, my lord Red. Azran counts the Seekers amongst his servants. Though they are reluctant slaves, they are deadly fighters."

"I look forward to the battle. I will summon the largest of my clans and crush him!"

"I meant no disrespect. Merely warned."

Gold looked to his brother. "Bring the corpses to me. They must be burned before all of us. Only then may we rest with the knowledge that the Bedlams are no more!" He rolled up the map and returned it to the warlock. Madrac drifted back into the shadows.

"Black has begun his assault on the City of Knowledge, hoping, obviously, to take it for himself. He is a fool! The Gryphon, half-breed that he is, is still more than a match for him! While both weaken each other, Kyrg will stay back, pretending to wait for Toma. Should Black somehow succeed, Kyrg will assure that it is my legions that occupy the city and libraries. By that time, brother Black's hordes of madmen will be depleted and his clans reduced in strength."

"What of Toma?" Storm, partially gray, partially yellow—at the moment—asked in curiosity.

"Mito Pica is the city that protected the grandhatchling of Nathan Bedlam during his growth. For that reason alone, it has forfeited its right to exist. Toma shall raze the city!"

Something that should never have been born cried out from the depths of Kivan Grath. Gold kept his face expressionless, but cursed to himself. The other three Dragon Kings looked about, openly startled by the eerie sounds. Madrac, half hidden, revealed no emotion at all.

The emperor improvised quickly. He leaned toward his brothers. "Know and remember this; I am ruler of the Dragon Kings! To disobey me is to suffer the consequences! To betray me is to die! The legions of Iron and Bronze discovered that!"

They visibly shuddered. Gold nodded, pleased. Let them wonder about the unknown servants of their master. It would help to keep them under tight rein.

"You are dismissed! Brother Red. See to it that you do not fail! Great rewards await you if you succeed, but great pain will be your only prize if you should fail!"

"I understand, my lord!" The master of the Hell Plains departed last of the three, his mind contemplating the rich life of the Dagora Forest and what he would do when it was his.

Gold was now alone. Alone, save for the warlock Madrac.

The emperor turned to his ghostly companion. In his mind, the sorceror was the only one he could really trust. Madrac spoke as if destruction and death were sustenance for him. They were kindred spirits in many ways.

"I have not forgotten you, Madrac."

"I merely await your pleasure, King of Kings."

"You shall be well rewarded for your services." Gold did not mention that the warlock would be rewarded with death soon after the present crisis was over. Kindred spirits, perhaps, but that also made Madrac dangerous once the present crisis was over.

"The destruction of the Gryphon and these new Masters will suffice."

The dragon lord nodded. His mind turned to other matters. "I have much to think on. You are dismissed for now."

Madrac bowed and drifted into the blackness. The eerie cry of Gold's most loyal servant issued forth once more. Lost in thought, the emperor wandered off to feed his pet. The few torches in the chamber were dying out. Soon there would be total darkness.

In what little light remained, a shadow was formed. The shadow took on the shape of a cloaked and hooded figure. Madrac. Though servants of the Dragon Emperor lurked in the hidden recesses of the room, none detected the presence of the intruder. The warlock laughed, a laugh of death and horror, and, for the first time, pulled the cowl from his face. What he had of a face, that is.

He may have smiled. It was difficult to tell with the blurred features of Shade.

XII

KYRG JUST SITS there. None of his force even received a scratch. I don't understand it, Lord Gryphon."

The lionbird turned to his companion, Blane. There had been a lull in the fighting. It was now a normal siege situation. The Lochivarites and their firedrake commanders were testing the durability of the city. The dragons obviously feared more attacks of the kind the Gryphon had used to destroy the initial aerial assault. That would change very soon if the lord of Penacles was unable to translate the words he'd read in the books. Why rhymes and poetry, of all things?

One consolation: the longer the firedrakes waited, the harder their human fanatics would be to control.

"Kyrg," he said, "awaits Duke Toma. Toma is, at present, destroying Mito Pica."

"What?" Blane dropped his helmet, which had been held under his arm. "Mito Pica? Can we do nothing?"

"Nothing. So many of the spells I thought useful are proving to be insufficient. Small wonder that the Purple Dragon was unable to kill Nathan Bedlam outright. Most who study the books think in terms of generalizations, not specifics. More and more, I am finding out that to receive what you really wish, you must be very precise. If not, the libraries will play games."

"Why has no one ever written down the spells in some simpler form? Surely, one of this city's rulers—"

"In three days, every copy of the page will disappear. Anyone who read it will forget what it said. Some sort of fail-safe, I would imagine."

The commander's scarred face became even uglier. "Bah! Magic! Give me a simple war!"

Looking out at the vast army of the enemy, the Gryphon shook his head. "There are no simple wars."

An aide stepped into the room behind them. When they did not turn to him, he cleared his throat nervously.

Blane looked at the man. "What is it?"

The aide blanched. The commander's visage had halted more than one man dead in his tracks. "Pardon, but I've come to speak to the Lord Gryphon concerning the Lady Gwen."

The lionbird became interested. "And?"

"I went to summon her, as you requested. I searched first in her room, and then in that of her missing companion. She was in neither."

"Indeed." The Gryphon was tugging at the hair under his beak. "What then?"

"I—I asked others to assist me. We searched several floors with no success. It was then that I discovered the truth."

"And that is?" Blane was growing impatient.

The soldier was white. "She talked to your spy before you yourself, Lord Gryphon. She heard that Mito Pica falls to the dragon forces of Toma. A servant overheard all this, but remained silent out of fear of the Lady's powers."

"Understandable. Go on."

"She flew into a rage. The spy shrugged and departed. Only the servant overheard her final words. She had planned to leave for Mito Pica!"

The growl of anger that escaped from the throat of the Gryphon caused both humans to step back. There was little reason in the mind of the lion-bird at that moment. Only after several seconds was he able to calm himself down enough.

"Are we a sinking vessel, that our allies disappear one by one?" The words were more to himself. "Mito Pica is finished! What she seeks is most likely no more! She might die for her folly!"

Blane asked cautiously, "What does she seek?"

"Cabe Bedlam grew up near Mito Pica. Over a space of several generations. The why and how remain in question since no one knew of this until one of the Dragon Kings accidentally discovered him. The Lady no doubt believes that she can glean some information about his past that may enable her to rescue him from Azran. Thin hope at best, but she is acting more with emotion than logic. I should have feared as much."

The commander from Zuu coughed hoarsely. "Now what do we do?"

The Gryphon stared at the room. The Gray Mists had drifted into the city. Every room was dim, despite more lamps than usual in those areas used by the military.

"I've heard several men who have that same wretched cough you do. It now strikes me that this is all too familiar."

"What is?"

"The Gray Mists are sapping our strength. We grow weaker while the Lochivarites inhale freely. I remain uninfected, but the rest of the city is in danger." He walked over to a window and peered out at the interior of Penacles. "This will be a short siege. We must either break them in the next week or two or fall to them like sick infants."

Blane managed to grin. "I will gather my men—"

"No. It would be a slaughter. The key is to find the source of the Gray Mists. If only I—" The Gryphon broke off. "It could be! Blane! Please inform General Toos that I will be in the libraries for the next several hours!"

"What is it?"

"I may have mistaken fire for air!" The lionbird rushed out of the room.

Behind him, Blane shrugged, coughed, and picked up his fallen helm. "He claims the Gray Mists don't affect him! Sounds like they've addled his head, Zuu-kala help us all!"

The tapestry had been moved to one of the deeper, more secure areas of the palace. Though he fairly ran through the building, the Gryphon felt as if he were crawling along. It was only a hunch, and probably wrong at that. Still, it explained a lot, such as how Lochivar had gone from a clean, peaceful land to a dreary, ghostlike wasteland. It amazed him that the thought had never occurred to him in all these years.

This time, the libraries were located in the center of the city. The dead center. He wondered if this was some sort of safety factor.

He found himself standing in the corridor of one of the libraries without having even noticed the change in locations. The gnome—or *a* gnome—waited patiently. This came as no surprise to the Gryphon, but what the little man held in his hands did. There, without having searched for it, was a blue book. It was open, and ancient script filled the two pages visible. The lionbird eyed the keeper of the tomes.

Without blinking, without hesitating, the gnome handed him the book. "To save you some much-needed time, Lord Gryphon."

A DAY HAD passed. Cabe was still in the chair. It was becoming painfully uncomfortable, but Azran's shock spell would have been much worse, no question about that. Still, it might have been easier if he had at least eaten. His father had apparently forgotten all about him.

Such was not the case now. With a trace of sulfur, Azran and his throne materialized no more than three feet away from Cabe. There was a smile on the black magician's face. It did not encourage his prisoner in the least.

"Well, my son, how are you feeling today?"

"Can I get out of this chair?"

"I suppose so."

Azran waved his hand. Cabe watched the area around him glitter and sparkle. When things returned to normal, he cautiously stood up. Every part of his body ached. He straightened up slowly—

—and leaped at Azran.

It is difficult to do anything while floating in the air. Cabe discovered this the hard way. His father frowned, whirled his finger, and watched the hapless victim spin around several times.

"I'm disappointed in you, Cabe. I really thought you might behave yourself." Azran's face darkened. "I can see that there is little hope in talking this out with you. Pity. I shall have to use more drastic means."

Cabe was unceremoniously dumped on the ground. The sinister warlock stroked the black half of his beard. This boy, he decided, was far too similar to Nathan.

"You know, yesterday, I found it difficult to face you. Family relations have never been my strong point, but I think you've heard about that already."

Equilibrium totally out of sync, Cabe tried desperately to separate the floor from his face. He was paying little attention to his father's words. Azran, lost in his thoughts, did not notice.

"Having tried again, I see no alternative but to introduce you to the darker side of the spectrum immediately. Once you've seen how much more efficient and satisfying it is, I doubt you'll ever want to turn away. I speak from experience." Azran's eyes glowed with a strange light.

Finally able to differentiate between up and down, Cabe pushed himself to his knees. Most of what his father was saying had escaped him, but one thing did sink in. Azran planned to turn him to the dark powers. He tried to stand up, his legs wobbling haphazardly. His head was still reeling from the spins.

"No!" The word came unbidden and in a voice that was his and not his.

The black-clad figure of his father was thrown backward, chair and all, against the stone wall. Only Azran's quick thinking saved the evil sorceror from a broken skull. Just before impact, he disappeared. Wood collided with stone. The chair fell to the floor, shattered into countless fragments.

Cabe collapsed.

Moments later, Azran reentered. Winds howled and lightning filled the room. A glowing shell encased him. He was crouched, ready for mortal combat. The crumpled form escaped his notice at first. Instead, Azran turned his head this way and that, looking for some new attack.

When time had passed and all remained quiet, the malevolent warlock finally calmed down enough to observe that his opponent was unconscious. The spells dropped almost instantly, much to the relief of several indescribable and quite agitated servants.

"My son—pfah! You're Nathan's, body and soul, and therefore of no use to me!"

Growling, Azran threw a bolt of pure force at the inert body. It glanced off, forming a new window in the far wall that it eventually struck. Puzzled, the warlock tried again. The resulting hole in the ceiling allowed several dark creatures immediate access to safer portions of the castle. Azran stood back and tugged at the silver half of his mustache. He knew that the boy had the potential for unheard of power, but that did not explain his use of abilities most adepts had to wait years to learn. The strike that had nearly ended Azran's career was no mere raw force. It was designed to nullify several defenses before reaching the target itself. The fact that he had escaped meant nothing save that, unlike some sorcerors, he always added a twist to his personal-defense spells. Only that had given him enough time to teleport away rather than shatter against the wall in an invisible and unbreakable magical grip.

It was very obvious that Nathan was responsible. The attack was as clear as a signature. The style was one that no one had ever attempted to copy. It required skill and costly power.

All this pondering, Azran realized, was getting him nowhere. His son was protected by the Turtle's Shell, a strong barrier that could be called up naturally. It would be a waste of time and energy trying to penetrate it. Besides, the boy—boy? After several generations?—was helpless. He could not leave unless the barrier was dropped, at which point escape would be impossible since Azran would set up spells that would strike immediately. No, Cabe was still a prisoner, despite his safety for the moment.

There was a flapping at the window facing out into the greatest expanse of the Hell Plains. One of the Seekers, behaving unusually. Azran turned his attention to the creature, permitting it entry with the pass of a hand. The avian flew through the window and landed, standing, on the floor. It kneeled before the warlock, the crest on its head bristling from excitement. Curious, Azran put a hand to its head.

Dragon pack. More than one, a divided army, in fact, with several groups coming from all directions. To—to the warlock's castle! Azran pulled his hand away. The Red Dragon was coming for him. Somehow the location of his stronghold was known. He had assumed the spells of the ancients powerful enough to hide him. That, it seemed, was not the case. Someone had informed the Dragon Kings. They now believed him unsuspecting and vulnerable. In both cases, he would prove them terribly wrong.

He dismissed the Seeker after ordering it to prepare its kind for battle.

Whether the avians would prove equal to the task was questionable. They had the will and the power, but they lacked numbers. No, Azran decided, he would have to enter this battle and make short work of the Red Dragon. For that, he would need the sword.

The body nearby remained motionless. Satisfied that his son would not escape the spells he had cast around the Turtle Shell, the dark warlock departed for his inner sanctum. This battle would announce to the world that here was a force to be reckoned with. Here, Azran would be seen as invincible.

Dreams of grandeur filling his head, he marched off. If—and only if— Azran had kept his mind, he might have seen the small glow of light that formed out of nothing in the middle of the room, no more than three feet away from Cabe. A spell of shunning deflected the various traps set for the figure on the ground. Then, as if unfolding from his very cloak, the shadowy sorcerer called Shade stood surveying his surroundings.

A smile may have briefly touched his lips. As planned, the residents of the ancient castle were now caught up in preparations for battle. The Red Dragon's hordes would be in sight any minute now. Once the battle started in earnest, Shade would take Cabe and depart. Who would prove to be the victor was unimportant to him. Both the Dragon Kings and Azran would suffer a loss of strength, and that was more than satisfactory.

Shade bent to awaken Cabe. He was instantly repelled by the shell of pure force. The blink of an eye would have missed a rare, clear look of surprise on the hooded warlock's face. This was something unexpected. It now put both men in jeopardy. Shade would most likely survive, but he did not care much for the idea of suffering at Azran's hands. For Cabe, there would be no hope.

Somewhere outside and above, the cries of the Seekers as they caught sight of the enemy filled the air. Whether ordered to or not, they would defend the fortress to the death. There was a connection to this land that went deeper than any spell. To invade the home grounds of the avians was to invite destruction. Only Azran's quick thinking had saved him from a grisly fate. The dragon packs would not be so lucky.

A slight groan alerted Shade to the fact that Cabe was regaining consciousness. He hoped reason would return just as quickly.

"Cabe!" Even a whisper seemed earthshaking.

Rubbing his head, Cabe forced his eyes open and looked bewilderingly at the strange cage of color around him. It was like a rainbow gone mad. Bright tones crisscrossed here and there, completely enclosing him. Turning, he was only barely able to focus on the figure next to him. When he realized who it was, he nearly tried to break his way through the shell. It was only a warning from Shade that prevented him from throwing himself uselessly against the side.

"That is not the way to go about it, Cabe. You must release the spell."

"Release the spell? Azran—"

The shadowy warlock held up a gloved hand. "Azran is not responsible. The Turtle Shell is a purely defensive incantation. If it was invoked, it had to be from you, and you alone!"

"Az—"

"Silence! Say his name one too many times and he may notice, despite the coming battle!"

"What battle?"

Shade growled. "I'll tell you later! *If* you ever free yourself!"

Cabe decided against mentioning that he had no experience or training and could hardly be expected to release himself unless he could merely wish the shell away.

The Turtle Shell vanished.

Mystified, Cabe stood up. Though his legs wobbled, he was able to stay erect this time. "That's all I had to do?"

His companion hesitated before speaking. "Yes, that's all."

The fierce roars of inhuman warriors engaged in battle alerted both of them. The dragon packs of the master of the Hell Plains had met with the Seekers and Azran's other servants. Sounds that chilled the marrow were constant. Cabe had no intention of viewing the slaughter outside.

"Come!" Shade extended a hand.

A rip in the very air itself emerged from nowhere and spread until it was large enough for both to step through. The faceless warlock led the way. Cabe was tempted to touch the edge of the tear, but decided that he might be risking a limb. Suppose the gap closed while his hand was still in the room? The thought was not pretty.

They were in a place that was not a place. Shade halted only long enough to give Cabe a warning.

"We are in something quite close to what men might call damnation. You must hold tight and ignore anything that you hear! If we should lose one another, you may never find your way out!"

The two continued on. Cabe stared down at his feet, trying to see what they were walking on. It was like staring into nothing. A misty nonland. If he released his grip, he wondered, would he fall forever?

The voices touched him. Calling to him. Pleading to him. Laughing and crying. Not loud. Far worse. They were just above the lower limit of his hearing. Whispers from everywhere. Each one catching his attention and trying to distract him.

One sounded like the stentorian voice of Darkhorse. Cabe strained to hear it, but his guide chose that moment to tug him forward. The voice was lost as new ones took its place. He prayed he would not go mad before they returned to reality.

Forever. They had been walking forever, it seemed. Shade was quiet and unusually harsh. The voices were apparently affecting him as well. Possibly even more so, considering his curse. He had, no doubt, spent some time here.

"There!"

The voice of Shade broke through the whispering. Cabe squinted in the direction his hooded comrade was pointing. He saw a tiny, almost insignificant speck of light. Insignificant, until one realized that no other form of illumination existed save a slight glow that had accompanied the two travelers as they entered this nightmarish nonworld. With renewed enthusiasm, both men moved toward the speck.

It grew in strange leaps. Distance had no real meaning in this place. What was far away one moment was near the next, and so on. They nearly walked into the patch of light without expecting it.

Shade reached into the light with his free hand. A tear formed in the light. From behind his companion, Cabe caught a glimpse of some rocky landscape. Whatever land it was, it sparkled. Sparkled like a diamond.

They stepped through. Cabe was more than happy to sit down. Shade sealed the rip in reality and turned to the younger warlock. The expression on the cloaked sorceror's face was, of course, unreadable.

"We will rest here for the moment." He sat down across from Cabe. The ground was rocky and uneven, but both managed to find a satisfactory spot.

Now that things had calmed down, Cabe had a few questions to ask the other. "Simon—Shade, what happened to you? We thought you dead with the Seeker!"

"I am not easy to kill. Though the spell was strong, my personal defenses were able to save me. Barely. I was flung into the void between universes. You might say that I did die."

Cabe, remembering the shadowy warlock's curse, shuddered. "Thank the gods you didn't!"

Shade may have nodded slightly. "Yes. Thank the gods."

"Who was attacking Azran's stronghold?"

A definite laugh. "The Dragon Kings. I passed on information to them, knowing that they would provide me with the smoke screen I needed to free you. Most cooperative."

"How did you know where Azran was and that he had me?"

"Mine are powers far older than those now in play. It gives me certain advantages. Disadvantages, also."

Cabe did not press what was obviously a distasteful subject to his friend. "Darkhorse disappeared when you did."

His companion hesitated before answering. "I am afraid that Darkhorse may have been lost."

"Lost? How?"

"The void between universes is vast. Though the dread steed is one with that place, he can be banished to it forever. An eternity could pass without finding the proper way out. It may very well be that we have seen the last of him." Shade lowered his head.

Cabe wished he had known the creature better. Despite the unholy appearance, he was sure the eternal's heart—if Darkhorse had one—was in the right place.

A slight movement caught his attention. The thing—it was too far away to see properly—was gone almost instantly. Whether it was animal or man was up for question. Cabe called to his companion, a low voice assuring that no one else would hear.

"Shade! Something is coming this way!"

The head of the hooded warlock came up slowly, as if nothing out of the normal had happened. "Can you describe it?"

Cabe shook his head. "It was large. Like a bear, but not quite so ungainly. Other than that, it was just a shape. Couldn't see clearly."

"We'd best be careful. I had little choice in locations."

"Why? Where are we?" Relief was giving ground to worry.

"The Legar Peninsula. Land of the Crystal Dragon."

Relief fled. The Crystal Dragon was one of the few Kings who did not deal with humans in any way. Of those, Ice hated mankind. Green had discourse only with the wood elves. Crystal—Crystal had no subjects save his clans. At least, that was the belief.

The thing was definitely not human. Cabe looked to Shade. The faceless sorceror was sitting quietly and apparently contemplating the nature of the multiverse. Before Cabe could say anything, though, Shade waggled a finger to silence him.

In quiet tones, the other whispered, "Let it get close. Trust me."

It would put his trust to the limit, Cabe decided, but he refrained from saying so. His companion may have smiled. The young warlock turned his attention back to the oncoming intruder.

It was gone.

He started to rise. Shade put an arm out to halt him. Cabe looked at him questioningly. In reply, the other pointed silently behind his younger comrade. Cabe whirled around.

An armadillo. An armadillo taller than a man, and standing upright. It was well protected by the thick outer skin and a pair of arms that ended in sharp, finger-length claws. Dusky brown, it was oddly tailless, a contrast to its otherwise similar appearance to the animal.

The creature glared back at him.

Shade stepped forward and began to emit strange hooting noises. The heavily armored monster eyed him patiently and, when the warlock had ceased, replied in the same sort of sounds, only much deeper. It then wandered off. Shade nodded and leaned toward Cabe.

"He says he will guide us to a better place. The patrols of the Dragon Kings come by here too often." There was a strange flatness to his voice.

"What is it?"

"A Quel. Once, they inhabited most of the Dragonrealms. Now, only the Legar Peninsula remains of what was once an empire rivaling the dragons themselves."

Cabe would have asked more, but the Quel returned abruptly. It was accompanied by another of its kind, nearly identical save that it was wider and slightly shorter. There was a look of malevolence in its alien eyes. Black as the void, it seemed to him.

Like the area around them, the Quel glistened brightly. Cabe first believed that it was natural, but then he was given a thin cloth cloak covered with small, sparkling diamonds. Merchants in Mito Pica or Penacles would have paid fortunes for it. The first Quel indicated that Cabe should put it on. Shade was wrapping a similar cloth over his hood and cloak. It was a wonder that the man did not die from the heat.

"What are these for?"

"The crystals bend and turn the light and, more important, spells. It also serves as camouflage. This way, the Quel blend into their surroundings.

Even the Crystal Dragon cannot locate them. Being human, we need the cloths; the Quel carry their protection in their outer shell. They put them on during early growth. The cracks in the shell eventually cover much, but not all of each crystal."

The creature with the sinister eyes motioned angrily. It wanted them to move on. They hastened to obey. Cabe noticed that the other Quel had lined up behind him. He did not think it was to protect them from the Dragon Kings.

For such ponderous beings, they moved swiftly. Cabe and Shade, physically and mentally weakened by their trip through the dark nonworld, were hard-pressed to keep the pace set. Neither human spoke, so as to conserve energy.

After traveling over countless and repetitive hills, by which time Cabe was more than half convinced that the Quel were purposely leading them in a circle, they came to a rather unassuming hole in a mound. The creature leading pointed at the hole and then at them. Its message was clear. Shade entered first. Cabe followed quickly.

It was a shock to discover that the tunnels and caverns of the Quel were far from the burrows the young warlock had assumed. Instead, it was only a short crawl before the first tunnel opened into a much wider one that was not only paved but also had walls smoother than any craftsman could have done. A little farther back, Cabe could see what he assumed was the edge of a large building in the cavern that opened up before them. He wondered how big the underworld dwellings of these armored creatures were.

Shade was becoming impatient. He started to pick up the pace, even catching up and passing the lead Quel. The great beastman stopped him with one armored, clawed hand. The shadowy sorceror slowed until he was back in his original spot in the group. When they reached the cavern city, all four paused.

Gwen's home had been partially natural rock, construction, and plant. It was a labor of legend, yet it paled before the sight that greeted Cabe. Here was a veritable metropolis cut from the earth and rock itself. Towers that began in the farthest depths rose until they met the high, flat ceiling of the cave. No castle or fortress was as tall as the nearest of the towers, but even this one seemed small in comparison to those farther inside. Gems glistened from every structure, a king's ransom on each. Oddly, though, there was no sign of life anywhere in the gleaming city.

The wider of the two Quel emitted a low hooting. His comrade answered rapidly. There was some disagreement. The taller wanted to head straight into the city; the other pointed to a path that ran along the cavern, opening often into passages in the rock itself. Shade angrily said something in the creatures' strange tongue. The wider of the two finally won. Cabe eyed the city wistfully, telling himself that he would no doubt see it later.

They walked on for what seemed forever. Cabe was amazed at the energy of the others; he was all for falling down and collapsing and had not eaten for a long time. Only pride, not to mention a little fear, kept him going. At some point, Shade, acting on some reserve of energy, took the lead. This time, the Quel did not protest.

These tunnels were worn and dusty, as if unused for some time. It brought up again the question of just how many of these monsters still lived. None had appeared in the city the few moments Cabe had viewed it, but that was hardly proof it was empty.

This particular tunnel opened up into another chamber, only a fraction of the volume of the one containing the city, but still huge. Man-sized lumps of crystal-encrusted rock dotted the cave walls by the thousands. It smelled of animals, a large number of animals. With a start, he noted that it was the same odor that clung to the two Quel.

"Where are we?"

He did not expect an answer, but Shade provided him with one. "The resting place of the Quel."

"This is where they keep their dead?"

"No, this is where they keep their race."

Cabe looked at him, but, as usual, it was pointless to try to read something from his companion. The faceless warlock pointed at the walls in explanation.

What he had thought ridges and lumps were, in actuality, thousands upon thousands of Quel, rolled up and clinging to the walls. Their crystal-specked shells were packed tightly together. Heads were barely visible, and limbs were not to be seen at all. Cabe could barely make out the fact that they were sleeping. Only a slight movement by each betrayed that fact.

"They sleep, Cabe Bedlam. Awaiting the time to rise once again to face their ancient foes, the Seekers. Only a handful of sentinels remain awake for any one period. The rest will sleep until the spell that binds them is broken."

"How do you know all this?"

Shade laughed. The humor escaped Cabe. "Some memories remain, despite the deaths of countless past personalities. I studied long and hard in some lives, seeking these creatures even as Azran sought the castle of the ancients."

"How do we wake them? If they could be used against the Dragon Kings—"

"The power that causes them to slumber is far beyond the ability of our kind—until now. You, my friend, are the only one with the potential to do it."

The two Quel had been standing nearby, quietly patient while the humans talked. Finally, though, one issued a questioning hoot.

"What's that mean?" Cabe was having second thoughts; the Quel did not seem to be very gentle in nature. There was a predatory look in their long-muzzled faces, and the eyes of the wider one were narrowed, as if suspicious of the two warlocks.

"He is merely impatient. This is the closest they've come to breaking the spell. None of them expected their sorcerors to die in casting it. With my help, however, we can remedy their mistake."

Cabe was unsatisfied, but he had no idea why. "Tell me what to do."

"Excellent. Wait." Imitating the sounds of their guides, Shade conversed with the Quel. After some discussion, the taller one departed on some errand.

While they waited—for what, Cabe had no idea—Shade surveyed the room in what seemed to be outright admiration.

"This is a place of power. This is the only place it can be done." The words were barely a whisper; the hooded warlock was talking to himself, carried away by the moment.

Something about his comrade's behavior was puzzling Cabe. A nagging thought fought its way into his head. It was lost as Shade turned his attention back to him.

"Come! We have little time!"

The Quel remaining led them to a stone slab in the middle of the sleep chamber. It was horribly reminiscent of the sacrificial altars Cabe had heard some savage races used. Shade stroked the slab with what might have been passion. Involuntarily, Cabe backed away—

—and into the mountainous body of the other Quel. With uncanny speed, the creature wrapped one arm around the hapless human. With the free hand, it placed an amulet around his neck. A bloodred jewel in the center of the piece began to pulsate.

Cabe cried out to the other warlock. "Shade—Simon! Help me!"

The shadowy wizard formerly called Simon turned—and chuckled. He bowed, flourishing his cloak. "Call me Madrac—this time!"

XIII

MITO PICA. ANOTHER name to add to the history of destruction. The dragon hordes of Duke Toma tore through the unsuspecting city. The guards manning the walls died quickly as lumbering, unthinking minor drakes batted themselves against stone until they or the walls gave in.

There were always more minor drakes.

Wyverns, firedrakes, airdrakes—all wreaked havoc, maiming and killing those who fought or fled. The worst were those firedrakes who assumed human form; they did not kill with the ferociousness of wild beasts, but with the sadistic calculation of a thinking mind. Even the minor drakes and their kind steered clear.

There had been some resistance, and a small part of that still existed. Troops stationed deeper in the city had gained enough time to prepare themselves. The first wave of the horde to reach the barracks found only death. Unfortunately, numbers were on the side of the invaders. Those human commanders still remaining opted to retreat to the lands around and, if possible, make their way to Zuu, Wenslis, or Penacles, if that city had not fallen by then. The citizens of Mito Pica did as citizens of any region under attack would do. They fled for their lives if they were swift enough and died if they were slow. More civilians died than soldiers, but there are always more civilians to kill than there are soldiers. It is the nature of war.

It was into this that the Lady materialized.

Her powers were still not up to par. She was forced to make two stops before reaching the countryside near the dying city. The term *countryside* was a euphemism at best; most of the nearby land had been torn up under the claws, hooves, and feet of the participants. Many trees were uprooted. The Lady had spent a day scouting the area. She did not want to run into any patrols or, worse yet, Duke Toma himself. It was said that Toma was a strong warlock in his own right, a throwback to earlier days. Only the pattern of his egg kept him from joining the ranks of the Dragon Kings. Nevertheless, he was second only to them and, with the authority of Gold and the power he himself controlled, he could even command them at times.

Questioning the displaced had given her a vague idea of her destination. It was away from the city, closer to a village that had remained untouched by this slaughter. Toma was intelligent and devious, but he had erred this time. It was not Mito Pica that had raised Cabe—not directly—but rather this nameless village. Her luck now depended on how close the huntsman's home was to the village. If it was near, then it might have been passed up. If not . . .

A small group of firedrakes, shaped as men and mounted, appeared from nowhere. They were chasing three riders on horseback, a family. An old man and two younger people, perhaps a recently married pair or the man's children. They would not be able to outrace the fearsome steeds of the dragon men. Already, the gap between the groups was closing.

Gwen was protected. She had cast a spell of invisibility around her. If she ignored the situation, she would be safe, undetected by Toma's powers. If she interfered, she threatened her own chances.

She interfered.

The path being used led into a patch of trees that had survived the fighting. The Lady smiled. Plants were her friends, her willing servants. She talked to them, told them what she wanted and why. They thrilled at the idea of serving her.

The humans and their horses passed through unharmed. The firedrakes were not so fortunate. The leader, confident that his prey was only moments from capture, pulled ahead of the rest. A stray branch struck him in the face; he brushed it aside. Another, stronger limb nearly knocked him off his mount. The firedrake barely ducked in time.

The third caught him in the throat even as he evaded the second.

With a satisfying crack, the leader fell from the saddle, his head at an awkward angle. There was no doubt that he was dead. One rider tried to avoid his fallen comrade. The enchanted drake under him tripped on a root that had not been above ground a moment before. The hapless rider was thrown to the ground, where he landed with a thud. He did not move.

Two of the remaining firedrakes dismounted. The others backed up, their half-shadowed eyes on the trees around them. Gwen called off her allies; she had already made her presence felt much too long. She hoped Toma was engaged in numerous matters and was not concentrating his powers.

The remaining riders picked up their fallen companions and dragged

them out of the dangerous path. From the safety of her spell, the enchantress could see that the second victim was also dead. The two bodies were
piled on the back of one of the two extra animals. The firedrakes had given
up on their prey; just as well, for they would have never caught them after
this long a delay. It was also obvious that none of them wanted to pass
through the small, seemingly innocent grove of trees. The Lady smiled.

The sense of victory did not last long. From here on, she would have to
go on foot. It would not do to go popping from place to place in search of
a cabin that might or might not be there. Toma would most certainly be
drawn to her then. Besides, she could easily miss her target that way.

Reinforcing her spell of invisibility, the Lady made her way through
the desolation, destruction, and—she thanked Rheena, the goddess of the
woods—the occasional piece of land that remained untouched by the horrors of Toma's butchers.

An hour passed. The land here was virtually untouched. Here and there,
mangled brush showed the movement of some large force, but Gwen lacked
the training to identify which side it had been. The path appeared to lead
in the general direction she was headed. An ill feeling crept into her heart.

Twenty minutes later, she spotted something that was definitely man-
made. That it was a cabin could not be verified; it had been demolished
by raiders. She nearly stumbled over the dead form of a minor drake, its
enchantment gone. No one could have mistaken it for a horse now. Or a
dragon, for that matter. It was well burnt. Gwen touched the remains and
detected something hauntingly familiar.

There was another form nearby. A third she discovered only a few feet
from that. Both were firedrakes, killed while in their human forms. It was
evident from the fact that their weapons were still sheathed that they had
been caught unaware.

What had happened to the rest of the attackers? For that matter, where
were the inhabitants of the cabin? Summoning to mind some of her more
potent defensive spells, the Lady moved cautiously toward the wreckage of
the building.

She found more traces of the firedrakes near what had once been the
front door. One had actually been in the process of shapeshifting at the
time of his death. Half-grown wings, arms that were too long, and clawed
feet. These had not been burned. They had been frozen to death. Instantly.

More and more, the handiwork dredged memories from her subconscious.

A groan. She stiffened, expecting any second to be attacked by the rest of the marauders. A second groan wiped away that belief; this was a human voice. A dragon's voice would have been raspy, even hissing. This was more high-pitched, like a minstrel.

Stepping over what was once the base of the northern wall, Gwen entered the remains of the cabin. The moaning had quieted down now. She began to worry that she had arrived too late. Moving with less caution than before, the sorceress made her way to the originator of the groans.

He was buried under the rubble that had been the roof. She tugged at one of the beams. It would not budge. Reluctantly, she gestured with her left hand, knowing as she did that each new spell would draw the duke's attention to her more and more.

When the last of the wood had been lifted away and deposited nearby, the Lady eyed the figure at her feet. His face was turned away from her, but the woodland clothes and the curly hair reminded her of someone from her youth. She turned his head slowly, so as not to injure him. Fortunately, the neck was not broken.

She had been correct. His face was more than familiar. The name that went with the face was Hadeen. He was part elf. He was also an elemental. Nathan Bedlam would have trusted no one more than this half-elf. Some claimed that Hadeen was once the tutor of Nathan himself. It could easily have been true.

Hadeen's eyes fluttered open. For the briefest of times, he looked at her directly. A smile played across his marred face. He muttered something, but Gwen could not hear him. She leaned closer.

"Lady of the Amber, daughter of the wood goddess." As if satisfied with that statement, the half-elf expired.

She looked down at him with shock. So close! Toma had succeeded in destroying her one thin clue.

"Gwendolyn."

The enchantress jumped. The voice was that of Hadeen, but the limp body was not the source.

"Here, Gwendolyn."

A tall, strong oak shook its mighty headdress of green. The Lady nodded to herself; Hadeen was still one of the forest dwellers, despite his human side. That which was elf had chosen one of the trees for its final resting place; its essence helped the tree and the surrounding land thrive. In such a way were the spirits of the elves always with their people.

It was almost as if the tree smiled. "Thank Rheena you came before I died, Gwendolyn. If you hadn't, I would never have fought for semblance of personality. For a short time, I can communicate with you."

"What happened here, Hadeen? Where are the rest of this dragon force?"

The branches of the oak quivered in triumph. "Earth, air, fire, and water! An elemental will not be beaten easily in his own home! I caught the first with the cleansing flame. A tornado disposed of the next attackers; they should be somewhere in the eastern seas. Water, in the form of the numbing ice, gave several of the monsters a preview of the underworld. Earth swallowed most others. Regrettably, I was unable to shield myself during the entire time. One of those I burned was able to let loose a spell before expiring. It struck while my attention was elsewhere."

The tree spirit was talking rapidly. It would not be long before consciousness gave way to the normal nature of the oak. After that, the Lady would have to deal with emotions. While she understood the way of the plants, the information she needed would be unattainable from a thing that thought by feeling, not by words.

"Hadeen—"

"There is no Hadeen; there is only the oak and the spirit that becomes one with it."

She reworded her statement. "That which was Hadeen, you cared for the young Cabe Bedlam, grandson of Nathan, your friend."

"I did."

"I seek him. I believe Azran has him. I would know—"

The disembodied voice cut her off. "Hadeen knew of the treacherous son's stronghold. They who you seek are not there."

Gwen could tell that the half-elf's spirit was incorporating itself with the very essence of the tree. She was running out of time, and now she didn't know where to look.

"Where is Cabe now?"

"He nears the beginning and the end. The ghost of two minds seeks his power, which is not his but theirs and theirs alone. If the power is passed, the Quel will wake."

Frowning in frustration, the Lady tried again. "Hadeen, listen—"

The voice struggled to pull what individuality remained back together. "Gwendolyn. The faceless warlock now has Cabe. The scale is now tipped to evil where the shadow sorceror is concerned. Go to Talak. Await your lover of two ages there."

"I don't—"

The spirit was becoming remote. "The child was dying. Nathan wanted to assure that at least his grandson survived. If he himself did, it would only be luck. He knew the Dragon Kings would win, but he hoped the seed would grow again."

She waited. At first, only the rustling of leaves in the wind answered her.

"Gwendolyn. Only the two who are one can succeed."

That was all. The half-elf Hadeen was gone. He had left behind more confusion than answers. Two who are one? She sighed. If time had permitted, she would have buried Hadeen's mortal body, but as it was, every extra second endangered her. The large number of spells in one small area was sure to attract Toma's attention, even if the loss of this force did not.

Something moved in the brush far to her right. She had dropped her spell to talk to Hadeen. Now, though invisible once more, Gwen sought the protection of the oak that now contained that which had been part of Hadeen. It was always possible that the firedrakes had some sort of enchantment that might counteract her spell.

A minor drake, in its true form, nosed through into sight. It did not care much for the foliage, being from the Tyber Mountains. The dragon tore up smaller trees and plants as it waddled toward the remains of the cabin. Two similar creatures followed close behind it. Hounds of the Dragon Kings.

She knew they could not smell her. Whether the wind was blowing or not had no bearing. Though she was no elf, the Lady was very much at home with the forests. She carried no scent that would mark her as human.

These, however, were not hounds in the normal sense. While two investigated the carnage, the original sniffed at the air, the direction it was headed too close for Gwen's tastes. It was homing in on her power. She knew that the Dragon Kings had been toying with the idea of a tracker capable of seeing the powers, but this was the first time she had seen that idea made into fact. It was not a pleasant discovery to make.

From the original path of the minor drakes came five armored figures. That they showed no fear of the trackers marked them as firedrakes even before they were close enough to identify visually. Four had swords drawn; the fifth was empty-handed. The enchantress noted him as the most dangerous. If he went unarmed, it was only because he had other abilities to protect him.

The dragon warriors poked around the cabin. The one without a weapon was evidently in command. He seemed more than interested in the corpse of Hadeen. Gwen tried to keep her breathing down. Three of the five fire-drakes and the one tracker were all within only a few yards. Without the sorceror, she would have had no difficulty. His presence might delay her just long enough for one of the others to make a vital strike.

After searching the grounds, the firedrakes seemed satisfied that there were no survivors. With nothing to be gained, the sorceror decided it was time to depart. The warriors and two of the minor drakes obeyed without question; the third continued to stare toward the witch's hiding place. It did not move closer, but it also did not give up.

The sorceror stalked up to the animal and hit it solidly with the back of his hand. The thick, leathery hide of the tracker protected its wearer from pain, but the action was enough to stir it from its duty. The beast turned and lumbered toward its companions. The firedrake stood staring at the oak, as if sensing its true nature. One of the others called to him. The sorceror blinked, red, raging eyes looking directly at the cloaked enchantress, and shook his head. Gwen breathed a sigh of relief as he spun around and joined his fellows. Not until they were out of sight and sound did she step away from the tree.

It galled her to hide like some helpless animal, but secrecy was of the utmost importance. Hadeen had given her a jumble of disjointed pieces of information. Somehow she had to make sense of it all. She knew that Cabe faced danger. She also knew now that Shade had been added to their list of adversaries. Ever a two-sided coin. It would have been better to not involve the blurry warlock at all. His new identity would retain some memory, and his ancient powers would provide much of the rest.

Now that she was alone, all that remained was for her to visualize a ma-terialization spot for her next hop. Talak was not far; it would require only one stop on the way. She prayed that her powers would be up to full soon. This sort of travel was far too untrustworthy for her tastes.

She remembered a dirt road that curved to the left. It was the only road to Mito Pica from the city near the Tyber Mountains. Even after all this time, Gwen was sure that it remained virtually unchanged. She pictured it in her mind and concentrated. The air shimmered around her.

The Lady vanished.

The Lady materialized. In a force sphere. A dragon warrior, clad in gold and wearing a helm almost as elaborate as that of the Kings, was seated be-fore her. There was a goblet of wine in his left hand. He raised it in greeting.

"Welcome, Lady of the Amber!" Lord Toma smiled and sipped his wine.

* * *

IT WAS TOO obvious.

Too dangerous, for that matter. It would mean confronting the Black Dragon himself. Only then could the Gray Mists be halted. The Black Dragon controlled the Gray Mists.

The Black Dragon *was* the Gray Mists.

The mistake was in making labels. Not all the Dragon Kings were fire-drakes. The Ice Dragon was proof of that. Why, then, must the master of Lochivar be one? The answer was that he was not; he was an airdrake. The most powerful one of all. What other could spread his deathly presence over an entire land?

To destroy the Gray Mists, the Gryphon would have to destroy the Black Dragon.

No easy task. The lionbird was a veteran of countless battles, but even he had never taken on one of the Kings face-to-face. Nathan Bedlam was the only one who had ever succeeded, and it had cost him his life. Yet if the Gryphon failed to halt the choking numbness of the fog, Penacles would fall for certain.

He began seriously considering retirement from politics.

Closing the tome, the Gryphon handed it back to the librarian. The gnome took it cautiously, his eyes lit with excitement. When the ruler of the City of Knowledge departed, the short, squat man would pore over the pages his master had read. What was written was not so important as the fact that it *was* written. The gnome lived for books alone.

The libraries faded from the Gryphon's sight, but he paid it no mind. Plain and simple, he thought to himself. The book had given him his answer in plain and simple words. No tricks. No rhymes or riddles. Questioning the gnome had proved fruitless; the librarian claimed only that he knew that his master needed that particular tome. Where that idea had come from, the little man did not know or care. It was the way of the libraries.

He materialized in the palace not a moment too soon. From the sounds outside, it was evident that the Lochivarites had resumed their attack. Though he disliked the use of magic for the most part, time was of the essence. Gesturing quietly, he disappeared—

—and reappeared near the eastern walls. The violence nearly over-whelmed him. Black-clad figures were trying to scale the wall. Some of them made it to the top, only to be cut down by a defender. Countless dead littered the area outside the wall. The fanatics paid it no mind. They kept coming and coming, an endless wave that seemed ready to engulf all. It was hard to believe they were really human.

The casualty count was not one-sided. Those of the enemy who managed to scale the siege ladders to the top made their marks. Too many defenders were dying. Though ten times the number of the foe probably lay dead or wounded, their legions were far greater in size. In a war of attrition, Penacles would lose.

Where were these invaders coming from?

Airdrakes and firedrakes soared high above. Though they let loose with a volley now and then, their effectiveness had been curtailed by the accuracy of the archers. If those men fell . . .

"Lord Gryphon!"

A burly, well-armored boar of a man shoved into him. Both fell to the side. Seconds later, the spot on which the Gryphon had stood was bathed in flames. Archers manning a nearby tower made short work of the daring reptile. The firedrake fell to the ground, crushing several empty tents in the deserted bazaar nearby.

Grimacing more from the weight on top of him than from his near-death, the lord of Penacles grunted at the figure who had saved him.

"My thanks, Blane, but if you wish to make your actions count, I must request that you remove yourself before I die from lack of air."

The huge bear grinned. "Apologies, Lord Gryphon! When you appeared, the dragons took a sudden, unhealthy interest in you! Likely that they've been given orders to stop you at all costs!"

"Most likely. What happens here, Blane? Can we hold out?"

"I think so. The zombies are running out of ladders even if they aren't running out of no-minds to climb 'em! Gods! Where did they get all of them?"

"Would that I knew. Perhaps . . ." The Gryphon's words trailed off as he watched the hordes of Lochivar start to pull back. Penacles had survived another day.

"Perhaps what? Lord Gryphon?"

"Where is the general?"

"That fox? Out near the southern gate. Group of blackies tried to sneak around to the west side. Imagine he's mopped them up by now."

The Gryphon put his hands on Blane's shoulders. The commander shuddered involuntarily; the lionbird's claws could have easily torn through his neck. There was still something of the animal in the Gryphon's nature. That had already been proven.

"Blane. I believe I have the key to breaking this war before we all perish from fog or foe." As if on cue, the commander coughed hoarsely. "We don't have much time. I have to do it."

"Do"—cough—"what?"

"I know the source of the Gray Mists. It's the Black Dragon himself!"

Blane's eyes widened. "Then to destroy the mists, you have to kill the Black Dragon?"

The other nodded.

The commander turned red. "I suppose you think you're gonna go in there all by yourself and take care o' him! Insanity!"

"A large force would never make it. Humans would succumb to the mists the nearer they came to the Black Dragon. Without Cabe, the Lady, or Shade, I have only myself to turn to."

"Suicide! I won't have it!"

The Gryphon pulled him forward by the collar of his uniform. Blane found his face perilously close to the predatory beak of the lionbird.

"You are not in the position to tell me what to do! Forgive me, Commander, but Penacles will not survive much longer! The Lochivarites nearly made it this time! Haven't you noticed how much slower the archers have become? We also lose far too many men with each renewal of the onslaught! I have no choice!"

He released the sweating soldier and turned to stare out in the general direction of the Black Dragon's lands. Dark masses were pouring toward that area, the remainder of the fanatics' armies. For the first time, the landscape did not appear so thoroughly covered by the hordes. The Lochivarites had sustained heavy casualties. That still left Black's clans, though. Many dragons had not yet entered the fray. It would not be long before they did.

There was also Kyrg to consider. No doubt he was waiting for both sides to weaken themselves, whereupon he would step in and attempt to capture the libraries in the name of the Dragon Emperor. How long would he wait?

Looking rather sheepish, Blane bowed before the Gryphon and presented him with his sword. "Apologies, lord, for my actions. Take my weapon. If you must face the Black Dragon, she'll be of good use to you."

The Gryphon smiled as best his avian mouth would allow him. "Rise, Commander." He studied the man. "Royal background?"

"Aye."

"Thought as much. Second or third son, no doubt. I've met your type before." Blane flushed. "Keep your sword. I'm sure it would serve me well for most needs, but few things can pierce the armor of a Dragon King. No, I will need something else."

"If his hide's so thick, you'll need magic. This would cut through anything normal."

The eyes of the Gryphon glittered. "Yes! I believe I have it! I shall let Azran's toy live up to its claim!"

If Blane had looked pale before, his countenance now took on that of a corpse. "The Horned Blade? It's said that Masters rather than Kings died on that accursed weapon!"

Grim, flat tones. "No tales that. At least three. It brought about the destruction of all they had planned. It gave the damned lizards several generations more! Azran has much to pay for; his creation will satisfy some small portion of that bill!"

Around them, survivors of the latest confrontation set about the task of locating the wounded, disposing of the dead, and removing the wreckage and rubble. There was an endless supply of each. The walls were becoming more and more sparsely manned. The Black Dragon was hastening lest Toma or Kyrg claim the prize before him.

Tearing his eyes away from the scene, the Gryphon turned once more to the commander from Zuu. "When Toos arrives, I want both of you to meet me in the stables. You'll receive your final orders then."

"You'll be needing supplies."

"I'll be carrying very little. I have to move swiftly if I hope to succeed at all."

Blane saluted. The Gryphon departed, his thoughts a raging, flooded river. The Horned Blade was a vile weapon; some said it could master the bearer. That was all supposition so far as the lionbird was concerned. Only three had ever held the hellish sword, the first two being Azran and the Brown Dragon. If they had been entranced, their actions had not shown it. The Gryphon wished he had had the foresight to question Cabe. Now it was too late.

Why was the weapon here? Azran would have wanted it. The lord of Penacles was not a believer in chance. Everything had a reason, especially this. No, he decided, the Horned Blade had been left for a reason. A trap? Perhaps. Why? Azran could not work on the assumption that someone would use it. Just as unlikely was the idea that the warlock's minions had betrayed him.

He eventually found himself at the door to his room. The two iron golems stared at him emotionlessly. At a slight nod, one of them opened the door. The Gryphon stepped inside.

Distrustful of the sword and unwilling to leave it in Cabe's room, he had ordered one of the golems to pick it up and deliver it here. That same creature now stood waiting, the ominous blade in its metallic hand pointed directly toward the lionbird. The Gryphon hoped that the sword had no control over unliving creatures.

He held out his empty palm. "Give me the weapon."

The golem grasped the blade in a way that would have left any man with one less hand. It held out the pommel to its master. Feathers and fur slightly ruffled, the Gryphon gripped the Horned Blade.

It tingled, but that was all. Strangely, he was almost disappointed. Almost. While the Gryphon enjoyed a challenge, he was not suicidal. Those who went fearlessly and wholeheartedly into battle lived rather short lives. Common sense dictated his actions. Up until now, anyway. He had to admit to himself that Blane was right; this mission could well be a disaster.

The Horned Blade was now in his right hand, though the lionbird was left-handed. Reaching down with his free hand, he removed his own sword and tossed it to the side. He then passed the sword to his left. A final motion placed the dark blade in his empty scabbard.

He would take only one of the emergency packs stored in the barracks of the palace guards. That and a sack of water would provide him with the sustenance he needed. The Gryphon prepared for a hunt; no animal would hunt on a full stomach. Despite his diplomatic ways, there would always be a part of him that belonged to the wild.

Bloody Styx and sister Hestia would pass near one another tonight. Not as terrible as nights when they met, but still a time to beware.

He laughed bitterly. When was there a night not to beware?

XIV

MADRAC/SHADE LEANED OVER him. Though the warlock's face remained obscure, the aura of evil surrounding him was quite evident now. That Cabe had missed it earlier said much for the shadowy sorceror's power.

"Time is not quite right yet. We must wait 'til the beginning of the eleventh hour." He may have smiled. "That gives us some time to talk, if you wish."

Cabe glared at him.

"No? Not even questions? How about this? How did I know all about you and your situation, hmm? I believe you know that I retain only partial memories after each reincarnation."

Despite his anger, Cabe found himself listening.

"We are entering a new age, Bedlam. The rule of the Dragon Kings is dying. Decaying. Gold is an emperor who moves between calm reason and ungoverning paranoia. Most of his brethren are treacherous and bickering. They are no longer the cold, efficient masters of the lands. They have caught your grandfather's final weapon. They have been infected with the disease called humanity. In time, all but the lesser drakes will lose their right to be called true dragons."

"What do you mean?"

A low chuckle. "He talks! What I mean is this. Have you noticed how the firedrakes, especially the dukes and the Kings themselves, almost always parade around in their near-human forms?"

"They've always done so."

"Incorrect. The first Dragon Kings never shapeshifted. Only after they delved into the magic of humans did they begin to take on the forms of almost-men. The females found this easier, though they could not master much of the other spells. It became so common among the firedrakes that eventually the ability became inherent. At the same time, they weakened those abilities that had been theirs originally."

One of the Quel came near, a large ornate crystal in the creature's arms. Cabe pointedly ignored it. "What does this have to do with what you were talking about?"

"Everything!" The one who now called himself Madrac gestured at the endless rows of sleeping Quel. "Before the age of the Dragon Kings, before the Seekers, even, this land was ruled by the beings you see before you. Their empire, at its height, was greater than that of the reptiles. As their might and that of the avians crumbled, the dragons entered the lands and grew. Powers shifted, some becoming dormant, others grasping more control."

He waved away the Quel who had brought the crystal. The armored monster hooted angrily, its huge clawed paws coming up in an obviously threatening attitude. Shade spoke back to it, his sounds higher, but no less angrier. The Quel finally gave in on whatever argument was taking place and backed away.

Shade turned back to his prisoner. "The Quel was anxious to get on with the ceremony. They don't understand that it must take place at a certain time." He leaned over and whispered to Cabe, though it was very likely that his nonhuman allies could not understand. "This will be a momentous time for all of us. For a short period, you will have power undreamed of. After that, the Quel will be released and I will achieve what has eluded me for untold years. Escape!"

Snapping his fingers, the warlock gestured to the creature. Cabe looked from one to the other. He did not like what was being done.

"What's going on?"

"The time draws near. We will proceed with the preliminaries in a moment. I fear I must cut my story short. Suffice it to say, the powers that control me are ones left from that ancient time. That which was dominant when Simon met you would prefer to leave this new world be, but that which now controls my actions awaits this new age. With the Dragon Kings waning in power, the Quel and the ancient ways will reestablish themselves and mankind will not take the reins of these lands. He will live only to serve."

"Like yourself?"

An open palm flashed across Cabe's face. There was anger in the other even though the features could reveal nothing.

"When the power takes control, I will be rid of this ridiculous curse! I will be Madrac! Only Madrac!" Shade glanced up. "But I'm afraid the rest will have to remain a mystery to you!" He laughed.

Insanity, Cabe thought to himself. From one madman to another! He turned his head and caught the sinister stare of the Quel. To confront the Dragon Kings was bad enough, but now people would have this threat hanging over them. He struggled to move, but to no avail.

Shade turned away from him. The hooded necromancer was uttering words that sounded hauntingly familiar to his captive, though he knew he had never heard the language before. Ominous tendrils of dark smoke materialized around Shade's head.

The Quel was staring at the smaller crystal on Cabe's chest. It had taken on a glow, barely noticeable at first, but increasing in intensity as the hour approached.

The cloaked figure was absorbed in his incantations. Cabe paid him no mind. His attention was riveted on the object on his chest. Everything else faded into insignificance.

As the eleventh hour neared, the crystal began to quiver. Worse yet, he could swear that it was slowly sinking into his chest. Yet there was no pain, no blood, just tingling.

The Quel shifted nervously. It was definitely unprepared for this incident. The long face turned to Shade, but the warlock was still occupied in his casting. The monster, more afraid of disturbing the ceremony, remained silent but eyed the sudden events with great trepidation.

Like some creature caught in quicksand, the gem sank deeper and deeper into Cabe's body. Horror was replaced by fascination—and something else. Cabe understood that this would not hurt him, but help him.

Looking the part of a wind-whipped specter, Shade moved swiftly in the midst of awakening powers, his hands darting to and fro, each movement adding to the swirling mists and things. The sleeping Quel shivered as one. Cabe's guard became distracted by the stirring of his people.

Something dark and nebulous formed in a far corner of the chamber. It was behind the creature that guarded, so only Cabe was aware of its presence. He, though, paid it little attention; the crystal demanded and received the vast majority of his awareness.

From within that ignored darkness, coming from eternity itself, laughter was emitted. It was low, almost beyond the hearing of any creature. Nevertheless, the Quel who stood shuddered and glanced about. It did not turn to the darkness.

Shade, however, did.

"Who laughs . . ." His eyes fixed on the hitherto unnoticed spot. Madrac cursed, glanced at Cabe, and began gesturing.

In one moment, it seemed the forces of all hells had been loosed. The laughter suddenly rose to great heights, cutting out most other sounds. The cowled warlock, alerted by senses far beyond the ordinary, unleashed his spell. It was not aimed at Cabe; rather, the powers were thrown at the darkness. The two forces met, fought for control. It was only a short battle. The darkness swallowed Shade's powerful spell as if it had consisted of nothing.

Through the blackness came a creature as dark and sinister as its home. Great hooves carved grooves into the rocky floor. Ice-blue eyes glared at those in its sight. The wild mane shook loose small particles of ebony night. The mouth was framed with a snarl, revealing very sharp and very unhorselike teeth.

Darkhorse leaped at Shade.

The Quel tried to block the rampaging form, but all that was accomplished was that the armored monster vanished into the void that was Darkhorse. The sleek equine shape was not even slowed. Warlock and eternal locked into combat.

Cabe was jarred from his fascination with the crystal by the appearance of his unearthly friend. He stood up, ignoring the sudden absence of his bonds. He only knew that there was incredible danger where two such powerful forces met.

Darkhorse kicked at the mage with his forehooves. What would have cracked mountains only jostled the shadowy sorceror. Shade rebalanced and threw a number of sharp black spears at the steed. Somehow the creature maneuvered around them, charging his opponent head-on as he did so.

"Cabe! Talak! Talak is your destination! Go!"

The eternal's words were not spoken, but rather came from Cabe's own mind. As if a puppet, his body moved swiftly toward the entrance to this chamber; behind him, he could hear the howls and explosions of powers unleashed. He had no desire to await the outcome.

Ignored in this was the crystal still buried deep in his chest. It had altered. The glow had changed color, and the gem was now as blue as the daytime sky and pulsating as well. Cabe did not realize it, but the more he exerted himself, the more the gem pulsated.

Whether it was magic or perhaps some hidden sense, something made Cabe duck. A huge, four-edged ax bit deeply into the rock on the level his head had been. The Quel holding it hooted angrily and pulled the weapon up for another swing.

Cabe was barely able to roll away as the armadillo-like horror tried once more to separate his head from the rest of his body, while within the sleeping chamber, the battle of titans still reigned. The hapless young warlock now found himself contending with falling rock as well as his murderous adversary.

In an act of desperation, he extended his left hand at the Quel. Simultaneously, unintelligible words flowed from his mouth. The tips of his fingers glowed. The color matched that of the crystal.

The Quel stepped back for a better swing, his ax high in the air— unnaturally high. The ax bit deeply into the ceiling above, its hapless owner pulled from the ground. The rock, already loosened by the battle between Shade and Darkhorse, fell. A cave-in commenced. Cabe managed to leap forward; the Quel was not so lucky and was buried beneath tons of earth and rock.

Not willing to discover whether the creature was dead or not, Cabe continued his departure. His magic had saved him once again. Better yet, he felt more comfortable, more confident. The fact that he should not have known the spell never occurred to him. With no past training, he was unfamiliar with the route other magic-users were forced to take.

He ran past the city. No other Quel made an appearance. Were there only two? He could not believe himself that lucky. Nevertheless, nothing impeded his progress. The entrance through which they had entered was only seconds away, and that caused him to think. Darkhorse had told him to flee to Talak, but Talak was far, very far, to the northeast.

Stepping out onto the surface, he scanned the area. The Legar Peninsula was misleadingly peaceful and beautiful. At any other time, it would have been fascinating to explore it, even barring the fact that it was controlled by the Crystal Dragon.

Night had fallen. Cabe disliked the thought of traveling by dark, but he could see no alternative. He had no light, and it was probably wiser not to carry one. In this area, a torch would stick out for miles. Cabe hoped that there were no large predators in the area, for this time he had no magic sword to save his skin. He would have to rely on his own powers and abilities.

By the stars that were visible, he determined the general direction he needed to go. The ground beneath his feet shook, reminding him of the fierce struggle taking place. With renewed effort, Cabe started off quickly from the mouth of the tunnel.

Seeing turned out to be little trouble. With both moons out, the lands fairly gleamed from their light. After a short time, he slowed his pace. This would not do. The battle between Darkhorse and Madrac/Shade might end at any moment. If the cowled sorceror proved triumphant, he would be close behind his intended victim within seconds. Cabe wished he could teleport or fly or summon something to carry him away. His powers, though, were apparently not ready for that stage yet.

No creature stirred. Were there no animals? It seemed strange. He had not even heard an insect or a night bird. Did the curse of the Barren Lands extend even farther than believed? To his knowledge, no one had ever mentioned traveling to this remote part of the Dragonrealms. That meant either that no one dared speak of it or no one had ever come back.

Time became a blur. Cabe remembered only running, then walking, and finally stumbling across the Legar Peninsula. At some point, he finally fell over, totally exhausted by his ordeal. He had paid no attention to the crystal in his chest; it was so much a part of him now. Nor did he know of the change in his hair, due partly to that gem. Not one trace of his original hair color remained. The silver had covered it completely.

He slept through the night, waking only once, and that for just a moment. That which disturbed him might have been a movement of the earth. It might also have been the endless struggle between two immortals. At the time, Cabe couldn't have cared less. He was asleep again the next instant.

Though he had seen none, life did indeed abound on the peninsula. One or two small plant-eaters scurried by his motionless form. A bird flew past overhead. None of the dangerous animals, especially the hill wolves who dominated this area, came near. In fact, those that sought to suddenly changed their plans and hurried on to other hunting grounds, unaware that there had been any alteration. Each time, the crystal glowed brightly.

MORNING CAME, AND with it surprises. First and foremost was the wonderful smell of bacon turning crisp over an open fire. Second was the realization in Cabe's mind that he was no longer alone. With speed that surprised him almost as much as the other things did, Cabe rolled away from the figures nearby.

"Moves almost like elk, he does."

"Huh! Moves more like newborn elk, you mean. Will get grass stains over his pretty clothes, he will."

There were two of them. Having lived fairly close to the Dagora Forest, Cabe knew what they were even if he had never actually seen their kind before. It was impossible to mistake wood elves for anything else.

Both were short and thin and almost completely identical. They came no higher than Cabe's shoulder, although he had heard of taller ones who sometimes infiltrated and even intermarried with humans. These two, though, were definitely completely of the blood.

They were standing side by side. The one on the left grinned and said, "Has a bit of the People in him, he does. Can smell it, can't you?"

His twin nodded, albeit somewhat reluctantly. "Stinks much more of human, though, and something else."

Cabe decided to interrupt. "Who——?"

"Course he does! Must be the mage we seek."

"Excu—"

"Must be. Doesn't look to be much, does he?"

"I—"

"Looks can be deceiving. Still, you have a point, I think. Doesn't look like much of a mage."

Anger swelled to the breaking point. Something gave.

"He's a mage, he is!"

"Quiet! He might do it again, he might!"

"Why does he have to blow holes in the lovely countryside, though?"

"Quiet!" Cabe was barely holding back a second explosion.

The two wood elves became silent. Motionless, they might have been a pair of statues for some lord's gate. All they were to Cabe, though, were two great annoyances.

"Who are you?"

The one on the left: "Allanard."

The one on the right: "Morgyn."

Cabe folded his arms. "You were looking for me?"

Allanard rubbed his elbow and winced. Both elves wore identical clothing: simple woodland outfits colored green with small areas of brown here and there. The outfits blended in perfectly with the landscape around them.

"Are you Bedlam?"

"I am."

Morgyn nodded. "Can see it in the face, I can. The grandfather is in you." He made a face. "Your father, too."

"Why are you looking for me? What do you want?"

Both of the elves started to laugh, but stopped when they caught sight of Cabe's face. Allanard smiled. "From you, we want nothing. This is a favor we do, it is. Favor for a half-blood relation and your grandfather, good Nathan."

Morgyn caught sight of the crystal. "Allanard, he's got a bloody gem poked in his chest, he does."

"Quiet!"

Cabe had not been listening. "Who is this half-blood relation? Why would he help me?"

"Why? He only watched you break the link with death and grow up! That's why! We're talkin' of the man who you thought was your father, we are!"

"My—"

"Hadeen was his name. He looked after you out of friendship to Nathan. There may be blood involved, too."

"Blood?" Cabe's face paled.

Allanard shook his head. Even his hair was tinted green. "We're talking relations here, we are. You might be our kin. That makes it doubly important for us to help you. Besides—" For the first time, bitterness edged its way into the merry voice. "—we owe the lizards for Hadeen."

Cabe did not catch the last part, his mind turning back to the danger beneath the earth. He hoped these two had good transportation. The more distance separating him from the Legar Peninsula, the better.

As if to emphasize his point, the ground quaked with unnatural fury.

Morgyn was thrown to the ground. "Has the nation of gnomes gone to war?"

Cabe regained his balance. "Worse! A wizard named Shade and a creature called Darkhorse fight somewhere below!"

The elves' mouths dropped. Allanard was the first to regain use of his tongue. "The black steed and the two-minded warlock at odds! Nothing was said of this! We must make haste, we must!"

"Where do we go? Do you have horses?"

"Horses? Are you not a mage and one of the blood as well?"

"That's debat—"

Allanard waved off any talk. "Swiftness we need, though I don't know if it's possible to escape the likes of those two should one come seeking you in evil! Morgyn! This is your specialty!"

"Aye, brother!"

The terrible combat beneath the surface was forgotten as Cabe watched in wonder. Morgyn took out a small piece of black chalk and was now outlining a shape in the air. Literally. Wherever he drew, a black line remained despite the fact that nothing supported it.

It took the young warlock some moments before he recognized the general shape of the drawing. It was definitely a bird, but it had to be one of the largest avians he had ever seen. If real, the creature would have been able to carry them all.

Morgyn finished the outline and then quickly added several details such as eyes and mouth. The last and oddest features were three man-sized seats on the back of the bird. When he was satisfied the bird was complete, Morgyn waved the piece of chalk and muttered in what had to be the elven tongue.

A brownish mass filled in the drawing. The eyes of the bird blinked. The beak opened and closed, a pinkish tongue momentarily protruding from it. Massive wings were tested and found satisfying. The great condor turned its head and peered at its creator with one of the staring eyes.

All this in less than a minute.

Allanard looked at Cabe. "Well? What are you waiting for, the fuzzy-faced wizard to give you a boost up?"

Somewhat warily, Cabe climbed aboard the back of the bird and sat down in the middle seat, it being the largest of the three. The two wood elves took their places, and Morgyn tapped the condor lightly on the head. The young warlock looked aghast at him.

"Aren't there any reins?"

The elf patted his creation and smiled. "Now, what would we be needing reins for?"

The condor took off. Cabe held on for dear life. It irked him that Morgyn sat up front, only his legs holding him to the soaring bird. He was laughing, and so was Allanard. Both elves were at home with this type of transportation. Cabe would have been more satisfied with a bumpier but easier-to-handle vehicle such as a wagon.

The condor rose higher and higher. Cabe caught himself just as he started to look down. Allanard chuckled.

"You can look down, you can. Won't see nothin' but clouds this high up!" His emphasis of their altitude only wracked Cabe's nerves even more.

Morgyn's voice came from in front. "Heads up! We're goin' straight into a dark one!"

The warlock had only a minute of surprise before the gray cloud was smack in front of them. The condor flew in without a care. Much to Cabe's annoyance, the wood elves laughed heartily as they entered. They had, he decided, a particularly strange sense of humor.

Beads of moisture formed all over him, despite the fact that he was not in the least bit hot. There was an unusual smell in the air. Cabe finally recognized it as the odor left after a spring shower. It was clean and helped ease his nervousness a bit. Seconds later, they departed the rain cloud. All three of them were wet, but his companions were not bothered by it at all. The wind quickly dried them as they moved on.

THE LONGER THEY traveled, the more accustomed Cabe became to such an odd mode of transportation. He even dared to look down now and then. It was the first of these glances that made him marvel at the speed they were moving.

Lest he lose his grip, he chose to speak to Morgyn rather than Allanard. "Is that the Dagora Forest below us?"

Morgyn looked down only momentarily. "Aye, that's home, right enough! When we've brought you to your destination, brother and I will return here!"

The lush forest, with its masses of greenery and ever-present wildlife, well hid the fact that it was the same forest through which Cabe had faced more than one peril. Somewhere, he knew, the Lady's manor lay.

"We've flown for no more than an hour! That's incredible!"

Allanard's chuckle reached him from behind. "Don't encourage him too much, Cabe Bedlam! You're liable to get us movin' so fast even I won't be able to hold on!"

His brother had turned to face the front once more. The condor increased its speed perceptibly. Morgyn let out a quiet laugh.

A dark, green form flew up toward them from the forest. Even from the tremendous distance, Cabe could see that it was at least as huge as the condor. By its color and shape, he knew it had to be a dragon—at this height, most likely an airdrake.

He alerted the elves and pointed at the swiftly rising figure. It was set on an intercept course. Both elves watched it closely but did nothing to prevent a confrontation. Cabe released the hold he had with his left hand and held it, palm forward, in the direction of the airdrake. He was not quite sure what he was about to do, but was now at least confident that he would do something.

Allanard reached around him and swatted down the hand. He whispered in the warlock's ear. "Do nothing!"

The dragon's wings flapped hard as it lifted itself higher and higher. At one point, it let loose with a challenging roar. The condor pointedly ignored it. Cabe wondered if the bird was capable of reacting.

Some fifty yards or so from them, the drake halted. For a full half minute, it hovered where it was, watching their movement. Then, as if totally uninterested, it tipped its body and dove with horrifying speed back toward the forest. It was out of sight almost instantly.

Cabe looked to his two companions, considering his position as best he could. Morgyn had resumed controlling the bird, but Allanard nodded to him.

"See? One must not be so hasty in proclaiming judgments, one must not."

Wishing he could turn around completely, Cabe twisted himself as much as was possible. "What do you mean? Why did that airdrake fly all the way up here and then depart without attacking?"

"Humans, even such as yourself, live near but not in the Dagora Forest. We live most of our entire lives there. Even still, we know little of our true monarch, the Green Dragon. When he commands, we obey, we do. When he says that you are to pass unharmed, even the strongest of drakes will not disobey."

"The Green Dragon allows us to pass?" Cabe had trouble believing that. Why would one of the Dragon Kings help him?

The elf shook his head. "Do not question good fortune, Cabe Bedlam, do not. More to the point, do not attempt to read the minds of the Dragon Kings. You may find yourself asking who your real friends and foes are."

Whether due to some joke of Morgyn's or some gust of wind, the condor dove abruptly. Cabe was forced to hold on tight. When the bird had leveled once more, the warlock did not resume his conversation with Allanard. He was too busy thinking about what had already been said.

Shade, Darkhorse, the Green Dragon, the Gryphon . . .

Whom did he trust?

Whom did he dare trust?

XV

Out in the midst of the Hell Plains, it was heard for the first time. Warlocks, witches, scholars—all those who dealt with the other realities heard or felt it. Had they been at the stronghold of Azran, they would have seen it in all its horror.

The hordes of the Red Dragon gazed upon it. Gazed upon it and died. Though servants of the dark sorceror died left and right, the firedrakes could not even so much as touch the master. Like the specter of Death, with his mighty scythe reaping steadily, Azran cut through their ranks with the Nameless.

Few dragons escaped, even though the warlock was only one man. With the sword screaming its bloodlust, he appeared here and there, striking opponents before they could even acknowledge his presence. The Nameless pulsated. Azran's face was totally devoid of all humanity. He laughed as he struck again and again.

Only the Red Dragon held his own. Summoning those powers he controlled, his true form swelled to mammoth proportions. A blaze of fire hotter than the core of the world covered all where it was aimed. Azran moved through it easily; he barely even felt the heat.

The lord of the Hell Plains summoned forth the substance of his very land. Though slightly less than his flame in intensity, the magma and steam overwhelmed through sheer abundance and force. The Dragon King cared little whether his clans died with the servants of Azran as long as he finally succeeded in destroying this wizard who was armed with Chaos itself.

The molten rock and earth slowed Azran only temporarily, and that was due mostly to the fact that he was forced to wade through it. The Nameless protected him from the effects, and before long, he was moving freely again. The boiling water from the geysers dampened him only slightly.

His magic failing him, the Red Dragon threw himself into battle. Great yard-long talons raked at the arrogant human; this attack Azran was forced to defend against. His deadly blade deflected the terrible claws, even slicing off the tip of one. No sooner had he fought off one massive paw then the other struck. The warlock was pushed back. Powerful though the Nameless was, it could not completely protect him from his own mortal frailties. Azran did not realize the contradiction this posed; though the source of the sword's power was the warlock himself, it was now much changed from his original intentions.

The crimson firedrake thrust its gaping maw at the momentarily imbalanced human. Azran was only barely able to meet him head-on. The Nameless swung screaming at the Dragon King. The great reptile snapped his head back out of reach, howling at the bloody gash now present along his nostrils. More angered than injured, the Red Dragon rose swiftly into the air, his tremendous bulk disappearing into the clouds with unbelievable speed.

Unperturbed, the black-clad warlock raised himself into the air and pursued his quarry. It mattered not that his stronghold was now in ruins and that most of his servants were either dead or dispersed. All that mattered now was the death of the other. Azran's face was the picture of berserker fury. It was the sword, not the man, who now dictated actions.

It should have been impossible for so huge a form to hide so completely among the clouds overlooking the carnage. Nevertheless, he could not see his adversary. That the Red Dragon still lurked about was obvious; no

Dragon King would run from battle, especially this one. Azran smiled. If hunt he must, hunt he would.

A shadow fell over him. Through its own volition, the Nameless arced upward, cutting deep into the thing above it. With an agonized cry, a drake who had survived the initial battle plummeted to the earth. The warlock grunted; he couldn't have cared less about such a minor creature. It was the ruler of this land he wanted.

Moisture and cool air calmed him down a bit. He became more aware of his precarious position. The dragon was a native of both land and air. Azran, on the other hand, flew occasionally, but was generally more satisfied land-bound. The crimson reptile knew how to move about in this aerial fog; the warlock had to make do with trial and error.

The more he regained control of himself, the more unsure he became. The Nameless, meanwhile, pulsated quietly and kept to itself. Its lack of evident power might have meant a thousand different things.

Silently, deadly, the Red Dragon chose that moment to strike. Its fore-claws were open to clutch, its jaws wide to crush. Azran was taken completely unaware.

The Nameless was not.

With renewed force, the sinister blade jerked its bearer around to confront the beast. Animal fury regained its hold over the sorceror's body. Laughing wildly, Azran flew straight toward the long, pointed fangs of the Dragon King. Neither would turn back now. The time for hiding was over.

Totally under the bewitching spell of his own creation, Azran soared faster and faster with no apparent intention of deviating from his suicidal course. The Red Dragon opened his maw to its limit; there was no way the human would be able to alter direction in time.

His reptilian teeth clamped together as the minute figure disappeared inside. The eyes of the firedrake gleamed with the joy of victory. That gleam was replaced almost immediately by a peculiar glazing, as if the creature were stunned by some thought.

No thought, though, ran through the mind of the Red Dragon unless, perhaps, there was realization of what had happened. The leviathan's body shuddered, only just realizing that it was dead. The hulking form twitched once more and then plunged earthward. As it did so, something burst through the back of the head. It was Azran; the sword had cut its way into and out of the skull. The swiftness of the weapon was such that there had been no time for the victim to react.

Covered with the indescribable remnants of his fallen opponent's skull, the warlock watched the bulky mass disappear below. Elation filled his very being. He had proved himself the master. Even his unlamented father had not succeeded in destroying a Dragon King and preserving his own life. Here Azran stood—or floated—nearly unscathed from a one-on-one fight with the deadliest of creatures.

He corrected that; it was obvious to him that he was now the deadliest.

Azran took in the deep breath of victory—not to mention the smell of his clothes and body in general. He coughed. So much for the sweet smell of success! He shrugged. It was a small price to pay for so satisfying a victory. He would clean himself up soon enough.

In his euphoria, he failed to take any notice of the Nameless itself. The demonic blade pulsated only slightly, yet it seemed to convey a feeling of newfound power. A power that would grow with each victory—

—regardless of who happened to bear it.

"And how arrre we today, sssorceressss?"

She almost expected a long, red ribbon of tongue, forked at the end, to shoot out from his mouth. There was something about Duke Toma that chilled her more than Kyrg or even the Dragon Kings had ever done. He was more the cold, inhuman reptile than any of the other dragons save the unthinking lesser drakes and their cousins. Here, Gwen decided, was what the first Kings had been like—save that Toma, by his birth, could never be one of them.

When she did not answer, the firedrake merely shrugged and smiled.

God! She could not help staring. Even his teeth were far more the sharp fangs of the dragon than his lords' were.

Toma walked slowly around the bubble, forcing his prisoner to try to rotate so as to keep the sinister warrior in view lest he pull some new trick. The dragon man was more than capable of such; his powers were at least as formidable as the Lady's—perhaps greater. Why, then, she asked herself for the hundredth time, had he always remained in the background? It was not like the Dragon Kings to waste a weapon of such potential.

The firedrake paused. As if reading her thoughts—it was highly likely he might be able to, even though Gwen always kept a shield up—Toma spoke.

"Has it occurred to you that a warrior of my . . . shall we say abilities . . . appears satisfied to serve those who are quite obviously his inferiors in power and leadership?"

"I assumed you were a craven coward at heart, like that sadist Kyrg."

The bubble became uncomfortably hot and severely stuffy. Gwen tried out a spell, but received only a headache for her actions. Her breathing became labored.

After watching her suffer for several moments, Toma casually waved a hand in her direction. Air circulation and temperature immediately returned to more tolerable conditions. The witch took in great gulps of fresh air and wiped the sweat from her brow.

This time, Toma did not smile, and the Lady saw that he did in fact have a serpent's tongue. He sat down in the only chair in his tent and poured himself a goblet of bloodred wine. By his slow movements, she knew that he was reminding her of her own thirst, something she had been unable to do anything about since her capture.

"You will avoid any such offensive outbursts in the near future, Lady of the Amber. They could prove quite breathtaking, at the very least." He took a long, teasing sip of the wine.

"You asked me a question. Yes, I have wondered. Why do you obey the Kings? Surely, even Gold is no match for you!"

Pleased by this comment, Toma poured some of the crimson liquid into another goblet. He passed a hand over it, causing it to vanish. Goblet and wine appeared almost immediately in one of Gwen's own hands. She forced herself to show restraint as she drank, lest the firedrake decide to take it from her in sport.

"Quite correctly put, milady! Still, I do not seek to unseat my father yet. His dreams are mine, though he swings from sanity to madness without warning. Only tradition prevents him from naming me as one of the successors. If one thing would unite the other Kings against him, it would be tradition." The duke spat as he spoke the last word; the ground sizzled where he had aimed.

"Surely, with your power—"

He raised a hand. "You are trying to determine the intensity of my abilities. I will tell you, quite freely, that it is insufficient to handle all of the Dragon Kings. That is why I have set about creating the basis for a new leadership!"

At first, the insinuations present in the remark passed over her head. Only after the words were allowed to sink in did she realize who and what she was dealing with. It altered much of what she had come to believe in the short time since her release from her crystal prison. They had all been fools, even the dreaded Kings, and—she felt a slight twinge of satisfaction on this point—the malevolent Azran had fallen so readily into the scheme of things.

"You. You started this chain of events! You've brought this new war upon the Dragonrealms!"

Reptilian eyes gleamed under the menacing dragonhelm that was and was not a part of the firedrake himself. He raised his goblet to her and drank. When he had finished, he smiled. It was more frightening than anything else he could have done.

"Yes! Through my agents, I stirred up several of the Kings. Blue was the easiest, the most pliant. Black was always harping about the Masters, although I must congratulate him for finding your companion, the young Bedlam hatchling. That was an unexpected bonus! It allowed me to twist Brown, who still held the Horned Blade. The fool! Call it foresight, but I knew the outcome of that meeting with the grandson of Nathan. Still, even if the boy had died, I would have played on the possibility that others might exist. I might have even released you, knowing full well that you would immediately set off to revive your legion of magic-users."

Toma's boasts were cut off by the appearance of a thing that was not exactly humanoid but close enough to make it a parody of men. It waited nervously for the duke to acknowledge it. Toma did so, barely nodding his head. The creature shuffled forward on legs that seemed uneven and much too short for the body. It handed its master a small, rolled-up piece of parchment. The item in hand, the firedrake dismissed his servant. Gwen noticed the eagerness of the thing to leave the presence of its lord.

For the first time, Duke Toma frowned in displeasure. He opened the parchment and studied its contents carefully. When that was done, the message was slowly lowered to the table bearing the wine. The firedrake stared into space, his mind temporarily occupied by the revelations he had just read. The Lady leaned forward, trying to scan the words from her magical cell. Whatever discomforted Toma was worth knowing about.

The duke noticed her straining to see the dispatch. He casually knocked it aside and out of her sight.

"Matters of which you can play no part, milady. I will deal with them should they prove troublesome. Now, then, where were we?"

Gwen did not answer him. Her mind was on the message. What had it said? Did it concern Cabe?

Dismissing her attempts to understand what he had read, Toma continued his tale of self-glory. "The Kings suffer from too much tradition. They believe that they and they alone command powers worthy for ruling." A laugh, disturbingly human, for once. "I sat among them, pretended to be one of them, even convinced one he had the power to resurrect his dying kingdom!"

A shapeshifter, too. More and more, the witch did not like what she was hearing. Even the Dragon Kings were confined to two forms. From what Toma was saying, he had taken on a third form as well.

"Does not this particular Dragon King ever suspect?"

"Hardly. The Crystal Dragon has never answered a summoning. Whether the rest of the lands destroy themselves does not concern him. He once told the council that he had duties far more important than bickering with his brethren. What those duties were, no one has ever learned." He shrugged. "It is unimportant."

Unexpectedly, he rose. "I have, up 'til now, supplied most of the conversation. While it has been interesting talking to someone other than ignorant rabble, I really should be receiving more information from you. That, sadly, must wait for a more attractive moment. If you will excuse me?"

Bowing in jest, Toma departed. The Lady watched him leave, curious. Not having been able to read the note, she could not know the concern that had suddenly sprung full grown in the duke's head. The sphere in which she was imprisoned did not float randomly; spells locked it in one specific location.

Whether the commander of the imperial hordes would return quickly or not was uncertain. Nevertheless, Gwen had to take a chance. She had narrowed down the field quite a bit; somewhere there was a flaw in this spell that was holding her captive. One of the first things Nathan had taught her was that any magic-user could counter a spell merely by knowing where its inherent weak spot was. Even some of the most powerful spells could be canceled by apprentices if they could identify the location.

Trouble was, the more complex the spell, the more difficult it was to find the weak spot unless one already knew where to look. That was one of the things that had made Nathan Bedlam so powerful; he plotted his spells carefully and made a thorough study of all others.

Her hands touched the bubble only lightly. It required a sensitive touch to find and move the various lines and colors that made up the basic "physical" components of the spell. What gestures or words were used did not matter so much. They would help, but she was confident that she could unbind the bubble without them.

Nothing. She lowered her hands to another spot. Still nothing. She shifted first to right, then to left. On the left, she felt a slight stirring. It was not much, but it was a sign. The fault was near.

Gwen wiped the sweat from her brow. She was so near! Pausing to catch her breath, she noticed now the real difference in temperature. Her breathing became labored. Immediately, the sorceress ceased all activity.

Something new was added this time. Slowly but consistently, her own body proved too great a burden to bear. She was forced to the smooth bottom of the bubble, her face pressed against its surface. The weight of several times normal threatened to crush her. Her only chance was to remain motionless.

In a flash, all was normal once more. Slightly sore, the Lady turned to face Duke Toma. He was shaking his head as a teacher would when scolding a troublesome student.

"The next time will be the final time, milady. Not that it would do you much good. While you were . . . lying down, I took the liberty of altering the nature of the bubble spell. I guarantee that you will not have enough free time to find the fault. We will be too busy traveling."

"Traveling? To Penacles?"

The firedrake looked at her, almost convincingly puzzled. "Penacles? Why should I wish to go there? It has nothing I want."

Now it was her turn to show puzzlement. "The libraries! The City of Knowledge . . ."

Toma shook his head. "City of Knowledge! By this time, the Gryphon has no doubt learned just how useful that knowledge really is. I have made a careful study of its past." He rubbed his leathery chin. "Do you know what I discovered? No ruler of Penacles has ever really been able to rely on the libraries themselves! It's all a lie, Lady of the Amber! A great hoax! The emperor, of course, does not believe that, and neither does the Black Dragon, who has always coveted the city. Kyrg, obedient fool that he is, was more than willing to take his forces there and wrestle the place from whoever survives. He expects me to meet him there, but I have already sent a message, changing his orders."

Gwen's eyes narrowed. "In what way?"

"He is to join in the assault on Penacles. Not right away, but soon."

It was what she had thought. Penacles could not possibly withstand the added onslaught of Duke Kyrg's imperial hordes. The firedrake had many faults, but his skill in leadership was near that of Toma himself. She suspected that none of the Black Dragon's commanders could even come close, which was why they had failed up to this point.

Something else struck her. There was always the chance that Kyrg, the master of the Gray Mists, and many of the other firedrakes in charge might be injured or killed. That would do well to cut down Toma's competition.

The dragon warrior waggled a finger at her. The bubble floated toward him without a sound or any means of propulsion. "Come with me."

As if she had a choice, she thought angrily.

The flaps of the tent spread widely apart as the bubble moved through. Once outside, the Lady was shocked to see that most of the firedrake's forces had already prepared for departure. They moved quickly and quietly, their inhuman speed cutting in half the time it would have taken many armies. She watched wagons being loaded and lesser drakes being hitched up. At that point, their new destination became evident. It was, after all, the only city to the north of Mito Pica.

She dared to interrupt Toma as he directed the efforts of his forces. "Why Talak, Duke Toma? Why turn back the way you came?"

The sphere glowed briefly with increased heat. It returned to normal only scant seconds later. The warlord studied her face, read her emotions. "I suppose there is no danger in telling you, since you are hardly in a position to do anything about it. My catalyst has served his purpose; to allow him to live might actually endanger my plans. Therefore, we return to Talak to remedy the situation. Cabe Bedlam will die before his powers are allowed to develop fully. His death will spell the end of any attempts to resurrect the Dragon Masters."

The Lady barely heard his last words. Cabe in Talak! How? Azran would not live so close to civilization. Therefore, as hard as it was to believe, Cabe had either escaped or was stolen from his treacherous father. There was still hope if the former was the truth.

Toma smiled coldly, his eyes gleaming. "I can assume, then, that you will be traveling with us? I should think you would be grateful at this chance to see your lover."

Her face reddened. "He's not my—"

The dragon warrior silenced her with a wave of his hand. "I will not discuss the idiosyncrasies of human behavior. We are ready to leave now. I think you will float slightly behind me, in case I should wish to talk to you."

He purposely turned his back to her. "Rest assured, I have the utmost confidence in my safety."

She did not argue the point.

Toma ordered his humanoid troops to mount up. The rest of his creatures were ordered forward. Those who seemed reluctant quickly felt the lash of the man-shaped firedrakes. Gwen wondered why the lower drakes did not rebel. They outnumbered their masters a hundred to one. She then remembered the duke's own words. The dragons as a whole were caught up in tradition. To turn on their rulers was unthinkable; only the royal factions would dare, but that was evidently something also considered tradition—save where a nonruling firedrake such as Toma was concerned.

It could also be that the dragons did not rebel because they were too stupid to. The witch decided that each notion was equal in validity. Without the Dragon Kings and their minions to steer them, most of the lesser drakes would be no more dangerous than the rogue wyverns and basilisks. Such threats were far easier to crush.

The army moved with amazing speed, considering the makeup of the bulk of its fighting force. Within an hour, the entire column was leaving what once had been the outskirts of Mito Pica. The Lady used this time to view what she could of the dying city.

Toma had based his camp on the eastern portion of the city. Because of this, she had not been able to see much of the actual destruction. The sounds and smells, though, created a vivid picture in her mind. If the bubble had not cut down her powers, she would have used farsight to discover the damage.

What the sorceress saw on departure was enough for her. Blackened buildings still smoked. Walls that had held countless foes back were shattered to dust. Gwen suspected that the warlord had had a major role in that portion of the battle. She could imagine the faces of the city's spellcasters as their walls crumbled despite their best efforts.

She had assumed that Azran or Gold would be the greatest threat. She had been wrong. At the moment, the witch was now only a few feet away from the real cause.

The lands around the ruins were oddly untouched, save where some beast of war had gone rushing after a hapless victim. Even the nearby villages had remained unaffected. The duke had seen that Mito Pica—only Mito Pica—had fallen. Hadeen's cabin was the only exception she could think of.

The warlord was sending out a message to those who might defy him. Obey and you would live. Disobey—and disobedience in this case was

rather loosely defined, she noticed—and you would suffer the consequences. Only a lack of information had saved the small village where Cabe
had been raised from joining the city.

The dragon hordes pushed on. Gwen wondered what Talak would do
when faced with the situation. Would they attempt to fight, or would they
turn on Cabe in the hopes that they would be spared? From what she had
recently gleaned of the current ruler, Rennek IV or something, she did not
think Nathan's grandson would receive a very courteous welcome.

Behind the swiftly moving forces of Duke Toma, the last smoking em-
bers of Mito Pica burned out.

XVI

"B ETTER EAT, CABE Bedlam, if you wish to keep your strength."
Cabe stared at the green mess in his wooden bowl—the same green
mess that he had been fed for the past four days—and poured it slowly on
the ground. He was convinced that the grass under the gruel died instantly.

"I'll pass, thank you. I've had more than enough of this . . . this . . . whatever! We've been here long enough! From what we've heard from passersby, I
don't think the Dragon Kings have any allies here."

Allanard swallowed a mouthful of food with great satisfaction. Cabe
nearly turned the color of the wood elves' clothing. "The Dragon Kings
have allies wherever humans are, if you'll be excusin' me for saying so. You
may be the most abundant of the races, but you're also the most varied, you
are."

The words brought Cabe's own father to mind. He nodded slowly.
"Nevertheless, Darkhorse said to go to Talak. I trust him. Remember, he
saved me from Shade."

Morgyn sighed. "The eternal's ways are his own. Mayhap he has some
dark deed in mind."

Disgusted, the warlock rose. "You two can make excuses until the end of
time, but I'm going in there. Thank you for your assistance in getting me
here. I think I'll be okay from here on."

The two elves stood up, their faces the most sober he'd ever seen them.
Allanard extended his hand. "Go with our blessings, Cabe Bedlam. It's
not that we don't want to help you, but think of our people. We're not
the fighters your kind are, we're not. If the Dragon Emperor thinks we

actively move against him, there's no doubt that he'll order us crushed like Mito Pica, he will."

"The Green Dragon—"

"—may or may not do as his ruler orders. I'm sorry, I am. We just can't do anything else. As it is, we hope and pray that none of those thick-skinned flying sentries recognized us. Might very well find the hordes breathin' down our necks the moment we touch home."

The other elf also extended his hand. "Good luck, lad. Pleasure knowin' you and your old man's old man."

Feeling somewhat guilty over his earlier words, Cabe took both proffered hands. "Sorry about what I said. Hope you have a safe journey back."

Allanard smiled grimly. " 'Tis not us who have the hardest ride ahead."

Bidding them a final farewell, Cabe turned and headed directly for the front gate. Behind him, he heard the sound of a large bird taking flight. He did not bother to look back.

Though darkness had fallen more than an hour before, people were still moving through the gate in both directions. Guards routinely checked them as they passed by. It did not appear that they made very thorough examinations.

Following a trader's wagon, he nonchalantly walked up to the first of the soldiers. The man's face nearly made Blane look handsome. Unlike the commander from Zuu, the guard struck Cabe as a rather unsavory sort of person. He decided to wait until he was inside before revealing his identity to anyone.

A hairy paw shoved him in the chest. "Here! Daydreamin' ain't any excuse to pass by inspection! Who are ya and why are ya travelin' empty-handed?"

Cabe became uneasy. He was sure his tale would go well above the soldier's head. If he had carried money, there would have been no problem. The warlock had seen this type several times while working as a serving man. He looked down at his clothes and came up with the only reasonable answer he could think of.

"I was by myself, coming here, when bandits ambushed me. I ran. Six-to-one odds I don't care for. Especially when they have bows." He was thankful that the gem was covered by his shirt. Allanard had suggested that a little magic could remove the article of clothing and replace it, more or less whole, over the crystal. After all, the elf stated, few people wandered around with gems in their chest, and it was more than likely that such a rock would only encourage the greed in many.

The guard nodded. "Yeah, we get that now and then. Be damned if I'm going out there to look for bandits, though. They tried that once. Lost seven men and never even caught one! Worse than wyverns!"

He waved a hand, dismissing Cabe, and turned his attention to the next cluster of travelers, which included several young women. Thieves and their victims were dropped from his thoughts completely. The warlock let loose a deep breath and wandered through.

It dawned on him that he might have used his powers to enter the city secretly. Almost immediately, it also dawned on him that he might have ended up sticking out of a wall or landing in a well. For the time being, normal methods would do.

Like most cities, Talak was surrounded by a fairly nondecorative wall. Cabe knew, though, that such walls could prove to be little defense against the Dragon Kings. Penacles was fortunate in that the Purple Dragon, as paranoid as his brethren, had rebuilt the barrier completely. Ironically, it had probably saved the City of Knowledge more than anything else.

While the city itself could not boast such wealth as Mito Pica or Penacles, it still impressed him greatly. Much of this was due to the fact that, being far away from most human cities and too close to the imposing Tyber Mountains, Talak was forced to depend more upon itself. It had, therefore, acquired a style all its own.

Where most cities were filled with spires, Talak was a place of hundreds of ziggurats, ranging from small shops to imposing edifices that seemed like half-grown mountains. Banners flew everywhere, and orderly soldiers, much more professional than those at the gate, kept guard over the population. It would have proved even more awesome had not Cabe known that the firedrakes had come in, demanded, and received tremendous amounts of meat without any argument.

Darkhorse's suggestion to come here was becoming more and more questionable.

The bazaars were shut down for the most part. There was, however, much activity coming from the various taverns and inns that seemed to dominate the first streets one reached on entering the city. Some were quite elegant, and all of them were far beyond the penniless state he was presently in. Involuntarily, one of his hands went into the pouch that he had always carried his few meager coins in.

He blinked. His fingers caressed a coin of some sort. He quickly pulled it out and examined it. The lighting out in the street was not the best, but the glint of gold was quite obvious. That came as a surprise; Cabe could not recall where and when he might have picked up such a piece.

One would be enough to buy him food and a night's lodging, though it would have been nice to have a few more. He shrugged; no sense cutting down his luck. The fact that he had somehow gained a gold coin should be enough satisfaction. Perhaps, he thought, one of the two elves had slipped it in his pouch when he was asleep or occupied.

Cabe chose an inn and took a step toward it. The pouch clinked against his leg. He stopped. A tentative hand reached in, felt the round, metal shapes, and pulled out again as if bitten.

There were at least a dozen coins in there, and he did not doubt for an instant that they were all identical to the one in his hand. This was not the work of the elves. Rather, Cabe's own powers were becoming more and more active, obeying his every thought. He would have to be careful about daydreaming.

The inn he chose was a cut higher than the one he had worked in, even if the customers were not. He sat down and ordered some food and ale from the matronly serving woman. His table was away from most of the crowd, save for four men and two women behind him. Cabe did not bother to pay any attention to them.

The center of the place was brightly lit, and in that area of light was a band of minstrels that played tunes from every major city. As they played, a scantily clad young woman somehow managed to dance erotically, despite whatever the tune was. The warlock suspected that she could have danced without music at all and hardly anyone would have taken notice. As it was, they could barely be heard over the general din of the people.

His food came. Cabe attacked it with gusto. He noticed that it was almost completely vegetarian. The armies of Kyrg and Toma had stripped Talak of most of its meat. The city would probably send the rare trading party to Wenslis or perhaps buy from the farmlands to the west. Despite the absence of meat, however, Cabe found the meal more than satisfying.

Intent as he was on the devouring of his meal, he paid little attention to the increasing weight near his leg. At some point, he pushed the trouble-some pouch so that it hung almost behind him. After that, he forgot about it completely.

That was soon remedied. There were shouts and grunts from the people behind him. Someone bumped him from behind. Cabe turned around to find all six people on the floor, scrambling as best they could to round up the endless shower of coins falling from a tear in his pouch. Cabe had not turned off whatever spell he had inadvertently cast. He quickly fixed that, just by hoping, but the damage was already done.

Without thinking, he reached to retrieve some of the gold. One of the men, a bulky character with a tremendous beard and muscles to match it, looked up. Caught in the act of picking up what was obviously someone else's money, the initial greed gave way to panic. He reached forward, dropping several coins, and pulled Cabe down.

Cabe's chin came within an inch of the floor before it stopped for no particular reason at all. He did not have time to make note of it. The bearded one was trying to hammer him into the ground. Reflexes came into action and the warlock rolled away before the blow fell.

Still distrustful of his wild powers, Cabe decided to run rather than fight. Unfortunately, he had become disoriented, and he moved toward the kneeling figures rather than away. He tripped over the bearded one, who was still clutching his hand in pain, and fell face-first into one of the women, taking her down with him. By this time, others had seen the loose coins. The back half of the place was turning into a free-for-all.

Cabe found his head lying nestled between two soft mounds. He quickly extracted himself from the woman, who seemed more disappointed than hurt. Finding himself a clear spot, he crawled away from the growing mob.

His gaze fell almost immediately on two uniformed legs. The owner was a gigantic figure dressed in the garb of the city's army. The face was akin to a bulldog, and the soldier's attitude was no better. He was also standing in front of a group of several similarly dressed men—the town watch, who had just happened to be nearby.

The soldier literally picked up Cabe, but it was more to move him out of the way than anything else. Turning the hapless young man over to one of the other guards, he commenced a roundup of everyone presently engaged in fighting for the loose coins.

The work was done with quick efficiency. In only a few minutes, nearly all those involved were divided into two groups, one male, the other female. To Cabe's surprise, some of the soldiers in back were not really men; he learned later that Talak's army was about fifty-fifty in terms of men and women. It was actually quite an innovation. He knew of no other land that had even proposed the idea.

All that was forgotten as they were herded out of the inn. Cabe did not think to use his abilities; it was still too easy to think of himself as a normal person. Magic would only draw attention to him, and this close to the Tyber Mountains, that could prove dangerous.

THE PRISONERS WERE all put into one holding cell. It was, in fact, the only cell in the place. The women had been taken to some other location.

Cabe settled down in the stained hay that covered most of the floor of the cell. If Talak followed the pattern of most cities, they would no doubt be released the next day, providing they could pay or knew where to obtain their fine. When that time came, he would carefully conjure up the exact amount.

Most of the other prisoners had settled down after the arrival of the newcomers. They were a mixed lot, including some particularly nasty-looking characters who appeared capable of every crime ever written up, but no one seemed in the mood to start trouble. Cabe closed his eyes to go to sleep.

"You!" The voice was rough and sounded of a man who had already drunk more than enough.

The warlock lifted his head. It was the bearded fighter, and with him were two of his companions; the fourth man was nowhere to be seen and might have escaped the town watch. These three, though, looked vicious enough without help from the other.

"Stand up!"

He stared at the drunken man. Surely, he wasn't planning on starting a fight here? The answer came swiftly as Beard reached down and pulled Cabe to his feet. It was becoming an annoying habit, the warlock decided.

"We're in here because of you, aren't we?" The last was aimed at his two companions, a short, weasel-faced character and a thin, dark-complexioned thug who had a mustache that drooped down past his shoulders.

"Thaz right," said Weasel. He was as drunk as the first. Mustache merely nodded, grinned at Cabe murderously, and appeared in no way to be intoxicated. That made him the worst of the threesome.

"Hold him for me!" The bearded man waited until his companions had jumped Cabe from both sides so that he could not escape. Each had an arm pinned.

The burly man pulled back his fist for an all-out blow. He grunted as he swung for Cabe. Due in part to his drunken state, his fist hit his intended victim squarely in the chest.

That turned the grunt into an ear-piercing shriek. Not only had the

Talakian used the same hand that had smacked against the floor of the inn, but he had also encountered a hard resistance on impact with Cabe's chest. The crunch that accompanied the scream was not from the gem. Beard had broken his hand this time. The warlock had felt nothing.

The cry was almost immediately answered by the guards. One unlocked the cell door and remained there, his eyes on the prisoners and his hand near his sword. Six others cut a path through to where Weasel and Mustache had hurriedly released their captive.

The captain of the guard looked them over. Cabe's attacker was on his knees, his face contorted into agony. The officer grunted and turned to Cabe.

"You look to be the center of this! What went on here?"

"He tried to j-jump me!" The words poured out quickly from Cabe's would-be assailant.

A boot struck the bearded man in the side, and he toppled over.

"I want an answer from you, I'll ask."

Catching the captain's attention again, Cabe looked him straight in the eyes. "It was my gold that they tried to take at the inn. For some reason, they blame me for their ending up here."

The soldier looked at him suspiciously. "Your gold?"

Cabe switched subjects. "Listen! I've got to see the King! Can you take me there?"

"Sure! Why not?" The captain suddenly smiled, something that did not improve his rather canine appearance.

"Wha—?" The warlock was taken aback. Was it this easy? Just ask?

He could hear more than one mutter of disbelief, and Mustache hissed angrily. The guard captain ordered his men to keep the other prisoners away. He turned back to Cabe.

"Follow me."

Confused but more than happy to escape his fellow inmates, Cabe did as he was told. The other soldiers looked at the commander with obvious curiosity, but no one dared question his actions. Within seconds, he was heading out the building with the captain and four escorts.

"You realize, of course, that I can only introduce you to the Master of Appointments. He'll determine whether you can have an audience with the king or not." He smiled again; it was very blank.

A spell, Cabe realized. He had accidentally placed the soldier under a spell. Eye contact, apparently. Something else to watch out for. If he was

not careful, he might shoot off spells left and right without even noticing it.

After a long period of walking, they arrived at the gate of the largest of
the ziggurats. This was the palace royal of the kings of Talak. Bright banners flew in the dim light of the Twins. Fanciful demons, imps, et cetera,
decorated the architecture here and there. An immense flower garden was
barely visible to the right. Cabe wondered how the palace might look in the
daylight.

They were met at the gate by two elaborately dressed knights. One talked
with the captain while the other kept an eye on Cabe, the obvious reason for
the encounter. The conversation lasted only a minute, at the end of which
the knight allowed the four to pass through.

Once inside the palace grounds, Cabe saw the archers and foot soldiers.
Again, it was easy to see that the palace was heavily defended, and again, it
was also disturbing that neither Toma nor Kyrg had been refused admittance.

They had to stop four times. Each time, the sentry on duty asked their
reason for coming. Only the captain's reputation got them through. Cabe
was thankful at not having to resort to another spell.

All of this just to see the Master of Appointments. Cabe might not even
be allowed to see the king—unless, of course, he made them see his way.
Remembering that rulers usually had court wizards or powers of their own,
he felt no desire to make himself noticed.

The dog-faced guard leader knocked loudly on a thick, ancient wooden
door. There was no sign proclaiming the function of this particular room,
but Cabe trusted the knowledge of his guide. Under the circumstances, the
man could not really lie.

"Enter." The voice was old and terribly scratchy. It reminded the warlock
of an old priest who had passed through the village. Every spare moment
had been spent trying to convince the young serving man that the holy
man's gods were the only ones worth praying to. It was quite evident that
he saw a potential priest in the young worker. Fortunately, guards from
Mito Pica came chasing after him. It seemed that he also had a fondness for
young males in general.

The door was opened, and the figure hunched behind the incredibly high
desk stared down at them. Cadaverous, he picked up a quill with one bony
hand and waited like one of the judges of the dead.

The captain spoke up. "Captain Enos Fontaine with one visitor to see
the king!"

The Master of Appointments pulled out a pair of seeing lenses attached to one another. These he put over his eyes. Another innovation.

"His name?"

Everyone looked at Cabe. As best he could, Cabe answered him. "Cabe. Cabe . . . Bedlam."

Gray eyebrows arched. Other than that, the Master of Appointments revealed no other emotion. The guards were all muttering to themselves.

"Relation to Nathan Bedlam, the Dragon Master?"

"Uh . . . grandson."

"Indeed." The quill was dipped into ink and then applied to parchment. The Master wrote for several seconds before turning his attention back to the warlock. "What is the purpose of your audience?"

What was his purpose? Did he wish help to attack the Dragon Emperor? No, that was preposterous. What could he say? Darkhorse had told him to go to Talak; he'd said nothing about what to do after reaching the city. Cabe had made the assumption that the ruling powers should be told. Was he wrong?

The Master of Appointments was an incredibly old man who had seen and been involved with more than he had ever mentioned to the kings he had served in one station or another. Cabe's background and silence made him draw conclusions of his own.

He waved his hands at the guards. "You are dismissed! I will handle things from here on! Go!"

They were more than happy to do so. Cabe had scarcely drawn another breath before he found himself alone with this rather enigmatic man.

The official sat up high. "My name is Drayfitt. Once, long ago, I was apprentice to a warlock named Ishmir the Bird Master. That apprenticeship was cut off by the Turning War. Ishmir was convinced by Nathan Bedlam to join the struggle."

Drayfitt, Cabe mused, must have been a powerful apprentice to have survived all these generations.

The old man continued. "If you come seeking aid in a new campaign, I will tell you that you will receive none. Talak is a shell. I have watched it wither under the baleful eye of the Dragon Emperors. I have seen King Rennek reduced to a babbling madman. His son now occupies the throne. Melicard, though, is new to the running of a kingdom. He can ill afford entanglements with a new generation of Dragon Masters."

Cabe thought to say something, then realized he had no idea what.

The Master of Appointments watched him with sad, tired eyes. "This is our home, regardless of the presence of dragons in the Tyber Mountains. If we join in some mad campaign, we will feel the crushing paw."

He held out the parchment he had been writing on. Cabe could make no sense of the writing in the dim light.

"I have here your admittance to see King Melicard. If you wish to meet with him, then I will sign it. If not . . ."

There would be no use in seeing Talak's ruler, Cabe knew. Drayfitt was right. The city had nothing to gain but instant retribution if it was discovered helping the enemies of the Dragon Kings. Mito Pica had been much farther away, yet it had fallen to Toma because it was suspected of being Cabe's home during growth to manhood. How might Talak suffer for aiding him?

He shook his head. "I have no wish to see the king."

Drayfitt crumpled the parchment in his hand. "I will make no mention of your presence in this city. I only ask that you depart as soon as possible."

Cabe nodded. The Master of Appointments summoned the guards back. He turned his attention back to his desk, not glancing up once until Cabe was gone and the door was shut again.

The old man pulled out a tiny statuette, a bird in flight. He stroked it lovingly, sadly, thinking of his teacher, his brother.

CABE WANDERED THE streets of Talak for more than two hours. The darkness did not bother him. Nor did any of the more inhospitable citizens. His mood was dark, and his powers reflected it. He did not even notice the faint glow from the gem on his chest. It had become such a part of him that he no longer thought of it unless something happened that pointed it out to him.

Why was he here? What did Darkhorse hope to accomplish? He was not even certain whether the ethereal steed still existed in this dimension. Might Shade have been able to cast him out? The creature had claimed that Gwen had the power; Shade was surely at least as strong and skilled.

Tired, irritated, and seemingly eternally confused, Cabe wandered into the nearest inn and asked for a room. Without thinking, he reached into his pouch and pulled out a gold coin. He followed the bowing owner up to a rather dingy and poorly lit room.

When the man had gone, Cabe locked the door and fell onto the bed. At any other time, he would have searched such a bed for lice and bedbugs, so rotten was it. Though it strained under his weight, he merely rolled over and slowly slipped into a troubled sleep in which faces he knew danced just out of his reach. Only one of them was unfamiliar, and yet it really was not.

A face of power, much like his own in features.

JUST BEYOND THE horizon, less than a day's journey from Talak, the hordes of Duke Toma made camp.

XVII

THEY HAD NOWHERE to flee, and because of that they perished. The deadliest of warriors, whether male or female. Whether in human form or their natural shape. They died, and few would mourn them, even among their own kind.

The green wave of death stopped only when it reached the borders of the Barren Lands. Within it, the bodies and skeletons of the last of the Brown clans slowly added to the rich new soil. Animal life came quickly, as if magnetically drawn to the lush plant life.

The spell had been cast; the sacrifice, albeit unsuspecting, had been offered up.

The Barren Lands were Barren no longer.

DUKE TOMA TOOK the lead as his army neared the city. The Lady was forced to ride alongside him, still trapped in the sorcerous bubble. She had accepted defeat where this prison was concerned, but she knew that there would come a time when the warlord released her from it. When that happened, he would pay, and pay dearly.

The firedrake had chosen early daylight for his arrival. He wanted the inhabitants just barely awake and only beginning their daily routine. Always best to catch your prey when it has just become occupied with something, he thought to himself. There was a human analogy about a man caught with one leg in his pants and the other out.

He turned to his captive. "Well, milady, we are nearly at our destination. Does not your heart beat faster at the thought of being so close to your companion?"

"I'd rather it was your heart that beat faster—until it exploded!"

"Such talk! Best that you practice your manners, Lady of the Amber.

Such comments can only heat up your present difficulties." Toma raised the temperature of the bubble just enough for Gwen to start sweating.

She forced herself to smile. "When will you tire of that little parlor trick? I used to use it to reheat my meals when I was only an apprentice."

The duke stiffened. Gwen noticed the heat die down almost immediately. Her captor turned forward, his interest in the city increasing quite suddenly. This time, she did not have to force her smile. Toma was not immune to emotion.

As they neared the gate, the Lady was shocked and dismayed to find it opening wide to receive the firedrake. At the very most, she had expected Duke Toma to meet with the ruler of Talak through some intermediary. To enter the city itself, his army free to charge in should there be trouble, showed the power the Dragon Kings had over this city.

During normal periods, the gates would have been open to allow travelers in and out of Talak. Today, people were strangely absent. All movement had come to a halt. No one wanted to even breathe around the reptilian warlord. A single wrong movement could spell death and destruction for all.

The bulk of Toma's inhuman army remained outside of the city walls, much to the relief of the citizens. Only a personal guard, albeit sinister and capable in appearance, followed the duke in. His only other companion was the Lady, who scanned the crowds restlessly for some sign of Cabe. She wanted dearly to see him, but prayed he would not show himself. If he fell into the Dragon Kings' clutches, no hope would remain.

No less than the commanding general of Talak's army rode up to greet the warlord. He saluted sharply, as one would do to one's superior. Toma did not bother to return the salute. He was direct in his desires.

"You will take me to King Melicard immediately. Understood?"

The general, looking very much unlike a soldier at the moment, nodded nervously. "Yes, milord! Please follow me!"

As they resumed movement, Gwen could not resist asking a question. "Melicard is king? What has happened to Rennek IV? I understood he was king of Talak."

There was the faintest of humor in the dragon warrior's voice. "Rennek had the honor of dining with Kyrg before my half brother made his way to Penacles. I assume that, being human, he was rather unsettled by the way we consume our meals."

It was enough to make even the sorceress pale.

They soon reached the tall ziggurat that was the palace. There was no need for the party to dismount and enter the grounds. Melicard, his features grim and only barely hiding his fear, waited for them outside the gate of his home. A half-dozen guards stood on either side of him, but Gwen doubted that they would be much help against the well-trained killers that made up Toma's protection. For that matter, with his skills, the firedrake did not really need his soldiers. They were there only for show.

"Hail to you, Duke Toma, First Commander of the Imperial Forces of the Dragon Emperor!" Melicard spoke with obvious distaste.

"Hail to you, King Melicard, who is hopefully a stronger man than his father."

The young king was visibly stung by these words. Though tall, athletic, and unquestionably handsome, he was barely into adulthood. Even Cabe seemed more experienced with life than this new ruler. The former prince had obviously led a somewhat sheltered life before his ascension to the throne.

Melicard choked back an angry response. He glanced with interest at Toma's prisoner and then asked the warlord, "What is it you wish of us? We have little in the way of meat at the moment, but we will do our best."

Toma dismissed the idea. "As long as there is one human in Talak, there is always meat. But that is not what I want. No, what I want has to do with my unwilling companion here."

"Who, if I may be so bold as to ask, have I the pleasure of addressing?" The young king had dared to speak to her directly.

"I am Lady Gwendolyn of the Manor. The Lady of the Amber."

The king's eyes widened; he had heard many stories of the enchantress, but he hardly expected to meet her in the flesh.

The warlord went on. "We seek a companion of this lady. He is a warlock. Young. A stranger in this city. His name is Cabe Bedlam. I want him before the end of the day."

It took some time for this to sink in. Melicard had just ascended to the throne. He had watched his father lose to madness, confronted a terrible dragon lord and a beautiful and legendary witch, and was now ordered to locate a foreign warlock somewhere in his city before the sun set.

"How am I to find this warlock? Have you a description of him?"

Toma's description of the sorceror revealed only that he could be one of countless males in Talak. The king bit his lip, both because he hated the thought of turning over a fellow human being to the lizard and because he could see no way of locating this Cabe Bedlam before the time limit had expired.

As if reading the young ruler's mind, the duke made a suggestion. "Have your servants spread the order throughout the city. Make sure that no area is left untouched. I believe it is very likely that the one I seek will do your work for you."

Unsure of the logic, but unable to come up with any ideas of his own, Melicard bowed graciously to his inhuman visitor. "It shall be done immediately."

"For your people's sake, I would hope so. They will pay if you fail. I will leave just enough of them in one piece so that they may personally bring their frustrations out on you for having failed them." It was evident that the duke was a student of human psychology.

The king's voice was quivering slightly. "Will there be anything else?"

"Not at the moment. You will clear out one section of your palace for myself and my retinue. You will have meals delivered to those rooms." Toma smiled, showing his sharp, tearing teeth. "That should save you from any unpleasantness our eating habits may reveal."

With almost-evident relief, Melicard excused himself. The warlord turned to his unwilling guest. "I should think that before the day is through, your companion will walk up to the palace gate and turn himself in. Wouldn't you agree?"

She shook her fiery hair. "I think you underestimate his abilities. You may find him more than you can handle."

"My dear Lady of the Amber, I do not care how amazing his abilities are. I have you and this city in my claws. It is his nature that I rely on. It is his inherent goodness that will send him to me. Nothing else."

He turned his attention to his men, thus allowing Gwen to think on what she knew of Cabe. Duke Toma was correct; Cabe would not let any harm come to this city, not after what had happened to Mito Pica and what might be happening to Penacles.

She lowered her eyes in guilt. No doubt the Gryphon believed that she had abandoned his people. From what the Lady knew of the Lochivarites, they would swarm and swarm against the walls of the City of Knowledge until either they were wiped out—highly unlikely—or Penacles fell.

It was against everything Nathan had taught her to leave a people in danger. Nevertheless, she would have done it for him as she had done it for Cabe. For the same reasons, she suddenly realized.

* * *

TWO THINGS NOW confounded the Gryphon as he stumbled over a well-decayed tree. One was, of course, the source of the Black Dragon's inexhaustible man-supply. He intended to do something about that, too, providing, of course, that he survived his encounter with the Dragon King. The second item in question dealt with the master of the Gray Mists himself. The mists extended for mile upon mile, even advancing to the lionbird's own city. How, he wondered, was the Black Dragon capable of emitting so much of the mind-twisting fog?

His initial confidence in his idea and the knowledge from the libraries was evaporating. It was unusual for the tomes to ever read straightforward. He should have mistrusted it from the start.

His foot came loose from the bog with a noisy slurp. If anything, Lochivar's countryside had turned even more repulsive and gooey since his last visit. He wished he had wings like the creature whose name he wore. As it was, two small vestigial stumps were all he could lay claim to. Normally, he kept them hidden under his clothing. It was a sore spot with him.

As he took another step, the distant sound of water slapping against solid ground was picked up by his superior hearing. At first he wondered how deep the swamp was, but a much more reasonable idea soon caused him to disregard that line of thought.

Two-plus hours of slow, dragging steps brought him to confirmation of his idea. Somehow he had completely turned away from his original target. The water he heard was that of one of the eastern seas. The Gryphon had wandered all the way to the coast.

At least, he decided, the terrain had improved. Neither his animal nor human aspects cared very much for the quagmire he had just crossed. On solid ground, he could now move quietly and quickly.

There were several dim torchlights out by what he could only assume was the harbor. In the glow they stubbornly emitted despite the mists, he could see three large sailing ships and more than a dozen figures who could have been dragon warriors, Lochivarites, or anything else that even remotely resembled a human. Most were standing guard near the vessels, crafts of unusual configuration, if he saw them properly. Two or three were wandering toward a building away from the docks.

He picked up the footsteps of the guard well before the soldier was in sight. Once again, the advantage was his; by the way the man ignored him, the Gryphon could tell that his own eyesight was better in this soup than that of any of his human adversaries. He crouched low behind a gnarled tree that seemed to be attempting to grow sideways.

The guard paused some four or five feet from the tree and peered uselessly into the mists. The lionbird's eyes narrowed; this was no Lochivarite zombie. The man's actions indicated that even before his unfamiliar uniform became obvious. The sight was both curious and satisfying to the Gryphon. This soldier, he knew, might be taken alive. A Lochivarite would fight until one of them was dead.

In the soldier's hands was a spear that ended in a wicked barbed point. A broadsword hung at his side. The darkness made it impossible to read his face, especially since most of it was covered by some decorated helm. The slow, ungainly movements were important. The guard was tired. That might mean that he would be relieved soon. If so, it made the Gryphon's chances slimmer. Not that he had much choice.

He waited until the guard had turned back. Then, with a graceful leap reminiscent of his feline cousins, the Gryphon was on him.

It was almost more of a shock to him than it was to the soldier. Tired or not, the man had the strength of a bear. Fortunately, the lionbird had one hand over the guard's mouth. He wanted to end this quickly, before he lost that small victory. Yet the soldier had to remain alive.

Hissing into one of the man's ears, the Gryphon whispered, "Desist or I will extend my claws and shred your face!"

He was not sure whether the other would believe him. He might be able to do what he claimed. Then again, the guard might throw him off. When the guard's body relaxed, the Gryphon held back from the temptation to breathe a sigh of relief.

Pulling out the soldier's broadsword, he pushed the point against his prisoner. At the same time, he removed his hand. The guard did not seem inclined to act, though his head did move momentarily to the spear, which had been thrown some distance away in the struggle.

The Gryphon tapped him with the sword. "Turn around."

The prisoner did so. He was a hirsute man and looked more like a bear than the lionbird could believe. The man muttered something that only faintly sounded like the Lands language used by all. It was coarse and sounded as if a dog had barked it. The word was recognizable, though.

He nodded. "Yes, I'm the Gryphon. As to who you are, that will have to wait. Do you know how far we are from the Black Dragon's lair?"

The man shook his head.

Putting the broadsword's tip to the guard's throat, the Gryphon asked the question again. This time, he received a better response. He was glad the man was so easy to read. The first answer had almost screamed its lack of any truth by way of the soldier's eyes and stiff movements.

He ordered the guard to kneel facing away from him. Taking a length of rope from around his waist, he cut it in two. One half was shaped into a noose. This was placed around the man's neck. The other went around the ankles, allowing the man to walk but not to run. The prisoner was then ordered to stand again.

Continuing to whisper, the Gryphon said, "I leave your hands free only to fool others. They will not see the rope around your legs, not in these mists. Try to yell, run, or fight, though, and I shall snap your neck before the first sound escapes your lips! Don't think for one moment that I don't have the strength to do so! Understood?"

The guard nodded cautiously. Satisfied, the lionbird prodded his captive along. He had debated throwing away the broadsword and using the Horned Blade, which was sheathed at his side, but decided that he did not care to draw undue attention to himself by utilizing the dark sword's powers too soon.

They walked for the space of nearly an hour. The soldier made no attempt to lead him astray; evidently, he believed everything the Gryphon had said, especially concerning the noose. A good thing. Every word was true.

Three times they had to halt for patrols. These were Lochivarites. They stalked with mad determination through the blinding grayness. Fortunately, the Gryphon's sharp ears heard them just in time. It was more difficult than when he had listened for his captive; the Lochivarites were as silent as the wraiths they so closely resembled.

It dawned on him that the tremendous size of the fanatics' army was probably due to the steady flow of slaves and prisoners from the unknown ships: The uniform of his captive seemed vaguely familiar, but, try as he might, the lionbird could not place it. If there was time, he would question the man. Right now, silence was of the essence.

Visibility was almost nil. The Gryphon rested the tip of his borrowed broadsword on the back of his companion. He knew that the lair of the Black Dragon could only be a short distance away. He also knew that neither of them would find it if the fog got any thicker. Add to that the fact that his prisoner was now starting to cough and his own throat was just beginning to feel scratchy. He was not immune to the Gray Mists after all.

Something large and heavy ran by. From the hiss it let loose, the Gryphon knew he had at last reached his destination. He tugged slightly on the rope encircling his prisoner.

"Turn around," he ordered.

The man crumpled to the ground. Rubbing his hand, the lord of Penacles peered through the mist for a place to hide the unconscious guard. He finally dragged the body over to a large, weed-ridden thicket. The broadsword went in for good measure. From here on, he would have to trust in Azran's little toy.

Whether the enshrouding mists would work to his advantage remained to be seen. He knew that the Lochivarites could move fairly accurately through the fog, and he had little doubt that Black's clans were long accustomed to them as well. They would, however, give him some cover, and that would be all he could really ask for.

His feet moved without sound through the rocky landscape. The Gryphon thanked various deities for the fact that the lairs were on solid ground. It would have proven difficult to sneak up quietly in the swamps.

As he neared the cavern entrance, the dim light coming from six torches was just enough to reveal what awaited him there. A dozen firedrakes in human form sat astride the largest and meanest lesser drakes the lionbird had ever seen. They were constantly sniffing the air, and he gave thanks that the wind was blowing to him. Oddly, the mists continued to float in the direction of Penacles as if the air was calm. The Black Dragon's magic evidently allowed him to control his life-sapping mists.

Undaunted, the Gryphon felt his way to the side of the hill that made up the visible portion of the Black Dragon's home. Making sure that the Horned Blade was securely sheathed, he revealed fully his sharp claws and dug his hands into the rock. His feet found footholds few humans would have been able to use. Slowly at first and then more quickly as he gained confidence, the Gryphon made his way up.

Trying to ignore the thought that he made a very tempting target to anyone who spotted him, he scanned the hill above. The lionbird did not see what he was looking for and forced himself to move on farther. He cursed each second that delayed him, not just for his own sake but for the sakes of those who had chosen him to lead. There could be no failure on his part if the city was to survive.

One hand struck only air, causing the Gryphon to nearly lose his hold completely. Gingerly, he felt around the opening. Its width satisfied him.

Caverns as large as the ones used by the Dragon Kings had to have ventilation shafts if air was to be able to circulate. Such a hole was rarely guarded since very few could reach them safely, much less fit inside. Only by twisting and turning would the Gryphon be able to do so. The thought of becoming trapped in the shaft did not faze him in the least. He would not allow it to happen.

Feet first, he lowered himself gently into the gap. The sheath had to be pushed against his leg in order for him to fit. When he was up to his waist, he lifted his arms and slid slowly downward into the heart of the hill.

It was not bad going. Long use had slowly eroded the sides, so that he sometimes even had to grab hold on both sides to prevent himself from falling too swiftly. His worst moment came when the shaft suddenly veered nearly ninety degrees. Only by contorting his body was he able to keep himself from becoming trapped at the turn.

The temperature had risen several degrees. The Gryphon hoped he had not chosen the shaft leading to the hatchery. If he survived the fall toward the magma pit, he would still have to contend with one or more angry dams. It would be a choice of being scalded to death or eaten. Even if he survived, the entire cavern system would be alerted.

Fortune was with him. The shaft ended in a minor chamber that appeared to have seen little use in many years. The Gryphon estimated himself to be several levels below the surface. He was probably no more than two or three away from the main chamber where the master of the Gray Mists held the Dragon King version of court. The Horned Blade was pulled from its sheath. It pulsated in anticipation. The lionbird resisted a sudden urge to go charging through the tunnels. He would not allow the weapon to warp and dominate his thoughts.

The caverns were amazingly empty of any grayness at all. The lack of a mist did not concern him. If it made him more visible at this point, it did the same to his foes. He also found his strength increasing, but whether that was due to the clean air or the bewitching effect of the sword he carried was something he could not afford the time to think about.

He heard and felt the rumble that was the Black Dragon's voice long before he neared the main chamber. The king was angered. Now and then, there was a prolonged silence, as if someone else were speaking.

There had been no resistance or even any sign of a guard. While the Gryphon knew that the reptilian monarch had thrown the vast bulk of his forces into battle, he also knew the Dragon Kings. Black would never allow himself to be unprotected; he was one of the more paranoid of the tyrants.

Sword ready, the Gryphon stepped quietly toward his destination. The other voices became apparent; men or, like the Dragon Kings, shapeshifters. One could never be sure. As he had assumed, they were arguing. He moved closer to the source and found himself in a small side tunnel that allowed him a good view of events.

Both the men and the horrifying monarch they confronted had their profiles to him. Like the guard, they wore dark, furry armor, their heads covered by fierce wolfhelms. One of the men was speaking.

"I have said all that I may, milord! There will be no more for at least three seasons!"

The ebony leviathan twisted a massive head down to near the speaker's face. Hot, fetid fumes issued forth from both mouth and nostrils. For that matter, the Gryphon realized, smoke had been spouting from the Black Dragon before that.

A hiss. The long tongue slithered out momentarily. "I do not think you understand, D'Shay! Time is of the essence! Given another week, I would crush Penacles and the accursed misfit who rules there!"

D'Shay stroked the tip of his well-styled Vandyke. What features were visible were distinctly foxlike. "While that would greatly please us, I fear that I cannot supply you with the necessary prisoners. The ones you received should have been sufficient."

"Sufficient? You have never tried to bring down the walls of Penacles!" The statement was followed by a swift pulling away of the head in irritation.

"Nevertheless, we provided you with the manpower that you requested. We have yet to receive anything from your end of the bargain."

"When the City of Knowledge is mine, my brother's power will follow! Then, you will receive your landssss, warm-blood!"

"We have fulfilled our part; the rest is up to you."

The massive beast lifted his head to gaze up to the ceiling. He considered before making his next statement. There was what passed for a smile playing on his face. "I wonder . . . could it be that the great Aramites are finding their neighbors stronger than earlier believed?" The head swung down again. "Is that it, D'Shay? Have you come up against resistance to your empire's expansion?"

D'Shay's companion shifted in place uncomfortably, but he himself did not. "They have not seen their way to joining us, I must admit, but they are running out of time even quicker than you are. Within a year, we will have pushed them into the northern seas."

"I cannot wait a year!" It seemed as if the Black Dragon were about to crush his guests, but he held back. D'Shay ignored the display, if not the words.

"We have done what we could, milord. The rest is up to you."

"What of your sorcerors?"

"They cannot be spared. Nor can any of our troops."

The master of the Gray Mists spread his wings wide and lashed his tail back and forth. His eyes glittered angrily as he attempted to control his fury. "Then go! I shall crush Penacles without your assistance! Fear not; when I am done, you shall have your lands!"

The dark-clad speaker bowed. "That is all we need know. May I assume, then, that our conversation is at an end?"

"Pfah! What do you think, warm-blood?"

D'Shay nodded to his companion, and the two turned and walked out without ceremony. The Black Dragon watched them disappear, rage only barely held back. The mists continued to rise from his mouth and nostrils. A small jewel, dark blue and shining, was strapped to the monstrous neck.

There would be no time better than now, the Gryphon realized. To wait any longer would only invite disaster. The Horned Blade throbbing, he leaped for the huge form of the Dragon King—

—and found himself held fast by some invisible web.

The airdrake turned his head slowly and confidently toward his prisoner. "I knew you would come! I did not know when, but I knew you would come! I have you!"

What a fool I am, the Gryphon cursed inwardly. Small wonder he had so few guards.

The entire bulk of the Dragon King's body filled the space before him. The lionbird hung helplessly in nothing, the deadly sword pulsating madly in his hand. Black laughed at him.

"I should summon back D'Shay! The pleasure of your death would no doubt give him incentive to replenish my thinning ranks! Then again, with your destruction, Penacles will fall for certain!"

The gaping maw moved toward him. In desperation, the Gryphon added all his will to that of the Horned Blade. It had tasted the blood of one Dragon King and thirsted for more. It would not be denied.

Arm and sword came free just before the jaws reached him. The blade sliced through the air. There was a harsh, guttural scream from the Black Dragon. The gigantic airdrake pulled back, red liquid dripping from within the mouth. The triumph and hate in his eyes had been replaced by a new emotion—fear. The Black Dragon backed away as his would-be victim freed himself and then stalked before him.

The Gray Mists had ceased to form. The Gryphon suspected that his cut had gone deep and that the blood was pouring into the beast himself. A monstrous hacking verified his notion. The Dragon King was in danger of drowning in his own life fluids.

The lord of Penacles knew better than to allow his admiration of the blade to get the better of him. To do so might very well put him under the weapon's entrancing powers. Besides, it had yet to prove that it could complete the task.

The reptile was still coughing up blood. The Gryphon caught sight of a huge gash in the back of the airdrake's mouth. The Horned Blade had cut without touching; its physical reach would not have been sufficient. Azran had been no fool. The warlock had found a way to fight without endangering himself more than necessary.

Still, the weapon had a way of overcoming such safety precautions. He did not doubt that it might try to pull him into the fray just for its own bloodlusting sake. Demon swords were known for that tendency.

The Black Dragon was only just recovering. The Gray Mists were strangely absent. At the drake's feet lay the shattered fragments of the jewel. The Gryphon came up with a number of quick hypotheses.

Several figures arrived from various entrances to the chamber. Among those first in were the mysterious D'Shay and his silent companion. The others were guards, both human and otherwise. The Gryphon was both irritated by their presence and eager to have more targets to strike out at. The latter thought was suppressed quickly as it smelled of the Horned Blade's desires.

D'Shay pulled out a menacing zweihander from what was definitely nowhere and was shouting out the lionbird's name along with a number of words that made little or no sense. His partner had out an equally deadly battle-ax. Soldiers and creatures filled every nearby exit. The Gryphon had lost any chance of escape, but he was determined to make his remaining moments count. Ignoring the others, he charged for the rising bulk of the Dragon King.

The screams and shouts that filled the room at that point were for the most part ignored by the Gryphon, as he assumed them to be concerning him. He did not hear the sound of steel cutting into stone, nor could he hear the roaring laugh until it finally managed to cut through his raging mind.

Between the two foes came a flash of ebony, a glimpse of the void. It wore the form of a horse, but it was easily much more. Both fell back from it, but only the Gryphon recognized it immediately for what it was. That made him back up even farther.

The ice-blue eyes targeted on him. "My Lord Gryphon! You are the one I seek!"

With that, the dark steed charged him.

"No!" He raised the sword to defend himself, uselessly, he knew, but the Horned Blade was still, cold. There was not even time to run as the specter touched him, pulling him—elsewhere.

Mocking laughter bid the inhabitants of the caverns good-bye. Through a portal that did not really exist, Darkhorse departed, returning once more to the Void.

XVIII

LIGHT POKED THROUGH the cracks of the shutter that covered the one window in Cabe's room. How long into the day it was, he could not say. His body still ached, and the only reason Cabe was awake now was the racket that echoed in his ears.

Someone was arguing outside the door.

Feeling oddly detached from everything, Cabe rose. He blinked, momentarily befuddled by the rather palatial settings that had only been there since shortly after his falling off into slumber. The original furniture, including the shoddy, moth-eaten bed, were gone.

As consciousness overwhelmed the last vestiges of sleep, Cabe smiled, for he remembered now—remembered everything. That he was not the same Cabe who had gone to sleep the night before did not occur to him. It was all natural to him now, even the reason for its being. The gem, once embedded in his chest, now lay on the plush blue carpet, shining like so much everyday quartz.

He picked up the gem and stared at it, thinking to himself how little Shade had truly understood what he was doing. The gem had served its purpose, unleashing the power that lay within, but not in the way the dark warlock had expected. It had served as a focus, or perhaps a catalyst, for the power's own purpose, not Shade's. The deadly mage could not truly be blamed; how was he to know that Cabe's secret had a mind of its own?

Cabe let the crystal slip from his hand.

Memories of a time long past overlapped memories of the last few weeks. Cabe, the look on his face that of someone entirely different, muttered, "Azran!" and "Gwen!"

The door shook as something heavy rammed against it. The memories faded to the background. The altered Cabe made his way to the doorway and reached for the handle.

He opened the door and found himself facing six or seven men, the owner of the establishment among them. It took them several seconds to realize the door was open and even more to recover from the shock.

"Grab him!" The words rushed out from the owner.

To Cabe, the scene bordered on the hilarious. In their eagerness to jump him, the group acted as one. Unfortunately, the doorway was wide enough for only a single person. The two largest in the party became jammed and could not back out due to the zeal of their companions. After much struggling, they fell through, missing Cabe, who had wisely backed away. The rest of the party, save the man in the rear, tripped over the first ones.

Cabe watched with amusement as his would-be assaulters struggled to rise, each causing his companions to lose their footing. The single standing attacker pulled out a long dagger and tried to leap over his comrades. He succeeded, but a glance from the warlock kept him floating helplessly in the air.

With the one man under control, the young warlock turned his attention to the others. He pinned each of them to the walls of his room and picked out the most fear-stricken of the bunch. The ruffian's face went pale as he was pulled close for questioning.

"Why have you attacked me? I did nothing."

Some small portion of courage returned to the hapless attacker. "Nothing? By Hestia, you've brought the wrath of the Dragon Kings down upon us!"

The quiet humor that had been an integral part of the new Cabe disappeared for the moment. "What do you mean?"

"That lizard, Duke Toma, says that he'll tear apart the city if you aren't handed over today!"

The mention of the warlord's name darkened even more the expression on the warlock's face. "I thought Toma was headed for Penacles. Why come here?"

"He says he wants you!" the man replied uselessly.

"And you thought to help me on my way there? Kind of you."

"What else could we do?"

Cabe nodded, remembering the Minister of Appointments' words. He could not blame them, not really. They had always lived under the fear of the Dragon Emperor. Besides, what was one man where the life of an entire city was concerned?

Smiling grimly, he cautiously released his captives. They eyed him but did not move against him.

"Forget this ever happened. You can even share that"—he used a thumb to indicate the gem—"among the lot of you. I have no more use for it."

Without another word, he stepped toward the open doorway. Those standing closest to it gave him plenty of room. No one tried to jump him from behind, useless as that would have been. By the time he had departed the inn, his sense of humor had returned.

A few citizens watched him, but Cabe pushed aside all thoughts of action from their minds. He did not want any delays, not now, not after coming to grips with the reality of his situation. Not with the Dragon Kings threatening the lives of all.

As he strode purposely toward the front gate of the city, word of his approach spread ahead of him. By his manner and appearance, there could be no doubt of who he was. It was therefore not surprising when he was confronted by Talak's new king and several guards, all on horseback.

Melicard nodded. "Greetings to you, stranger. I take it that you are the warlock that scaly abomination desires?"

"I am Cabe Bedlam, yes."

The king studied the head of silver hair. "What a powerful sorceror you must be, Master Bedlam. Powerful enough to slay an army of shapeshifting vermin, I think."

Cabe gave him the ghost of a smile. "Perhaps. What do you want with me, my liege?"

"I wish to see those creatures dead! Kyrg is far away, but his master awaits your presence. The city will pay if you do not show!"

The warlock resumed walking. "Then I'd best be going."

Melicard maneuvered his steed in an effort to block Cabe's path. "Go? Will you attack them? Shall I summon my troops?"

Without pausing, Cabe stared the horse down. It moved away, trying to avoid his gaze. "No. It would only bring you the same fate it brought Pagras in the Turning War."

The king paused, his schooling bringing forth the meaning of the warlock's comment. Pagras lay to the east of Talak. A strong, proud sister of his own kingdom, it had been reduced to ruins that had never been reinhabited save by wild animals.

"What will you do?"

"Give myself up."

Face reddening, the monarch practically screamed. "Give up! Are you a coward?"

Cabe did not look back. "I'm no fool, if that's what you mean, my liege."

Melicard made to follow, but his steed did not move. Not that it had no such desire, but because it could not make any headway. It was as if rider and mount had run up against a brick wall. He turned to his men. They were sitting on their horses, watching him. He became furious.

"Don't sit there gaping! After him!"

The commander hesitated before answering. "We—we have tried, my lord! Neither our animals nor we ourselves can move to aid you or catch the warlock!"

The young ruler slumped in his saddle. All the aggression had gone out of him. He sighed. It had been so much simpler when he'd merely been a prince. At least then he had not had to contend with sorcerors and dragon warriors.

Duke Toma found the palace irritating. It was too civilized, too elegant. The warlord was a born warrior and a powerful necromancer. His own caves reflected this. The heads of foes and animals decorated the walls. His personal laboratory took up nearly half of his dwellings. Here, much of the scenery consisted of paintings and sculptures and rich, varied furnishings. Only an occasional statue or suit of armor interested him for even the briefest of times. Even the fine meal he had just finished had failed to relax him. It was almost a waste of a superb, freshly killed ox. For all he remembered of it, it might as well have been cooked or something.

He pondered his adversary's movements. Nathan's grand-whelp had proven to be the fool in the deck, and those who played the games properly knew that the fool was no fool. It could topple opponents with even the strongest of positions. If only that cursed warlock, Shade, had not interfered. Whether good or evil in nature, the sorceror had clouded up Toma's knowledge of the young warlock for reasons of his own. Reasons that apparently had little to do with the situation in hand.

Finding himself near the ballroom where he had been forced to leave the enchantress—the sphere would not fit through the hallways, and he had had no desire to remove the spell—Toma opened the door and entered.

The Lady was sitting quietly in the bubble. Such a scene did not lull the firedrake into complacency. He knew that her mind, if not her body, had been working on the forces that held the spell together. He increased the temperature abruptly by several degrees and watched with sadistic pleasure as she shifted here and there in a futile attempt to escape being burned. When she had twisted around for several seconds, he returned the sphere to normal.

She glared at him. "One day you will suffer tenfold for that, oo—duke!"

The enchantress had stopped just short of calling him by the name of one of his very distant cousins, a swamp-dweller that built its den from its own excrement. Duke Toma smiled his cold smile as he nodded like an instructor pleased to see his pupil learn.

"If that word had escaped your lips, milady, the heat would have gone up much higher. I would not have killed you, as you have hostage value to me, but your suffering would have been greatly prolonged."

"How much longer must I live in this thing?"

"That depends on your companion. He has not revealed himself as yet. I'm more than half tempted to raze this city now."

"He might not be here. Have you thought of that?"

Toma bared his predator's teeth. "You and I both know he is in the general vicinity, milady. We are too well trained not to feel him, especially with the power he carries."

She smiled. "Knowing his power, you still think to stop him?"

"He is unskilled. Most of what he knows is only the instinctive part of sorcery. It will not save him when he is brought before the emperor."

A horn sounded. Toma hurried to the window and peered outside. Gwen wished dearly that she could push the rest of him through. The warlord pulled away from the window and turned back to his prisoner.

"Your companion has arrived! Come! I want you to be there to greet him!" He rushed out of the room. The Lady's spherical cell flew off after him, throwing its unwilling inhabitant against one of the sides. The enchantress muttered words normally reserved for use by the more unsavory elements of the city.

The duke swept past his aides, who had come to tell him the news. One was nearly bowled over by the bubble, something that gave Gwen at least momentary satisfaction. Moments after, both warlord and captive were outside the palace.

The object of everyone's attention was just entering the gate. Clad in a dark blue garment of perfect fit, his silver hair seeming to gleam, Cabe walked quietly toward the dragon warriors.

Toma frowned and muttered something the Lady could not hear. She could feel the pull of the darker part of the spectrum as the warlord made use of it. A slight reddish glow surrounded the firedrake commander.

"You will halt right there, Bedlam!"

Cabe stopped. He looked closely at the warlord's captive, shock and concern flashing across his features. Toma regained his confidence.

"Yessss, human! I have your female! A wiser move on my part than I imagined, now that I sssee you again!"

The young warlock barely contained himself. "You have me! Let her go!"

"I don't think so. Her presence assures me of your good behavior during our trip!"

"Trip? Where are we supposed to be going?"

The duke smiled, flashing his white, pointed teeth in dramatic triumph. "Where? Why, to the Tyber Mountains, of course! We mean to see an end to the line of Bedlam!"

"Aren't you forgetting my father?"

"Azran is the type to sit, trying to hatch insane plots. He will be little trouble as far as my plans are concerned."

This brought curiosity. "Your plans?"

"As I have already told your companion, much of the events of the recent past are due to my efforts." The tone was far from modest.

Cabe nodded. "I see. The misfit would be ruler. That explains much of the infighting of the Dragon Kings."

An almost human look of pleasure passed over Toma's face. "You grasp quite quickly! I instigated Brown and the others, either from behind the scenes or in the form of the Crystal Dragon." Pleasure gave way to mistrust. "You seem far more intelligent and informed than my spies indicated. Glad I am that I sought you out now rather than later." To an aide he said, "Ready our mounts!"

The two eyed one another. "Am I to walk, Duke Toma? I have no horse."

"Much as I like that idea, I fear it would delay things far too much. I believe in speed foremost."

Uttering in a language long unused by any but those who trafficked in the arts, the warlord pointed at his adversary. A bubble like that holding Gwen surrounded Cabe, who studied it but said nothing.

"That is how you will travel to the halls of the emperor! You may discover from the Lady the advantages and disadvantages of this mode. I suggest you heed the disadvantages with more care than she has." Toma waved a hand, causing Cabe's globe to fly over to float next to the other.

The duke eyed them both. "An odd pair of paperweights. One of a kind, I'd imagine."

Toma turned his attention to organizing for departure. Gwen chose that moment to speak to Cabe, but he quieted her with a finger to his lips and a shake of his head. She looked on in confusion, wondering how he, being untrained, could take command. Cabe said nothing but made a signal to her before turning back to watch the dragon warriors act.

The signal did not reassure her. Rather, it only confused her further. She understood its meaning but not its origin. Only two people in the recent past had ever known that particular sign language. She was one, having studied it in a rotting old tome many, many years before. The other was the owner of that book, the man, the teacher, the lover. Only Nathan, who had recovered the tome from its centuries-old resting place, would have known the signal.

PREPARATIONS FOR LEAVING Talak did not require much time. The bulk of the army still waited outside the city and had not bothered to settle down yet. Duke Toma's retinue carried little in the way of supplies and equipment. Thus it was that the party neared the front gate only a half hour after the confrontation.

The warlord looked around as he departed the city. "It seems that Melicard will not be seeing us off. Curious."

At mention of the young king, Cabe's head snapped up and his eyes closed momentarily. Gwen recognized his actions but pretended not to notice, though her puzzlement had increased. She dared a glance at Toma, hoping his mind and eyes were on other matters. Fortunately for both humans, he had already dropped the thought and was now concerned with moving his forces.

The massive bulk that was the dragon forces began to move, slowly at first, then picking up speed as the seconds passed. The duke, his retinue, and the two humans took their places at the front of the great column. Citizens of Talak lined the walls to watch them depart. Cabe glanced at the throngs and thought he could pick out Melicard. He could not see the young king's face, but he was fairly certain of his feelings.

Already the Tyber Mountains loomed overhead like so many titans of legend. Higher than the rest, Kivan Grath stood proud over his subjects and almost seemed to dare the puny creatures who would enter his domain. The closer the column came to the mountain range, the more imposing the Seeker of Gods appeared.

There were no animals along the path leading into the mountains, though Cabe spotted what looked to be the skull of a horse at one point. A few creatures flew lazily overhead, but their skins were leathery, marking them as servants and distant relations of the firedrakes.

No one spoke along the way. Toma was too deep in self-glorification; he was basking in the praise he believed his father would give him. There would be little opposition to his becoming one of the Dragon Kings, especially with most of the others dead. Once a King, he could openly re-structure the empire so as to ensure its supremacy over the warm-bloods for millennia to come.

Lady Gwen watched the vanishing distance with much trepidation. To her mind, this was the stuff of nightmares. Here was a place she had known from her childhood as a bastion of evil, a land unfit for men. Her training under Nathan had not changed her image of the range; rather, it defined the form of the evil. She looked to Cabe for some reassurance, as she had his grandfather so many years ago, but he was absorbed in the study of his sphere and had his face away from her. She remained quiet, not wishing to accidentally catch the reptilian warlord's attention.

The sphere, Cabe had discovered, was a complex creation that constantly altered its general design. He suspected that his was far more advanced than that holding the Lady, since it seemed that the duke was more worried about his presence than that of the enchantress. Nevertheless, it was not difficult to identify the pattern of the changes. Cabe did not think for one minute that another magic-user would have been able to do this, especially so quickly. All that concerned him was being able to escape in a hurry should the action prove necessary.

Satisfied that leaving would prove simple, he leaned against the side of the bubble and, much to Gwen's shock, closed his eyes. It would be best right now if he conserved his strength. Despite his new feelings of confidence in his abilities, the warlock knew that entering into the emperor's lair was even more dangerous than falling into a pit of venomous serpents while unconscious. He had no desire to arrive in anything other than peak condition. Fortunately, the sphere seemed to negate both hunger and thirst, so this would not be a problem.

Kivan Grath loomed far over their heads.

BECAUSE OF THE massive size of the army and the fact that its route was mostly upward, passage through the mountain range would take several hours. Gwen shivered, but not from the cold. She could feel as well as see the colors of the powers that dwelt here. She also sensed other forces, lesser, equal, and greater than those she knew, whether dark or light. They were older, far older, and filled with the touch of beings neither men nor dragon nor any creature she had ever encountered. Some emitted an indifference to all around them, while others felt almost benevolent. These the witch tried to contact, but with no result. Communication with such as these was beyond her.

It was probably fortunate, she decided. For there were also powers perverse in nature. Powers that seemed to want to crawl into her mind and twist her to their wills. She shunned any mental contact with these. A few probed, but apparently they lacked the strength to do anything else.

She noted that neither Toma nor Cabe appeared disturbed in the least by these specters of the ages. Cabe, though, had no reason for remaining so calm. The Lady knew from experience that apprentices and untrained magic-users were far more open to contact than those who had learned to shut their minds from intrusion. Yet her companion slept as if he were in his own bed. She grudgingly tacked it on as one more mystery about Nathan's grandson. She would live long enough, she hoped, to solve some of those mysteries.

But it was turning out to be all for naught, she realized. When first freed from the amber prison, Gwen had believed that this would be her chance to live up to Nathan's dreams and deliver the lands from the Dragon Kings. She had met Cabe and saw in him the beginnings of a warlock at least as powerful as her lover. Yet with the addition of Darkhorse, the Gryphon, and, yes, even Shade, the enchantress had come to believe in the realization of everything the Dragon Masters had planned.

Her face darkened. Once again, it was Azran who had destroyed the hopes of men. They could have held against the fanatics of Lochivar with their combined strength, even minus the enigmatic but tremendous powers of Shade. Azran, though, in his petty quest for domination over men and dragons, had kidnapped Cabe for reasons she still could not discern. It could not have been for fatherly concern; of that she was certain.

Neither she nor anyone at the front of the column noticed the single figure rushing through the air at a madman's speed. The intruder was coming up directly behind them, the tail of the army only scant minutes away from him. He seemed not the least bit worried about the tremendous size of the forces below. If anything, his pace increased.

A single scout, flying up for a routine check, spotted the figure. Curious and completely confident that no threat could exist in the Tyber Mountains, it flapped its leather wings and moved in for a closer scan.

At recognition, the scout gave out a startled squawk, but it was far too late. Grinning evilly and totally under the spell of his sword, Azran slashed at the air. Though far, far out of reach of the Nameless, the airdrake twitched and plummeted limply down the long distance toward the ground, a great gash across its throat.

Though the blood and lives of countless creatures had already been tasted by the warlock's devilish blade, it was not sated. Rather, its craving increased, and as it did, the hold over Azran solidified. The long, twisting, crowded column presented a target that could not be denied.

Azran dove, sword outthrust for assault against the hordes of the Dragon Emperor.

A cry rose up from the back end of the army. Duke Toma and the Lady whirled around. Cabe was startled out of his slumber.

Gwen was the first to recognize the wielder of the sword, and nearly spat out the name. "Azran!"

Toma turned his beast so that he was facing the action, and glared. "Most of those in the rear are earth-bound or too stupid! They are also much too close together!" He stared at the marauding warlock intently. "Still, I did not think Azran would dare something such as this! I wonder . . ."

The whisper was only loud enough for Gwen to hear. "The sword! He's created another sword!"

She looked at Cabe, looked back at the berserker diving up and around and through the ranks of the Duke's army, and nodded. Even here, she could feel its malignant presence.

The warlord had come to the same conclusion. There was a frightening gleam in his burning red eyes as he watched. He had seen the Horned Blade, but Brown would allow no one else to touch it. Some of the other Kings had suspected that the lord of the Barren Lands was not totally himself. This did not bother Toma in the slightest. He considered the others much weaker than himself. If he could not have the one sword, then he would have this other one.

He could not rely on his forces; of that the duke was certain. Already, many were in panic. Other than the ruling members, there were few competent sorcerors among the intelligent clans. Thinking of that, Toma recalled that Red had gone out after the warlock. Evidently, the ranks of the Dragon Kings were now more depleted than ever before.

Glancing at his captives, the warlord ordered the two spheres to journey on. His father would see to their disposal and only add more praise when Toma showed him the new prize. With the enchanted blade, the duke's right to rule could not be challenged by any of the surviving kings.

THE SUDDEN FLIGHT of their bubble-like cells threw both magic-users wildly around. Gwen regained her balance first and looked to see how her companion was doing. Cabe rolled for a few seconds longer and then lay still, one hand on his head. He grinned at her. She could see little humor in their situation and let him know it without speaking.

To her surprise, he continued to smile and pointed up as if telling her to wait. The Lady watched him cautiously. This was not the man she had come to know; this was a completely different person, and one with so many alarmingly familiar expressions.

He caused all movement to cease, astounding her with his seemingly experienced control. The two spheres came to a halt, out of sight of Toma, but much too close to their intended destination. Cabe then placed his left hand on the inner surface of his own bubble and slowly ran it over the surface. Abruptly, he reached out with his right and touched another area, totally away from his original choice. With a slight hiss, the prison floated to the ground. As it landed, the entire sphere evaporated.

Cabe repeated the process with Gwen's cell, the time to do so twice as long since he was forced to walk around it and then had to rediscover its exact weak point. When the bubble had dissolved, the two dropped into each other's arms without thinking and remained that way for several moments.

With some awkwardness, he finally broke the embrace. "We have to move on."

They looked at their surroundings. The land dropped off quite abruptly in front of them. Though dwarfed by the nearby Kivan Grath, the mountain on which their ledge was located was still a leviathan in its own right. The ground below was a bleak and disquieting place, uninhabited by anything larger than a few pale-green bushes and one or two twisted firs. The mountainside was little better. The Tyber Mountains were as inhospitable as those who dwelled in them.

Gwen had lost all sense of direction. "How do we find our way out of here?"

"We don't. We have to go into the caverns inside Kivan Grath."

She went pale. "Into— Yes, you're right. We may never have another chance."

"It's not as bad as all that. If the Gold Dragon is expecting us, he'll be expecting us as prisoners, not free and willing fighters."

That relieved her. It also made her think. "Yes, that reminds me. How did you free us?" Her gaze demanded an answer.

Cabe shifted uncomfortably. "I'll explain later. I don't dare upset the balance between me now."

"What?"

He turned to face the Seeker of Gods. "We'd best get moving if we want to keep the element of surprise."

"Hold it! You mean you're going in there—" The Lady stopped short as Cabe turned away and marched on toward the lair of the Dragon Emperor. Furious, she hurried after him, praying to her patron goddess that she would give all the aid she was capable of giving—

—and doubting that it would be enough.

XIX

THE CITY OF Penacles was cautiously hopeful. The Gray Mists had thinned, enough so that sunlight easily cut through. Scouts were reporting great unrest among the remaining legions from Lochivar, and many of the fanatics were visibly exhausted, having been running on their addiction alone. To most of the citizenry, it meant victory.

To Blane, it meant that the worst was yet to come.

"What do you think?"

His words were directed at General Toos. The general, his foxlike features in profile, watched the enemy forces through his seeing lens. "I think that they are trying to organize for an attack. Every minute that they delay saps their strength and restores ours. Also, if they move swiftly, they might hope to catch the city while it still relaxes."

Blane nodded. "I've ordered all the men to stay alert for one more massive encounter. I think they'll be ready."

"They'd better be." Toos put down the seeing lens and looked squarely at his co-commander. "The Lochivarites are moving even now."

"Damn!"

"Indeed."

Blane was about to return to his soldiers when Toos stopped him with a raised hand. The general took up his lens again and turned so that he was facing more northerly. His attention became fixed on the large mass that had not moved since its arrival several days before.

It was moving now.

"Summon all able men—and women—Commander Blane."

"Why? What is it?"

"The sadist Kyrg is moving his inhuman army against us. Apparently, all the waiting is over. This is to be the final assault!"

Horns were already being sounded on all walls save the southern. The city returned to its deathly quiet, that most terrible sound of any war, in the expectation of horror.

Both commanders had gone to rejoin their men. Toos would be confronting the greater number, but Blane would be facing fresh, battle-hungry troops with a hatred for all that was human. His would be the near-impossible task. Fewer men lined the northern and western walls because the brunt of the attacks had always been on the eastern side. No doubt that was one of the reasons Kyrg was attacking now.

It might be that they knew the Gryphon was away. For all their abilities, neither commander could inspire the army the way the city's ruler could. The Gryphon had a force of spirit about him.

As one, the invading forces spread relentlessly toward Penacles. To the defenders, the tide seemed as endless as in the beginning. The landscape was covered by moving forms.

The frontmost Lochivarites came into range. Archers let fly with arrows, the air filling with a deadly rain as they did so. The first blow had been struck by the city, but the enemy would soon answer with violence of their own.

THE SHADOWY FORM of what might have been a great ink-black steed materialized at the abrupt edge dividing the Legar Peninsula and what was once the Barren Lands, its eyes scanning the terrain for signs of unwanted strangers. Satisfied that all was safe and secure, Darkhorse raised his head and let loose with a roar that could never have come from a true animal.

From that which contained his essence and was also contained by him, a small speck appeared. It grew larger and larger, like a rash spreading over the creature's side. When it was large enough, it fell out rather than off the steed and dropped to the ground with a fierce and angry grunt.

The Gryphon scrambled to his feet, the enchanted sword ready in one hand. He growled as any large cat might, save that it ended in a rather birdlike squawk. The Horned Blade went out before him as warning to the eternal.

If Darkhorse had been capable of rolling his eyes, it would have matched the tone of his stentorian voice quite well. "Please! I did not bring you here so that you could uselessly attempt to skewer me! Time is running out for all of us!"

Still cautious, the Gryphon lowered the blade only slightly. "What are you talking about, demon? Why have you taken me from what must be done to save my people?"

"Demon? Why— Never mind! I have need of your assistance! You and the sword, that is!"

"To what end?"

Darkhorse snorted in annoyance. "Ours—or at least yours, if I can't convince you! Only with your help can I banish Shade!"

"Banish Sh— He's alive?"

"As far as those terms can be used with one such as he! No longer does he go by the name Simon! Call him Madrac and place much of the emphasis on the first half of his new title!"

The tip of the sword went down, not without some objection from the weapon itself. "I feared as much. When we could find no trace after his battle with the Seeker, I was sure the worst had happened!"

"Well should you fear! This Madrac is the quickest and the strongest incarnation I have seen since knowing the warlock! I was barely able to contain him, and I do not know how much longer I can hold him! He remembers nearly all of his past lives, especially that concerning Cabe! If I had not broken free from the trap he set for me upon his reincarnation, the young warlock would have been used as a power source to free him from his curse!"

The Gryphon finally nodded. "Better we should let the Dragon Kings maintain their tyranny. All right, but you must return me to Lochivar as soon as the deed is done!"

"There may be no need. Black will be unable to emit his horrid mists for some time, and he has lost the crystal that amplified and controlled the mists that he had. It was a precarious idea to begin with and only served to weaken him physically and twist him mentally! He was no more master of his existence than his fanatic humans!" His wild mane shook violently as he tossed his head. "Come! Time is wasting!"

With that abrupt change in the conversation, Darkhorse reared, turned, and trotted quickly into the crystal lands. The lionbird sheathed his unwanted weapon and hurried after the eternal. He hoped the creature did not intend to lead him all the way along the outthrust piece of earth that the crystal Dragon claimed as his. He would be little use for anything, and he had no desire to be left alone in this most unknown of all the Dragonrealms save the northern wastes of the Ice Dragon.

Fortunately, or unfortunately, the ebony steed halted before what appeared to be a small crater that dropped far down into the depths of the inner world. The Gryphon came up from behind his guide and gazed down, both fur and feathers bristling in anger.

"You expect me to climb all the way down there? The sides are as smooth as glass!" He paused at realization of what the statement could mean. "Did one of you do this?"

"Shade. I can only feel that luck was with me on that one! Though I would not have died, there would have been great pain! The warlock knows me better than any other and now may call upon most of the memories of his past lives! I already know he recalls some of my weaknesses!"

The Gryphon could not imagine what weaknesses the spectral horse might have, and refrained from asking.

Darkhorse went on. "As to climbing down there, you are correct! Even if it were possible, it would take you hours that cannot be afforded! That is why you will ride me!"

"Ride you?" There was no questioning his courage, but even the Gryphon was tempted to draw the line at the thought of climbing on top of this rather ethereal stallion. He dared not, though.

Mounting proved to be no more difficult than with a real horse, since the eternal had no desire to lose his passenger for any reason. Once balanced, the lionbird gave his wraithlike companion the go-ahead.

Darkhorse jumped into the hole and plummeted straight down.

The Gryphon had both arms wrapped around the massive neck. He had, in his folly, assumed that they would be flying down. Only now did he recall that Darkhorse, for all his power, was confined to the earth when in this dimension.

Four steel hooves struck the bottom with force that should have shattered each of the legs. Darkhorse pawed the ground for a moment, getting his bearings, then sped down one of the tunnels that riddled the earth. Glancing left and right as he held on, the Gryphon soon realized that these tunnels were not natural. There was that about them that spoke of a time before the dragons. A feeling of age. That calmed him; the inhabitants were, no doubt, long dead and of no concern.

With no warning whatsoever, Darkhorse came to a halt. The Gryphon blinked at the sight before his eyes and had to be reminded by his mount that there was still work to be done. Never tearing his gaze away, he leaped off and pulled out the Horned Blade, which pulsated in anticipation.

"What is that?"

A glob of constantly changing clay, a mass of liquidy blackness. It twisted and shaped itself without pause. The Gryphon grimaced as well as his face might allow. The nebulous form smelled as disgusting as it appeared.

"That is the prison I have created to hold the mad sorceror. It is of the essence that I contain and that contains me. No more did I dare unleash into this dimension, lest it tear the fabric of reality asunder."

"How do you know he's still in there?" The lord of Penacles could make out nothing that seemed human.

"I know."

"I see." He did not, but there was little sense in saying that.

Darkhorse stepped up. "The Horned Blade lacks the power to kill him unless it touches him directly in the heart. Therefore, banishment is all we can hope for. Were he his other side, Shade would want this."

"What do I do?"

"Thrust into the very midst of the mass. The sword will do the rest. I would have done this myself, but it would have meant my banishment as well."

The Gryphon, who had been readying himself to thrust, held up. "What?"

Eyes of frost gleamed. "Worry not. It is only because I am not completely attached to this plane. You are very much a part of this reality; I am of the void! Do it!"

Raising the demonic blade once more, the lionbird readied himself.

Who is it?

The words were not spoken but felt. The Gryphon turned and started to say something to Darkhorse, but the voice interrupted, this time with more determination.

Gryphon! Friend! Help me!

He stared at the glob in front of him. Could it be . . .

"Shade?"

It is you! Beware! Darkhorse plots evil!

"Evil? No, Shade—or rather, Madrac! I know about you!"

Madrac is dead! I am Benedict—this time.

"Benedict?" The sword hand wavered.

Darkhorse will unleash ancient evils that still live in this land! You must release me before he realizes!

The Gryphon wavered. He had little trust in the steed. Shade had always been a friend, as close as was possible for him, and an adviser as well. Yet he had always talked of his faith in Darkhorse, who understood the warlock more than anyone else could ever possibly.

"Why do you hesitate?" This was spoken in loud, commanding tones, even as a question.

He glanced at the eternal, unsure whether to trust or not.

Gryphon! In a moment of panic, the tone had changed. It was no longer the Shade he had known.

A hand burst forth from the blackness, grasping for something. Most of the arm continued out after it.

Darkhorse roared. "He's loose!"

Acting with a swiftness beyond the ken of man, the dark steed leaped forward. The black mass, including the arm, was swallowed up. Darkhorse stood alone, but he was wavering, as if part of him did not exist.

"Run the blade through my side!"

"Won't you be banished?"

"There is no choice! I cannot hold him like this and banish him at the same time! He would escape! No more explanations! Run me through!"

Without further hesitation, the Gryphon plunged the Horned Blade into that which was Darkhorse. There was a scream of pain, but it was not from the eternal. The lionbird released his hold on the sword and fell back as the tunnel shook with the violence of conflicting realities.

His form fading, Darkhorse laughed, though it was a laugh tinged with some other emotion. The phantom stallion looked longingly in the direction of the sky, and his voice was strained as he whispered, "Now we ride together forever, my one true friend!"

The walls and ceiling cracked, and the Gryphon feared he would be crushed under tons of earth. The tunnel held, though, for it had been designed to stand through the roughest of earthquakes.

Little remained of Darkhorse. With each passing second, he was less noticeable. Only the piercing blue eyes seemed to have any reality at all. They looked to the Gryphon only momentarily before vanishing with the rest of the shadowy figure. The laughter stayed only as an echo.

The quivering sword was the only evidence left of what had happened. The Gryphon dusted off the brown, dry dirt from his body and reached forward to pick it up. It fairly screamed in his mind. The power contained within had nearly doubled. Rather than risk loss of his freedom to the Horned Blade, he sheathed the weapon. Even then, it shook.

He had no intention of exploring these tunnels further. With Darkhorse gone, the place took on a new feeling, one of a waking evil. The ebony steed's presence had either masked it or kept it under control. Whatever the case, he knew that it would not be safe to stay here much longer.

THE TUNNEL SYSTEM held little difficulty for him. Like the animals that composed his namesake, his hunting and tracking skills were always on a level far above that of men. Timewise, it turned out to be much longer than he had originally estimated. Darkhorse had been going very fast.

At the bottom of the hole, the Gryphon stared up in dismay. The sides were almost like glass. He could make out very little in the way of foot- and handholds. Still, he realized, his only other option was to turn back. Better to chance a broken neck.

Sharp, ivory talons dug into earth baked rock-hard. He contemplated using the Horned Blade, but it would be much too awkward and he did not want to rely on the sword any more than he had to. Pulling the paw free, he reached high above his head and gouged out another hole. In this way, he proceeded slowly but steadily toward the top.

Some two or three lengths from the surface, he had his worst moment. The earth here was softer and gave way more than he would have liked. Stretching his one arm up, the Gryphon suddenly felt his other paw slip away from the wall, the loose dirt in his grip all that was left of his hand-hold. Only quick action saved him. As he slipped, the lionbird shifted his body and managed to reach his previous hold. He teetered somewhat, but this one did not give way. The rest of the journey was made much more cautiously. At the top, he fell to the ground and took several deep breaths.

When he was finally able to look up once again, his eyes widened. His head cocked to one side. The horizon was tinged in green. The Gryphon had not looked at it earlier. He stumbled toward the lush vegetation, half interested and half concerned.

His first good view of the landscape before him confirmed what he had guessed. These were the Barren Lands. *Were* was the correct term. If any place contradicted its own name, it was this untamed but peaceful meadow. There were birds in abundance. Trees dotted the meadow here and there, though there was a forest off to the northeast. Now and then, movement in the brush told him of wildlife, most likely rabbits and other small animals.

Fascinated, the lionbird wandered into the fields. There was such a change to this land. It was more beautiful than it had been those many years ago, before the Turning War.

His foot hit something hard. He pushed away the tall grass and discovered a broadsword half buried in the earth. It was decorated with serpents, identifying it as a weapon of a firedrake warrior. The Gryphon tried to pull it out, but the ground would not yield its prize. He finally gave in and resumed his journey.

The next discovery shook him. From a distance, he had been unable to identify the objects. Only up close did he know them to be the bones of a fully grown dragon. The skeleton, what was left of it, was fully entangled in the innocent-looking grass that spread as far as the eye could see. The back of the firedrake was broken, and much of it was already buried beneath the soil. It had been completely stripped of flesh.

Now that he knew what to look for, he came across several more during his travels. The most disturbing was the find consisting of five armored warriors, two still astride their minor drake steeds, smothered by the greenery. All were quickly in the process of returning their basics to the earth and would be gone before the coming of winter. Each corpse bore the mark of the Brown clans.

Having heard the tale of Cabe's struggle with the Brown Dragon, the Gryphon did not have to ask what had happened. It was not encouraging. He did not care much for magic, even that which he himself had. The sword at his side weighed on him with more than physical discomfort. Right now, though, he dared not leave the Horned Blade anywhere. It must not fall into the hands of a weaker mind.

A trembling in his stomach reminded him of the fact that he had not eaten in quite a long time. The Gryphon pondered the danger of seeking food in such a place. None of the animals appeared in danger, though they most certainly had done their best to decrease the amount of plant life. Would he be attacked as the dragons had been if he dared to steal some fruit or killed one of the rabbits? The westernmost border of his kingdom was several days' journey. He could not hope to complete the entire distance without food. Despite his hunger, no attempt at hunting was made. It would not do to end up like the hapless clans of Brown.

The riders appeared only moments later.

Six they were. The Gryphon's bird-of-prey eyesight identified them even from afar. There was no mistaking the glint of sunlight on armor or the faces covered mostly by helmets. The mounts were not horses but minor drakes. Here, in the middle of nowhere, there was little reason for dragon warriors to disguise their cousins, though they usually did so out of pure force of habit, a trait picked up with enthusiasm from the warm-bloods they despised so much.

The grass was tall and wild. That would hide him from the warriors, though their mounts might be trained to sniff out a foe. As of yet, the Gryphon's hand made no movement toward the devilish sword by his side. He would rely on the Horned Blade only if necessary.

They were riding with purpose, but they had not seen him. Their path would take them quite near his hiding place, and the wind was blowing his scent in their direction. Cautiously and quietly, the lionbird made his way to safer ground. He had no desire for battle; the delay would cost Penacles and his friends even more time. Time that could not be spared.

The leader of the pack was decked in an elaborately ornate dragonhelm. He rode purposefully toward the very spot the Gryphon had chosen. There was no question as to the rider's identity; the sense of power that flowed out before him, magnified by his oneness with the plant kingdom, marked him as the keeper of the Dagora Forest, the Green Dragon himself.

The Gryphon drew Azran's terrible toy, though it would also alert the Dragon King to his presence as if a beacon had been lit.

All six riders pulled up abruptly. After a brief pause, the leader moved slowly forward. With eyes fire-red, he stared straight at the hidden figure.

"Stay your foul tooth, Lord Gryphon! I come to speak, not to hunt warm-bloods!"

It seemed pointless to remain in the high grass when they all knew where he was. The Horned Blade ready, the lionbird rose to confront the reptilian monarch.

"What would a Dragon King have to say to me? I do not surrender to words." He kept his words low and monotone to underscore his disbelief and contempt.

Some of the warriors stirred uneasily. The Green Dragon raised a four-digited hand to silence them. "I am not asking for surrender. Rather, I seek an alliance."

The thought was so unbelievable that the Gryphon almost jerked his head back in shock. Fortunately, he was able to hold his composure and revealed no more than a slight widening of his eyes.

"An alliance? With a Dragon King? Why?"

The burning orbs dimmed as a look of weariness overtook the firedrake. "I am a realist, Lord Gryphon. The Kings are a thing of the past: The Age of Mankind is upon us. I would have it that some of my kind survive rather than fall to a rightfully vengeful race of humans! No longer will I follow the folly of the emperor and my brethren!"

The sword tip pointed directly at the Dragon King's throat. "A sudden change of heart. Why should I believe you?"

"If you want proof, consider this. Bedlam's grandhatchling was forced to travel over the Dagora Forest on his way toward Talak—"

The Gryphon interrupted. "Talak?"

"Talak. I did not intercept him, even though I had standing orders to do so. As a matter of fact, it was I who provided him with the transportation."

It might be true. The Gryphon could not recall any tales of evil concerning the Green Dragon. The master of the Dagora Forest was one of the few Kings who did not interfere with his subjects' lives if at all possible. He generally remained neutral, allowing nature and its children to take their own courses.

"Assuming that I take your word, what do you propose?"

"The greatest threat to your rebellion does not come from my brethren. I know this. We have one in our midst who is a master of the darker side of the spectrum, though he himself cannot rule."

"Toma? I've heard the stories—"

The Green Dragon let out a hiss. "They are not stories, warm-blood! I have watched and studied. There is reason to believe Toma has been among us at our councils, cloaked by the form of a Dragon King!" He did not have to elaborate on that point. A firedrake that could metamorphose into more than one form would have to have tremendous control over the powers.

Absorbing every word spoken, the Gryphon studied the Dragon King closely. "I think much of your newfound enthusiasm comes from a greater fear that Toma may rule. Humans you could fight, if necessary. Toma, though, would probably kill you when he was sure you were no longer needed." One of the warriors reached for his weapon. "I wouldn't do that unless you desire a new monarch!"

The hand moved away.

The Green Dragon leaned forward. "If that is not enough, then I shall also tell you that Azran is also loose and destroying all he finds. I need not tell you what rule under one such as he would be like! If the information I have is correct, he may be a bigger danger than Toma!"

"What information?" The Gryphon's first thoughts concerned Cabe and the Lady.

In answer, the other pointed to the ebony demonsword in the lionbird's grip. "You bear the Horned Blade, Azran's curse. Rumor has it that he carries a new one that makes this look no more deadly than a hunter's knife."

The weapon pulsated, as if angered at this insult. The Gryphon, meanwhile, was rapidly trying to assess the possibilities of the warlock's creating such a fiendish device. Unfortunately, the odds were good. Azran had skills far beyond most of his kind. It would explain his lack of action all those years.

He sighed, a strange half purr, half squawk. "All right. I'll take your word—for now!"

"How kind. How fortunate, also. Know this last bit: I am one of the Lady's patrons, though I lacked the power to break Azran's wretched spell. I will permit no harm to come to her."

"Do you know where she is?" The Gryphon did not bother to ask about Cabe; he was positive that the two were together.

He was correct. The Green Dragon pointed to the northeast. "There. In the Tyber Mountains. Everything nears a conclusion."

"I assume that you have something in mind, seeing as you've come far from your own territories."

"I have. These lands, though, are not out of my territory; they are now part of it. . . . Unless you wish to make a claim?"

Thinking back to the scattered remains of Brown's clans, the Gryphon shook his head.

"I thought not. Very well, I shall explain what I have in mind."

The Green Dragon's features twisted into a predatory smile.

XX

THE BRONZE GATE was a fitting entrance to what, for all practical purposes, was a visit to the underworld. Its incredible age was apparent from the first, a relic from a time long before even the Dragon Kings. That age did not prevent it from being a very real barrier to the two magic-users.

Gwen looked up the entire height of the door. "Now what? Toma was ready to send us here unattended. There must be a way in."

"How about knocking?"

She wasn't able to decide whether he was joking or simply at a loss. She chose the latter as he suddenly reached forward and banged hard. The noise overwhelmed all else.

They both waited for a tide of devilish creatures and indescribable things to come rushing out at them. Nothing at all happened, however, save that the massive gate swung slowly open. No one stood by. All that could be seen was a vast darkness.

With little other choice, the two entered. Almost instinctively, the Lady surrounded herself with a soft green glow. It allowed her to see while not spreading unwanted light. To others, it would be nonexistent. She extended it so as to cover Cabe as well.

Above them, things that should not exist fluttered here and there, disturbed by the two beings they dared not face. These were lesser servants, the spies and messengers. Cabe shifted their sense of reality in a way he did not understand. The shadows quieted, no longer noticing that there were intruders.

In the dim glow of the few lit torches, something stirred up ahead.

The enchantress sought it out with the glow, stretching it before them. A mockery of shape, just close enough to be considered humanoid, tried to shamble away from light it felt rather than perceived. It was not designed for speed, though, and Gwen was able to expel it from this dimension before it could escape to the cracks and corridors that lined the caverns.

Cabe grabbed hold of the hand that was nearest to him, squeezed it, and leaned over to whisper. "We're there, aren't we?"

She felt it as he had, and nodded agreement. There could be no hiding a place of such power as the master chamber of the Dragon Emperor.

Again, there was the feeling of age beyond belief as they entered the chamber. Ominous guardians of stone peered down at them, some recognizable, some hopefully only the products of nightmares. How many ages had passed since this place had first been carved out was questionable. Those who had built it were surely no longer known to this world.

Seated in the midst of all was the huge, savage figure of the Gold Dragon.

"Welcome, Bedlam. It hasss been a meeting too long put off. Decadesssss too long."

The great wings spread wide, almost touching the walls to each side. The Dragon Emperor stood on his hind legs, fore-claws at the ready, his head near the ceiling. He roared his amusement.

Gwen could not help but step back in open fear. Even the new Cabe appeared daunted, his body shivering momentarily.

"Well? Have you nothing to ssssay, Dragon Massster?"

Cabe's companion looked at him. "He thinks you're Nathan!"

"Thinks? Enchantress, you of all should know your lover, despite his new appearance! Perhaps this will help!"

There was a pulling on the darkest parts of the spectrum. Cabe felt something cover him, but there was no attempt to harm him. He allowed it to complete.

A gasp arose from the Lady. The warlock looked down at himself, mildly interested in the blue robe and hood that he now wore. He turned to Gwen. Her mouth was open and she was pale from shock. Cabe smiled to reassure her.

Then he turned back to the beast. "Right and wrong."

The huge, gaping maw was rushing down at him. Cabe pushed Gwen aside and jumped back, barely clearing the massive head. Grunting, the dragon pulled back.

The powers were twisted as Cabe's towering adversary unleashed his strength. Golden the reptile might be, but his sorcery was of the darkest kind. As he fended off a crushing wall of pure force, the warlock realized that everyone had underestimated the Dragon Emperor.

The Lady joined him, melding her power with his. The great leviathan was forced back onto his throne. He roared and let loose with a sea of flame. Cabe shielded them both, but the heat was nearly unbearable. They lost the momentum they had just gained. The dragon moved in once again, adding physical threat to his magical attack.

Claws raked at both humans. The tip of one caught Cabe on his arm, but it did not cut. In reply, the warlock released a burst of light, which both startled and blinded the firedrake. Roaring angrily, the monster swung wildly with his claws in the hopes of catching one of his opponents off guard. Cabe and his companion were forced to back up against a wall.

The Gold Dragon's vision cleared. He spied the two tiny humans and gave them the smile of his kind just before attacking head-on. Two or three statues that had stood for countless ages tumbled over as he passed. The two magic-users readied themselves.

The ploy was so unexpected, it almost succeeded. The shift was so sudden, it might have seemed instantaneous. From enraged gargantuan to battle-ready warrior in the blink of an eye. A gauntleted hand reached for Cabe's throat even as he was casting a spell against the beast that was no longer there. The enchantress was shoved aside by the hand that carried a gleaming, sharp sword.

Cold laughter filled Cabe's ears as the Dragon King thrust forward with his blade. The warlock barely twisted aside and was only cut superficially, though that hurt more than enough. Fiery orbs glared angrily from under the dragonhelm as the firedrake tried once again.

Though he managed to shove the sword tip away, Cabe was running short of breath, and the hand on his throat threatened to snap his neck. It made concentration almost impossible, yet he had to try.

He reached forth and pulled the brightest colors to him. When they had melded together, Cabe thrust the pure power into the Gold Dragon's mind and prayed his own neck would not snap first.

The reptilian warrior shuddered. He was trying to cast out the attack, but it was too unusual and too deeply entrenched. Mouth open, fangs gleaming, the Dragon Emperor put both hands to his head and fell half to the ground. The eyes lost all appearance of sanity. The twisted mind of the

Gold Dragon could not tolerate the flood. Cabe remained where he was, one hand massaging his throat as he regained his breath.

Writhing, the Gold Dragon dropped. His face was frozen in a silent scream. Only with the greatest of efforts was he able to call out. The words, though, made little sense to Cabe.

Something shrieked in anger. Out of one of the many passageways that dotted the chamber came a creature only remotely resembling a dragon. Its head was too large for its body, and it had spindly arms of little use for anything. The face was partially covered by what seemed to be whiskers that drooped straight down.

The Lady covered it with darkness. It howled even more loudly, and the darkness dissipated. Cabe surrounded it with a field of cold. The thing fought with astonishing strength. There was a tug on the minds of both magic-users, but the misty cold held.

Fear-struck, the monstrosity turned. The move caught Cabe off guard, and the creature freed itself. It loped off into the endless caverns, burrowing into and beneath Kivan Grath. The Gold Dragon collapsed into a semiconscious state with its departure.

Cabe rubbed the sweat from his face. "What was that?"

"A Jabberwock. Rare and deadly. A mutation that may occur only once in a hundred generations, if that often. I once studied an ancient tale concerning one."

"Is it dangerous?"

"If it had seen us clearly, we would have burst into flames."

He cocked an eyebrow. "Burst?"

"Unless you're a snowman, you contain some amount of heat. Don't ask me how, but the Jabberwock's gaze will increase the intensity of that heat at least a thousandfold! Poof! Spontaneous combustion!"

"What about the scream?"

"Probably to disorient its victim. I know I have a terrible headache now."

He nodded, his face becoming more and more that of another man, though it still retained just as much of his original features. When Gwen started to say something, he turned his attention to the quivering form at their feet.

"I find it hard to believe that it's all over so quickly." He shook his head.

"He almost had you."

"A brilliant idea. Caught us both by surprise."

The Lady nodded suspiciously. "Yes, but you recovered quite nicely. As if you'd been well trained." She paused, eyes moist. "How, Nathan? How and why did you come back?"

The warlock turned to her, smiling grimly. It was Nathan . . . yet it was also Cabe. "As I said to our scaly friend, you're right and wrong."

"I don't—"

"I am Nathan, as both of you suspected, but I am very much Cabe. Even more so, in fact. Call part of me an angel on Cabe's shoulder. That's more than I meant it to be."

"Meant it to be?"

Eyes half closed. Memories that pained. "You know most of this, but I'll say it all. Three weeks before the assault on Penacles and what I thought was the knowledge leading to victory, I—Nathan, anyway—discovered the birth of a son to Azran's woman at that time. What her name was, I don't know. She died in childbirth."

His form shivered, as one part was only just now realizing what it had lost. "The child was dying, due mostly to neglect. His only chance was a spell that had been located some years back in a pile of old manuscripts. There would be one chance and one chance only."

Images passed briefly through Gwen's mind. Of Nathan carrying the small bundle and locking himself into his study, allowing no one, not even the woman he loved, to enter. Of the mage days later, emerging haggard and drawn, bearing the same bundle and summoning a spectral servant to transport him away because he no longer had the strength. Finally, the memory of Nathan preparing for battle, still pale. If he had not saved the child . . .

Cabe nodded. "The Turning War might have gone differently. Selfishness, however, is a human trait. I—that is, Nathan—would not allow his own grandson to die! There was a chance, too, a chance that something might be preserved from all of this should the battle go awry. So Nathan, out of both love and duty, gave more than half his life force—his soul's essence—to his grandson. Until now, I—he didn't realize what that would mean. You know the rest better than we remember." The warlock frowned, the mixture of personal pronouns only one sign of his deep confusion over his true personality.

"Hadeen took care of Cabe—you—and pretended to be your father. Nathan and he must have foreseen a day such as this."

"Perhaps. So much of it's muddled in my head. . . . But that's unimportant for now." Cabe straightened and scanned the area. "We've still got things to take care of."

The sounds of inhuman movement had built up steadily, though neither had noticed until this moment. The warlock motioned for silence. Summoning forth the powers, he looked where mortal vision could not pass.

"We have nothing to fear from the denizens of these caverns. They are few now, know their master is defeated, and are fleeing to the safety of this twisting mountain range. Without him, they have no courage." He stared at the form near his feet. The Emperor of the Dragon Kings lay still, only his breathing relaying evidence of life.

Gwen wrinkled her face in disgust. "Azran and the firedrake Toma must still be engaged in struggle outside, though. Would that they would kill one another."

"I doubt very much whether Toma can defeat Azran. This new sword bears a blacker taint than the Horned Blade, if such a thing is possible. I doubt very much whether he even controls his own mind anymore."

The Lady paled.

Cabe turned toward one of the countless passages sinking into the land. "We've one more thing to do."

Gwen jerked her head around. "What?"

"Somewhere down there is the hatchery."

She put her hands on her hips. "Somewhere down there is a beast that just needs to see us to kill us!"

He smiled grimly. "Would you rather take the chance of fighting a whole new generation of Dragon Kings someday in the future?"

"That depends on whether we have a future or not! What about him?" She pointed to the still motionless body of the Gold Dragon.

"Leave him. I doubt whether he's capable of even standing." There was almost a sadness in his voice, as if Cabe would have preferred a different conclusion to their fight.

Reluctantly, she moved to join him. When they stood face-to-face before one of the tunnels, she impulsively put her arms around him and kissed him. When eventually they separated, she looked deeply into his eyes.

"Before anything else happens, I want you to know that I love you, whoever you may be."

"I'm still the same man who's been in awe of you since I broke through the amber. I just know the truth about myself now."

"Yes, that's one of the things I mean to talk to you about. How you just happened to come to know yourself in the nick of time."

He chuckled as he led her into the passageway. "Good planning and dumb luck!"

THE CAVERNS SEEMED determined to run forever, possibly to the bottom of the world, if not the deepest of the hells. The fetid smell of generation upon generation of dragons sometimes threatened to suffocate them. Irritated at her own stupidity, the Lady finally covered them both with a sense-altering spell that made the tunnels smell strangely of lilacs. Cabe said nothing but smiled at the touch.

They encountered only one warrior. Every species has its scavengers, and the firedrakes were no different. This one was bent over a precious hoard left by a dead or fleeing relative. What the scavenger planned to do with it after it had all been gathered together was unknown, for he pulled out a wicked ax and charged the two.

Cabe had no patience left for delays. The dragon warrior froze in midstream. His form twisted and shrank, and the reptilian features became dominant though he was no longer a drake of any kind. The tiny lizard scurried along its mindless way, the warlock not even pausing to watch it depart.

There was no sign of the Jabberwock. To keep such a beast hidden from the eyes of the Kings, Gold would have secured it deep. Few creatures visited the lower tunnels. It was rumored that things of past ages still roamed down there.

That they had originally taken the wrong passageway was obvious. The hatchery would normally be located higher than this and nearer to underground volcanic activity. Now, though, they sensed a rise in the temperature. Their path would, after all, lead them near their destination. It was the loss of time that concerned Cabe. Azran and Toma could not be expected to battle forever.

The sudden appearance of the hatchery entranceway was not so surprising as the burnt and torn corpse of a firedrake warrior lying just outside of it. Gingerly, they stepped up to it and then peered around into the room.

Blazing red eyes met theirs.

The old dam who guarded the young was far too massive to leave the hatchery. She was almost as large as Gold had been and much more savage-looking. Cabe suspected she could not shapeshift. It would be important if they had to run.

"Sssstep no farther, warm-blood! I have already protected the children from one ssscavenger, and he wasss one of my own kind!" Beneath her massive wings she sheltered a number of firedrakes, three of which were clearly marked as new Kings. There were even a few lesser drakes, who stood in front, hissing at the strangers. They were too small to be anything more than an annoyance.

Both humans looked at one another, and then Cabe slowly stepped inside. He was instantly bathed in flames.

When the fire had ceased and the smoke had cleared, he raised both hands in a gesture of peace. "We will not harm the children. I seek only to take them elsewhere. They will be fed and well educated."

"To be used asss ssslaves by your kind!"

He shook his head. "No. I will give them every right we give our own children. At least then, they will have a chance to live in peace. Nothing remains for them here but death."

The dam raised her wrinkled head and glared sharply at the small figure. "I will raissse them asss I have raisssed countlessssss othersss!"

"With what? There will be no more food! The Gold Dragon is defeated; what remained of his clans have fled in the face of the battle between Duke Toma and the warlock Azran!"

"Toma will feed the young! He—"

"—cannot win! Why else would the others flee? His army is already decimated! Would you have the warlock come for the children next?"

That struck a chord. The dam shivered. It was as if a human nanny had just been told that her charges would be fed to a wild animal. There was pain in her eyes, but she at last relented.

"Take them!" She unfolded the wings and shoved them forward. They waddled around uncertainly until she crooned to them in a startlingly sweet voice. Even the young minor drakes obeyed her, although they continued to hiss at the two humans.

"I trussst you for sssome reasssson, warm-blood. You appear honorable, sssomething lacking from most of your kind, and mine asss well lately." She folded her massive wings around her head as if to go to sleep. "Leave me now."

"What will you do now?"

She lifted her head momentarily to peer at him with one eye. It was older than it had first appeared. "My function isss no longer necesssssary. The other dams fled. I, though, I will sssssleep. A very long sssleep, I think."

The dam refused to say more. With one last look at her charges, she covered herself again. The two humans said nothing and started herding the various young into the tunnels.

Pushing a wandering firedrake back into the bunch, Gwen muttered, "What do we do now? I wasn't planning on playing nursemaid!"

Cabe stopped. He listened for something that his companion could not hear. The dragon young stirred nervously. She was annoyed that they had some inkling of what Cabe was doing while she herself did not.

"I'm afraid you'll have to play nursemaid a little longer."

She started to say something but never had the chance. Surprise was with the warlock. With skill that spoke of years of training, he encircled everyone but himself in a blue transparent sphere. The last thing he saw was the look of indignation on the Lady's face. He only smiled sadly.

The sphere winked out.

This time, the voice was loud enough for all to hear. It echoed through the tunnels, carried along by a wave of power so that it would reach anywhere. Cabe had not had to hear it even the first time. He could only feel too well the presence of the other. It was as much of him as anything else could be. Nevertheless, he listened to it a dozen times before taking a step.

"Cabe! My son! Come to your father!"

XXI

WITH ALMOST CHILDLIKE glee, Azran chopped apart one of the ancient stone monitors decorating the chamber. The Nameless sliced through without touching. Fragments flew here and there.

Once again, Azran shouted, his spell carrying his voice to the deep tunnels beyond. Still his impertinent son did not answer! In sudden anger, he destroyed a relief upon one of the walls, shattering through two feet of stone as he did so.

Writhing at his side, Duke Toma looked on in a mixture of hatred and fascination. The bonds that held him were not physical. Azran was taking special care with this, his greatest of prizes so far. The dragon warlord had come very close to nearly overpowering the sorceror despite the presence of the sword. His mind was fuzzy as to exactly why he was keeping this one prisoner. When he tried to remember, the warlock experienced a severe headache.

The demonsword glowed brightly at those times.

It was a vast disappointment to find the emperor of all dragons lying on the ground like some helpless babe. Even the sword had not bothered with him. The condition of Gold was, however, definite proof that Cabe had been through here. Therefore, it was only a matter of time before the two of them met.

The Nameless pulsated hungrily. Even the hordes of Duke Toma had not been sufficient to appease it. Besides, many had escaped during the battle with the warlord.

One part of Azran's mind had an almost overwhelming desire to go charging through the mazes, but the slightly saner part knew the risk that meant. The point was made moot, however, by the arrival of the warlock's greatest desire.

The figure who stepped from the passageways startled him. The robe was more than familiar, and the physical resemblance was so close as to leave a great distaste in his mouth.

"Greetings, Azran."

He growled, almost giving in to the sword's impulse to leap forward and cut down this . . . this . . .

"You do little to endear yourself to me by wearing that outfit, my son!"

A smile. All too familiar. "I have no intention of endearing myself to you. At least, not until I've brought you back to reality."

Toma was dropped to the ground unceremoniously. The firedrake watched both warlocks closely, knowing all too well that his fate most likely depended upon which of them won.

Azran's voice dripped with evil intent. "You should show more respect for your elders, my son. I shall have to reprimand you."

Cabe's eyes turned a misty gray. "You were always an arrogant child, Azran. Nothing moved you. I was negligent; you should have been punished long ago."

Despite its hold on the mind and body of Azran, the Nameless almost fell from his grasp. The face was dead as comprehension slowly seeped its way into the twisted mind of Nathan's son and Cabe's father. Almost was the battle won there. Almost.

The dark warlock recovered. Arrogance had given way to pure hatred and . . . a hint of fear.

"Father." He whispered, the word sounding like the blackest curse of the hells. The grip on the mind-numbing sword tightened frantically.

Cabe sighed. It was a twofold sigh. That which was Nathan sighed for a family torn asunder, while Cabe himself sighed for the coming of more useless bloodshed. Both parts came to an agreement.

"There has been enough blood. This will be decided another way." He gestured quickly, catching Azran by surprise.

A moment later, the chamber was minus two warlocks.

"WHERE ARE WE?"

The scream was Azran's, but the question had its origins in the blade in his hand. It pulsated unevenly, caught in a situation it could not comprehend completely.

Cabe/Nathan spread his arms out solemnly. "This is nowhere. This is that commonly called 'the Void.' The existing equivalent of death, some say."

The Nameless was brandished. "Take us back!"

"No. One way or another, this shall be decided here and now."

"I can kill you so easily!" The sword flew this way and that as if cutting up some imaginary foe.

That which was Nathan consulted with Cabe. How to separate what was still Azran from what was really the Nameless was debatable. The demonsword was his creation; much of it was the warlock himself.

"Azran, my . . . son, do you remember your departure from my keep?"

The face changed. The memories took dominance. "Of course! You were sending me far! Never trusted me the way you trusted Dayn! Couldn't teach me this or that because I always reached too far, wanted to learn both sides!"

"Especially the darker side."

"Of course. Far more efficient. I tried to tell you that." Azran smiled a childlike smile of satisfaction.

"You've done amazing things with it."

The Nameless quivered. "I've done things few other sorcerors could even imagine! I proved you wrong! There is no danger!"

"Not even from something like the blade in your hand?"

"This? Do you like it, Father? I've dubbed it the Nameless. Shall I tell you why?"

Cabe/Nathan shuddered. "I think I know why."

Like a young child seeking praise from his father, Azran went on. "You should have seen it, Father! Nothing could withstand its power! It slew the Red Dragon! It destroyed two armies, even defeated the lizards' best warlock! Nothing can stop it!"

"Not even you."

That took Azran aback. "What?"

"Are you certain that you can control it? How do I know it doesn't actually control you?"

The Nameless pulsated wildly. Azran's face emptied of almost all emotion. "Of course I control the sword. I created it just as I created the Horned Blade, only much better."

That which was Cabe asked, *What are you doing?*

Sword and sorceror must be separated if we hope to win!

A new tactic had to be applied. "I never meant to alienate you, Azran."

The demon weapon's control diminished as emotion surged through the sinister warlock. "You hated me! Dayn was always your favorite! Dayn did everything right! Dayn was so perfect! I showed both of you!"

Sadness crept into Cabe/Nathan's voice. "Dayn looked down at you, then? He taunted you?"

A pause. "No. No, Dayn never did."

"He showed off in front of you? He laughed at your attempts?"

Childlike, sulking. "No."

"Did he never help you, try to teach you when I no longer had the time?"

"He—he taught me many of the beginners' spells. Tried to encourage me when you were gone."

"That's why you killed him."

". . . Killed him." The Nameless wavered in his grasp. It had yet to learn how to control shifting emotions. Azran's change had left it unprepared.

Or, Cabe/Nathan pondered, *is it more of its creator than we imagined? Is it that it cannot cope with what we say any better than Azran?*

"What about your instructors? Did they prove haughty, disciplinarian?"

Eyes widened in anger. "Yes! Always pushing! Never letting up on me!"

"It is the way of magic. They often told me how strong you were and the potential you had. If not for their training, you would have never survived your delving into the darker side of the spectrum."

Pride. "I did it all myself!"

"Did you? Did you never use the wards they taught you nor incantations of preserving they'd made you memorize for countless hours? I have studied both sides, you know."

This time, there was only silence.

"Why did you kill them?"

Just barely was Cabe/Nathan able to avoid the spell fired off by Azran.

The silence had been twofold; the warlock had retreated to some inner part of his mind, confused, while the Nameless had taken the opportunity to regain control of the host body.

A nebulous green cloud floated away into the eternal emptiness of the Void. Cabe pointed at Azran before the possessed warlock could attempt any further attacks. The sorceror floated helplessly, his arms pinned to his sides and his form surrounded by a blue glow.

Too close, that which was Nathan said. Thank you for watching, Cabe.

It's my body, too.

Azran struggled, though his face was totally impassive. It was not complete control. The sword was losing once again, but each battle brought it closer to total domination of the body.

What now?

Good question.

The bound warlock blinked. He struggled until it was obvious that the bonds would hold him.

"Father?"

Cabe/Nathan could not hold back the surprise. "Yes, Azran?"

"I—I'm sorry about Dayn . . . and about my instructors, too."

"Good." Neither Cabe nor his grandfather knew what to make of this. If it was a trick of the Nameless, it was an abrupt change in strategy. If it was Azran, it could very well still be a trick. Either that, or the demonsword had taken its toll on whatever sanity had remained.

Caution slipped ever so slightly.

"Father!" Azran vanished.

Cabe whirled around. Despite the vast emptiness, there was no sign of the other. Nor did a glance using other senses locate any trace. Azran was far, far away.

Can't we just leave him here?

With the combined abilities of sword and host, they would find a way out. It might be to our plane of existence or to another. Neither is acceptable unless we control Azran. Pause. We were so close! I'm afraid he finally lost his struggle with the sword.

So what do we do?

Drift.

Drift?

Which is exactly what Cabe did. With a slight boost from his powers, he pushed off into the blankness of the Void.

* * *

MUCH LATER, IF time could be reckoned in a place such as this, they were still searching. Around them, the nothingness went on forever.

Neither personality had spoken much during the flight. The Void was not a place conducive to conversation. It was more to ease the growing tension that Nathan spoke to Cabe.

I am saddened by Shade. I knew him once when he was a good man, though he later changed in a way similar to that of the recent past. It is a more terrible curse than most think.

What happened in the underground city? Why did the crystal placed on me by that Quel help us? I know that was not Shade's intention.

Though he understands much that we do not, Shade had never come across the type of spell I used. He did not know that his catalyst would function as well with my magics. We can thank him; you would still be unprepared if not for that. I meant for you to grow up in a much quieter environment.

What does that mean? Cabe was curious about his long childhood.

The spell required an . . . incubation period. Hadeen watched over you for many years while you slept. When all was done, you were released. Only then would you start to grow. I'd hoped by then that things would be more peaceful. My mistake. It cost Hadeen and almost cost you.

A small, alien object floated by. Cabe broke off the internal conversation to look at it. He had come across things now and then. So far they had been artifacts similar to this.

The Void is as near to the center of the multiverse as is possible for anything other than Chaos itself. You will see debris now and then. Gates exist everywhere.

If that is true, why is it not more crowded?

The Void is endless. It is not bound by the laws of Order, nor is it bound by the randomness of Chaos.

What is it?

The Void. It is a thing totally of itself.

Darkhorse comes from here.

There are a few native creatures from the peripherals. They would be just as lost as we if thrown into the midst of this place. We are anchored firmly to one location. The only other means is to find a gate. That could take anywhere from a second to all eternity.

Cabe developed a sweat.

Something!

Both parts cried out in unison, an action that gave Cabe's body a massive but swiftly fading headache. He squinted, trying to make out the figure in the distance. It did not look like Azran. In fact, it did not look human at all once it became more visible.

What is it?

The thing had four arms and an almost owlish face. It was clad in a shimmering robe of silver and was most definitely dead.

A traveler from some other plane or universe. Either dead when he entered or unable to withstand the shock. It happens.

The creature was a dusky brown and well over six feet in height. Cabe wondered what its home might have been like and why it had come here. He watched it drift away and thought about how precarious his own position was.

Interesting that we should run across so many objects.

Why?

One could go for centuries without sighting a single thing. We must be near a focal point.

Focal point?

An area—if one can use the term—containing two or more gates, thus the larger number of items or people one runs across. We must find Azran before he falls through or finds one of those gates!

Adding a little to his speed, Cabe moved in the opposite direction of the floating corpse.

There!

Cabe's arm shot up to point at a small speck slightly to his right. He veered toward it, moving cautiously. It was humanoid, though one appendage seemed much longer than the others and somewhat distorted. On closer examination, the appendage proved to be a sword clutched in a hand.

Azran.

He was drifting limply. Despite the awkward angle of the rest of his body, his sword arm looked ready.

Move closer, Cabe.

Closer?

Closer, but below!

He did so. The sight he saw shocked both personalities. Azran's face was a twisted, maddened picture of horror. The eyes stared blankly into the Void. Glancing at the Nameless, Cabe noted that the demonsword was vibrating only faintly.

Extreme shock.

From what?

The Void is dangerous for those unprepared. Nathan would say no more.

What now?

A sigh. We take my son and your father back with us.

And the sword?

Unless we decide to cut off his hand, we'll have to take it with us.

Cabe could feel almost nothing from the Nameless. It had apparently exhausted itself in the attempt to escape. The decision was to return to the caverns and then to a place of safety where warlock and blade could be dealt with with minimal risk.

Taking one last look, which showed him nothing, of course, Cabe tugged mentally at his link. Both sorcerors vanished from the Void.

DISORIENTATION.

Holding his head, Cabe first stumbled and then tipped forward. He was alone in his head. The sudden emptiness only made him even dizzier. Everything was swimming. Barely visible to his eyes was a crevice in front of him. The warlock twisted as he fell, avoiding the deadly fall.

His new view was no better. Azran, his face still frozen in shock, stood near him, arm raised.

Pulsating violently, the Nameless swept down in triumph.

A blur of white blocked the way. The demonsword was forced to twist in an attempt to block the attack on its host body. It failed. An ebony blade cut through Azran's chest, spilling out his life and sending the body into convulsions.

The two swords met. The Nameless shattered its adversary into several fragments, but was knocked free from a grip that was by now almost nonexistent anyway. It bounced oddly, at angles that defied logic, and fell into the crevice. It was out of sight almost immediately.

Cabe looked up at his savior. The Gryphon stared at him with his avian eyes.

"If it's all the same to you, warlock, I would dearly like to go home."

XXII

CABE STARED DOWN at the limp, twisted body. He was alone in his mind. Nathan was gone permanently, it seemed, either from the machinations of the Nameless or through some choice of his own. The knowledge and skill were still there, for they were as much a part of Cabe as anything else. Still, even that did not seem like enough at this moment.

"I wanted to stop the bloodshed."

"It was out of your hands. I saw Azran. There was nothing left in him but the sword itself. He was only a tool." The Gryphon tossed away the hilt, all that remained of Azran's other devilish blade. "I'm sorry."

The warlock had turned away, his thoughts now on the Nameless. He peered down the crevice, trying to discern the presence of the demonsword, but other powers, their origins and uses long forgotten, interfered with any real chance of finding it. Cabe stood up and frowned. It would be futile to search.

He sighed, hoping the Nameless was lost forever. "I'd hoped to contain the parasite, but it's beyond my powers to find it down there."

The Gryphon was eyeing him intently in his avian manner. His visage failed to mask the curiosity the lionbird was feeling. There was a difference in Cabe that he was interested in knowing much more about.

Cabe surveyed the chamber. Two other problems immediately became evident.

Both Toma and the maddened emperor were missing.

When asked, the Gryphon answered, "There was nothing in this chamber when I appeared. I hid, assuming you and the Lady to be here somewhere. When you and Azran materialized together and I saw that sword ready to strike, I charged."

"None too soon. Thank you."

"If I may ask, where is the Lady?"

Sudden realization flashed over Cabe's face. "I teleported her and several dragon young back to Penacles! You're here! Does that mean—"

The Gryphon cut him off. "I cannot explain now, but I've made a deal with the Green Dragon. But I had no time to discover how badly off the city is. He may arrive too late. It was enough trouble for him to teleport me here."

"Then I may have just sent Gwen into the heart of destruction!" He began gesturing. "We've no time to lose!"

His companion had just enough time to shout a protest before they disappeared.

THEY MATERIALIZED IN the midst of chaos.

Soldiers were everywhere. They were all running. Some were dragon warriors, many were human. They did not fight one another. Rather, they chased after a common foe.

These, the two realized with a start, were the forces of Penacles and the Green Dragon. The objects of their pursuit were the remnants of the Lochivarite horde and the few living members of Duke Kyrg's own army.

The Gray Mists were nowhere to be seen. The Lochivarites, ragged and worn, stumbled away. Kyrg's firedrakes, vastly outnumbered by those of the keeper of the Dagora Forest, tried to make a stand, but were only minutes from being completely overwhelmed.

An unfamiliar banner, held by one of a number of riders, went by. Belatedly, Cabe recognized it as the flag of Mito Pica. Survivors of the overrun city, here to make sure that their city would not be so soon forgotten by the servants of the Dragon Kings. They were particularly bloodthirsty, having little left to go back to.

The Gryphon chuckled. It came out as something resembling a cough. "Never trust a Dragon King! While he made deals with me, his army was already on its way here along with other reinforcements!"

Cabe nodded, his mind only partially on the advancing soldiers. He was looking at the walls of the city and finding that portions were missing. What little he could see of the inside told him that the enemy had managed to break through at some point in time.

He tapped the Gryphon on the shoulder. "Hold tight. We're going inside the city."

"Wha—

—AAAT?"

A closer view proved no more comforting. A path of destruction led purposely toward the palace. Many buildings to the far left and right had not even been touched. The attackers had come with only one thing in mind: capture of the libraries. The Gryphon would have liked to tell them how foolish they had been.

Nervous, Cabe gave no warning whatsoever for the next jump.

* * *

"It's about time you arrived!"

The Gryphon inspected his palace for damage while he waited for the two to separate. There were a few cracks in the walls and stains on the floor. Here and there, bodies of fallen warriors from both sides lay sprawled in death. One of the golems was scattered about and another was missing an arm and was covered with dents. The lack of real damage indicated that fighting had been sporadic by this point.

Gwen was the first to speak. "I was afraid Azran had killed you!"

"No. He's dead. The Gryphon had to kill him."

She looked down. "I'm sorry for you, but not for him."

"I understand. Another thing." He took a deep breath before continuing. "From here on, it's only Cabe."

A pause. "That's fine. Nathan and I—that's a thing of the past. I realized that when I thought Azran might have killed you."

They kissed again.

The lord of Penacles cleared his throat. "Excuse me, both of you, but I was wondering if the Lady might know the extent of the damage."

The tone of the lionbird's voice only caused their faces to redden further. After that, Gwen became quiet.

"That bad?"

"The northern and eastern walls need heavy rebuilding. So does the northern corner of the west wall. Have you seen the trail leading here?"

They nodded.

"Most of the carnage was reserved to that path. Fortunately, that means a great many of the people were unharmed. Casualties are high among the army, though."

"I shall see that their families will be cared for. No one will suffer while I rule. Have you seen General Toos or Commander Blane? I'd like to talk to them."

Gwen took time before answering. Both Cabe and the Gryphon shifted anxiously.

"Toos is in control of the mopping up. Blane . . . Blane died defending the libraries."

Cabe shook his head in sadness. The lionbird hissed. They had not known the commander from Zuu for very long, but he had always been friendly and helpful. Without his assistance, the city would have surely fallen.

"How?"

"That lizard Kyrg chose himself a squad of handpicked murderers. They tore through the streets with only one destination in mind. Blane apparently managed to gather his own men and halt them. They took heavy losses, and a few managed to get inside. I don't know what they planned to do if they succeeded in finding the libraries."

"Kyrg believes in crushing all opposition to his goal whether he can attain it or not." The Gryphon's tones spoke of nothing but contempt for the firedrake warlord.

"Blane and the few remaining men with him battled it out with Kyrg here. The commander personally put an end to the lizard before going down from an ax."

That was it, then. The tragic part in their minds was that so many had died fighting over a thing that few could even understand. How much use would the Dragon Kings have gained from it? In the end, it had done little to save the Purple Dragon, and he had studied it far longer than any. Even the Gryphon had gleaned nothing much in all the years he had ruled, though that had been more than a human life span.

The libraries were of secondary importance now. Their secrets would still be waiting long after the dead had been buried.

The Gryphon summoned a servant and ordered food. "Come tomorrow, we will begin rebuilding this city. For now, I think we could all do with a little rest."

Neither argued with him.

THANKS TO A preservation spell, the bodies of Blane and the rest of the dead from Zuu were carted off to their homeland. Survivors of the band and escorts from Penacles rode along to protect them from damage. Also with the caravan were dukes of the Green Dragon who had vowed to openly take the side of humanity from here on. That alone would slow Toma's plans should the firedrake attempt to garner support from his kind.

The dead of Penacles were burned, as ritual had always stated. The Gryphon placed honors on each of the dead, whether warrior or civilian. Cabe went about the task of easing the rebuilding of the city, while Gwen helped with healing and food. Both were only human and had their limits; they assisted but could not wipe out the problems.

When not helping the people, most of their time was occupied with teaching the young turned over to them by the dragon dam. The firedrakes proved as capable and as unruly as human children. The minor drakes were no more intelligent than dogs or horses, and were eventually turned over to the stables. A request quickly followed for the building of a separate stable, as the regular animals were having trouble sleeping so near to the predators.

The Green Dragon gave suggestions but declined when asked to take over the training. It was his feeling that the young should be raised as human as possible. Only that way could his kind have a chance of surviving in the world to come.

Scouts reported that the Gray Mists had completely vanished from Lochivar, along with the Black Dragon and the few fanatics and drakes left to him. The Gryphon looked into explorations across the eastern seas. Something nagged him about the sinister, wolfhelmed agents from the lands beyond. Something he felt he should know. Much of his past was shadowed even to him.

Through some encouragement by the Lady Gwen, Cabe finally summoned the Sunlancer bow. It was now evident that his subconscious, perhaps through Nathan, had been responsible for his narrow escape from the Brown Dragon. The bow was the final legacy of Nathan. To Cabe, it meant that he was prepared to follow the path of his grandfather. That pleased him almost as much as the presence of the woman at his side.

OVERLOOKING HIS KINGDOM, the lionbird was interrupted by the two magic-users. He knew why they were here. They were looking for a chance to get away for a short time. By themselves. The Gryphon laughed quietly. It was the least he could give them. The city could run on its own.

Cabe offered his hand. "Have a minute?"

"I believe affairs of state can wait while I talk to two good friends."

The two smiled at him. Cabe paused before going on. "We were wondering if you could spare us for a while. We'd like some time to ourselves."

The Gryphon stroked his chin as if in thought. "The food supply has stabilized. The treatment centers are starting to empty out. The walls are seventy-five percent completed. I think I can spare you for a day—" The look on their faces reminded him of children who had just missed dessert. "—or even a month or so."

They both thanked him at once. Cabe was shaking his hand and patting him on the back. Gwen pulled his head down slightly and kissed him on one side of his beak, an action that ruffled both fur and feathers more than he would admit. He quickly excused himself and turned back to the task of running a city.

Outside the Gryphon's room, they kissed again.

Cabe grinned. "So. Where do we go?"

"I thought the manor would be a good place. I'd like to restore it to what it once was."

He pretended to grimace. "I thought this was supposed to be a holiday!"

Gwen held him in a long embrace before replying, "It will be."

A sudden, terrible chill ran through both mind and body.

When it had passed, Cabe was frowning. "What was that?"

Though she still shivered at the memory, Gwen rejected any unhappiness. "I don't know and I don't care. Not now, anyway. We are going to enjoy ourselves and rest for a change. After that . . ."

"After that?"

"After that"—she held him close—"we'll just have to save the Dragonrealms again. That's all."

This time, nothing disturbed their embrace.

ICE DRAGON

I

THE BONE-NUMBING WINDS of the great Northern Wastes tore at the cloaks of the two riders, seeking to remove their only real protection. One rider paid the wind no mind though it often threatened to thrust him from the back of his steed. The other rider, his form, like that of his companion, hidden by the enveloping cloak, would glance from time to time at the first one as if seeking some response. After a moment or two, he would return his gaze to the endless white world before them—and specifically to the jagged, treacherous range of ice-encrusted peaks near the horizon.

He urged his steed forward, knowing that the other would follow if he could convince his own. His urging however only succeeded in gaining a slight increase in speed; the mounts had suffered greatly and were, in fact, the last of six that he had started out with.

The slow movements of the steeds angered him, but he knew his choices had been limited. The mounts he would have desired would have been dead long before, the cold of the Northern Wastes having an even more pronounced effect on those creatures than the horses he and the other rode.

Already he felt sick of the cold, sick of the snow and ice—but what choice did he have? The others were fighting among themselves or, worse yet, were dead or turned traitor, which was the same thing in his eyes. He let loose a hiss of anger, disturbing both horses. It took him several moments to calm them down. His companion made no move despite the jumpiness of his own steed. There was no need to. His legs had been tied to his horse by the other rider.

It was a necessity.

They rode on, and as they moved closer and closer toward the mountains, the one rider's anger turned to uncertainty. Who was to say that he would gain aid here? This land was ruled by the most traditional of his kind and that tradition conflicted with his own desires, namely the rule of his own and other races by himself. Under the laws governing birth for his kind, he was ineligible. As his father's warlord and the ruling duke of the clan, he should have been satisfied. He was not, however, knowing as he did that his command of the power was greater, far greater, than many of his father's brethren.

But for a few birth markings . . .

The snowbank before him rose, and continued to rise.

It towered over him and his companion, blotting out the landscape before them.

The snowbank grew eyes, pale, ice-blue eyes—and tremendous claws designed for digging through frozen earth and easily tearing through soft flesh.

The first of the guardians of the one he sought.

He had now two choices, it seemed. Either kill the guardian or be killed, and neither was particularly wise.

The horses began turning and bucking. Only the rider's skill kept his own animal from throwing him and only the rope fastened from his own animal to the other kept him from losing his companion. The other rider teetered back and forth like some toy, but his hands were also tied to his mount's saddle, preventing him from falling too far.

The lead rider raised his hand and made a fist. He could not, of course, allow either of them to die, which meant he had to halt the guardian. He began to mutter under his breath, knowing that it would require a strong spell to turn, much less destroy, this creature.

"Halt."

The sorcerer paused, checking but not canceling his magical assault. He peered through the snowstorm the guardian had caused in rising and finally noticed the figure to his front right. The mage blinked.

It walked stiffly toward him, one hand holding a staff which he was sure controlled the great snow beast. A blue gem pulsated on the top of the staff. The figure holding the staff was not human.

"You are in the domain of the Ice Dragon." Its voice was emotionless and reminiscent of the whirling wind. There was something about it, something that made it difficult to see until it was practically on top of the sorcerer. "Only one thing prevents your death . . . and that is that you are one of the master's kin, are you not, drake?"

The lead rider reached up and pulled back his hood. As he did so, he revealed the dragonhelm that should have been noticeable, hood or no hood. The magical cloak which had hidden it allowed him to travel through the lands of men, but that function was no longer necessary here.

"You know who I am, servant. You know your master will see me."

"That is up to the Ice Dragon."

The firedrake hissed. "Tell him it is Duke Toma who awaits!"

The declaration did not impress the odd-looking servant. Toma studied it with narrowed eyes—narrowed eyes that widened when he saw the thing's true nature. His estimation of the Ice Dragon's powers grew and the nagging fear of the Dragon King, which he had kept safely locked in the back of his mind, poured over his mental barriers.

Necromancer!

The servant turned. It was a thing of ice, a caricature of a man made all the more horrible because its binding structure, its skeleton, was a figure frozen within its core. The corpse, whether man or drake or elf or some other creature of similar form, was impossible to identify and moved within the ice man like a twisted puppet. Leg moved with leg, arm with arm, head with head. It was as if someone was wearing an all-encompassing suit—save that, in this case, the suit was wearing the someone. Toma wondered about what had occurred here in the months since his escape from the battle between the human mages, the cursed Bedlams.

Thinking of the Bedlams, Azran and Cabe, reinforced the drake's resolve. He knew that Cabe had won and that the Dragon Kings were in disarray. Black was secluded in his domain, Lochivar, and the Gray Mists, which covered that land, were so thin that there had been talk of confronting this one particular King at last.

The servant raised its staff toward the behemoth, which had remained silent and unmoving since its initial rise. The tip of the staff was pointed at where Toma estimated the huge creature's head might be.

The leviathan began to sink back into the snow and ice. The two drakes' horses, only barely under control, now panicked. Duke Toma had to raise his hand and draw a pattern in the air. The horses calmed.

Turning back to the two visitors, the servant indicated Toma's companion. "And him? He also wishes to visit my lord?"

"He wishes nothing," said Toma, pulling the other horse over to him. He then reached up and took hold of his companion's hood, and pulled it back so the face and color of the other drake could be easily studied. "He has no mind with which to wish for even the smallest of favors. Yet he is your lord's master, your lord's liege, King of Kings, and he will be treated and cared for until he has recovered. It is your master's duty!"

Nearly identical to Toma in form save in height and color, the Gold Dragon stared forward mindlessly. A bit of drool flowed from the left corner of his mouth and his forked tongue darted in and out at random. He would not, or perhaps could not, return to his dragon form, and so Toma had also remained in his semi-human warrior form. They were two scale-armored knights with helms topped by intricate dragon faces, their true faces. Within the helm itself, bloodred eyes stared out. Though harder by far than any normal mail armor, what they wore was not clothing but their own skins. Long ago, their ancestors could have assumed some other form, but continual contact with humans and the realization of the advantages of a humanoid form had made this second shape something learned from the time of birth. It had become as natural to them as breathing.

The Ice Dragon's servant bowed its head briefly in the direction of the Kings of Kings, acknowledging or mocking the mindless monarch's sovereignty. Toma hissed loudly.

"Well? May we go on, or are we to make camp here and wait for spring?" Spring had not come to the Northern Wastes since before the rule of the Dragon Kings. Now, the land was buried under a perpetual coat of snow and ice.

The creature stepped aside and pointed the staff at the mountains toward which the drakes had been riding. "My lord knows of your presence. He is coming to meet you." This, at last, seemed to impress the servant. "He has not come to the surface since returning from the last Council of Kings."

The surface?

The chilling wind picked up, going from a constant annoyance to a howling, storming, chaotic whirlwind before Toma could even pull the hood back over his father's head. The temperature, already distressingly uncomfortable for a firedrake, became truly numbing, almost threatening to lower both riders' temperatures below a safe minimum. Visibility dropped to nothing, so that all that Toma could see was snow. He only knew his father's horse remained near thanks to the rope.

Something *very* large came to rest before them. Toma reinforced the restraining spell he had laid on the horses.

"Myyyy greetingsss to you, Duke Toma, hatchling of my brother, my king. My home issss open to you and our majesty."

The wind died down, though not to the level it had been previously.

Visibility improved to where the firedrake could see his host. Yet another surprise met his eyes.

The Ice Dragon loomed tall, wings spread, maw open wide. He was huge, greater in length than even Gold. This was not the Ice Dragon who had last visited the King of Kings just prior to the chaos. This was a creature in every way more frightening than either of his bizarre servants. Thin to the point of emaciation, so much so that each rib was apparent, the Ice Dragon might have been some ghoulish thing risen from the dead. Even the eyes, which never seemed to settle on dead white or icy blue, were those of something that measured life by other standards. Its head itself was long and lean and from its maw clouds of cold air erupted regularly.

A transformation had been wrought on the Lord of the Northern Wastes in the months that had passed since that last visit. This was not the Dragon King Toma had expected and almost definitely not one that he wanted, either.

It was too late to turn back and the firedrake could not have even if he had wanted to. This creature was his best hope of restoring his father and, therefore, Toma's own dream of rule from behind the throne. The question now, however, was how similar his goals and those of the Ice Dragon actually were anymore.

The frost-covered leviathan spread its ice-encrusted wings and smiled as only a dragon can smile at his tiny relations. There seemed no real emotion behind that smile, though. Nothing.

"I've been expecting you," the Ice Dragon said at last.

II

*T*O HIS HORROR-STRICKEN *eyes, the blade seemed twice the length of a full-grown man. From the handle, two horns, much like those of a ram, curled outward, giving the sword an evil appearance. The weapon was called the Horned Blade, a creation of the mad warlock Azran Bedlam, and it was evil. Cabe knew that all too well, for not only had he wielded the demonic sword himself, but he was also Azran's son.*

"Your blood is mine," hissed the figure now wielding Azran's toy. He stalked without difficulty toward the young mage who, in his panic, could not seem to find his footing. Cabe stumbled away from the huge, armored figure, trying to recall a spell, trying to find a way out of the lifeless stretch of baked mud called the Barren Lands. How long he had been running, he could not say. It did not matter. In the end, his foe had stayed with him.

His pursuer laughed mockingly, blazing scarlet orbs the only portion of his visage not buried in the murky depths within the dragonhelm. A false helm at that, for the face within was less the visage of his pursuer than the intricate dragonhead crest was. Even now, the glittering eyes set in that reptilian visage watched with growing anticipation.

This was a drake, one of the creatures that ruled the lands known collectively and singly as the Dragonrealm. More so, this was one of those chief among those who ruled—and who now chose to give the human his personal attention. There were only a dozen like him and only one of the others would this one call lord.

Cabe was alone and at the mercy of a Dragon King.

Something caught him by the foot and he went crashing down onto the centuries-old, stone-hard earth. He was blinded momentarily as his face swung toward the relentless sun. When his eyes cleared moments later, he saw what had brought him down.

A hand. A huge, clawed hand that had emerged from the ground itself. Even now, it refused to relinquish its grip.

Cabe struggled and struggled and only after several seconds did he remember the greater threat. Only when the one shadow for miles draped over him did he recall and then it was almost too late.

"Your blood is mine," the Dragon King repeated with a satisfied hiss. He was as pale a brown as the dried earth below him and this made no sense to Cabe.

The demon sword came rushing down—only to miss by inches as the young sorcerer succeeded in rolling aside despite the hand gripping his ankle.

His new point of view found him face-to-face with a long snout and narrow, savage eyes. A creature reminiscent of an armadillo—but no armadillo grew this large. The thing hooted once and then rose from beneath the ground, revealing a form taller and wider than any human and huge, clawed hands identical to the one holding Cabe by the ankle.

"Shall I let them rend you limb from limb?" the Dragon King asked sweetly. "Or would you prefer the kiss of this blade, Cabe Bedlam?"

Cabe tried to recall a spell, but, again, he failed. Something had severed his ties to his power. He was helpless and unarmed. But how?

In his mind, there suddenly came an image—an image of hate and fear. An image of his father, Azran. He was as Cabe had seen him last, handsome with a groomed beard and his hair exactly half silver, as if he had dyed one side of his head. The silver was the mark of a human mage and Cabe had such a mark in his own hair, a vast streak that seemed ready to devour the dark color of the rest of his hair.

"You would not be mine, my son; therefore, you will be theirs." Azran smiled benevolently for no other reason than that he was very, very insane.

As if on command, the Quel who had risen from the earth took hold of his wrists. Cabe struggled, but the tremendous strength of the creature was too much.

He heard the rasping breath of the Dragon King and for the second time the sun was blocked by the armored form. The drake lord spat at him, the sword already positioned for a deathstroke. "With your death, I bring life back to my clanssss!"

Cabe shook his head in disbelief. He knew which of the Dragon Kings stood above him now—one that should not have been able.

"You're dead!"

The Brown Dragon, lord of the Barren Lands, laughed—and plunged the Horned Blade into Cabe's chest. . . .

"YAAAH!"

With a start, Cabe woke from the dream, only to stare straight into the inhuman eyes of another drake, which resulted in a second shout. The drake ducked down and scurried out of sight as fast as its four legs could carry it.

Light burst forth from everywhere, bathing the room in brilliance. He caught a glimpse of a green, leathery tail disappearing through a half-open doorway. A hand gripped his shoulder. He only barely succeeded in stifling yet a third shout.

Gwen leaned over, her hair a long, fire-red tangle, save for a great streak of silver. Even though it was dark, her emerald eyes captured his attention as she sought to calm him. He briefly wondered how she always managed to stay so perfect. It was not all due to her magic, which, in its own way, was greater than his and certainly better honed.

"It was one of the hatchlings, Cabe. It's all right. The poor thing must've gotten loose. Probably nibbled through the grate." She moved toward his front side and he saw that she had conjured up a robe of forest green. Lady of the Amber, she was called, because of her imprisonment within that substance generations before by Cabe's father, but she might well have been called the Green Lady or the Lady of the Forest, such was her love for nature and the color which represented it best.

With a quick gesture, she made the door shut. This time, it would take more than a curious young dragon's bumping to open it.

"No." He shook his head, as much to clear it as to correct her misconceptions concerning his screams. This was not the Barren Lands, he kept telling himself. This was a room in the palace of the Gryphon who ruled Penacles, the City of Knowledge in the southeastern portion of the Dragonrealm. He and Gwen, friends and allies of the inhuman ruler, were here as the monarch's guests.

"That's not what I yelled about—not the first time, anyway. I—" How could he describe what he had dreamed? Did he dare? Gwen, too, had suffered at the hands of Azran and the Dragon Kings, yet, the sort of dreams he had been having of late—dreams in which he had been helpless, bereft of his own abilities—might very well mark him as insane as his father. Would she understand?

The Dragon Kings. He thought of the one in the dream and shuddered anew. The reptilian creatures were now trying to reclaim their once-mighty power from the human vermin. Though their power had been absolute once, there had always been few of the intelligent drakes and, therefore, they had allowed, perhaps even trained, the first humans in the duties of trade and farming. From that point on, there had been no stopping the growth of the younger race. Only after it was too late did the Dragon Kings realize that they might have trained their own successors—and the drakes had no intention of surrendering control without a fight. Were it not for the fact that they lacked numbers and even needed the humans, the reptilian lords would have started a full genocidal war long ago. The only thing that had held the humans back was the incredible, savage power of the drakes that more than made up for there being so few.

Gwen looked at him, the picture of concern and patience. Cabe chose to downplay the dream. It was something he must deal with alone. Instead, forcing his voice to a semblance of annoyance, he said, "I'd like to find something that will keep those lesser drakes penned up long enough for us to arrive at the Manor. They'll escape one time too often during the journey and it's important we don't lose even one."

"Another dream?" The concern in her voice was as evident as that on her face. She had had no trouble seeing through his poor attempt at deception and refused to be sidetracked by anything else.

Cabe grimaced and ran a hand through his hair where the silver which marked both him and his love as magic-users vied for dominance with the darker strands. Of late, the streak in Cabe's hair seemed to have taken on a life of its own; it was difficult to say what pattern his hair color might take each day. Sometimes it was nearly completely silver, sometimes it tended toward the dominance of his original hair color. As entertaining and amusing as the sight might seem to some, it definitely worried the young magic-user. The shifting had begun soon after he and Gwen had married two months before. She could not explain it and he could draw no knowledge from the memories of the archmage Nathan, his grandfather, who had bequeathed to him, at birth, much of his own soul and power.

"Another dream. This one was a bard's epic. There were the Brown Dragon, my father Azran, and one of those Quel things. The only one missing was Shade."

"Shade?" She arched an eyebrow, something she did quite beautifully, so Cabe thought. "That could be it. That damned no-faced warlock might have escaped from wherever the Gryphon said Darkhorse had taken him."

"I don't think so. Darkhorse was a powerful demon and if anyone could keep Shade trapped in the Void, it's him."

"You have too much faith in the monster."

He sighed, not wanting to be drawn into the same useless argument they always had concerning the two. Both Darkhorse and Shade were unique, tragic figures to Cabe. Darkhorse was a shadowy steed, part of the Void itself. Shade was a sorcerer who had been too greedy far back in history; he had attempted to harness both the "good" and "bad" aspects of the powers, two contrary pieces of nature, but instead had become a pawn between the two forces, an immortal who served good during one lifetime and who worked hideous evil in the next. Each incarnation sought to break the curse. For that, Shade had attempted to use Cabe as a conduit in a great spell, and only Darkhorse had saved Cabe, but apparently at the cost of his own freedom. What was sad was that Shade and the demon had been the closest of friends during the former's more pleasant lives.

"It's not Shade," Cabe finally decided, "and before you suggest it, I doubt this is Toma's style, either. I think this has to do with what I am—a warlock, mage, whatever. This is still all too new to me, that's all. Sometimes my fears return. Do you know what it's like to be as confident as—as Nathan, the Dragon Master, was—and then suddenly revert to my untrained self in the midst of doing something?"

There. He had said it. His self-doubts were returning and, with their return, the confidence he had gained from being the legacy of Nathan Bedlam was retreating rapidly. Cabe yearned for the days when he had simply been an innkeeper's assistant, before the Brown Dragon had sought him out as a sacrifice to return the Barren Lands to the lush fields they had once been.

Gwen leaned forward and kissed him lightly. "I do know what it's like. I have them myself. I saw them when Nathan learned of the death of his elder son by his younger son, Azran. I experienced them through my training and all through the Turning War over a hundred years ago, up to the day that pig Azran ensnared me in my amber prison near the end of that war. I still feel them now. When you stop having doubts about your prowess, you usually make a fatal mistake. Take my word for it, husband."

Men and women were shouting and Cabe realized they had been shouting for some time. It was not the shouting of men in battle or people under attack, but rather the curses of those seeking to herd a frightened minor drake back into its holding pen.

"Do we really have to do this?" The thought of what they would be attempting come the next day was almost as frightening as the nightmares.

Gwen gave him a look which brooked no argument. "The Gryphon made an oath with the Green Dragon and we're the best ones to see that it holds. When we're sure that Duke Toma and the remaining Dragon Kings can be kept at a safe distance, then we can move them elsewhere. Right now, the Manor is the best place for the Gold Dragon's hatchlings. Besides, I think the Gryphon has other worries to deal with besides the Dragon Kings."

The shouting died down, indicating that the wayward drake was once again under the control of its keepers. Cabe wondered how the other drakes were holding out. Among the young there were seven major drakes, the species from which the Dragon Kings had come. These were intelligent dragons, the true enemy as far as many were concerned. Wyverns, lesser drakes, and such were merely animals, albeit deadly.

He was not fond of the drakes, but neither could he abandon them. The Green Dragon, Master of the Dagora Forest and the sole Dragon King thus far to make peace with humanity, wanted them raised as human as possible. The Gryphon, Lord of Penacles, had agreed in part, but only if, in addition, the hatchlings received equal training from their own kind—a request which both astonished and pleased the reptilian monarch. The Gryphon, who seemed to have little or no background of his own, as far as Cabe knew, was determined that the drakes learn about their own heritage as well as that of mankind. It was a grand experiment, but one that *had* to succeed if the lands were ever to be at peace.

It fell to Cabe and Gwen to care for them for the time being. As much as the powers of the two were welcomed by the Gryphon in his struggle to raise a people that was not his own, he knew how important this long-term project was and who was best suited for the potential dangers. As long as Toma lived, the hatchlings stood the chance of falling into his hands and being subverted to his cause. The two mages would not be babysitting. If the Gold Dragon was dead or died later on, Toma's only hope was to plant a new puppet on the Dragon Emperor's throne. . . .

There were three such potential puppets.

"Cabe?"

"Hmmm?" He had not realized he had been ignoring her.

"If nothing else, consider this a trial for the real thing."

Puzzled, he studied her face. She was smiling devilishly. "Trial for what?"

"Silly." She settled down next to him. "For when we have children of our own."

Gwen laughed quietly at the look on his face. For all he appeared physically older than she, thanks to the properties of her amber prison, there were many things he was still naive about.

It was one of the things she liked best about him. One of the things that set him apart from her first love, Nathan Bedlam. The enchantress put a finger on his lips in order to still any further comment. "No more talk. Go back to sleep. You'll have plenty of time to think about it once the caravan is on its way."

He smiled and abruptly reached up. Taking her head in his hands, he guided her mouth to his. Even as they kissed, she dismissed the light.

PENACLES WAS PERHAPS the greatest human city in the Dragonrealm, even though its rulers had never been human themselves. From time immemorial, those drake lords who had chosen purple as their mark had ruled in a steady succession. There had always been a Purple Dragon, and so it had been believed that there would always be one. The Dragon Masters and the inhuman mercenary called the Gryphon had succeeded in at least changing that, and it was now the Gryphon who ruled here in the place known as the City of Knowledge. Through his efforts, Penacles rose to new heights, but, because of that success, he was diligently watched by the brooding, angry Dragon Kings. They had still not recovered from the Turning War with the human sorcerers—but watch they did. Waiting. Waiting until Duke Toma rekindled hostilities between the two races for his own ends. Now, even the previously untouchable merchants, they who dealt with both drake and man, were not safe.

It was only one of his many concerns. The Gryphon, accompanied by the guards General Toos, his second, had demanded always be with him, strode majestically toward where Cabe and Gwen were supervising the last bit of packing. Watching the two was frighteningly like watching the witch and her first love, Nathan Bedlam. The lad (anyone below the Gryphon's two hundred odd years of age could be considered a lad) was so much like his grandfather that the lionbird was often tempted to call him by the elder's name. What truly prevented him from doing so was the fear that Cabe would respond. Something of Nathan literally lived within his grandson, and though he could not describe it the Gryphon knew it was there.

Heads turned in the courtyard. The Gryphon was a startling figure in himself, for he was as his name implied. Clad in loose garments designed not to impede his astonishing reflexes, he almost looked human from the neck down, if one ignored the white, clawed hands so much more like talons or the boots that did not totally hide the fact that his feet and legs were more like those of a lion. The swiftness of his movements came not just from his years as a mercenary but also because, like the savage creature whose name and appearance he bore, he was a predator at heart. Every action was a challenge to those around who might dare to oppose him.

It was the head, however, that grasped all attention. Rather than a mouth, he had a great, sharp beak easily capable of tearing flesh, and instead of a normal head of hair, he had a mane like a lion that ended in feathers like that of a majestic eagle. And his *eyes*. They were neither the eyes of a bird of prey nor the eyes of a human being, but something in between. Something that made even the strongest of soldiers turn away in fear if the Gryphon so desired it.

Cabe and Gwen turned just before he reached them, either due to some power to sense his coming or a chance glance at the awed faces around them. The lionbird was pleased that the two mages showed no such awe. He had enough followers and all too few friends as it was. Waving the guards back, he joined the two.

"I see you have just about everything ready," said the Gryphon, studying the long caravan.

Cabe, looking worn despite what the Gryphon would have assumed was a good night's slumber, grimaced. "We would have been done long before now, Lord Gryphon."

"I have told you time and again—you two need never call me lord. We are friends, I hope." He cocked his head slightly to the side in a manner reminiscent of his avian aspect.

Gwen, a radiant contrast to her husband, smiled. Even the fierce visage of the Gryphon softened at that sight. "Of course we are your friends, Gryphon. We owe you too much for what you've done."

"*You* owe *me?* You two seem to have forgotten all the work you've done here, and now you are even taking those hatchlings off my hands. I owe *you*. I doubt if I will ever be able to repay you properly."

"This is silly," Cabe finally decided. "If we're all such good friends, then nobody owes anybody."

"Much better." Even as the lionbird nodded, an unwelcome thought squirmed its way into his mind. *They may be lying. They may be anxious to be away from the monstrosity that rules over their fellow humans.*

"Is something wrong?" Cabe put a hand on the Gryphon's shoulder. The monarch forced himself not to brush it away.

"Nothing. Exhaustion, I suppose." What sort of foolish thoughts had those been, he wondered. There was no reason he should think of such things. He knew these two too well. They were honest about their emotions.

"You should rest more, Gryphon. Even *you* need sleep."

"A king's work is never done."

"It is when he tumbles over from lack of rest."

The Gryphon chuckled. "I won't hold you any longer. The sun is already fairly high in the heavens and I know you want to get started." He glanced toward the caravan. "How are your charges doing today?"

Gwen indicated the cart that was a little behind their horses. In it were several reptilian figures coiled about one another in slumber. Other than by color, it was impossible to tell where one creature ended and another began. Behind that cart was another one likewise packed. "Last night's escapades wore them out. They should sleep for at least part of the journey today."

"If I ever let you begin." The Gryphon reached out and took the Lady of the Amber's hand. His features contorted, then blurred. When they re-materialized, they were human. By most human standards, the Gryphon's new face would have been considered quite handsome. His features were, appropriately, hawklike, the kind that young maidens dreamed their heroes had. He kissed the back of Gwen's hand.

"Should I be jealous?" Cabe asked innocently.

The enchantress laughed lightly, a sound like tiny bells—at least to the two males near her. "If you aren't, maybe I should find a reason you should be."

"This is where I definitely part company with you," the Gryphon said. He stepped away and his features returned to their normal state. Gwen smiled toward him and then had Cabe help her mount her horse. Cabe then mounted his own steed and took the reins from a well-trained page who had been waiting quietly all this time.

Farewells were said by those in the caravan to friends and relatives standing nearby. Cabe finally looked at Gwen, who nodded. Raising his arm, the young mage signaled to the rest of the travelers and then urged his steed forward. The Gryphon waved once and then stood silently watching.

It will fail, he realized. *The experiment will fail. The hatchlings should be back with the drakes. With their own kind.*

The Gryphon swore. That was *not* the way it was going to be! This experiment *must* succeed! It had every chance of succeeding—didn't it? He felt the uncertainty grow. Oddly, it was not restricted to this one thing. If his judgment concerning the young drakes was incorrect, then so might his judgment concerning any number of things.

He shivered, belatedly realizing it was not from his thoughts. It *was* cold! Bone-numbing, mind-chilling cold.

As quickly as it had come, the intense cold vanished.

"Milord!" A page, little more than a dozen years in age, perhaps, rushed over to the Gryphon. "General Toos is looking for you! He . . . he makes it all sound so urgent, your majesty!"

"It will wait a few minutes longer." He would wait until the caravan was out of sight. The lionbird was astonished at how hard it was to part company with those two. Being both ruler and an outsider, even after all this time, he savored the few close companions he had—and with the Dragon-realm in such turmoil of late, there was always the chance he might not see them again.

When the caravan was out of sight, the Gryphon still stood staring, and only when he heard the messenger fidgeting next to him did he recall that one of his oldest companions, perhaps the one who knew him best, had urgent news for him.

He sighed and turned to the page. The boy was, of course, in awe of the being before him. Most likely his first time delivering a message to one so important as well.

"All right, lad," he said in his friendliest voice, his worries forcibly pushed to one corner of his mind. "Show me where Toos is so that I can reprimand him for the hundredth time on proper chain of command. After all, *he's* supposed to come to me, not the other way around."

The page smiled and, if only for a moment, the Gryphon's worries seemed pointless.

III

B Y HORSE, THE center of the Dagora Forest, where the Manor was located, was several days journey to the northwest of Penacles, and with a party of more than thirty—the Gryphon had insisted on supplying Cabe and Gwen with all sorts of servants—the time tripled. Wagons had to maneuver around obstacles, people kept losing things, and there were even children to consider. (If the young of the Emperor Dragon were to be raised among humans, they had to be made to understand human children as well, and if the barriers could be broken between the young, there was hope.)

From their carts, the drake hatchlings watched with guarded expressions. Occasionally, one could tell when the hatchlings grew curious because their eyes would widen to literally twice their normal size. Excitement was the easiest emotion to read. Those of the intelligent drake race, looking like bizarre, two-legged lizards, jumped up and down in copy of the human young they had observed, while the young lesser drakes, pure animal, swayed frantically from side to side, hissing all the while.

As they were doing now.

The forest was suddenly alive with men. Masked men.

They all wore baggy traveling outfits and Cabe suspected that beneath those outfits was armor. It was obvious that this had been planned in advance. The caravan was more than a day's journey past the borders of Penacles' lands, and there was nothing in sight now but more and more trees.

"The fools!" Gwen hissed. "The Green Dragon will never tolerate this assault in his own domain!"

"He may not find out about it. We're far from where you said he makes his home."

She looked Cabe squarely in the eye. "The master of the Dagora Forest knows everything that happens anywhere in his domain."

The apparent leader of the band urged his horse a little closer to the group, seemingly unconcerned about his safety, even with two mages present. He was a tall man and probably a veteran of many a fight, judging by his stance and the way his eyes took in everything. There was little else that could be said about him since much was covered to preserve his identity.

"We only want the damn lizards! Give them to us and the rest of you can go on your way!"

Cabe tensed, having recognized something in the tone of the man's voice. He was fairly certain that the spokesman was from Mito Pica.

"Well?" The spokesman was growing impatient.

Gwen spoke up. "The hatchlings are under our protection and will not be turned over to the likes of you! Depart before it is too late!"

A few of the marauders chuckled, which did nothing to ease the disturbing feelings Cabe was experiencing.

"Sorcerers' spells won't touch us, witch, not with these." He lifted a medallion out of his clothing. From such a long distance, Cabe could make out very little other than that it appeared to be quite worn. Gwen let out a slight gasp.

"Those things are the work of the Seekers," she whispered. "I've seen one or two, battered and broken, but if they have more. . . ." She did not have to complete the thought. The Seekers, avian predecessors to the drakes, had left behind more than one secret which hinted of a power once far greater than the Dragon Kings at their finest.

"So you see," began the hooded figure once more, "we don't have to be nice. We've no quarrel with you unless you give us trouble. That'd be bad, considering we have you surrounded and outnumbered."

"Are those things really that effective?" Cabe muttered.

The Lady of the Amber nodded sourly. "Try casting something and the spell will go haywire some way. I don't know about prepared spells, but I think it works for those as well."

"There's only one way to find out. . . ."

The marauders were stirring. The leader shifted in his saddle. "You've had all the time you need to discuss it. We'll take them by force if need be. . . ."

"Touch them and not one of you will live to sssee the morrow. Your bonesss will be picked clean by the birds of the foresssst."

Marauders and caravan alike jumped at the commanding voice. The spokesman looked this way and that before seeing the single figure riding atop a fierce-looking lesser drake. The riding beast hissed hungrily, disturbing all the horses in the area.

"You are not wanted in or near my forest," hissed the Green Dragon. Like his brethren, his humanoid form resembled an armored knight wearing an immense and elaborate dragonhelm. He was covered by glittering green scale armor (which was really his own skin). Gleaming red eyes stared out at the assembled examples of humanity.

It was evident that this was one of the last beings the leader had expected to see. Nevertheless, when he spoke, there was only a hint of uneasiness in his voice. "These are not your lands. You have no control over this region."

"I share a common border with the lord of Penacles and I am his ally. I protect hisss side when necessary and I would expect no lessss from him. As for you, the east or the north is where you should be, human. Fight Silver or the remnants of Red's clans. Challenge the Storm Dragon, but do not presume to hunt in or near my domain. I will not permit it. Tell your bene-factor King Melicard that."

"Melicard?" Cabe whispered to Gwen.

"A rumor, nothing more. They say he supplies them. He hates the drakes as much as they do. Remember, it was Toma's half brother, that sadistic Kyrg, who drove Melicard's father, Rennek, mad."

Cabe nodded slowly, recalling the incident. "Rennek thought he was going to end up as part of Kyrg's dinner."

The hooded spokesman started laughing. One could almost picture the sneer hidden by his mask. "There's nothing you can do against us. These things have put a damper on your powers. I know how to use these. You can't even shapeshift to your dragon form."

The Green Dragon was not put out by this news. He reached slowly into a saddle pouch and pulled something out. "Would you care, gelding, to match your bits of bird magic to mine?"

The Master of the Dagora Forest held up something in one clawed hand and muttered sounds akin to the constant call of some raven.

There was a yelp from the marauder leader and a second later the man was working desperately to take the medallion from around his neck and cast it away. It was a waste of time, though. The medallion crumbled as all watched, until all that remained was the chain. The hooded figure quickly removed the chain and tossed it as far away as he could.

"I have not kept control of this domain for so long without reasssson. Did you think my brethren approve of the freedom the people of my landsss have? Those concessionsss were hard fought—and I ussse the last word literally." The Green Dragon returned the item to the saddle bag. "De-part now and we will forget this incident happened. You serve a purpose to me, but only to a point. Rest assured, I have other tricksss, if it comes down to it."

The intruders looked to their leader, who in turn looked from the Dragon King to the two mages to the cart where the hatchlings watched with agitated interest. Finally, he turned back to the Green Dragon. "If they leave your lands, we will seek them out."

"Your war isss with the Council, not hatchlingsss." The Green Dragon took a breath. When he spoke again, his words were measured and the hiss inherent to his kind was all but unnoticeable. "Now go, or do you wish to test your trinkets against a full-grown dragon again? Be assured that I have eyes watching you even now. They will continue to watch to make certain that you do indeed depart and never return unless invited—which I doubt you would ever be."

The spokesman hesitated, then finally nodded in defeat, and signaled to his men to retreat. Reluctantly, the marauders departed, the leader last. He seemed to spend most of his time studying the two magic-users, as if they were traitors to their own kind. When the last of his men had disappeared into the forest, he followed.

The Master of the Dagora Forest hissed, but this time it was in satisfaction. "Fools grow rampant these days. The only reason they made it this far into the border lands at all is because I was forced to reprimand one of my own for plotting to take the hatchlings from you just before you reached the Manor."

"Your own clans?" Gwen's surprise was evident.

"Drakes will be drakes, as humans will be humans. I have dealt with that one as I have dealt with this one. I suggest you and yours follow close behind me for the rest of your journey. We will save time if I lead you through the secret ways of the forest."

"Milord . . ."

"Yes, Cabe Bedlam?" The emphasis on the last name struck hard. The Green Dragon still remembered Nathan and the Dragon Masters, the group of mages who had fought the Kings in the Turning War and reduced the power of the drakes to its present state despite losing in the end.

"That disk . . ."

"This?" A clawed hand brought forth the item in question. "I have had many an occasion to gather and study the artifacts of our predecessors. The Lady Gwendolyn is not the first to stake claim to the Manor. That place has housed many since it was abandoned in the waning days of the Seekers. I believe the lower levels may even predate them.

"They planned well—perhaps too well. The dampers like those marauders wear are excellent creations, but, like all Seeker magic, those were created with a countermeasure already in mind. That, I believe, is what led to their downfall. They planned too well and someone took advantage of that."

The Green Dragon nudged his lesser drake toward the front of the group. As he passed them by, Gwen whispered into Cabe's ear. "You will find that the Seekers are a pet project of his. It was the original reason he dealt civilly with Nathan. They both wanted to know how such a powerful race could fall so rapidly."

"Like the Quel?"

She nodded. "These lands have seen many races rule. Each has had its cycle and it appears the time for humans is close at hand. Nathan didn't want us falling as the others had and the Green Dragon wanted to preserve as much of his people's ways as possible. For the sake of both races, they shelved their differences."

It was not what Cabe would have expected from the stories he had heard, but it rang true in his memories, which were partly Nathan's as well. There was some knowledge of the Seekers back in there, he realized, but it was like trying to find one's way through a thick fog. He could not dredge out anything specific from the past.

The hatchlings were growing extremely agitated. The presence of the Green Dragon was something new to them, having spent all of their short lives either under the watchful wings of the great dams who guarded the hatcheries or under the untrusting eyes of the humans. They had never seen a male adult of their kind so close, but they knew kin when they saw it.

One of the royal hatchlings, the one Cabe reckoned as eldest, stood confidently on its hind legs. His face seemed punched in, less like a beast and more like a man. The tail had shrunken as well.

He's learning, the young mage realized. He's starting to shift from dragon form to manshape. All he needed was an example to get him started.

With one to lead them, the others would soon follow suit. First the other two royal hatchlings, then their unmarked brethren—who would be the dukes or soldiers of their species—and finally the single female (Gwen had assured him it was indeed female; he had not wanted to find out close up). That the female would take longer was no fault of her own. Female drakes had a different metabolism and, while she would take much longer, her human form would be near perfect, perhaps more than perfect, Cabe remembered, having almost fallen prey to three such enchantresses who had once taken up residence in the very place they were now heading.

He did not look forward to the future where the drakes were concerned. He knew that the Dragon Kings, while silent now, had not yet given up.

Cabe guided his horse as near as he could to the drake lord. "Why didn't you destroy the raiders while you had the chance? They may choose to ignore your warning."

The Green Dragon's eyes narrowed to two tiny pinpoints of red. "With as many as there were, there was too much of a chance for something to happen to the hatchlings. A lucky shot by an archer might have struck down the heir to the dragon throne. I chose the best way to avoid all of that. If they try again, *then* they will forfeit their lives. Not this time, though."

Satisfied, Cabe slowed his horse until he was even with Gwen. The rest of the caravan slowly trudged forward again. Despite the Dragon King's words concerning eyes that watched over them, more than one person could not help glancing around from time to time. Regardless of their renewed vigilance, however, no one, not even the Green Dragon, who prided himself on his skill, noticed the single figure perched high in the trees. No wyvern this, but an avian creature who watched all with arrogance and something else.

The Green Dragon had been correct when he had said the Seekers designed with countermeasures already in mind. The watcher wore one such measure now and kept it quite well hidden from the mages and drakes below.

The observer waited until the caravan was lost from sight before finally moving. Then, silently and swiftly, the Seeker spread its wings and rose into the heavens, its destination to the northeast.

ALONE IN HIS chambers, the Gryphon sat quietly, his mind on a number of scattered items of interest. Like someone putting together a puzzle, he maneuvered the pieces around, trying to see if there were any relation between them. It was the way in which he ruled this city. He had learned more through this process than a hundred meetings with the various ministers that protocol demanded he pretend to listen to. He doubted any of them would be able to help him with even one of the problems he now considered.

A servant brought him a goblet of fine red wine. The Gryphon's face twisted and contorted as he formed a human visage in order to drink without spilling it all over his person. The wine was excellent, as usual, and he nodded to the servant, a half-seen shadow that immediately thereafter melted into the walls. Such servants unnerved many who lived in the palace, but the Gryphon refused to do anything about them, for he needed them in more ways than one. They were not only servants, but his eyes and ears as well. Merely with their presence, they made him feel as if he were not the only unique creature in all of Penacles.

His keen hearing detected the sound of someone walking purposefully and he turned toward the doorway. Two huge, metallic figures stood next to the doorway, one on each side. Rough conceptions of men. The Gryphon waited expectantly.

Suddenly one of the figures opened its eyes, revealing nothing but an iron-gray blankness where the pupils should have been.

"General Toos requests admittance," it grumbled.

"Let him enter." The golems made very effective doormen, since nothing short of the most powerful magic would stop them if they believed he was in danger.

The doors swung open of their own accord and a tall, thin, foxlike man stepped into the chamber. Most noticeable in his hair was the silver streak, a surprising thing since most people believed the general to be unable to perform magic. He was, however, noted for shrewd hunches and last-minute miracles. Though human—he also claimed a bit of elfin blood, but that was debatable—Toos was by far the Gryphon's oldest companion. More than that, he was a close friend.

"Milord." The man bowed in one smooth, sleek action. Age had done nothing to slow him. He was already far older than most humans ever got—almost *twice* as old, the Gryphon realized with a start.

"Sit, please, Toos, and forget formalities." It was always this way. The general was of the sort who always followed protocol even when dealing with those he had known for years.

Toos took the proffered seat, somehow managing to sit without wrinkling his dress uniform. It amazed the Gryphon that his comrade should go around so unprotected—even Penacles had its assassins. Yet, though there had been attempts, Toos had survived most without a scratch.

The old soldier pulled a parchment from his belt and reluctantly handed it over to his lord.

"More concerning . . . what you showed me?"

"No. I suggest you read the report first."

The Gryphon unfolded it and studied the contents. A report from one of his spies who passed as a fisherman in the coastal city of Irillian by the Sea, the main human habitation in that region and a city that was controlled by the aquatic Blue Dragon. It was not the location that the Gryphon would have expected news to come from.

He started reading the portion he knew Toos had wanted him to see and ignored everything else. Two figures wearing the distinctive black armor and wolfhelms of eastern continent raiders had been spotted traveling out to the caverns which served as the aboveground entrance to the palace of Irillian's true master. One matched the description the Gryphon had given his spies of a raider named D'Shay.

D'Shay.

A name, but one the Gryphon felt he should know, and remember. An aristocratic raider from across the Eastern Seas.

D'Shay was a wolf in human form, though not in the literal sense. Still, the Lord of Penacles would have felt safer with a pack of ravished wolves than alone with the raider. With wolves he at least understood what he was up against.

His uncertainty returned. D'Shay in contact with the Blue Dragon. The Lord of Penacles did not care for the potential that such an alliance might offer. The Master of Irillian had raiders of his own and they were a constant problem even to some of his fellow Dragon Kings, yet nothing had been done because they were too swift, too skilled. Dragon Kings did not wage true war with other Dragon Kings; that was a stated fact, though there had been rumors to the contrary occasionally.

He had not realized that he had uttered D'Shay's name out loud until Toos spoke up. "Please reconsider this, milord. We cannot afford any new campaigns at the moment. There is no telling when the Black Dragon will recover completely. Now would be an excellent time to rid ourselves of him. His fanatics are weak and the Gray Mists are merely a wisp right now. Lochivar is visible for miles inward."

Shaking his furred head, the Gryphon rejected the suggestion. "We can't afford such an action. Despite the weakness of both the Gray Mists and the Black Dragon, the Lochivarites and those that the raiders brought over will indeed fight. That's all they know anymore. The Mists only enforce Black's will even more. Most of those people have grown only knowing servitude to him. If he says fight, they will."

"But D'Shay is . . . Gryphon, I know what's forming in your mind, dammit! Don't even consider it!"

They stared at one another and it was finally Toos who turned away. The Gryphon stared down any further comment before reminding his second-in-command, "D'Shay represents a threat we know nothing about. The wolf raiders want to set up some permanent base in the Dragonrealm, either because they are expanding their hunting grounds or because they are losing whatever war they fight across the seas. It may even be that D'Shay is simply after me. He knows something about me, and I would like to know what it is. One of the puzzles I've been mulling over of late." The lionbird patted the report. "This gave me the extra piece I needed. Lochivar is too volatile at present for them to consider as a port, but Irillian is perfect. I should have realized it sooner."

Toos looked at him darkly. When his lord spoke like this, it meant he was about to do what most rulers would imagine unthinkable. "Who will lead while you are away? We are not speaking of some local journey. We are speaking of the realm of the Blue Dragon. Other than the Master of the Dagora Forest, he holds the greatest respect of his human subjects. You will not find so many allies there. You could be gone for months or—yes, I'll say it, dammit—forever! Dead!"

The Gryphon was unmoved by the emotion. The idea of journeying to Irillian in order to seek out the wolf raider D'Shay was becoming more and more of a priority. Carefully, so that his growing obsession did not show, he asked a question of his own. "Who leads when I am away?"

Another unseen servant brought forth sweets, but the general irritably waved away both bowl and creature. "Damn you, I'm a soldier, an ex-mercenary. Arguing with politicians is your specialty—and what do I care about the price of wheat as long as my men and their horses get fed? You've ruled here so long that no one can imagine any other as lord! Only those like me still remember that there ever was a Purple Dragon!"

"Are you through?" The Gryphon's face had reverted to that of a bird of prey, but his voice indicated amusement.

"Yes," sighed Toos.

"You'll take over—as usual?"

"Yes—dammit. You could have at least mentioned our other problem to the sorcerers while they were here. Then, I wouldn't be so worried."

"The frost incident appears to be isolated. No one else has reported any animals found frozen solid or fields of ice-encrusted oat. I've already contacted those with the resources to investigate more thoroughly. If I'm not here, they will find you."

A crafty look crept over the human's face. "Why not send these—hell, they're elves—to Irillian?"

"Because there are no elves in that region, save the seagoing kind, and they, like the people there, are loyal to the Blue Dragon." The Gryphon rose with the ease of a cat. "Why do you always persist in this show of reluctance?"

"Because old habits die hard and I always have this feeling you're going to stick me with this king business and run off permanently."

"It would serve you right, you old ogre."

The general chuckled, then recalled what he had shown the lionbird the day before. "I still wish the Bedlams were here. They might know something. That mule was as solid as a chunk of iron, Gryphon! What could freeze a creature so?"

The Gryphon found that he no longer cared about mules, fields, and sorcerers. Now that he had decided to depart the city, he was anxious to get away as soon as possible. It was not like him to be so uncaring about such puzzles, but perhaps that was because he had never before been offered such a chance to capture the wolf raider D'Shay. At the very least, the information D'Shay could give him concerning the wolf raiders themselves would surely be more valuable. The ice was probably the error of some fledgling sorcerer or witch. Perhaps even some sort of insane joke by sprites. Yes, that made some sense, he decided. Now, there was no reason to hesitate.

Turning to his aide, the Gryphon outlined his thoughts. General Toos did not seem taken with the ideas, but he soon gave in. The lionbird knew that Toos would understand as time went on.

"Now that that's settled," he continued, "there is no more reason for me to hesitate. Toos, I have full faith in you and your men, but this is something I have to do myself. D'Shay once claimed a connection to me; I want to find out what that connection is or whether he spouted it purely in jest."

"I could stop you no more now than when you led our company in battle, though, now that you are king, I would have hoped for different." The general looked highly displeased with the situation, but knew better. "How soon will you be departing?"

"Before tomorrow morning. Have someone saddle a horse for me."

"*Before morning?* You—" The soldier broke off at the look on his monarch's face. "Aye, dammit, as you say."

The Gryphon dismissed his oldest companion with a gesture. Toos sputtered, but said nothing. It did not matter to the Gryphon, anyway. The complaints of Toos or the ministers did not concern him. Only his journey to Irillian did. That—and the man called D'Shay.

He felt a brief pounding in his head and started to question its cause, but the pounding ceased and, with it, his curiosity concerning it. All that mattered, he reminded himself again, was Irillian and D'Shay. Nothing else.

IV

TOMA ENTERED THE frozen hall of the Ice Dragon with great trepidation. From the first, he had come to loathe this cold, dead citadel and its even more gruesome inhabitants. This was not the Dragon King he had expected. The Ice Dragon who ruled here was nearly as dead as his kingdom—but far more powerful than any of the other Kings. Something was afoot and Toma doubted he would care for the answer when he found it.

He shivered, and not just from the cold.

The Ice Dragon lay across the remains of some ancient structure. It was a thin, cadaverous creature but still larger than any of his kin. A gigantic corpse, the firedrake thought. I am dealing with a gigantic corpse.

At first, there was no acknowledgment of his presence. A lone drake warrior stood nearby. Had Toma not seen the chest rise and fall, albeit slowly and shallowly, he would have thought the drake a frozen ghoul much like the unliving thing that had first met him. The guard ignored him, instead staring straight ahead at something that, to Toma at least, was not there.

Slowly, as if rising from some grave, the Ice Dragon stirred. Massive frost-covered wings spread with a crackling sound that the firedrake realized was the breaking of thick layers of ice that had formed on the leviathan while he slept. The eyes opened, revealing a chill blue hue much like the skin color of a human long frozen. It reminded Toma all too much of some of the Dragon King's servants. It was also wrong. When last he had visited the Dragon King in this hall, only the day before, those eyes had been white as the eternal snow outside.

The Ice Dragon studied him with a total lack of interest. "There is something you wished of me, Duke Toma?"

They were not speaking as equals, that was something the bone-white dragon had established soon after their first meeting. The Ice Dragon was one of the Kings; Toma was merely a drake whose duty was to serve.

"My father, your *emperor*," Toma began purposefully. His only authority existed when it concerned the King of Kings. The Ice Dragon seemed oddly unused to warm life these days and the few of his clans that Toma had seen were of a similar attitude. It was as if they had completely forgotten what life was.

"Yesss?" A trace of impatience escaped the Dragon King. Toma was pleased, as it meant at least some of the old Ice Dragon still remained. Where there was emotion, there was life.

"I've yet to ssssee any aid for him. He hasss ssslept—" Toma cursed inwardly. He was becoming unsettled. "—he has slept as you suggested, but there has been no change. I lack the knowledge and skill for what ails him, though I think a little more warmth could certainly not hurt. You, though, are a Dragon King. I came here because of your power and experience; you must know something that will aid in his recovery!"

The Ice Dragon jerked his head up and, for a brief moment, Toma thought the leviathan had remembered something that would help. Much to the firedrake's disappointment, it was immediately apparent that his host was now concerned with something totally unconnected to the present situation.

"The sssstupid creaturessss!" hissed the Dragon King. His eyes were alive with rage. "Not now!"

Suddenly, the chamber became the center of a massive snowstorm. Toma cried out in surprise, then pulled his cape about him in a feeble attempt to protect himself from the elements. Snow blew about wildly. There was thunder and lightning. The wind whipped things around so much that the firedrake could not see. He could only hear the howling of the wind and, above it, the angry voice of his benefactor as that one roared his frustration out on some unfortunate.

As spontaneously as the storm had erupted, it ceased. He realized with surprise that it had lasted for barely a minute.

Brushing the frost and snow from his face, Toma gazed up at the Lord of the Northern Wastes. There was a momentary glow about the Ice Dragon so short that the firedrake would have missed it had he blinked. He did notice how much more energetic his host became after the glow faded.

The massive head swung back to face him and Toma could not help stepping back a few feet. He still had not reverted to his dragon form and had no desire to even now. It was too difficult to keep from losing body warmth when he was in his birth form, and if the Ice Dragon truly wanted him dead. . . .

"Someone invades my domain—with sorcery yet," the great dragon suddenly told him. "My children will deal with them. It will give them a taste to savor."

He could feel the chilling breath of his host and frost gathered on his brow. The Ice Dragon looked beyond the chamber and then at the firedrake. The incident of the moment before had already seemingly been forgotten.

"You may rest assured, Duke Toma, that my loyalty is to the throne. Everything I do here is in his name, for what he represented. My emperor will be cared for. You will see. Now, I must rest more. . . ."

"If I may . . ." Toma began.

The Ice Dragon's eyes narrowed to slits. "Is there something more you wanted?"

The firedrake stared into the cold, dead eyes of his host and shook his head. He knew well enough the signs of danger. Now was not the time to pursue *any* subject. The Ice Dragon, satisfied, laid his head back down upon the ruins. For the first time, Toma looked at them closely. The rubble had once been a temple, he decided. A temple which still housed something, for there was a pit or hole within and it was over this that the ghostly leviathan rested.

The Dragon King watched him with one baleful eye, then closed it. Toma whirled and departed the chamber, realizing that his earlier fears of something going on had been all too correct. In fact, he suspected that he had greatly underestimated how wrong things were. His whole trip here had been a waste of time and now quite possibly threatened his existence as well.

The trouble was, he doubted very much that the Ice Dragon was about to let him leave the Northern Wastes alive.

SOMEHOW, SOME WAY, the lord of the Dagora Forest led them along a hidden path that took half their travel time off. The Manor crept up on them and then seemed to spring into existence full grown. Cabe stared at the edifice and wondered how it had grown so large. His memories of this place were only months old and, while his visit had been short and hectic, he was certain that he would have noticed all of this.

The Manor was a magnificent blending of nature and construction. Much of it had been built within a great tree, yet just as much had been constructed by artisans of great skill and care. It rose several stories high. In many places it was difficult to see where exactly the two portions mixed. The latest of more than a thousand generations of vines enshrouded some portions, but most looked as if someone had been living here just yesterday.

The grounds were equally as fascinating as the Manor. Here, instead of clearing the land, the creators had sculpted the surrounding regions so that what they built actually benefited from the hills and plant life. If the Seekers had built this, which Gwen believed, then it revealed a side of the avians that no one else had ever seen before.

From his right, where Gwen sat on her own steed, he heard a tiny, muffled gasp. The memories she was experiencing were not ones that Cabe cared to dwell on, for he knew too well who many of them revolved around. It did not matter that she loved him and loved him greatly; Nathan was her first love and a tragic one at that. She had gone from Nathan to Cabe with hardly any gap in between, at first drawn by the similarities, then ensnared by the differences.

Still, Cabe could not help feeling some jealousy.

The Green Dragon reined his drake to a stop and dismounted. The party came to a halt behind him and waited. It was clear that the Dragon King was in the midst of something. A few of the humans muttered uneasily, but Cabe waved them quiet.

Raising his hand and forming a fist, the Green Dragon called out something that neither Cabe nor Gwen could hear. A moment later, the forests around them were filled with drakes of the humanoid kind. Cabe, fearing that the Dragon King had lied all along about his part of the oath, readied himself for a swift but bloody conflict.

Surprisingly, it was Gwen who held him back. He turned his head and looked at her in amazement, thinking, ever so briefly, that she was another of the King's pawns. Hurriedly, she corrected his misconceptions.

"I'm sorry, Cabe, we thought it best to wait until we arrived here."

"We?"

"The Gryphon, the Green Dragon, and myself."

He suddenly felt surrounded by enemies—all because his name was Bedlam.

"It is not like that!" she added quickly, evidently able to read his mind. "It was decided that we should have an equal number of drake servants. This way, both races will learn."

"Drakes?"

The two parties eyed one another uneasily. The humans muttered to one another, not caring for the thought of sleeping in a den of dragons. The drakes, on the other hand, knew that the lord and lady of the Manor were human mages of great power and that their own lord was turning their well-being over to the grandson of the greatest of the Dragon Masters, which was akin to being turned over to their worst nightmare.

"Cabe?"

He finally nodded. The two reluctant groups began to merge as Gwen dismounted and commenced supervising the unpacking and organizing. The tension was so strong one could almost see it, but no one wanted to anger the magic-users or the Dragon King. Cabe dismounted his own animal and began to walk off into the forest. Trying somehow to come to grips with everything. He had gotten used to the hatchlings—somewhat—but an entire clan?

Somehow, the Green Dragon was suddenly standing in front of him. Cabe had not even noticed when the Dragon King had dismounted, much less how he came to be here.

"I feel, despite the differences between our races, that I understand some of your fears. That is why I place the responsibility for any actions by any of my clan members on my own shoulders, Bedlam. Whatever happens, I will share the punishment. I want you to know that."

Cabe nodded slowly, not comforted in the least. The Green Dragon proffered a scaled, four-digited claw/hand. The human mage stared at it for some time before finally taking it. The Dragon King's grip was strong and hard and Cabe thanked whatever deity was watching over his fingers.

"Lady Gwendolyn will not need you for the moment, I think. Please walk with me. I would like to discuss some things with you, yes?"

He tried to read the burning eyes within the dragonhelm, but they were as enigmatic as everything else concerning this firedrake. Cabe turned to look briefly for Gwen, but she was nowhere to be seen.

"The servants know what to do and both sides will keep as much apart as possible for now, so there is no worry. Your mate is altering the spells that surround the Manor. The original protective spell was decaying. When she is finished, only those with the permission of the Lord and Lady will be able to pass." When Cabe did not apparently plan to ask one question in particular, the Master of the Dagora Forest added, "Even I will require permission. Your home will be secure."

The boundaries were to be closed to the Dragon King? It made sense, as the spell could not possibly differentiate between one King or another and both Silver and the Storm Dragon were close neighbors. So was the Crystal Dragon, but no one knew what his intentions were.

"Pleassse, Bedlam. That is not why I came to speak to you. If we may walk and enjoy the forest."

He followed the drake lord as the latter began to walk the boundaries of the Manor's grounds. Cabe could not tell where the borders were, but his inhuman companion seemed to know when not to step too far to the left or when to turn.

"There are," the Green Dragon began abruptly, "bad feelings between the drakes and those who bear the name Bedlam. That is understating the fact, actually. There are those in my own clans who have dared almost to defy me completely because there is a Bedlam now living in the midst of my kingdom."

It was always comforting to know that the forest was filled with friends, Cabe thought wryly.

"I had discussions on more than one occasion with the Dragon Master Nathan, you know. I suspect I have been tainted by humanity far more than any of my brethren. Even my speech patterns have degenerated."

The Dragon King paused and turned his head toward Cabe. The fierce dragon visage atop the helm seemed ready to make a meal out of the human, but the words of its owner belied that image. "I have learned to welcome what the others call the human threat. We were never numerous, never imaginative in the ways of your kind. Our rule is one of stagnation; I suspect that nothing would have prevented our fall soon."

Such bald truths from what was supposed to be a hereditary enemy made Cabe stumble as he tried to follow every word and, therefore, paid little attention to the path before him. The drake seemed not to notice.

"You fight among yourselves, you lie, you destroy, you run, and you steal. Despite that, you have become our superiors. You also create, look beyond the future, refuse to give in to impossible odds, and pick yourselves up when you've been defeated. We can only touch upon these qualities at present. That's why I requested that the hatchlings be raised as human as possible. To give my race a second hope. To give both races a place in these lands."

There was nothing Cabe could say that would have felt sufficient at that moment. The two continued to walk, gradually moving farther away from the boundaries of the Manor. In his days at the inn, he would have never been able to imagine himself walking side by side with one of the horrifying Dragon Kings.

He froze. The drake looked at him.

"Is something—"

"Gwen!" Cabe whirled and started running, not caring whether the Green Dragon followed or not. She was in danger. Briefly, her mind had touched his. What sort of danger threatened her, he could not say. Cabe had only felt her panic, nothing more.

He leaped over a small rise and felt a tingle through his body. It lasted barely a moment and he surmised that it must have been the barrier. From behind him, he heard an angry shout. The Green Dragon called out his name. Despite the urgency he felt, Cabe stopped and turned quickly.

The drake lord was standing behind the rise, his hands pushing against the air. Apparently, Gwen had already altered the protective spell and now the Dragon King had no way of entering the Manor grounds without help. Cabe recalled how he had once let in the demonic Darkhorse.

"Enter freely, friend!" The words were not the same he had used that last time, but the meaning was clear enough. He saw the drake stumble forward. Satisfied, he turned and began to run again. The Dragon King would either catch up or meet him there—wherever there was.

Cabe ran, passing by startled drakes and humans. He was on the right path, he realized. Gwen had once told him how close relationships between magic-users sometimes formed a link. It was not always a steady one, but there would be times when one felt the need of the other—as he had this time.

He was beyond the immediate grounds of the Manor before he realized it. The barrier had to be near. Where—

She lay crumpled in a heap on the outer edge of what Cabe would have called the garden, close, it dawned on him, to the place where her amber prison had once stood. She was alone and facedown next to a long overgrown row of bushes. Rushing over to her, Cabe gently turned her onto her back. From memory, he reached out with his mind to what he perceived as a spectrum and manipulated one of the soft, reddish bands. His spell washed over Gwen. A sigh of relief escaped his lips when he was able to determine that, at least physically, she was unharmed.

"There isss nothing here."

Cabe shook. His thoughts buried in concern, he had not heard the Green Dragon approach. "She seems unhurt, but . . ."

". . . we will know when she wakes," the drake finished. "Which she appears to be doing now."

Gwen was indeed stirring. She shivered and slowly opened her eyes. When her gaze found Cabe, the relief in her eyes was nearly overwhelming.

"I was afraid . . ." The enchantress paused as if unsure of what she had been afraid of.

"What happened?"

"The spell. I completed it, didn't I?" Suddenly, she was very much frightened again.

"Yes." Cabe could not help glancing around. Had something slipped inside beforehand?

"Nothing lurks within that I can discern," the Green Dragon added. "I have been searching since Cabe first felt your danger."

"What was it, then, Gwen?"

She blinked. "The ground is untouched. The—thing—is not here. Nor is the Seeker."

"What thing? What Seeker?"

"There is that," the drake suggested. They followed his gaze to a statue poised near the top of the Manor. It was a Seeker in mid-flight. There were other such statues scattered around the Manor and the grounds. As with this one, they were amazingly lifelike.

Gwen frowned. "No, it couldn't have been that—I think. That would still not explain the abomination that I saw."

"What did it look like?" Cabe asked softly.

She shivered. "Huge. All white fur and great claws like some digging creature. I swear, it tore up the area!"

Cabe and the Green Dragon studied the area, but saw nothing. The young mage looked up at the drake lord.

"It isss possible," the reptilian monarch began. "That, in reworking the ancient spells, you unleashed some old Seeker magic, perhaps something meant to frighten away outsiders."

The enchantress did not seem convinced. "They were fighting one another! It was as if I felt the avian's thoughts—even its death! It did—did succeed in killing that thing, though."

The drake gave a very convincing copy of a human shrug. "I can think of no other reason. No one else ssseems to have noticed it."

"Am I going mad? Is that what you're saying?"

"By no means. I believe my theory isss—is sound. Not perfect, perhaps, but sound."

Gwen looked off into the distance. "I was so certain it was real. . . ."

A few drakes and humans had gathered behind them. Curiosity—and possibly uncertainty—had drawn them together as nothing else had so far. Cabe looked at them and frowned. This was not the way to start out.

"It's all right," he shouted. "Exhaustion, nothing more. Back to the unpacking."

The servants slowly dispersed, but Cabe knew that they were not completely satisfied. What could he have said?

Gwen struggled to rise and both Cabe and the Dragon King aided her. She was still staring off into the distance. "I'd swear that—that at one point the Seeker actually saved my life. Not for altruistic reasons—but because it was a necessity, I think. I remember falling, being grabbed—and then blanking out."

"Forget that for now," Cabe suggested. "You need rest. Later, we can discuss it again."

"I suppose so."

The Green Dragon put a gauntleted hand on her arm. "For you, Firerose, I will send word to my servants to investigate the area. Though Seekers are cunning, there is a good chance they will discover if one has been nearby."

She shook her head. "It's not necessary."

"I think it isss."

Gwen smiled and then started to sag in Cabe's arms. Both he and the Dragon King were forced to assist her to the Manor. She made no protest.

Had they spent even a few more moments studying the area around the spot the Lady of the Amber had fallen, it was likely they would have found nothing. It was also possible that, if they had looked a little closer at the bushes, they might have seen the two feathers that Gwen's weight had buried deeper in the branches of those bushes. Feathers from a very large bird—or possibly something else.

V

IRILLIAN BY THE Sea was a city that thrived on fishing. War or not, the plentiful bounty its fishermen brought back was bought by all those neighboring regions too far from the Eastern Seas to do their own fishing.

While scores of boats moved outward seeking the first catch of the day, only one boat was headed in the opposite direction, to shore. Its path was one avoided by the fishermen, for that path led to the Aquias Maw, the vast caverns, partially submerged, which were the entrance to the undersea world of the one the human Marshal of Irillian called master.

The Blue Dragon.

In the weak light of predawn, it was barely possible to make out the three figures in the boat. One was the boatman, a figure shrouded in a soaking cloak woven from plant life taken from the seas. The passengers knew that he or she or it was not human and had probably never been, and did not really care. The boatman performed its function without complaint and that was as it should be. There was no reason to think about the being further. Both men had observed stranger things in the spans of their lifetimes.

The two passengers were like leaves on the same branch. Both were clad in furred armor, black as a moonless night, and upon their heads they wore tight-fitting helms with broad noseguards and a stylized wolfhead. A tail of fur ran from the back of the wolfhead down past the bottom of the helm and another hand's length further. Both were veteran fighters, yet both had airs about them as only ones who were born to lead can have. One was slightly shorter than the other and clean-shaven. The other, his apparent superior, sported a small, well-trimmed beard, a goatee.

The boatman brought the craft ashore by itself, displaying amazing agility and strength yet never revealing any portion of its person, including hands or feet. The two wolf raiders disembarked and watched silently as the boatman set out once more.

D'Shay raised his helm and wiped the mist of the seas from his face. "We have been sighted, D'Laque."

His companion followed suit while asking, "How long ago, Lord D'Shay?"

"At least a week, maybe two."

"Could he be here already, then?" D'Laque began to eye the beach.

"It's possible, but I think not. The animal is too good a hunter and too mistrustful of his prey to move like that. No, I think he's near, but not quite here yet. Scouting, perhaps."

D'Laque eyed his superior. "You make it sound as if this is some sort of game between you two. He is secondary; a permanent place for our ships is what we need most. The Pack Leaders are growing impatient, even D'Zayne, who, of all of them, should mirror your desires."

D'Shay was unmoved by the thought. "We shall accomplish that mission, my friend, but think how well we shall be received if we bring the Gryphon's head back with us. The news of his survival did not please the Pack Leaders. D'Morogue's . . . dismissal . . . is proof of that. He was supposed to assure our success, if you remember."

The other wolf raider swallowed hard. No one liked to think about what little the Runners had left of the hapless D'Morogue. Raiders in command who failed Pack Leaders in something of such importance never rose in rank and usually ended up as part of the Runners' feast. D'Morogue's name had been stricken from the Pack Commanders' ranks, the caste designation R' replacing his former caste designation D', and he had been tossed, bound and gagged, into the lairs of the toothy Runners.

Eyeing D'Shay as the other replaced his helm, D'Laque could not help but wonder why that one had not risen to Pack Commander. Certainly, his unofficial authority was known to all. No Pack Commander moved if D'Shay spoke out against it, and no Pack Leader approved new front strategies unless he was assured that D'Shay would have no major objections. Here, across the seas, was a man whom even the assembled Pack Leaders respected—yet he was not one of them, despite his superiority.

"Was there something you wanted, D'Laque?" asked the aristocratic raider. He had not so much as glanced anywhere near his companion.

"No." D'Laque quickly shook his head. "Nothing, D'Shay."

"So. I thought you might be having second thoughts about joining me. I know how much you fear Senior Keeper D'Rak." D'Shay turned away from the seas and faced Irillian. The city was still buried in the shadows of pre-dawn, but signs of life could already be heard. "Soon, we shall have a treasure trove with which to present the Pack Leaders. New ships, new lands, riches, allies, and the last great stumbling block in our war with the Dream Lands served on a platter. At last."

D'Laque hid the frown that crept up onto his face. He had the distinct feeling he was in the dark about certain decisions and was not going to find out about them until it was too late to do anything about it. He suspected that D'Shay *needed* to capture the Gryphon, or else lose valuable influence. It would be just what D'Rak would want.

It would also leave D'Laque defenseless against the master he had secretly betrayed.

NIGHT-CLAD RAIDERS AND wolfhelms. They now haunted the Gryphon's dreams, haunted his every thought. The closer he got to his destination, the worse it became. There was no way he could have turned back now. This was his chance to capture and question the wolf raider D'Shay. It was not the first time he had undertaken such a mission; there had been several during his years as a mercenary. This was different in one way, though. He knew that this time he was obsessed. He even knew the fallacy of such a feeling. Obsession generally led to death and often it was the death of the one obsessed. His head pounded briefly and, for a moment, he questioned this obsession and its sudden growth. Then, the pounding went away and his determination to continue on returned. He forgot his confusion.

The Gryphon shook his head and then studied the map of Irillian's—or rather the Blue Dragon's—lands once more. Some places were just too damn far away, he decided.

He looked up. The landscape around him was chaotic. While there were fields and trees that grew as if undisturbed for generations, there were also the occasional enigmatic craters, as if something had once happened here.

To reach Irillian by land, one had to pass through the uncharted domain of the Storm Dragon. The Gryphon's fur and feathers ruffled. The Storm Dragon was one of those Kings who revealed little about his full strength. The lionbird had never encountered him during the Turning War or the years after even though he and the leviathan were neighbors. The extent of his knowledge was a passing glimmer of Wenslis, the human city on the western edge of these lands and the nearest major human settlement to Irillian, which was not saying much. Wenslis was as far from the seaport as it was from Penacles, but, while it would have been an excellent place to stop, it would have taken him several days out of the quickest and shortest path.

I hope you're not expecting me for dinner, D'Shay, the Gryphon thought wryly. *I'm going to be late.* If the charts that he had succeeded in wresting from the libraries were correct, the trip got no better. Supposedly, this land had many swamps, and the worst of those was in his path and large enough that it was pointless to try and go around it.

Lochivar had looked bad, but much of that was due to the mindnumbing Mists. These lands were soaked the deeper one wandered.

This is the kingdom of the Storm Dragon.

As if the last thought had been a cue, the skies began clouding up with unbelievable speed. The winds began to howl. He quickly rolled up the charts, returned them to their case and packed the horse. This was not the place to be caught out in a storm, not by these trees. There was an overhang off to the right, perhaps an hour's journey. He'd be high and dry if he could make it there before the first rains fell.

His steed, having long ago learned to trust its rider, allowed him to choose its path and pace. The Gryphon envied such trust, hoping against hope that he could return that trust by not leading it into some hidden gap or straight into the den of some hungry minor drake.

It was almost as dark as night, now, with both moons being hidden. The horse's hooves sloshed in the increasingly wet grass and the Gryphon knew he was coming to the outskirts of the swamp sooner than his charts had indicated. He prayed it would not be too rough going before they made it to the overhang—providing he had not read the charts wrong about its location.

The sky rumbled.

Small, half-unseen creatures flittered, darted, and loped around him. Where had all these blasted things come from? Even despite his predatory background, he had had the worst time attempting to catch food. It was as if the oncoming storm was drawing them from the earth itself.

Or something was chasing them, he realized all too belatedly as the huge, ugly head rose from the swampy fields.

The horse sought frantically for dry, speed-slowing earth, but found only slick grass and mud. The Gryphon was nearly flung from the saddle as his mount spun in nearly a complete circle.

The minor drake turned its weak gaze toward the commotion. This was an older one, the Gryphon determined. A younger drake would have been on his tail already, jaws wide, claws fully extended. The elderly dragon, though, was only just realizing that the huge thing before him was the food he sought. Much bigger and better-smelling than the tiny marsh creatures it was normally forced to eat.

The heavens were split asunder as the first bolts came home to the earth. Its prey was momentarily forgotten as the minor drake looked upward and shivered. By the brief but brilliant light, the Gryphon could see that the thing was a mottled, unhealthy green. It was very old and probably dying, but evidently it was going to live long enough to give him trouble.

He'd wanted to avoid using any magic for fear that would draw the Storm Dragon or one of his underlings to him, but now was no longer the time to worry about that. Old or not, the dragon was a threat he could not avoid. At the very least, he would probably lose his horse if be attempted to go around it. Old and infirm though it might be, the thing only needed one sweep of its claws to decorate the landscape with bits of horse and rider.

The beast put a massive paw down in the direction of the two, then nearly fell forward when that paw sank deep into the mud. The dragon roared in annoyance and began the task of pulling the leg back out, the action accompanied by a loud slurping noise as the mud fought until the very end.

The Gryphon's eyes brightened. He raised both hands, keeping his balance by locking his legs against the horse's sides.

The spell was a simple one that might easily escape notice. Essentially, he was allowing the absorption of water by the soil to speed up. At least, that was what he was hoping he was doing. Generations of experience did not necessarily make a mage a master of the natural elements. All it meant was he knew how to manipulate the powers to create the end result he desired.

And this time it worked. The minor drake put its massive paw down on what it knew to be safer ground, only to have it sink even further than it had at the other spot. The beast howled with rage and the Gryphon was barely able to keep his horse from bolting into some of the muck itself.

The creature struggled in vain to release the one leg, working its remaining three into the mud as it pulled the fourth. Now, it was completely trapped. It hissed and glared balefully at the Gryphon, as if realizing that he was the cause of its misfortunes. When it opened its maw, he raised a fist in sorcerous defense against its flame, but nothing came out. The dragon was too old, too spent. Had it been younger, it might have freed itself or managed a flame stream long and intense enough to do the lionbird some damage, but such was not the case. Slowly, cautiously, the Gryphon began to urge his horse around the right of the thrashing obstacle.

The rain was starting to come down. The Gryphon shook his mane in disgust. He hated dampness and he hated rain even more. There was a place for cleanliness, but this was not it. Silently mouthing a curse at the Storm Dragon, he eyed the distant overhang. The old drake ceased thrashing, either worn out or finally realizing it was better off for the moment if it made no move. The mud was already up to the bottom of its body.

As the rain continued to come down in an ever-increasing fury and the ground threatened to suck horse and rider beneath it, the Gryphon once more began to think obsessively about the problems. Obviously, he thought morosely, it wasn't something to keep you warm and dry at night.

The overhang did not seem any closer. If this were any indication, the Gryphon suspected he was in for a very long, very slow, and very *wet* journey.

MUCH TO HIS misfortune, his suspicions proved all too correct.

More than a few days had passed and, at last, the border between the domain of the Storm Dragon and his aquatic brother was only another day's journey away. To the Gryphon, however, it seemed more like a hundred days. The rain had let up only once in the days it had taken to cross this land and that meant that it had taken even longer to make that crossing. Both the lionbird and his mount were sick of water and mud. It was a wonder anything could grow before it drowned, the Gryphon thought. What sort of life must the inhabitants of Wenslis have?

The weather was not his only problem, however. Twice, dragons had flown overhead, obviously on patrol and perhaps on the lookout for him in particular. He knew that the Dragon Kings had their eyes and ears in his domain. He had not expected his departure to be kept a secret. He *had* hoped to be nearer to the outskirts of Irillian when that happened, though.

Ahead of him lay more soggy fields of marsh grass and one more swamp. Up until now, he had been lucky. Both patrols had missed him, but now he faced the watchful eyes of the Blue Dragon's servants as well. If he was *extremely* lucky, he thought sourly, maybe a patrol from each would spot him and the two would kill each other in the fight over who should claim the prize. He knew how much each of the Kings desired his death and the prestige that such a kill would bring both patrol and King.

He sighed, knowing that nothing would be accomplished until he moved on.

The horse trod carefully on the half-sunken path, aware from the past few days that even the safest-looking piece of ground was treacherous at times. The Gryphon knew the odds were that he would lose his horse at some point on this journey, most likely in Irillian if he made it that far, but he was determined to do his best to see that, if it came to that, the animal might be "accidentally" found by someone who would care for it. He realized that it was a foolish, romantic notion, but it had always been his nature to reward those who had proven themselves, be they men or whatever. A good hawk or steed was sometimes more valuable, more worthy, than a hundred soldiers.

It was clouding up again. The clouds seemed almost alive, so perfectly did they gather over his head. He contemplated the possibility that he was being stalked, but decided it was his paranoia. The rain began to fall again. The horse snorted in disgust, as did the Gryphon.

The sky thundered. There were flashes of lightning. The Gryphon had become accustomed to both. Neither had, as yet, swayed him even in the least from his goal.

The bolt struck not more than twenty yards from him. The shock threw his horse off the path and into the boggy field. The animal cried out in alarm, but its rider had troubles of his own as one foot was caught in the stirrup and the Gryphon nearly ended up having his leg crushed. Only his inhuman reflexes allowed him to pull himself free in time.

The horse landed on its side with a loud splash and the Gryphon was enveloped by a muddy wave.

Another bolt struck, this time a little closer.

He *was* being stalked.

They were there now, flitting in and out of the cloud cover. There were at least two, maybe more; it was difficult to say since only two were visible at any one time. He did not recall much about the clans of the Storm Dragon, save that they were very protective of their lands and they were capable of producing something very much akin to an actual lightning bolt.

Why wait until now? Or had they just discovered him? Somehow, he did not think so. He was being set up for something.

His horse was struggling unsuccessfully to rise, but the mud was proving too slippery to support it. The Gryphon started toward it, then glanced up quickly when he heard a sound he recognized all too well.

One of the dragons was diving toward him, maw open in a frightening display of teeth.

The speed with which it dove was shocking. The distance between it and the earth shrank rapidly. The Lord of Penacles was forced to leap away from his steed and land once more in the marsh. He knew that nothing would save him now. There was no time to utilize a spell, no time even to pull out the tiny whistles that he kept around his neck for such life-and-death situations. He could only hope that somehow the dragon would miss. A near-miss was not sufficient; the claws of the dragon would probably take most of his backside with it.

There were shrieks from both the dragon and the horse and then waves of rank water were washing over everything, including the lionbird. Several seconds rolled by and when the Gryphon still felt nothing, he cautiously rolled over. His eyes widened as he realized that his luck had changed considerably.

The dragon had struck, but against the horse, not the rider. The gallant mount hung limply from the claws of the dragon as the latter made for the cloud cover. From the angle, the Gryphon knew the animal was dead already.

It was still raining, but not half as heavily as it had prior to the attack.

The Gryphon stood there, water up to his knees, and pondered what had just occurred. The dragons had stolen his mount, but had left him unharmed. Very strange. It was almost as if he was meant to continue on, but not without knowing that the Storm Dragon had *allowed* him to pass.

Curious.

He located the path and stood there, almost defying the dragons to return. They did not. He was going to be allowed to continue. Out of one fire and into another. The Gryphon succeeded in locating one saddlebag, but that was it. He now had no rations and only a few essential items. The idea that someone was trying to manipulate him increased. Still, if they wanted him to move on, they certainly could have planned better than this.

By all rights, it would have been more intelligent to turn back. He was expected and that could only mean trouble. Everything within screamed for him to return to Penacles . . . yet he found he could not. Each time the thought of going home entered his mind, the image of D'Shay in Irillian reared its head again and crushed all other ideas. Sighing, he slung the bag over one shoulder and stared in the direction of the port city. If he was lucky, he might reach the seaport by the end of his lifetime. The Storm Dragon's domain was swampy; the Blue Dragon's domain was dotted with countless lakes, ponds, rivers, and any other body of water one could think of. Even with a horse it would have been difficult going. On foot, it was going to be nearly impossible to make good time; most of the journey would involve going around places rather than across them.

The Blue Dragon had little reason to fear attack along his western borders. No matter how one looked, the land itself was a natural defense. Armies would become mired down. Only the skies seemed open and free, but the Gryphon suspected that they too were defended. Irillian's master was nothing if not thorough.

Briefly, the Gryphon thought of the tiny, inconsequential wing stubs on his back and what they might have accomplished if they had been full-grown. Only a few knew they were there. Useless for flight, he saw them only as another flaw and therefore kept them hidden. It was at times like this that he truly wished he had all the attributes of the creature he so resembled. Flight out of the question, the lionbird contemplated daring a teleport, but, since he had no way of knowing what lay ahead, the risks tended to outweigh the gains. He might very well end up at the bottom of a lake or in the middle of a bog—or worse.

The Gryphon adjusted the pack on his shoulder and started walking.

VI

DESPITE THE INCIDENTS of the first day, life at the Manor went on fairly smoothly. True, the drakes and humans there did live an uneasy peace, but that was all that could be hoped for. It was not surprising that, for the most part, the two races remained separate whenever possible. Cabe was just happy no one had tried to kill anyone yet.

There was no news concerning the vision Gwen had suffered through. The Green Dragon's eyes in the forest reported little unusual. There were almost no traces of Seeker activity, but both Cabe and Gwen knew that meant nothing; the avians were a secretive race and quite adept at covering their trails.

However, one bit of news passed along by the monarch of the Dagora Forest interested Cabe. Here and there, portions of the forest had been found dead or dying. The apparent cause was the extreme cold—yet winter was still far away and would only barely affect the Green Dragon's domain when it finally did arrive.

Cabe stood in the garden, his eyes on the forest, though he did not actually see it. His mind was elsewhere. Becoming a mage, he had once decided, made one paranoid. Perhaps he was overly anxious, but he could not get the freak incidents of frost out of his mind. They nagged at his memories, both the ones from his own life and those passed on to him by his grandfather, and he was fairly certain now that there was a connection between that and another brief incident not so long ago. A chill wind it had been then, one both he and Gwen had felt in the very palace of the Gryphon. The chill had not just been physical; it had struck at their very souls.

Oddly, that made him think of his dreams. He could not say why, but he felt there was a connection with them as well.

He smiled ruefully. The thought was too wild. Cabe forced the idea away and began strolling about the grounds in the hopes of clearing his mind of such irritating puzzles.

He saw a few drakes and humans working to clear what a lifetime's worth of unimpeded plant growth and general disuse had wrought on the Manor grounds. The drakes seemed fairly calm, despite the fact that their powers were nearly nonexistent within the confines of the protective spell, something new to them. They could not even shift to their dragon forms unless they departed the area. Even then, the spell would probably prevent them from returning unless they became humanoid again. The complexities of the spell amazed him at times and he was quite thankful for them, especially when arguments flared between the two groups.

The Manor was almost livable now. The garden, the spot where Gwen's amber prison had stood, was nearly cleared. It was the one place in the Manor where drake and human associated freely at all. There was a peacefulness to the garden that Cabe had not noticed on his prior visitation, most likely because he had been assaulted by drakes, pelted by magically flung chunks of crystal, and dropped on by Seekers. It was hard to believe that it was the same garden.

It had not originally been the Green Dragon's news that had brought him here so early, but yet another nightmare, this one a futile flight from his ever-present father over countless mountains and through hundreds of deep, damp caverns. Each time, Azran was waiting for him. Each time, Azran slashed at him with one of his demon swords. The Horned Blade, which Cabe had even carried for a while, had been bad enough. The enigmatic thing that his father had called the Nameless . . . Cabe did not even want to think of that weapon. In the end, it had proven to be his father's master. That was the way with demon swords. That was why only madmen like Azran Bedlam created them.

Cabe touched his head. He knew without looking that most of his hair was silver. It generally was after particularly strong nightmares. Again, he found himself with a connection between two events, but with no cause. Cabe scowled. It was bad enough that the nightmares had started again after having abandoned him right after the start of the journey here. It was almost as if they had tracked him down like bloodhounds.

The young mage sat down on a bench and stared up into the heavens. Again, he thought about how simple his life had been before the Dragon Kings had sought him out.

There was a sudden hiss of indrawn breath. No human was capable of making a sound like that. Cabe leaped from his seat, hands ready to cast a defensive spell—any defensive spell.

A drake stood crouched before him, preparing to be struck down by the powerful sorcerer for entering his presence.

"Who—" Cabe took a deep breath and started over. "Who are you? Why are you sneaking about?"

"Milord," the drake hissed. "I am only one who ssserves you. I did not sssneak up on you. I did not even sssee you until I almossst fell over you."

The mage studied him. From head to toe he looked no different from any other humanoid drake. Cabe quickly corrected himself. There was a difference, all right, one that he realized he had seen on most of the other male drakes who now served him.

"Your crest," he said, indicating the dragon's unadorned helm. "Where is it?"

Though it was dark, he was certain the drake looked at him in curiosity. "I am permitted no crest. I am a ssservitor."

"Servitor?"

"We perform the duties unfit for the drake lords."

So, Cabe realized, yet another caste. First and foremost were the Dragon Kings and the royal dams. Then came the ones such as Toma or Kyrg, who belonged to drake aristocracy by virtue of having been born in a royal clutch. These made up the soldiers, the warriors.

No one had ever told him of servitors, and the memories he had inherited from Nathan only hinted that his grandfather had known of such things.

The drake was waiting, no doubt a bit annoyed at the human's curiosity, Cabe assumed. "What're you doing out here?"

"I will depart if my presssence disturbs you, milord." The servitor began to turn away.

Cabe surprised himself by putting a hand on the drake's shoulder to halt him. When the creature whirled, Cabe fully expected to lose that hand and therefore jerked it back quickly.

The drake merely looked at him questioningly. "Was there something else, milord?"

"I didn't say you had to leave. I only asked why you were out here."

The other looked uncomfortable. "It is easier to think here."

Cabe nodded. "About what?"

"What is to be expected of us? Only the royal drakes have had any true contact with your kind, milord. You are—forgive me—odd, weak creatures that we are superior to—so it is said, milord." The last, Cabe noticed with some wry amusement, was added swiftly when the drake realized he was insulting his new master.

"What's your—do you have a name?"

Now it was the drake who was insulted. "Of course! I am no minor drake. I am Ssarekai Disama-il T—"

Cabe held up a hand to quiet him. "How long are full drake names?"

He thought he saw what might have been a smile, though on a drake that might have a different meaning. "The sun will have risen before I am finished. All clan members deserving honor are incorporated into the name."

Considering how long the Dragon Kings had ruled, Cabe suspected the drake was not joking about the length of time it would take to repeat his name. Another tiny fact he had never known about his new servants. "Ssarekai is what I shall call you."

"Sssatisfactory, milord. That isss how I am called by my own kind."

"What is your function?"

"I train and care for those minor drakes utilized for riding—though"—the drake hesitated—"horsesss have been of interessst to me of late."

Cabe grimaced, misunderstanding at first. "You are not to touch the horses. They're not meant for food."

"They are sssaid to be somewhat coarssse, milord, but I meant asss—as riding animals. A swift horse has great advantage over a riding drake, milord."

An idea was beginning to form in Cabe's head. One that might warm relations between the two groups and ease his own worries. "Have you approached the human who trains the horses?"

The drake shook his head.

Smiling more to himself and feeling at least a little brilliant for once, Cabe said, "See me in the afternoon. We'll go together. I want you two to meet."

Ssarekai shuddered. "Mussst I, milord?"

"Yes." Cabe hoped it sounded blunt enough.

"As you wish. If I may be excusssed, milord, I have duties to perform. The day ssseems suddenly busy."

"Then go."

Cabe watched him depart, pleased with himself for a change. Perhaps he was finally coming around to this. Perhaps the nightmares would finally stop if he came to grips with his own abilities.

He made a mental note to remember his appointment with the drake. He also made a note to request that the staff as a whole cease calling him "milord" so much. It smelled of hypocrisy.

Something moved near the garden gateway. At first, Cabe thought that Ssarekai had returned, but then he saw that the figure was too small and not quite right for a drake.

An elf? There was more than one type—some tall as men, some short like dwarves—and the Dagora woods was home to a great many.

"Who is it? Who's there?"

There was a slight intake of breath and then the figure was darting through the shrubbery. Cabe swore and followed. He remembered Gwen's fear that whatever she had seen might have gotten in before she was able to complete the spell. If something had indeed gotten in then everyone might be in danger.

He caught a glimpse of the figure again. A child? The glimmers of sunlight were now peeking through the trees. It could not be a child; the shape was distorted, too narrow and hunched over oddly.

There were still two Dragon Kings whose borders touched those of the Green Dragon. One of their minions, perhaps . . .

He was close to the edge of the spell when the tiny intruder suddenly veered back in his direction. Momentum kept Cabe going and suddenly he was tumbling over the figure.

There was a whining hiss, a jumble of limbs as the two of them became tangled together, and then Cabe's world spun madly. He spouted a stream of phrases enriched by his years at the inn.

When the world had at last stopped rolling, Cabe was staring upward, and into the face of—a drake?

It squirmed in his arms, but his grip, despite his astonishment, held fast. It was a drake—and it was not. The face was pushed in and more human than any other male. The dragonhelm was missing; there was no false helm at all. The head was like an incomplete and ugly doll, a doll that hissed and whined its fear.

One of the hatchlings. The eldest. A royal hatchling, but shifting like no drake he had ever seen. It was more like the females of its species, so much better was it at mimicking the human appearance than its adults.

"You," he finally managed to say, "are going to be a problem."

"Prrroblemmmm," it hissed back at him.

He almost lost his grip then and there. He knew from the Green Dragon that drakes grew rapidly and had to learn certain essentials before those few years were over with. Shifting was the most important of those essentials. Speech was another, and one he had forgotten.

A four-digited hand swatted his face and he forgot for a moment that it was a firedrake he held. The hatchling was losing its fear. Cabe knew he was considered clan leader by the young—at least as far as they understood the term. He was in charge, despite his alien appearance.

The young drake swatted him again and this time he recalled that it was not a human child he held, for one of the hatchling's claws scratched a line across his cheek.

"That's all the playing for now," he muttered. Cabe rolled over and, clasping the squirming drake to his chest—at the expense of his robe—stood. . . .

And noticed the irregular mound beyond the trees.

"Hold still," he absently mumbled to the hatchling. Cabe moved toward the mound and felt a tingle. He had passed the barrier. His grip on the young drake tightened, which only made it squirm more.

This, he thought ruefully, is not going to be a good day.

The mound, unidentifiable beyond that for the moment, stretched far beyond the boundaries of the spell. Any other time, Cabe would have not noticed it or would have thought it a part of the landscape. Close up, though, he could see that something—something huge—was buried here. Cabe continued to stand there, the hatchling still squirming—and occasionally mumbling something that sounded like "prrrobllmmm"—and debated whether he should go and get help or not.

"Cabe?"

Gwen's voice, soft but still commanding, came from the direction of the garden. "Cabe, where are you?"

That settled it for him. He tucked the annoyed drake under his arm and made his way back to the Manor. The way seemed slower, trickier than before, but that was probably due to the fact that he had been too busy chasing "the evil minion" under his arm to notice.

Gwen, clad in an emerald hunting outfit, was waiting for him in the garden and she was not alone. There was another female with her as well, one with the incomparable look of beauty that a few years of maturity can bring and dressed in a shimmering gown. Cabe was sure he would have recalled such a woman in the party and then realized why he could not. This was a drake. He swallowed uncomfortably.

"Looking for this?" he asked casually and held up the yawning hatchling. Let them think he had risen with this in mind.

The drake let out a gasp of relief and took the hatchling, which instantly clasped itself to her. Gwen smiled in relief and some pride, making Cabe feel more like the schoolboy who had pleased his favorite teacher than a master mage.

The female drake was eyeing him in another way. If there was one thing they loved more than wrapping males around their fingers, it was power.

Cabe represented an opportunity to gain both. He ignored her as much as was politely possible.

Fortunately, Gwen was speaking. "The dams stepped away only briefly to check on some of the other young. He was gone in that instant." She looked with interest at the hatchling's humanoid form. "Now I see how. Remarkable."

"More than remarkable. Look at the face."

Both women did and Cabe was pleased to see the knowing look vanish, albeit briefly, from the dam's face.

"Have you ever seen that before?" he asked her.

She used his question to give him a look which had nothing to do with the present situation but rather hinted at other possibilities. When Cabe's face remained frozen she finally replied, "Never, milord. I've heard it once in a while. Only old stories. They say Duke Toma did something similar to that, but I know of no one else."

"Toma. It figures he would be special."

Gwen nodded. "We're going to have to watch this one closer. All of us. This is a royal hatchling with amazing potential if its shapeshifting is already better than an adult's."

No male drake could assume more than one shape other than its true dragon form and that shape was always of an armored warrior, possibly because it had been the one first chosen by earlier Dragon Kings. The females could become several women of human appearance, but they would always retain certain physical features, making them look like sisters of their former forms. That was the extent of shapeshifting save for one such as Toma. Toma, it had been discovered, was capable of not only assuming his warrior form, but he had on more than one occasion copied the form of one Dragon King or another and had secretly joined in council meetings. Toma confessed to not being able to retain such a form permanently; still, it was far more than even the Dragon Kings were capable of.

The two women were beginning to turn back to the Manor when Cabe remembered the mound. He allowed the dam to depart with her charge, but asked Gwen to stay. When they were alone, he led her back toward where he remembered seeing the thing.

"What is it?"

"I think—it's only a hunch—I think I found something you should see."

She glanced around them. "If we go much further, we'll be out of the protection of the spell, Cabe. What is it you have to show me?"

"I really don't know." He did know, however, that something about the mound disturbed him.

Gwen followed silently. It took longer to reach the mound than it should have, for Cabe was suddenly having trouble remembering exactly where he had last seen it. That should not have been possible. Then he happened to look down and saw the spot where the plant life had been crushed by the combination of his body and that of the hatchling. He looked out into the woods and, after some scanning, finally noticed the mound again. That he still had only barely noticed it unnerved him even further.

"There." He pointed toward it and, unmindful of the barrier, walked through. Gwen, after some initial hesitation, followed after, swearing to herself that, love or not, she was going to take Cabe to task if this proved to be nothing.

As they moved nearer, Cabe felt the ghost of a chill that even touched his soul. It made him pause momentarily, but curiosity proved stronger in the end. Gwen, too, paused, but for another reason. The mound was striking at some memories of her own. Terrible, recent memories.

"Cabe." Her voice was tinged with growing apprehension.

He looked at her, worried.

"Stand back." As he obeyed, she raised her hands and gestured. Earth began to fly away from the mound, as if invisible diggers were at work.

Cabe frowned. Gwen waited nervously, biting her lip as the first traces of—something—were uncovered. She immediately cut off the spell and, to Cabe's surprise, rushed over to examine the find. Gwen moved near it, but did not touch it. He could not blame her. There was a feeling so unreal about the thing that he almost wanted to shrink away from it.

After a few moments, she rose. The expression on her face frightened him. "What is it?"

She did not answer at first, merely stood there shaking her head, both frightened and repulsed by what lay beneath the soil.

"Gwen?"

"It's my vision, Cabe," the enchantress finally whispered. "It—it's that abomination from my vision. I know it is!"

When she then collapsed, he was so surprised he only barely succeeded in catching her before she would have struck the ground. He stared over her prostrate body at the deathly white form that his wife's spell had partially uncovered.

He shivered again.

VII

CABE TORE HIS gaze away from the mound and looked down at Gwen. Her eyes fluttered open and she met his gaze. The fear was still there, but she was trying to cope with it.

"Help me up, Cabe. I—I have to stand."

He aided her to her feet. The moment she had her balance, she pulled away from him and stumbled back toward the object of her fright. Gwen paused an arm's length from it and stared. Cabe remained where he was, but readied himself should she faint again.

Gwen continued to stare at the mound, her eyes wide and red and one hand covering her mouth. She began whispering, "It's real! It's real!"

Cabe stepped up behind her, trying to soothe her as he, too, studied the mound. "Whatever it is, it's dead. There's nothing to fear. Nothing at all."

It would have helped if he could have felt that way. Regardless of the absence of life, the creature continued to fill him with an uneasy fear. He knew what that fear was now. It was the feeling that the abomination would suck him dry of everything he was. An irrational fear, yes, but a powerful one.

"No dream," the sorceress muttered to herself. "No dream after all."

"Dream?" Cabe recalled suddenly the entire vision that Gwen had described. The attack by the digging creature and the rescue by the Seeker. This was the thing from that dream? He shuddered, thankful that most of it was still buried beneath the ground. How long had it been roaming around the Manor? Had it actually been within the boundaries of the old spell? Why had it been so difficult to find?

There were shouts from behind them. One of the servants had evidently seen the Lady of the Amber collapse and now several figures, both drake and human, stumbled uneasily toward the two mages. Cabe made them halt out of sight of the creature. He wanted as few as possible to know about this. He spotted the drake known as Ssarekai and summoned him.

Ssarekai eyed the unmoving mound with great trepidation as he hurried over to Cabe. "Milord, what is—"

Cabe cut him off. "You can handle riding drakes well, I suppose—or would you be faster in your true form?"

"Riding drakes are riding drakes because they are swifter than personal flight, milord. We lack the stamina for long, sustained flights and tire quickly. Patrols are fine, but—"

"Then take one of them and hurry to your lord. Tell him for me that we have something requiring his attention. Describe it if need be."

"Milord, the forest—" Ssarekai sighed and shut his mouth as he noticed Cabe preparing to cut him off again.

"Will the news move faster than you can ride—and as accurately? How many will know about this by the time it reaches him?"

The drake shook his head, but he understood. "I will depart immediately."

"Thank you." As Ssarekai departed, Cabe gazed at the others and grimaced. He was getting too excited over what might not be anything. All he had so far was a dead creature and Gwen's too-real dream.

The others waited expectantly, murmuring among themselves on what might possibly be the cause of the lady's collapse. Some thought to question Ssarekai, and Cabe realized he had not exactly ordered the drake to remain silent. Ssarekai apparently took such a command for granted, for he ignored all questions and continued running.

"A Seeker."

"What?" Cabe spun around, expecting to see the avian leaping at him from atop some tree. There was nothing to see, though, only Gwen kneeling near the great corpse, studying it without touching it.

"A Seeker." Gwen's voice was low. Even distressed as she was, she did not want to spread further panic among the others. "There was a Seeker in my—vision. I wonder what happened to it? Why did it save me?"

A point that Cabe had not even considered. If the mound creature was real, why not the Seeker? And why had it rescued Gwen and fought the monstrosity that now lay before them?

"It had to be real, Cabe. There had to be a Seeker here." She stood up, her eyes never leaving the corpse, her body never touching it.

"What makes you say that?"

"The vision. It must have been an involuntary transmission from the Seeker. Distorted, since it neither sees nor thinks as we do. You remember."

He did remember. He remembered the Seeker who had come to him while he had been a prisoner of his father. The Seekers had served Azran, but they hated him more than any other human and this one had tried to convince Cabe to strike out against Azran if it freed him. Cabe, barely understanding his powers at that point, had refused. Not once had the Seeker spoken; it had touched his head with its hands and revealed its thoughts through emotions and images. Images of Azran murdered a thousand hideous ways. Cabe had never mentioned that to Gwen. It was what had made him refuse, aside from the obvious fact that he lacked the confidence if not the skill.

"I'm still certain the Seeker died killing this thing, Cabe. I think that's what made me black out in the end."

"Why you? Why would it speak to you?"

She still had not looked away from the creature. Her arms were wrapped about her, as if she were freezing. "I was trained to feel the land, Cabe, even better than those that live their lives here. I feel things you don't. I suspect the Seeker was projecting randomly, possibly to any of its ilk that might be near. Perhaps the 'rescue' was never real. It may have actually been only how I perceived the Seeker's thoughts. I do know that its actions saved me, intentionally or not. I—I'm guessing all of this."

Cabe nodded. The noises of the gathering were growing stronger and closer and he turned back to the assembled group. "Go back to whatever you were doing. You and you." He pointed at a human he knew to be a soldier and one of the drakes who wore a crest. "This area is forbidden to everyone until the Master of Dagora arrives. See to it."

What sort of mind was he developing, he wondered belatedly, that even during this chaos he was still striving to improve relations between his people and the drakes? Choosing one human and one drake to guard an area he could have thrown a spell around smelled more of foolishness than anything else, but he stuck to the idea. Use the potential for danger to draw them together, something had whispered from the back of his mind.

Advice from Nathan?

Something else was nagging at him. Something about the creature. He had not really come in contact with it yet, but, unlike Gwen, the desire was starting to grow within him. He felt he should know something about it. Touching it, though . . .

It would take the Green Dragon some time to return here. Even at top speed tomorrow was the soonest. He might have asked Gwen to question the inhabitants of the Dagora Forest, but he suspected they knew little save perhaps the path the creature had taken. That no one had sought to warn them before led credence to that. This creature had been a mole, a digger, and probably had passed unseen for the most part.

"We should destroy it," he heard Gwen say.

"Not until the Green Dragon has a chance to see it."

She eyed it with disgust. "I suppose so, but it disturbs me. I—I still feel like it wants to drain me."

Drain her. That was the feeling Cabe had had. This was not an ordinary creature. This was something that had been perverted by some power. This creature was an abomination to nature, to life itself.

Was this Toma's doing?

Cabe shook his head. A possibility, but no more. There were other threats than that one drake. Far too many other threats.

If I could touch it, I would know.

His hand was nearly upon it before he had realized what was happening. With a start, he jerked it back. Gwen, who had turned away, looked back and gasped.

"Cabe! Don't touch it!"

For a brief time, the old Cabe returned, unsure and unwilling to commit himself to such a potentially dangerous task. Then his face hardened, resembling another more and more, a face that Gwen knew well, for she had once loved that person as much as she now loved his grandson.

He muttered something under his breath and the sorceress felt the tug on the powers. The tug became a wrenching, threatening to cut her off from them. Whatever spell was being cast, its potential was far more than any she had ever cast.

The palm of his hand touched the snow-white fur of the creature.

To Cabe it was as if someone had opened up a book to the past and he was watching a story unfold. He was in the Barren Lands, but they were lush, much like they were today. This was long ago, though.

This was the Turning War and he was Nathan Bedlam.

There were others with him. Yalak, who disliked what was about to occur, but had abstained in the voting. Tall Tyr, cloaked like a priest; he heartily approved this measure. Somber Salicia, a tiny woman of tremendous power. Basil, the true warrior of the group. It was up to him to keep the enemy away if they should come before the spell was cast.

There were others, too, but they lurked beneath the ground. Horrible things, twisted from what they had originally been. A spell that Nathan and his companions would never forget; their greatest shame and sin.

The picture vanished, to be replaced by one of the Barren Lands more as Cabe had known them. What remained of life was shriveling fast. Somehow, Cabe/Nathan knew that some of the clans of the Brown Dragon had yet survived; the Dragon Masters had been too human to make full use of the ancient spell. Yet, even as much as they had called forth might be too much, for now the hunger was turning outward, seeking new lands, and the horrible thing was that Cabe/Nathan, as the focus of the spell, hungered with them.

They were a tired and tattered band now. Salicia was dead, torn apart by the hunger as she sought to halt it on her own. Cabe/Nathan felt the revulsion within him as he realized that he had grown stronger with her death, with the . . . the . . .

The revelation refused to come.

Then, the Dragon Masters were combining their might, seeking to turn the flow back upon the creatures that they had twisted. Only with the cessation of hunger could they hope to destroy them all. Yalak had tears in his eyes; he had foreseen all but the death of Salicia—that hurt him the most. Basil was supporting Tyr, ever the faithful companion.

Cabe/Nathan stood with his back before them, haggard, guilt-ridden. If he had known what it was he had unleashed, he would have never suggested it. Better that the spell remain locked forever in the darkest recesses of his subconscious. Better that they lose the war with the Dragon Kings than ever let loose the hunger again.

The mounds of earth were moving toward them, some as great as the dust-covered hills of this region. The Dragon Masters prepared themselves.

Great digging claws broke through the surface and a mountain of white death rose.

Cabe shook violently as that which had been Nathan wrenched him from the horrors of the far past to the terrors of the present. These new memories, however, were drawn from a creature only remotely intelligent, though far older than the ones unleashed by the Masters. The memories were fragmented pictures, much like the communications of the Seekers—not a surprise, considering that the first of this monstrosity's kind had probably been brought forth by the avians themselves. A last-ditch effort to defeat some foe—but the Seekers came to realize that the abominations they were about to unleash were far more of a threat. Better to bury them within the cold, frozen earth and hope there would never be a need. Better to let the lands become the domains of . . . the Draka? The Seekers would wait centuries, if need be.

More disjointed images appeared before Cabe. Long periods of sleep, of darkness, of a tiny, gnawing hunger. Awakening in the cold, hearing the rasping voice of the new master. Knowing joyfully that soon there would be a chance to appease the hunger—if they could appease the hunger of their master first.

A few had been given freedom. They had only to obey the cold ones, the dead ones of the master.

Disobedience! The hunger had been too strong and there was life to the south—but the One They Served had known and punished most of those who had disobeyed! It was not yet time, He had cried angrily at them! Better to flee to the horrid warmth than face the punishment inflicted by that one. There was life there. Life to feed the hunger . . .

Cabe fell back as if lightning had coursed through his form.

Gwen was at his side before he realized it. Her hands passed over his body, seeking any damage. He knew he was unharmed . . . merely drained, exhausted. As if the memory of the creature alone had been enough to pull his life from his body. It had not been Cabe's choice to break contact; he had become engrossed in the images.

It had been Nathan who had broken the link. Almost too late. It had been that part of Cabe which was also a part of his grandfather that had realized that the beast was a conduit and, even dead, it retained some of that facility.

Given a little more time, it would have drained him of everything—all for the one it still sought to serve in death.

Death, cold, and magic of the highest, most dangerous caliber. The images explained much to him. This creature, Cabe knew, had been unleashed by the Ice Dragon to feed a greater spell—but what?

Then, he recalled the frost again.

TOMA WOKE TO find a somber, bone-white figure standing near his chamber. One of the few of Ice's clan that he had seen. Like his lord, the warrior was as thin as a cadaver long dead. The eyes, bright ice blue, were those of a fanatic, a reflection of the Ice Dragon himself. Toma would find no allies with his cousins here. They seemed little more than extensions of their lord.

"What is it? What do you want?" Toma bared his teeth to show that he had no fear, only disdain for this poor excuse for a drake. The warrior ignored the look. Outsiders were to be tolerated as long as the Ice Dragon desired that. Other than that, they were nothing. Even Toma knew that.

"My lord wishes to speak with you." The drake's voice was flat, dead. The ice servants had more life in them.

This was not what Toma had sought. These were not allies, but threats to his existence and that of his parent. Time and time again, the Ice Dragon had made promises concerning the Gold Dragon, promises which Toma saw now were actually twisted threats. What the Lord of the Northern Wastes saw as aid was just the opposite of what the firedrake had sought.

Madness! I am surrounded by a sickness, he realized. *A sickness more dangerous than a hundred Dragon Masters.*

He looked to his parent, but there was no change. The Gold Dragon lay still, his humanoid form stretched across a furred couch with more furs wrapped around the body itself.

Toma rose silently and followed the other drake. He was led along the same corridors he had traversed countless times before and knew now as well as his own mind. He was forbidden to travel them alone now and that was another change that disturbed him. Whatever the Ice Dragon sought to accomplish, it was coming to a head. Already it might be too late for Toma to escape—if escape was what he should do. It was possible that there still might be some way of twisting his host's plans to his own needs. Toma had not become a power behind his father's throne for nothing. What he lacked in a few silly markings he more than made up for in all else.

At last, the two entered the central chamber. For once, the great leviathan was not perched atop the ruins. Toma now saw what had been hidden. There were the remains of the building—a temple, yes—and there was a hole. A vast hole. Far more vast than Toma had imagined. The entire temple must have covered that hole.

He felt a chill run through him the longer he stared at the hole. It was the chill which ran through the soul and so he quickly turned his eyes away, only to find his gaze ensnared by that of his host.

"You have been wondering for some time about that, haven't you?" There was no curiosity in that voice, no emotion whatsoever. The Ice Dragon might very well have been asking Toma if he was enjoying the weather.

Here was another change. The Ice Dragon had transformed to his humanoid form, looking like a drake warrior left frozen in the ice for centuries. The dragon crest had taken on a haunting quality and Toma could not make out any of the features within the false helm. Ice clung to the white drake's form, so much that he looked almost like one of the unliving servants.

Toma finally found his voice. "Yes, I admit to some curiosity. I admit to being curious about a number of things, though by this time I no longer expect to get answers concerning them."

The Ice Dragon chuckled dryly, but the brief display of emotion only served to put Toma more on his guard. His host was playing at life for the firedrake's sake. The master of the bitter Northern Wastes had no more a sense of humor than the snow itself did.

"Spoken like the Toma I know. Still, I can answer some of your questions now, for the time has come for the Final Winter."

"The what?"

"The Final Winter—the answer to the human problem. The cold that will sweep them from the Dragonrealm forever."

Glancing around, Toma noticed suddenly that his guide had been joined by five other drakes, all of whom were positioned strategically near their master's guest. Toma was no fool; he knew his odds of surviving a battle. Best to continue playing the part of audience.

"I admit my ignorance, milord. Tell me of your Final Winter."

It was a mistake. He had asked the very thing that the Ice Dragon had wanted him to ask. He had not played the fool after all. He had *been* a fool.

"I will do better than that, Toma. I will show you."

Strong, cold claws gripped him. He thought to shift to his true form, to take the battle to them, but something held him back. Something prevented him from changing his form.

He was trapped.

"Rest easy, nephew. My warriors only hold you in the extreme possibility that you might lose courage before you look down. I want you to see what it is that I have discovered. I want you to see what I have wrought for the glory of the Dragonrealm!"

Insanity! Toma's mind cried out. He did not want to go near that pit. He did not want to see what was down there, but he seemed to have no strength. The Ice Dragon's warriors dragged him forward much the same way Azran had toted him around after defeating him in the Tyber Mountains. There, Toma had only felt anger and shame at his defeat. Here, he now felt fear for what the humans called the soul.

The steps of the temple were nearly as ruined as the building itself. Bits crumbled as the drakes moved upward. Toma found himself counting each stone step, as if he were heading to his own execution—which was a possibility. Yet, the Ice Dragon had no reason to lie to him. Perhaps, his host merely wanted him to see what lay at the bottom of the pit. The thought did not soothe the firedrake; he had no desire to see the contents of the hole. Not when each step nearer made the chill more numbing.

At last, they stood at the top. His "companions" appeared ready to go no further and Toma almost sighed in relief. That was before four of the undead servants stepped from—somewhere. Within each was some unfortunate creature, at least one a drake not of these clans. The macabre puppets came and replaced the drakes as his guardians and once more the procession moved toward the pit. Toma did not even struggle, despite a voice within that shouted for some resistance. Belatedly, he knew he was under some powerful spell of his host, more powerful than he had imagined the Ice Dragon to be anymore.

They stood at the edge of the pit and it was then that the Ice Dragon spoke. "Lean over, Duke Toma. The hole is deep and only by being directly over can you see my surprise. Rest assured, my servants will prevent you from falling in."

Had he a choice, Toma would have refused. As it was, two of the unliving creatures bent him forward until the upper half of his body was stretched out over the hole. The firedrake's eyes were sealed tightly shut.

When he was not thrown in immediately, he dared to open his eyes a crack. From a crack, they widened, then shut quickly again. One glimpse was all he needed. One glimpse, even from this height, was more than he wanted.

Toma knew things were far worse than even this portended, for then the Ice Dragon was speaking again and his words were nearly as chilling as what the firedrake felt from the thing below.

"She is my queen, hatchling of my brother! She is the future of the furred vermin that have risen to defy our rule! A very short future and a very definitive one! Through her and the children, I will bring a winter down upon the Dragonrealm such as no being has ever seen! A *final* winter! One that shall *forever* cover this land!"

As Toma was dragged back from the pit, he noted with nervousness that, for once, the Ice Dragon spoke with true emotion.

VIII

IT WAS NEARLY noon the next day when he finally trudged over what he knew to be the border between the lands of the two Dragon Kings. There was no sudden change, no marker that proclaimed the sovereignty of one drake over another; it was merely something the Gryphon felt—which meant that there were forces in play here that went beyond the five obvious senses. Subtle ones, he realized, but strung across the land like a great web.

Even before his journey here had barely begun, they knew he was coming—or rather that someone had invaded the lands of Irillian. The Gryphon could only marvel at the spell that draped across this land; it was far more than he would have ever expected. This was a spell of such potency that he suspected it was not part of Dragon King lore. Rather, it was older, perhaps something from the Seekers, perhaps something from one of the races that had come before them, such as the Quel.

Whatever the case, his mission appeared hopeless. D'Shay was no doubt laughing at him even now. Yet he *had* to continue on. He could not say why he was so determined and, when he tried to think about it, the headache returned again. It did not vanish until he put the question from his mind.

"The bird stands in puzzlement; does the bird think to wait for a dragon, perhaps?"

The words were spoken in a tone reminiscent of a drake's hiss but they were accompanied by the sound of water being spewed, as if the speaker had swallowed some liquid beforehand. The Gryphon scanned the area, but all he saw were the damp fields of high grass, several ponds of varying sizes, and a few marsh trees.

"The bird is blind; does the bird need a hand to guide him, perhaps?"

Something tugged at his right hand and the Gryphon jumped away, landing in a combat position with his daggerlike claws extended. His eyes narrowed as he saw the thing slink out of the water of the deepest of the ponds.

It was and it was not a drake. More like an amphibian, a salamander possibly. The Gryphon cursed himself for missing the obvious. The Blue Dragon was a creature of the seas; it should not be surprising that his servants included all sorts of water creatures.

This was it, then. He waited for others to join the first. They would no doubt seek to overwhelm him with their numbers, for the first creature stood no higher than his shoulders and was sleek but not well-muscled. Like drakes, it was scaled and of a greenish tinge.

No others joined it. The creature waited expectantly, its long snout pointed at the Gryphon, sniffing his scent possibly.

"The bird jumps around like an anxious chick seeking food; does the bird think to attack, perhaps?"

Its sentences were almost nonsensical and seemed to flow with a rhythm. It stood in what was almost a squatting position.

The creature sighed and blinked its very large eyes. "The bird is mute as well; does it plan to stand here until the dragons come for it, perhaps?"

"Dragons?"

"The bird speaks; does it plan to speak anymore, perhaps?"

The Gryphon lowered his hands but did not sheathe his talons. "What are you? Are you one of the Blue Dragon's servants or not?"

A long, forked tongue darted out of the water creature's mouth, and caught a passing insect. "The bird is mistaken, obviously; does it not know about the Sheekas, perhaps?"

"Sheekas?" The lionbird puzzled over the unfamiliar title. Possibly . . . "Not—Seekers?"

It grunted. "The wet fowl says 'Seekers'; does it not know their proper name, perhaps?"

The Gryphon bristled. The odd speech patterns of the creature were beginning to tell on his nerves. "Are they the same? Nod yes or no, please."

It nodded.

"You serve them?"

"The bird does not know that all Draka once served the Sheekas; does it think all betrayed the masters, perhaps?"

This was becoming unnerving. The Seekers—or Sheekas—were becoming unusually active. Perhaps their long enslavement by Azran had stirred them to greater action than in the past. Perhaps they were no longer satisfied with watching the world that had once been theirs.

"Are you here to help me?"

The creature nodded.

"At the Seekers' request?"

"The wet one—"

"Yes or no will do."

The amphibian nodded again. Through a pattern of questions, the Gryphon pieced together a story of sorts. The Draka, as the thing was called, had been created to serve the Seekers or Sheekas—obviously the name had been corrupted at some point in the dim past. There were even fewer Draka than Seekers now and most remained hidden unless summoned, but the avians had sent this one to await the Gryphon's coming. The Seekers knew about the warning spell that laced across the land; it was indeed one of theirs.

Much of what the servant spoke of made little or no sense to the lionbird, but he did come to understand that the Draka would lead him along the safest path until they neared Irillian. It refused to say what bothered the Seekers so much that they had decided to deal with an outsider.

"What about the warning spell? They'll know where we are at all times."

"Bird thinks Draka stupid; does bird think Sheekas not prepared for own spell, perhaps?"

The squatting creature held out one webbed hand, revealing a symbol etched into its palm. "Loyal Draka will never be seen by the hatchlings of nest vermin."

It was said as bluntly as was probably possible for the amphibian, and it was filled with hints of past events the Gryphon would have liked to discuss.

"The bird is silent again; does that mean we can move on, perhaps?" It was quite obviously annoyed at wasting so much time.

The Gryphon opened his beak and then shut it tight. If the Seekers were coming to his aid, he would not turn such a powerful alliance down. He knew, though, that it was temporary at best, for the Seekers would always have their own interests at heart first and the Gryphon suspected said interests did not coincide with those of the humans.

With something resembling a cross between walking and hopping, the Draka led the way. The ground was soft and moist and stable footing was at a premium. The Gryphon hoped that his mysterious guide was correct and that he was now invisible to the all-seeing spell that the Blue Dragon had shrouded his domain with.

He almost hoped D'Shay had been there to see his quarry vanish. It was a minor but very satisfying thought and he held on to it for much of the journey.

In the first hour of their journey, they passed several streams, two or three lakes, a marsh, and, at last, a raging river. The Draka was very specific about the path they took, so much as to chide the Gryphon for stepping too close to one of the lakes. The lionbird would have asked what the danger was, but then the lake had started bubbling and the Draka had ordered the Gryphon to keep his beak shut tight. After a few seconds, the bubbling ceased. The amphibian signaled for him to follow once again.

The river was more of a problem. It was obvious that the Draka normally would have swum across it and, despite his aversion to any task that forced him into a body of water larger than a pond, the Gryphon could have done the same. Still, the Draka seemed to think that it was a bad idea.

Too many Regga was the answer that he finally got out of the amphibian.

The Draka did not bother to explain what Regga were save that they had almost met one back at the lake.

The Gryphon's guide located a tiny body of water and proceeded to wipe water over its skin in order to keep it from drying out. It stared at the river and then at the lionbird.

"Regga watch the lands; do they watch the misty paths, perhaps?" it mumbled to itself.

"What are the—"

He received a hiss in response. The Draka glared at him with its huge, round eyes and motioned for complete silence again.

"Misty paths," it mumbled again after several seconds of thought. In the Gryphon's eyes, the creature seemed confused, as if it had made a decision it was not certain about. As if—

His own head started to pound. This time, the Gryphon tried to hold on to the feeling, despite the annoyance of it. There was something not right about the way he had been acting. In all his years as both soldier and ruler, he had never made so many abrupt decisions.

The Draka chose that moment to seek his attention and all of his thoughts vanished as he remembered how urgently he had to get to Irillian. The pounding ceased.

"No talk from bird; does bird think that possible, perhaps?"

The Gryphon nodded. Not completely satisfied, the Draka nonetheless began to lead his charge once more—but away from the river. The Gryphon hesitated. He might not know the land the way this creature did, but he did know they had to cross this river if they wanted to get to Irillian. The lionbird almost opened his mouth to speak, but finally decided to let the amphibian have its way for the time being. It could not be so stupid as to believe he did not know which way to go; therefore, it had an alternate route in mind. Something about "misty paths" . . .

They were almost out of sight of the river when the Draka came to a dead halt before a tiny pond. Tiny frogs and crabs moved about the area and water bugs skittered on the pond floor. It could not have been more than two feet at its deepest point. Though the Gryphon could see no reason to stop here, his guide seemed very satisfied with what it saw. It began drawing patterns on the surface of the pond.

Just when he was about to finally say something, the Gryphon froze and stared. The bottom of the pond was shimmering as if it really was not there. He blinked and it was *not* there. Instead, he saw a stairway that led down so deep that he could not see the end of it. It was old and made of crude stone blocks left unadorned, but it was a stairway nonetheless.

"The path is open; does the bird wish to take it, or wait for the Regga or some other servant of the blue one, perhaps?"

The Gryphon's mane bristled. "Down there? I don't breathe water too well, friend."

"The Draka is not stupid; can the bird say the same, perhaps?"

In other words, the lionbird thought, *the stairway will protect you, idiot.* Where was his mind?

His guide glanced toward the river. The Gryphon followed his gaze and saw that the surface of the river was frothing.

"Regga!" the amphibian hissed, forgetting his usual singsong speeches. He pushed his charge toward the stairway. The Gryphon did not argue, but he could not help moving with some trepidation. It still *looked* like it was covered by water. His first step did nothing to help the situation. His boot came down on the first step with a *splat* of water. The Draka urged him on. The river, meanwhile, frothed even greater, as if something were seeking to manifest itself.

Taking a deep breath, the Gryphon ran down the steps.

Water closed about his head and he briefly felt a dampness. He almost panicked, but then the water was gone and he found himself a dozen steps down a walled stairwell. Looking up, the former mercenary saw nothing but ceiling. The stairs seemed to lead down directly from it. He could see no opening. Turning his attention to the lower steps, he saw that they ended about twenty feet lower at what was probably a hallway.

"The stairs move nowhere; does the bird think they will do the walking for him, perhaps?"

He almost stumbled down the entire flight. The Draka stood on the higher steps, grinning its malevolent-looking smile. It practically sat on the steps, so wide was its stance.

"Where are we? The name only, if you please."

The amphibian snorted, but it merely said, "The misty paths."

"A portal of some sort?"

This time, the Draka only grunted. It waved him on and started waddling down after him. The Gryphon followed the stairway to the bottom and then paused. A single hallway met his gaze. While it was not gloomy—or, as he had figured, completely dark—it was still not very inviting. Menacing was the word he would have chosen.

He could see how this path had gotten its name. Less than five feet down, the entire corridor faded into a white mist so thick that he wondered whether he would have to chop his way through it. What was worse was that it seemed to beckon to him, to be inviting him to enter.

Behind him, he heard the Draka snort in derision—and then moist hands were pushing him forward. The mist enveloped him.

The walls, the ceiling, everything was gone. The Gryphon wondered briefly how he was supposed to find his way through this fog. Then, he saw a vague figure in the mists ahead of him. It beckoned to him, slowly at first and then impatiently when he did not move. The Draka, he realized. It had gotten ahead of him and was trying to lead him. He followed after the creature, but, despite his best efforts, he could not catch up to it. He thought about calling out, but was not certain that would not attract some denizen of this region that he would regret meeting.

Always his guide succeeded in staying just ahead of him. The Gryphon never saw more than a vague arm or backside. If he ever completely lost sight of the Draka, the lionbird doubted that he would ever find his way back.

How long he wandered, it was impossible to say with any certainty. Two or three hours—maybe. The Gryphon hoped they were at least far beyond the river. Whatever the Regga were or was, they or it seemed to be well respected by the Draka. Respected enough to be avoided.

The path was unearthly silent. The Gryphon could not even hear his footfalls. He even tried slamming one boot on the ground, but all he achieved was a muted thud that no one who was not standing right next to him would have heard. The silence and lack of sights made him turn to his thoughts.

His desire to reach Irillian had dwindled to little more than a shadow of itself. The Gryphon began contemplating all the dangers of entering a city directly controlled by a Dragon King. Irillian by the Sea was one of the most loyal human cities in existence. He could really not blame them. The Blue Dragon had always treated his subjects fairly and he could not be condemned for the ways of his brethren. The Dragon Kings did only what they themselves chose to do; the only other being who had any say over them was their emperor—and no one, save Toma, perhaps, knew whether he still lived or not.

The more he thought about it, the more he wondered about his sudden decision. When the throbbing that had previously prevented him from continuing such a line of thought failed to do so this time, it finally dawned on him what had happened.

Like a fish on a line, he had been played with and led to the net—and the claws that held that net undoubtedly belonged to the master of Irillian.

He would have tried to turn back then, but it came to him that his guide had vanished while his mind had wandered. The Gryphon took a step forward and tripped. He put his hands up to stop his fall and met resistance. Stone, but not a wall. The mist began to dissipate.

His eyes focused on another stairway, this time leading upward. The Gryphon's first thought was that he had somehow turned around in the mists. He looked around for the Draka and discovered the creature just exiting the misty path.

"How did you get behind me?"

"The Draka has always been behind you; does—"

The Gryphon cut him off. "You were in *front* of me. You led me here!"

"The Draka has always been behind the bird; does the bird not know of the mist dwellers?"

"Mist dwellers?"

Snorting, the amphibian lumbered past the Gryphon and up the stairs. He turned back to his charge just long enough to say, "Follow."

Evidently, the Draka was not going to elaborate on the mist dwellers. The Gryphon came to the conclusion that it was probably best he did not learn more. There were probably dangers on the path that he would not have wanted to know about.

He stopped momentarily when the Draka vanished from the steps, then realized that this was the same way that both of them had entered. Bracing himself, he continued up, trying to ignore the ceiling that he appeared about to walk into head first. The ceiling—and the stairway—vanished just as the top of his head was about to touch stone. The Gryphon now found himself standing near a dark, damp tunnel.

It stank, too.

The Draka waited impatiently while he got his bearings. "Where are we?"

"Destination," the creature mumbled. It cared for the stench as little as the lionbird did. Talking meant having to breathe more.

"Destination?" Had he a nose to wrinkle, the Gryphon would have. Where would—

The tunnel was part of a *sewer system*. A vast sewer system. The Gryphon turned his gaze upward. A huge wall encompassed nearly all of his view. It ran on as far as he could see. A city, then. He sniffed and recognized at least part of the source of the stench. Rotting fish. More than that. A smell he recalled from the past with disgust. The smell of the sea.

"Irillian!"

The Draka nodded slowly. "Destination," it muttered again.

"Where is he?"

D'Shay was furious, almost insanely so, and D'Laque knew better than to answer him now, at least with the unhelpful and unnecessary answer he had to give him. The Gryphon had simply disappeared. The crystal which monitored the spell lying across all Irillian and her surrounding lands was blank where the lionbird was concerned. The few things it did reveal were the occasional border crossings of drake patrols from the domain of the Storm King. These were tolerated by the lord of Irillian so long as they lasted no more than a few minutes.

"He is not to be found," rumbled a voice akin to a wave breaking on the rocks.

D'Laque winced and prayed that his superior would not say something to offend their host. D'Shay's mouth, however, was clamped tight as he sought control over his emotions. He was not quite so far gone that he was willing to snap at what was most definitely a potential ally.

"Is there, perhaps, something wrong with the spell? Does it no longer cover the land?" Both questions were asked with the greatest politeness and only D'Laque read the sneer behind them.

May the Ravager guard us if he loses his reserve, the wolf raider thought.

The Dragon King raised his massive head, water still dripping from his muzzle. The Blue Dragon was at home in the Eastern Seas and it was there that he conducted the business of ruling both the land and the waters of Irillian. He was sleeker than his brethren, more like a serpent than a dragon. His paws were webbed so that he could swim and he was longer than any other Dragon King, though that length did not make him the largest in terms of mass. His eyes seemed to have no color save whatever was reflected to them by the water. It was disconcerting to D'Laque, who understood that some of the other Dragon Kings had features which made those of the Blue Dragon look rather ordinary and commonplace—which he most certainly was not.

"The spell is perfect; I cast it myself."

"Then, where is he?"

The dragon eyed him coldly. "There are other powers than those of the Kings. They may, for a time, be an annoyance. He will be found."

"He must be."

D'Laque flinched. The Blue Dragon leaned forward so that his head was no more than an arm's length from the two men. The smaller raider took a step back, overwhelmed by the size. The room was suddenly filled with the smells of the seas.

"The Gryphon's capture is of as much importance to me as it is to you, manling. He owes for the death of at least one of my royal brethren."

Reality had at last reached D'Shay. He nodded quickly and then added a bow. "Forgive me, milord. There are certain—passions—which I normally keep in check, but have of late found difficult to do. I apologize if I have appeared impertinent."

No one believed the apology, least of all the Dragon King, but it was accepted by the drake with a tip of his head, bringing his snout to within a foot of his "guests."

The Blue Dragon pulled back and closed his eyes as if in contemplation. Both wolf raiders were familiar with this routine by now, as they had observed it countless times. It was the Dragon King's way of organizing his thoughts, of deciding which matters were of the utmost importance. On the surface, it seemed trivial. Yet, the Blue Dragon ruled most securely of all the Kings, save one.

It was that one which concerned the dragon now. "There is no news from the Wastes. Your agent and my guides have ceased to be."

D'Shay looked at D'Laque, who cleared his throat and replied, "If D'Karin is dead, we would have known."

"Hmm?" The dragon seemed to find this mildly humorous. "Ah yes, your little tokens. Paltry pieces of power when compared to the glories of my kind."

This time, it was D'Laque who almost lost control. D'Laque was a trained keeper and carried a Ravager's Tooth, which marked every wolf raider under his Pack Leader's command. Anyone marked by a fragment—a scratch was all that was necessary providing there was blood—was attuned to it. Pack Leaders used it to keep in contact with their spies and their staffs. One only had to think of the person. The keepers, made highly attuned by continual marking, were guardians. If something happened to the fragment, the keeper reacted as if someone had stolen part of his very soul. Needless to say, D'Laque and his kind were very sensitive about their duties.

D'Shay put a hand on his companion's arm. "Explain to our host why we cannot verify what he says."

The other raider nodded gruffly. "D'Karin's death would leave a shadow of his soul within the Tooth. It is that part that each of us owes the Ravager and at death we willingly give it up. When I think of D'Karin, there is only blankness; he is invisible to us, yes, but I have neither seen nor felt that bit of his soul pass within."

The Blue Dragon looked on with mild interest now. "I should like to see this—tooth—sometime. Perhaps it is like a Demon's Cup, a spell for ensnaring the souls of one's enemies."

"It is nothing of the sort!" shouted D'Laque. The sudden look of anger on the Dragon King's massive visage sent a shiver through him that broke the rage. "It is from the Ravager."

Having no interest in what he considered the worship of a lump of rock, the dragon returned to his original thoughts. "Whether your man is dead or not, he, like the Gryphon, is hidden from our eyes. I like it not. I am sealing the north shores of my domain from all. I am sending an emissary of my own to my brother. The time for games is far past. With the chaos created by the emergence of this new Bedlam, there has been too much trickery, too much treachery. If the Northern Wastes are now a threat to the security of my kingdom, I must deal with that threat first—and I cannot afford to become your back door at the same time."

"What?" shouted both men. D'Laque turned to his superior. D'Shay stroked his finely clipped beard. "We have an agreement."

The dragon laughed mockingly. "So far, I have only seen and heard of your wants. I have seen nothing profitable. Brother Black dealt with you. See how his lands fare now. I cannot afford to waste my time if my chilling brother has become a danger."

"The Gryphon—" D'Shay began.

The eyes of their host burned through them. The two raiders fell silent. The Blue Dragon studied them, especially D'Shay, for some time before speaking again. When he did, it was with a knowing smile.

"Let me offer you a . . . deal. Bring me the Gryphon, manling, and I will reconsider your request. Yessss . . . My emissary to the Northern Wastes must bring a gift to my brother. What better to open the gates than a prize like the lionbird?"

D'Shay almost turned down the second chance, but he thought better of it. There was one that he had to answer to if he failed—and the death of the Gryphon, regardless of who was responsible, would please that one greatly. "Very well, milord. I will give you the Gryphon. We know he is coming here; the only question is when and where in the city. You'll have his head before long."

The Blue Dragon chuckled again, for D'Shay's true desires were evident. The drake drove in another nail. "No, raider. Not just his head. I want the whole body, alive and breathing. More or less unharmed, in fact."

The aristocratic visage of the wolf raider darkened considerably.

"That is my offer," the Dragon King continued. "Take it or leave it."

After a moment, D'Shay finally nodded curtly. Without another word, he turned and stalked from the cavern. D'Laque quickly bowed and followed.

The Blue Dragon watched them depart, a savage reptilian smile that D'Shay would have questioned spreading across his visage.

IX

A S HE STARED at the quite sturdy walls of the city, walls which appeared to stand taller than two full-grown dragons and which were remarkably smooth—climbing was out of the question—the Gryphon thought seriously about turning around and demanding that the Draka lead him back to Penacles.

Irillian by the Sea had always had walls; he knew that long ago. He had never known that they were so incredibly high or that the smoothness of the sides could only be compared to a well-formed pearl. The comparison was more apt than he knew. The Blue Dragon did, after all, have the resources of the Eastern Seas to draw upon.

"The bird goggles at the walls of the city; does the bird really intend the folly of scaling the walls, perhaps?"

Even in the darkness, the Gryphon could tell the squatting amphibian was smiling as best as his jaws permitted. It ruffled his feathers, but he held his peace. The Draka had, after all, performed the function he had promised. The Gryphon was safely at the edge of the city. Not only that, but, thanks to the paths that the creature still refused to explain, he had covered in mere hours what should have taken days.

"You have another way?"

"The bird must be a fish; does he dare be a fish, perhaps?"

"A fish?"

The Draka indicated the grate behind them. With his webbed hands, he removed much of the rotted plant growth on it. "The bird is strong; does the bird have a stomach to match, perhaps?"

It was not necessary to ask what the thing meant, for removing the generations of rotted plant life released an even more foul stench than the Gryphon would have thought possible.

"This *is* part of the sewage system, I gather."

The Draka nodded, chuckling throatily at the other's predicament. "The Draka goes no further; does the bird think he can find his own way, perhaps?"

Coward! thought the Gryphon wryly. The stench was almost enough to keep him from moving on. Years and years of decaying garbage, much of it fish, had given the sewage system a unique, powerful scent. Yet, he had no choice. He had to go on.

"Draka." The creature gazed up at him. "Why are the Seekers willing to help me? Why did the Storm Dragon allow me to pass through his lands? He knew I was there."

Shaking its head as a parent might do when asked inane questions by a small child, the Draka replied patiently, "The Storm Dragon does what the Storm Dragon desires; does the bird think such arrogant creatures obey the Sheekas, perhaps?"

Much as it tore at him, the Gryphon had no time to question the creature about the exact relationship between drakes and the Draka.

His guide raised a webbed hand as if indicating a major point. "Manlings differ on many things of import; does the bird think the Sheekas are any different?"

Meaning that not all Seekers were in favor of this assistance and that the lionbird should be moving on. The Gryphon nodded understanding and, taking a last deep breath, stepped into the sewage tunnel. The tunnel was a hand's width higher than him and about half his height in width. Brackish water rose over his ankles.

Behind him, the grate closed. He turned to see the Draka replacing the dead foliage with great care. The Gryphon cocked his head and chuckled. How infuriated the Blue Dragon would have been had he only known his vast defenses could be penetrated at any time by a creature such as the Draka—which was not to put the amphibian's abilities down. He could certainly not deny it himself.

He expected some last word from the Draka, but perhaps that was an expectation originating from his years in human company, for his guide merely shuffled off, perhaps to return to its home. If the Gryphon survived, which he never took for granted, he planned to see what the libraries beneath Penacles might have to say about the Draka—and how they might relate to the Dragon Kings.

He wondered if once Dragon Kings had served the Seekers? Small wonder, then, that the ruling drakes often inhabited former dwellings of the avians.

The odors of the sewage system began demanding his attention and he suddenly realized that it might be hours before he was out of here. The thought sent both fur and feather up in disgust and the lionbird set out without further hesitation, less concerned with locating D'Shay specifically as he was with finding a good, safe place to depart this underworld. Preferably the sooner the better.

His passage was preceded and followed by numerous ripples as he sloshed his way down the tunnel. As if the odor was not bad enough, he now had trouble remembering the last time he had been, if not dry, at least minimally damp.

He was several minutes into the depths of the system when it dawned on him that he was no longer protected by the spell carried by the Draka. His thoughts turned to treachery, to carelessness, and then puzzlement. If it had been a trap, it was certainly an intricate and confusing one. There would be no reason for such a charade. They could have had him long before now.

The Gryphon continued on, but there was always the nagging doubt in his mind, strengthened by the idea that he truly could not say he understood the workings of the Seeker mind. For all he knew, such a convoluted trap was normal for them. They were certainly unpredictable.

An odd ripple in the water told him suddenly that he was not alone in the sewers.

It slithered down a side tunnel, but in the very dim light that slipped through the occasional vent, he made out what could only be its hind quarters and tail. The tail was incredibly long and probably thicker than his arm. Unless the creature was mostly tail—and the short glimpse of the back legs did not back up that assumption—the lionbird's temporary companion was about twice as large as he. He hoped it was a plant-eater or, at the very least, something satisfied with rats and other tiny scavengers that made their homes down here. Whatever the case, it soon became evident that the thing was not headed back his way. The Gryphon gave a sigh of relief, but kept a sharper look out just in case his visitor had a mate or family.

The terrible odor seemed to lessen as time went on, though it might have been that he had just become more used to it. Light was rare at best; more than once he stumbled, but fortunately never so that he fell face-first into the muck. At one point, the object over which he had stumbled proved to be a corpse of something—human, drake, or whatever—but the Gryphon had no intention of discovering its true identity. It was possible that what had killed this creature, and made off with most of the lower half of the body as well, was still near.

The Draka had not given him any directions, and the Gryphon had assumed that meant he was to find a safe exit as soon as possible. He had passed two already, but both of those had been rusted shut and to open them would have required much more noise than he was willing to make. The third door proved in better condition, but he was forced to ignore that one because feet kept rambling across topside.

After what he estimated to be a little over two hours, he found a functional, deserted exit. Peering through a vent, the Gryphon assured himself of that before climbing back to the surface. After getting this far, he had no intention of turning back and spending even more time in the sewer. The memories he had already were more than enough.

There was a slight sea breeze which irritated his system. The sea always reminded him of that day so long ago, a past memory too deep to forget. His battered figure on the beach, the mind never fully recovering. Fortunate it was that he had not drifted to the shores of Irillian. The Gryphon's tale would have ended before it had begun.

He found himself in a street not far from the seashore itself. A few figures moved slowly in the distance. The Gryphon shrank against a wall when he recognized them for what they were. Guards. A patrol, perhaps.

This was insane, he knew. Insane, but highly invigorating. The chase always was, regardless of the obstacles. It was one of the things he missed as ruler. It was one of the reasons he sometimes contemplated leaving Penacles to Toos.

At first, he was tempted to go back into the sewers and see if they could bring him nearer to where the maps had said the Marshal's residence was. If anyone knew where D'Shay might be staying, it would be the Dragon King's human aide. The Gryphon doubted he would have too much trouble getting inside. Security was more slack in this city than in his own.

In order to move about on the surface, he would have to risk shapeshifting. It was a chancy thing; even inherent form-change, such as he or the drakes were capable of doing, disturbed the lines and fields of power—or the spectrum, if one believed in that theory of magic. There was a chance that the Blue Dragon would be observant enough to catch it. Still, it *would* be easier than trying to skulk about the city or, worse yet, returning to the sewer for a second engagement with the aroma of city life.

The Gryphon moved around a corner and *changed.*

It was over in less than a minute. He peeked back around the corner, but the guards were no longer in sight. Drawing his cloak about him, he stepped out into the open. How much time he had until dawn he could not accurately say, but he knew he had more than enough to make it to safety, if necessary. As far gone as he had been during his "obsession," he had remembered to check the maps for places of safety, places that sentries and such assumed were too obvious to check thoroughly.

For the first few minutes he passed only a few people, late-night revelers and those who made their money in the night—how was debatable. A few were cloaked like him. This was not, he decided, one of the better districts of Irillian, which was probably to his advantage.

One patrol passed by, but far enough away that they did not even notice him. His worst moment actually came when a rather seedy creature he assumed to be a female stumbled up and offered to show him tricks that would have required amazing flexibility on both their parts. His first refusal fell on deaf ears and only when he gave her a coin did she leave. Much to his surprise, he discovered that the commotion had disturbed no one. This district was apparently seedier than he had first imagined.

His decision to locate the Marshal's home for the information he needed vanished as he turned the next corner. It was a credit to the Gryphon's years as both king and mercenary that he did not stop in his tracks and stare open-mouthed. The six wolf raiders stumbling out of the tavern would have spotted him in a second.

Stumbling was perhaps the wrong word. It was true that they were definitely inebriated, but they were not so drunk that their guards were completely down. Their uniforms were still in good order and they studied their surroundings with clear eyes. One of them mumbled something about there being no hurry; the ship was not going out until dawn. The other, an apparent officer, reprimanded the first.

"The serpent's fur's up," the officer reminded his companions, unmindful of the fanciful image he had created. "He's decided we should have the ship out of port by sunrise."

"What about the Fox?" From the way one of the other raiders asked, the Gryphon took the last word for a name, not merely an animal.

"That shifty one'll be staying here, along with the keeper. There's something up, and I think it'll make the difference between us staying here and having to go back and face the Pack Master with nothing but empty holds."

There was an almost simultaneous shiver from the six. None of them was eager to face their superiors.

Little more was said than that. Talk of the one called the Fox and the danger of returning home empty-handed to their superiors had dampened the spirits of the group. Now they were all eager to return to the ship and make preparations. If they made a good showing for Irillian's master, it might help in their efforts to secure a port here. The Gryphon debated on continuing on his present course or following the six black figures. He finally chose the latter.

Wolf raiders permanently based in Irillian. The thought did not settle well with the lionbird. He knew who the Fox was without even guessing; D'Shay would be the one in charge here, just as he had been when dealing in Lochivar with the Black Dragon.

There was something about the raiders' mood, though, that hinted of a change in circumstances. Now and then they talked of home as if things were not going as expected. The enemy, whom they did not name other than by colorful metaphors, was still holding its own, and there was talk that this port here was actually an emergency measure should the tide really turn against the Aramites—which was what the wolf raiders called themselves.

Aramites? The name struck a chord far back in the deep recesses of the Gryphon's memories. He knew them, knew of them, but, whatever he knew, it would not as yet come to him. He cursed silently and continued to shadow the six figures.

They were heading toward the docks. The lionbird slowed, knowing he could observe them from a longer distance and thereby lessen the chance that they might discover he was following them.

Behind him, a boot scraped against stone.

The Gryphon did not whirl, did not give any indication that he had heard anything. Instead, he moved on after the Aramites, but more slowly than before. When they turned a corner, he waited a count of twenty and followed suit.

The wolf raiders were already some distance ahead. The Gryphon gazed around and smiled.

Only a minute or two later, a dark figure stepped quietly around the corner—and paused. The wolf raiders were long hidden by the night, but the one following them should have been visible. Immediately, the figure looked upward, but, if he had expected to see his quarry clinging to one of the walls, he was disappointed.

One hand opened and suddenly there was a knife in it. The figure pressed against one wall and took a step forward.

A longer, much sharper blade than the one he carried flashed before his eyes and then came to rest against his jugular vein.

The Gryphon reached from behind his prisoner and took the other's knife. "You were," he whispered, "looking for me, I assume. I know you are not a common mugger, so it may be that you work for our six friends. Anything to say?"

"Urk."

"Not too loudly. I have sharper tools than this little blade at your throat." He relaxed the touch of the knife just a bit.

"Know—knowledge is a danger—dangerous thing."

"Eh?" The Gryphon whirled his prisoner around. "Where did you hear that?"

The man, who looked and smelled like a fisherman, clamped his mouth shut.

Understanding dawned. The Gryphon nodded. "But only if misused. That's what you are waiting for, isn't it? Has to be. Toos made that up."

"No names, you fool!" the man hissed. "Didn't they teach you that?"

"You're right." The Gryphon studied the man closely. This was one of his spies, apparently. His nose, now that he had one, wrinkled at the smell of fish. Evidently, spying meant you did not have to bathe too often—if at all. "Why were you following me?"

"I wasn't, idiot. I was following them. Orders. I saw you and knew that no sane mugger would go after six of those hounds. You had to be like me. How'd you get around me? Who set you on them?" It was obvious that the man's opinion of the Gryphon was getting worse and worse. The lionbird was tempted to tell him who he was, but thought better of it.

"My secrets," the Gryphon said with a thin smile. With his agility, even as a human, it had proved no problem to climb up one side of the building and climb back down another—behind his shadow.

"Is it a secret why you're on my mission?"

"I have my own mission—which is to find the one called D'Shay. They were my guide."

That made the fisherman's eyes widen. "I wouldn't wish that for anything—but you're wrong, my quick friend, about that one. No one's seen him for days, except maybe the Lord and Master of this city."

"I—" The Gryphon froze. It occurred to him that he might find information concerning his adversary down on the beach.

Down on the beach? He shook his head. Where had that thought come from?

A familiar pounding filled his head. The grubby fisherman/spy took hold of his arm. "You okay?"

Not this time, the Gryphon thought madly. *Not this time!* He had been found much sooner than he had expected! Perhaps his earlier transformation *had* been noticed.

"Eye of the hurricane!" the other whispered in shock. "You're—you're changing into something!"

The lionbird glanced down at his hand as he tried to fight off the mental thrust. He was losing his human form and, in the eyes of his compatriot, that meant that the powers-that-be in Irillian had discovered him.

Go to the beach of your own free will, then, something boomed in his head. *You will be unharmed. You have come this far. Will you back out now?*

"Get out!" rasped the Gryphon. His nameless associate took this to mean him and darted off. Under other circumstances, the Gryphon would have been disappointed in the man, but now it was better that he had departed.

Come to the beach. The beach facing the sea caverns.

His mind was suddenly his own again. He stared at his hands and felt his face. The transformation was now complete. He was once more the creature that had, during his first encounter in the Dragonrealm, caused an entire village to run off in fear and panic.

I'm coming, he thought at his would-be master, *and my mind will stay mine or else.*

He received no acknowledgment.

The shoreline was not difficult to find nor was that particular beach, but it was getting too close to daylight as far as the Gryphon was concerned.

A boat might prove necessary, the Gryphon determined with a shudder. Over the years, he had grown more or less accustomed to rivers and lakes, but the sea still unnerved him. He could now suddenly recall the taste of salt in his mouth; the horror of fighting for each breath as all the water in the world seemed to be forcing its way into his lungs.

These were not memories he was familiar with. These were memories he had blotted out over the years. Now the vivid terror of those memories came back as well. The feathers and hair on his body rose in shivers.

He was afraid. Afraid that this time the Eastern Seas would take him for good. Afraid that this was what D'Shay had planned for all this time, though that was likely not to be the case. Had his mental adversary chosen to strike again at that moment, he could not be certain that he would have had the necessary concentration to fight back successfully.

The night was slipping away. Come the dawn, he would be trapped. There was nowhere to hide unless he returned to the sewers, and he doubted there was time to reach them. Long before the first rays of light struck the rippling water, the fishermen would begin their day. It was the best time to catch in this region. There was some saying about that, but the Gryphon forced such trivial thoughts from his mind and wondered impatiently if he had walked into the dragon's jaws of his own free will after all.

He gazed at the boats that dotted the shoreline, large black lumps in the dark that might have been an invasion of giant slumbering turtles, and then turned his gaze once more to the moonlit water. *Well?* he projected.

As if in answer a tiny black dot appeared on the sea, between the jagged caverns out in the distance and the beach he now crouched on. It was a boat, he knew, but who was in it he could not say. A single figure, that was all he could make out.

The boat grew only a bit in size, becoming large enough to hold perhaps six or seven people. It had one lone sail, which was open and full despite the wind blowing in the wrong direction. The boatman was still a mystery.

When it became apparent that the boat would go no further, the figure climbed out and began to pull it in by hand, which spoke volumes of its strength. All the while, it gazed—at least, the Gryphon thought it gazed— at him. At last, he was able to see that the being was wrapped from head to foot in what resembled a shroud. Even the hands and feet were not visible. No simple fisherman this. Likely not even human.

The Gryphon rose. "Are you the one who has tried to lead me around like a puppet?"

The formless boatman shook his head and indicated for the lionbird to board. He did so without hesitation, knowing it was foolish to attempt any-thing else—and was this not what he had wanted all along?

When he was aboard, the boatman, seemingly unhindered by the added weight, shoved the vessel back out to sea. The Gryphon sat down and stared out in the general direction of his destination. Effortlessly, the shrouded figure maneuvered the boat around. Once more, the sail was full of wind, though the single passenger could feel nothing.

"How long will it take?" he asked the boatman.

The being did not respond, intent now on the sailing of the boat. He turned his attention to the sea caverns, where the vessel was indeed headed. The Blue Dragon had gone through a lot of trouble to bring him here and, judging by the tone of the last attempt, that meant that he needed the Gryphon. Desperately.

Why?

The thought of what would disturb one such as the Blue Dragon was almost as unnerving as the thought of entering the citadel of the Dragon King himself.

X

THE GREEN DRAGON arrived without warning. No one, not even those of his own clan, knew it until he called forth from the outskirts of the protective spell. Ssarekai was with him, the drake looking as important as he could in such august company. They were not alone. By the crests, a good six of the royal drakes of the Clan Green were there. Cabe identified only one of rank duke but quickly realized someone had to be in charge when the lord was away. The others served as commanders.

He glanced around at the hastily assembling throng. "You wished to see me concerning something of great import. Coincidentally, I wish to see you for the same reason."

Not encouraging first words, Cabe thought.

As the minor drakes lumbered in, the inhabitants noticed for the first time the bundle on the back of one. It was man-sized and there was no question as to what was wrapped within. Cabe and Gwen stared at each other and then back at the bundle. Definitely not encouraging, Cabe re-peated to himself.

The Green Dragon dismounted and handed the reins of his beast to

Ssarekai, who bowed as low as possible, which was difficult considering he had not yet dismounted himself. The drake lord made directly for the two magic-users and his walk indicated that he was disturbed. Greatly disturbed.

"Well," he said upon reaching them. "Shall you begin or shall I?"

"What—who is that?" Gwen finally blurted out.

"I do not know." From his tone, that bothered the drake at least as much as the corpse's presence—wherever that had been. "If I may be permitted to include one more member in our party?"

Cabe nodded.

Snapping his fingers, the Green Dragon summoned forth an individual that no one had managed to notice before now. A tall, narrow fellow who reminded Cabe of the man who had pretended to be his father for so many years, Nathan's friend and with elf blood to boot. His true name had been Hadeen something, so Gwen had said. This was Hadeen again, only more so. The blood was pure in this one.

"This is Haiden, one of my—eyes in the north."

The similarity in names startled Cabe, but he suspected there was no further relationship between this elf and Hadeen save the blood of that older race.

Haiden bowed, he, like Hadeen, a definite contrast to the tinier, more annoying sprites that Cabe had encountered in the past. Cabe understood that the taller elves were very sensitive about maintaining the distinction between the two types. Like many humans, they found their smaller cousins troublesome.

"Lady of the Amber, Cabe Bedlam." He looked up at both of them—admiringly at Gwen and in slight awe of Cabe, not only because he was Nathan Bedlam's grandson, but because his hair today was nearly all silver. It had remained that way since contact with the creature. Both sorcerers assumed there was a connection.

"It was Haiden's people who I sent to scout the rim of my brother's domain."

"The Northern Wastes?" Cabe blurted out. The Northern Wastes and their monarch were the kind of places he had heard about in fright stories as a child. No one save the Dragon Kings really had any traffic with the denizens of that numbing place.

"Yes, the Northern Wastes." The drake lord eyed Cabe with unease. "It was there that they found this."

Two drakes carried the bundle to the little group. One of them began to untie it until Gwen raised her hand. A number of servants had gathered, as they had when Cabe had discovered the creature. She looked from her husband to the Dragon King.

The Green Dragon gazed down at the bundle and then at the assembled group of humans and drakes. He turned his attention back to the lord and lady of the place. "It is your decision. In my opinion, they should be made aware of this. The unfortunate within is only one of many."

Cabe nodded agreement and Gwen indicated for the drake to continue.

They almost regretted that decision. The corpse was perfectly preserved, and the look on the man's face—what remained of it—revealed that he had not died easily. Haiden, who surely must have seen the body several times, turned away after a few moments. Many of those assembled stepped away and an uneasy murmur grew. The Green Dragon and Cabe both stared at it with the greatest intensity. Gwen found herself looking away and then forcing herself to look back again, only to repeat herself twice.

She finally dared put a hand near it. "It's cold. Colder than . . . than *death*."

Cabe understood what she meant immediately, though not because of her emphasis. He understood because, as with the creature, he was seeing another time, another place, and things similar to the dead monstrosity.

There had also been corpses such as this in the memories of his grandfather. He had not understood them at the time, but Cabe knew now that they had suffered the same fate as the drake clans of the Barren Lands.

"Don't touch it," Cabe finally muttered.

Though she had no intention of doing such a thing, Gwen still asked, "Why?"

"You wouldn't like it. It—it's like the absence of all life force. As if everything including the soul had been yanked out and replaced by—nothing. Absolutely nothing."

Gwen pulled her hand away for fear she might accidentally brush the body with her fingertips. "What happened to him? Who was he?"

"A wolf raider. Look at the crest on his helm." Cabe recalled a conversation he had had with the Gryphon after the final encounter with Azran. The story of the lionbird's encounter with the Black Dragon and the dark wolf raiders and how the Gryphon had felt a connection with the plunderers from across the Eastern Seas. He explained the tale to the others.

The Green Dragon was the most interested. "I've heard a tale or two about such."

"What he was isn't important for now," Cabe remarked as he bent near the corpse. Unknown to him, his manner and look resembled Nathan Bedlam more and more. "It's what happened to him that is."

"He was, as I mentioned, in the Northern Wastes. Haiden?"

"Milord." The elf bowed. "He was one of at least three riders. We found no physical trace of the others save some tracks before the attack and some scattered objects near this one. Whatever killed them was fairly thorough about cleaning up afterward—to a point. For some reason, they missed this one. Possibly because he had been thrown some distance."

"What?" Gwen forced herself to look at the body again. The wolf raider had not been a tiny man. "How—how far?"

Haiden grimaced, remembering the elves' estimates. "Far enough. We think at least one of the . . . the attackers . . . must have been taller than the trees."

Cabe did not raise his eyes from the corpse. "How so?"

"When one of us went to the top, to get a view of the surroundings in case there were more, he found traces of fur. As he came back down, he noticed that there were traces all the way down that he just hadn't noticed."

"What color was the fur?"

"White. Deathly white, like some undead creature."

Gwen turned pale as Cabe stood. She glanced back in the direction of where the large mound creature lay. "Then, it's the same thing!"

He wanted to say "You don't know that," but he knew she was correct. He knew it with far greater conviction than she did.

"Those three were not the only victims," the elf reluctantly added.

The mages stared wide-eyed at him.

Haiden looked at his master, who nodded slowly. He took a deep breath, forced himself to glance once more at the sorry remains of the wolf raider, and began. "The northernmost lands are all in the midst of winter."

"We're not even out of summer yet," Gwen protested.

"Be that as it may, Lady, in the domain where the clans of the Iron Dragon still cling to life, the hill dwarves have burrowed deeper into the depths of the earth. The drakes themselves have moved southeastward to join their brethren in Esedi, where the clans of Bronze still hold sway. Many there are who did not survive the trip and some simply . . . died, such as this one."

"The confusion is made greater by the fact that neither has a king anymore," the Green Dragon added. The Dragon Kings of those two regions had attempted the unthinkable—open revolt against the emperor. Nearly the entire army, including the traitorous rulers, had died at the claws of the Gold Dragon.

"What of the humans?" Cabe asked quickly. In the scheme of things, it was almost always the humans who were overlooked by the other races, possibly due to jealousy in some cases.

Haiden shrugged. "There are humans on the coast of Iron's domain, off the Seas of Andromacus." Such was the name for the western seas. Andromacus was the demon who supposedly had instigated the gods into creating the world, for reasons no one knew. The seas had been so named because they were far more turbulent than those on the eastern side. "I cannot say what has happened to them or any in the northeast. My brothers and sisters do say that the cold had reached past Talak and is fighting its way into the Hell Plains and the lands of Irillian. They also say that something follows it, something they could not get close enough to discern at the time."

"Of Talak I have no pity," the master of the Dagora Forest commented. "Let the human king Melicard freeze with the rest; but, the Hell Plains? Haiden, you made no mention of this before."

The elf looked chagrined. "Forgive me, lord. I—I fear the lack of sleep is finally catching up to me."

"How long has it been?"

"I have not slept since we discovered this one." He pointed at the icy corpse. "I forced two faithful steeds to death to bring this to you as soon as I could. I am ashamed."

The drake shook his head, "You are loyal, Haiden. When we are through here, you mussst rest. I fear I will need you again before long."

Haiden looked relieved.

The Green Dragon's eyes burned crimson. "The creature. The mound of fur. Yes, I want to see your catch now." To the drake who had untied the horrid bundle, he added, "Wrap that up again. No one comes near it unless I say so. There still may be something to learn from it, and it really is not necessary for it to lie revealed, disturbing everyone further. Haiden, you will accompany usss."

"Milord." It was difficult to tell whether the pallor of the elf's face was all natural, or due to exhaustion or distaste at what he had seen of late.

Gwen was already turning. She was not eager to return to the abomination's corpse, but she wanted the drake lord to see for himself, so that hopefully he would recognize it and know what to do. Cabe and the Dragon King followed closely behind, the former caught up in ancient memories of another, the latter silent and brooding. Haiden remained respectfully in the rear.

"You know," the Dragon King hissed, "that the frost which my domain hasss sssuffered isss only the beginning. I believe thessse little—ssspatterings—are the first sssigns that the magic isss extending even farther to the sssouth.

"I tried to contact my brother to the north. He hasss not resssponded. I am—a traitor in hisss eyesss."

Cabe knew it was best to say nothing about that.

The latest pairing of drake and human stood guard near the spot, their differences losing substance what with the boredom of guard duty and curiosity about what exactly it was that they were guarding. The drake heard them first and quickly assumed a position of attentiveness. The man, who had been in the midst of saying something, followed suit a moment later.

Cabe set them at ease. The Green Dragon stepped past Gwen and over to the hole she had created. He caught his first glimpse of the beast and came up just short of the huge form. He squatted and hesitantly held out a clawed hand toward the thing.

"Don't!" The cry was Cabe's; he assumed that the Dragon King meant to touch the monstrosity. The drake lord looked at him and held up his hand to indicate he was planning no such thing.

The mages joined him. "Thisss—this was once a harmless digging beast, I think. Their kind is—was—fairly common some time back, but they've become rare now."

Gwen could not believe what she was hearing. "That thing was harmless?"

"Not as it was just before it died, by no means. This is, as you said, a 'thing.' An abomination of the highest order. Someone has perverted its nature. Just being near it, I can feel it attempting to leech out my—this is old, old magic. Seeker magic at the very least, I'd say. Amazing how much of that is around of late. One would almost think the birds were on the rise again." The drake lord's tone indicated he thought it more than just a possibility.

"It was horrible," Cabe muttered without realizing it.

"Hmm?" The Green Dragon looked up at him.

The young sorcerer blinked. "I'm sorry. Nothing."

The drake rose and glared at him. "The Barren Lands. You are remembering the Barren Lands."

"I—"

"You told me what occurred with you and Nathan Bedlam, Cabe. I know you recall things that had happened to him. Things like the Turning War and the Barren Lands."

"They didn't understand what it was they had released!"

The Dragon King seemed to tower over Cabe. The armored figure was obviously fighting with various emotions. At last, the drake let out a very human sigh. "Many things happened in the Turning War that both human and drake feel shame about. I apologize, especially considering what I believe is happening up in the Northern Wastes."

Cabe nodded. "The Ice Dragon knows the spell, the same spell that my grandfather used. That's what I think."

Gwen, who had lived in that time, put a hand to her lips. "Rheena!"

"Woodland goddesses will be of little use to us now," commented the Dragon King dryly, "and I fear, Cabe, that my brother to the north knows more than the Dragon Masters did."

"How so?"

"What Nathan Bedlam discovered was only a fragment of the whole spell. That may have been why they were able to stop it as late as they did. My knowledge of our predecessors—most especially the Seekers—is greater than that of most who study them. I may say that without prejudice. Nathan knew much and knew that this was not the entire spell, but what did exist served the purpose he needed it for."

Cabe's eyes widened. "You sound as if you knew about it in advance."

The Dragon King looked down. "I did. I hoped he would not use it, but I knew that he had little other choice at the time. They were losing. Brown's clans were fierce, every drake a fighter until death. Even sorcery can be hard-pressed against such fanaticism. When I discovered that Nathan Bedlam had gone ahead and used the spell, I was revolted—as much by my inactivity as I was by his use and the fact that we Dragon Kings had forced him into it. There had been possibilities of peace, but the Council had rejected them. We did not deal with humans; we ruled."

"What about the Ice Dragon? How does he enter into this?"

"You know of the Northern Wastes." The drake lord glanced at both of them, assuring himself that they did indeed know before continuing on.

"What you probably do not realize is that, of all the Seeker ruins—and they left many, being a once vast race—it is the ruins within the mountains of the Wastes that are the oldest. The region of the Northern Wastes, you see, is the true home of the avians."

Gwen's eyes scanned the trees, as if she thought the Seekers might be listening. The avians always disturbed her. "They lived in that cold land?"

The Green Dragon chuckled, but there was no humor in his voice. "You've seen what the Barren Lands became. That was with only a fragment. Once, so I believe, the Northern Wastes had been more lush, more lively than even this forest. Until the Seekers created the ssspell."

"That was when the Wastes began to spread."

Neither of the mages could say anything. The images in their minds were too overwhelming, too horrible for mere words.

"The worst yet," the Dragon King continued—and there was a touch of fear in his voice as well—"is that the Northern Wastes are the results of an incomplete spell themselves. I know nothing of the circumstances, but it appears that the Seekers chose whatever befell them over what the end results of their experiment would be. They brought the process to a halt, but too late for so many."

"And now the Ice Dragon may have the complete spell."

Cabe turned his gaze northward, though this far south he did not expect to see the edge of the Dagora Forest, much less the Tyber Mountains and the Northern Wastes far beyond. Talak was in there somewhere, too.

"The Ice Dragon knew nothing about the spell before Nathan discovered it," he suddenly stated flatly.

Gwen and the firedrake looked at him and then the Dragon King nodded slowly. "That is as it seems."

"Then I—we—he—was responsible for this."

"It would have been discovered eventually."

"Perhaps. Perhaps not. As it stands, the responsibility is still my family's."

Gwen was the first to understand the look in his eyes, for it was identical to that of the first man she had loved. It was a look filled with determination. Determination to step into the jaws of the Ice Dragon himself if that was what it took to set things right. She knew what he meant to do.

"Cabe, that would be foolhardy! We need to know more!"

"We don't have time. I know that. What little I recall shouts that in my face. The Ice Dragon is ready!"

Now, the Dragon King understood as well what Cabe planned. Unlike

Gwen, however, what the sorcerer intended seemed necessary to him. "Haiden will guide you. I will see to that."

"I only need him to lead me to the edge. I will take it from there."

The elf frowned, but held back from saying anything.

"I'm going with you!" Gwen added suddenly. She raised a hand when Cabe began to protest. "There are others who can watch the hatchlings, and I hope that my lord drake will see to the safety of the people here. The memories you inherited from Nathan are incomplete; I may be able to help. Besides," she added with a grim smile, "no one is separating us again if I can help it!"

The Green Dragon nodded. "Do not argue, Bedlam. While you are away, I will spread the word to human and drake rulers alike—even Talak, if need be. This is something that goes beyond our differences. It seems to me that Brother Ice is intending to create one kingdom, one Dragonrealm, where he and his frosty clans will be the only rulers. The Dragon Kings will not stand for that."

"So that's it then," added Cabe, pretending to be more confident than he actually felt. Despite everything, there was still within him the young inn worker, the one who would have preferred to turn away from such danger and let others handle it. Cabe knew that was beyond him now. He was the one who had to handle things. There was really no one else.

"Tomorrow we set off for the Northern Wastes—and the Ice Dragon."

TOMA COMPLETED THE spell and waited.

The wall before him crackled a little, as if someone had poured warm water on its icy surface, but nothing more.

I still have my power, he thought coldly, *but it has been rendered ineffective here. I am a prisoner of madness.*

He had been separated from his father. The Ice Dragon would not say what had happened, but Toma suspected that either he or his parent was going to be a part of this depravity before long. Perhaps both.

"Duke Toma."

The firedrake turned to find one of his northern cousins, a torch in one hand, awaiting him at the entrance of his new "room." After witnessing what lurked at the bottom of the pit, Toma had tried to convince them that their lord was mad and would bring about their own destruction. They seemed not to care a bit. They were as emotionless as their master.

He could still see it. A vast . . . mass . . . of white fur that never ceased moving. It had no claws, no eyes, no sharp fangs—not even any legs. Yet, it frightened him as nothing else had. Just to stand near it was to endanger his life, Toma realized. The thing could feel his presence, sense the life within him. That was what it wanted. His life. It wanted to suck it out and discard the husk like the leftover shell of an egg.

Even in here, far away, he could feel it stirring.

The other drake was still standing there. Duke Toma finally looked at him again and asked, "What is it now?"

"Your presence is required in the royal chamber." Three more of the icy drakes, one with a torch, materialized behind the first. Toma was being given no choice in the matter.

"Very well." If only his magic would work! This was madness! An eternal winter would be the death of these drakes as well, did they not see that?

With two guards before him and two behind him, there was little he could do. The frost-covered halls glistened as the torches brought light to the depths of the ice caverns. Each step echoed forever and ever. Toma realized that in all this time he had still not seen either a female drake or any young. For that matter there were only a handful of minor drakes, and those creatures generally bred to great numbers unless strictly controlled.

He suddenly wondered just how they had been "controlled."

Like a corpse on display, the Ice Dragon was once again draped over the pit, eyes closed. Unlike Toma, he seemed to draw strength from the leviathan below, the thing that the Dragon King insisted on calling his "queen."

The dragon raised his head as the five stepped forward. To each side, an ice servant stood like a marble statue.

"Aaaahh, Toma. So good of you to come so quickly."

"I just couldn't stay away," the drake retorted angrily.

One of the icedrakes reached for him, but the Dragon King shook his head. "Leave him. Despite his outspoken manner, he is as dedicated to the race as any of us. Is that not so, nephew?"

My madness can in no way compare with yours! Toma wanted to shout, but thought better of it. Instead, he bowed slightly and replied, "The reign of the Dragon Kings has always been utmost in my mind, milord."

"I thought as much. That is why I hope you will forgive me as time goes on. I know that eventually you will see that what I do is the right decision—the only decision—where our race is concerned. This foul system of cycle after cycle—one race overwhelming the previous only to be eventually overwhelmed by successors of their own—must cease. Humanity will never rule the Dragonrealms; they will not survive another year!"

The Ice Dragon's eyes glistened, the most life Toma had seen yet in the behemoth. He turned to one of the unliving servants and nodded. It and its counterpart made their way to the small group of drakes and Toma was certain it was now his turn to be fed to—whatever that thing was. He quietly cursed all those he felt responsible for his presence here: Cabe Bedlam, the Lady of the Amber, Azran Bedlam, the Gryphon, the cowardly Dragon Kings—everyone but himself. He even found himself blaming his father.

It was a shock then, when, instead of taking him to the pit, the servants instead merely held him by the arms. They needn't have bothered with that measure. Toma knew that without his sorcery he was helpless here. He could not even shift to his true shape.

Things grew even more puzzling when the four icedrakes marched forward and up the crumbling steps of the ruined Seeker structure. As they neared the top, the Ice Dragon crawled off the pit and over to one side. The drakes did not turn to watch; they continued to march until they were at the edge of the hole.

Toma shook his head. This could not be happening! They wouldn't!

"For the glory of the race," the Ice Dragon whispered, though his words carried through the entire chamber.

One by one, the four drakes stepped off the edge of the pit and vanished into the depths. There were not even any screams, Toma noted with great unease. It was as if . . . this was what they'd wanted.

The Ice Dragon was addressing him. "There is loyalty, Toma. There is the faith that will mean the end for our would-be successors. The last four have given themselves over so that my power can grow."

"The last . . . four?" The firedrake's eyes were wide crimson suns and his mouth gaped open, revealing long, sharp teeth designed for tearing and a forked tongue that darted nervously to and fro. "All of your clans—dams, warriors, and hatchlings—all of them?"

"The last of the minor drakes went no more than an hour before. These were my most trusted warriors, these four. They were to be last so that they could witness the culmination of my researches, researches begun in the days of the Turning War."

Hands of the coldest ice gripped Toma harder, though he had made no move.

"I have decided that it is time to release all of my children, my selves, out into the realms, nephew. They will draw the life from the land and make me stronger. Already my spell spreads across the northern countries and even touches as far south as the forest lands of cursed Green. With all my children loose, I will bring forth a winter like none has ever witnessed before. . . .

". . . And that none shall live to witness ever again."

None . . .

Toma hissed nervously. None. Not even the clans of the Ice Dragon—which no longer existed. This was not a mad plan of conquest. This was death for everything. Everything. If the Dragon Kings could not rule, the Ice Dragon was saying, then no one would.

He had to escape, had to find help. All of his dreams were dying and he would soon be joining them, he knew, unless he found allies of power—like Cabe Bedlam.

All he had to do first was escape from the chilly depths of the Dragon King's caverns.

The Ice Dragon chose that moment to rise to his full height. The servants pulled Toma's head back, so that he was forced to watch the drake lord's face, which was the picture of death itself, so lifeless did it appear.

The Ice Dragon hissed something that, even with his booming voice, was unintelligible to Toma.

The thing in the pit began to stir. Toma briefly felt the touch of the leeching force, but something—his host, he realized belatedly—turned its attention elsewhere.

Toma screamed as thousands of hungry minds cried out at the shock of being fully wakened and freed. The two unliving servants strengthened their grip on him—a good thing, for he nearly lost consciousness.

It's too late, he thought through a battered mind, *it's too late.*

XI

THE GRYPHON HAD been promised things, but all he had received so far was food, wine, and countless glares from the drakes that served the Blue Dragon. He was not even in the main caverns; the boatman had deposited him in what could only be termed a waiting area.

Waiting for what? he wondered idly.

Left to his own musings, he turned his attention to other things. The Draka may have lied or perhaps been lied to. Maybe the amphibian had indeed believed it was serving its masters or maybe its true master was a Dragon King. The speculation was pointless, but it kept creeping into the lionbird's mind. It had seemed to believe what it said.

The Storm Dragon, on the other claw, *was* indeed a part of this. That much the Gryphon knew. The other dragon had toyed with him, revealed to him that he could have had the Gryphon at any time yet had let him pass. The lionbird doubted, however, that the two drakes were working that close. None of the Dragon Kings really trusted one another or else some of them would have answered Silver's call for unity. The Storm Dragon had also always been one of the most independent.

His surroundings were extravagant, albeit a bit bizarre. A cavern decorated with items that had been scavenged from the seas, by the looks of them. Treasures that would have otherwise vanished from the sight of all, ancient statues, magnificent coral displays, even tapestries of such superb quality that the lionbird almost had the feeling the merpeople depicted were about to leap out at him. For his comfort, chairs and cushions had been provided.

It had almost been sunrise when the boat reached the rocky formations that were the above-water portion of the caverns. The Gryphon had expected the boatman to drop him off on one of the jagged shoals, but, as they rounded the caverns, he saw that there was a tiny beach on one side, with a cave that was not the product of nature lying about ten yards in from the shore. The boatman brought the vessel ashore, once again displaying remarkable strength but not one bit of his form.

At that point, two drakes had ushered the Gryphon into this place. They were sleeker than their cousins and possibly taller, with a hint of blue in their skin color. His needs would be taken care of, one of them had finally said with slight disdain, while he waited for the summons of the lord. He had waited almost an entire day so far.

He heard someone approach but, after all this time, he had no intention of standing up unless he had to. There had been too many disappointments already.

They were drake warriors. The nearest one carried a wicked barbed spear that was pointed directly toward the Gryphon. "You will come with us."

"Your lord wishes to see me at last, I gather."

"He has found time for you, yesss. Please ssstand ssso that we may assure ourselves of your goodwill."

They had searched him earlier, but he relented in the name of time, which he knew was running out. He had been stripped of his weapons and his few surviving supplies already; they had examined but had not taken the chains around his neck, thinking them perhaps religious ornaments or signs of vanity. The lionbird refrained from showing any pleasure, as they had left him his most powerful weapon if it came to fighting. Even the Blue Dragon's sorcery was not enough to fully contain the power within the charms. One such charm had devastated the first major assault by the drakes during the brief siege of Penacles.

When the guards were satisfied that he had not succeeded in hiding some weapon from the first search, he was led deeper into the caverns to a staircase which spiraled downward, ending somewhere in the blackness of the earth. The view reminded him uncomfortably of the misty paths the Draka had unveiled. The Gryphon looked at the drakes expectantly. One produced an unlit torch and offered it to him. He tried to start a fire, but nothing happened. His powers, as he suspected, were being suppressed. The Dragon King was taking no chances. The lesson over, one of the guards took the torch and lit it with an odd flint apparatus. Whatever the Blue Dragon was using to suppress the lionbird's powers evidently affected a general area and not him specifically.

The torch was almost shoved back into his face. The blue pallor of the drakes was more evident now, as was the fact that their armor was smoother, less scaled than their landbound cousins. Other than that, they were similar to any other drake.

"Down. All the way."

That surprised him. "Alone?"

One of the drakes grinned evilly. The Gryphon, who had faced Dragon Kings, was not impressed. Like many drakes, this one had teeth that were sharp, but more human than predatory. Its tongue, which darted out once, was only slightly forked.

The scholar within him was taking too much control, apparently, because the guard with the spear poked him in the side with the blunt end. "Frightened or not, you will go down now if we have to throw you!"

The Gryphon glared at them and began to descend, his scholar's mind making one last note concerning the well-trained speech patterns. There was more interaction between drake and human in Irillian than in most of the other areas of the Dragonrealm, and therefore the drakes spoke with either little or no hiss, save when terribly excited.

Down and down he went and the stairway continued to spiral with no end in sight. Wryly, he wondered whether this was some mind-numbing test on the part of his host, a test to see if the Gryphon, or any other visitor for that matter, could be worn down in advance. Certainly a tired foe was preferable to one ready for any trick.

To his surprise, the bottom of the stairway materialized only a few minutes later. The Gryphon refused to give the Blue Dragon a sigh of relief, though he knew the drake could probably sense his emotional condition with whatever it was he had used on him.

"Halt."

Two more drakes, identical in every way to the two above, blocked his path with the same spears as the one above had held. The Gryphon stood there, torch in hand, and waited.

"Let him enter." The voice was booming, and sounded as if the speaker had not quite finished swallowing a long drink of water.

The guards pulled back their spears, one of them holding out his free hand for the Gryphon's torch. There would be no need of it here, for something in the walls ahead glowed. The Gryphon relinquished the torch and stepped forward to meet the Blue Dragon.

There were those who thought the master of Irillian might be the basis for the Dragon of the Depths, the closest thing to a ruling god for the drakes. That was foolishness, of course; the other Dragon Kings would certainly not have worshipped one of their own brethren, and the legend of the Dragon of the Depths, said by some to be the progenitor of all drakes, would have been far older than the Dragon Kings. However much they might deny it, the drake lords were mortal in the end.

"Welcome, Lord Gryphon. Thank you for coming so . . . willingly," the great dragon bellowed politely.

The polite tone was what worried the lionbird most now. There was no reason for the Dragon King to be civil with him. "Greetings, Lord of Irillian by the Sea and her surrounding domain. I should like to discuss my rather *extreme* willingness with you at some point in the conversation—once, that is, we have dealt with the matters you wished to discuss."

The Blue Dragon gave him a toothy smile. It was not quite as bad as facing the Black Dragon, but not much better. He was surprised by the more serpentine form of the Dragon King, but not very much so. It made sense, considering his domain.

"The Aramite called D'Shay will be sorry he missed you," the drake lord added.

"Where is he, then?" The Gryphon expected the aristocratic raider to step from the shadows at any moment, but the only things he saw were the dragon and glowing walls. Walls that had been carved out by someone.

"Out in Irillian's countryside, I imagine, searching desperately for you and trying to think of some excuse to murder you while still satisfying my demands—which were to keep you alive for the moment."

The Gryphon was perplexed, but calmly answered, "I'm supposed to be grateful to you, I guess."

"Yessss . . ." The Blue Dragon slipped momentarily into a more drakish mode of speech. "Ssssimpleton! The one called D'Shay thinks too highly of himself."

"Many are like that."

The dragon eyed him, pondering whether he should feel insulted or not. At last, he decided to ignore the remark. "Your pasts have intermingled more than once, I understand. I could say more, but then I would lose one of my bargaining chips." The Dragon King closed his eyes and seemed to concentrate.

"Bargaining chips?" The Gryphon finally said, in order to fill the void of silence, "Bargaining for what?"

The eyes opened and they seemed to have no color of their own, for they matched the blue-green glow of the walls perfectly.

"First I shall prove my honesty by explaining what has brought you here. Please, have a seat." With his head, the leviathan indicated a chair that had not been there a moment before.

The Gryphon shook his head. "I prefer to stand for now."

"The poised hunter. Excellent. You will need to be sharp."

"You were explaining . . ."

The dragon nodded. "I have been planning for weeks. My plan was aided by the sudden appearance of the Aramites, who no longer felt secure with their deal with brother Black. Lochivar. As *you* well know, he is not very stable at the moment."

The lionbird inclined his head momentarily. The Black Dragon's problems stemmed partly from a throat wound that the Gryphon himself had delivered with one of Azran's demon blades.

"To continue . . ." The Blue Dragon stretched his wings, which seemed more appropriate for swimming swiftly through the water than for flying. "I had detected something amiss in the Northern Wastes. Brother Ice refuses contact, and every spy, including an arrogant raider sent by D'Shay to negotiate with him, has disappeared. I know a little more than the Aramites suspect and I know that whatever Ice plans, it will be the death of us all."

The dragon paused, as if awaiting a response from the Gryphon. The lionbird finally shrugged. "You say we face a threat from the master of the Northern Wastes. Nothing else. I suspect you are correct in that assumption, but I could do with a little more background if you truly desire my aid, which is what I gather."

"You gather correctly. I know a little and what little I know frightens me. My powers are strong and I am aided by a number of artifacts left behind by the Seekers and, before them, the Quel: the spell which covers like a sheet my domain, and a crystal which allows me to see anything that has disturbed the spell and also can reach out and touch the minds of others. In the latter case, it can either draw knowledge from you or emphasize some emotion that I choose; in your instance, your desire to capture D'Shay and find out what he truly knows about your past. It was wearying and I cannot do it for very long, especially with a mind as strong as yours. Still, once you set out, you worked partially under the assumption that you were in your right mind and that made my own task easier."

"What of the Draka?"

The Blue Dragon grimaced; a disturbing sight, as it appeared as if he had just eaten something or someone that disagreed with him. "The Draka thinks it obeyed its masters—and perhaps it did, since once I felt the touch of a Seeker's mind, only to have it pull away with a sense of satisfaction. Who knows? I, too, may be being manipulated. I found the creature useful when I discovered that he had a way of getting you here without the wolf raiders knowing. Tell me—what are the misty paths like?"

Waving the question aside, the Gryphon asked, "What about D'Shay? What purpose was there in including him?"

"That should be obvious. D'Shay was bait. You certainly wouldn't have come here if he had been in Lochivar. You almost certainly would not have come here if I had asked you. At the same time, his presence gave me a bargaining chip to use against my brethren, Black and Storm. Storm wanted your head, but not if it meant allowing the raiders to establish a permanent base, which I would never have allowed anyway—not that he needed to know that. Black needs the Aramites' prisoners for his armies and if I give them a port here, the raiders will not bother to deal with him again. In return for my 'promise' to turn them away, Black would neither hinder you nor attempt some foolish assault on Penacles—which might have worked, much to our detriment."

The Gryphon nodded, a conclusion forming. "It sounds, then, as if it's actually the libraries you want."

"I hope you do not feel offended." The Dragon King gave his "guest" a brief, toothy, smile. "In the end, yes. The libraries are the oldest artifacts in the Dragonrealms. They actually predate the Seekers and the Quel and two other races I know. I often suspect that when the final day comes, the only thing remaining will be the libraries."

"Then it's a truce you want."

"Yesss, a truce. A temporary one, for now."

Cocking his head to one side, the Gryphon eyed the dragon. "If you'd have offered anything more I wouldn't have even considered it."

"I can still give you D'Shay, if you like. I have no use for him and I have no desire to see a wave of wolfhelms marching across the countryside."

"Now, you're pressing your credibility." They had slipped into an exchange between two heads of state rather than two mortal enemies. The Gryphon had great respect for the Blue Dragon's capabilities, even his leadership, for the people of Irillian were probably nearly as satisfied with the rule of the dragon as those who lived within the domain of the Green Dragon or the Gryphon. Certainly, it would have been difficult to convince them at this time that overthrowing the drake was to their benefit, especially since their city would then become a battlefield.

"Let me offer this, then," the lord of Irillian replied. "I shall deport the raiders from my domain. Whether you pursue them from there is up to you."

He would go that far, the lionbird knew. No one but the Black Dragon had any interest in the foreigners, and Black was only interested in replenishing his armies of zombie-like fanatics, slaves to the Gray Mists.

"My abilities are at your command, Lord Gryphon. I don't know what Ice plans, but my loyalty is first and foremost to my domain, despite what you might have heard."

The Gryphon considered. The libraries could indeed be of assistance and, if what the Blue Dragon said was true, time was of the essence. With the last thought came a sudden disturbing notion. His eyes narrowed as he looked up at the leviathan. "How do I know you are not attempting to influence me now?"

The dragon laughed wholeheartedly. "You are as distrusting as they say . . . which is probably why you still rule. Wait."

Rising to near his full height, the Blue Dragon made his way to the center of the chamber, forcing his guest to back up considerably. The dragon closed his eyes.

The chamber became terribly warm. The Gryphon's eyes widened, for he saw that the Dragon King was literally melting away before his eyes . . . yet, the flesh which flowed from the drake lord seemed to dwindle to nothing before it touched the floor. The massive wings folded, then shriveled, shrinking to nothing. The tail pulled into the dragon's body and the legs and foreclaws straightened and shrank, the claws becoming sharply nailed hands. The chest sank in, then readjusted itself, taking on the aspect of an armored human chest.

Most disturbing of all was the face. The neck shrank to nothing as the Blue Dragon's features slid *upward* from his face, leaving in their place a hollow depression which gradually formed a face-concealing helm. Two reflective eyes stared out and a humanish mouth formed, from which sharp teeth could be seen. The dragon visage, shrunken to less than a tenth of its size, continued to slide upward until it was now almost at the top of the pseudo-helm. In a moment the skin of the figure adjusted itself, looking for all the world like the finest scale armor.

The now-humanoid Dragon King studied his temporary ally with some curiosity. "You have never seen us shift form before?"

"Not this close. Not in this much detail. Battle doesn't allow the time to study."

"How true, how sad." There was no mockery in the drake's tone. "If you will now follow me, I will give you the proof of your free will in this matter."

The Blue Dragon led him behind the space where earlier his dragon form had lain. There was a passage there that the Gryphon had not been able to see before. Like the chamber they had just departed, the walls glowed. It gave them both a rather sickly pallor, he noticed for the first time.

"What makes the walls give off such light?"

The drake stopped, reached out, and rubbed a finger against the wall. Some of the glow came off on his hand. He showed it to his guest. "A sea moss, from the dark depths. The light is part of its living process, though

I cannot say exactly what purpose it serves. I only know that if the glow is gone, the moss is dead. I have used my power to adapt it for this use. As long as it serves my purposes, I am satisfied. This"—he held up the finger covered with moss—"is only the least of the treasures of the seas. The beauty of the land is nothing compared with the beauty beneath the waves."

With that said, the drake gently wiped his finger off and continued on. He had his back turned completely to the Gryphon, as if offering such trust as proof of his good intentions. The lionbird reminded himself that even if he should succeed in slaying the Dragon King, he would still have to fight his way out and swim to shore, not something which appealed to him. So far, he trusted the drake.

They entered a second chamber, this one larger than the first, and the Gryphon heard the sound of waves breaking against the rocks. The reason became evident immediately, for apparently the far end of the chamber was part of the sea itself. The chamber was actually an underwater grotto.

The walls were lined with books, artifacts, and equipment of all sorts. This was where the Blue Dragon actually maintained control of his domain. Here was where he worked his spells and watched over Irillian.

A large crystal sitting in the middle of a wooden tripod caught his notice and it was to this the drake lord led him. The crystal seemed to glow brighter as they approached.

"What I call home is all that remains of Old Irillian."

"Old Irillian?" As far as the Gryphon knew, Irillian was one of the oldest cities in the Dragonrealms. He knew nothing of a predecessor.

"Before the Seekers, before the Quel, this city was the finest in all the land. But it fell victim to a quake of monstrous proportions, so great that vast areas of the city sank near intact. The inhabitants were much like the Draka, so some survived and made use of the area. They were still essentially land creatures, though, so they began work on the present Irillian. After they vanished, the Quel came along and ignored the city. They used these caverns, dug many of the tunnels. After them, the Seekers came. Most of the artifacts here are theirs, some belonged to the Quel. After the Seekers died out, the first drakes discovered these caverns. Much preferable to the city, which they left for the first manlings."

The Blue Dragon dropped a hand lightly on the crystal. "This is what I used, my—Lord Gryphon. This is the power that bound you to my will for a while." He stepped away from it. "Take it. Use it. I give you leave."

If the Dragon King assumed that such an offer would make the Gryphon trust him completely, he was sorely mistaken. The lord of Penacles had already learned how dangerous overtrust could be. He strode forward with determination, one eye always on his host, and carefully touched the crystal with his right hand.

It was cool to his touch. He felt doorways opening within him. He sought out Penacles and saw it through his mind. Toos. He wanted to see Toos. The general was arguing with two advisers, men who kept trying to bring up a needless tax which the Gryphon knew would go more to lining their pockets than aiding the city. Toos rose and pointed at the door, his voice calm but authoritative. Defeated, the two stumbled out.

Good old Toos, he thought. *I was never able to make them bow so low. You should be leader.*

He returned his attention to a more immediate subject. The Blue Dragon would be waiting. He could not play with this all day. One test should be sufficient.

He focused his mind on the drake and concentrated.

The Dragon King began to pace. Then the pacing turned into a nervous pounding of his fist against the wall. At last, the drake lord was quivering, shaking so badly that he could hardly stand.

The Gryphon let him remain that way and then released control.

His reptilian ally was breathing heavily and the lionbird found he was as well. The Dragon King glared at him momentarily, then calmed.

Several guards came rushing in, all evidently intent on spreading the Gryphon's bodily parts throughout the caverns. The Dragon King ordered them out immediately. Such was his command of his subjects that they departed without protest. The drake focused his attention on the lionbird.

"You—you did not have to do that! I—I thought . . ."

There was no sympathy. "You thought I would be so noble as not to make use of your toy. You led me around by the beak for days, made me forget my duties, built up an obsession that might have killed me!" Had the Dragon King thought it a simple test of control? "Now you've felt its touch! Now you know something of what I've been through so you could play games.

"Now we know where we stand."

Blue nodded, his breathing nearly normal at last. "Are you then prepared to accept this truce?"

"Of course."

"Only as a temporary measure, you understand?"

"What do you think?" the Gryphon asked wryly.

XII

S LEEP DID NOT come easy at the Manor that night. Cabe found himself staring at the ceiling more often than not and knew from the sounds beside him that Gwen was faring little better. He said nothing to her, however, and pretended to sleep. If his play-acting gave her a moment's more rest, then it was worth it. To increase her worries by knowing how much he was worried was pointless.

Poring through what books he had been able to gather over the last few months gave him no more insight into what he faced. Some of the books had supposedly been written by one or two of the Dragon Masters themselves. Yalak, in particular, seemed to think it important to put what he knew down in script. After puzzling through the man's handwriting for three hours, Cabe had come to the conclusion that the ancient mage had been in bad need of a scribe, and finally gave up. Besides, most of what the mage had written down seemed more concerned with obscure predictions and how to interpret them. The unfortunate thing was that most of what Yalak wrote needed interpreting as well.

Why must magic be so mysterious and muddled, he wondered. Why can't it be straightforward and tidy?

It was all up to him, apparently. Most of those who could have told him something had died during or immediately after the Turning War.

He rose before dawn, having at last given up for the night, only to discover her waiting for him. As he had done, she was staring at the ceiling. When she noticed his movements, she turned to look at him.

"Morning," he said lamely. It would have seemed rather odd if he had added "good" before that. Neither of them was looking forward to the journey.

By the time they had dressed and breakfasted—their appetites were unsurprisingly light—their mounts were saddled and packed. Ssarekai and his human equivalent, Derek Ironshoe, were waiting. The two appeared almost companionable to Cabe—as companionable as people can be at such an early hour. It served to brighten his day a little, at least. Gwen, seeing him smile, was able to smile as well. Things were not totally dark.

No one else was up, though that would not last long. Cabe and Gwen intended to be gone before then rather than become part of a scene. Gwen had already left instructions for the coming and going of the Manor's staff, and the Green Dragon had promised to watch over them. The mages took the reins from the two servants and mounted. Cabe gave Ssarekai a nod, which made the drake smile slightly—not a pretty sight—and turned his horse. Gwen followed on her own mount.

That the lands were threatened by something horrible seemed more like a rumor to the two as they rode. The sun was shining, birds were singing, and the forest overall seemed teeming with healthy life. Cabe recalled how dull his own life had seemed just prior to the day the Brown Dragon had come seeking him out. Appearances could indeed be deceiving.

Though these woods belonged to the Green Dragon, that by no means meant that the two were careless in their riding. Things such as basilisks made no distinction between those under the Dragon King's protection and those not. Such creatures were always too hungry to care, since they had to catch their prey just at the right moment. Basilisks, for example, ate the stone figures which were their victims, somehow deriving nourishment from them, but only during the first half hour or so. After that, the only use for the petrified corpse was as a statue in a garden. Cabe had yet to understand the purpose of a basilisk.

Only ten minutes into their journey, the horses came to an abrupt halt. All the encouragement in the world would not make them continue, and Cabe's first thought was that they had run across yet another of the furred abominations of the north, only this time it was still alive.

Such was not the case. From beyond the path, a figure emerged, tall, silent, and clad in green, the favorite color of elves.

"Haiden!" Both mages relaxed, canceling their spells quickly. Haiden, who had been smiling at the way his skill had surprised the two, suddenly realized that he had stood a good chance of being changed into something unsavory. The look that crossed his face made the other two laugh.

"You shouldn't do things like that. Not around magic-users," Gwen chided him.

"I'll remember that," Haiden swore. "I wouldn't want to wake up crawling on my belly, looking for mice."

"Oh, I'd never turn you into a snake. . . . Something else, perhaps, but not a snake."

"How comforting."

Cabe scanned the forest. "Are you alone or do we have more surprises?"

"I'm alone save for one companion." The elf was carrying a long bow; he put that aside for a moment and reached behind the trees. He led out a sleek, pale horse. There was a look to it that no ordinary horse could have duplicated. This animal had been raised by elves to be ridden by elves. It was as different from their own mounts as they were from the elf.

"It's not necessary for you to come with us," Cabe commented.

Haiden stroked his horse. "There are things elves can do that you might find handy. I need to ride north, regardless. I still have companions up there. They decided to stay behind, lord, in case there was anything else to report. They'll meet us at the edge of the Wastes."

There was no sense in arguing. Cabe finally agreed to let the elf join them.

"Which path would you recommend?" Gwen wanted to know.

Haiden smiled, this time with a touch of grimness. "We have the wonderful choice of crossing the Hell Plains lengthwise or passing through the domains of Bronze and Silver, the latter of whom is still very active."

The Hell Plains was a volcanic region southeast of the Tyber Mountains that had once been the home of both the Red Dragon and Azran. Both were long dead now, though some of the Red clans still lived. It was not an easy path, for it meant traveling within sight of Wenslis, the edge of the Storm Dragon's kingdom. There was also the possibility of running into the marauders who had assaulted them on their way to the Manor, or even the scattered remnants of the Red Dragon's people, out for vengeance of their own. One also had to be prepared for the abrupt eruption of a volcano or two.

Going the other way meant the certainty of facing all of the Silver Dragon's minions, not to mention survivors of three other clans, including those belonging to clan Gold.

Cabe sighed. Either way, it was going to be a long, hard trip. "We go through the Hell Plains."

Haiden nodded. "I thought you'd see that. I cannot say I'm pleased with either route, but those were the best—unless you would care to climb the Tyber Mountains. . . ." He grinned at their expressions. "I didn't think so."

Something which had nagged Cabe in the back of his mind finally came to the surface. "Haiden, has your lord mentioned anything about the other Dragon Kings? Surely, they cannot condone something like this. What the Ice Dragon is doing *must* affect them as well."

The elf looped the bow about his neck and shoulder as he replied, "The Lord Green has said nothing about them. I do know he is disturbed by their inactivity—at least what we assume is their inactivity. None of the remaining Dragon Kings trust one another anymore, at least not since Iron and Bronze sought to betray their emperor, and they certainly do not trust my liege, who turned from them and made peace with the Gryphon."

"No, I suppose not." There was nothing more that Cabe could add to what Haiden had said. They were on their own, unless they had allies they knew nothing about.

"Well . . ." Haiden grinned, and his face again reminded Cabe of the half-elf Hadeen, the one he had assumed for years to be his father—*was* his father as far as he was still concerned. Azran had been his father only biologically. "We might as well be on our way. Can't keep the lizards waiting, can we?"

Their ride was uneventful for the greater part of the day, the only nerve-wracking moments coming when waves of cold seemed to pass through the region. No one had to say out loud what the cold was; they knew now. It did not keep them from clutching themselves tight, useless as that was. The cold was within them as well.

"It's stronger," Gwen said after the final time. "It's pressing south."

Cabe nodded. "It's begun."

Haiden, the least informed of the trio, glanced at Cabe anxiously. "Are we too late, then?"

"No, not yet. Soon, though."

They pressed on harder.

EVENING SAW THEM near the northeasternmost edge of the forest. There was a slightly sulfurous odor in the air and the trees and bushes were thinner here, as if the soil was tainted. Haiden sniffed the air with disdain and finally announced, "We'll be entering the Hell Plains some time in the morning."

The Dragonrealm was such a hodgepodge of different lands that some believed they had been designed that way. Certainly, each Dragon King had done his best to shape his kingdom to his liking, but even they did not possess the power needed for such extensive changes. Some blamed past races; others thought it the work of some god. No one knew and it was likely no one would ever know. The Dragonrealm was what it was, and questioning its origin did nothing to change that fact—which meant that the trio had to cross the volcanic region whether they desired it or not.

Sleep came easier this night, if only because they were so exhausted. Haiden offered to keep guard, but Gwen arranged a protective spell which she assured him would be more effective. Besides, they all needed a full night's sleep.

That soon proved impossible. They were unable to sleep for more than two hours before some great eruption threatened to burst their eardrums or some tremor shook them like helpless infants. Worse, it was obvious that there would be no letup.

At one point, Cabe used words he was sure must date back to his grandfather—although he himself might have learned them in the inn—and asked sourly, "Do we have to sleep in this domain for the next few days?"

Spells proved ineffective—unless they wanted to totally isolate themselves from their environment. Cabe suggested it, but Gwen pointed out that such spells would drain them considerably, forcing them to travel slower—meaning more days spent in the Hell Plains.

Haiden brightened at one point. "Can either of you teleport?"

"Both of us can," Gwen replied.

"Why don't we teleport ahead? We'd save days."

Cabe hated to burst his enthusiasm. Gwen had explained it often enough for him to know it by heart. "Neither of us knows this area well enough. If we teleport in the Hell Plains, we might end up above a crater. If we attempt to teleport as far as the Wastes, we run the risk of coming face-to-face with the Ice Dragon's horrors. Or even if we don't, we would be too exhausted if something came across us soon after we arrived. We can't afford being less than one hundred percent when we enter the Wastes."

Gwen nodded in agreement, pushed thick hair from her face, and added, "We can't even afford to do short hops. They'd have to be so short that we would tire ourselves out quickly. There is also the outside possibility that we might teleport into something, such as a tree or a mountain. It *has* happened."

Haiden quickly dropped the subject.

They were silent after that, hoping that they might get more sleep before the next eruption or tremor.

Very early the next morning, they spotted the Hell Plains. The name was a bit of a misnomer, for there was nothing really flat about the region. To be sure, some areas were stable—especially near the caves of the drakes—but for the most part, the Hell Plains was an area of hills and ridges, most of them including live or recently active volcanoes. As Haiden put it, this was a land where the Dragonrealm's sorrows were given true form. Here, the earth was revealing its pain.

The horses protested, but eventually the trio entered the land. The last trees had vanished long before and the grass here was thinly spread. The Barren Lands had looked more hospitable than this, Cabe decided. He then recalled that the soil in this region was actually richer than anywhere else, for the eruptions often brought up a variety of minerals and nutrients to replenish those lost. It was in the stable areas that the plant life flourished, encouraged by the drake clans who fed on the wildlife there. Oddly, it was in the Hell Plains that the drakes came closest to being called farmers, though no one could ever have doubted their savagery. The trio had been fortunate. What little remained of the Red clans lived mostly to the north, and it was possible that they might travel through the Hell Plains without ever confronting a single drake.

It was very hot and, as the day passed slowly, Cabe contemplated removing his shirt. Haiden shook his head as the sorcerer suggested it. "You would not like the touch of a cinder on your back, and I think your magical abilities would be worn to nothing if you attempted to protect yourself so during the entire journey."

"Besides," Gwen added with a smile, "I don't think it fair that I'd have to keep my blouse on."

"In the forest, the nymphs run without any sort of covering," Haiden commented.

"If my wife does likewise, my first act will be to remove any prying eyes from the area—permanently."

Haiden smiled at the friendly rebuke, then frowned as he spotted something far off to the northeast. "We appear to have caught the notice of the drakes after all."

The other two followed his gaze and saw them. A large body of riders. Humans, it turned out, not drakes. It also turned out that the other riders had not noticed them, for they continued on their way, their path roughly parallel to that of the trio, but headed south instead of north.

"Who would be out this way?" Cabe wondered out loud.

"Could they be from Wenslis? Maybe Talak?" Gwen suggested.

Haiden shook his head. "If they come from Talak, then they are taking a strange route. Much easier to have gone directly south. No one in their right minds would traverse the Hell Plains willingly. Wenslis might be a possibility, but they have little traffic with either Zuu or Penacles. Mito Pica and Irillian got most of their trade."

"Mito Pica . . ." Cabe muttered to himself.

"What about it?"

"Nothing—except they might be heading home—sort of. It's possible that those are some of the marauders."

"The self-styled drakeslayers?" Haiden took hold of his bow with his left hand.

"The same. It makes some sense. Mito Pica was their home, and it's also a good reminder of why they fight. I'm surprised no one thought of that before."

"Maybe no one wants to think about that," Gwen suggested, a dark look on her face. "Toma destroyed their home simply because you had lived there. I think even some of the Dragon Kings were angered at that. After all, Mito Pica was not in Gold's domain. Emperor he might have been, but invading another drake lord's domain was still a bad move."

Cabe nodded. "But that wouldn't keep them from attacking the ruins now. Any Dragon King would know that the only ones remaining in the city now are either scavengers or the renegades. Either one the drakes could do without. Still, it was only a guess. I could very well be wrong."

Haiden encouraged his horse to move on. "We'd better keep going, lord and lady. No sense testing our luck too greatly. They still might see us. You were the ones who told me you had to conserve yourselves as much as possible."

The two mages followed him, with Cabe temporarily taking up the rear. The riders still disturbed him, but there was nothing he could do. The thought that they might be on their way back to the Manor entered his mind, but after the last encounter that seemed a foolish notion. The leader of the marauders was no fool; Cabe had seen that. The man knew when he was beaten. At the very most, he might travel around the perimeter of the Dagora Forest. With the Green Dragon watching for him, to do any more would be to invite disaster.

By late afternoon, the riders were a distant memory. There was still too much land to cover and too little time to do it to be concerned about dangers that might exist only in his own mind. Cabe forgot about the riders, especially when they came across the first of the skeletons.

He had heard of something similar to this, but that was far to the southwest, in the lands once belonging to the Brown Dragon. It was there that Cabe had once almost been sacrificed, only to have his own latent powers put an end to the Dragon King. The Gryphon had told him later about the end results of that action, for the Brown Dragon had received his desire in death—almost. The Barren Lands became lush once more, but with a deadly twist. The plant life that grew there was inimical to the clans of that drake. A twisted perversion of the spell that he had sought. The plant life sought out the drakes, making no distinction between drake lord and the lowest of the wyverns, so long as they were of Brown's blood. Only a handful that had fled to the lands of Bronze and Crystal still survived—so rumor said of late.

This was also a slaughter, they saw. The first skeletons, picked clean by the various scavengers of the region, led to others which led to others and so on as far as they could see.

They reached a stable rise, rode up, and looked down upon one of the few true plains regions in this domain.

"Rheena!" Gwen gasped. "It's a sea of death!"

Cabe nodded sadly. He knew what they were near, though it was hidden by two active craters of recent origin. Without spells to protect it, this area would eventually become unstable. Someday, the citadel which these drakes and creatures had fought over would be torn apart by the violence of the earth.

They would have to find another path around here. The scattered remains of leviathan after leviathan literally covered the landscape. Skulls gazed up mockingly at the sky. Some creatures had apparently fallen in struggle together with their foes, unless the movements of this volatile land had flung their skeletons into one pile somehow. The bones of the drakes mixed freely with the dead of the defenders and it was impossible to believe that any creature had survived this massacre.

One had—for a while—and it was his abandoned citadel which stood nearby. Cabe did not want to see it, but he felt that it might be wise to stop there, if only to let the horses rest in shade before they continued. Perhaps there would even be some book or clue that would be of aid to them, for the master of this place had been one of the most powerful mages alive.

Azran.

TOMA STRUGGLED AT the ice that held him prisoner against the wall. He was furious. Furious at himself, furious at being herded from one thing to another like some mindless minor drake, furious at the Ice Dragon—who would rob him of the throne that was justly his. . . . He could not put into words most of the things which angered him. He did know which angered him most, however.

He was powerless. He could not shapeshift and could not cast a spell sufficient enough to light a twig on fire. That was what was needed now. Warm, cleansing flame. To free him and destroy this overgrown icicle. To wreak vengeance on the lord of the Northern Wastes.

The drake shook his head. Anger was getting him nowhere, despite how easy it was to give in to it. He needed to escape, to regain some measure of power. Allies would be necessary, too. Silver would join him if it was known that his emperor was prisoner here. Blue might also aid him. The others were questionable. Storm did what Storm desired, whether that coincided with his brethren or not. Black was a misfit, a failure. The Crystal Dragon . . . Toma knew nothing. Crystal had come to the early councils, said little, and departed each time without any farewell. Crystal was an enigma that Toma could not trust, although that had not stopped him from utilizing the Dragon King's form so that he could spy on the council and see that his words were heard by those who otherwise would have spurned him.

Silver and Blue, then. They could be allies. He had the glimmerings of a plan; now he needed to escape. Toma hissed in frustration. That was the problem he had started with. His logic was going in circles, most likely because his brain was half frozen.

There was a noise akin to fluttering, but Toma paid it no mind. Like many of the Dragon Kings, Ice had servants that hid in the shadows—unthings that flew and chittered or crawled and hissed—and none of them was of any interest to him.

Toma stared at the single torch that hung from the wall across from him. His "host" had claimed it was so that the firedrake would not have to wait in darkness. Toma suspected it was some little quirk, some remaining bit of emotion in the Ice Dragon, and that the torch was there as some sort of torture. Only a few moments with that flame would have been sufficient to free him, but the torch was out of range.

I am going to be sacrificed to some abomination so that a demented drake lord can fulfill his deathwish! Toma thought madly. He had yet to speak out loud to himself, but he knew that time was coming soon—provided the unliving servants did not come for him first.

Something fluttered again and this time a shadow passed him. Toma blinked and stared. Before him stood a Seeker where none could possibly have been a moment earlier. It was gazing at him with arrogant eyes, as if deciding if he was worth the bother. Then the avian reached for the torch, removed it, and brought it toward the drake's head.

Toma had visions of himself being burned alive, for even firedrakes have only a limited tolerance to open flame. Instead, the Seeker pulled the torch back and reached up with its free claw. It put the claw across Toma's face.

There were images then, of Toma fleeing the citadel, seeking aid to the south. Toma almost shouted agreement before it dawned on him that whatever he thought was open to the Seeker's mind.

Seemingly satisfied, the creature brought the torch near the drake's right wrist. The ice sizzled and Toma struggled to break free before his wrist did the same. Time dragged horribly slow, each second an invitation to discovery. At last, Toma wrenched his right arm free. While he fought the ice manacle on his left wrist, the Seeker freed his ankles.

When it was done, the avian handed him the torch and pointed to one of the walls. Toma saw nothing. Impatient, the Seeker pointed up. The firedrake saw it finally, a hole near the ceiling, the secret method by which the bird creature had evidently infiltrated the Ice Dragon's home. Toma was to use this hole as his escape route.

When he turned back to the Seeker, he found himself alone. The torch was back in its normal location. Toma cursed quietly, almost expecting to wake and find himself still fastened to the wall. He shrugged finally. If this were a dream, at least he would escape his captors in one way. Perhaps they would find him here later, as mindless as his parent.

Thoughts of his father and liege made Toma hesitate, before he realized that neither of them would be free if he attempted to take Gold with him. It would be better to return with aid. The Ice Dragon was not yet ready to sacrifice his own emperor; the timing apparently had to be just right. His "host" was, after all, still a traditionalist.

That settled, Toma made his way up the wall, his clawed hands turning to ice as he dug deeply. He wished his savior had thought about taking him with it; that would have been much simpler. The Seeker's thought process was as frustrating as the race itself.

He reached the hole and pulled himself through. He did not doubt that the servants would be coming for him soon, and now a new worry entered his mind as he realized how easy it would be for them to follow him through the tunnel.

Having pulled himself all the way in, he twisted round to see if there was any way of blocking the entrance—only to find that there was no entrance anymore. A solid sheet of ice left no trace of his passage and undoubtedly no indication from the outside that this tunnel existed.

There was no turning back now. Toma grunted and began pulling himself forward, his mind awash with many thoughts: how a race as resourceful as the Seekers could have ever fallen; in what way might he regain his own powers; and what the odds were of slipping past the roving packs of Ice's soul-seeking abominations.

Most of all, he wanted to know how long he was going to have to pull himself solely by his arms, a process which, he knew, would have the muscles in his arms screaming before long.

XIII

THE BLUE DRAGON chose to act on the Aramite situation quickly. Before long, he had most of the wolf raiders on their way to their vessels. It was a fairly smooth operation; the raiders seemed to be prepared to move at a moment's notice and therefore there was little time for them to organize and stow away. Finding D'Shay and his companion was a bit more difficult, but in the end they were led by a guard of some eight drake warriors to their ship. D'Shay argued all the way, claiming that the word of the Blue Dragon was obviously worth little more than the sand on the beaches. The Dragon King bristled when he heard this later on, but by then the wolf raiders were out at sea.

"I should have turned him over to you," he commented sharply as he returned to the Gryphon.

The thought had occurred, over and over, to the lionbird, but he had forcibly reminded himself that the Aramites were a minor problem compared to what they possibly faced from the Ice Dragon. "As pleasant as that may be, I have no time for him—and we have no more time for this. I was going to suggest that perhaps you should use this crystal to study the Wastes."

"A useless task, bird. My brother shields his domain, and my power is insufficient to pierce the barrier. . . ."

The Gryphon noted the pause. "What is it?"

The drake lord had closed his eyes. When he opened them again, he smiled. "If you are willing to link yourself to me, our combined strength might be sufficient to break through. I suspect that between us we represent a great degree of power."

It was still difficult for the Gryphon to accept working with this

Dragon King, much less linking with him, but the lionbird understood the importance of what his temporary ally was suggesting. If they intended to use the libraries, it would help greatly to have some idea of what it was they were up against. Blue had explained earlier that he believed Ice's plan had something to do with the desolation of the Barren Lands by Nathan Bedlam, but beyond that he did not have a clue. The Ice Dragon had always kept to himself, appearing at councils only when it might be to his advantage.

"What do we do?" The Gryphon's feathers and fur ruffled slightly. He was not looking forward to this.

The Dragon King was already standing on the other side of the crystal. The combined illumination of the crystal and the walls made the drake resemble something risen from the dead—a shadow person. "I realize that this is distasteful for you. I care for it even less. Perhaps if I tell you that I was just informed that raging blizzards have struck my northern borders, you will be more willing. Perhaps if I also tell you that something follows the cold and snow, something numbering in the thousands, apparently, you will see the need for haste even more. Drakes are dead—and so are members of other races, including the humans you care so much about."

"I wasn't planning to back down," the Gryphon responded coldly. "Whether or not I like the thought has nothing to do with what I feel is my duty. Enough nonsense. What do you want me to do first?"

"Stand across from me on the other side of the crystal."

The Gryphon obeyed. Blue raised his arms, his hands opened with the palms pointed away from himself. "Take my hands and stand as I do."

When they were both in position, the drake closed his eyes. The chamber became deathly silent save for the water lapping against the rock. The Gryphon felt nothing and wondered if perhaps the Blue Dragon had failed.

Then, a shock went through him. Everything stood on end. He closed his eyes tightly and tried to suppress the pain. There had been tales of people struck by lightning who had lived to tell of it. Trying to explain what it felt like to have such raw, elemental power coursing through your body for even a brief instant was impossible. Now, the Gryphon understood why.

He felt the flow of his own power as it was drawn from him through his hands. It did not flow into the Dragon King, as he had expected, but instead seemed to gather, like a cloud, around the crystal. He noticed then, even though his eyes were still closed, that the same thing was happening to the drake. The Blue Dragon was creating a field of power around the crystal, building it up to a level he believed would be sufficient to cut through the Ice Dragon's barrier.

As the field grew, the Gryphon felt great warmth. He dared to open his eyes and suddenly found himself staring in awe at the crackling glow about the crystal. The pain was gone now, only a sense of exhaustion remained. The lionbird knew that it would be very soon; neither he nor the drake lord could long withstand such a draining before one of them collapsed.

"Now!" the Dragon King shouted. The Gryphon was not sure whether his companion was speaking to him or not, but he allowed the drake to keep control of the situation rather than take the chance of disrupting everything.

The field began to shrink—no, the Gryphon corrected himself, it was not shrinking. Rather, it was entering the crystal, feeding it.

He looked up to see that the Blue Dragon was now gazing at the center of the crystal with great anticipation. He followed that gaze but saw nothing but milky white within the gem. His shoulders slumped a little. They had failed.

"Do not give in to defeat!"

Even as the Dragon King shouted those words, the Gryphon saw the milky-white substance thin until something else became vaguely discernible. It did not seem to be shaped like anything either of them recognized, but considering how poor an image it was, that meant little.

The Blue Dragon tightened his concentration, hissing in response to the challenge facing him. This was the best he had done; he refused to give in now. He had to know, if only for himself.

Despite that, the Gryphon felt the Dragon King wavering slightly. The strain was greater on the drake, for he was both originator and focus of this spell. The lionbird clamped his beak shut and consciously added even more of his strength to the flow of power.

The drake lord's eyes gleamed as he realized what his ally was doing. Skillfully, he manipulated the power, using the new flow to cut through his brother's spell as a knife cuts bread.

The veil was pierced. In one instant it fell away, revealing . . . a thing of monstrous size with claws as large as either of them! The Blue Dragon briefly lost control and the image began to dissipate. With a hiss, the drake pushed back the gathering mists and strengthened the connection.

It was cold, they knew, horribly, terribly cold. The cold seemed to be both a part of the creature and to be moving parallel with it. As it moved through the countryside, the few trees became first frost-covered, then brittle as the chill increased. The thing tore up four or five with one blow and both watchers shivered as they saw the trees first wither, then solidify. The abomination threw them aside, ice-hard corpses. Behind it, they came to realize, was a trail of death. Whatever had lived there before was now like the trees, be it plant or animal.

Even as the first moved away, another came up from behind and to the right of it. It was larger than the first and no less eager. Try as he might the Gryphon could discern no mouth on the thing, and for eyes there seemed to be two little black dots, perhaps, but no more. This was no natural creature. This was the creation of the Ice Dragon. Living death. Monsters that sucked all life from what they touched. The Gryphon recalled what little he knew about the devastation of the Barren Lands. Something about it struck a sinister, similar note, but he could not say what.

"They cover the landsssscape!" the Dragon King whispered in open horror. He was correct, and the Gryphon bristled. They were everywhere, these creatures, and if the landmarks around them were any indication, they were already well into the northern areas of the Blue Dragon's kingdom and still heading south.

South to the rest of the Dragonrealms.

He had trouble concentrating after that and felt the drake lord waver as well. If the strain was telling on him, how badly did the Dragon King feel? He watched as the image faded away, to be replaced by the milky white once more. They had lost the image for good.

With a gasp the Blue Dragon released his hands, and both of them were collapsing to the floor of the chamber.

"My . . . my apologies, Lord Gryphon. I'm afraid my concentration wavered too much." The drake was gasping for breath. The Gryphon felt little better himself.

"Understandable . . . drake lord."

They both sat there, sprawled on opposite sides of the crystal, which had returned to the same dim glow it had had originally. Neither of them wanted to speak of the terror they had just observed, as if that would make it go away.

"It would seem we are too late already. Those things move well beyond the borders of the Wastes. They will be near the northern edge of the Tyber Mountains before long. If any more of them turn east, they will enter the central regions of my domain in three to four days and join up with the others. I must ready my defenses." The Blue Dragon struggled to his feet.

The Gryphon followed suit. "What can you do? What sort of defense can you prepare?"

"I have legions. . . ."

The lionbird shook his head. "You've felt the hunger; I know it. You know what those things are doing. Your legions would barely whet their appetites."

"I have spells!"

"How long before you tire? They flow like a river, drake lord. There must be thousands of them. The Ice Dragon has had time to prepare—or don't you think him capable of planning ahead?"

The Blue Dragon hesitated, then nodded his head slowly. "As you say. Ice is devious. He will have planned for measures such as I would use. The libraries are still our best hope. I will prepare a blink hole."

"That could be dangerous."

Blink hole. The tunnel through the Void, some called it. A blink hole was a passage beyond, which one could use to transport large objects to another destination in only a few minutes, regardless of distance in the real world. The Gryphon recalled the misty paths and wondered if they were related in some way.

"Azran knew how to control them and some of his secrets are now mine." Noting the expression on his associate's face, the drake explained. "Did you think that I would leave such a treasure trove as his citadel alone? It was abandoned, Gryphon, by those who by rights could have claimed it." It was obvious that the Dragon King knew that his "guest" was responsible for the blow that had actually slit Azran open, though Cabe had fought the bulk of the battle.

"You really can create a stable blink hole?"

"It is easier than you think. With it, we can move back and forth from your domain and mine."

"Can we be assured that no one will enter without our knowing?" He did not voice the thought that a tunnel to his palace would be a perfect way for the Blue Dragon to invade Penacles. The Gryphon shook his head. Old suspicions died hard, although . . .

"I can take care of my end. You will have to deal with where we exit." The Dragon King smiled, revealing all of his teeth. "Don't you trust me?"

"Barely."

"Give me time to rest—and decide where you want the exit to be. Be as precise as possible, because it is from your mind that I will draw the image."

The Gryphon nodded. The Blue Dragon bowed and departed, leaving him alone once more. It chafed him to be forced to wait; his instincts were those of a hunter and waiting only increased his frustrations. He was not certain that the magical libraries of Penacles, which when they did reveal answers tended to be obscure at best, would be of any assistance, nor was he totally secure with working with a foe such as this.

There was nothing else he could do. Until they returned to Penacles, things were more or less up to the Blue Dragon. He settled down to relax, expecting a long, boring wait, and fell asleep only moments later, the spell having drawn more from him than he had imagined.

THE SOUND OF marching feet woke the Gryphon. There was no way of telling exactly how long he had been asleep, save that the water level in the back of the chamber had lowered slightly. Tides in an underwater cavern? Not knowing anything about the sea—and not especially wanting to—he dropped the thought. There were, after all, more important things to settle.

He rose to his feet just as the Blue Dragon entered, the latter accompanied by two other drakes, possibly the guards who had confronted the Gryphon earlier. It was always difficult to tell one from another as far as he was concerned.

"Have you kept yourself occupied, lionbird?" By the Dragon King's tone, he knew exactly what the Gryphon had been up to.

"What time is it? I lose track in these underground chambers. I look forward to seeing the countryside of Penacles once again."

"Charred as it is?" The drake lord smirked. While much of the land controlled by the Gryphon remained as it always had, most of the countryside to the east of his city still suffered the effects of the siege by the Black Dragon. That was by no means the only area, but it was most definitely the worst. It was doubtful that the land would recover for several years at least.

The Gryphon's claws extended involuntarily. "Don't test the limits of our truce too often, reptile! You'll find my claws as sharp as yours!"

"Temper, my lord, temper! Merely a little humor in these dark times!" The Blue Dragon sobered. "Dark, indeed. While we—I—slept, the creatures of my brother have chosen to divide themselves into two main packs, each pack taking one side of the Tyber Mountains, thereby, ironically, giving Talak a brief reprieve."

"They can dig. Why go around the mountains?"

"Think, lord Gryphon! There's very little in the Tybers that they desire. In the time it would take them to find something satisfying—if they can truly be satisfied—they could be well beyond the Hell Plains in the east and the lands of the hill dwarves to the west! Irillian would already be theirs."

The Gryphon sheathed his claws. "They are remarkably capable for such brutish creatures. Surely they cannot reason that well."

"They cannot. I'm sure of that. Which means that they are controlled completely by brother Ice. They move like his left and right hands. One wonders if they truly have any will at all."

"Feeding a hunger . . ."

The Dragon King looked at him keenly. "You've thought of something?"

"Only something that should have been obvious to us. We've felt the hunger, the driving force that keeps those things moving. Big as they are, their hunger should have been sated by now. No creature eats that much. It isn't efficient. Why would Ice bother with such a creature? Surely, he could devise something more to his benefit? It is the constant hunger that is the key!"

"You are suggesting that the lord of the Northern Wastes is feeding off of the abominations, are you not?" the drake to the Dragon King's right blurted out. It was the first time either of the two had spoken. The Gryphon realized that these were not guards; these were Blue's dukes, most likely his own hatchlings.

"He is suggesting that, Zzzeras, and it is a suggestion to be taken to heart, yes?" the Dragon King snapped. The duke nodded quickly and quieted, though his stance seemed to be that of a child sulking.

"For what purpose, Gryphon?"

"I would say to keep the spell going, though I may be wrong."

The Blue Dragon hissed. "Whatever the case, it would be wise if we departed soon."

He snapped his fingers and the other two drakes stood back. Zzzeras seemed to hesitate briefly, then thought better of it. The Dragon King raised his hands and began an intricate pattern. The Gryphon watched in total fascination, the scholar in him once more taking control.

As the drake lord completed the pattern, what could only be described as a rip in reality appeared. The Blue Dragon nodded to himself and then began a second pattern. As he formed the pattern, the rip grew, becoming circular as it did, until it was taller and wider than a man—or drake warrior, in this case.

The Dragon King turned back to his ally. "I hope you don't mind, but I had Zzzeras draw the memory of your personal chambers from your mind while you slept. Rest assured, he sought nothing else. He knows better than to disobey, and I need your trust. It is possible to ascertain what I have said."

The Gryphon made no reply, not trusting himself to keep to civil words. He was tired of being used, tired of the invasions into his mind. Had it not been for the madness being perpetrated by the Ice Dragon . . . "Let's get on with it."

"Kylin." At the Dragon King's summons, the other drake stepped forward. "This gate is to remain open for as long as necessary. While I am away, I expect you to keep things running smoothly, yes?"

"Milord."

"Zzzeras, you will assist us here. We'll need the crystal and those items over there." Blue pointed to various items that he had gathered together at some point previous to the Gryphon's appearance. This revealed the confidence with which the Dragon King had plotted his course of action.

"I will have one of the servitors take it through."

"No, I want you to do it. The fewer who know what we do, the fewer with the capability to interfere. Perhaps, though, I will take this." He removed the crystal from its base. "Lord Gryphon, I must ask you to lead the way. If someone should somehow be in or near your chambers . . . or if my planning is faulty and we arrive elsewhere in your city, they will not take kindly to the intrusion of a drake."

"As you wish."

"Kylin, you are dismissed. Zzzeras, follow us."

The Blue Dragon reached over to a shelf and pulled a small case from it. He handed this to the Gryphon with a warning to be careful. He did not bother to explain why, but the lionbird took his word.

Zzzeras stood ready, his fingers tapping on the former resting place of the crystal. He seemed very impatient. The Gryphon doubted he liked playing servitor. Like many drakes, this one was arrogant and self-centered. He wondered whether Zzzeras had been born with the proper markings on his egg. Hopefully not. This one would make an impatient, dangerous Dragon King.

"Lord Gryphon?" The master of Irillian was waiting by the blink hole, the crystal nestled in his right arm.

His thoughts once more turning back to the misty paths utilized by the Draka, the Gryphon stepped forward. He felt a slight tug as he moved through the blink hole.

The world evaporated, to be replaced by a vast field of nothing. A great white nothing. Directly below his feet, he saw what resembled a path—only there was nothing below *that*, either. His mane bristled. Behind him, he heard the Blue Dragon and then . . .

. . . The path vanished beneath his feet and he was floating with nowhere to go.

XIV

THE CITADEL OF Azran was an ominous sight. It stretched high. There were turrets that jutted here and there for no practical reason that any of the trio could think of, save that this had perhaps once been a domicile of the Seekers. Cabe shuddered to think that the avians had once been so widespread. He wondered if any still remained in the ruins. It might have been a mistake to stop here.

"Fresh horse tracks," Haiden suddenly commented.

Cabe looked down. The only things he saw were more bones. It seemed impossible to avoid them completely. Granted, there were marks that might have been made by hooves, but at the same time it was impossible for him to differentiate them from tracks left by the countless scavengers who had picked this bounty clean after the battle. "How can you be certain?"

The elf looked at him solemnly. "It is one of those things my people can tell." He broke into a grin. "Actually, some of the horses left rather obvious reminders behind and our mounts have chosen to step on the reminders."

Cabe sniffed and realized Haiden was correct. He had assumed the odor was merely something left over from the carnage. "But how—"

"I've worked with horses long enough to tell the difference—and no wild herd would bother to be out here. If you want further proof, we passed some garbage that someone left behind."

"If you're not careful, Haiden," Gwen interjected, "you're going to give away all the secrets of your people."

"Small loss. Too many of my people think too highly of themselves."

The longer he rode with them, the more human the elf seemed to grow. Haiden had explained that one of his duties had been to act as liaison with the city of Zuu, which lay near the southwest portion of the Dagora

Forest. Cabe recalled a warrior he had met, Blane, the prince-commander of the horsemen from Zuu, who had died in the fighting within the walls of Penacles. Blane, a large, burly fighter, had died the way he wanted to and had taken the sadist Kyrg with him. There was a monument to Blane and his men in Penacles now.

"Are we going inside?" Gwen asked in general, though both she and Haiden looked at Cabe for an answer.

This was the sanctum of his father, the castle in which Cabe himself had been held prisoner for a short time. The only memories he had of this place were evil ones . . . yet, there might be something here to help them. Azran had been one of the most powerful necromancers—the undead creatures that had kidnapped Cabe from Penacles were proof of that. With the entire Plane of the Dead from which to draw knowledge, it was possible that they would find a solution here.

The citadel was also a nightmare Cabe felt he had to face if he was ever to have Azran's shadow lifted from his soul.

"We go inside."

Gwen especially was not pleased with the answer, but she nodded. Haiden's smile had diminished to a mere memory.

"You don't have to go in," Cabe suggested.

She shook her head, sending a luxurious wave of red hair flying. "No, I think it might be a good idea after all."

"Has anyone bothered to think that someone else might be inside?" Haiden asked.

Cabe turned to him. "You're the elf; you tell me."

Haiden grimaced and their mood lifted a little. One of the first things that Cabe had done on their way to the citadel was to seek out possible inhabitants. One did not go into the former home of a mad sorcerer without some precaution. That he had thought of that before the others had made him a bit proud. Despite all the knowledge he could draw from his grandfather's memories, he was still somewhat of a novice when it came to actual experience.

The elf moved to obey, but Cabe shook his head and informed them that it was indeed an empty building. Even as he said that, however, a slight hesitation caught him. He hoped he would not be proven wrong.

They entered the gate and the first real evidence that someone was using this as a base of operations became evident, for the stables were clean and there was fresh hay and water for the horses.

"Now we know where those riders came from, anyway." Gwen muttered. Having entered the grounds had subdued her.

"We'll only stay the night, Gwen. If we cannot find anything of use by then, it's either gone or somewhere we won't find it. Besides, we've run these horses into the ground these past few days. Unless they get some rest now, they're likely to die before we reach the Northern Wastes."

They dismounted and Haiden took the mages' horses. The elf was more than happy to be in the stables for now; it was the most mundane place in the citadel. Gwen and Cabe, hand in hand, took their belongings and walked across the yard to the massive iron doors which marked the entrance to the actual building itself.

"I wish we could have taken another path," the enchantress muttered. "One that would have avoided this *place*."

"This is the quickest and safest region and I forgot this would be here. I'm not that happy with entering a place that was home to Azran and built, as far as I know, by the Seekers." Cabe stared at the iron doors again.

If this was truly a Seeker relic, he started to wonder, why bother with doors and such? Why not make it more of an aerie? Had the Seekers in fact taken over a relic of some earlier race? Where did the list of dominant races begin? When were the lands that were now called the Dragonrealms first inhabited and by whom—or what?

So many questions. Nathan, he knew, would have told him that it was a sorcerer's duty to continually ask such questions, even if it proved impossible to answer them in his lifetime. Not a satisfying way to look at things, Cabe thought.

The doors were not locked; there was no real reason for them to be. As far as most were concerned, Azran's home had been stripped of everything useful. It was said that the Blue Dragon had been the first to stake claim, though others mentioned the Storm Dragon, Talak, and even the Crystal Dragon, though that last one seemed unlikely considering the reclusive nature of that drake lord and the great distance between the Hell Plains and the Legar Peninsula, which jutted out on the southwestern corner of the continent.

As they wandered through the abandoned building, their respective fears diminished. There was nothing here but dust and cobwebs now. The marauders had left a few things behind, but it was obvious that this was not a permanent camp. They would not have left it unguarded, otherwise.

Decay had set in. After standing for so many ages, the citadel was now without preserving spells. Azran had drained those away at some point for his own use, most likely during the slaughter of the Red Dragon's horde.

Cabe glanced at a stairway leading down. He turned to Gwen, who was inspecting a few tattered tomes that had been left behind. Judging by her expression, which might just as easily have had to do with the tremendous amounts of dust, they had been left behind for good reason.

"I'm going to have a look down here. I shouldn't be long. It looks like a storeroom."

"Do you want me to come with you?"

He shook his head. "Wait for Haiden. When I come back up, we'll eat. I'm sure that whatever sort of room is down there has been cleaned out."

As he descended, he tried to identify what he saw with what little he knew about the citadel. For the most part, he had remained in one room. Only briefly had he seen the outside. As far as he knew, he had never been down this way.

As he suspected, it was a storage area of some sort and one that had been picked clean. Even shelves were missing, though the brackets remained. Still, he felt that there might be something here. . . . Cabe ran his hands along the walls, thinking to himself that if there was indeed a secret panel, someone would have discovered it by now.

He touched the far wall, the obvious choice, but felt nothing. However, touching the wall on the right side made him tingle. It was an odd sensation, almost as if the wall was trying to identify him and was having some difficulty.

Cabe concentrated, seeking out the point of origin. It was not hard to do, but somehow he suspected now that others would have had a rougher time. He reached with his mind and forced his will on it.

The wall was no longer before him. He fell face-first into a room from which a terrible stench rose. It was as if all the dead outside were still rotting. Cabe quickly covered his nose and looked up.

There was a pool, but water certainly was not what filled it. A brackish liquid of some sort, with a greenish ooze overlaying it. It bubbled and belched. Cabe rose to his feet, his nose still covered, and turned back the way he had come. There was a blank wall behind him.

Uneasily, he returned his attention back to the pit. Azran would not have hidden it if it were not something important. He remembered his own thoughts about his father's dealings with the dead. This room would certainly qualify as ideal for that.

The bubbling was slowly growing more intense, he realized, as if something were coming to the surface. Cabe had no desire to see what that something was. He tried to relocate the spot that had allowed him access to this godforsaken room, but it was nowhere to be found. Evidently, that was not the way to leave.

The pool was frothing now and Cabe noticed that the stench was becoming even more nauseating. He was almost ready to throw up.

The—a description escaped Cabe for the moment—rose out of the muck and ooze.

"Who do you seek?" it rasped. The voice kept changing, as if there were more than one speaker attempting to take charge.

Cabe tried to avoid looking at the odd collection of limbs, eyes, mouths, and indescribable appendages as he gasped out a response. "No—no one! It's a mis-mistake!"

"The summons was clear—though whether it was you or another is not." There was just the slightest hint of puzzlement in the—its—voice(s).

Several thoughts flashed through Cabe's mind, including, of course, Azran, who . . .

"I will bring him forth."

Bring him forth? Cabe forgot about the stench, forgot about the horrible appearance of the other, and shouted, "No! Not that one! That's not the one I want!"

Azran! He had come that close to facing the specter of his father! Great caution was called for here, Cabe realized. If he was not careful, he might next summon the Brown Dragon or—he quickly squelched the last thought. He did *not* want to speak to the Brown Dragon!

Another idea occurred to him. "Bring me Nathan Bedlam!"

The—*guardian* was the most reasonable title Cabe could give it—hesitated. "That proves . . . impossible for the moment." It was silent for several seconds, then: "There is one who hears you, who wishes to speak to you."

"Not Azran!"

"No. He calls himself . . . Tyr."

Tyr! One of the Dragon Masters! One of the two undead forced to kidnap Cabe for Azran! "Yes! That's the one!"

The guardian sank slowly into the muck. It vanished and with it went some of the potency of the stench. That did not mean that Cabe was not having trouble breathing.

The pool bubbled again. A head slowly broke free from the ooze. Cabe watched as a tall figure rose above the surface. The remnants of a dark blue robe covered him. Unlike the guardian, he was free of muck.

The skin was wrinkled and dry and overall the man had the appearance of one who had died violently. Tyr had not survived the Turning War and he showed it. Once, he might have been thought of as handsome, but only the memories of that remained.

The eyelids of the unliving mage opened, revealing blank, white, sightless orbs. Yet, Tyr turned his head and looked directly at Cabe. The dead, it seemed, saw things with a different sort of vision.

"Cabe—Nathan. You came as I hoped. When I felt your presence near, I tried to reach out, to draw you here." The macabre figure folded his hands. "I rejoice in seeing you. I rejoice in knowing that Azran has come to us to pay for his misdeeds."

Cabe shifted uncomfortably. He did not want to even think about Azran. Tyr apparently saw this and smiled. It did little to reassure the young sorcerer. Part of Tyr's jaw was loose.

"When the gatekeeper felt your touch upon the wall, it was confused. You were too much like Azran—yet, too little as well. If you had been other than you are, one who is two, it would have recognized you as only a relative or an outsider and forbidden you entrance. But that which Nathan has bequeathed you gave you the key."

"This place," Cabe finally managed to blurt out, "this place is where he summoned you from."

"And forced us into misdeeds. There are penalties for abusing the sleep of the dead, but Azran thought he would live forever. Now, he will suffer for some time before he is given his rest. But that troubles you. Let us instead speak of why you came to this place. The lord of the Northern Wastes has unleashed the Void."

"The Void?"

"Not the actual Void, but something that can only be thought of in those terms. The Void is a place that is the absence of matter. Open a hole to the Void and matter enters. You have seen the place. You have seen the debris that litters it."

Cabe nodded, thinking of an owl creature he had seen. A mage or something from some other world, dead most likely because it had been careless. There had been fragments of other things as well. "I remember."

"The Void can never be filled. The Dragonrealms as a whole would not diminish its hunger by a single iota. So, too, is the hunger that the Ice Dragon now contains within himself."

"Within himself?"

Tyr nodded, shaking loose a bit of flesh from the right side of his face. It struck the murky liquid below with a dull splash and sank quickly beneath the surface. Cabe paled.

"There must be a focal point, a place for the power to gather. You know that. Nathan knew that."

Nathan had been the focal point for that spell. Yet . . .

As if anticipating Cabe's thoughts, Tyr added, "Soon there will come a time when the Ice Dragon will be able to release himself from the spell. Then, he will control it completely and no one will be able to turn it back. It is only while he himself relies on the spell that he is vulnerable—I think. My mind is not what it was. For all I know he may be unstoppable now— but no, that can't be right. . . ."

Tyr was losing substance, both fading and deteriorating. Cabe started to reach out, but thought better of it. He did not want to chance falling into the pool. There was no telling whether he would be able to climb out again. It was not yet his time to cross over to the Plane of the Dead—at least, he hoped not. Besides, Tyr seemed unconcerned with the loss of his physical body. Being dead, it might not hurt him. Perhaps this form was only one he had re-created to speak to Cabe.

The dead sorcerer shook himself from his stupor. "This is all unimportant. The reason that I wanted to speak to you concerns you alone, Bedlam." Tyr was transparent, and much of his flesh had already fallen from his body. Cabe could barely keep from looking at the skeletal figure, but he knew that the Dragon Master would not have sought him out if it was not important. "I shouldn't warn you, but when I knew that you were here, perhaps because I hoped you would come, I knew that I must defy the rules. . . ."

"Rules?" Cabe watched Tyr fade away, then reappear, little more than a smoky blur. "Tyr, what rules? What do you mean?"

"They've done this, the guardians. I . . . should have known better. They wanted me to speak to you of other things, albeit important things, until my time was gone from here. . . . A pity you do not have the knowledge of the dead that cursed Azran had; I could walk the earth and tell you in my leisure. . . ."

Tyr faded away again.

"Tyr!" Cabe stared down at the pool. It bubbled obscenely. The odor became very noticeable again.

"Wait!"

The very force of the voice made the young mage stumble back against the wall. With an effort obviously taxing for one of the dead, Tyr brought himself back to full corporeal existence. It would be a momentary thing, Cabe knew. The strain was probably as painful as anything a living creature could feel, if not worse.

"Damn their games! Damn their melodramatic ways! Damn all petty gods or those who think themselves gods! Bedlam!" Tyr's eyes were burning into Cabe's mind. "Your destiny lies in the Northern Wastes, but . . . if you go there, you will almost surely at last die! I—"

Tyr vanished; this time for good, Cabe knew. The pool bubbled, but nothing more. Even the horrid guardian did not reappear.

He was going to die.

He was going to die and the dead Dragon Master had tried to warn him, tried to prevent him from going on . . . but no! He had said that Cabe's destiny lay in the Northern Wastes! Did that mean that they were going to fail? No! Tyr had said nothing of the sort!

I'm going to die, Cabe repeated to himself.

Cabe.

He felt his own name in his mind. His first thought was that Tyr had found the strength to reach out to him again.

Cabe. This time, his name was followed by a low chuckle. He knew then that it was not Tyr.

Somehow, his groping hands found whatever it was that would allow him to exit this chamber. He fell forward even as the low chuckle began again. Only when he was completely through the wall did it seal and, with that action, cut off the mocking voice.

He recognized that voice, and thanked the heavens and the earth that he had not had time to think upon its owner for any length of time. Had he still been in that chamber, he might have died right there—unless something worse could have occurred.

Cabe stumbled up the stairs, where he fell into the arms of a startled Gwen. She held him tight, only comprehending his shock and not understanding what had caused it. Haiden was nearby, but he kept his peace.

He was going to die in the Wastes. That must have been why the voice had chuckled. He knew that voice, knew it for Azran. Azran was mocking him.

Azran had told him, only with Cabe's own name and that laugh, that he was expecting him soon.

AT LAST, TOMA thought to himself. *At last I have found the exit to this blasted labyrinth of a tunnel!*

While he did appreciate the aid the Seeker had given him, he cursed it for making him crawl through a maze of ice for who knew how long. His hands were numb; most of his front side was numb from crawling along without rest. Toma had not dared rest. There was no telling when the Ice Dragon might decide it was time to check on him. Even now, there might be scores of the unliving ice servants searching for him along the outskirts of the mountain range. There might even be a number of them crawling through the tunnel system like a multitude of rats. How could the Ice Dragon not possibly suspect such a complex system of tunnels within his own citadel? Was this merely a trap? A game for the Dragon King's entertainment?

Toma longed for the time when he would regain his own sorcerous powers. Then, he would be ready for a fight. Then, he would crush the Ice Dragon once and for all.

He closed his eyes and hissed quietly. His mind was addled. He had to escape first. All his boasts would be for naught if he perished in the Wastes. It was cold out there, far colder than it had been since his arrival. It had something to do with the mad plan of his "host." There would be a winter like this everywhere, apparently. No domain would be untouched.

He shivered, the tatters of his cloak no more protecting him from the onslaught of the cold than if he had not been wearing a cloak at all. He continued to try to wrap it around himself out of reflex action. A part of his mind told him that he was slowly losing touch with reality, but the other part went on with life, such as it was. After all, there was now the Wastes to conquer.

It took some maneuvering to keep himself from falling headfirst from the hole into the ice and snow below. He wondered vaguely how the Seekers did it. It probably helped that they could fly; they did not face the risk of falling to their deaths. Headfirst was probably normal. They would need to go that way in order to gain the wind currents and fly.

How long before the Ice Dragon was on his trail? At the moment, he no longer saw this as a game played by the Dragon King. Ice had no desire for games such as this.

With the greatest of difficulty, he made it down to a ledge some three-fourths of the way to the bottom. He was honestly amazed that his hands had any sort of grip left at all. Turning around, Toma gazed at the great expanse of the Northern Wastes. It had changed since last he had seen it. No longer was it a flat, dead land. The ice, snow, and earth had all been churned up, as if great worms had dug their way up to the surface after a heavy rain. He hissed an oath that would have shocked even the Ice Dragon. Now, the going would be even worse. He would have to climb and climb and climb.

The image of great worms digging was not far from the truth, it suddenly occurred to him. He had seen how one of his captor's monstrosities had risen from beneath the earth. This was merely a case of more than one.

Many more than one.

Toma scanned the horizon as far as he could see in every direction. Not one area of the Wastes had been left unscathed by the digging creatures—and the drake could see the landscape for miles away. There had to have been thousands.

He had to cross this alone and without his magic.

Toma shivered. Not for the first time since his arrival here and not, certainly not, from the cold.

XV

"THE BLINK HOLE! Someone hasss disssrupted my ssspell!"

Both the Blue Dragon and the Gryphon floated helplessly in the nothingness of the Void. The drake lord spent the first few moments cursing those who had placed him in this predicament—whoever that might be. The Dragon King had not gotten that far in his cursing yet, though it sounded suspiciously as if he had a notion.

The Gryphon was trying to be more practical. This was his first true visit to the Void; he had glimpsed it more than once, but had been fortunate never to have needed to travel through it more than briefly. He would have been happier if he had never had a reason to. Nevertheless, he was not going to let the Void overwhelm his emotions.

The two were slowly drifting from one another and, since the Gryphon had no real working knowledge of the blink hole, he determined that it was very much to his benefit to stay near the drake.

Magic, it seemed, was unaffected for the most part. Utilizing the bare minimum of raw power, the lionbird pushed himself toward his companion, whose curses were quieting down. At first, the Gryphon assumed he would come to a gradual halt, as would have been natural under the laws of his normal plane of existence, but in fact he lost no momentum whatsoever and very quickly was heading into a collision. Before he had time to react, the Blue Dragon was boosting himself to the side, one clawed hand out to grab hold of the Gryphon. More experienced, the drake caught him and brought both of them to a spinning halt.

"A dangerousss maneuver, Lord Gryphon," Blue commented. "You should have waited. I wasss not about to lose you."

"At the time, it was hard to say what you planned to do at all."

"Forgive my outburst, but I have alwaysss prided myself on thinking things through. It never occurred to me that there might be those among my clans who would so actively betray me like this. They must feel very confident to make such a move."

Revolt by drakes against their own ruler? The Gryphon knew of lesser kings who had revolted against the Emperor Dragon, but that was a completely different scale. Clans never overthrew their clan leaders—did they?

Blue was laughing mirthlessly. "You know less about our race than you think. In some ways we are as violent, as unstable a race as the humans. We are also pragmatic, though. Long-term revolts against our own kind are not common. When it is known that a leader has been overthrown, the clans do not continue to fight among themselves. They accept that new duke or even king as their proper one. After all, with few exceptions, the antagonists are both of royal markings. No one will accept the rule of an unmarked drake—not even if that drake is Toma or Zzzeras."

"It was Zzzeras, then?"

The Dragon King did not reply, already considering their options. "Blink holes always leave residual traces. I've never had to try to find one from within, but there's always a first time."

"What about the crystal?" the Gryphon suggested. "It served us well in your chambers."

The drake lord showed him an empty hand. "I fear that the crystal is now merely one more artifact floating in the Void. I relinquished my hold when the path vanished and I have no idea in which direction it was hurtled. Trying to find it will take away precious time. I cannot say how long the traces will remain noticeable."

Since his work required the use of both hands, the Blue Dragon made his companion take hold of his belt from the back side. He also gave the

Gryphon a warning; there was a slight chance that they might face some sort of danger here in the Void. Not everything was dead and even the unliving objects might prove hazardous, as some of the larger ones might be floating at speeds several hundred times faster than what the Gryphon had been moving earlier. Impact against a soaring, hill-sized chunk of earth would easily shatter their skeletons and leave no more trace of either of them than two messy spots.

The Gryphon got the point.

It was difficult going at first. The drake's gestures kept moving both figures this way and that, making concentration almost impossible. The Dragon King was finally forced to gesture very slowly, making him look more like a dancer. The Gryphon refrained from commenting on this to his companion, knowing all too well the unpredictable humor of the drakes.

"Damn!" Blue hissed at one point. "I can barely feel it! We are running out of time!"

Frustrated, the Gryphon spoke out. "Let me try!"

"You don't know the spell!"

"You can show me, can't you?" When he saw that the drake was reluctant, he added, "Preserve your secrets all you like, then. It'll give you something to think about while we spend the rest of all time floating about like leaves in a pond!"

The other hissed, then agreed. "You have a point, my friend. Very well, see if you can locate it. It's much like trying to tap into a source of power."

The Gryphon nodded and then closed his eyes as he concentrated. For some time he felt nothing, and his confidence began to slip. All he felt was the blank nothingness of this undimension. It was like having another Void within him. It was almost too much.

When he was on the verge of giving up, he caught hold of something tenuous. The Blue Dragon had said it would be like tapping into the powers. That was the way this felt. His mind traced it back a little. This was indeed the blink hole; there were still mental after-images of the hole itself.

"I have it!"

The drake lord hissed again, but this time there was a note of triumph in the sound. "Open your eyes, then. I'll have to do this physically rather than possibly make you break your hold on it."

Releasing himself as slowly and carefully as possible—in order to minimize drift—the master of Irillian began to repeat the spell. The Gryphon watched, matching the movements as precisely as he could. The two were beginning to float apart, but he tried to ignore that fact. All that was important was for him to complete the spell.

There was suddenly resistance from the other plane, as if someone definitely did not want them coming back. That was nearly the case, for, involved with this new problem, the lionbird almost missed a movement. He was able to correct himself barely in time.

"Someone . . . someone's fight-fighting me!"

"Ignore them! They cannot stop you at this late point. They can only hope to slow you down or make you miscast!"

The Blue Dragon revealed the last part of the spell.

The Gryphon completed it.

They were standing on the path again. The drake wasted no time. "Hurry! Back the way we came!"

In the next instant they were leaping through the blink hole and back into the mortal plane. The Dragon King came down in a pile, striking the floor hard. The Gryphon, attempting to jump over him, struck one of the walls with his shoulder. He fell to ground, groaning as every bone and muscle in that side of his body shouted out in pain.

Through watering eyes, he saw two other drakes. One was even now slumping to the floor, a savage blow from the other having ripped out his throat. The victor looked at the injured lionbird and there was bloodlust in the burning eyes. Then the drake turned and gazed at Blue, who was rising to his feet. The other drake sank to one knee.

"Milord! I thank the Dragon of the Depths that you have made it back!"

"Kylin." The drake lord looked down at his duke, then at the corpse.

"Zzzeras," he whispered.

"Milord." Kylin dared to stand. The bloodlust had vanished the moment he knew his monarch had been looking directly at him. "I returned here to have a last-minute word with him, only to discover him standing here laughing, claiming that he would now be ruler. He was certain of his success and certain that I would bow to him once I realized you were gone. I did not."

"Zzzeras hoped to rule, unmarked as he was?" the Blue Dragon asked, his voice low and even a bit sad.

"We knew his ambitions, milord. Before the chaos that tore your council apart, he often met with Toma."

"I remember. It seems that wherever he goes, Toma spreads madness.

Had he not been protected by the emperor, I would have challenged him—as dangerous as that could have been." The drake lord looked down on the corpse. "A pity. I wish truly that it had not come to this."

Kylin was reaching out a supporting hand when the Blue Dragon, claws extended, caught him by the throat, ripping the entire area out with that one blow far more cleanly than Kylin had done to Zzzeras.

The other drake did not even have time to look puzzled before he fell to the floor, to join his counterpart.

Blue turned his attention to the Gryphon, who was rising slowly, eyes glued on the Dragon King. "As I said, lionbird, you know less about my race than you think."

"You . . . you killed him. Ripped out his throat like a madman—for serving you loyally?" It was incredible. Unbelievable.

The drake shook his head. "I killed him for betraying me . . . and for murdering Zzzeras, whose greatest fault was playing the dupe. It was Kylin who sought to abandon us in the Void."

"Kylin?"

"Does that surprise you?" Blue shook his head. His voice was tinged with disgust. "Zzzeras did not have the skill to cut us off. Kylin did not know that Zzzeras also only dealt with Toma on my orders. Toma was always one to be watched. Poor Kylin. He never realized that I used the crystal to spy on him. To spy on all of them. How else does one remain ruler in troubled times?"

In the short time since his first meeting with the Blue Dragon, the Gryphon had learned much about drake society—more than he would have wanted to know. He could not say that it differed greatly from the human society that he, in all honesty, had to consider himself a part of. It did not give him any satisfaction to know that the drakes were no better.

"He must have thought this the chance of a lifetime. I played the fool perfectly, imagining that his delusions of power were only that. I didn't think he would actually do something like this."

The Blue Dragon shrugged. "Enough of this! I would say that the guards Kylin sent elsewhere should return in a matter of moments. In the meantime, we have new things to consider, most important of which is the loss of the crystal. I had hoped that, if we discovered something, it might prove of use for focusing our power."

At the moment, the only thing on the Gryphon's mind was to leave this domain and never return, but he knew that such a move would solve nothing, and the Ice Dragon was not a threat to be dismissed.

"Our greatest concern, drake lord, is the libraries themselves, not your crystal. We can worry about possibilities later on, but the first thing we need to do is discover what avenues we may take. There may be nothing in the libraries, or there may be some reference so obscure that we won't find it in time. It may be possible that we have to confront the Ice Dragon face-to-face, though I cannot fathom what we might do then. One thing I do intend to do is to contact Cabe Bedlam and your counterpart who rules the Dagora Forest."

The Blue Dragon glowered, and the hiss that escaped from his frowning mouth held no love for the last suggestion. Blue cared little for his turncoat brother and even less for anyone of the surname Bedlam. From his point of view it might make sense, but the Gryphon was having none of that now.

He pointed a taloned finger at the drake lord. "Hear me on this. This is a time when enemies will have to embrace, much as you and I have had to do—at your suggestion. Whether that enemy bears the name Bedlam, it is nothing compared to the danger we presently face. I would have dealt with Azran himself if it meant saving the Dragonrealms from the frosty lord of the Wastes. Do I make myself clear?"

"Clear. Perfectly so," the Dragon King admitted. "If I may, we shall depart as soon as I have rectified this situation." With one hand, he indicated the two still forms.

"I have no qualms about that."

"It will not take long. When things have been settled, I will open a new blink hole . . . unless you wish to try."

The Gryphon shook his head. "I have no desire to revisit the Void for any length of time, and that is what will probably happen if I attempt that spell. My concern was less with memorizing it than getting us back."

"Then, I shall construct the hole. We should have no interruptions this time." As the Blue Dragon finished speaking, several drake warriors and servitors came running in. One of them apologized profusely for having been duped by Kylin, and offered his life. The Dragon King did not take him up on the offer.

An eye on the proceedings, the Gryphon's mind returned to the libraries. He was certain that something concerning what they faced was located in the libraries; as far as he knew, *everything* was in the libraries. The question was, whether they would find the answer and understand it before it was too late.

The more important question was: would there be a solution at all? Was this one case where the Seekers or whoever had designed the spell had not had time to create a counterspell?

The Gryphon pictured himself wading in volume after volume in search of a ghost that might be standing right before him. He wondered whether the builders of the libraries had considered this when they had built it. Had they designed the structure just so? Was it intentionally confusing or was there a pattern that neither he nor his predecessor, the Purple Dragon, had discovered?

In frustration, the lionbird began to silently curse the madmen who had built the libraries. He stopped up short, though, considering then the sudden notion that those mysterious builders were watching him even now and that to curse them would only be inviting new complications when he began his search.

"I am about to open a new hole," commented the Dragon King. Somehow he had walked directly up to the Gryphon without the latter's noticing him. "All will be under control this time."

The Gryphon's mane ruffled in uneasiness. A more idiotic statement he had never heard.

GWEN LOOKED AT Haiden and shook her head. "He still won't tell me what it was he came across down there."

They were in the main hall of Azran's citadel. A small fire was burning itself in the fireplace and a meal had been left half prepared on a table that the elf had dusted off. They had given up searching the building after Cabe had come screaming through the wall. Gwen had searched for some sort of passage, but even her abilities could detect nothing behind the stone blocks. Yet she knew Cabe had come from somewhere. There had to at least be some trace of a dimensional gate or a blink hole. There was not; at least, none that she could find. It did not surprise her. This had been the home of Azran, and she already knew too well how devious he had been. For a moment, she even thought she heard him laughing at them in that mocking tone of his.

Cabe had calmed, almost so much that both his companions worried that much more. He seemed almost indifferent at times, though that could change any moment. It was almost as if he were of two minds—which he was in a way, but not the way Gwen thought him now. On the one hand, he seemed to accept everything they planned as inevitable. On the other hand, he hesitated when it came to actually doing anything that would further their efforts.

Haiden walked over to the stairway and peered down. "Maybe I can discover something."

"Don't bother," Cabe finally muttered. "Only Azran and I have the ability—and I shouldn't. If you do manage to break through the barrier, I wouldn't doubt that my father left a few surprises before he departed for the last time."

The elf turned back to him, frustrated. "Then why don't you tell us what is in there—and where 'it' is, for Rheena's sake?"

Cabe stood and seemed to shake himself out of his stupor. "It wouldn't matter. We can forget about searching any further. There's nothing here that would be of assistance to us. We leave as early as possible in the morning. I want us at the edge of the Northern Wastes by the next day—which will mean teleporting at some point, I guess."

The elf whistled and Gwen stared deeply into Cabe's eyes. She did not like what she saw—or rather, did not see—in them. It was as if he was purposefully cutting her off from a part of him, something she had never known him to do so adamantly.

"It will be a terrible strain on the horses. I don't think they'll last into the Wastes, then," Haiden commented.

"Then we'll get fresh ones from your companions up there. At the very worst, we only need one horse." He did not have to elaborate on what that meant; if it came down to it, Cabe planned to go on alone.

"Two," corrected Gwen. Cabe did not even try to argue with her—which did not mean he agreed. She knew that the closer they came to their destination, the more she would have to watch him. It was not unlikely that he might try to slip ahead of them. He was beginning to really frighten her now. "If you plan on trying to teleport, you'll need someone to assist you. A spell like that is liable to leave you helpless."

Haiden sighed. "Very well, lord and lady, if we are to rise early, I had best get our meal taken care of. That way, we can call it an early evening." He studied the hall, taking in the shadowy corners, the dust-covered walls, and the grotesque reliefs that lined the walls.

"I could not ask for a more peaceful, pleasant abode," he added dryly.

They spoke little over their meal and even less afterward. Gwen cast a protective spell, as she had so many times before, but Haiden was not satisfied this time. Azran's former home disturbed him. He volunteered himself for watch, assuring them that he would remain alert all night if necessary.

* * *

THEY WOKE EARLY that morning . . . That is to say, Cabe and Gwen did. Haiden was rolled in a ball on the floor, oblivious to everything. It took several attempts to wake him, which said something about the tales of elves' legendary stamina. Haiden confessed that he had remained awake for most of the night, dropping off an hour or so before dawn. The red in his face did not vanish for the next half hour.

It was noticeably colder, an unusual climatic change for a land aptly titled the Hell Plains. Even here, they could feel and hear the eruptions of minor volcanoes. Gwen was the first one to put the thought into words.

"The Ice Dragon's powers are growing. He can already maintain a steady cold this far south in the Hell Plains. What must Irillian and Talak be like?"

"This is more of a natural cold," Cabe commented almost emotionlessly. "The soul-numbing cold hasn't reached this far yet, at least not with any regularity."

"And how long will it be before that happens?"

Cabe gave them that look that reminded Gwen so much of Nathan. "Far sooner than we can hope."

They were on their way a few minutes later. None of them was displeased with leaving the crumbling citadel of Azran behind. As far as they were all concerned, the sooner the Hell Plains tore the place apart, the better. There was nothing good about the structure, and whatever or whoever had built it no longer mattered; Azran had tainted it with his presence.

With the exception of a handful of times when they were forced to go around unstable ground, they met with no difficulties for the better part of the day. The cool weather remained steady save when they were forced to ride extremely close to some of the more active craters. Only then did the land live up to its name. Despite the fact that there were very fertile areas in this domain, no one could see why anyone, even a drake, would want to live here.

As if in response to that thought, riders materialized on the horizon.

They were not men. No man rode a minor drake unless his life depended on it . . . and even then many would have hesitated.

"Haiden," Cabe whispered. "You mentioned nothing about drake activity."

"That's because there hasn't been any, sorcerer. From this distance, I cannot say what clan they are. Gold's, perhaps, or maybe remnants of Red's."

"We'll find out in a moment," Gwen added. "They seem to be coming in our direction."

The trio readied themselves for the worst. They could not possibly out-run the riders at this point and it was obvious that they had been spotted. The ground behind them was too unstable for a reckless retreat. It would be child's play for the riders to pick them off from behind.

As they neared, it became evident that these were indeed remnants of Red's clans. A whole clan, in fact, for there were dams and young as well as warriors and servitors like Sssarekai.

"Refugees," Cabe muttered.

"Which still won't prevent them from running us down," Haiden added.

Astonishingly, the riders did slow. By the time they were within hailing distance, the drakes had slowed their mounts to a trot. It was probably a dif-ficult task; minor drakes had big appetites and these looked as if they had not been fed properly for the last couple of days. They eyed the horses with growing interest.

"Cabe." Gwen's voice was tinged in uneasiness. "Isn't it said that the Red Dragon died battling Azran?"

He nodded, already having seen the reason for her question.

The crimson dragon warrior raised his hand, bringing a halt to the drakes. His helm was the most intricate Cabe had ever seen, save those worn by the Dragon Kings themselves. That, more than his color, proclaimed what he was.

"Apparently, the previous Red Dragon planned in advance. He had an *heir.*"

"A new Dragon King . . ." That was all Haiden could say. The mixture of disgust, hatred, and fear in his voice was enough to jolt even Cabe.

The Red Dragon—for there was no denying him the title of his prede-cessor—urged his mount slowly forward until he was close enough for Cabe to see the burning eyes.

"An elf. An elf and two humans . . ." The new lord of the Hell Plains studied them closely. "Two human mages, at that."

"Milord—" Haiden's attempt at diplomacy was cut off by a sharp wave of the hand from the drake.

"I have not given you permission to speak, leaf-eater. Besides, it is the humans I wish to speak to."

Cabe urged his own mount forward a little, no small task considering the animal's quite natural urge to be as far away from dragons as possible. He bowed his head and waited for the Dragon King to speak again.

"You do not have the look of murderous raiders about you, but humans are a treacherous lot. I could attack you; I would probably kill you, but possibly at the loss of my own life and that of some of my clan."

The arrogant boasts almost made Cabe smile before he realized that there had to be some truth in them. He was King by birth, or else the others would have never followed him. That meant that he controlled the forces of his predecessor, which made him a formidable opponent indeed. The last Red Dragon had been known for a fierceness that had rivaled his brother Brown.

"I would know, human, to whom I am speaking. You look to be of some importance, despite the fact that you ride with only a dam with hair nigh as red as fire and a worthless tree-dweller."

Haiden made a choking sound, but the drake lord ignored him.

Cabe took a deep breath. Matters had been hanging heavy on him and now this had to be added. He might have tried to lie, but somehow he suspected this new ruler would recognize a lie. "I ride with my wife, Gwendolyn, known as the Lady of the Amber, and Haiden, a worthy guide and scout. My surname is familiar to you, as my first name may be. I am Cabe Bedlam."

The Dragon King hissed loudly, causing much unrest among his followers. For the briefest of times, Cabe thought he saw fear in the drake lord's eyes. He could imagine what it might be like, a new ruler who suddenly finds himself confronted by a name synonymous with the darkest evil as far as his race is concerned.

To his credit, the drake quickly recovered. Sitting as tall as possible, he stared directly into Cabe's eyes. "Have you come, then, to complete the destruction of our clans by both your sire and the soul-stealing death to the north?"

The Ice Dragon's creatures were moving quickly. The horror the already-battered clans of Red had faced must have seemed to them a sign that their extinction was demanded by the powers. Now, just when they might be safe, they faced an older fear—a mage whose name was Bedlam.

Cabe shook his head. "My only desire is to see the Dragonrealms at peace, with both drake and human coexisting. The death of your predecessor was due to the madness of one of my kin." He decided against pointing out that it was the old Dragon King's fault as well. "What I am concerned about is the death from the north that you just mentioned."

"And why is that?"

"I hope to put an end to it."

The drake lord was silent at first; then, a low laugh escaped him. There was only pity in that laughter, pity for what the Dragon King thought surely must be a madman.

"Have you seen what comes from the Wastes? Have you seen the gift of my brother, the lord of the Northern Wastes?" Evidently, Cabe realized for the first time, all Dragon Kings considered one another brothers once they held their respective thrones."

"I've seen them. One wandered south long before the others."

"One?"

Cabe could see the false mouth of the drake smile, revealing teeth almost human. Actually, he realized that this new Dragon King looked more human than any of the others.

"One?" the drake repeated. "You have not seen horror until you have seen hundreds—thousands—digging their way through the soil, reaching out to devour, not our bodies, but the life-force within us! You have seen nothing!"

Gwen dared to urge her own steed near Cabe's. "We know more than you think. We know something of what's going on up there. We mean you no harm, drake lord. If you have information of value to us, we would appreciate it. If not, we have no quarrel with you and would wish nothing else than for both parties to be on their respective ways."

The Dragon King listened intently, though his eyes never left Cabe. "I have more than you see here, Bedlam. Most of my kin have gone to Silver's domain. We are the last, the most northern of the clans and the wall of defense behind which the others were able to depart. I started out with a group nearly a third again this size, but those ungodly leeches caught them either one or a few at a time. My scouts report that they have penetrated even farther south in Blue's Kingdom, no surprise since there is a much more bountiful feast awaiting them in Irillian. How do you plan to stop an unliving wave that devours all life before it? Are you going to pull demons from another dimension? Can you cleanse the Wastes with fire?"

"There is a possibility, but I have to go deep into the Wastes. I have to confront your counterpart himself."

"Madness!" The Dragon King shook his head. "I see no reason to hold you from your task, then. It only brings the abominations closer to us and prevents you from fulfilling your deathwish any sooner."

Cabe had gone pale at the last statement, thinking that perhaps the drake lord knew something, but the latter was only mocking what he felt to be a fool's quest.

The reptilian monarch sobered. He started to turn his mount around in order to rejoin his subjects, then twisted so that he faced Cabe once more. "If there is truly something you can do, I wish you the best. I have no love for your race—and especially your clan—but I have no desire to see the lands under the icy claw of that cursed colddrake who rules the Wastes. Better we all be dead than bow to his rule."

Cabe bowed his head briefly, with Gwen and Haiden following suit. The Dragon King turned away and returned to his party. At his signal, the group moved to one side, allowing the humans and the elf to pass by. Cabe nodded his gratitude to the drake lord, who suddenly called to him.

"The lair of my most damned brother lies within a mountain range toward the west. Beware. His servants blend with their surroundings—and avoid the elves' paths!"

Haiden stiffened and would have questioned the Dragon King regardless of their mutual dislike, but the drakes were already riding south. He turned quickly to the two humans, seeking some sort of comfort. Cabe could only shake his head; he had no idea how the elves up there might be faring. Gwen pointed out how skilled they were at not being seen.

The last did not encourage the elf. "We are good when we have something to work with. Where will they hide if the trees and earth have been torn asunder?"

Neither of the mages could answer his question with any conviction. Cabe pulled his cloak tighter around himself, noting with some apprehension that it seemed to be getting colder.

Something white as snow and very large rose over the horizon and then vanished before he could see it clearly.

"We have trouble."

"What sort of trouble?" Gwen asked.

He pointed toward the horizon. "The Red Dragon erred when he thought there was more distance between his band and the creatures of the Ice Dragon."

Haiden and Gwen followed the direction his finger pointed. They saw nothing at first, then another white mound materialized momentarily.

"They're heading this way."

XVI

"THEY'RE EVERYWHERE!"

Cabe nodded, his mood darker and darker by the moment. Tyr had talked about his death in the Wastes and, as far as Cabe was concerned, any place where the Ice Dragon's behemoths roamed could be considered part of that domain.

"Cabe!"

At Gwen's call, he broke partially free from the darkness. "What?"

"We have to try to teleport!"

"Where?" Haiden asked hesitantly. "Those things are all over the horizon." He did not add that there was no doubt now that they must have overrun his fellow elves. No one was willing to bring that up.

"It would have to be in the midst of the Wastes itself. There's a chance that by now they're all beyond the original bounds of the Ice Dragon's domain! We could jump behind their lines!"

Despite himself, Cabe could not help feeling hopeful. It would mean a respite. Nathan would have approved of such a move and, judging by the feeling within him, Nathan did. It was at times like this that the younger Bedlam was grateful for the link he had with his grandfather. Things would have been so much more difficult if he had no one to turn to.

"Can you teleport other objects?" Haiden looked worried. Both mages realized then that one of them would have to carry the elf. There was also the problem of the horses. At such a great distance, the power needed to drag a mount as well as rider would be tremendous. At the very least, neither of the mages would be able to defend themselves very well.

Gwen took a deep breath. "Let me do it, Cabe. It will *have* to be a blink hole. I was never very experienced at those myself, but I think it better if I do it than you. I'll need a few moments. You two will have to keep an eye out—and pray that it works."

She dismounted, gave Cabe the reins of her mount, and chose a spot behind them. Closing her eyes, she began to draw a pattern with her hands. Haiden and Cabe measured the distance between their party and the creatures and saw that they should have some time. Something small materialized in the air before Gwen. Cabe belatedly realized that he *did* have the knowledge with which he could have formed a blink hole himself, but then decided that in his present state of mind it was probably safer for them all that Gwen was casting it. One of his would probably have proven unstable.

"How long does this take?" Haiden whispered.

The ground to the front of their party erupted. It was an eruption of white fur and daggerlike claws as long as Cabe's body. One of the Ice Dragon's abominations, more anxious than the rest, judging by how it had outdistanced the rest of the pack. Gwen shook violently, but she succeeded in continuing her spell. It would only be a few more seconds before they had their escape route—if the monster would give them that long.

Haiden's maddened steed turned in circles as he tried to regain control. Cabe put a hand on the head of his own mount and that of Gwen and cast a false illusion in their minds. As far as the horses were concerned now, everything was peaceful. They readily would have stood where they were, even up to the point when the digger would have leeched the life from each of them. Cabe, however, had no intention of letting things get that far.

It was almost reflex action. The gleaming bow was before him in that same instant, the shaft, which glowed like a piece of the sun itself, ready. He only had to look at the target; the bow did the rest. With a precision that would have been physically impossible for an inexperienced bowman such as Cabe, the shaft sought its target's most vulnerable spot. Cabe watched the arrow disappear into the thick fur. He had a momentary fear that there was no vulnerable spot.

The digger had one great clawed appendage high in the air when suddenly the creature's entire frame shuddered. It moved forward a bit more, as if trying to deny that anything was amiss. Then it began to tip to one side, seemingly unsure in which direction to turn. It did not stop tipping, however, and in seconds it was down on its side.

Lifeless.

Haiden finally succeeded in calming his horse. He turned to gaze at the hulking corpse and shook his head. "I have heard tales of the sun-spawned bow that some mages can form, but never did I think to see a Dragon Master actually use it. One shot."

Cabe watched the bow vanish. He hoped there would not be need of it again for some time. "That was only one creature. If we're attacked by several, the bow won't be able to save us. I don't know if I could do it again, either. It seems to come when it wants to."

"It's done!"

They both twisted around. Gwen looked proudly at the blink hole, then, with a bit of an uncertain stagger, returned to her horse. When she had remounted, with a little help from the other two, the trio wasted no time in riding through the gate. Cabe wondered briefly if the Ice Dragon would notice the loss of one of his vampiric monstrosities and whether he would realize what had killed it. If so, they might arrive in the Wastes to find an army of the creatures waiting for them. Or something worse.

WHAT THEY EMERGED into was a terrible, horrible cold. Haiden called it an obscene cold, and neither of the mages argued. It tore not only at their physical bodies but at their minds and souls as well. This was the ultimate goal of the Ice Dragon; this was what all the domains would be like if the lord of the Northern Wastes was not stopped. Nothing would remain but a lifeless, chill landscape where even the mountains and hills would eventually be worn down by the rough winds.

They had planned in part for this moment, and each of the trio now pulled out furs. These they wrapped tightly around their bodies. The furs protected them fairly adequately from the physical cold, but there was little they could do about the other. The horses shivered. Physical cold they could understand; the soul-numbing cold was something new and frightening. It was only training and trust that kept them from trying to turn back.

Cabe took some time to cast a small spell about them. It lessened the wind and warmed up their immediate environment a little. He would have preferred to avoid casting such a spell so near to the Ice Dragon's citadel, but Gwen was in need of help. Her initial enthusiasm over the success of the blink hole had given way to exhausted depression. If they were forced to fight in the next hour, she would be of little use. The blink hole had been a chancy thing; Gwen had never been to the Northern Wastes. The extra effort needed to ensure their safety had drained her.

It was as she had suggested. The Wastes were riddled with the burrowing trails of the monstrosities, but there appeared to be no more of them. The thought that there might be a second wave was not spoken out loud, though each of them knew that the others had thought of it as well. Such thoughts had a nasty way of coming true if one was not careful.

Far ahead, Haiden could barely make out a jagged range of mountains. For all practical purposes, they were on the Ice Dragon's front step. It was not unlikely that the Dragon King had servants other than the nearly mindless leviathans moving south, and that meant that each step closer increased the chance of discovery. In no way could they relax their guard now.

Haiden whispered something in a language vaguely familiar in Cabe's memories. "What is that?"

"A death call. Mine or the Ice Dragon's. If that's what it takes, I'm prepared to give it."

Cabe shuddered, reminded again of his own future. He dared not dwell on it much, fearing now that he would bring Gwen and the elf with him. "I hope that won't be necessary."

The elf shrugged. "There are worse ways of dying. I could become trapped in a cell with a dozen sprites—those things you insist on calling wood elves—and die of insanity."

Haiden broke into a slight smile a moment later. Cabe was amazed at his companion's ability to joke even now and it raised his own spirits a little. Gwen smiled but said nothing; even conversation was too tiring for the moment.

The stark emptiness of the landscape overwhelmed them for the first hour, then merely became yet another obstacle in what was becoming an endless list. The cold continued to gnaw at both body and soul and the horses began to stumble. Even increasing the potency of the spell around them did little good. It was, they knew, because they were moving ever nearer to the caverns of the Ice Dragon. They also knew that, with each waking hour, the drake lord was growing stronger. Soon, it would be doubtful if anything could overcome him.

A mist was developing, further hampering their progress. The mountains loomed more like indistinct specters than actual peaks. The ground, torn asunder by the marauding behemoths, was proving treacherous. The mist was low, forcing them to ride carefully. Often, they found that they had arrived at some gully or unstable hill formed by the creatures; that meant turning back or seeking another route. Once, the earth began to give way beneath Cabe's steed, but he was able to back the animal up before the last of his support crumbled and fell into a new ravine some two or three hundred feet deep. No one wanted to hazard a guess as to the actual size of a beast that could bore such a vast tunnel. Their pace picked up for some time after that.

Something began to nag Cabe on the edge of his consciousness. It was as if Nathan were taking an active part, watching for something that Cabe did not understand. It comforted him until he realized that to draw that which had been his grandfather from his own being must surely be a threat of the direst proportions. If he was to die in the Wastes, Cabe was at least hoping for a swift, painless death. Not the sort of thing he suspected his guardian was watching for.

There was a tickle in his mind and at first he believed the dire threat was upon them. Then, Cabe came to understand that it was his own innate senses—the difference between one and the other was debatable, but he was not inclined to contemplate it here and now—and that he was feeling the touch of another mind. Not one of his companions, either.

Very near, he decided. *Just—next to me?*

Swift and silent, the attacker pulled Cabe from the saddle. He had a glimpse of reptilian features and then was locked in a life-or-death struggle. His mind, dulled by constant exposure to the Ice Dragon's numbing spell, could not ready a proper defense. He was forced to go hand against hand with his adversary.

"Bedlammmm!" the drake hissed. His voice was chillingly familiar and the young mage decided then that his death was fast approaching.

This was Toma.

On reflex, his hand went up in a basic defensive spell. The drake should have seen it, should have reacted, but all he did was laugh and attempt to throttle the human. Cabe's spell was only half complete when another form joined the battle, wrapping strong arms around the drake.

Toma lost his grip and began cursing wildly. Cabe surprised himself; instead of continuing the spell, he formed a fist and lashed out at the drake. Every bone in his hand vibrated and the pain was probably worse for him than for Toma, but he succeeded in driving the air from the warrior's lungs. Haiden assisted with a great bear hug. The drake fell to his knees and a simple spell bound him so that even at full strength he would have a long, tedious time escaping. Time they would not give him.

When they felt it safe, they turned him over. Toma's eyes blazed and his sharp, tearing teeth were quite visible. He was suffering from exposure and moved in a slightly drunken fashion. The assault had taken the last of his energy reserves. It was obvious that he had been out in the Wastes for days.

"Toma." Cabe sought the drake's attention. Toma's eyes kept wandering to the horses and it was very evident that he was not thinking about them as riding animals.

The reptilian warlord turned to gaze steadily at the speaker. When his mind acknowledged that it was Cabe, Toma's eyes narrowed and he spit, not an easy feat for one with a long, forked tongue.

"Bedlam."

"You've obviously been through a lot. Cooperate and we'll treat you fairly."

"What are you saying?" Gwen, partially recovered, stood ready to slay the drake. She had not forgotten the days she had been his prisoner. Toma had chosen to torture her each time she spoke back or attempted escape.

Cabe understood her—a part of him wanted to see Toma die slowly for everything he had done—but this was a time when, distasteful as it was, there were priorities. The warlord who had been the driving force behind the massacre of Mito Pica had to be wandering the Wastes for good reason. That reason could only have to do with the Ice Dragon.

"Well?"

"Cabe . . ." Even Haiden was protesting. Cabe quieted both of them with a look. Before him was the drake responsible for the death of the man who had been the only father he knew, the half-elf Hadeen. Having an elf with him did not make his present decision any more pleasant. Yet, the Ice Dragon was a far greater threat, for his success meant the destruction of everything and everyone and a land where only the clans of the Waste would rule—if even they survived.

A semblance of sanity returned to Toma. "You've bound me. With sorcery that should not work. What a fool am I! I could have struck you all down from a distance!"

That was doubtful, considering the drake's present health, but Cabe said nothing about it. "Did you come from the Ice Dragon's citadel?"

Toma closed his eyes briefly, as if there were memories he did not want to bring up, and then nodded slowly. The three exchanged looks of consternation. If this was what contact with the lord of the Northern Wastes had done to as powerful and deadly a nemesis as Toma, then what could they expect?

"He's mad," Toma added quietly. "You probably think this is some conquest, some master plan to make all the lands become one—his own."

"It's not?" Gwen had to force the words out. She knew already that she was not going to like whatever answer their prisoner was about to give them.

"No. We've all been fools, humans. I came to him for aid for my parent, my emperor."

Cabe remembered. Toma had been a prisoner of Azran, and the dragon emperor had been reduced, by Cabe himself, to a near-mindless child. Both drakes had been missing when he and the Gryphon had succeeded in destroying Azran. Now, he knew where they had headed.

Toma continued, the story spilling out now. Difficult as it was to read his features, there seemed to be great relief; for days he had sought to tell someone. "He offered me a place to stay while he sought a cure. The Ice Dragon has always been the most traditional of the Dragon Kings, even if he is more concerned with our ruling race as a whole and may despise the emperor. If the emperor is in danger, he would be the first to step forward to offer aid—so I thought."

Bloodred eyes began studying the horses once more. Cabe quietly signaled Haiden to bring something from the packs. While the elf hurried, Cabe urged the prisoner on.

His eyes switching to Haiden, Toma said, "I waited . . . and waited. Always there was something that prevented him from aiding me. Then, he began talking about his grand plans, always only a little at a time. As with you, I saw a plan of conquest and worried that I had made a fatal mistake; I had delivered the one stepping stone he needed. My parent. He placed a handful of his warriors near me—to assist me, he said—but in actuality to watch me. I wondered then why these were the only members of his clan that I ever really had contact with."

Haiden returned with some near-frozen meat. He was set to at least warm it when, shedding his dignity, Toma lunged forward in a desperate attempt to pull it to him with his teeth. Disgusted, the elf tore off a chunk and held it gingerly before the prisoner, suspecting with each passing second that Toma would take his hand with it. When the piece had been devoured—Gwen had turned away—Cabe blocked an attempt by Haiden to feed Toma further.

"You've more to say. Then, we'll feed you." Cabe did not like what he had become, but he justified it by telling himself that much of it was really the drake lord's fault.

Toma nodded. "Agreed. I will cut to the meat of it, so to speak, so that I can satisfy a bit of my hunger even as I satisfy your curiosity.

"This is it, then. Those four and a few others were all that remained of Ice's clans. The rest had been sacrificed—no—the rest had sacrificed themselves to his grand experiment."

Cabe shuddered. "His own clans fed the source from which he draws his power, the power that he uses to turn the lands into one great Waste."

"Something like that. There is a thing . . . much like those creatures out there, but horribly more so. It draws from them and he, in turn, draws from it. He calls it his queen. Dragon of the Depths! The mad lord intends to turn the entire land into one Waste, yes, but not so he can rule! There will be no one, not even the Ice Dragon. In the end, he will unleash the full force remaining within him. The backlash will kill that monstrosity that is so much a part of him and that in turn will kill those other things, they being only parts of the whole. By then, though, the upstart vermin, you humans, will be dead—as will every drake, elf, dwarf, Seeker, and whatever else is a part of the Dragonrealm."

There was more the drake intended to say, but exhaustion had made him pause for breath. Cabe stood up and looked at the others. "This is far worse than memory indicated. Whatever Nathan discovered, it was only a minute portion of what the Ice Dragon has. I thought I understood, but—I was wrong." Briefly, he was the Cabe who had never known life other than as a huntsman's inept son. "I—I don't know what to do next."

He heard laughter then. Laughter that mocked him; laughter not quite sane. Cabe looked down and stared into the eyes of the smiling Toma.

"In the end, you are as weak as all your kind, Bedlam," the drake said disdainfully. "One wonders how the Ice Dragon could believe you warm-bloods will inherit our kingdom. If we were not so close to death, I would rejoice that the greatest threat of the manlings is a coward and a fool."

Toma shrieked in pain, for Gwen, at the limits of her patience, had decided to give him back some of the agony she had suffered at his hands. Cabe reached out with his mind and canceled her spell. She whirled on him.

"He's said all that he has to say! You know he's too dangerous to leave alive. The Gryphon has ordered him slain on sight. The Dragon Kings will certainly not miss him! None of them want anything to do with this . . . this *pretender*!" She virtually spit out the last word and Toma, recovered from her assault, bared his teeth and hissed. Had it not been for the cold and a lack of food, he might have become a threat. As it was, his brief surge of fury was followed immediately by a collapse. He was barely able to stay conscious. His eyes closed and then opened.

"A truce, Bedlam. I see it now. There is only one way that we might overcome the mad monarch of the Northern Wastes. We—we must work together. I know the caverns. I know where that 'bride' of his lies and some of the things he has for servants. I will swear by the Dragon of the Depths if need be!"

Cabe did not look at Gwen, for he knew the response she wanted. Instead, he waited for Haiden to respond. The elf shifted uncomfortably. No matter what answer he gave, he knew that someone here would not be for-giving. Haiden, well versed at reading faces, also knew what Cabe's decision was going to be, regardless. What the sorcerer wanted was for the elf to tell him why that decision was not right.

Haiden shook his head, also refusing to look at the Lady of the Amber. "He's right, lord and lady. And if he swears by the Dragon of the Depths, he will keep his word."

Gwen said nothing, but her face was pale. At last, she acquiesced, albeit very reluctantly. "Make sure he swears first, at least."

They waited. Toma cleared his throat and slowly said, "I swear, as one of the living line of the Dragon of the Depths, he who is sire of us all, that I shall abide by the truce until this threat to all of us is at an end." He stared up at them defiantly. "That is the most I can promise."

It was not much, but Haiden nodded satisfaction. With some hesitation, they removed the drake lord's bonds. Toma stood up slowly, hands before him, and brushed himself off. His legs were shaking and all three of them could see that he lacked even the power to walk for very long, much less at-tack or shift his shape. He was also covered with splotches, possible signs of frostbite, though not one of them knew if drakes suffered that prob-lem. Toma eyed the meat in the elf's hand and then glanced at Cabe. The young mage nodded and Toma reached out a hand for the ice-covered food. Haiden gave it to him, being careful not to hold on to the meat any longer than necessary. It was a wise move, for the drake jerked it out of his hand and began gorging himself on it. Cabe sourly reminded him of the dangers of eating too much too fast after starving and then purposefully turned his back on their new ally.

Cabe wandered over to the horses and petted them absently. Gwen joined him a few seconds later.

"I can see something is bothering you. Can't you tell me?"

He sighed, watching vaguely as his breath floated away in a cloud of mist. "There are a lot of things bothering me, Gwen. Most of them I can't even name. A couple I don't want to even mention because I'll really start to think about them." He turned and took her in his arms. "I want you to know . . . I'll always understand if there's a part of you that will always love Nathan. I try to be everything he was; I try to be the pillar of confidence I know everybody is looking for."

"That's not—"

"Shhh. Let me finish. I'm not always those things, but I will promise one thing. Whatever it takes, whatever it costs, I'll make sure that the Ice Dragon fails . . . if only to save you."

"Cabe . . ."

He refused to let her say anything, instead holding her tighter and kissing her. They did not separate until a mocking hiss alerted them to the presence of another. "How . . . warm-blooded. You can say your good-byes when we confront my dear 'uncle.' Time is, I promise you, running very, very short."

Duke Toma had regained enough strength to walk, but little else. "I regret also that I will be in need of your powers, Bedlam. My own, now that I have them again, are still far less than perfect. I could use, indeed, I need, something to keep me physically warm."

Cabe shook his head. "No more spells. We have to conserve." He pulled a blanket off his horse, hating himself all the while for depriving his mount so that one like Toma could keep warm. Another thought occurred to him.

"Much as I dislike it, I'm going to let you ride, drake. I can walk for a while and then Haiden can take a turn. We'll need you coherent and your powers at some level of usefulness."

Smiling, Toma reached for the reins of Cabe's horse. "My thanks, Bedlam."

As he struggled to mount, some of the human's anger died. The warlord was barely able to climb up, despite his bravado. Again, Cabe found his thoughts turning to the caverns of the Ice Dragon and how little time remained—for the Dragonrealm and for himself.

XVII

HOW MANY MORE days of this? General Toos ran a hand through his thinning hair as he sat down upon the chair he had ordered his men to place in the audience chamber of the Gryphon's palace. He had the men place it a level below and to the right of the throne, so that any who came would know without a doubt that he was acting on behalf of the Gryphon and was not entertaining thoughts of a coup.

As much as they argued, he could see that with very few exceptions the ministers and various functionaries were relieved to know that it was he who would command them in their ruler's place. They knew the general for what he was, an honest and blunt man who played no favorites, no matter how obvious the bribes might be. Toos understood the nuances of politics, but he had developed such a system of honesty—which he always claimed he had learned from the Gryphon—that even those ministers with the dirtiest pockets generally dealt with him fairly. It was, they had long discovered, to the best of their interests.

A page announced the captain of the guard, a fellow who had served under Toos for nearly seven years. Alyn Freynard was from the hill men of the western coasts. His people were the most secluded of the major human settlements and generally preferred to keep it that way. They proved industrious in their own right, which was why they had never been disturbed by the Iron Dragon, who had ruled that region until his fatal attempt to usurp all power from Gold.

Freynard had been different than most. His father was a trader from Zuu, a tall, burly man, much like the late Prince Blane, who had chosen to stay his winters with one of the local women. Freynard's people tended to be more open-minded about such things, which had caused no end of grief the first time the young mercenary had chanced to bed the unhappy wife of one of Talak's leading merchants. In the years since joining the guardsmen, however, Freynard had become more a younger copy of the general and incidents like Talak were left behind. Unlike Toos, he had eventually taken a wife, something his former countrymen would have looked at in almost as much shock as the merchant had upon finding the tall, sandy-haired man with the clean-looking face in his bed with a supposedly ill bride.

The captain saluted sharply. The sandy color of his hair had begun to give way to speckles of pure white, even though he was several years younger than Toos. His visage remained much the same as those earlier days, still the clean look of a green recruit, but there were a few scars. It was rumored he kept his own wife very contented and several other men's wives very disgruntled because of Talak.

Toos would have trusted him with his life—and had several times.

"What is it you want, Captain?"

Freynard approached the general respectfully. "Sir, I have received reports that two men, perhaps more, from the List have been reported in the city walls."

That caused the general to sit straighter. The List, as it had come to be referred as, was a sheet outlining the known facts concerning several humans and nonhumans that the Gryphon or Toos felt should be watched out for.

Most of them were cutthroats or renegades from some mercenary group. A few others were known traitors who had sought escape from Penacles but who might return. A few, like Azran and Toma, were in a different league altogether. It was because of the List that the Gryphon had had the captain of the guard also trained as a sort of secret law officer.

"Who?"

"The description of one matches the foreigner that our majesty has been so concerned with of late. He has at least one accomplice who matches the description of the other raider who arrived with him in Irillian."

Gripping the arms of the chair so tightly that one cracked, Toos leaned forward. "Let me understand this, Freynard; D'Shay is in Penacles—not Irillian?"

"If the watchers were correct—and I have no reason to doubt these men."

"I see." The general's mind raced. Somehow, for some reason, the wolf raider who had obsessed the Gryphon so much was now in the city—which meant that he had gotten past a very well-trained unit of guardsmen.

"Where were they seen?"

"At the Silver Unicorn." The Silver Unicorn was the most expensive of inns, a vast place that catered to merchants and diplomats. Toos blinked. Odd that D'Shay should pick so vulnerable a spot to hide.

"Has anyone moved to pick them up?"

"No, sir. I ordered my men to continue watching while I sought instructions from you. This seemed a special case, General."

Toos nodded. Freynard was correct. D'Shay was about as special a case as there could be. From what little the Gryphon had told him, the man was very dangerous. Toos had the impression that much of what his lord had told him had come from some buried memory, that the Gryphon knew more, but could not recall anything but impressions.

"Have them continue to watch. Find out if there are only two of them or if we have a nest of vermin developing here. Also find out how they got past the city gates."

"Sir!" The captain saluted and turned to leave.

"Alyn . . ."

"General?"

Toos turned his head, revealing to Freynard the foxlike profile. "If it looks as if D'Shay is slipping away from us, I want him captured or killed. Use your own judgment. A trial is not necessary for this one."

"Yes, sir." The captain departed. Toos knew that Freynard understood. If D'Shay did die, that would be the end of it. The Gryphon's obsession would be no more. He would settle down and rule the city he had freed from the tyranny of the Dragon Kings.

That was the way it should be, Toos decided. Both he and the Gryphon had gone beyond the point where they had personal lives, personal obsessions. Penacles was their duty now.

Nothing else mattered.

THE BLINK HOLE had opened into his personal chambers.

The Gryphon stepped out, once again very relieved that he was free of the void. He glanced around. It was night. Nothing had been disturbed since his departure save where servants had cleaned up after him. His books were still in place, the iron golems were still guarding the door on this side, and he assumed that meant that there were two more on the outside.

He stepped to one side and and waited for the Blue Dragon to follow. It had proven harder for the drake to correctly locate the new blink hole than he had thought. After several attempts, each followed by several hours of recuperation, he had finally succeeded. It was about time, too, as far as the Gryphon was concerned. Precious time was slipping away.

Still, the days had not been wasted. They were now certain they had every parchment, every artifact from the Blue Dragon's collection that might be of use to them.

The Dragon King, one arm filled with scrolls and whatnot, stepped out. "Well, I—"

Whatever the drake lord was about to say was forgotten, for suddenly two heavy figures reached for him. The scrolls spilled to the floor as the Dragon King sought escape. One attacker failed to reach him, but the other caught hold of one of his legs.

The iron golems were fulfilling their purpose: defending their master from any enemy, including drakes. In his relief to be in his own quarters again, the lionbird had forgotten that an enemy did not have to attack him; he or she merely had to be there. Some portion of his mind had assumed that since the Blue Dragon was acting as his ally, there would be no attack.

Before the situation grew any worse—for he knew that the Dragon King would defend himself and then where would the palace be?—the Gryphon shouted "Stop!"

The iron golems hesitated, but did not halt.

"Gryphon!" Blue shouted. One hand was already going up. If the Gryphon did not hurry, his ally would be unleashing something particularly nasty at any moment.

"I command you! Cease all movement!"

This time, the golems froze. Another command allowed the Dragon King to free his leg. After that, the Gryphon was able to order the unliving creatures back to their normal locations.

"My apologies, drake lord. I had no idea that would happen."

The Blue Dragon studied his leg for broken bones. "Indeed. Remind me never to attack you in your private rooms."

"Or in the hall. Any more commotion, and there would have been twice as many."

"I am impressed. Iron golems are difficult to make. Golems in general are, but iron is one of the most difficult holding cases for the elemental spirit."

"The work in creating one is made up by their efficiency, such as it is," the Gryphon added.

"So I see."

With calculated movements, the drake lord carefully picked up the scrolls. He straightened and looked at the Gryphon expectantly. "It would be best if we went straight to the libraries. Are they far from here?"

The Gryphon could not help smiling a little. At present, the tapestry, which was the only entrance to the libraries, hung on the wall behind the Dragon King. "Not far at all. If you will follow me please."

While the puzzled drake watched, the lionbird walked past him and over to the tapestry.

It was the most perfect combination of needlework and sorcery that the Gryphon had ever seen. Each and every detail of the city was included. Everything was up to date. A small shop was missing from the merchants' district. The Gryphon suspected that he would hear about a fire in a day or two.

The symbol for the libraries, of late an open book in red, was in none of the usual locations. There were always a few surprises, it seemed. He finally located it underneath, of all things, one of the schools he had instituted during his early years as ruler of Penacles. For a city legendary as the seat of knowledge, the general population had been one of the most ignorant in all the realms. The Dragon King who had ruled here had been no fool; it knew that a learned citizenry would be a troublesome citizenry. It was one of the first things the Gryphon had changed and the results had shown. Penacles was not only an oasis of knowledge, but it was the cradle for new thought. More innovations came from the Gryphon's domain than all the others combined, save perhaps Mito Pica before it fell.

He turned toward the Blue Dragon, who was admiring the tapestry but growing impatient. The Gryphon placed a finger on the mark of the libraries. "See how this compares with your blink hole."

His concentration was broken by the sounds of men outside. At least one of them was shouting.

One of the golems suddenly announced, "General Toos demands entrance."

"Demands?" The Gryphon glanced at his companion. He did not think Toos would take kindly to a Dragon King standing in the royal chambers themselves, a Dragon King about to depart for the precious libraries.

"If I may, drake lord, I'd like to suggest that you perhaps step into the next room for a moment. I want to break the news of your presence to my second, but I want to do it calmly."

"As you wish." There was a touch of disdain in the drake's voice. In his own domain, he would have shouted down any protest; either that or he would have killed the protester.

When the Blue Dragon was out of sight, the lionbird said, "Toos alone may enter."

His exact words must have been repeated, for there was some debating. A minute later, the doors opened and the general entered, very anxious and not a little bit angry. Several other figures stood outside, trying to see what was going on. The doors closed in their faces.

Toos bowed. "Your majesty—Gryphon. I am relieved to see you once again."

"Relieved? You looked as if you were about to kill me, Toos. I have to admit that my actions were not entirely my own before my departure, but everything is satisfactory now."

"Not your own?" The ex-mercenary studied him closely. "Who was responsible? D'Shay? I'll—"

The Gryphon shook his head impatiently. He did not want his aide getting worked up. It would not do the introduction of their new ally any good. "It's over with. Speaking of D'Shay, the wolf raiders have departed Irillian. You can sleep easy tonight, old friend. I won't be running off after him for the time being."

He expected the news to satisfy Toos at least a little, but the general only looked even more unhappy. Evidently, the last few days had worn him down. It was probably best to bring out the Dragon King now, before matters worsened.

"You are aware of trouble to the north?" When the human nodded, the Gryphon continued. "The Ice Dragon moves, Toos. He's mad and even his brethren have no use for him anymore. It turned out that the true reason for going to Irillian had to do with that."

The Gryphon had always counted on his second for his ability to grasp situations and make the best of them. It was one of those skills which some said were the sorcerous abilities he seemed to lack even though the man was marked by a silver streak in his hair. Toos did not disappoint him.

"Blue sought a pact with you."

"Correct."

The foxlike visage turned grim. "You wouldn't be telling it the way you are unless you were considering accepting it—or you already have."

"I have."

The narrow figure turned and gazed about the room. "Someone reported noise up here and thought they heard your voice. They also thought they heard another voice." Toos swiveled and asked, "If I may be bold, Gryphon, how did you return here? I knew when you left; it's part of my job. The trouble is, I didn't know when you returned. I expect many things from Freynard, but some things I do myself and I should have heard. While I know you have the power to teleport, even you would think twice about teleporting from Irillian. Too much chance of something going awry."

"I came through a portal. A thing called a blink hole."

"I see." Toos shook his head. "There is nothing I can say that will change the situation, Gryphon. You've made your decision and, as your aide and subject, I will abide by that decision. From the way you talk, I assume you did not come alone. The Dragon King need not hide; it is unbefitting for any being of his stature, enemy or ally."

Heavy footfalls told the Gryphon that the drake lord had indeed stepped out of the other room. "Well said, human. I approve of loyalty, especially when seasoned with reason. You are to be commended. My spies were not wrong in their judgment of you."

The last was said with a touch of humor, but all three knew it to be true. As the master of Irillian had profiles on his enemies to the south, so too did the Gryphon have profiles of many of his adversaries. Only a handful, such as the Storm Dragon and, most especially, the Crystal Dragon, were nearly total unknowns. The Gryphon wondered how much more the Blue Dragon really knew about the last two. They were fellow Dragon Kings, true, and there was some contact between Blue and Storm, but that meant little in the long run. The Ice Dragon was an example of how little even the other Kings knew about one of their own brethren.

"Milord." Toos bowed.

The Gryphon walked over and put an arm over the general's shoulders. "Toos, you trust me."

"Yes . . ."

"I'm going to take him with me to the libraries."

The human tensed. The lionbird's grip on his shoulders tightened before Toos could get out of control.

"You said you would abide by my decision, friend. Hear me now. The Dragon King is a master sorcerer and a historian as well. Those are the two greatest qualities one needs when facing the absurdity of the libraries."

"Forgive me, milord. It is your decision and, as I said, I will obey."

The Gryphon would have been more satisfied if the look on his second's face had not been so sullen. He made the best of it, though. "Fine! We will be popping in and out. There's no telling what will happen. I want you to keep an eye out in the north, though. Alert me to everything."

"Yes, milord."

A few of the Gryphon's feathers ruffled, but he said nothing more. He released Toos and returned to the tapestry, the Dragon King close on his heels. As the lord of Penacles placed his finger on the symbol of the libraries, he turned to Toos and added, "Contact Cabe and the Lady Gwen. Tell them I need to speak to them as soon as possible."

The Gryphon and his drake ally became blurry. Toos instinctively blinked, trying to get them back into focus. He knew better, but he did it every time. Gradually, the two dwindled away until the human was alone in the room. He shook his head and departed.

The others were still waiting for him; the news of their monarch's return had everyone in an uproar. Toos patiently raised his hands and waited for the hall to quiet.

"His majesty the Gryphon will not be available for the near future. He is conferring with others on a matter important, not only to Penacles, but to other domains as well. If there should arise any problems of such magnitude that I myself cannot give approval, I will speak to him. That is all."

Everyone wanted to ask more, but the soldier was not having any of it. He barged past the ministers and assorted bureaucrats, his greatest desire to be as far away from the royal chambers as possible.

It was a rare thing for him not to divulge information to his lord. The Gryphon had come to trust him as a brother and Toos felt that he was now betraying that trust. He had not told the Gryphon about D'Shay's sudden presence in the city, a sudden appearance made even more suspicious when it coincided with the lionbird's own return, something even the general had not known until after it had happened. It had also proved impossible to speak of the plague of horrors coming out of the south; already, they were well into the Hell Plains and, more importantly, into Irillian.

Toos knew it was wrong, but he wanted the Dragon King weakened before he spoke out. If the Blue Dragon became desperate, he would be more open to influence by the Gryphon, which meant more influence by Penacles.

He had neared his own chambers when one of Freynard's aides came rushing up. The man was out of breath; he must have searched almost the entire palace, Toos realized. The general gave him time to calm down.

"Sir . . . sir, Captain Freynard sent me to report that the wolf raider and his companion are on the move."

All thoughts of his dealings with the Gryphon were pushed aside. "Clarify."

"Several minutes ago, both figures—they'd been eating—suddenly rose as if something they'd been waiting for had happened. They hurried upstairs, supposedly to their rooms. One of our men went up to investigate and did not return after the allotted time. Captain Freynard himself went up, came down a couple of minutes later, and shouted that they had slipped away. They'd discovered our man and knocked him senseless. The captain ordered some of the others after them and sent me to tell you what happened."

"*Damn!*" The guardsman jumped from the sheer intensity in the general's voice. The ex-mercenary knew it was not fair of him to take out his anger on the guard, but stopping now was impossible. "You return to Captain Freynard and remind him of what I said earlier. He'll know what you mean. Tell him to make sure that those two and any accomplices do not leave this city in one piece! Is that clear?"

"Sir!" It was impossible for the young soldier to stand any more at attention than he was already.

Toos took a deep breath and counted to ten. In a calmer voice he said, "That's all, get going."

The guardsman practically left a smoking trail behind him. Toos could not help smiling despite his troubles. He needed sleep now. This day had been far too hectic, especially the last few hours. If he wanted to be sharp, at least a couple hours of rest would be needed. Since the Gryphon's departure, the number of hours he had rested collectively added up to less than the sum total of the digits on both hands. Most of those hours were cat naps.

He hoped tomorrow would bring some sort of peace, but, judging by past experience, he knew that was wishful thinking.

"General, sir!"

Evidently, he was not to get sleep after all. Toos wondered if some god had it in for him. With more bite than he intended, he snapped, "What is it *now*?"

The soldier, who had been on sentry duty and knew nothing of the sort of day Toos had been having, was forced to take some time to regather his suddenly scattered thoughts.

"There . . . there is an . . . an elf waiting without, sir. A messenger from the lord of the Dagora Forest, so he says."

"Does he? What does this messenger want?"

"He says that his words are for the Lord Gryphon and he will not speak them to any other unless by his orders."

"*That* might prove a bit difficult. While the Gryphon has returned to Penacles, he expects to be . . . to be in negotiations for quite some time with one of his counterparts."

"Sir?" The soldier had not understood a thing.

Toos waved the matter aside. "Never mind. Bring him to me. If I can't convince him to tell me what's so important, he'll just have to wait until the Gryphon is available. Go get him, lad."

"Sir!"

As the young guard hurried off, Toos tried to calculate how long it would take him to return with the elfin messenger and whether or not there would be at least enough time for the general to restore a little of his depleted energy reserves.

"Manaya," he muttered, thinking of a particularly volatile wine he drank. Manaya would wake him up—though he would regret it come the next day. He hoped the message from the Green Dragon warranted the elf's attitude. If not, it was possible that the Dragon King would be short one obstinate messenger before very long.

✻ ✻ ✻

THE SEEKER ADJUSTED its balance and closed its eyes, the avian's mind searching the thoughts of those within the palace. It was a difficult task; contact worked better for the transmission of alien thoughts. Still, the patterns of the primitives within were easy enough to pick up once it located them. Only staying in contact for any extended period of time might prove a real hazard. More sensitive primitives might detect the intruding presence.

One of the arrogant ones was here, as was the hybrid who ruled here. The Seeker had not yet made up its mind about the hybrid; its avian qualities did it justice, but it continued to ensnare itself in the workings of the humans. This was something the Seeker mind could not fathom. Lesser races were to be used. They were rewarded if they did well, as one rewards an intelligent animal, but they were to be punished or forgotten if they failed.

Both the arrogant one and the hybrid were gone. They could only be in the libraries. This Seeker had never seen the libraries, only the eldest had ever seen them, but it knew that the libraries were worthy of the respect of even the elders. That meant that things were progressing as they should be. All the Seekers needed was time.

The avian stretched his wings momentarily, secure that its hiding place on the roof would not be suspected by a race that could not fly.

The Seeker allowed itself a moment of satisfaction concerning its appointed task and then readied itself for the night's wait. Beginning the morrow, it knew, things would happen of great interest to all.

XVIII

THERE WERE FEW things capable of truly impressing a Dragon King, but the Libraries of Penacles had most definitely succeeded in doing just that.

Staring down the endless corridors of books, the Blue Dragon had shaken his head and muttered, "Astounding!"

"You've never seen them before?"

"Never. Brother Purple was quite protective of his power. He did not trust us."

The Gryphon squawked. "I wonder why."

After that, it was a case of hit or miss as the two sought out clues. A gnomish librarian—the lionbird was never certain whether there were several or just this one—was waiting to assist them. He seemed undisturbed by the presence of the drake, taking his requests as he would the Gryphon's.

Unlike previous visits, the librarian did not lead them to particular books; instead, he brought them to a table and two chairs, something the monarch of Penacles had never encountered in all his time down here. The presence of these three pieces of mundane furniture bothered him, because they were an indication that this might be a long, involved search. Even before they had made any specific requests, the little man was bringing them an armful of thick, distinguished-looking books.

After going through the first hundred or so and discovering some of the libraries' tricks—such as nonsense verse and unanswerable riddles—the Dragon King threw one of the heavy volumes against the shelves. The Gryphon watched with annoyance.

"This is preposterous! What madness built this place?"

The Gryphon sighed and closed the tome he had been perusing. "From what I gather, even the Purple Dragon, with all the time available to him, never discovered that one fact in here."

Standing, the drake lord began to pace; a scholar though he was, he was also a warlord of his kind. Inactivity, or worse, useless activity, made him nervous. He eyed the Gryphon. "Tell me something that I have grown curious about. I have heard conflicting tales concerning the Purple Dragon's death. Some attribute it to you, some to Nathan Bedlam. Which is the case?"

"Both. Nathan had weakened himself with other activities. A stalemate was the best he could achieve. He needed an opening. By sheer accident, I brought him that opening. I discovered the key to the libraries and, being as possessive as he was, the Purple Dragon turned his attention to me. He underestimated me, apparently, because he left himself open for too long. Nathan was able to summon a Sunlancer bow. The action left him depleted, regretfully, and your fellow drake turned back in time to prevent a killing shot. I struck, adding yet another wound. He knew then that he was dying, and he meant to take all of Penacles, including his precious libraries, with him to wherever it is Dragon Kings go. Only Nathan's quick thinking prevented that. The force he contained destroyed both of them. . . ."

"Leaving you the spoils . . ."

The Gryphon glared at his temporary ally. "Someone had to help these people. Apparently, some people decided they preferred a living hero to a dead one, which is why many of them think I alone was responsible. There are those with the opposite view. As far as I'm concerned, the glory can all go to Nathan Bedlam."

"Some of my brethren would be interested in this, though I doubt I'll bother to enlighten them. I meant no disrespect, Lord Gryphon. It is as I thought; Purple was arrogant and self-serving to the end. He was missed for his mind, but none of us were sorry he perished."

The gnome was bringing yet more books. The little creature looked aghast when he saw the one tome that the drake had tossed in anger. He retrieved it as soon as his hands were empty. The glare he gave the drake would have done one of the reptiles proud.

"Why do you persist in bringing us these useless volumes?" hissed the Blue Dragon.

The gnome, book in hand and anger seemingly gone, stared at him blandly. "It is my function."

"These books are filled with gibberish!"

The librarian shrugged. "To those without the knowledge—yes. It must be admitted that the specifics you seek are no longer among the contents of the libraries, but the other volumes do contain important refer—"

"Cease!" The Gryphon stood up and turned on the elderly gnome. Even that did not disturb the librarian. "You are saying that we've been wasting our time?"

"No, present lord of Penacles. What you seek can be inferred from the sources I have been bringing you. Specific information no longer exists."

"What happened to it?"

Puzzled, the gnome replied, "You do not recall? A good two dozen volumes were utterly destroyed some months back when you requested information on winds."

Winds . . .

The Gryphon stared at the books lined along the entire wall. The libraries had been invaded—somehow—and, as the gnome had said, several books were destroyed and many others damaged. At the time, the Gryphon had assumed it was the work of either the Black Dragon or Azran, both of whom would have had good reason. How stupid he had been!

The Dragon King had caught the gist of what the gnome was saying. "All of these books have some clue, then. We've just failed to understand. We should take these back to the palace and pass them among your learned men. . . ."

"We cannot. If we try to remove them, the pages will turn blank. Occasionally, some scrap of information will remain, but usually because I've taken the time to really understand it. That seems to be the only way to retain anything. Also, the more potential contained within the information, the less of a probability that we will succeed in remembering it once we've used it once."

"Such twisted thinking is the Seekers' way."

"Neither the Seekers nor the Quel, who succeeded in keeping their civilization at least partially functioning all through the avians' reign and the early years of your kind, had any knowledge of the true functions of these libraries. I can only hazard a guess at what the builders had been like. I know a few rulers have added to the structure, but most of the growth seems to be self-generating—as if the libraries were an entity."

The Blue Dragon looked around uneasily. "Not a pleasant thought, even if it is impossible—I hope." He pointed a gauntleted hand at the gnome. "You! You know nothing of this place's origins?"

In a patient voice which indicated that he had heard this question countless times before and repeated the same answer as many times, the tiny creature said, "I have always served the libraries. I only remember the libraries. I have no interest in anything else save my duties."

The Gryphon nodded. "Undoubtedly. I think, drake lord, that we should retire to the palace. There are duties which I would like to discuss and the time spent down here only serves to increase my appetite."

"A fair suggestion. I've found it difficult to concentrate on the last two volumes."

To the gnome, the lionbird said, "Leave the books we have. When we finish with those, I'll want the other ones we had before."

The librarian acknowledged the command only absently, already hard at work straightening and organizing the books on the table. The Gryphon and his reptilian ally departed.

THEY MATERIALIZED IN the Gryphon's chambers. The golems did not assault them this time, but one spoke. "General Toos left a message. He wishes to speak to his majesty upon his return."

The Gryphon did not reply at first, amazed to learn, as he glanced toward a window, that it was daylight. "What a coincidence. Did he say where he would be?"

"Message ended." The golem stared blankly ahead.

The Dragon King slowly moved toward them. "I cannot help but admire them. The secret of their manufacture came from the libraries. . . ."

"Yes, and it's well hidden. Trust me."

Turning, the drake revealed a dark smile. "As you should trust me. I was merely wondering what other treasures those books contain—if we could understand them."

"Occasionally, I get a straight answer. Why, I don't know. The whims of the libraries, I suppose."

The last statement made the Dragon King frown. "I would prefer to cease speaking about that structure as if it had a mind of its own. It makes one feel like they are in the gullet of a beast and don't know it."

"As you wish." The doors opened and the Gryphon turned to leave. He paused halfway through the doorway. "If it's all the same to you, Dragon King, I would prefer you with me. As great as the shock will be to some of my people, I would rather have you with me—in case the golems forget you are my ally."

They both knew that the Gryphon did not want to leave the drake alone with the key to the libraries. When this business was past them—providing they were alive—the lionbird would take steps to ensure the safety of the tapestry. For now, however, he lacked the time.

"I understand completely." Blue's tone matched the Gryphon's exactly. Once more, they were rulers vying in the treacherous battle of diplomacy.

The golems outside stirred briefly, but the Gryphon waved a taloned hand and they subsided. No guards were stationed in this hall. That did not mean it was undefended. At the moment, several pairs of eyes watched the progress of the two. The Gryphon knew that word would be spreading to Toos even as they walked. He doubted that they would have to be forced to walk all the way to the general's quarters.

Someone did meet them at the corner, but it was not the Gryphon's second. Rather, it was Captain Freynard and one of his men. They came to attention when they realized it was their king. Both Freynard and the guard, who must have been his own aide, gave the Dragon King a long, steady stare.

The Gryphon cleared his throat. "This Dragon King is allied with us for the moment. I trust, Freynard, that you will be discreet and tell only those who need know."

"Yes—sir."

This was proving easier than he had expected. He nodded approval to the two soldiers. "Have you seen General Toos?"

"Last time I saw him, he was in his chambers, majesty. 'Getting some rest at last,' he said. May I say it is good to see you." Freynard smiled broadly.

"I appreciate that. That'll be all."

Both men saluted, Freynard's companion with evident relief. It must have been difficult to keep calm in the presence of one of the legendary Dragon Kings. Mothers in Penacles used tales of the drake lords to frighten bad children. The lionbird wondered what Blue would think if he knew that. Then again, the master of Irillian probably already assumed such things.

The Gryphon and his companion continued on only a little farther before they found themselves confronting Toos. The foxlike man might have been standing there waiting for them. He was in uniform and his breathing was very even for someone who no doubt had been running—unless he really *had* been waiting for them.

"Your majesty."

"You never cease to amaze me, my friend. I understand you wanted to see me."

The ex-mercenary glanced momentarily at the Dragon King. "I would have preferred a more private audience, milord."

"Unless it really concerns something our 'comrade' should not hear, you can tell both of us."

"As you wish. In fact, it's probably proper that he hears it as well. A messenger came from the Green Dragon."

"A messenger?" Beside the Gryphon, the Blue Dragon hissed.

"An elf. I . . . there's been trouble . . . bad trouble . . . at the Manor, Gryphon." Toos hesitated and then finished, "The three royal hatchlings . . . and the other four . . . uh . . . smart ones . . . are . . . are *gone!*"

"What??" The Dragon King took the human by the collar and raised him high. "The emperor'sss get are gone? How? Why?"

"Put him down!" The Gryphon did not threaten and his hands were at his sides, but the drake unconsciously obeyed him regardless of that.

"My . . . apologiesss, General. Please. What happened?"

Toos rearranged his shirt and, clearing his throat, he explained. "Marauders. The band from Mito Pica. It took me some time to get the answer out of the messenger; he was only supposed to speak to you."

"Was the Green Dragon at the Manor?" asked the Gryphon.

"He was, which makes him all the more shamed. They were protected by medallions of great power. It hid them from the sight of his eyes in the forest and allowed them to slip through the protective spell surrounding the Manor grounds."

"I do not like thisss," the Dragon King muttered. "For such rabble, they are remarkably well armed."

"Melicard probably supplies them."

"With Seeker magic as well? We have sorely underestimated that human, then. I'll rip his . . ."

The general dared speak out. "There's more. . . . And your kind is partly responsible for Melicard, drake lord. It was Kyrg who drove Melicard's father, Rennek IV, to madness."

The Blue Dragon hissed.

Toos ignored it. "As I was saying, Gryphon. They succeeded in getting in unnoticed, but then everything seemed to go wrong for them. One of the servitor drakes, a Ssarekai, I think the elf said, noticed one of them. The alarm was raised and it became a full-fledged battle."

"Surely, Brother Green and his clans were able to overwhelm them instantly! Either through magic or sheer brute strength . . ."

"The protective spell, *my lord*, apparently prevents shifting of form—and the marauders were again *protected*."

"What happened, then, Toos?" The lionbird hoped that his draconian companion would stay silent until the rest of the story was told.

"It becomes a bit confusing. Some of the marauders got into the Manor. One, who the lord of the Dagora Forest seems to think was one of the leaders, broke into the rooms set aside for the hatchlings. At the same time, the entire area was plunged into what . . . into what the Green Dragon says can only be described as a . . . I admit it sounds foolish, but an explosion of *utter darkness!*"

"Darkness?" This time, it was the Gryphon who interrupted. Darkness?

"A darkness in which the marauders in the Manor stole away with Gold's young!" the Dragon King concluded angrily.

"*That* is the confusion." Toos frowned. "The explosion was an accident. So the hapless instigator claimed—before he passed out again. Lost an arm and part of his face. It won't heal properly, either. Talak's going to have one ugly king if Melicard survives."

The Gryphon could not believe the last. "Melicard? Melicard was *with* them?"

"It was to have been his glorious victory. He wanted to rally his own folk and any others who had suffered under the—under the drakes." When the

Blue Dragon said nothing, the old soldier pushed on. "Melicard said that the medallion was supposed to blind his enemies, not everyone."

"And the hatchlings?"

"They found the marauders dead and the female drakes who acted as guardians in a daze. Something had thrown the one marauder who broke in out the window. They were three floors up. He won't tell anything to anyone; he's dead. The young drakes—no one knows what happened to them in the confusion."

"What isss my brother doing to find them?"

"The messenger didn't know. I *did* ask."

The Gryphon nodded approval. "Where is the messenger now?"

"He's waiting your summons in the guards' quarters."

"Have someone get him. I want to question him and see if there might be anything he held back, though I doubt it, knowing your luck." He started to turn, but Toos was still standing there. "Was there something else?"

Toos was embarrassed. The Gryphon finally realized that, though it would have been impossible to tell that from the man's visage alone. The general had an excellent face for betting games.

"Milord, I fear that the wolf raider D'Shay is somewhere in the city."

"What?"

"Impossible!" added the Dragon King.

Toos shook his head sadly. "He was seen in the city several times. I finally had Freynard dispatch some men after him, but he and a companion escaped. No one's sighted him since."

"Freynard mentioned nothing of that when we encountered him a moment ago, but then, it wasn't his place to, I suppose. Why didn't you tell me, Toos?"

"I should think that's obvious, Lord Gryphon," the drake commented.

The lionbird turned from one to the other. Rare though it was, both man and drake were in agreement. "You were afraid I was going to go after him and forget everything else."

His oldest and dearest companion, the only man remaining from his original mercenary army, bowed his head. "I am fully prepared to be dismissed from my post and suffer whatever consequences you deem necessary."

He was being sincere, too, the Gryphon realized. "Don't be absurd, my friend. Anyone who replaced you would be no more efficient and probably a lot less capable than you. If you want to redeem yourself, keep your post and find D'Shay, hard as it is to believe that he is here."

"He must know," the Dragon King remarked. "He must have discovered our alliance."

"Which explains the speed and relative lack of resistance when his people departed *your* city."

"Point taken. It seems we both have been remiss, Gryphon. All the more reason to make haste. A pity we lack my crystal; it would have proven useful in our search, not to mention as a means of spying."

"There's . . . Yalak's Egg!"

"I beg your pardon?"

The Gryphon shook his head. "I'll tell you in a few moments. Suffice to say, I think it best we return to my chambers. Toos! I am not trying to demean you in any way, but could I ask that, when you send someone for the messenger, you also have someone bring food to my rooms, food for both of us? Make sure it's prepared and delivered by someone you trust completely, please. Oh, and make sure you have them give us something strong to drink."

"You can be sure of that. Does the— Do you have any preference, my lord?" Toos addressed the Blue Dragon politely, but there was a hint of mockery in his eyes, as if he expected the Dragon King to order raw meat.

"Fish, if you do not mind. Well salted. You need not remove the bones." The Dragon King smiled at him, predatory teeth fully displayed.

The general was not disturbed. He saluted the Gryphon, bowed very quickly to the drake, and went on his way. The lionbird turned and headed back to his chambers, a curious and annoyed Dragon King trailing him.

"We have only just departed from your rooms! Why the haste to return?"

"Yalak's Egg." When the Blue Dragon only looked more confused, the Gryphon asked, "You have heard of Yalak, I hope?"

"A Dragon Master. One of the worst of the scum."

"Yes, I suppose you would have seen them—and myself—that way. Yalak had a knack for visions. He studied the process and, when he believed he had captured the essence of such abilities, he created the Egg, a way for him to bring forth hints of the future, events of the present, and glimpses of the past."

"You have this Yalak's Egg."

"He asked me to watch it for him, not knowing his foresight would fail him and he would be one of many to fall at Azran's hands." They reached the doors, but the Gryphon did not enter immediately. He was glimpsing the past himself. "You should have made him an honorary drake, my 'friend.' Azran did more than any of your kind to bring defeat to the Dragon Masters."

"I would rather have had a human victory than deal with that shark spawn."

"Hmmph." The doors opened and the Gryphon stepped through. He felt a tingle and his mane stood on end. The Dragon King followed him, apparently unaffected by anything.

How odd, the Gryphon thought. He scanned the room, but nothing seemed amiss. The doors closed behind them. He caught sight of the Egg.

"There it— Awk!"

Impossibly strong fingers caught him by the neck. The Gryphon tried a spell, but nothing happened. *The Blue Dragon has betrayed me!* was his first thought. Then, he heard a struggle and saw the drake lord thrown across the room by the other golem. The hapless Dragon King struck the opposing wall with incredible force, cracking the wall itself and falling limply to the floor. A moment later, one golem had the Gryphon's left arm while the first one shifted its grip so that it held his right arm and his mane. It pulled his head back.

Someone stepped into the chamber from the other room. Slow, measured footsteps. More than one being, actually. Even without seeing them, the Gryphon knew who at least one of them would be.

"Things could not have turned out better," D'Shay commented to his unknown companion—most likely the other wolf raider he had been seen with. "We have the Gryphon, the vast libraries of Penacles, and even a soon-to-be-willing ally who will give us the permanent base of operations our dear commanders desired. Quite satisfactory, eh, D'Laque?"

The other raider, D'Laque, replied, "Very much so, Lord D'Shay."

A hand, a human hand, gripped the Gryphon beneath his beak. "Now. Shall we commence with plucking this prize bird?"

THE GREEN DRAGON hissed in frustration. He could not tell whether the resistance he felt was due to exhaustion on his part or defiance on the part of the one he was attempting to contact. Certainly, it would not be the first time they had refused to talk to one another. It was even worse now, with the Dragon Kings all at one another's throats.

Blue was nowhere to be found. For some reason, he had departed his kingdom. He was not the type to run, of that Green was certain. There had to be another reason.

To his surprise, somone else had answered his summons. A new Red Dragon, an heir to the one who foolishly believed he could destroy Azran. This new one would be no help to him; the few good lands of the Hell Plains had already been overrun and the remaining clans were fleeing southwest to Silver's domain. The new Dragon King's only words had been that he had come across Cabe, the Lady of the Amber, and an elf on their way north at some point. From what was babbled as Red broke the connection, the three were riding into a huge pack of the soulless creatures from the Wastes.

Silver refused his summons with a sense of pure hatred. Silver saw himself as Gold's successor, and his brother to the south as the darkest of traitors for having made peace with the human mages. Green did not bother to point out the contradictions, such as the fact that the other Dragon King still allowed Talak to remain an open city. He suspected that Silver was still having trouble bringing the domains of Iron and Bronze under his control and now had the horrors of Ice to contend with as well. In the end, the other drake cut contact off as if he had been wielding an ax. The withdrawal made the Green Dragon's head throb.

Storm deigned to speak to him, but only long enough to say he would defend his own realm and that the concerns of Green were Green's alone. The last was said with the typically flashy trait of that King; thunder and lightning punctuated each statement. He, too, left the master of the Dagora Forest with a throbbing head, but more because of the noise than anything else.

That left the Crystal Dragon.

He had avoided contacting this drake. What the Crystal Dragon had been once was certainly nothing compared to what he was now. Now, that Dragon King was a remote, enigmatic figure whose very presence at the Council of Kings always had stirred up uneasiness. Part of that uneasiness, Green had discovered, had been due to the fact that Duke Toma had apparently used the Crystal Dragon's form as his way of spying on his masters. Even still, there had been times when it could only have been the true monarch of the Legar Peninsula, the land that glistened even from the Dagora Forest.

The resistance continued, but he was not about to give in. He suspected that, in his own way, the Crystal Dragon was possibly at least as powerful as Ice was to the north. Legar had been the last bastion of the Quel race; it was rumored that some still existed, though the Green Dragon had taken Cabe's tale of thousands of sleeping creatures as pure fiction from a strained young human mind. There had never been more than a few, but they were savage and crafty fighters, invisible to many senses. The thought of thousands of the sleeping creatures was the thing of drake nightmares.

"What is it?"

The other might have been standing behind him. The Green Dragon jumped, not out of fear, but because his mind had started to drift to other things. He found it difficult at first to formulate a response.

Unlike contact with the others, he could draw no clear image of the other Dragon King. That was by the Crystal Dragon's choice. Nevertheless, it was disconcerting. The only image Green had was of a vaguely reptilian form in the midst of a blinding field of light. One of the crystal caverns. Even the ice caves of the Northern Wastes could not compare to the elegant beauty of the Crystal Dragon's home. They did have one thing in common, though; both were so alien that the lord of the forest knew he would never have any desire to visit them.

"Well?" The voice was deeper than most drakes' and it seemed to shimmer and echo as if part of the crystalline structure itself.

"You know of the doings of our brother to the north."

"Yes."

"Have you seen what he has unleashed on us? What even now makes its way south through the Hell Plains, Irillian's lands, and Silver's domain?"

"I have. I have seen everything."

"I fear that he will soon have Gold's three royal hatchlings as well."

For the first time, the glittering figure stirred. "How?"

"A ploy by the Seekers, we think. Either working with Ice or intending to use the hatchlings in some bid of power with him."

"A dangerous bid."

"I can gain no support, no combined effort from the others. I have turned to you, because you and Ice are the eldest. You two are from very ancient hatchings, whereas the rest of us are from later ones, some of us by more than a few human generations, and can only call you brother because of our status." It was true. Humans believed all the Dragon Kings to be true brothers, born at the same hatching or from the same progenitors. In truth, the use of the word "brother" was more as an honorary title, an indication of the so-called equality between the kings. The drakes did not discourage those beliefs.

The Crystal Dragon was quiet and, in his mind, Green saw the indistinct figure stare off to one side. At last, the glistening drake said, "I will take your words under consideration. It is possible that I may have to take an active role and, then again, it is possible that I may not. For now, I will continue to observe."

"But—"

Contact was broken. This time, the drake lord knew an emptiness, as if his world would soon cease to exist—a very real possibility, he decided. The Crystal Dragon had taken his last chance for cooperation and left only the crumbs of hope. He might or might not act and even if he did it might be only when his own kingdom was threatened.

The Green Dragon's eyes blazed. Ice was as much the antithesis of his existence as was possible. The master of the Dagora Forest had no intention of giving up his domain without a struggle. His subjects were already prepared, should the abominations come this far. There did remain one other hope, too. The Gryphon.

The lionbird would not deny him. Bedlam and the Lady would not run and hide. They were his true allies, more so than the other Dragon Kings had ever been. In truth, those three were something he could never have considered among his own kind.

Friends.

And his brethren wondered why their own kingdoms crumble about them. He smiled grimly at their ignorance.

FIRST ONE LANDED. Then another. Then four more. They came in groups and they came alone. Regardless of how many arrived at once, the citadel of Azran was soon covered with them.

These were not the only Seekers in the Dragonrealms. They did, however, represent the opinions of the majority. It was the choice of that majority that had led the Seekers back into the activities of the realms at large. It was because of that majority that the Seekers in general were risking much of what remained of their civilization.

More than a dozen of the avians arrived together, landing in the midst of the open courtyard. They carried seven bundles among them and each bundle wiggled and howled. The leader of this band reached down to a medallion hanging from its chest and concentrated. The bundles quieted.

There was still some debate between the Seekers as to what exact use the contents of the bundles would be put to. A few still wanted to destroy the contents as an example of the power the avians still held. They were quieted down by the cold stare of the leader of the late arrivals. This was too precious a cargo to waste so, his eyes said. The original plan would continue.

The Seekers had no true leader at the moment, their last one dying during the battle for this citadel. This one and others vied for that spot now and, if this plan succeeded, there would be no difficulty guessing who would be chosen. Yet it was a double-edged claw, for failure in such an important project would mean death at the claws of those gathered here.

In a fit of vanity so unlike its kind in general, the Seeker in charge of the newcomers had some of those in its flock unbind one of the bundles. It pointed specifically at the largest one.

Unwrapped, it revealed the eldest of the hatchlings—but not as any of the avians had expected to see it. Calmed by the Seeker artifact, it gazed out at the creatures, more human than drake. The hatchling had not yet learned to form the helm, which the adult males used to cover their incomplete and alien visages. There was little need; while it could not pass for human, it lacked the reptilian horror of the male drakes and the sensuous, inhuman beauty of the females. Given time, the hatchling might succeed where its elder brethren had failed in their shapeshifting.

The young drake reached out with one hand, but the Seeker swatted it. Hurt, the hatchling held itself tight, as if that would make the monsters around it go away.

The Seeker in charge indicated for the drake to be bound once more. When that was done, it picked several other avians from the gathering and indicated that they should join with the original band. No one hesitated.

Satisfied, the leader spread his wings and rose into the air. Two by two, the ones carrying the kidnapped hatchlings followed. When they were all aloft, the others in the band followed.

The remaining Seekers watched until the group was gone from sight. There was no discussion, no comment at all. One by one or in groups, the remaining avians departed for their respective nests. The reckoning was close at claw. It was now the time to wait. Wait either for success or possibly the beginning of the end.

XIX

WHILE THE GRYPHON had pored over leagues of ancient script, Cabe and his companions had slowly pushed their way over a much longer and equally frustrating track of land that even the hardiest of creatures would have normally shunned. Now, pausing for a moment, they stared at their destination.

The ice-covered mountain began to loom overhead, even though it was still some distance away. It was by far the largest of the chain, a jagged behemoth approaching the height of Kivan Grath, the greatest of the Tyber Mountains.

Toma laughed mockingly. "Don't let appearance make fools of you. The Ice Dragon would like to think that his citadel compares to that of my sire, but, as with the dreams of many, this frosty edifice is more a house of glass—or should I say ice?"

It was certainly imposing enough to Cabe. "What's that supposed to mean?"

"Merely that most of this mad drake's home is nothing more than ice. The mountain is very small and as much a glacier as it is earth. I know. Stripped of its glorious mantle, the Ice Dragon's citadel would be a tall hill in comparison with the giants of Tyber."

"Which makes our adversary no less weak," commented Haiden. "I doubt that making disparaging remarks about the cold one's hearth and home are going to defeat him. He does not strike me as a sensitive soul."

Gwen agreed and added, "Doesn't it strike anyone as strange that we've not come across any defenses or even felt the touch of his power—besides that damned chill of his?"

"I have noticed a bit of snow and wind."

"Don't be sarcastic, Haiden. You know what I mean."

Cabe looked around them. White. Cold and white. It was beginning to disgust him. "I daresay that the weather to the south of this is far worse. Remember, the Ice Dragon has no need to cover his own domain completely, only those he wishes to overcome."

"If what you sssay is true, we may be in one of the more attractive ssspots in the Dragonrealm, Bedlam. Ssstill, I could do without this chill that shroudsss me within and without."

The cold was getting to all of them, but the chill within was doing more damage. There were long periods of time where no one wanted to speak nor wanted to be spoken to. There were times when they were surly with no reason, though that was debatable in the case of Toma.

The drake experimented, causing a tiny flame to burst from one hand.

"We ssstill have our powers. I have felt the touch of Ice. I would know if he wasss observing usss."

It was the elf who discovered a likely reason. He had been scanning the Wastes from ground to sky, ever cautious, and his persistence was finally paying off.

"Look there!"

At first, it was only an indistinct shape coming from the south. Toma turned to the others. "We should take cover!"

Cabe felt the touch that he knew was more Nathan than him. He shook his head. "There's no reason. They don't care about us. In fact, I get the impression that, if anything, they would approve of our actions."

"They?" Gwen concentrated, then, even as the shape separated into a number of smaller ones, she gasped. "Seekers!"

Toma nodded to himself, remembering how the one had aided him in his escape. The avians *were* plotting something. Perhaps his escape had merely been a delaying tactic while they prepared this. It may have been that they cared little whether he succeeded in crossing the Wastes. Certainly that was within Seeker thought as he knew it.

Now they could see that there were probably at least two dozen of the creatures, more than any of them had seen at one time, save Cabe, who recalled the day when the former Red Dragon had assaulted Azran's citadel, and how the Seekers had risen in a frenzy only partially caused by their forced servitude to the mad mage. The areas near the castle had contained one of their ancient rookeries, their breeding places.

The Ice Dragon had indeed made some dangerous foes.

The avians appeared to be carrying a number of litters with them, though what they contained was beyond the imagination of anyone in the party. The creatures were flying slow, sinking occasionally, and Cabe hazarded a guess that they were forced to make frequent stops. Whatever the avians carried, it must have been valuable.

Nothing impeded their flight. The foursome watched as the Seekers flew past, not even acknowledging their presence with so much as a glance. Cabe knew better, however; he had felt the skilled touch of more than one alien mind. The Seekers knew why they were here and, as he had suspected, they approved. It was their combined opinion, though—and the arrogance of the creatures surprised the young sorcerer—that the humans and their party would not be necessary. Cabe and his group were considered just one more plus. Something else to encourage the Ice Dragon to see their way.

"What's the matter?" Gwen asked. She, too, had felt the touch of Seeker minds, but could not read them so clearly.

"I don't know. Nothing, maybe. I just wish I knew what they were up to."

"We may find out soon enough," Haiden added.

"Why?"

"There are things moving through the Wastes. Heading in our general direction."

They had visions of the huge, digging creatures coming to steal their lives. The elf, seeing their expressions, shook his head. "Not those. These were smaller, manlike. Any more than that, I can't say."

"Drakes?" suggested Cabe.

Toma cut in. "There are no more drakes out here save the lord of this land. No, Bedlam, I think these are his unliving servants, as horrible in their own way as those things moving south."

"We can't afford to wait for them."

"Which means we have to fight them, yesssss." There was anticipation in the drake's voice. A chance to strike back at his former captor.

"If we can avoid it, we will." Cabe glared at the warlord until the latter finally nodded. "Purposely trying to fight them will do us as little good as hiding. We'll waste time!" In the back of his mind, Cabe almost wanted to give in to hiding. Anything to avoid what Tyr had predicted. He wished the dead Dragon Master had not warned him.

They rode cautiously, avoiding as best as possible places where Haiden claimed to have sighted the Ice Dragon's minions. Their minds reached out to seek any hostile presence nearby, but they felt nothing but the continuous scourging of their souls by the spell. It was becoming more and more difficult to get the horses to continue; they were cold within and without and frightened by their surroundings.

Another hour passed. The icy home of the monarch of the Wastes grew impossibly taller. Mostly ice, yes, but it was unnerving in a way that the towering Kivan Grath was not; it was cold with death, that was the only way to put it. Kivan Grath, home of the dragon emperor, had an overwhelming dignity, despite the fearsome awe most felt. Here were only the dead. The Northern Wastes were as much responsible for their fatalistic attitudes as the decay of their power.

Cabe shook off some of his melancholy. He began to wonder which would get them first, the induced weariness of life or their shadowy watchers.

Time passed, the mountains stood just before them, and they still were not attacked. Toma, presently walking, tested his powers by melting a hole into a snowdrift.

"This is sssome game. The Ice Dragon would not let us come ssso close otherwise."

"Maybe he just has his mind on other matters," suggested Haiden.

"The Ice Dragon is far more capable than that. Besides, his servants watch our every move."

Cabe looked around. "I'm beginning to wonder about that."

Gwen understood. "The Seekers?"

"The confidence I felt was strong. Very strong. I don't think those creatures would put all their hopes into one attempt."

"You're suggesting that those things watching us belong to the birds?" Toma shook his head. "This close to the lair of Ice himself?"

"Why would the Ice Dragon leave us be? Why not take us before we come too close and possibly risk all?"

"I told you . . . The damper spell!"

"You have your powers. I've been . . . prepared." He felt this was one aspect of the protection from Nathan. "Nothing."

"The Seekers must be inside by now," Haiden commented. "Perhaps they are responsible after all."

"Unless we have an ally we don't know about," added Gwen quietly.

At that moment, two ice-covered creatures stepped miraculously through the mountainside. Toma jumped back and Cabe and Gwen both began casting spells. Haiden's longbow was out and ready.

They were the unliving servants of the Ice Dragon. The party studied them with revulsion, for their nature was quite apparent. Within each were the stiff forms of some hapless being. One was human, that much Cabe could tell. The other might have been an elf or a half-elf, but the distinction was pointless. Both of these unfortunates had died and now their corpses gave these monstrous forms existence. Clear, icy fingers moved. Blind eyes saw.

The servants did not attack. They did not even look in the direction of the party. Instead, they each moved to one side of the hidden gateway and stood there, completely at attention, but entirely unconcerned with the nearness of the enemies of their master.

Cabe turned to Toma and whispered, "Do you understand what is going on?"

"Either we are like vermin being led to the trap by a piece of cheese or, asss you mentioned, we have an ally of incredible strength. Could it . . . No, not possible."

"What?"

"He doesss not interfere."

"Who?"

Gwen came up behind them. "Wouldn't it be better to talk about this when it's a bit safer? There's no telling how long this will go on!"

"She is correct," Duke Toma said reluctantly.

"What about the horses?"

"We leave them. What else can we do?"

The animals will be removed.

Cabe blinked. "What was that?"

The others looked at him curiously.

They cannot hear. They are not necessary. Follow my words if you wish to defeat the lord of the Northern Wastes.

Gwen, worried, put a hand on his shoulder. "What's wrong?"

Do not waste my time. Tell them nothing. The less they know, the safer.

He shook his head. "Nothing. Let's go."

They walked past the oblivious ice creatures as quickly and carefully as possible. Gwen closed her eyes briefly as she passed next to one and Cabe quickened his own pace. When they were through, he turned back to see if the servants had noticed anything. What *he* noticed was that the horses were indeed gone. Even at their fastest pace, there was no possible way they could have disappeared yet. There was a chance that one of the others had cast a spell, but when?

Ice entertains himself with the avians. They believe their prizes will tempt him from his madness. I have my doubts. It keeps him from noticing certain things, though.

Who are you? Cabe thought.

There was no answer. This was not Nathan, he knew that immediately from the sense of foreboding that enveloped him, a feeling in no way related to the Ice Dragon's spell. Nathan had spoken to him before, in his own mind, but his grandfather's spirit had always emitted a . . . humanity . . . that this intruder did not.

Toma, as the only one who had ever been in here, led the way. From the glares he gave the halls, the others knew that, had he his own way, the firedrake would have seen the icy portion of this citadel reduced to a lake.

"This is preposterous!" Toma hissed quietly. "There is no possible way he could not be aware of us!"

"Perhaps," was all Cabe dared to say. Gwen stared at him briefly, understanding, it seemed, much more than the drake.

"This place is so dead," whispered Haiden. To an elf, such a place as this, where only the darker aspects of nature existed, was an abomination as horrible as the creatures the Ice Dragon had let loose on the rest of the realm.

The comment made Cabe come up short. The words of Tyr had thankfully slipped his mind for the past few minutes, but the elf had brought them back to the fore. Almost, he turned back.

Of what point would that be?

He did not answer the voice's question and knew that the entity expected no answer. Both knew that Cabe had no real intention of turning back.

They walked for what seemed a mile of twisting tunnels. Toma assured them that they were on the correct path. The voice within Cabe's mind did not add anything.

Three figures suddenly crossed their path from an adjoining corridor. Toma froze and the others followed suit. Two of the unliving servants were leading someone by the arms and he followed obediently like a newborn pup.

Gold, the dragon emperor. His mind still suffered the emptiness caused by his struggle with a desperate Cabe so many months ago. The young warlock stared at the once-omnipotent drake lord with some pity. Better a clean death . . .

"No!"

Before anyone else could react, Toma was racing around the corner, hands outstretched in preparation of some spell. This time, even with someone shielding them, the group could not go unnoticed. The two horrors turned with amazing speed and grace for such bulky, awkward-looking creations. One raised a previously unseen staff about two feet long.

Toma did not give him a chance to use it. The firedrake stretched his left hand forward and a carefully aimed streak of flame enveloped only that creature. The staff exploded, sending the Gold Dragon and the other unliving servant backward. Toma's hapless adversary literally melted, until all that remained was the blackened corpse from within.

A fool! This one would rule us!

That was all the voice said to Cabe. He felt the connection between himself and the entity vanish, as if that other had decided this small band was of no further use to it. Cabe could not blame it for thinking that way.

Gold whimpered and the other servant rose to fight. Toma pointed at it, but before he could do anything, the creature cracked into several pieces and collapsed. The drake turned and found Gwen matching his gaze.

"You've probably brought death to us all now, Duke Toma!"

"Bah!" The reptilian warlord stalked over to his fallen parent. Close, his demeanor made a complete turnaround. Cabe and the others watched in amazement as Toma gently tried to help his sire up from the ground, his voice soothing the frightened piece of wreckage that had once ruled all the Dragonrealm.

Once Toma looked up at Cabe, and the sorcerer knew there and then that the drake had not forgotten who had turned the Gold Dragon into this. It had been a distasteful maneuver, and Cabe had used it only when nothing else could save him. He was not even sure he could do it again.

"Don't struggle!" Toma hissed at the other drake.

The floor beneath his feet seemed to melt. He sank a couple of inches.

Gwen pointed at the floor of the corridor. "The ice! It's moving!"

Ice had already spread up the duke's legs. Toma put out a hand, seeking to melt it before it spread any higher. Nothing happened. "Gone! Again!"

Ice was encroaching on the warlord's knees. He tried to pull his legs free and failed. Cabe tried to go over to him in order to assist, but found his own feet frozen into the floor . . . and . . . Was it his imagination? Were there icy fingers grasping his legs?

Gwen and Haiden cried out also. Cabe recalled a simple spell that should have torn the ice from his feet and legs. Nothing happened.

"I knew it!" Toma cried. "A trap all along!"

Had circumstances been more peaceful, Cabe would have corrected him. They had been abandoned and with reason. Their guardian—and Cabe knew that he, she, or it had been with them since long before they had entered the Wastes—had given up on them. All because of Toma.

The Gold Dragon was already encased and only one of Toma's arms was free. Cabe could no longer turn to Gwen, for the ice was already past his waist. Both his wife and the elf were silent now. Dead or soon to be dead, he thought.

Tyr had not spoken the entire truth. It was not Cabe alone who would die. Because he had not known any better, Gwen would die, a victim once more of a glistening prison, this time permanently.

Fools.

That was the last thing Cabe heard. The ice rose and covered his head with alarming speed. Cut off from the air, he blacked out.

* * *

AIR. PRECIOUS, WONDERFUL air.

Light. Light burning his eyes, burning away the comforting darkness.

He dared open his eyes.

The nightmares of childhood sprang to life.

Cabe was hanging on a wall in a vast, ice-covered chamber. His feet and hands were frozen into that wall—if they still existed. He could not feel them. From the moan next to him, he knew that Gwen was there also. He wondered if the same was true for Toma and Haiden. Turning his head was impossible, for he wore a brace of ice there as well. All he could do was stare at the one he had sought all this time, only to fail in the end. Stare at the triumpant lord of the Northern Wastes.

The Ice Dragon lay across a gaping hole on what Toma had said were the remains of a temple. Somehow, he was even more overwhelming than the drake's vivid description had made him sound. He was of gargantuan proportions, but so emaciated it was like facing a gigantic corpse. That might have been an apt description, for when the Ice Dragon noted that Cabe was awake, the ice-blue eyes ensnared his own. Cabe recalled the eyes of the demonic entity Darkhorse; those eyes, too, had been icy blue in color, but Darkhorse had conveyed a touch of life despite his nature while here there was nothing but the emptiness of something worse than mere death.

"Bedlam. The last of the clan. The last of the cursed. The last of the Dragon Masters."

The Ice Dragon rose and spread his wings, creating a frost that covered his prisoners. Somewhere Toma cursed, but not too loudly.

Cabe heard a squawk from somewhere to the Dragon King's left. The great leviathan turned his attention there. The Seekers, Cabe thought. They were still negotiating with the Ice Dragon.

The huge drake lord inhaled sharply and the room grew steadily colder. Was it his intention to freeze them to death?

"At last, all things have come together. It is fitting that the last of the Bedlams be here, along with the Lady of the Amber, and the misfit who would rule the dragons as *Emperor*. The Seekers and an elf, representing pasts that will never repeat themselves. And the emperor's hatchlings, they who would have been kings if not for the human plague."

It was impossible to say what was more horrifying, the absolute finality of the Dragon King's words or the total lack of any emotion save perhaps a cold fanaticism.

Again, there was a squawk. This time, the demand for attention was something even Cabe could understand.

The Ice Dragon swung his head toward Cabe and, with false politeness, said, "You will forgive me, but apparently this must be attended to now."

None of them, save perhaps those who hung at Cabe's extreme right, could see what was happening. They could only watch as the huge form of the dragon shifted so that he could face the Seekers. The Ice Dragon gave his avian visitors the barest of smiles, not something pretty on the massive visage of such a creature.

"I have put up with you this long because I wished to see what it is you plotted. I see now. Artifacts to dull my senses and weaken my power, hatchlings to bribe me with, spies within my very walls, and unseen mages in my citadel. An interesting bag of tricks and, in any other circumstance, an effective bag of tricks. But"—the Ice Dragon rose, overwhelming all else with the sheer magnitude of his size—"you have miscalculated. There can be no future for the hatchlings, not with the sea of vermin that now covers the Dragonrealm. The day of the drakes is over. The day of the Seekers has been over for far longer, and I will emphasize that by pointing out the decay within your minds. Your trinkets are still useful when dealing with my brethren or the disease known as Man, but, as all your vast powers eventually do, they have failed you in the end."

The Ice Dragon inhaled again and Cabe was struck by the image of someone drinking in pure power itself. The Dragon King literally grew, though he seemed to become more gaunt at the same time.

"I have no need to waste any more time on you."

A flash struck the Dragon King. It did nothing, apparently, but make him laugh humorlessly at such a weak effort. Thick black smoke rose about his massive paws, seemed to ensnare him much the way the ice had ensnared Cabe and his companions. The Ice Dragon seemed to watch the deadly smoke with mild curiosity. When it had risen to cover the lower half of his body, he shifted ever so slightly.

The smoke *shattered*. Pieces fell all about the leviathan.

Cabe felt fear. Not his own, but the emanations of creatures shocked that their supposed superiority had just been tested and found lacking.

The Ice Dragon smiled broadly, revealing frost-covered fangs at least as long as Cabe's arms. As with the laugh, it was false. "*That* was your last chance. Now, I will be done with you."

The walls shook, banging the prisoners against them again and again. Vast chunks of ice fell from the ceiling. There were squawks and shrieks recognizable as Seeker noises. They rose to a deafening high that coincided with the worst of the tremors and then died, the voices cutting off one by one until there was silence.

All this in less than a minute.

The massive head of the Ice Dragon turned to one of his unliving servants. "You know what to do with them. Take my emperor's young to their sire, so that they may enjoy a moment together.

"Senile birds." His attention focused on Cabe again.

"Irillian is nearly half overrun already. The Hell Plains will be gone in another day. Foolish Silver's domain is already enshrouded in ice, and my children move on both him and the arrogant human city of Talak. Within two days, the packs will converge on the lands of Penacles and the Dagora Forest. Soon, the Final Winter will cover the Dragonrealm. Soon, it will be cleansed of the human disease. There will be no successor to the drake race. We will be the last and the greatest of all the civilizations birthed here. When my children reach the southern shores, my duty to the memory of our forebears will be completed."

He eyed Cabe closely. "But before I can rest at all, before I can join my clans in the last sleep, I will see the last of the Bedlams become the pivotal nail in the coffin of his people. I will make your power mine—and with it, irreversibly draw forth the life-force, the heat . . . everything . . . from the human race. From the Dragonrealm itself.

"There will be nothing; nothing but an emptiness—within and without."

XX

As the Ice Dragon ranted, so, too, did the wolf raider D'Shay. "Let him see us!"

The command was not to the Gryphon's golem, though in the end it was that creature that obeyed. When the iron grip had relaxed, he looked bitterly at his captors.

D'Shay he recognized. The handsome, bearded face—similar in its foxlike aspect to that of Toos—tinged with a cruel arrogance worthy of a Dragon King. D'Shay was clad in the now-familiar ebony armor, the wolfhelm on his head and the long, flowing cloak that the Gryphon immediately knew was for more than wear. Briefly, he recalled the two-handed sword that the wolf raider had pulled from nowhere.

The other Aramite was slightly shorter than D'Shay but no less dangerous-looking. At the moment, he seemed to be concentrating on a gleaming fragment of something that the lionbird realized was what was controlling the iron golems. Strong magic, then, and one he was totally unfamiliar with.

D'Shay smiled, looking more like the predator that served as the crest of his helm. After their initial encounter, the Gryphon had wondered whether the raiders might be like the Dragon Kings—that is, shapeshifters. He now knew that that was incorrect and that the Aramites were human, but that did not mean they could be defined in the same way as the humans of the Dragonrealm. Not at all.

He realized he knew even more about them than he had thought and that they, in turn, knew far, far more about him than he had hoped.

"The last of the old, the last of the tainted. With your death, the fools at Sirvak Dragoth will surely give in and accept the inevitable. The Dream Lands will become a memory. The Ravager's will will extend over all!"

The Gryphon could keep quiet no longer. "*What* are you talking about?"

Near him, the other Aramite momentarily lost his composure, causing the iron golems to loosen their grips a little. The raider quickly regained control, but the lionbird found he could move and breathe a bit easier. He caught a glimpse of the Blue Dragon. The drake was still unconscious, having been taken totally by surprise by a magic both he and the Gryphon had apparently underestimated by a vast margin.

"You don't know?" The look on D'Shay's visage was almost amusing, until his eyes narrowed and he smiled. "You don't remember! D'Laque! He does not remember the Dream Lands, Sirvak Dragoth, probably not even the guardianship!"

With great difficulty, the Gryphon prevented himself from showing too much emotion. With each mention of some bit of his past, it was as if a door was being opened. He did not yet understand the minute glimpses of memory, but, given time, it would come to him. Time he probably did not have.

"This will certainly be a tale to tell, eh? All those years of wondering, all those years of watching. Only a few of us are left from so long ago, bird, but we remember well. I remember well. And all for nothing! You were building yourself a kingdom over here and didn't even have a thought to spare for the lands of your birth! Ha! What a grand jest!"

Another door opened and the master of Penacles was suddenly filled with such a loathing for the aristocratic raider that it shocked him. D'Shay's words had released something, some horrible memory of sadistic brutality, murder, from one who had been trusted.

The words were blurted out before he knew what he was saying. "You'll pay for all the friends you betrayed, D'Shay!"

All humor drained from the Aramite's face. "So! You *do* remember a few things, misfit! Perhaps you would have even if we had never met again! All the more reason to put an end to you—but slowly. Only one thing prevents us from ending this and that is the secret entrance to the libraries. We have discerned that it must be in your chambers somewhere, but so far we've drawn a blank."

The Gryphon merely glared.

"No answer? I suppose we could question the Dragon King. He really has nothing to lose—except his life. Still, even despite this incident, it may be possible that we can deal with him. After all, the balance of power seems to have shifted now. We have control of matters now."

At that point, a powerful, bitter cold swept the room. The raider D'Laque nearly dropped his talisman and D'Shay went pale. The Gryphon writhed as the chill tore at his insides. This was by far the worst he had felt.

Gradually, this new wave of cold lessened. It did not dissipate completely, however, and the Aramites were forced to pull their cloaks about them. Frost enshrouded those portions of the room nearest to the windows.

"I will be glad to return to our homeland, misfit, not only to bring back your head, but to escape this miserable cold. I do not look forward to your winters."

It appeared that neither of the Aramites knew the true cause of the cold, and the Gryphon doubted that they would believe him. Time, he felt, was running out for more than just him. With the cold reaching this far south with such intensity, the Ice Dragon's creatures could not be far behind. Irillian was probably under siege. He did not even want to think what might be happening to the farmlands to the north. Toos had already reported refugees coming south by the hundreds. That might swell to the thousands, providing they survived that long.

"You have just this one chance, bird. I can promise to make your death swift and relatively painless if you tell us how to gain entrance to the libraries. Well?"

One of the golems holding him suddenly stiffened and spoke. D'Shay was backing away, expecting a trick. Instead, all the creature said was, "The food requested by the Lord Gryphon is here. The manservant requests entrance."

"What?" It took a few seconds for the message to sink in. When it had, the Aramites laughed in relief. D'Shay smiled and replied, "Tell the manservant to leave the food and depart. The Lord Gryphon will retrieve it later."

The golem was silent, but there was a sense of the message having been delivered nonetheless.

"Well, so much for that."

"The manservant still requests entrance," the iron golem uttered.

The two wolf raiders exchanged glances.

"A ploy?" suggested D'Laque.

D'Shay nodded and turned back to the golem. "Describe who is out there."

There was evident communication between the golem who spoke and those outside. "One human of later decades, low mass, average height. Facial—"

"Enough!" D'Shay studied the Gryphon. "Remarkable products of alchemy, misfit, but there is a great deal of room for improvement. Your servants also show excessive tendencies, it seems. Watch him, D'Laque. I shall deal with our overzealous friend."

The other Aramite looked worried. "Wouldn't it be better to just keep ordering him away until he left?"

"Possibly, but he may alert others about this turn of events. Better to take care of him and keep him quiet until we are away."

"As you say."

D'Shay stood to one side of the doors. He pulled out a long, wicked dagger as deathly black as his armor. The Gryphon struggled in vain. Without speaking, D'Laque had evidently ordered the golems to silence him, for one of them reached up and held his beak tight. This meant that one leg was free, but the lionbird would have welcomed any suggestion right then, for he could think of nothing to do with it. The Aramite with the artifact was too far away to kick, and striking the golems would only hurt him, probably break his foot at that.

Glancing back at the imprisoned Gryphon, D'Shay whispered, "Let him in."

D'Laque looked about in confusion, but apparently he did not have to command anyone, for the doors began to swing inward.

D'Shay lunged forward, but found himself impacting against a solid, blue-gray arm. With a gasp, he tried to shout something. He did not have time. The Aramite was thrown backward with inhuman force and the knife flew from his grasp. D'Shay struck a wall much the way the Blue Dragon had and slumped to the floor. Unlike the Dragon King, he groaned loudly.

The two golems from outside stalked in, behind them what appeared to be the manservant. There were voices in the hallway and the sound of several armored figures rushing toward the open doorway.

Mouth wide open, D'Laque held up the glowing artifact in his hands and stared at the golems holding the Gryphon prisoner. One released the lionbird's arm and turned toward the newcomers. The other one tightened its grip on the Gryphon and prepared to twist his head off. Against such an opponent, the lord of Penacles stood as much chance as a newborn chick did of defeating a hungry, adult minor drake.

A familiar voice barked out a word in a language only three others in the room recognized. The golem stiffened, but did not release its prey. The creature that D'Laque had turned against the others also froze. The wolf raider gaped and reached into his cloak. He was too late. One of the remaining golems was already across the room and reaching for him. The Aramite succeeded in ducking the massive arms, but he stumbled against the wall and lost hold of the item he had used to control the golems. It hit the floor with a clatter and rolled away.

D'Laque reached for it. An iron foot applying several hundred pounds of pressure stepped on both the artifact and the raider's hand. The black-clad figure howled loudly, stared at the red mess that had been his hand, and collapsed on the floor, writhing and moaning in agony.

"My apologies, my lord, for taking such a chance."

The manservant stood before him, grinning. He ordered the golem to resume normal functions. As if horrified by what it had done, the iron creature released its prisoner and stepped back several feet. The Gryphon began rubbing the sore points on his body—sore points which constituted *most* of his body—and then patted his rescuer on the shoulders.

"Damn, it was you, Toos! I was beginning to wonder just how many people had free access to my quarters and command of my bodyguards!"

The general grinned, looking some twenty years younger. Escapades like this had been part of the original reason he had become so valuable to the Gryphon in the early days. "It was your own precautions that helped us succeed."

"True, but there are very few people I would trust with the one command word capable of overriding all previous orders of my metal friends here. Only one, in fact."

Long ago, when the first of the iron golems had been created, the Gryphon had contemplated the possibility, however rare, that someone might turn his creations against him. He had, therefore, added a fail-safe. A word—a name, he believed—from some language that floated in the back of his mind. A language he knew was as much a part of his past as D'Shay was. Unless one searched deeply into the essence that was the iron golems, the code system was safe. It required a great deal of skill and time, the latter of which the raider D'Laque had lacked. Spells within spells, ploys within ploys. Years as a mercenary had taught the Gryphon that.

Guards were assisting the still-stunned Dragon King to his feet. A physician was checking on D'Laque, who was now deathly still. Other guards were chaining D'Shay's wrists behind him. The Gryphon's nemesis had still not recovered completely from the swing of the golem's arm and his subsequent crash into the wall. The lionbird turned his attention back to Toos. The urge to smile was too much for him, and a beak could not possibly convey the feeling. He shifted facial appearance, becoming, for the moment, the handsome, hawk-faced man that only a few had ever glimpsed. The smile spread freely across his visage.

"Well, worker of miracles, explain to me how you came out of the blue—if you'll pardon the choice of colors—and rescued us in the proverbial nick of time! One could have not staged a better rehearsal."

Toos shrugged modestly. "Again, it was you who gave me the clue. I was off duty. It is Captain Freynard's responsibility to take charge when that occurs. When you said that you and he had met in the hall, it took me a few moments to realize that he should have been nowhere near here, especially with the hunt for D'Shay on. Admittedly, I reacted by expecting the worst and assumed there might be trouble in your very chambers."

"Your 'infallible' talent for making the right decisions again. You still claim you have little sorcerous power?" The Gryphon chuckled, his face slowly reverting to that of the astonishing creature he was named for.

The ex-mercenary, long used to the facial alteration, gave him an innocent look. "If I have so much power, milord, it is as much a mystery to me as it is to anyone else. I will admit, though, that it does come in handy."

"To be sure. So you countermanded the golems outside and—" He paused as the physician who had been examining D'Laque walked up to him and waited patiently. "Yes?"

"Your Majesty, I apologize profusely but there is nothing I can do for the wounded one. He is dead."

"Dead?"

The physician was a veteran of many a conflict and his expertise was beyond questioning. He nodded morosely. "The hand was cared for almost immediately and was not, at least directly, the cause of death. It seems he suffered some massive shock or withdrawal unrelated to it."

"That thing in his hands."

"Lord?"

"Nothing. Pity. He might have told us much. Now we'll have to rely on D'Shay for that." D'Laque, the Gryphon thought to himself, had died because his artifact—why did the name Ravager's Tooth come to mind?—had been crushed. There was a link between one such as he and the object.

Another door in his mind had opened.

Someone alerted him to the fact that the Blue Dragon was recovering. The Gryphon excused himself from Toos and the physician and joined the drake, who was apparently well enough to chase those assisting him away. He looked up at the lord of Penacles.

"Are those egg-eaters gutted? If not, I want D'Shay so that I can skin him alive!"

The Dragon King was definitely recovered. The Gryphon shook his head. "The other one is dead, but D'Shay is my prisoner. It was my palace and my life he was after."

The drake tried to rise. "How did you turn the tide? I was struck down by one of your supposedly loyal metal men."

"General Toos acted in his own indomitable way." He was not about to tell a Dragon King about the one word that would override whatever command the golem was following. He did, though, tell the drake that his second had taken control of the two outside before they could react and, since the golems only contact one another when they have to relay information or questions, informed the creatures of what they had to say. The golems within, limited in their thought patterns, would not suspect. Toos knew that the Aramites might suspect a trick, but not one that included retaking control of two rampaging creatures easily capable of tearing them apart. The arrogance of the wolf raiders had done them in.

"There are too many 'if's' in that plan."

The Gryphon's face had reverted to avian, but he seemed to radiate a smile of some sort. "Not where General Toos is concerned. I've found his instincts to be more or less infallible since I've known him."

"You are not telling me sssomething."

"Our truce still exists, if you're worried about that."

The Blue Dragon shook his helmed head. His eyes then focused on D'Shay, who had, in the time the Gryphon had taken to talk to the others, fully recovered. He was struggling with his bonds—quite unsuccessfully. Four guards stood near, two holding the prisoner, and Toos was already attempting to question the dark-clad figure. Judging by the look on the ex-mercenary's face, he was not making any progress.

The Gryphon made his way to the prisoner, the Blue Dragon right behind him. D'Shay's eyes left Toos and impaled the lionbird. There were anger, frustration, and some emotion the Gryphon could not identify but which made him uneasy. He was not at all satisfied that the wolf raider was completely harmless now.

"I hope you searched him thoroughly, Toos. Last time, he pulled a two-handed sword from nowhere." It was debatable whether D'Shay was a sorcerer or not. That was the only time the Gryphon recalled him doing anything truly magical, but his recent memories of the wolf raiders, the Aramites, would not have filled even a page in a book. Two face-to-face encounters. He wished dearly he could remember what part D'Shay had played in his past and why he knew the man for one who had betrayed friends.

"The misfit." The aristocratic marauder smiled coldly. "You always seem to have a knack for survival."

Toos was bristling. "I was attempting to find out what had happened to Captain Freynard and the other man."

"They never left the inn, did they, D'Shay? At least, not by conventional means."

D'Shay said nothing, but his eyes darted from the Gryphon back to Toos and back again. The general was red; Freynard, the lord of Penacles knew, had been almost like a son to his comrade. Both had assumed it would be the captain who succeeded the general, if he retired. Now, that would never be.

The soldier's eyes darkened and the look he gave the raider was one that had unnerved more than one prisoner, so much that confessions often spilled out. D'Shay acknowledged it as one might acknowledge a light spring rain. Toos slowly pulled a knife from his belt.

"This is my responsibility now, majesty. My men will take the prisoner to a cell where he can be interrogated thoroughly. I'll also have that other piece of refuse disposed of while we're at it." He nodded toward the still figure of the other ebony-armored figure.

This caught D'Shay's attention. "D'Laque is dead?"

He might very well have been asking what the time was, but the Gryphon caught a brief flicker of emotion that the Aramite was unable to conceal immediately. It was not fear—never fear from D'Shay, he suddenly remembered—but bitter anger. The man D'Laque had been an important piece in whatever game he was playing.

Toos, however, misunderstood. "Your friend with the rock is dead and his trinket is in a few thousand pieces. Let that be a warning."

The aristocratic raider shook his head. "Poor D'Laque! He warned me of the folly of doing this, but I convinced him otherwise. Keepers aren't supposed to be so near the action, but they dislike that. Certainly, Senior Keeper D'Rak disobeys his own rules. Ah, D'Laque. He trusted me—I have a reputation, you know." D'Shay had been smiling coldly and the chill in that smile was nearly as numbing as the Ice Dragon's spell. "Another thing you will pay for eventually, misfit. You can depend on it."

General Toos made sure that each of the guards had the black-clad figure in a tight grip. "You won't have anything to do with that, friend. We're going to lock you away somewhere that even the rats refuse to visit. Then, we'll pry a few answers out of you."

D'Shay continued to smile. The Gryphon was tempted to slap the smile off his face, but he knew the Aramite would have taken satisfaction in that. "We have much to talk about, D'Shay. I remember more and more and, with your help, I'll remember everything before long. Then, maybe I'll see to your masters."

"I see."

The prisoner scanned the room briefly, his eyes taking in everything, especially the tapestry. The Gryphon braced himself for some escape attempt, but D'Shay merely smiled in self-annoyance. "A lesson to be learned. I should have been more careful. I underestimated you, misfit, but I've learned from that as well. Perhaps . . ."

Still smiling, D'Shay suddenly broke into spasms. He coughed and some blood dripped from his mouth.

"No!" someone shouted, and the lord of Penacles realized belatedly that *he* had. This was *not* from some injury his prisoner had sustained! He knew what D'Shay was doing, knew that his nemesis was seeking an escape of a sort from which there was no return.

The Gryphon took hold of the shaking figure even as Toos turned and summoned the physician. The wolf raider's teeth were clamped tight against each other and his lips had curled back somehow, giving him a truly feral look as he continued to smile in open mockery of his captors' efforts. The eyes stared through the lionbird.

With horror and anxiety, the Gryphon knew that he was losing the only source of information he had concerning his own past. D'Shay was snatching a victory even in defeat.

"Damn you, carrion!" he squawked angrily. "You can't do this! Not now!"

The physician joined them, but by then it was too late. With one final jerk and a sigh that hinted at satisfaction, the wolf raider slumped like a marionette deprived of its strings. Not trusting the Aramite, the Gryphon had the guards secure his shoulders and legs while the physician inspected him.

After a thorough examination, the man rose. "I have no doubts whatsoever that this man is dead. I believe he's ruptured something. I'll know more given time to cut him open."

Staring down at the corpse, which somehow still retained its former tenant's arrogance, Toos shook his head. "With your majesty's permission, I would like to burn this rot immediately. It would help us both rest easier, I think."

The lionbird nodded. He was no necromancer; he could not raise the dead and he suspected that, even then, D'Shay would have found some way to cheat him. Besides, as Toos had said, he would be able to relax only if he knew that D'Shay was truly gone. "Do it, Toos, then scatter the ashes somewhere where they won't poison the animals."

Guards were already removing the other body. The Gryphon caught the Dragon King watching, with something in his demeanor that approached satisfaction.

"Not what I was hoping for, but a satisfying conclusion, nonetheless. The Aramite can have his little victory. I would rather be alive and fighting."

The Gryphon snorted. The Blue Dragon might be satisfied, but this turn would always leave a bitter taste in the lionbird's maw. "We might have to enjoy that little victory—or have you forgotten we still have another battle on our hands?"

"I had not, but it is still pleasant to watch one's defeated foes being dragged lifelessly away."

"Revel in that, then." The Gryphon picked up Yalak's Egg, which had been resting comfortably on a shelf all this time. He studied the crystalline artifact briefly, forcing D'Shay to the back of his mind, and then added, "And let us hope that it keeps you happy even if we fail, because we won't have anything else to think about except how long it will be before the Ice Dragon's abominations come looking for us."

XXI

THE SEEKERS IN the aeries about the Hell Plains knew the moment their emissaries had failed. The ones who represented those and the aeries scattered about the continent argued with one another in the decaying citadel of Azran. Not a sound issued forth from any of the Seekers, save for the occasional involuntary squawk. They spoke in the language of their minds, the only true way each could profess its opinion.

As set as they were in their ways, they could not conceive of yet more danger to them. When the first rumble occurred and the entire structure shook, many of the avians froze, not understanding in the least. Only when the first heavy pieces of the citadel began to fall on them did they finally react. The Seekers rose into the air as quickly as possible, but for many it was already too late. The first of many great diggers rose through the courtyard, grasping a number of confused and dazed avians before they could fly above its reach.

The Seekers had played their hand and it had proven insufficient. Now, the Ice Dragon was revealing to them the utter lack of concern he felt about their once-great power. They, like all his foes, were as nothing. It had meant delaying the process of the Final Winter to urge his creatures to concentrate on the avians, but the lord of the Northern Wastes was not concerned. His enemies were nothing now. This interruption would not last long. A few minutes, maybe more. Nothing could halt the nightmarish tide.

Some of his children, the things that were extensions of his being, would die. The Seekers, being what they were, would not take the destruction of their lives complacently. Yet there were so many of the beasts, and each one required the efforts of several of the bird-people.

Even to the arrogant Seekers, it was obvious what the outcome would be.

*   *   *

IN THE CAVERNS, to the confusion of his prisoners, the Ice Dragon laughed.

With each passing moment he continued to grow taller, and more gaunt. A veritable skeleton sheathed in parchment. The Spell of the Final Winter, as the Ice Dragon had come to call it, surged toward the point where it would be impossible to reverse.

Absently noticing the puzzled, cautious look on Cabe's face, the leviathan grinned as only a dragon can grin. The young warlock stared back defiantly. He no longer knew how long he and the others had hung here. The Ice Dragon appeared to be waiting for that proper moment to dispose of his "guests." Evidently, it was his desire to assure that his power, when needed, would be at its peak.

"The avians are in total chaos. The last obstacle is crushed. Destiny merely waits now."

This new show of emotion was so foreign to the demeanor of the Dragon King that it shook them all. That he could take pleasure in something showed how close to total success he was.

"Brother Ice."

The voice seemed to echo all about the caverns. There was an odd quality to it, as if the very ice about them were the source.

"Brother Ice."

The Dragon King's head shot up and ice-blue eyes flared coldly. "How is it you come unwanted into my chambers, Brother?"

"Is not part of your domain mine? Do not your caverns glisten with lesser reflections of my power?"

"What is it you want?" There was menace in the Ice Dragon's voice, showing once more that he had not become completely unemotional.

"This must stop."

"I offered you a place in this once, and you refused."

Toma started to say something, but Gwen quieted him.

"Ritual suicide serves no purpose," the voice replied.

"This does!" The Ice Dragon was warming to his cause. "There will never be a successor to our kind! We are the pinnacle, the epitome of power! To let the human vermin rule these lands would be to shame the glory that was! Better there be nothing!"

"I cannot condone this."

"What will you do?" The frost-coated dragon gazed around, as if trying to place the other in some certain location.

"I will do nothing. Your own actions will condemn you."

All of them waited for more, but the walls were silent. Toma finally whispered, "We are dead. Even the Crystal Dragon will not stand against him."

"That didn't sound like surrender," Gwen retorted, but the tone of her voice indicated that she, too, had given up hope.

Cabe would have spoken then, but an intruder familiar to his mind returned in force. He felt also the overwhelming presence of that part of him which had been Nathan Bedlam, as if it still sought to protect him against some dire fate—which he apparently was going to suffer regardless of that protection.

Bedlam. I believe you to be less of a fool.

He did not know what to make of the statement or why the other had returned.

The secrets brother Ice uses; they came from two sources. One is destroyed. The other is you.

I know, Cabe thought to the other. He wondered if this was the Crystal Dragon. Could the conversation before have been a ploy? He felt annoyance from the being in his mind, as if this was not the time to wonder about such insignificant things. The mage could not argue with that logic.

I am no longer strong enough to aid you directly, but, if you agree, I will borrow from you the very same secrets that Ice stole. I lack the tools to take them by force, as he did. I need your agreement. There are those that can still aid you, but they run short on time.

There was an anxiousness that Cabe had not detected before and he suspected that his mysterious ally was hard-pressed by other matters—matters, no doubt, whose tremendous forms were dwarfed only by their appetites.

"Do it," Cabe muttered.

IN PENACLES, THE Gryphon and the Blue Dragon, immersed in the books of the libraries, stiffened as Yalak's Egg began to cloud up and vibrate.

"Is that . . . normal?" The drake lord, having suffered more than one assault in the past few days, now looked at every odd occurrence as a possible threat. The Gryphon could not really blame him, for he was feeling the same way.

"No, it's not." The lord of Penacles gingerly lifted the crystal. When nothing out of the ordinary occurred, he studied the Egg.

The cloud gave way briefly to the image of an abyss. Things seemed to be drawn to the abyss. More and more until then, as if nothing would satisfy it, the abyss began to warp and twist. The Gryphon realized that it was swallowing itself. He watched until the abyss was no more.

The hunger grows and will ever grow until it must devour itself. The life feeds it, but the life kills it. The source is the beginning, but it is also the end.

The Gryphon blinked. "What was that?"

"I felt nothing," the Dragon King replied in puzzlement. "I heard nothing. I saw only mist in that crystal of yours."

"Does this sound at all familiar to you?" The lionbird repeated the phrases and then described the scene that Yalak's Egg had revealed.

"Sounds like something one of these cursed tomes would say," Blue commented.

"Sounds like . . . It probably is!" The Gryphon whirled around.

"Yes, lord?" The gnome was already standing there, a massive book in his arms.

The Gryphon eyed the tome critically. "Is that what I was about to request?"

"I overheard you as you spoke to that one." His nose was pointed toward the Dragon King.

"And you wanted to save me some time."

"Yes, milord."

"You knew exactly what to look for."

"Those phrases are in this book. Similar phrases may be found in some of the other volumes."

The Gryphon carefully studied the tiny librarian. "*We* have to have a talk if we survive this."

"If you think it will do any better than the last nine, present lord, I will be happy to tell you what I can."

The lionbird grimaced. He *had* spoken to the gnome before. So far, he had not gained a thing from the talks. Still, there was always hope. *If* they survived the Ice Dragon's assault.

"Of what use *are* these libraries?" muttered the Dragon King in response to the librarian's answer. The Gryphon did not have time to respond. He had already taken the book from the gnome's hands and was thumbing through what seemed an endless number of blank pages.

"There's nothing here but—" He held his breath. The phrases that had been revealed to him were at the top of the right-hand page. Below them . . .

Ignoring the gasps from the elderly librarian, he tore off one of the blank sheets and used it to keep his place. Slamming the book shut, he jumped to his feet. His eyes focused on the Egg.

The Blue Dragon was already on his feet. "What is it? What did it say?"

Yalak's Egg nestled in his arms, the Gryphon murmured, "It said we may already be too late. I can only hope. . . ."

"WHAT IS HE waiting for?" Gwen whispered. "Why isn't he doing anything?"

Cabe twisted his neck so that he was able to see her. Beautiful as ever, even after the trek to the Wastes and their subsequent capture by the Ice Dragon. It was a silly notion, but it made him smile briefly. Then he remembered her question, and the answer came to him instantly. He was surprised that he had not seen it before.

"He's waiting for the Twins to align themselves."

He saw that she understood. The two moons, Hestia and Styx, when aligned, created a period when access to power was far easier. "You mentioned that the Brown Dragon did the same thing. An increase in the sensitivity of the powers."

"It'll give him the push be needs. The Ice Dragon is still in great danger from his own spell. He would be a fool not to know that."

Gwen closed her eyes. Knowing that they had no access to their own power, Cabe watched her in puzzlement. She was concentrating, he could see that, but, without power, what did she plan to do?

Several seconds passed. The Ice Dragon ignored them, seemingly preparing himself for the grand moment to come. His unliving servants, with their gruesome interior forms, seemed oblivious to the enchantress's actions. If they understood anything, they probably knew that she had no magic to work.

At last, exhausted, she sighed and opened her eyes. There was a look of disgust on her face. Disgust at her own failure. "I'm sorry, Cabe. I didn't realize how difficult it would be."

"Difficult?"

"I was seeking out some kind of life, some creature that might be able to aid us."

"Without sorcery—"

She cut him off with a shake of her head. Assuring herself first that the Ice Dragon was still concerned with his own needs, she continued. "I have some rapport with nature that goes beyond mere magic. That was why the Green Dragon allowed me to enter Dagora Forest when I was younger. I thought it might work here, but I—there's nothing out there, Cabe! Nothing! Everything has either been killed or has fled!"

"The hour is near." The voice of the Ice Dragon suddenly echoed through the chamber. The leviathan turned toward them. "The hour of glory. The hour of the Final Winter."

"Does he have to go on like that?" muttered Haiden.

"No one will be able to stand against me. The Twins are almost in position. When the alignment begins its first phase, your time will be at an end." The icy blue of his eyes had given way to the dead white they had seen before. Soon, Cabe realized, the eyes would stay that dead white. It was all the result of the spell.

Tiny ice storms danced around the form of the Dragon King as he began to study the prisoners before him. His eyes focused on one after another until they finally fixed on Gwen. "I think . . . Yesss, I think *you* will be first."

Cabe struggled uselessly. "No!"

"Yesss. I undersssstand your kind well, I think. Let the last of the Bedlams watch his dam be the first to give her life. It isss . . . appropriate."

One of the servants straightened. "Hestia is in position."

"Excellent. Take the Bedlam's female."

Two of the creatures lumbered forward. Cabe screamed silently for his supposed ally.

I hear you. I cannot promise much. Ice's abominations are within my domain. Prepare yourself. If his control drops, your power may return. Shield yourself if you wish to maintain control of it. I cannot guarantee much more than that.

The voice had departed. Cabe held his breath and watched anxiously. The creatures were slow, but Gwen had only a couple of minutes of life left at best.

One of the unliving servants reached toward the icy manacle that held Gwen's left hand. The dead creature within seemed to stare at her. The enchantress, to her credit, tried her best not to look frightened.

There was a crack like thunder and the servant was reduced to flying bits of ice that somehow avoided the prisoners, instead blowing into the visage of the Ice Dragon. He snarled, more out of annoyance than pain.

"Do not interfere!"

There was another crack and this time Cabe knew that it was indeed thunder. Thunder and lightning. A bolt struck the floor of the chamber, charring the spot and creating a fissure in the ground a good ten yards long. One of the ice creatures stumbled and fell in. There was no sound of it hitting bottom.

He had been wrong, the young mage realized. His ally had not been the Crystal Dragon, but another Dragon King entirely—Storm, master of the marshy lands in and around Wenslis. Storm, as much a master of the elements as the frost-covered behemoth before them.

Lightning bolts ripped through the caverns, striking the Ice Dragon's minions with deadly accuracy. They seemed, however, unable to strike the drake himself. Bolt after bolt struck around the huge white dragon, sometimes missing by no more than a few feet. Pieces of the cavern flew about in fantastic whirlwinds that seemed to snap at the dragon. Oddly, through the entire assault, the lord of the Northern Wastes only looked . . . irritated.

Still, his control had slipped, if only a little. Cabe felt the tugging of power, but it vanished almost instantly.

I . . . am . . . buying time. There are others. They are almost ready.

They? Cabe did not know who "they" were, but he did know that the Storm Dragon was tiring. The bolts were coming with less and less frequency and the Dragon King's aim, if it could still be called that, was now so erratic at times that the prisoners were in danger of being roasted.

What was worse, though, was that the Ice Dragon was striking back at his counterpart. The four could not see the results of his counterattack, save that the lightning bolts dwindled until only a few succeeded in striking anywhere. A miniature snowstorm overwhelmed the lightning and thunder, seeming to devour it.

"Traitor," the Ice Dragon was saying to empty space. "You would rather the manlings rule. Well, then, suffer with them."

In Cabe's mind, he felt rather than heard the scream of the Storm Dragon. Then, the master of Wenslis spoke to him in a voice wracked with pain.

Another . . . mo . . . moment. Prepare! I cannot . . .

They were blinded as one more grand assault was unleashed on the Ice Dragon. Bolt after bolt of lightning struck the floor around the leviathan. Gaping fissures opened everywhere and water flowed from half-melted walls. The entire mountain shivered as the heat generated by the lightning storm weakened ice that had rested here for longer than even the Dragon Kings had existed. The Ice Dragon's footing slipped time and again. A great block of snow and ice fell not twenty feet from Cabe. Once, a lucky strike slipped past the lord of the Wastes.

It is up to . . . to them—and you.

The cavern was filled with smoke and steam. The Ice Dragon was breathing hard, and it was evident that the final attack had cost him more than he would admit. Cabe knew that many of the Dragon King's hungry abominations had died—had been burned out—by the excessive amount of energy the huge drake had been forced to draw from them. Not enough, though. Cabe could feel it. The Ice Dragon still had more than sufficient strength to see his dreams through.

It was unlikely that the Storm Dragon was dead, but Cabe knew that there would be no more assistance from him. His own kingdom was under attack and he himself was undoubtedly severely injured from the other dragon's reprisal.

Who was left?

Who were "they"?

Better yet, *where* were they? If there was anyone left to fight the Ice Dragon, Cabe estimated that they had only a few more minutes before any further assault would be pointless.

The lord of the Northern Wastes returned his attention to his prisoners. "A minor delay, at best. Come to me now, Lady of the Amber."

With no servants to perform his will, the Ice Dragon was forced to utilize his own power. The wall where Gwen hung twisted and re-formed, more like something alive than mere ice. Still holding her prisoner, the ice became an appendage. A hand of sorts, controlled in the same manner that the floors of the corridor where they had been captured had been, carried her forward to the waiting Dragon King. She struggled, but uselessly.

"Lady of the Amber," the drake lord was saying. "You who stood beside the foulest of the Dragon Masters and now stand with his heir and incarnation. You represent the rise of the manlings almost as much as the Bedlams. Your sacrifice will truly be symbolic, as well as useful. You are strong, and your life-force will contribute greatly to the spell."

This was it—and Cabe had no power to save her! Without thinking, he shouted, "You're a fool, Lord Ice! You don't realize the mistakes you are making!"

The gigantic head turned toward him, no hint of amusement or annoyance visible now. He was too close to victory. "What say you, *last* of the Bedlams? I have made no mistakes worth worrying over."

"Haven't you?" The words came from Cabe out of their own volition. He listened in amazement at himself.

"Amuse me, spawn of a mortal demon. Tell me."

Cabe smiled, though the smile was not his doing. He was disturbed, because he could not even hazard a guess as to where Nathan—it had to be Nathan's presence making use of him—was leading things.

"Something similar to this was used to create the Barren Lands."

"I know that." The Ice Dragon was looking at him closely, as if wondering whom exactly he was speaking with.

"It was to be a complete and final destruction by the Dragon Masters."

Gwen was staring at him, realizing who was actually talking.

"Yet, the Brown Dragon brought the Barren Lands to life, though it cost him his own life and that of all but a handful of his already nearly extinct clans."

"What are you driving at?" hissed the dragon. He had gone from complete indifference to slowly growing anger and confusion.

"Do you think that your spell will be so final? Do you really think that the *winter* you plan to spread across the lands will hold forever?"

"It will. The knowledge came from the books in the libraries of Penacles and even from your own mind. I know *everything*, Bedlam!"

"And you think the latter went unnoticed. You think that everything you learned from this mind was the truth or was not distorted in any way."

There is a cold so intense that it burns. The Ice Dragon's eyes burned with such a cold. Cabe shivered involuntarily, feeling just a touch of that cold. He had thought *the spell* agonizing!

"I know you now for certain!" the Dragon King roared with sudden rage. "The Grand Deceiver! The Dragon Master himself! I'd heard the tales, but not believed the extremity of them!"

"Then you know that what I say can be true."

Within his own mind, Cabe worried that the Ice Dragon would see through what had to be a bluff. Wasn't it? That which was Nathan, which had, after Azran's death, seemed to have melded with Cabe forever, now controlled him. Was it truly possible that Nathan had been prepared for this?

"I think you lie," the Dragon King muttered, but his confidence had slipped. He glanced at the captive Gwen and then at the pit beneath him.

The cadaverous dragon hesitated. His guard dropped for only a second.

Cabe tried to cry out as he felt himself yanked from reality. The cavernous citadel of the Ice Dragon appeared to pull away from him, shrinking and shrinking until it was . . . *gone.* He floated in nothing. It did not even resemble the Void. He was just . . . elsewhere.

The decision is yours, a part of his mind seemed to say. It was impossible to say whether the thought was his own or that of his grandfather.

He did not hesitate. Gwen was back there. If nothing else, he had made a promise to her. If it meant his own death, as the unliving Tyr had predicted, then so be it.

"Yes."

Without further thought, he was thrust back into reality. This time, he *did* scream.

XXII

IN THE DAGORA Forest, the Green Dragon prepared. While his lands were far south compared to the Hell Plains or even Wenslis, the first forerunners of the unholy packs let loose by the Ice Dragon had already made their way into his domain. Overenthusiastic, the drake thought sourly. They had been destroyed, but the cost was far more than he would have liked. He could only imagine the suffering to the north. From his eyes around the Dragonrealm and from those who had sought refuge in his forest, he knew that many fields and forests were withering and hundreds of animals and people—drake, human, whatever—had perished from exposure, hunger, or, worst of all, the voracious hunger of the Ice Dragon's children.

New attempts to contact his brethren and plead for cooperation had achieved little. Storm did not acknowledge him, though the Green Dragon was now of the opinion that his brother to the northeast was planning steps of his own—providing he was still alive. Silver's domain was under assault; that one had no time to speak with him, though it was hastily hinted that any aid would not be rejected. Lochivar's master was silent, as was the enigmatic lord of the Legar Peninsula. How the Crystal Dragon could still remain indifferent puzzled Green. Then again, the Crystal Dragon had always puzzled him. As for the Black Dragon, he apparently seemed to think that if he hid in his domain and did nothing, the Ice Dragon would leave him be. Hardly.

Penacles, however, proved to be an even greater enigma than his fellow Dragon Kings.

He had discovered the Blue Dragon's presence there and the temporary alliance forged with the Gryphon. That in itself was still amazing, but now they were in the midst of something that the lionbird would only say was as much a danger as it was their only hope. Even word that a band of Seekers had, at one point, been sighted ferrying several large bundles toward the north had not bought more than a few seconds of the lionbird's time. The young of the drake emperor were of little import at a time when the entire realm might cease to be. Muttering under his breath, the lord of the Dagora Forest had felt the Gryphon break the connection with such finality, he knew it would be useless to seek further enlightenment.

And somewhere in the Northern Wastes, in the lair of his mad counterpart, the hatchlings which might have given his race a future alongside that of humanity were now probably moments from death themselves. At the claws of one of their own.

He stalked the perimeters of the central chamber of his citadel, helpless to do anything but fight off the abominations and pray that either the Bedlam whelp or the Gryphon could succeed. Placing his future—his very life—in the hands of such was unnerving, even though he had done something akin to that when he had made his original pact with the Gryphon.

As the true abodes of many of the Dragon Kings reflected their respective natures, the Green Dragon's citadel was the bonding of nature with civilization on a scale even more grand in its own way than the Manor. A vast King of oaks, larger and older than any other tree in the forest, had been shaped by the Seekers—at least, he assumed it was the Seekers—so that there were rooms and hallways, some of the former quite immense, throughout the plant even though the oak itself was strong and healthy. If the Green Dragon harbored any superstitions, it was that his domain would crumble the day the tree died. Not surprisingly, one of his predecessors had made daily care of the oak top priority. It still was.

"Lord Green!" a voice rasped.

The Dragon King froze.

A tiny dot before him seemed to unfold continuously, quickly gaining a humanoid form that focused into the very human form of Cabe Bedlam. Drake guards, alerted by the unfamiliar voice, came rushing in, one leading a pair of half-grown minor drakes. The Dragon King waved them away.

Cabe's face was pale and he was panting. He paused briefly in amazement at what he had just done and then remembered why he was here. Ignoring protocol, he gripped the Green Dragon by the arms and asked hurriedly, "My lord! You've amassed a great treasury of artifacts from the Seekers, the Quels, and other civilizations, haven't you?"

"I have." There was a tremendous buildup of energy within the human and it was such that the drake lord had every intention of treating him with nothing but respect.

"I must see it! Do I have your permission?"

"Yes, I—"

"Teleport us there! I . . . I have a balance I must be careful to maintain!"

Stunned as much by the demanding tone as the very idea of being given orders by any human, the Dragon King still only hesitated for a second. This was, after all, a Bedlam. One who should even now be in the Northern Wastes. If Cabe was *here* . . .

He wasted no more time on words. They were gone before either of them could take another breath.

"IT ISN'T WORKING," the Gryphon muttered. "We're too late!"

"Hestia has only just entered the first portion of her phase. Both moons have to be in position, Lord Gryphon. It cannot be too late!" The Dragon King sounded as weary as the lionbird felt. They had given it their all and the only results had been a drain on both of them. As far as they could tell, the Ice Dragon had probably not even felt their assault.

"Something is missing. . . ."

The drake hissed. "Obvious! What, though?"

They were sitting on the floor of the Gryphon's chambers, Yalak's Egg between them. The Egg glowed with energy; it was the only thing that had thus far benefited from the spell. The Gryphon could not help thinking that it was waiting for them to do something else—but what?

There were many passages in the book that hinted at other possibilities. Had he missed one? The Gryphon was reaching for the book when a hiss of indrawn breath from his draconian ally made him turn back.

Cabe's *face* peered out at them from within the crystal. This was not a vision of things to come; he was actually looking at them. His eyes lingered questioningly on the Blue Dragon, then fixed on his friend.

"Gryphon, have you followed the passages in the book?"

The two in the chamber glanced at each other before the lord of Penacles replied. "Yes, how did you—"

Cabe smiled, but it was a tired, worn smile. "I guessed, actually. I've also been in contact with a few of your . . . associate's . . . counterparts."

"*Have* you?" There was restrained curiosity and even a mild bit of instinctive distrust emanating from the master of Irillian by the Sea. Cabe ignored the Dragon King.

"You've failed. Don't ask how I know that; I do. You've misunderstood one section, I think, because you really didn't understand it. Don't worry. I know what to do. I just need you two to continue on with it. As long as you have the will, the power. Don't stop until exhaustion makes you collapse. It's the only way."

Even as he spoke, Cabe was beginning to fade. The Gryphon called out to him. "Cabe! What are you going to do?"

There was some hesitation and then, in an almost wistful tone, Cabe's now wraithlike voice answered, "What the Brown Dragon tried to do to me once—more or less."

Yalak's Egg was once more a foggy, glowing shell.

"What did the Bedlam whelp mean when he spoke of Brown? Brown died at that human's hand in the Barren Lands!"

The Gryphon was brooding. He had a good inkling of what Cabe meant. Absently, he answered the Dragon King. "The Brown Dragon took Cabe into the Barren Lands; it was he who brought Cabe's powers to the fore. He . . ." There could be no mistake. Cabe's captor had had only one thing in mind that night, a night when the Twins were high in the sky. In just about the same locations they would be shortly. In mere minutes. "He intended to sacrifice the boy's life to twist the curse around."

At last, the Blue Dragon understood. "Until now, I had trouble believing a human capable of such an act."

"Then let's make it work. For him." The lionbird shifted back into position. "We only have to give our strength. Cabe Bedlam intends on giving his life."

THE ICE DRAGON'S rage at Cabe's escape—due to his own overconfidence—was as short as it was terrible. The walls of the chamber, already weakened by the assault of the Storm Dragon, began to crumble more. The ceiling creaked and threatened to collapse. Snowstorms burst into life about the form of the chill monarch. Gwen, closest to the dragon, turned away as best she could, her body already half buried by the magically created snow.

Toma felt the grip on his right hand loosen as ice clattered to the floor. He made no sign, however; the Ice Dragon had regained control, and none of his remaining prisoners could utilize their skills. It was not even possible for Toma to shift to his natural form.

"Bedlam!" The name, spit out in a burst of frosty smoke, marked the end of the Dragon King's tirade. The cold, lifeless mask returned once more. "No matter. Even if the last of the Bedlams is nothing but a cowardly hatchling, I still have his dam."

His gaze turned to Gwen, still caught in the grip of the ice. To her credit, she stared back.

"You show more teeth than your mate, little one. Your power, your spirit, will increase my strength greatly. If there are no *further* interruptions, we shall begin again."

The gaunt leviathan rose on all fours and moved to the side of the pit. The thing within that pit stirred, and Gwen had a glimpse of something at least as large as the Dragon King himself. Her defiance gave way to uncertainty and, regardless of her attempts to hold it back, fear.

There were hisses and shrieks from the dragon's far left. The hatchlings had gotten loose from their guards and were now swarming around the indifferent figure of the Gold Dragon. They seemed to be trying to urge him to some action. Their hisses were of anger and fear, not for themselves, it soon became evident, but for the Lady. Belatedly, Gwen realized that they must have felt her call before. There was nothing they could do to help, however.

A grunt of annoyance escaped the master of the icy Wastes. "Perhaps, since they are so tainted by interaction with humans, I should give them to my queen now. It will wash the shame away so much quicker."

"No!" Gwen shouted. "At least let them live! They're your own kind! Your emperor's young!"

"And humanity's future puppet rulers. I think not. I think they will join you shortly. Better they give their lives for the glory of our race than ever bow and call warm-blooded vermin 'master.'"

Gwen was carried toward the pit by the icy pseudopod. With each foot closer the despair generated by the Dragon King's spell grew even more oppressive, until she could do nothing to fight it any longer.

And then . . .

And then, the despair was gone. The fear was gone. The cold was retreating. The storms swirling around the cavern dwindled away before a summer warmth and the entire chamber was illuminated as it had never been.

And there was Cabe Bedlam, arms outstretched, a small object in his left hand, looking all the world like his grandfather. The Ice Dragon's monstrous queen moved uneasily, suddenly cut off from its feeding, cut off from that other link that kept it acquiescent. A link that now spread its massive, frost-encrusted wings wide and glared with eyes filled with death at the tiny human.

"What have you done?"

The Ice Dragon seemed to fill the chamber. Both magnificent and terrible, he rose above all else. Far longer than any of his brethren. Parchment-like skin that barely covered his bones. An anger so great that it lent the dragon a calmness nearly as chilling as his lifeless, emotionless attitude of late. The light, the heat, began to fade. New storms blew into existence.

"Bedlam."

"I warned you that you did not know everything, Dragon King. I did not lie."

"There was nothing that I missed. Nothing."

Cabe shrugged. A part of him was as indifferent as the rest of him was frightened, but he had no choice. Things had to be played out this way. Even if in the end it meant his doom. "As it pleases you. The truth is evident enough."

Fooled once before, the Ice Dragon increased his dampening spell. His other prisoners remained shackled, harmless, but Cabe still glowed with the fury of his own power. Disbelief began to gnaw its way into the dragon's iron-hard heart. He needed more strength.

The thing in the pit protested. He ignored its annoyance and drew forth that power, unwittingly causing the deaths of countless of his creatures, his extensions, by literally starving them as he took what energy they had and made it his own. He glowed now, but it was a bitter, lifeless glow that made him appear as some huge harbinger of death—which perhaps he was.

Still the Bedlam whelp did nothing but wait.

A mocking laugh escaped from the throat of the Dragon King, a coarse sound that shook the fragile ceiling further. The ice about Cabe suddenly took form, took a false life of its own and twisted about him like a giant claw. Cabe looked about, saw his danger, and rose into the air. He only barely succeeded in dodging a second hand of ice coming from above. Free of both, he turned the powers to his own command and brought the two hands together so sharply that they shattered in one massive clap. Tiny fragments flew with great precision at the Dragon King.

"A wasted effort," Cabe remarked casually, hoping that the Ice Dragon did not know how close that attack had really come to achieving the drake lord's goal.

Cabe was now closer to the Ice Dragon, closer to the pit. He could feel the unseen assault of the Dragon King, the constant battering at the shield that protected the young mage's tenuous connection to his powers. The energy drain, Cabe knew, must be massive. The lord of the Northern

Wastes was seeking to maintain the spell of the Final Winter, prevent his other captives from regaining their own powers, control his remaining creatures' actions—all while still assaulting the human before him with both invisible and quite visible threats. There was also to be taken into account the massive level of energy that the Storm Dragon had caused him to utilize. If the latter had not also been fighting a battle on more than one front . . .

"Ifs" did not matter. Results were what mattered. Results that needed to manifest themselves when the moons were at last in position. Hestia was already there. Styx still needed a few minutes. Minutes Cabe was not sure he had.

What would the master of this snowbound domain fear? Heat, of course. But heat alone would not be sufficient, unless . . .

Nathan, he thought, *if you know what to do . . .*

"What isss—" the Ice Dragon began. The entire mountain was shaking again. Steam rose from the largest of the crevices. The temperature of the chamber grew noticeably. A thick, red-hot substance began to spew from the cracks in the earth.

The dragon hissed. Molten earth rose steadily, urged from the depths of the world by Cabe/Nathan. Fear emanated from the abomination. Heat was deadly to it, would bring pain to its children.

The Ice Dragon flapped his mighty wings, inhaled sharply, and blew on the encroaching lava. With horror, Cabe and his companions watched the molten earth cool and freeze in a matter of seconds. Enhanced by the drake lord's power, the cold seemed to spread down into the crevices. The cavern became even colder than before. Cabe shivered momentarily and knew that the others, who lacked any magic, must be suffering terribly.

A wave of chilling frost suddenly enveloped Cabe while he still floated in the air. Perhaps at one time it would have been enough to stop the human, but days and days of enduring the inner chill of the Dragon King's soul-numbing spell had inured him to this at least enough for him to counter it with more heat of his own. Even as the Ice Dragon again pulled back from the warmth it despised so much, Cabe prayed that it would not realize what a price he himself was paying. Unlike the dragon, he had nothing to call upon but his own reserves and what little he dared to steal from the drake's abominations—and in that last lay his hopes for victory.

Great chunks of ice came clattering down as the dragon stumbled against one of the chamber walls. This was taking a toll on him as well. How much longer before the leviathan's control over something slipped? The breaking point had to come soon! If not, then Cabe had seriously overestimated his own chances.

While the two fought a war of wills, Gwen found herself aswarm with worried, fearful hatchlings seeking to pull her away. Only the eldest seemed to understand that it required more than tugging at her clothing and hair—the latter action one she quickly reprimanded them on—and began to scratch at the ice that gripped her. His claws, however, were pathetic excuses; he had not yet learned to shift completely from one form to the other and still wore a shape that was three-fourths human and one-fourth drake. His claws were little longer than those of a person and not very much sharper. He hissed and uttered something that he could only have learned from one of the manservants back home.

The Lady looked up as a shadow covered her. Almost she let out a gasp that would have surely caught the attention of the Ice Dragon. Standing near her was the dragon emperor himself, red eyes vacant of any true thought, only here because he had been led by the hatchlings. Yet she could still feel power coursing through him; the Ice Dragon had not bothered or would not bother with his own lord. As she had inadvertently done with the hatchlings, Gwen began to seek out what remained of the mind of the King of Kings and soothe it.

ALL OVER THE lands, the sudden and inexplicable deaths of so many of the ever-hungry diggers brought hope to those under siege. The Storm Dragon actually began to beat back the still impressive hordes and, in the domains of the dragons Blue and Silver, defenses began to hold. All knew that it was not through their doing, that some miracle had been wrought. They also knew that there were more than enough of the monstrosities remaining to overwhelm them once they tired more—and, at the present rate, that would not be long.

THE THING WITHIN the gaping hole was active now, its hunger greater than ever. The Ice Dragon continued to draw from it, and was now forced to turn some of that power drawn against the very source lest he lose control.

Hestia waited high in the sky, also hungry. Her brother, Styx, was only now coming into his proper position. Both moons had risen in the sky early, as was their custom in this time of the year, but to those who waited, it seemed as if the second would never reach his destination. Cabe could see neither of the two moons, but he felt their pull, felt their collective hunger even as he felt the growing hunger of the Dragon King's "queen."

And then, the sign he was waiting for revealed itself. The sign that the Ice Dragon was faltering.

Toma burst free of his bonds, his power returning to him in a rush. Long green tendrils rose from the wall behind him as he pointed toward his "uncle." His eyes burned with vengeance. The tendrils gathered and shot toward the huge, pale drake. The Ice Dragon had finally reached his limitations. He could not hold everything together.

He was not, however, by any means defeated. A wave of intense cold buffeted Toma even before he was more than an arm's length from the wall. With a crackling sound, the hapless drake was tossed against the ice. He was not unconscious, but any advantage he had had was now long gone. The tendrils withered and died in an instant, no trace remaining.

"You cannot stand against me!" the Ice Dragon was shouting almost calmly. "I have seen my duty and I know it just! The reign of the drakes will be the last such of these lands even if I must sacrifice myself now!" He turned back toward the last of the Bedlams.

Time! The Twins were in position!

Cabe glanced briefly at the object he had held in his hand all this time. The crimson blade with its beaklike point was not quite suited for his human grip, having been designed by the Seekers. Still, it was the proper tool, the one that Nathan had chosen not to use in the Barren Lands, thereby condemning it to its deathly state until the Brown Dragon's mad attempt to sacrifice Cabe. Nathan refused to make such a sacrifice. That he had been able to stem the tide had proven sufficient—then. The spell was too far advanced for that now. Now, only the sacrifice of his own life could reverse what the Ice Dragon had done. It was such a sacrifice that the Brown Dragon had attempted and it was Cabe who would have been the victim.

With a final whisper to Gwen, even though he knew she could not hear him, he clumsily thrust the blade through his own heart.

BACK IN PENACLES Yalak's Egg shuddered, and the energy gathered within was sucked out by a force so strong that it brought both the Gryphon and the Blue Dragon to the point of total collapse. They fell back from the crystal simultaneously, both, in those brief remaining seconds of consciousness, wondering if they would wake.

A storm of overwhelming proportions whipped across Penacles, throwing objects and even a few inhabitants about like so many leaves in a wind. It was a storm that covered nearly all the Dragonrealm save the Legar Peninsula. It was a storm that raged in magnificent fury—for no more than half a minute.

When it suddenly ceased to be and everything had settled to the ground, those that could opened their eyes in order to see what, if anything, remained of the world.

IT WAS GONE.

The Ice Dragon understood that, but the realization was so overwhelming that all the leviathan could do to acknowledge it was to blink. The Final Winter had been reversed. He knew that it would require a sacrifice of such potential that only a master sorcerer's existence would satisfy the requirements. It was a sacrifice that he himself had been about to undertake—but someone had beaten him to it and, by doing so, had twisted his spell so that nothing he did could undo it. He had spent everything on the creating, building, and maintaining of the spell; there was no way he could begin again.

The creatures were cut off from him, but not from that which was the true source. Without his control, without the Dragon King to act as a focus, she was becoming wild, drawing the life-force from her children—his children—so that they died by the dozens, by the hundreds, until soon, so very soon, they would all be dead. She did not even know that she did it, actually believing, as far as her mind could comprehend, that she was working to save them.

Worse yet, the damage they had done would eventually repair itself, even as the Barren Lands had when the Brown Dragon had become the victim of his own folly. Not even the Wastes would be exempt. They would still remain, but the cold would dwindle. Life would push farther north than it had in millennia.

He had failed. His massive head turned this way and that in a mad frenzy—until his eyes at last found the slumped figure at the far end of the chamber.

"Bedlam."

The figure did not stir. If the human had done his work properly, the dragon knew, then this was only a lifeless shell—which did not mean that the Dragon King would not tear it apart nonetheless.

"Cabe!"

His spell sundered, the Ice Dragon's captives were freeing themselves.

The behemoth forgot the still figure, realizing now that he still had a chance to avenge himself on living, fragile creatures, most especially the mate of the Bedlam whelp.

"Damn you, dragon lord!" The enchantress rose into the air. Below her, the hatchlings crowded around the Gold Dragon, who stared vacantly in the general direction of his frosty counterpart. Toma was rising at last and, seeing that Cabe was down and Gwen was preparing to take on the Ice Dragon, turned his attention to his sire. There was a time to fight and a time to flee, and with his father unable to defend himself Toma realized that his best choice was to depart in haste. Once he had the emperor safely hidden again, he could return to settle things with the survivors.

A fist backed with elven strength struck him hard across the back of his neck. The drake stumbled forward and fell to his knees. From behind him, he heard the voice of Haiden.

"Since you consider your alliance with the Bedlams at an end, drake, I see no reason not to count you as another foe—one worse than the Ice Dragon at that."

Toma turned so that his helmed visage faced the elf. Haiden turned pale but held his ground.

"You should stay hidden in the background, tree-eater," the firedrake hissed. Toma waved his hand and Haiden found himself completely surrounded by a bubble of some soft substance. He punched it, but it held. What magic he had did little more than create a temporary aura as it burned itself out on the bubble.

The firedrake watched as the elf dulled his knife on the inner surface of the sphere. He laughed and turned to find his father.

THE KNIFE.

The knife which Nathan had known would be in the Green Dragon's collection of Seeker artifacts, for, after the creation of the Barren Lands, he himself had planted it where the drake lord would find it. Without the knowledge of its use, it was merely one more odd piece. As those who studied them knew, the avians formulated no spell without having already conceived a counterspell. The knife was the focus of that counterspell, and to utilize anything else was to invite the same sort of disastrous side effects that had resulted in the carnivorous plantlife with a taste for the flesh and blood of the Brown Dragon's clans and no others.

Nathan could not bring himself to destroy the blade. Not because he had believed that someone like the Ice Dragon would resurrect the spell, but rather because he was, in the end, a lover of history. A fortunate flaw as it turned out.

Cabe had understood all of this. Cabe had understood everything, thanks to Nathan, including the fact that he would have to die to save the Dragonrealm.

Then, why was he still *alive*?

Anyone glancing at him might have differed with his opinion. He was haggard, at least thirty years older in appearance, and, at the moment, as weak as a newborn puppy. Yet he *was* alive.

But he had succeeded! How?

How?

The Seeker blade lay on the floor before him, not one drop of blood on it. Slowly, he put a hand to his chest, not actually wanting to feel the gaping wound, but still attracted to it in much the same way many people are fascinated by death itself. It *had* to be there.

Nothing. No wound, no blood, not even a rip in his shirt—but something had been torn from him nonetheless.

Only then did he realize that things were far from over. The ground shook, throwing him down again, and he turned over to see Gwen desperately battling the Ice Dragon, who, though worn, was still a Dragon King.

More than a dozen bright blue rings circled the behemoth. They seemed to be trying to loop themselves over him, but something held them back. One by one, the dragon *breathed* on them. As he did, the ring he chose would pale and fade away. Gwen was running out of rings and her face was almost as pale as the snow.

Cabe rose, picked up the knife, and stumbled toward the pit, which the lord of the Northern Wastes had abandoned in his quest for vengeance. It was really not that far a walk, he thought absently, although there were portions of the short trek he would not even remember making when he was finally at his destination.

One of the Ice Dragon's few remaining servants staggered into the chamber and Cabe, still weak, prepared to defend himself with the knife as best he could. The creature, however, made it only a few steps further before it began to crumble before his very eyes. Cabe felt another presence, and realized then that the thing within the hole was still trying to feed the hunger within it, a hunger which the Dragon King no longer controlled and which was even now searching about for new food.

Somehow, he found the strength to deflect the searching mind. The horror below was desperate now, taking even the energy which animated the Ice King's servants, foul as that probably was to it. It was that desperation that Cabe hoped for—for there was one obvious source it had yet to draw upon.

Gathering himself up, Cabe turned toward the Ice Dragon and shouted, "Dragon King! Lord of the Northern Wastes! Have you forgotten me, then? Are you so frightened of the name Bedlam?"

"Bedlam." The behemoth said his name quietly, calmly, but his reaction was anything but that. As the last of the rings ceased to be, the Ice Dragon whirled, forgetting a desperate Gwen. "Bedlam? Will you *never* cease to annoy me?"

The gigantic, gaunt dragon lumbered toward him, frosty smoke issuing from his nostrils in great, constant puffs. To the Dragon King, Cabe must have looked like the dead come to life—and only barely, at that. Certainly no threat, but a chance at last to make the sorcerer suffer for the blight he represented in the drake lord's mind.

It was not until he neared the pit that the Ice Dragon realized there was another hunger possibly stronger than his own. Cabe stumbled back as the dragon shook his head in disbelief and confidently sought to regain control. That confidence turned to uncertainty and then frustration. The ice-white leviathan began to twist as he sought in vain to overwhelm that other mind, a mind with a desire he understood all too well.

"Nooo!" the Ice Dragon hissed angrily. "Not yet! Not until the Bedlam whelp is mine! Not until the vermin are cleansed from the Dragonrealm!"

The dragon began to flail about. His tail was nearly as long as the chamber was tall, which meant that when it swung to and fro, there was little place to hide. Gwen succeeded in dodging the massive appendage, but Cabe could not tell whether any of the others had been as lucky. The fiery-tressed enchantress came to rest not far from him and chanced the tremors that the Dragon King was creating. She tumbled into his arms, both shocked by his appearance and thrilled by his survival. Great spears of ice embedded themselves in the walls as the lord of this frozen land struck out blindly. Both mages were forced to duck.

"Cabe . . ."

His legs and arms were losing sensitivity. "Help me to somewhere safer."

"The Ice Dragon . . ."

". . . will take care of things for us, I hope." He pointed in the direction of the massive drake.

The Dragon King was only half the size he had been earlier and he moved with a stiffness that reminded Cabe of the unliving servants. As his strength faded, the dragon's gaze fell on a figure walking aimlessly in the midst of all the rubble. The Gold Dragon. Clinging near him were the hatchlings, who innocently believed that their sire would protect them from anything. The eyes of the behemoth narrowed.

"No!" Battered, Toma rose from rubble that had once made up a good portion of the ceiling. Haiden, inadvertently protected by the bubble, could only watch. . . .

"My emperor." The Ice Dragon's voice was haggard. "My lord. I am failing you, failing the glory of our kind."

As if drawing strength from the other drake's presence, the lord of the Wastes straightened to the limit of his much-diminished height and added, "But your hatchlings will never lick the boots of human masters. Never."

Cabe felt the sudden rush of energy from the mad Dragon King as the latter, briefly surrounded once more by his pale aura, roared, "Feed one last time, my queen!"

A full-fledged snowstorm overwhelmed them. It was the Final Winter contained in the one chamber. Gwen cast a spell, shielding herself and Cabe. Jagged knives of ice shattered against it. The crevices widened further and she had to grab Cabe as the icy floor beneath him tumbled away. They heard a strangling cry from Toma, then nothing. Of Haiden, the Gold Dragon, the hatchlings—even the Ice Dragon—they knew nothing. The storm raged for what seemed like hours, though they knew that, in reality, it was only a few brief minutes. But those brief minutes seemed more terrible than the days spent riding north, constantly buffered by the Dragon King's spell.

And then . . . it faded to nothing.

XXIII

CABE WAS THE first to understand what the silence meant. He could not believe it any more than he could believe he was still alive after Tyr's words and his own sacrifice—although he had a frightening suspicion that he now understood the true meaning of the ghostly Dragon Master's warning.

"Gwen." He put a hand on her shoulder. Her eyes flew open. She had not been unconscious, but the effort of protecting the two of them had been so great that she had been forced to tune out the real world. Her eyes stared uncomprehendingly for several seconds, then focused on her husband.

"We're alive?"

"Yes." Something—many things, actually—had changed. Without even being able to see yet, Cabe knew that the thing in the pit was dead. Somehow Cabe had the feeling that it had, in the end, fed upon itself. He would never know for sure. At the very least, it saved them the trouble of dealing with it. As for its master . . .

Cabe felt some of his strength returning. He dared to create a ball of light, knowing that the Ice Dragon was no more threat, but fearful that he might be in error. He commanded the light to flitter to what remained of the ceiling of the chamber and turned his gaze toward the platform and, in particular, the pit.

"Rheena preserves us!" Gwen whispered from his side.

Cabe could only nod, both fascinated and revolted by the spectacle.

The Ice Dragon stood there, wings outstretched, in his full glory. He had not had time even to fall before every bit of life, energy, heat—whatever it was the creatures truly had extracted—had been drawn from him. Like the victims of his "children," he stood a lifeless, rock-hard corpse.

Now, Cabe thought idly, *now he truly is an ice dragon.*

That was so. The remnants of the Dragon King's last assault had left him covered with a second skin of pure frost. In the light of Cabe's spell, he glistened. A monument to what once was. A monument to obsession.

A monument to madness and wholesale death, Cabe concluded bitterly.

"The others . . ." Gwen rose. "Where are the hatchlings and Haiden? Where's Toma?"

Toma? Cabe scanned the wreckage of the chamber. The storm had broken loose countless chunks of ice and rock from both the ceiling and the walls. The fissures created by the Storm Dragon's earlier attacks had widened even more and then been filled by falling fragments from above.

There was no sign of anybody.

A hapless, reptilian hiss rose from near the center of the chamber. Gwen hurried down. Cabe followed, sure that, considering how aged he felt, his bones would crack from the slightest fall.

Tyr was right and wrong, he thought to himself. *I did die . . . yet . . . I didn't.* Nathan—what had once been Nathan—had realized the truth long before. Small wonder his grandfather's personality had begun to emerge, had begun to exert itself once more.

Cabe's powers still remained, but his memories—Nathan's memories—were little more than half-seen shadows now. When Tyr had said there would be a death, he had meant Nathan. Cabe was alone in his mind now, and would always be. Nathan had understood what his former comrade had meant, understood the tangled web the lords of the Other had spread, and that was why Nathan had encouraged the sacrifice.

He had known that it was not his grandson who was going to be sacrificed, but his own essence. He was long past his time and Cabe no longer needed his . . . essence . . . to survive.

It had been so different when his grandfather had supposedly merged with him after the death of Azran. He was gone, yet still a comforting presence. No more. Nathan Bedlam had relinquished his power and his hold on life for both Cabe's and the Dragonrealm's sake. He knew that his grandson was no longer the sickly child or the totally ignorant young boy.

There was no more reason for Nathan to stay.

His musings—for that was all he knew they could truly be called—were interrupted by Gwen's summons.

The hatchlings were safe, but only by a miracle almost as unusual as Cabe's. In the end, through either reflex action or some long-buried memory, the Gold Dragon, King of Kings, had protected his young from the raging storm. Death had taken him while he was still more humanoid than dragon, but his growing form had created a barrier, a shield for the hatchlings. Whether he had been trying to protect himself or them was anyone's guess. They were unharmed, albeit confused and, like Cabe, more than a little dazed.

That left only two.

"Haiden?" Cabe turned to where he had last seen the elf and Toma. "Haiden?"

"I'm not coming back in there unless you promise me it's finally finished."

"There's nothing to be worried about."

Both Gwen and Cabe turned to the corridor which led to and from the master chamber. Disheveled, shivering, his clothes in tatters, and his face an odd blue color for an elf, Haiden stepped gingerly back in the room.

"Well?"

Cabe pointed at the Ice Dragon. Haiden's eyes widened and he whistled. "And his . . . 'queen'?"

"No more."

"I wish I could say the same for Duke Toma."

Anger washed over Gwen's face. "Again? He's run off again? Will we never be free of him?"

Haiden grimaced. "I have to thank him, really. It was because of him that I survived. He trapped me in a sphere of some kind, one meant to imprison me, but one that ended up saving my life by protecting me from the brunt of that last . . . madness. It finally collapsed near the end, which is why I look like this." The elf indicated his battered appearance. "It's not *quite* as terrible as it looks, though I am feeling a bit cool." He sobered. "I saw him duck out of the chamber when the fury broke loose. My first re-action after I was free was to chase him, knowing what he might do if he escaped. I regret to say he knows these chambers better than me."

"He also has his powers back," Cabe reminded him. "He would have killed you easily. You're lucky he didn't kill you before."

"There is that."

"What now?" Gwen asked. She had herded the young drakes into an almost manageable group.

"We put an end to this," a voice that seemed to echo from everywhere suddenly said. The devastated chamber lit up with a brilliance that burned out Cabe's own humble spell.

The Bedlams and the elf formed a triangle around the hatchlings. Nei-ther the mages nor Haiden could find the source of the voice. Cabe was the one to finally recognize it.

"You . . . you're the Crystal Dragon."

"I am."

In that instant, wherever there was a reflection, there was a glistening image of an indistinct dragon shape. It was beautiful, terrible, and enig-matic all at once—and somewhat like seeing the world through the multi-faceted eyes of an insect. They could not help blinking wildly at first. Here was a sense of power so totally different from any Cabe had encountered. Greater in its own way than that of the Ice Dragon.

Were they to fight this menace as well?

An amused chuckle reverberated through the chamber, loosening yet more chunks of ice. "I am no menace to you. I have merely come to add the final touch to the end of my brother's insanity."

The reflections seemed to contemplate the towering form of the Ice Dragon. At last the voice said, "I warned him about his folly. I warned him that he would do little more than bring drake and human closer together, if only temporarily. He refused to let me shatter his illusions. Well, now I shall do more than that. It is only fitting and what he certainly deserved."

The brilliant light increased. Hatchlings hissed and the two humans and the elf were forced to shade their eyes. The gleaming form of the late master of the Northern Wastes quivered as if life were returning to him once more. A kaleidoscope of color whirled about the chamber. Cabe briefly looked down at his hand and watched it change from green to blue to red and so on. Gwen's hair turned black, orange, violet. . . . It was not merely a change of color, either; he could feel the distinct power represented by each as it washed over them. This was what the Ice Dragon only pretended to be. He had been an imperfect replica of *this* Dragon King.

The living rainbow began to gather about the huge, icy form. The Ice Dragon vibrated more violently, bits of snow and frost falling in showers from his body. Just when it seemed that the motions of the leviathan's corpse would bring down what remained of the cavern, the Ice Dragon *stopped* quivering.

Cabe and Gwen realized what was happening and fell to the ground, the latter forcing the hatchlings down with her. Haiden was already on his stomach, no fool he, not when Dragon King magic was running amok.

The Ice Dragon *shattered*.

A sea of fragments flew in all directions, but those that neared the tiny, huddled group in the center of the chamber melted into a fine mist.

When the last pieces had fallen to the ground, the voice of the Crystal Dragon, somewhat less poised than before, whispered, "*Now* it is ended. You need not have feared for yourselves; I was watching over you."

The humans, their elven companion, and even the hatchlings gazed around in newfound respect—respect that grew to awe when the Crystal Dragon added, "Soon, the Seekers will come to claim their home of ancient. There has been enough strife and I have things of greater interest to do. As you are understandably torn by your ordeal, I shall allow you to conserve your strength. You will have enough to do after I send you home."

Which he then did, with no more than a nod.

THE NEXT FEW days passed quickly. There was so much to do. They were not as bad as the weeks that had followed the siege of Penacles, but they were days that Cabe would have enjoyed doing without.

One major problem solved itself. Once the Ice Dragon's spell had been reversed, the countless corpses of his abominations began to decay at an alarming rate. They did not even leave time for scavengers to take their fill, though it was said only the worst scavengers even bothered to sniff the remains. No one and nothing wanted anything to do with the late Dragon King's creatures.

What to do with Melicard was a situation that took three days to discuss. In the end, the crippled sovereign was returned to his city in the hopes that his people would take the cue and make peace. His marauders were scattered all over the countryside. Whether they would continue their fanatical slaughter of drakes was questionable; their ranks were depleted and they no longer had the Seekers or Melicard to provide them with supplies and protective devices. Besides, most people were, at the moment, more interested in rebuilding their own lives than aiding some mad cause.

The Gryphon talked with the others about some sort of expedition to the continent on the other side of the Eastern Seas, but nothing definite was planned. He had mentioned it once before, after his first encounter with D'Shay in the domain of the Black Dragon. Toos, who had just gone through one session as "temporary" ruler and now saw the possible nightmare of another, longer period, protested the idea.

"Dammit, bird, I'm too old to do this on a regular basis." The general's eyes flared, but there was a hint of humor in his voice.

"Old? Toos, you con artist, you've more sorcery than you either think or pretend to think. You've lived longer than most men and you still have the reflexes you had in your prime. You once claimed your line was long-lived, had elven blood, but you've pushed past the point of reality. If anyone who knows your past is still fooled, it must be you alone. Only powerful sorcery can keep anyone with human blood alive and fit for so long. You have special abilities, my friend, so subtle that we tend not to notice unless we force ourselves. I think your powers would keep you fit and running this city for several decades to come—if the need arose, of course. You might even consider marrying and fathering a few young." He raised a hand as the ex-mercenary turned red. "Don't protest; I've seen some of the ladies of the court eye you, *old man.*" The Gryphon laughed, an odd-looking sight, considering his avian visage. "Don't worry so! I haven't said I was actually going!"

The general mumbled something that no one could hear and everyone decided was better left a mystery. The lord of Penacles nodded imperceptibly. He had lightened what had otherwise been a fairly dreary mood on the part of his companions. After what they had been through and accomplished, they deserved better. He formed a human face and sipped some wine a servant had brought them. Cabe was the only one who truly worried him now. He watched as Gwen took her husband's hands. The two had hardly even gotten a chance to become used to their lives together. The Gryphon hoped and prayed that things would finally calm down a bit.

Hoped, but did not expect. Expectations in the Dragonrealm had a way of turning inside out before long.

He took another sip of wine.

CABE AND GWEN eventually stepped away from the others. The Gryphon was speaking to the Green Dragon about the possibility of extending the truce with his counterpart in Irillian. Haiden, invited with the Bedlams, was talking to General Toos about places the two of them had seen during their lengthy lifetimes. They were both men of the land and had more in common than Cabe would have thought possible.

When they were far enough away, Gwen finally pulled him to one side and asked, "What's wrong, Cabe?"

His face was pale, drawn. "He's gone, Gwen. This time, there's nothing left of Nathan. I'm entirely alone. The power is there, but it's me now. Whatever he was—soul, essence, my own imagination—he gave that so I would live. It's hard to be alone, though, after becoming so used to having another presence *always* there."

The Lady of the Amber said nothing, instead choosing to put her reply into a long and lingering kiss. Cabe knew what she was saying and his misery slowly faded.

"You'll never be alone, Cabe. Not as long as I can help it."

He felt a twinge of guilt that his sorrow for his grandfather was dissipating so quickly, but, knowing Nathan as he had, he doubted the elder Bedlam would have minded a bit. Possibly, he would even have reprimanded his grandson for moaning and groaning when there was a beautiful woman waiting who also happened to love Cabe dearly. He should be taking her in his arms and returning that love.

Cabe smiled slightly and did just that. Perhaps, he thought just before he allowed the present moment to carry him away, Nathan Bedlam was *not* completely gone after all.

A breeze danced briefly about them, but it was warm and they did not even notice it, caught up as they were in more important matters.

WOLFHELM

I

R'DANE CAUGHT HIS foot on the uncovered root of the huge oak, tripped, and fell flat on his face. It was not that he was a clumsy man; it was simply impossible to keep one's mind on the path when there were Runners on one's heels.

He could hear them now. Not the sounds of their great clawed paws striking the ground with each lope or the snap of their toothy jaws, but rather their growls of anticipation, their hunger. The Runners were always hungry, if only for blood and violence. Were they not, after all, the *true* children of the Ravager?

Rising to his feet, R'Dane once more pleaded silently to his master, the true one. It was not his fault that the latest excursion toward the Dream Lands had ended in complete and utter failure—well, not entirely his fault. He *had* led the expeditionary force, but the plan had been approved by his superiors.

"Come on, you fool!" he muttered to himself. There was no time to dwell on past mistakes. This was a time to run and keep running in the hopes that maybe—just maybe—his former enemies would be his salvation.

Why he hoped for any assistance from the lords of Sirvak Dragoth was beyond him, but the desperateness of his plight made their aid the only possible solution. No one outside of the Dream Lands was about to come to his rescue. Nothing existed on this continent now save the Dream Lands and the empire he had once served, the empire that now demanded he pay the price, stripped of his rank, reduced to the R' of the common soldiers, and let loose as prey for the Runners in a race that no one to his knowledge had ever won.

He had begun running again while thinking of this. What was most frustrating was that he did not even know if he was near the Gate. He was just running in the general direction of where he believed the Dream Lands to be, hoping that someone would see him, realize his plight.

The Runners were closer. He imagined he felt their hot, fetid breath on his neck.

THE PACK MASTER and a handful of his aides sat watching the lone figure stumble through the wooded region that separated the eastern edge of the Aramite empire from the outskirts of the Dream Lands. Occasionally, something would interest the Pack Master and he would lean his huge, armored form forward as if in anticipation. All but one of his aides would follow suit, hoping they, too, would see whatever it was that interested their emperor so. Only one aide—the only one standing—seemed to have little interest in the doings shown by the keeper's crystal.

The room was dark, the better to view the scene in the crystal, and the darkness gave those within the chamber the look of fearsome specters, for all wore armor of the purest ebony and blended in with the shadows. Physically, the Pack Master looked no different from the rest, save for his incredible size and a long, flowing wolfskin cloak. He wore no other symbol of his station than that. The armor was plain, flexible—very well made—and covered every square inch of his body. No one had seen him without it for years, and, if any of them had been asked, it was doubtful they could recall his face.

He leaned forward again, and none of those present could say exactly what the Pack Master might be thinking, for he, like the rest, wore the face-concealing wolfhelms that were a symbol of the Aramites' devotion to their god, the Ravager. The leering wolf-head design on the helm was only a depiction of what their god supposedly looked like; only the Pack Master and one other possibly knew the true face of the deity. Most of the others had no desire to know. They were quite satisfied to serve and leave it at that. Small wonder. There were few, if any, with the courage, let alone the power, to challenge the somber dictator. On a physical scale alone, the arms of their leader, twice as thick as anyone else's, revealed the strength that could snap a man in two—whether he wore armor or not.

One helmed figure sat away from the rest, his hands above the crystal, guiding the scene along. There were no markings to differentiate him from the others, but no one in the room would have mistaken him. Keepers were just that way. They could be nothing else.

"How far is he from the estimated borders of the Dream Lands, Keeper D'Rak?" one of the Pack Leaders grumbled.

Keeper D'Rak was the only one in the room, other than the Pack Master, who could, if need be, flout tradition during council. Whereas the others were required to wear the ceremonial helms during such meetings, he was allowed to wear the more open helm, with the wolf's head a crest rather than part of the face mask. A length of fur ran down the back. This helm was preferred when not in council, for it was much cooler. In this instance, D'Rak, a slightly overweight Aramite with a mustache and one long brow across his forehead, had chosen the open helm in order to concentrate better on the manipulating of the crystal.

"He might already be within the borders; it is impossible to say with the Dream Lands." D'Rak could not keep the irritation out of his voice. The Pack Master would have not asked such a stupid question; nor would have the aide standing near him. Of all those in the room, only they understood the difficulty in pinning down the borders of a place that existed as much in the mind as it did geographically. That had been R'Dane's problem; he had acted as if his foes were as precisely located as, say, the Menliates had been. The Menliates had had an obsession with precision that only conquering them had finally been able to cure. The lords of Sirvak Dragoth, on the other hand, controlled a region that appeared as flexible in form as mist.

"Let us see the Runners." A hand fully capable of containing *both* of D'Rak's own clenched tight, the only other indication of the Pack Master's growing interest in the chase. The *voice*, on the other hand . . .

More than one member of the council stirred uneasily at the sound of that voice. Even the keeper shuddered. There was something about the Pack Master that disturbed even the most formidable of the Leaders and Commanders. It had an echoing quality, as if the man actually sat elsewhere. Again, the only exception to this uneasiness was the aide who stood near the Master, but then, there were enough stories about that one as well.

Nodding, D'Rak whispered something and waved his hand over the crystal. Keepers were attuned to their respective talismans and, as one of the seniormost keepers, D'Rak had control of the Eye of the Wolf, one of the most powerful of the artifacts of the raiders. The Eye of the Wolf had many abilities; its present use involved one of the most minor of those abilities.

The picture shifted. At first, the scene appeared to be little more than a dark blur. It was a moment before even the keeper realized that the blur was actually the Runners. Focusing the power of the crystal did little to increase the detail of the creatures. It was that way with the Runners.

A thing fairly lupine in shape hesitated a moment by a tree's roots, apparently on the scent of its prey. It was darker than the armor of its masters, darker than the night. An impossibly long, narrow maw opened wide, revealing daggerlike teeth that glistened in harsh contrast to the monster's form. A tongue, more like that of a serpent, lolled. It raised a splayed paw and scratched at the tree with arched claws as long as a man's fingers. The claws ripped easily through the roots. The Runner should not have been swift, built as it was, yet there were few creatures it could not catch.

Another joined it, and then three more sought to share the discovery. There was no way to see where one creature ended and another began; they seemed to blend into one another. All that was evident was that the Runners had very good noses and very large jaws. At points, there seemed to be nothing but teeth and claws.

The discoverer of the new trace left by their prey bounded off in the same direction R'Dane had gone only a minute or two before. It was joined by the second one and then the others. A number of the creatures howled or barked, alerting their fellows nearby.

"Return the view to the hunted."

"Yes, Pack Master." D'Rak manipulated the power within the Eye and turned the scene once more to the fleeing man. R'Dane's face—which D'Rak thought sourly was too ruggedly handsome for his own good—was a study in fear. He knew that the Runners were only a short distance from him and that sanctuary was nowhere to be found.

"How long has he been out there?" the Pack Master asked almost casually.

"More than a day, milord," said one of the commanders.

The huge figure shifted in his seat, apparently contemplating. However, only a few seconds had passed when he leaned back to the aide behind him and said, "End this game now."

"Milord." The aide brought his wolf's-head mask forward as he stared at the crystal. D'Rak suppressed his irritation. He, like all keepers, disliked when outsiders, especially this particular outsider, fooled with the talismans the keepers were bound to. A keeper's talisman was his existence. The Pack Master had chosen to honor this one with the kill, though, and there was nothing the senior keeper could do.

A frenzy of howling built up among the Runners as something stirred them. The Pack Master's aide continued to stare, and, as seconds passed, the howling rose to such a level that some of the raider leaders were forced to put their hands over their ears.

"Enough."

The armored figure stepped back, bowing to the Pack Master as he did.

TURNING TO LOOK behind himself despite knowing he should not, R'Dane stumbled over uneven ground and tumbled down a small slope. He rolled to a stop only when his body collided with a tree. The shock of the collision knocked the air out of him, and he was unable to rise.

They have me! Curse the Ravager! What kind of god—

Softly but surprisingly, strong hands took hold of him. At first, he thought that the Runners had reached him at last, but those creatures would have torn him to pieces by now. His eyes refused to focus, and his lids were, in fact, becoming too heavy for him to keep open. The last thing he saw before the world faded to black were two indistinct figures who seemed to be without faces. Then, nothing.

ODDLY, THE ASSEMBLED wolf raiders did not see this. What they saw was a hapless former comrade who had failed his lord. They saw the Runners come upon that failure and, with great glee, circle the fool. Then, one by one, they jumped at R'Dane, snapping at him, biting him, cutting him with their foreclaws, but always retreating, though their circle grew tighter each time.

At last, the lead Runner broke from the circle, snarling and glaring at the man with what could only be described as both anticipation and disdain. It circled him once and then stepped back a few paces before coming to a halt.

The cowering figure in the middle might have bought himself a few moments more if he had stayed motionless, but such was not the case. R'Dane took a step away from the lead Runner, a sign of weakness to the creatures.

The lead Runner took three steps and leaped at the former wolf raider. The other creatures, howling wildly, followed suit.

WHEN THERE WAS nothing left, not even a piece of bloodied cloth, the Pack Master rose, indifferent to the horrible execution he himself had ordered and then watched. "D'Rak, recall the Runners. The rest of you—remember this."

The Pack Master departed without fanfare, followed immediately by the one aide. D'Rak watched the others file out. He could have controlled the Runners himself all that time. His lord had only had the other raider do it to show that the latter was once more in his good graces.

No surprise. D'Shay had always been his favorite.

The keeper made contact with the Runners, who were reluctant to return. Probably in a blood frenzy. One rabbit was not enough for so large a pack. Perhaps it could be worked out so that they had two or even three. Now, that would be entertaining.

THE RUNNERS MILLED around aimlessly, their prey suddenly lost to them. When the keeper's summons reached them, they hesitated, baring their teeth and disliking both the fact that they had been cheated and the thought that something out of the ordinary had happened.

Fear and loyalty won in the end. The lead Runner howled and began the run back to the kennels. The rest of the pack followed close behind.

They did not see the two figures standing beside them, carrying the unconscious Aramite between them. Even when one Runner brushed against the pale gray cloaks they wore, it did nothing more than unconsciously move aside to a clearer path.

When the last of the Runners had vanished in the distance, the two figures turned to the east. The air before them shimmered, and a gaping hole opened up in the fabric of reality itself. Had D'Rak still been watching, he would have glimpsed a great tower in the distance and a massive gate around which unidentifiable things swarmed, protecting the Gate to the Dream Lands from outsiders.

The two carrying R'Dane stepped through, and the hole vanished.

D'Rak had been essentially correct in his assumption. The Dream Lands were indeed as much a state of mind as anything else. And R'Dane, in those last seconds, had finally become attuned to them.

II

ARE YOU CERTAIN that this 'safe harbor' of yours is truly that?"

Beseen, the captain of the Irillian privateer *Korbus*, smiled, revealing his sharp, draconian teeth. Most Irillian ship captains were either members of the ruling drake clans or humans who had served faithfully under other drake captains. Unlike many of his kind, Beseen was a short, almost stout drake. While his appearance was that of a bluish, humanoid, armor-clad warrior whose face was nearly completely obscured by a helm, he was far more comfortable commanding a vessel than fighting wars—odd, considering that the *Korbus* was one of the most successful privateers.

"Truly that, Lord Gryphon, truly that. My crew and I have used it more than a dozen times. The Aramite wolf raiders, who pride themselves on their own enterprises at sea, decided that this place was useless, being too far south of the bulk of their empire and lacking any unconquered villages to plunder. Then again, their needs differ from ours."

The Gryphon did not ask him to elaborate. Too often, drake needs consisted of things he would rather not hear about or even try to imagine. It was difficult enough to comprehend why drakes would want to become sailors. Overall, the race seemed to have an unconscious obsession to become more and more like the humans they sometimes so despised. Why risk their lives as privateers when they could shift into their original forms and swarm over their prey as dragons?

Beseen, more open than most of his kind, had given him several reasons over the course of the voyage. Odds were, he had said, that a dragon attacking a foreign ship would have to be so careful that his powers would almost be useless. There was nothing to be gained from a drifting pile of smashed timber. It was also extremely tiring for most dragons of his clans to be airborne for very long—and where would a full-grown creature land in the middle of the ocean? The drake would drown while trying to shift back into humanoid form. Dragons did not float very well for some odd reason. While the Blue Dragon's clans were seagoing, they were still land-based creatures like their cousins.

There were other reasons as well, and the captain had gone into them in some detail, but the Gryphon found the explanation as a whole somewhat suspect. He had studied the drakes aboard the *Korbus* throughout the entire journey, and Beseen's tone more than his words had finally convinced the lionbird that the true reason was that the drakes had actually come to *prefer* their humanoid forms. From their manner and some careful questions, the Gryphon knew that some of the crew could not even recall the last time they had shifted to their original shapes. More important, drake hatchlings, especially after contact with humans, were learning to transform themselves at a younger age and with more success. He could foresee a time, not too distant, when all drakes would be able to pass for humans—even better than some humans themselves.

He thought of suggesting this to Beseen, but quickly decided against it. The crew already watched him warily. Telling a drake that he wanted to be more human was an invitation to disaster, and the Gryphon knew how low his odds of surviving were with so many of the race aboard.

The past weeks on the ship had been grueling ones. Putting aside his theories for a more leisurely time, the Gryphon squeezed the rail with both clawed hands as a light spray dotted his face. Both his fur and feathers were damp, and he could not blame the crew when they sometimes chose to stand to one side of him when the wind blew. It was enough to rankle even the lionbird's senses, and he had lived with the problem all his life.

All his life. That was another problem, possibly the greatest. Over a hundred years before, the Gryphon had washed up on the shore of the Dragonrealm region belonging to Penacles, the City of Knowledge. A creature human in form, but with the face of a bird of prey, a mane like a lion, and clawed hands that sometimes were covered with fur, other times with feathers. He was truly a human version of the beast, with vestigial wings and lacking only a tail.

He had power, though, as well as fighting skills from some forgotten past. With his magic and his ability to command, he raised a mercenary army. Despite his appearance and his decision to avoid working as much as possible for the reptilian Dragon Kings, he and his men had prospered. Throughout all that time and the turbulent period following those mercenary days, he had always avoided the sea whenever possible. It brought on a chill within him that few things could match. He knew his past lay across the Eastern Seas, but only until recently had he discovered both bits of his past and the courage to cross the vast body of water separating the Dragonrealm from the lands of his birth.

That courage had not made the crossing any easier. Memories of being tossed about the seas before finally washing up on land, three-quarters dead, remained with him even now.

The privateer turned so as to make its way into the hidden harbor, forcing the Gryphon to move to another part of the ship. To all appearances, he walked as any human, elf, or drake did. His boots seemed a bit wider, but, other than that, he moved like a well-trained hunter. The loose clothing he wore served another function than the obvious, for it hid the tiny knobs that were his wings and covered the fact that, like a cat or bird, his legs bent the opposite way at the knee. His wide boots hid the fact that his feet more resembled a cross between the paws of a lion and the claws of an eagle than they did those of a man. After all these years as ruler of Penacles, it mattered only to him, but it mattered. His subjects had accepted him as one of their own, and he tried to return the favor by dressing the part. A silly notion, to be sure, but no worse than many he had seen.

Recalling Penacles, he closed his eyes. What must they think of him? he wondered. Abandoning them when the whole continent was caught in the midst of change. The Dragon Emperor was dead, killed by one of his own kind—who was also dead. The northern lands had been ravaged by that same Dragon King before his death and were still recovering. A total of six of the ruling drake lords were dead, and only one had had a ready successor. Despite their sudden surge in influence, the human kingdoms within those regions were little better off. Mito Pica still lay in ruins, its citizens slaughtered or scattered by the would-be drake usurper Duke Toma, who was still at large. Talak's king, young Melicard, was a crippled fanatic who had lost part of a face and one arm during an attempt to kidnap the hatchlings, the children, of the late Dragon Emperor. The hatchlings had been under the care and guidance of Cabe and Gwen Bedlam, two of the most powerful mages living and close friends of the Gryphon. They were also under the protection of the Green Dragon, the only Dragon King allied with the humans on a friendly basis.

Beseen was shouting orders to the mixed crew of humans, drakes, and assorted others. The *Korbus* entered the tiny harbor slowly, almost tentatively. The captain liked this harbor because one had to follow a straight path or else take the risk of running across one of the many underwater ridges. Beseen claimed his divers had uncovered countless traces of hapless ships that had tried that trick.

"Duke Morgis on deck!" someone shouted.

The Gryphon turned. After the wolf raiders, specifically the aristocratic D'Shay, had attempted to assassinate both the Blue Dragon, master of Irillian, and the Gryphon, the Dragon King had extended his temporary truce with the lord—now former lord—of Penacles. The Blue Dragon had ships that now and then harassed the Aramites, and he had the *Korbus* make room for the Gryphon, who was determined to discover the truth about himself after the final confrontation with D'Shay had revealed things the Gryphon had been unable to remember before.

D'Shay had died in that encounter, willing himself to death apparently. The lionbird still had trouble believing that, but he had witnessed it with his own eyes. Yet, each night, he thought he saw the wolf raider's face as D'Shay laughed at him. The Aramite was an important link to his past— even dead.

Duke Morgis stepped into sight. The Blue Dragon trusted his ally only so far, and had sent one of his newly appointed dukes along as companion and adviser to the lionbird. Like his predecessors, Morgis was one of Blue's own hatchlings, though lacking the markings that would have allowed him to succeed his sire if something occurred. Dragon Kings were sticklers about the royal markings. It had been that which had nearly killed the Dragon King and had resulted in the death of two of his other sons—one by the hand of the other, who had then died from a single blow by the Blue Dragon. A blow that had torn out his throat.

Morgis was a true drake lord, despite the lack of markings. He stood almost a foot taller than the Gryphon, who was above average height himself. He was green with a tint of the sea blue common among his clans. Many of the drakes not marked tended to be green in scale color unless their clans chose to do something about it when the hatchling was young. Some bred for the colors or symbols their clans represented. The clans of the Red Dragon—the new Red Dragon, since the old one had perished long ago at the hand of Cabe's mad father, Azran—were all bloodred in color.

The helm and armor effect was just that—an effect. The armor was actually the scaly skin of the drake, fashioned through natural draconian magic into the form of an armored knight, the closest most male drakes could come to human shape, although it improved with each successive generation. Morgis, like many of the younger drakes, preferred the handier humanoid shape so much over the one he had been born in that he, too, refused to shift unless it was a life-and-death situation. And even then he would have hesitated.

"My Lord Gryphon," the drake rasped. The Gryphon admitted that some of his dislike for the duke was due to the fact that, other than color, Morgis resembled Toma too much. Like Toma, the lionbird's companion was a throwback, having the long, forked tongue and sharp, tearing teeth that in no way could be described as human. The dragon-head crest was also elaborate, though that was more a symbol of the drake's power than anything else. The Gryphon had seen drakes shapeshift before; had Morgis done so, the dragon's face would have melded into his own, eventually becoming his true visage. Morgis, he suspected, would be one large dragon.

"Duke Morgis."

"Have you made a decision as to where you wish to head once we land?"

That had been troubling the former lord of Penacles all trip. Should he attempt to sneak into Canisargos, the sprawling capital city of the Aramites' empire, or should he seek out the Dream Lands and Sirvak Dragoth, two places that D'Shay had mentioned and that now nagged at memories still locked away?

"East, then northeast."

"You want to find these mythical Dream Lands, then." It was a statement, not a question, and an indication that the drake had known the Gryphon's decision before even he did.

"I do—and I don't think they're mythical."

Morgis turned to Beseen, who, satisfied his men had the situation under control, was coming to see to his two passengers. "What do you say, Captain? Do *you* know where the Dream Lands are?"

Beseen hissed in thought. "They mussst exissst." He concentrated harder. Drakes, being perfectionists at times, were determined to speak the common languages without flaw. That was sometimes difficult for a reptilian race, especially when emotions soared. Lapses were common. "They must, or else the wolf raiders would not spend so much time and manpower trying to conquer them."

"Spoken like a realist. I concede the point." Duke Morgis smiled. It was not a pleasant sight.

The Gryphon cocked his head to one side, the better to view the shore. He could, if he greatly desired, shift temporarily into a human form with human eyes, but his own vision, similar but far more advanced than that of a true bird, was more than satisfactory. Better to leave form-shifting for when he needed it. It was a tiring spell if kept up for long periods of time, and he suspected such a situation would materialize before his quest was completed—*if* it was completed.

There was a good possibility, a definite possibility, that he would die before he even found a trace of the mysterious Dream Lands and Sirvak Dragoth—and a gate, it suddenly dawned on him. A gate of some importance. Another door in his memory, long barred from him, had opened. While he welcomed the return of such memories, they also annoyed him, because, more often than not, he could not connect them with anything else.

One day I will remember everything, he swore.

Beseen was speaking: ". . . shore, the boat will return. We cannot afford to stay here too long. There is always the chance some adventurous raider will head this way, perhaps thinking his predecessors have missed something. We also have a quota to make. You'll find a friendly village some ten miles due east. They'll sell the two of you horses."

That stirred the Gryphon to full attention. He turned on the drake lord, focusing on the glittering eyes within the false helm. "The two of us?"

Morgis was smiling slightly. He refused to return the Gryphon's glare. "My sire's orders were to accompany you. He felt it would be inopportune to mention it to you then."

"Because I would have refused in very graphic terms."

The drake's tone was one of amusement. "That was mentioned, yes."

"I still refuse!" The fur on the Gryphon's back rose.

Morgis shrugged indifferently. "Then Captain Beseen will turn the *Korbus* around, and we will head back as soon as we pick up supplies."

From what the Gryphon could see of the captain's face, the stout drake had not been consulted about this second choice. It was not his place to protest, however.

There was no turning back. The hint of memories still locked away haunted the lionbird day and night. To return to the Dragonrealm now would drive him to madness. Even now, the land before him called to him with a siren song so compelling that he was half tempted to swim the rest of the way, regardless of his intense dislike for the seas.

"All right, but just you." He pictured himself riding with a fully armed party of drake warriors and trying to look inconspicuous. Even disguised, such a party would have drawn attention.

"Of course. I'm no hatchling, Lord Gryphon."

We'll see about that, the ex-ruler thought wryly. He, at least, could cover himself with a cloak or shift to human form when necessary. How was he to hide a tall, massive drake lord resembling a fully armored knight?

The duke was ahead of him. "My sire gave me two of these. To ease our trek, he said."

One of the crew, a human, brought forth two cloaks. The Gryphon had to admire the choreography. Morgis, or perhaps the Blue Dragon himself, had set everything up so that his "ally" would have no time to think out any solid argument—if there was one.

"Illusion cloaks. They took quite some time making, I understand, but they should give us the safety we need." The cloaks would provide them with the appearances of whatever they mentally imprinted on them. Simple in looks, the cloaks were difficult magic.

For a brief moment, the Gryphon contemplated the new possibilities opened by the use of the garments. With one of these, he could probably enter Canisargos without too much difficulty, and from there . . .

From there, what? Surrounded by enemies, some of whom probably had greater power than he did, what would he do? No, better to continue with his original plans and seek out the inhabitants of Sirvak Dragoth. The wolf raiders could wait—but not forever. They owed him, if only for the memories they had stolen from him.

Beseen took the cloaks and handed one to each of his two passengers. "The styles of clothing vary as much here as they do on our own continent. If you choose clothing from, say, Penacles or Irillian and avoid distinctive markings, you should be fine. The physical forms I'll leave for you two to decide."

The Gryphon studied the cloak. It was loose-fitting but cut so that it would not interfere if they had to fight. There would be no trouble wearing weapons. It was possible to imagine weapons, but, should trouble rear its ugly head, illusionary swords tended to prove pretty useless.

Morgis and the Gryphon donned their garments. For several seconds, the lionbird found it hard to focus on his companion. The duke was an indistinct blur that eventually reshaped itself into a tall, dark-haired man with arresting blue eyes. There was, however, a self-confident smirk on Morgis's face, and the Gryphon could not help thinking how, even disguised by illusion, the true personality of the wearer so often revealed itself. That made him wonder what it was that the duke saw when looking at him.

Captain Beseen, ever helpful, called for a looking glass. Someone located one among the "treasures" the privateer had yet to sell and brought it on deck. Morgis inspected himself first, seemed satisfied, and handed the mirror to the Gryphon.

It was a slight variation on the face he normally used when shifting his form. His memory apparently had proven faulty, but he could not complain about the look. He had what could appropriately be called a hawkish look. His nose was aristocratic, but fortunately falling in the region of size where it enhanced his appearance rather than detracted. His hair was blond, almost white, and his eyes were narrow and dark. Unlike the drake, who had chosen to go clean-shaven, his illusionary self sported a thin, well-groomed beard.

That brought up a notion. "We'd best not be with anyone untrustworthy for too long, else they'll wonder why we never have to shave or why our hair is never out of place."

"Agreed. We shall also keep the mirror—just in case." While the garments should keep their present forms locked into whatever spell had been cast, a strong will, either conscious or sleeping, could alter one perceptively. That was the danger of such a cloak. It was far from perfect.

The Gryphon adjusted his garment. The illusionary powers of the cloak extended to itself. Instead of the oddly cut cloth it was, it now appeared to be a normal riding cloak with attached hood. The Gryphon could only marvel at all the work the Dragon King or his mages had put into it.

A crewman walked up to Beseen, stood at attention, and saluted. "The boat is ready, Captain."

"Excellent. My lords?" The drake bowed and indicated which direction they were to go.

The boat was large enough for a good dozen men, though only the Gryphon, Duke Morgis, and four rowers were going to make use of it. Their supplies were already in the boat, and the vessel itself had been lowered to the water. The four crewmen waited patiently while their charges climbed down.

Above them, Beseen shouted, "May the Dragon of the Depths watch over you!"

The duke returned the farewell, and then the tiny boat was moving toward shore. As it rocked, the master of Penacles shivered inwardly. Water! The last time he had been in a situation such as this, it had been on his way to confront the Blue Dragon. He cared for this no better. The *Korbus* at least gave him some sense of security. This boat—this boat was so light that he expected each and every wave to be the one that would capsize it. It did not capsize, however, and soon the crew was preparing to pull it ashore.

They waited until one of the crew signaled that it was all right to climb out. The Gryphon silently cursed the feel of seawater around his boots and the spray in his face. Morgis, human or not, looked no more pleased— an odd thing considering his was a maritime domain. Unlike the ruling Dragon King, Morgis was evidently land-oriented.

The crew members transferred the supplies to shore, saluted the duke, and then pushed the boat back out to sea. The Gryphon and his companion watched them row out to the ship, then picked up their gear and turned to scan the land around them.

They were at the bottom of a gently sloping ridge dotted with grass and a few trees along the side. Had it not been on such a precarious angle, it would have made good grazing land. Beseen had said that a friendly village lay ten miles east. A fair walk, but nothing terrible. Had this been some region in the volcanic Hell Plains, ten miles might have proven an impossible task.

Glancing briefly back at the *Korbus*, which was just now beginning to get under way, the Gryphon sighed and, making certain his gear was secure, he sunk his clawed hands into the earth. The ground was firm and gave him a good handhold. Morgis followed suit, and it then became a sudden contest to see who would reach the top first.

The drake won, but only because of his relative height and the sudden realization to the Gryphon that the first one to the top might find himself staring at the boots of some wanderer who might not prove to be friendly.

Standing at the top of the ridge, they discovered that the grasslands gave way to a lightly wooded region that seemed to thicken the farther one went east or north. The grasslands themselves extended only about a mile or two in any direction. The Gryphon thought it beautiful; the drake thought it dull and turned back to glance at the *Korbus*, which should have been out in the open sea by then.

"Gryphon!"

The lionbird whirled at the surprise in his draconian companion's voice.

The *Korbus* was just out of the natural harbor and heading west. Unfortunately, there were three other vessels on the horizon and, though it was impossible to say from so far away, both of them doubted that these were drake privateers.

"They must see him," Morgis cursed. "Look! They're trying to cut him off!"

It was true. Vast expanses of sea separated the three newcomers from the privateer, and the captains of the trio were moving to block all paths of escape for the *Korbus*. If Beseen attempted to return to the Dragonrealm, he would have a ship coming from all sides. He could hope to outrun them or turn to the south and keep going until they gave up. If there were other choices, the Gryphon could not think of them. He was, admittedly, in the dark where naval warfare was concerned. It couldn't be *that* different, could it?

"Why don't some of them shift to dragon form? They're close enough to the land that they could return here when the battle's done."

Morgis shook his head. "A dragon would make a very nice target for the Aramites. They *do* have surprises of their own, I understand. Beseen is a good captain. If he thought he could win the other way, he would have already begun."

"Oh." The Gryphon grew uneasy, wondering what sort of countermeasures the wolf raiders had that would make a dragon reluctant to attack.

The drake froze, then hissed angrily.

"What is it, Morgis?"

"We'd best not wait around to see if Beseen can pull his ship out of this mess. Better to give ourselves as much distance from here as possible. They know the *Korbus* came from here. I don't doubt that they'll want to see what its business was."

The Gryphon nodded. It was wise for them not to underestimate the Aramites. Doing so had cost more than one life. Only General Toos, the lionbird's former second-in-command and now his successor, had saved both the Gryphon and the Blue Dragon from a slow death at D'Shay's hands.

Tearing their eyes away from the scene, the two started east. From the captain's explanation earlier, they assumed the village would be easy to find, which, of course, meant that any wolf raiders following them would find it, too. That meant that they had to reach it, buy some decent animals, and move on. Only when they were deep into the dark woods that Beseen claimed were much, much farther east could they truly rest.

The trek was a quiet if unnerving one. The Gryphon could not say just what it was about the ever-thickening woods around him that so disturbed him. Whatever it was, it had put Duke Morgis on edge as well. The closest the lionbird could come to describing it was the feeling that there were a million eyes—no exaggeration—watching them from all around. Eyes that were not necessarily friendly, either.

The two weary travelers were more than a little thankful when they finally came across the village.

Resal was the name of the village, a pitiful-looking place even from where they first spotted it. This was the village that Beseen had said would sell them horses—if they had any. There were no more than a dozen or so structures that could loosely be called buildings, and several others that should not have been but evidently were. Most were made from stone, mud, and thatch, and the closer the duo got, the more haphazard the buildings looked. It was as if someone had thrown Resal together without care. There was nothing in the way of a road; the Gryphon and Morgis chose to walk in the wild grass rather than trudge through the muddy stretch running through the village. A few worn-out animals wandered aimlessly about, but none of them were horses. No horses were visible anywhere. The people were clad in simple cloth outfits and, while everyone seemed to be actively involved in some task or another, many appeared just to be going through the motions, as if they cared very little about their lives. That changed when someone finally noticed the two newcomers.

Friendly was not the way the Gryphon would have described the unfortunate inhabitants of Resal. Morgis saw nothing wrong with their attitudes, but that was most likely due to the fact that they practically fell over their feet to help the two. As a member of the ruling drake family, this was what he was sometimes accustomed to. The Gryphon wondered how helpful the people would have been if Morgis had revealed to them his draconian form. From brief conversations with Beseen, he gathered that the drake captain sent only a few trusted humans in to deal with the inhabitants.

These were a conquered people, he realized for the first time. They had little spirit when encountering anyone with any true self-confidence. Children who had been playing when they entered had stopped to stare with sullen eyes. Adults ceased all activity and women went inside while men stood silently, expecting the worst. When it was learned that the two would not be staying the night and all they wanted were a couple horses, supplies, and food, the people were all too happy to give them what aid they needed—quickly, so as to get the strangers out of their lives as soon as possible.

The privateers obviously did not care about these people, but the Gryphon did. When one elderly man, apparently parting with a prize animal, almost tried to give it away, the lionbird was forced to almost threaten him in order to make him take more.

This was what the Aramites had wrought. Perpetually frightened children and cowering adults willing to give up everything. His mane bristled as his anger grew. One more mark against the wolf raiders—as if he needed any more reasons to despise them.

"We should be moving on. We can't have more than two, maybe three hours until sunset." Morgis was already mounted. He, too, had seen more than enough of the village. It was too dirty. Better to chance the unknown woods than stay in such a filthy place—even if the people did know how to show respect.

The Gryphon read some of what the drake was thinking in his face, again amazed at how the illusionary visage revealed as much as the real thing—which suddenly made him realize that his own disgust at the duke's attitude was probably just as visible. He forced himself to relax.

They told no one where they were going, though they did hint they were moving north. There was no way of knowing for certain whether there were spies or loyalists in the village, but it might at least throw anyone pursuing them off the track for a short while.

As they rode out of the village, the inhabitants greatly overdoing their farewells, Morgis spotted an odd pole sunken into the ground. It was as thick as a human's trunk and at least a foot taller than the drake. On the top was a crudely carved representation of a wolf or some similar creature.

"An interesting piece of work, wouldn't you say?"

Its eyes seemed to draw the Gryphon's attention. He stared at it even after they passed it, turning away only when it became impossible to see it without riding the horse backward.

Another door opened, releasing yet more memories.

Morgis, who had been moving ahead, looked back and slowed his mount, no easy task since, unlike the humans, it could tell the difference between what the drake looked like and what he actually was and continually fought him. "Gry—what's wrong?"

"Ravager."

"I beg your pardon?"

"The Ravager. The Aramites' chief god. They call him the living god." The Gryphon felt cold. He urged his steed to a faster pace. Morgis's horse matched it.

"It's just a totem. Besides, why worry? It's been my experience that most gods tend to let things run themselves. What's the point of being a god if you have to work so much?" Morgis smiled, looking no less pleasant than he had before the illusion.

The lionbird shook his head, trying to lose the feeling he'd had when caught by the thing's gaze—no, that was ridiculous! It was, as his companion had said, only a totem. Yet, something in his new memories bit at him—and he knew what it was though he had no memories to back it up.

"The Ravager," he finally said, "is different, then."

"Different?"

Something . . . a story someone had told him long ago. A story he could not remember. "The Ravager takes a personal interest in his people. Controls them quite well. All in all, the ultimate source of the wolf raiders' actions is said to originate from the Ravager himself."

Morgis frowned. "You're not suggesting . . ."

The Gryphon nodded, his eyes on the vast expanse of land before them, a land all under the eye of one being, so it was said. "I am. We may soon find ourselves stepping on the feet—or paws—of one very real, very dark god."

III

H AD IT NOT been for the fact that they were on a foreign continent where anyone or anything had to be counted as a potential threat, both riders might have been bored. There was a certain uniformity about the country-side that sometimes made it seem as if they were traveling in a circle. Every-thing tended to look the same. The Gryphon almost looked forward to the coming sunset, if only for the fact that it would give the land around them a different look.

Morgis leaned back in the saddle. "Shall we make camp here, or would you prefer to go on for a little while? I have no desire to stop, and the horses certainly seem eager to keep moving on."

That was certainly true. Both riders were experiencing some difficulty in maintaining control of their mounts. The horses wanted to run. Neither the Gryphon nor his companion had any intention of allowing them that. Riding wildly through a darkening wood was not the wisest of moves.

The Gryphon considered the duke's question. "Let's ride on for a little longer." He pointed up at the sky. "Only Hestia is going to be out in any strength tonight, and she won't even be half there. I've no desire to travel through these woods too long if I can't see."

"We've seen nothing. These woods are empty."

"Then ask yourself *why* they're so empty."

Morgis quieted at that, and the Gryphon was once more able to concen-trate on the situation at hand. What he had asked the drake was what was troubling him a bit. The woods *were* fairly empty. Even the normal sounds of nature—the birds and the night animals—were muted. Was it just such a sparsely populated area that this was normal? Perhaps the Aramites' initial conquering of this region had so decimated the wildlife that they had not yet returned in great numbers. That seemed odd, for he would have ex-pected the landscape to have suffered as well. With so many warriors in his hypothetical army, there should have been wide-scale destruction. Trees cut or burned down, items such as that.

These trees were far too old. In the length of time it had taken them to grow to such heights, the animal life should have long replenished its numbers.

He stiffened then, for the forest had become completely quiet. Dead quiet.

In the gloom, he could make out Morgis, who had reined his steed to a halt, signaling to him. Something to the north. The Gryphon came to a stop, concentrated, and, thanks to the quiet, he heard it. A very faint sound, but unmistakable. The clink of metal against metal.

Running would be foolish. The lionbird peered around, his eyes coming to rest on some heavy foliage to the right of him. Indicating what he wanted to the drake, he dismounted and slowly led his animal toward the spot. Morgis followed with his own mount. They led the creatures around and then forced them down.

Visibility was nearly nonexistent, but that worked to their advantage as well. In their present position, it was more likely that they would spot the newcomers than the other way around.

They did not have to wait long. Now the clink of metal against metal was more obvious, as were the sounds of both men and horses. Morgis put a hand on the Gryphon's shoulder to alert him. The first of the riders, resembling only an indistinct blur, passed by.

He could not see their helms, but he knew they were wolf raiders. There was just a way about them, a way so much a part of them that, even now, he could picture what they must be thinking. There were at least ten, probably twice that many. It was difficult to say, but he doubted his estimate was off by very much.

At one point, he felt a probing in his mind. Subtle, almost unnoticeable. The Gryphon formed a barrier, diverting the probe so that it seemed he did not exist. He turned anxiously to the drake, but Morgis was already nodding; he, too, had felt the probe. A sorcerer of some sort was riding with the patrol. Like the one with D'Shay that last time. The one who had seemed to wither up and die when one of the Gryphon's unliving bodyguards had accidentally crushed the talisman the man had been utilizing. Keeper? That was the term. The Aramites had a keeper with them.

He also knew where they were going now. They were on a direct course for the village where the two had purchased the horses, which meant that they were, at the very least, trying to determine whether the *Korbus* had left anyone behind.

The last of the wolf raiders went by. The duo waited, the Gryphon mentally counting the seconds. Morgis finally tired of waiting and was about to stand when the Gryphon pulled him back down. It was a fortunate turn, for no sooner was the drake back behind the foliage than several more wolf raiders appeared, their route identical to their predecessors'. It was as the

Gryphon had suspected. The second group served as backup. It was a way to draw a foe from cover and then hit him from two sides. Let him think the patrol had passed and then catch him by surprise when he rose from cover.

It was clear they had even less of a start than they had assumed. Somehow, word had traveled from the raider ships to one of the outposts in less than a day. The lionbird had no doubt word would travel equally fast around the area the moment the patrol discovered the existence of two unknown travelers who had been forced to purchase horses only ten or so miles from the harbor. They could not even assume that they had the time needed for this patrol to reach the village, question the inhabitants, and turn around to pursue them. If communications were this efficient, another patrol might already be waiting to cut them off at some point ahead.

This time, they waited much longer before even thinking of standing. Finally, the Gryphon rose silently, scanning the surrounding woods. A strange feeling coursed through him—as if they were not alone despite the certainty in his mind that all the Aramites had passed by. It was similar to when he had felt as if they were being watched by countless eyes, only this time it felt as if they were surrounded completely.

Morgis rose, stretching sore muscles. The drake was not one built for skulking. "I suggest we go on for as long as the horses are comfortably able. We *have* to give ourselves as much breathing room as possible."

"We could use the illusion cloaks. Make ourselves resemble the foliage— No, we'd have to give up the horses, then." The Gryphon nodded. "No choice. We keep riding—but we stop the minute one of us begins nodding off. No carelessness for fear of losing face. If one of us grows too tired, he tells the other."

The duke nodded. "Agreed."

They mounted and, after only a short debate, continued directly east. Morgis suggested the southeast, but the Gryphon was certain that what he sought lay more to the north, if anywhere. Moving northeast, however, was chancy, as it would take them too close to the more populated regions of the wolf raiders' empire.

Hestia continued her way across the skies, shedding only a little light. The duo was thankful for the cover it gave them, but, at the same time, they would have liked to have been able to see more than a few yards ahead at a time.

All the while, the feeling of being watched continued to nag at the lionbird.

Time dragged. The Gryphon glanced up at the single moon now and then, trying to estimate both their speed and how long it was until sunrise. On the third glance, his eyes narrowed. Hadn't the moon been on his left all evening? What was it doing behind them? A moon was nothing if not constant. It followed a path and stayed on that path. It did not go traveling this way and that like some errant youngster.

So, if the moon was not at fault, that meant that they were now heading . . . south?

"We have a problem." The words were the Gryphon's, but they were uttered by Morgis. The lionbird pulled his gaze away from the misplaced moon and stared ahead where the drake was pointing.

"There's no way we can get through that tangle."

"Tangle" was a kind word for what blocked their way. There was no path. Instead, they found themselves facing a vast, twisted growth of tree and vine so thick that it would have taken days to clear it.

"Don't use magic," the Gryphon warned.

"I know better than that," Morgis hissed. "Any spell sufficient to break us a path through this mess would be like blowing a horn so that our friends in black can find us. Likewise, fire is out. Do you recommend we chop our way through it?"

"I recommend we go around it."

"Where?" The duke spread his arms. "It goes on and on. Why didn't we see this before?"

The feeling of being watched was growing even more intense. "I . . . don't know."

A sigh. "We'll have to . . ."

The Gryphon did not bother to ask. Morgis was staring behind them. The lionbird turned in his saddle—to find himself face-to-face with a wall of vegetation as thick as the one in front.

"Dragon of the Depths!" the drake cursed quietly. "A trap!"

They turned their horses to the right—west. Another wall greeted their narrowed eyes. Reversing direction, they found that their last route of escape had vanished as well.

That was when the whispering began.

At first, they ignored it, more concerned with finding a way out that did not require the use of magic powerful enough to alert the Aramites. Then they thought it was the wind creating sounds through the tangled limbs and vines. Only after a few minutes of frustration did they come to notice that there was no wind to speak of.

"We *have* fallen into a trap," Morgis muttered.

"Not the wolf raiders', though."

"Then who?"

The Gryphon did not answer, more concerned with trying to make out what the voices were whispering about. It was impossible, however, for the voices spoke so quickly that he could make out only one or two words, and even those he was not certain about.

. . . have . . . Tzee . . . certain it is . . .

. . . why . . . dead . . . Tzee . . . back . . .

. . . chance . . . redeem . . . revenge . . .

. . . revenge . . . Tzee . . .

. . . power . . . offer . . . Tzee . . . gain . . .

There was no order to the whispers, and most of the time they spoke simultaneously. It was as if one person had been divided into several parts and was trying to hold a conversation with himself.

He heard the rustling of cloth and turned to see the drake removing his cloak. The illusion of a human vanished as the duke pulled the cloak over his head. The whispering came to an abrupt halt, as if their captors had not been expecting this.

"Take this." Morgis threw the cloak at him.

The whispering picked up again, although now there was a different tone to it—as if the speakers were being forced to come to a rapid decision.

. . . dragon . . . one of his . . . Tzee . . .

. . . both then . . .

. . . I/we will . . . grow . . .

. . . power . . . Tzee . . .

. . . power . . .

. . . power . . . Tzee

The whisperers grew ominously silent once more.

Morgis dismounted quickly and handed the reins of his horse to his companion. "Pull back. I'm going to shift my form."

The Gryphon would have protested, but the drake was already transforming. The armor softened and twisted. Arms and legs bent at impossible angles and grew. Hands became claws. Tiny wings burst from the duke's back, unfolded, and continued growing. Morgis fell forward so that he was now on all fours. Already he was taking up most of the space they had available.

The intricate dragon face on the duke's helm slowly slid downward, gradually revealing itself as the drake's true visage. Morgis, almost completely now a dragon, continued to expand.

Looking heavenward, the Gryphon frowned as he watched a canopy of twisted vegetable matter form across their prison. The invisible whisperers continued their odd conversation, a new intensity, a new confidence, in their voices. The lionbird suddenly had a terrible feeling about all of this. Fighting the two frantically struggling horses with one hand, he pointed the other at the nearly completed canopy and manipulated the fields of power.

Nothing happened.

There was a scream, and then the voices of the whisperers took on a tone of triumph, of mastery.

. . . ours . . . Tzee . . . . at last . . .

The Gryphon's horse bucked suddenly, throwing him violently into the air. He had not survived years of mercenary service, however, without learning to adapt whenever possible. Striking the ground, he rolled to soften the impact. His momentum threw him against the side of their living prison, and he collapsed there. The Gryphon opened his eyes and rolled to the side just in time to avoid being accidentally trampled by the drake's steed.

As for Morgis himself, the Gryphon found him where he had originally stood, hands clutching the earth, moaning. He had reverted completely back to his humanoid form, and the shock of the sudden reversal had nearly thrown him into a catatonic state.

The whisperers were practically gleeful, and their constant, now completely undecipherable patter began to weigh unnaturally heavy on the ex-monarch's mind. He began to withdraw within himself, to seek some escape from them. His hands, fumbling aimlessly, came across a ring with two tiny whistles that had fallen from a pocket. A memory of another time, when the Black Dragon's clans and his fanatical human followers had laid siege to Penacles. Dragons had covered the sky one night, and all of them belonged to that Dragon King. Penacles would have surely fallen that night if he had not used the third whistle that had originally hung with these two. That had summoned birds from all around. So many that the dragons could not hide. Dragons had destroyed birds, but they had destroyed each other as well. Vast swarms of birds enveloped whole dragons, a thousand tiny knives cutting away at the hapless monsters.

The attack had failed miserably. With it had gone the Black Dragon's possibility for a swift victory.

He did not care which of the two whistles he had in his hand. The Gryphon brought the whistle to his beak, knowing all too well how much easier it would have been with a true human face rather than an illusionary one. Like the writhing Morgis, however, he could not bring about a change, especially now, when it was hard even to stay conscious. All he had to do, he remembered, was force air through the whistle. Just force air.

It proved to be much more difficult than he could have imagined, and he knew that their unseen captors had something to do with that. Every time he nearly made it, his head would begin to pound uncontrollably from the mad mutterings of the hidden creatures. Once, he almost dropped the whistles.

With what little conscious thought remained, he forced himself to build a mental barrier across his mind. It was much more difficult than it had been earlier, when he had blocked the random probe by the wolf raider. Nevertheless, it slowly took shape, gradually strengthening faster and faster until control was his once more. He tightened his grip on the whistle and even succeeded in shifting to a semihuman form.

The whistle planted firmly in his newly created lips, he blew. Blew until he nearly passed out from lack of air.

Its work done, the whistle crumbled in his hand, leaving nothing behind but a light ash.

The whispering pounded with renewed force at his barrier, but there was now an uncertainty in the maddening whisper pervading everything. The Gryphon wondered whether any wolf raiders had heard either his whistle or Morgis's shriek of agony. He was still certain, somehow, that this was not one of their traps. No, the Gryphon and his companion had stumbled into some dark corner of the very Dream Lands he sought.

A memory blossomed. More of a sentence, actually. *Sirvak Dragoth guards the Dream Lands, but it rules only those who wish to be ruled.* A way of saying that the lords of Dragoth welcomed all and hindered no one who did not care for their ways.

Caretakers, that's what they are, the Gryphon decided.

The constant mumble of the whisperers suddenly became a disjointed babble of anger and anxiety. The pressure on the lionbird's mind ceased abruptly. A stirring nearby told the Gryphon that Morgis was also no longer under attack. The horses, though, stood frozen where they were, their sides heaving in and out in fear. Herd instinct had taken over and they were now side-by-side, waiting for something to come at them, something they could lash out at to relieve their terror. The Gryphon made a note to watch them if the living prison weakened. In their present states, the animals might bolt off at the first chance, forcing their riders to travel on foot in a most definitely unfriendly forest.

Something snarled outside, something feline, thankfully. That meant that the whistle had done its work, for whatever was outside there was a symbol of a part of him. As the Gryphon rose cautiously to a sitting position, he fingered the remaining whistle. What was the third one for? The first had been related to his avian aspect. What did that leave?

The walls of the prison heaved inward. As the Gryphon once more flattened himself on the earth, his hands covering his head, he realized that he still might find out before this was over—providing he lived.

When the massive wall of vegetation did not crush him after several seconds, he dared to open his eyes and look around.

There was no evidence that the prison had ever existed. The feeling of being watched by all those eyes had vanished. The whispering had ceased.

Sharp ears picked up the faint noise of something moving through the brush, something moving in all haste to the east. The Gryphon leaped to his feet and immediately regretted it. The struggle for his mind had given him a powerful headache. He swayed but did not fall.

"Gryphon?" Morgis had avoided calling him by that name for fear it would reveal their true identities. They had never agreed on another name, something the lionbird planned to take care of the moment the world stopped having it out with him. He clutched his head and turned to his companion.

The drake was on his knees, his first act being to scoop up the cloak that the Gryphon had dropped at some point. Other than being a little dirty, it was fine. The moment Morgis donned it, he once more became the tall, burly human. "What happened? What did you do?"

Carefully pocketing the remaining whistle so as not to reveal it to his "ally," the former monarch replied, "I . . . called on a onetime spell for aid, a spell from my oh-so-murky past. With it, I was able to summon something from my feline cousins."

It was not quite a lie, yet it was not the truth either. Regardless, Morgis seemed to take it at face value. Not knowing of the final whistle, he had no solid evidence that his companion might have omitted anything.

"What happened to our unseen friends or our green prison?"

"I really don't know."

"Have we found the Dream Lands, then?"

Seeing that the drake was all right after all, the Gryphon turned his attention to their mounts, which surprisingly enough had not run off when the trap vanished. The Gryphon stared off in the direction that he had heard their savior depart. "Not a part we wanted to find. I'm having some new thoughts on the subject."

"New thoughts or old memories?" Morgis asked wryly. He was on his feet now, seemingly no worse for his ordeal. The lionbird knew better, though. Whatever pain the drake felt was going to be kept a secret from the Gryphon. Too much pride.

"What were those things?" the duke asked as he took the reins of his steed.

"I don't know. I feel I should, but I don't know. Not all my memories are so willing to come back."

Morgis hissed his understanding. "You were saying something about new thoughts. . . ."

"I was thinking that we should follow this path." The Gryphon pointed east along their mysterious benefactor's path.

"Any special reason?"

"Our savior went that way. I've gotten the idea that he, she, or it is definitely linked to the Dream Lands—the part we want to find."

The drake mounted with more than a little grunting. He was hurt far worse inside than his companion had first supposed. "Then let's be gone from here, friend. I've no desire for a return match with our soft-spoken acquaintances—at least not during the night. Let them come in the daytime. . . ."

He indicated what he would do by slowly squeezing a fist tight.

The Gryphon refrained from commenting on the drake's chances, considering what they had already faced. Instead, he mounted and said, "Forget about that for now. I want to put some distance between us and this place—maybe an hour. Then I recommend we set up camp, taking turns. We're both going to need some rest soon."

Even though it was barely visible, Morgis's face seemed to radiate relief. He was definitely worse off than he was willing to reveal. The Gryphon had already decided that the drake could have second watch—which would not start until the lionbird was absolutely certain his own exhaustion was starting to get the better of him.

With a backward glance that was supposed to assure himself that they were free of the presence of the whisperers, the Gryphon urged his horse toward the east. Morgis followed suit immediately, hands tightly gripping the reins. They had little trouble encouraging the horses; the animals had no desire to remain in this area either.

It was fortunate, then, that they were far from the spot when the two figures stepped out of what could only be described as a tear in reality. Tall, slim figures, who moved with arrogance where the unseen, whispering creatures had lurked. Had the Gryphon been there, he might have recognized the two for what they were, recognized them even though they had no faces. Only a white, blank area where eyes, nose, and mouth should have been. The two did not seem to be gazing at their surroundings so much as waiting for a third being.

They were joined but moments later by that third, a sinuous, feline shape that blurred as it neared the two, at last becoming something human—or at least humanoid. She—there was no mistaking that even in the dim light of Hestia—pointed to the east where the two riders had gone in the supposition that they were following a trail. A trail that she had purposefully laid.

No word passed between her and the two faceless ones, but they nodded. The female blurred again and became once more a menacing cat of some sort. She loped off into the woods, trailing behind the Gryphon and Morgis.

The other two watched until she was gone, then reentered the rip, which healed itself the moment they were through.

A moment later, the whispering began again. There was a new tone to it, and one word—a name—was repeated over and over, a sign of their anger and eagerness to someday soon wipe the smug arrogance from those who had just departed.

Tzee. It was their own name for their kind, the only one they knew. It was a power of sorts itself, and they drew strength from it.

Tzee. The Gryphon would have remembered that name had he heard it. Remembered what they could do when their full strength was marshaled, which was being done even now. The Tzee remembered the Gryphon as well. They had made the mistake of believing surprise could overwhelm him. Past experience should have reminded them of that fallacy. The misfit had always proven tricky. He had apparently even risen from the dead.

Soon, the Tzee promised themselves, it would be different. *He* had said so—and *he* had the power to *make* it so.

IV

THEY WERE NOT disturbed the rest of that night or the following day. The trail of their mysterious benefactor had, admittedly, vanished long before, but they continued in the same direction regardless. The woods eventually gave way to hilly fields, which proved to be the grazing areas for a farming settlement. The sun burned bright in the sky, and the land was alive with the wonders of nature—small animals, birds, flowers. Only the people seemed incongruous to the beauty of the region. Morgis actually sniffed in disdain upon sighting them, an act that the Gryphon was certain he must have practiced often to achieve such perfection. It would have been almost comical under other circumstances.

Here the people moved listlessly, completing their chores but seeming to take no interest in the work they did. No one really spoke, and it was amazing that there were even any small children, all things considered. The townspeople paid no attention to their appearance, some wearing clothing that obviously served little practical purpose, while others had definitely not washed in weeks.

"Living dead," the Gryphon muttered.

"Scum," retorted Morgis. "These people are scum. Do we have any real reason to stop here?"

"No."

"Then let's move on. I'd rather not spend too much time in their company. They probably carry something."

The lionbird shook his head at his companion's uncaring attitude but acquiesced. There was nothing they could do to help these people. Like the others, their spirit had been broken by the wolf raiders, so much so that they did whatever their masters wanted them to do. The Gryphon understood what was going on. These villagers and others like them were probably the supply source for the Aramite forces in the southern regions. The fields were too vast to be merely for the use of the settlement. Odds were that patrols made regular stops at each such settlement, which was another good reason to depart. The patrol that had passed them during the night might head this way as part of its normal routine.

They urged their horses to a faster pace and soon left the dismal place behind them. Ahead, they saw, lay more woods and, if it was not a trick of the eye, there was the faint outline of a major town or small city to the northeast. The Gryphon slowed his mount and turned to his companion.

"We've . . ."

What he was about to say vanished from his mind as he stared at the thing behind Morgis. A gate—no, the Gate—loomed beyond. The Gryphon had seen it before, though the memory was still a shadow. He had passed through it, too, though when also escaped his grasping mind. Long ago. That was all he could say with certainty. That and the belief that this portal was the path to and from the Dream Lands. The path the Gryphon had been looking for.

He felt a tie with it, a thin, tenuous tie, but one that stretched farther back than his fragmented mind could accept. What link could he possibly have with . . . with such as this? The Gate stood perhaps twenty yards back and was taller, far taller, than both riders combined. It was an ancient thing, but the only visible sign of its age were the slight traces of rust at the hinges of the two massive wooden doors. Its appearance suggested marble, but that might not be the case, he felt. What caught his interest the most, though, were the fanciful and frightening sculptured figures—

"'We've' what?" Morgis broke the seductive spell of the artifact. The Gryphon blinked and saw the Gate fade away much like the morning mist. By the time the drake was able to turn, it was gone.

Morgis turned back to the lionbird. "What was it? Did you see something? Are those damn things back again?"

Despite arguments to the contrary, the duke was still not fully recovered from the wrenching agony of being forced to shift his form.

"It—the Gate! The way into the Dream Lands! It was over there!" The Gryphon looked to his ally for some sign of understanding. Morgis studied him curiously and then squinted at where the Gate had supposedly been. His eyes widened, and at first the Gryphon thought the doorway to the Dream Lands had returned. When he turned to see for himself, however, his mane—fortunately disguised—bristled.

"I see no gate, but I do see something I'd rather not."

A wolf raider patrol was riding toward them at a more than moderate pace. There were at least twoscore men, a very massive patrol indeed.

They could only have been looking for one thing—spies dropped off by the drake ship. The Gryphon felt the gentle probing that he now knew was always the work of a keeper. He allowed the false surface thoughts that he and Morgis had discussed to be tapped. The keeper would find two men of slightly dubious background traveling about in search of new opportunities—opportunities of any sort. Beseen had told the Gryphon earlier that the Aramites encouraged free enterprise of the illicit sort if it profited them. They were also acknowledged as being of the lowest of the free castes, not even worthy of the low-ranking R' designation that all Aramite warriors began with. Insignificant beings to the patrol—unless, of course, they were on a recruiting raid. If that were so, the two were about to become involuntary volunteers, an irony that the Gryphon could have done without.

Neither fighting nor a foolish attempt at flight would have profited the two. Therefore, they remained as still and as calm as they could. The touch of the keeper had withdrawn, but both the Gryphon and Morgis knew better than to assume that it might not happen again.

The apparent leader of the patrol, a wide, muscular figure, raised his left hand in the air, a signal for the group to come to a halt. The entire patrol was clad as the Gryphon had last remembered seeing D'Shay, including the visor so akin to that of the drakes but that, in the case of the Aramites, served only the normal functional purpose it looked to be designed for. The wolf raiders were human—as far as the broadest definition of the word was concerned.

Several, including the leader and one who must have been the keeper, removed their helmets during the halt. The leader was an ugly, scarred veteran with a beard as ragged as his face was ravaged. A complete contrast to the impeccably groomed D'Shay.

The keeper—it *was* the keeper, for he held something tightly in one hand that emanated power of great potential—was something of a surprise. He was barely into his adulthood, but his eyes radiated a confidence and knowledge that told the lionbird that here was the final authority on matters involving the patrol. The Gryphon wished briefly that his golems had not turned the other keeper's artifact to so much dust during the struggle in the former monarch's former quarters.

"I am Captain D'Haaren, Fifth Level, working out of Luperion, the gateway to the southern regions." He indicated the city off in the distance. "Your names?"

"I am Morgis, of Tylir," the drake replied first. No one here would recognize the duke's name, and Beseen had often commented that Tylir was a good place to claim to have originated from because it was so far north that few people had ever visited it. It would be just their luck if the captain or the keeper hailed from that region.

"I am Gregoth, also of Tylir." For safety's sake, the Gryphon had chosen a name beginning as his did, but common enough, again according to Captain Beseen, on this continent to prevent someone who had knowledge of him from making the connection.

"You are of the pack," the keeper suddenly uttered in what they supposed was his way of awing two civilians. They pretended to be properly awed, nodding their heads slowly but saying nothing. The keeper seemed satisfied.

Captain D'Haaren was not. "Where have you two come from? Recently."

The Gryphon shrugged. "Here and there, Captain. We've traveled the country a lot lately."

In his mind, the lionbird created a layer, a shield, of false memories of a deal gone bad and the need for a quick retreat to the south. Far south. He had discussed the possibilities with Beseen, who had suggested the sort of things that would lose a keeper's interest. The memories were colored in favor of the Gryphon's character, who, naturally, would be somewhat biased. If the keeper believed those thoughts, he might not delve deeper. This young one, though, fresh to his duties, might push just to prove himself.

A tingle went through his mind. The keeper, though he looked almost bored, was actually probing them once more. A moment later, he could tell by the slight curling of the young raider's lip that the keeper had taken the bait and was now sympathetic.

"Forget them, Captain. They're all right. I, for one, would like to return to Luperion and get some rest. We've been out here for almost a day."

The patrol captain grunted, but said nothing that might have endangered his position. He did not care for the keeper, that much was obvious, but he knew better than to push one. Physical appearance was nothing compared with the strength of a keeper's mind in proper conjunction with his chosen tool.

The Gryphon blinked. He was remembering far more about such things than his experience with D'Shay's comrade, the keeper D'Laque, warranted.

"Very well, then," D'Haaren said politely. "Since both parties are headed for the same destination, I invite you to ride along with us. I *insist*, in fact."

Morgis might have been able to settle this entire matter by shifting to his dragon form and overwhelming the entire patrol, keeper and all, but such an action would not only have aggravated his injuries, it would also have alerted anyone with power that they were here.

It was also not a certainty that they *could* defeat the patrol. The keeper might not be the only one with powers. D'Haaren lacked the silver streak in his hair that marked sorcerers in the Dragonrealm, but such a trait might not exist on this continent.

"We shall be happy to join you," the lionbird replied politely in turn. He hoped that the captain would not insist on accompanying them once they were within the city itself.

The Aramite donned his helm, his men following suit immediately. The keeper took more time, brushing his own helm off and even taking a moment to admire the wolf's-head crest before finally putting it back on. The captain was visibly annoyed, but pretended not to have noticed the act of independence.

D'Haaren raised his arm and signaled his men to move. The Gryphon and Morgis were given a place of honor, so to speak, next to the captain. The keeper, much to the annoyance of the three, urged his mount forward so that he could join them.

"Have you ever been to Luperion?" D'Haaren asked much too casually.

"No," the Gryphon replied. "Nor have we been to Canisargos. I understand the capital is quite impressive."

"It has its points," the captain returned somewhat sourly. "You'll find that Luperion is quite a place itself. The only decent bastion of civilization in these parts. Like stepping into another world, you might say."

The Gryphon hoped that no one was paying too much attention to him, or else they might have noticed how he twitched at the last statement. D'Haaren evidently meant nothing by it, but the lionbird's mind had immediately turned to the Dream Lands. It was ridiculous to think that the wolf raider was *that* suspicious of them—wasn't it?

The captain continued asking seemingly casual questions that both newcomers knew were an attempt to cross them up and reveal them as something else. It took a while to realize that Captain D'Haaren's major reason for this was his desire to be transferred north, preferably to Canisargos. He was no doubt hoping that he could find something important enough to gain him notice from his superiors—the same superiors who obviously knew enough about him to have a longtime veteran shipped to some place where he would be out of their sight.

A bitter man was a dangerous man.

Luperion slowly became a distinctive form. It was a fair-sized city, about two-thirds the size of Penacles, and surrounded by a protective wall. They could tell little more about it at this point. A few tall, rectangular structures rose above that wall, one bearing a banner unreadable from this distance.

"Have you two run across any strangers in your travels during the past few days?" D'Haaren asked abruptly.

The Gryphon felt a sudden probe, barely discernible, at the edge of his conscious mind. Fortunately, it was a ploy that both he and Morgis were familiar with, and they replied easily and calmly.

"We met a few of the villagers. Unpromising bunch."

The keeper's probe withdrew, having obtained only false thoughts of superiority concerning cowering farmers—typical Aramite attitudes.

The patrol captain chuckled. "You wouldn't have said that if you'd fought them way back. The T'R'Layscions gave us a worse fight than anyone in the south. We had to set the keepers on their magic men. Almost failed, too."

"Not our fault," the keeper added smugly. "*Someone* decided not to wait until we were done. A third more casualties than we were supposed to have. The Ravager hates stupidity."

"Then he should do something about some of his keepers. Laziness is also a failing in his eyes."

Everyone had quieted completely. From the looks of the other Aramites, this was not the first time these two had argued so.

"There was no one out there. I checked."

"They have to be." D'Haaren glanced back at the two newcomers and then returned his gaze to the path before them. No one spoke for some time afterward. Suddenly, Luperion seemed quite an attractive place to the Gryphon and his companion. Anything to be away from such a volatile situation. Nothing good could come from being caught up in the personal confrontation between a bitter veteran soldier and a smug, young keeper.

It was the keeper who broke the silence, and his choice of subject worried the two almost as much as the argument had.

"Do they talk of the Dream Lands where you come from, friend Gregoth? Tylir, you said?"

"A little. I've never really paid attention. Who cares about some blasted place that isn't always there?"

It was apparently the right thing to say, because more than one Aramite, including both the captain and the keeper, nodded their heads in agreement.

"There you have the gist of the matter," the keeper continued. "They want us to fight shadows. Nothing. Why bother? The Dream Lands, wherever they are, have no armies as we know them. They rarely take the offensive. We'd be better off sending an armada across the seas and striking at those new lands they keep talking about. Of what use do we have for a place like the Dream Lands?"

Morgis innocently asked, "These new lands, do you know anything about them? We've heard rumors about monsters, but you're the first one to mention the lands themselves."

The young Aramite shrugged. "A bunch of petty, barbaric kingdoms, I hear. Monsters—nothing the children of the Ravager cannot handle."

It took both Morgis and the Gryphon a moment to realize that the "children" the keeper spoke of were the wolf raiders. Fortunately, no one realized the reason for their confusion, putting it down instead to talk of the new lands.

The two nodded agreement. The Gryphon would have asked another question, but his eyes were suddenly drawn to a figure far off to the right of the patrol. A figure clad in gray robes with a hood that covered the face. It seemed to stare at the party for several seconds, then calmly turned away.

He pretended to be looking over the landscape. The figure might have been someone or something from the Dream Lands, or it might have been something else. What memories he had regained drew a blank on this incident, and no new memories had arisen because of it. Best not to speak of it to anyone until he and Morgis were alone.

"Can you tell us of Luperion, Captain?" Morgis asked. "What sort of entertainment we might find—or better yet, good food and drink?"

D'Haaren went into amazing detail about the sights of the city, an indication of how long he had been stationed here. The Gryphon listened with only one ear. His concerns were with getting out of the city as soon as possible.

As the gates of Luperion came into sight, a chill coursed through him and his concern grew even greater. It was not the city itself that disturbed him so much as the single sculpture adorning the top of each gate. A savage wolf's head. Not just a normal wolf, either, but something almost manlike. That was the horrible thing about them. Each head revealed a combination of savageness and cunning that promised terror and destruction. There was no question as to what the heads represented. The feeling that washed over the Gryphon was the same as the one in the village.

The twin faces leered down at him, inviting him to join in the delights of the city.

The Ravager's city.

"SHE CLAIMS SHE was summoned," the two identical voices harmonized, "by one with guardian whistles."

"Impossible. All major guardians are accounted for. None of them made use of their talismans." The new voice belonged to a tall, narrow figure who seemed to glide across the room, though the effect was actually the result of the long, flowing robe of white and red he wore. His face was veiled, for it could prove hazardous to those around him if they happened to glance his way. Such was the price of power.

"Could it be, Haggerth," the two voices continued, "that someone found those of a past guardian? There have been those who died, or at least vanished."

"If a guardian dies, his personal talismans—all of them—die with him. The whistles would have been nothing more than ash. They could have found a way to copy the sounds, I suppose. . . ."

"Come now." The twin speakers scoffed at such a thought. "You know that true communication with the Dream Lands is beyond the Ravager. It is against the laws set down in the beginning."

"There is Shaidarol. That one knew the secrets. That one was one of us once."

"Shaidarol forfeited the knowledge when he allowed himself to be seduced by the Ravager's promises. The Brotherhood of the Tzee are also unable to make use of those powers, having put themselves beyond the normal boundaries of nature in their own mad quest for dominance. I understand that they were, in fact, the ones seeking to capture or kill those two."

The veiled figure called Haggerth reached up a gloved hand in an unconscious manner and tugged the masking cloth in thought. "Does Troia have any suggestions?"

The twin figures nodded simultaneously. "She thinks we dare not hesitate. The problem must be *dealt* with in a very final manner. Better to be safe than lose all."

"A bit drastic, wouldn't you say?"

"No."

"That would make us little better than the wolf raiders. Doesn't that bother you?"

"We often become our enemies in time of war. When the Aramites and their mad dog of a god are washed away into the seas, we will forget this terrible time and remember again the pleasures of life—all of us except the annoying Tzee, that is."

Haggerth sighed. "I think that your dreams of a return to the ways of the past are too much for even the Dream Lands. I have a suggestion. The not-people have entered Luperion. I think they will help us in this matter. It will mean summoning the aid of the Gate. Then, when the ones we seek are alone . . ."

The twin figures leaned forward as Haggerth explained his plan. In moments, they were both smiling identical smiles.

FOR JUST THE briefest span of time, it woke. The bonds still held it prisoner, as they had done for ages. Why, then, it wondered, had it awakened? It reviewed the past, which was always open to it, and discovered the presence of a mind of a type it was familiar with. Far away, but nevertheless the closest any had ever come. Perhaps, it thought briefly, the time of release would soon come. Perhaps.

One portion of its mind became active. It was a trick the prisoner had long been skilled at. That part of the mind would monitor and inform while the prisoner as a whole would continue his age-old slumber. If the faint trace went away, that portion would also return to sleep. If it moved nearer . . .

. . . The game would begin anew.

The great leviathan closed its eyes.

V

THE CITY WITHIN the walls was indeed impressive, but more so for the throngs of people and animals than anything else. There were groups of all sizes, and they were packed together so tightly that the riders looked as if they were leading their mounts across a river.

"Is it market day?" Morgis finally asked.

"Market day?" The keeper smiled smugly. "Hardly. This is what it looks like every day in Luperion!"

"Oh."

Though darkness was descending, Luperion had no intention of settling down. Torches, lanterns, and such lit most of the areas already. People continued to haggle or wander about, and the Gryphon suspected that the crowds would still be here hours from now.

Luperion was a contrasting mixture of function and fancy. In the market areas, tents and structures of all shapes and sizes abounded. Beyond, where the military might of the wolf raiders watched, the buildings became boxlike and dark. Banners with wolf-head emblems fluttered fiercely in the wind. Ebony-armored figures stood watch or marched back and forth. Everything seemed to be either black, gray, or white, a distinct difference from the open market region where countless colors vied with one another, including even the skins of the inhabitants themselves. Most were familiar to the Gryphon, but the blue men gave him pause. Beseen had mentioned them briefly, but the lionbird had assumed the blue was merely some sort of dye. It was not, he discovered. What proved more important was that they were from a place near Tylir. Beseen had chosen that area because visitors from there were supposed to be rare here in the south. Apparently, the drake's information had been sketchy. The Gryphon wondered what else Beseen had missed.

He expected hard going through the living sea of people, but the crowds flowed away from the patrol whenever it neared and flowed back after it passed. They moved with such precision that it almost seemed they had practiced for this—which, in a sense, they had. That said something about the Aramite empire, that the patrol should be so accepted an obstacle.

It was D'Haaren who suggested an inn, the Jackal's Way, where the two might find a room and food. The Gryphon thanked him for the information, careful not to reveal his suspicions about the captain's more tolerant attitude. The inn, no doubt, housed a spy or two, but it was not a great danger as far as he was concerned. There were ways to evade spies.

As they broke off from the Aramites, only one member of the patrol—the keeper—bid them farewell. He simply nodded and said, "May your endeavors reach an appropriate end."

Neither the Gryphon nor Morgis cared to dwell on the implications of the statement.

"Do you have something in mind?" Morgis hissed once they were out far away.

The lionbird nodded, pretending to comment on some sight. He whispered, "Yes. We'll go to the Jackal's Way and pay for a night's stay, but we won't be coming back. I want to leave here before dawn. Just in case we need to separate for a time, I want to find another inn—or some other crowded place—for us to meet at."

"Sounds reasonable, providing your plans also include an honest meal in the near future. I have a yawning chasm for a stomach."

The Gryphon knew how he felt. "It does . . . believe me, it does."

AFTER EATING AND drinking their fair shares at the Jackal's Way—the ale was good, but, in this case, the spice was uncalled for—they wandered deep into the city with the pretense of looking over the local entertainment. Under this guise, they studied the city around them and, during their sojourn, located the second inn. The going was rough; without the patrol or even their horses to break open a path for them, they were forced to go around and about the waves of pedestrians.

There was one close encounter. Morgis, trying to wheedle information from a merchant, mentioned Tylir in passing. Only after that did they realize that one of the blue men was nearby, looking over some animal skins. Fortunately, he appeared not to hear them. After that, they tried to mention the region as little as possible and always kept an eye out for the distinctive color of the northerners.

THEY WERE ON their way back to the second inn when the Gryphon again spotted a long, robed figure like the one standing in the field outside of the city. The hood obscured all traces of the person's head, and the lionbird was briefly reminded of Shade, the warlock who had been cursed to live an eternity of alternating lives, good and evil. But Shade was gone now, exiled to the endless Void by the only creature capable of defeating his darkest persona yet.

Morgis, too, had seen the figure. As they watched, they noticed one thing in particular: no one blocked the path of the hooded one for more than a second. Even Aramite soldiers on horses steered clear. It was quite obvious as well that the mysterious figure was not popular with the citizenry, though he or she was definitely respected.

"Someone we should know about, perhaps?" the drake whispered.

"Several we should know about. Look." The Gryphon pointed down the street.

Two more hooded figures strode through the crowds with the clear intention of joining the third, who stood waiting for them. In size, they were identical. Shape was debatable; it was impossible to say just what might be under those robes. Whatever it was, people avoided it like the plague.

The Gryphon studied the crowd. "It might not be a good idea to talk to anyone about this right now. From what I've seen, they're all too worked up about them. Besides, we're supposed to know who they are, apparently."

"I know one thing about them," Morgis commented, eyes on the now-distant trio.

"What's that?"

"They're heading toward the other inn, the one we're staying at."

They were, indeed. Worse yet, one had detached himself—again, the Gryphon could only assume they were men—and was now standing outside, gazing at the crowds from the murky depths of his hood.

"I think we have a problem," the duke hissed.

"I *know* we have a problem. To your right."

Much to their dismay, Captain D'Haaren and a handful of his men were making their way toward the duo. The look in the veteran raider's eyes was not one that appealed to them.

Slowly, casually they turned away, pretending not to have noticed the Aramite soldiers.

"What now?" Morgis hissed. Had it been up to him alone, he would have been sorely tempted to pull out his sword and fight. True, there were more than half a dozen of the soldiers, but the crowd would slow them long enough for him to take care of one or two.

The Gryphon frowned. "Down that side street."

The side street in question was no less crowded than any other avenue of the city. The former ruler of Penacles hoped that they could turn off into yet another side street before the Aramites got too close. It was his hope, a slight one, true, that they might lose the patrol long enough to recover their belongings, including the horses. The next problem would be to see if they could escape the city itself.

"What gave us away?" the drake whispered. It did not seem to matter how loud they spoke; everyone else was too caught up in their own activities.

"I really don't know. Maybe they ran into some of our neighbors and questioned them," he replied, thinking of the bluish men. Maybe there was something about Tylir Beseen had forgotten to tell them or had not known at the time. The Gryphon's eyes settled on another side street, almost an alley by the looks of it. "Down that way. Hurry, but don't run."

They turned the corner—and found themselves facing an oncoming party of four wolf raiders.

The knife was into and out of Morgis's hand before the Gryphon could stop him. The Aramites coming toward them were obviously on routine patrol and not part of any concerted effort to capture the two. They probably could have walked right past the soldiers.

It was too late for that now. The lead soldier went down without a sound, the hilt of the knife sticking out of his neck. The other three hesitated only a moment from surprise and then drew their swords, long, wicked blades that curved slightly.

Cursing, the Gryphon pulled his own weapon. Morgis already had his out and was moving swiftly toward the trio. One of them shouted something, but whatever it was became lost in the noise. The drake matched blades against two of the Aramites while the Gryphon arrived barely in time to save his companion from the third. The street was very narrow, and the lionbird was able to catch the man at an awkward angle. The point of his blade cut a deep gash along his opponent's shoulder where the armor of necessity had a break. The wolf raider gritted his teeth and switched hands, proving himself to be just as excellent a swordsman with his left as with his right.

Morgis thrust his blade through one of his two opponents, but got his sword stuck in the collapsing form. As he struggled, the remaining Aramite pressed his advantage, cutting the drake on the left side near the collarbone. The duke hissed more out of anger than pain, but his response so startled the soldier that Morgis had enough time to free his blade before the wolf raider pressed again.

With each breath, the Gryphon expected Captain D'Haaren and his men to cut them down from behind. Even if the captain had lost them, the noise of the battle would surely have been enough to alert him or some other patrol. If not the noise, then the crowd of people rushing from this particular street would have been a good sign that something was amiss.

The Gryphon parried a wild attack by his adversary, who apparently felt his left-handed assault would throw the other off, and followed through with a death-dealing thrust of his own. As the soldier fell, the former monarch turned and caught the drake's opponent from the side. The Aramite parried, but in doing so left himself wide open to Morgis. The duke dispatched him with ease.

Still D'Haaren and his fellows did not appear.

They were, however, being watched from the direction that the wolf raiders had come. A lone woman, there was no denying *that* form was feminine, studied them from behind a veil. When she realized that they had seen her, she stepped back gracefully but did not flee. It was almost as if she wanted them to chase her.

Morgis took a step forward, sword raised. "We have to take her. She'll warn the patrol captain."

"Will she?" The Gryphon matched gazes with her. She did not seem like any Aramite. Even through the veil, he could see that she had large, dark eyes. Entrancing eyes, but not like those of most women. More like a cat. A predatory cat.

She stared back with equal curiosity, almost as if she knew what actually lurked behind the illusion. The Gryphon might have stood there for hours if Morgis had not broken the spell.

A heavy hand gripped his shoulder as the drake tried to shake him back to awareness. "If you can tear yourself away from that woman, I thought I'd warn you that we have more company."

"What?" The lionbird whirled, expecting to face Captain D'Haaren. Instead, two of the hooded figures stood at the intersection, calmly waiting. Their hands were buried within their cloaks, leaving no portion of their bodies uncovered. It would have been impossible to tell whether these two were part of the trio that had gone to the inn they were staying in or whether they were two new ones.

The Gryphon turned his attention back to the woman. His eyes widened. She was now accompanied by two more. The Gryphon found himself hoping that D'Haaren and his men might show up after all. The Aramites, at least, were a fairly familiar danger; these cloaked figures, figures whom even the wolf raiders gave wide berth to, were not. Given a choice, he preferred the known to the unknown.

The two figures with the woman stepped past her and walked side-by-side toward the duo. At the same time, their counterparts moved forward from the other side.

"Back-to-back," Morgis hissed. "And if you have a spell ready, please use it. Shifting my form in this narrow place could prove quite uncomfortable."

Nodding, the Gryphon raised his free hand—and found he could do nothing else. He was frozen in place. When he tried to say something, nothing happened, not even a moan.

"So interesting," a distinctly female voice near his ear said. "Not one of the Ravager's kind, but something different."

She moved to his front. The veil was gone and, while she was breathtakingly beautiful, she was certainly not human. Her eyes were indeed dark and like a cat's, even down to the pupil. It added to rather than detracted from her looks. Her hair was short and pitch-black, and she had a tiny, well-formed nose that twitched on occasion for no apparent reason. Her lips were long and full—quite inviting until she smiled. It was not a smile of friendship, but rather the smile of a cat as it plays with its prey.

Of her form he could tell little, since she stood too close. The Gryphon did not doubt that she was lithe and strong, and under other circumstances he would have been very attracted. Even now, it was impossible to totally ignore the flirtatious looks she gave or the caress of her hand on the side of his head. He reminded himself again of the feline toying with its meal.

"I can feel the true shape of your face; your illusion does not completely fool my eyes. A strange creature you must be, but no less strange than your companion, I notice."

She ran her long fingers along his cloak. "It would be a waste to destroy this. I'll let you keep it for the moment."

The female stepped away, and the Gryphon saw that his assumption about her form was correct in essence but had not done her justice at all. Though she was looking at the two hooded figures before them, she seemed to be walking for his benefit—or perhaps it was just natural for her. If she was what he thought she was, then everything she did was a normal part of her nature.

"You won't tell me anything, will you?" she asked both of the figures. Neither responded with so much as a shake of the head, but the woman shrugged and turned to look once more at her two prisoners.

"They want you alive—not these, the Master Guardians. The not-people never say what they want. You just ask them something and hope they respond in the way you want. Sometimes I wonder who really runs the continent."

She frowned and then pointed at the Gryphon and Morgis. As if on cue, the others removed their hoods. It was fortunate that neither the Gryphon nor Morgis could move, for what met their eyes was one of the strangest sights either of them had beheld. The not-people, as the woman had called them, looked human in form—as much as was visible—but they lacked any feature on their head. No hair, no eyes, no mouth, no nose, no ears—nothing. A clean slate upon which anything might be added. It was impossible to imagine how they breathed, let alone how they ate or drank. They had to have something related to sight or hearing, for they moved in smooth motions that even the Gryphon, excellent as he was in matters of stealth, would have found impossible to copy.

When they were no more than an arm's length away, the two creatures raised their hands high. He could not see them, but the lionbird suspected the other two were repeating the process behind him.

The tremendous tug on the fields and lines of power astonished him. Surely, the use of such intense magic would alert every keeper in the vicinity—wouldn't it? That train of thought was cut off as a familiar sound briefly reappeared. A chill ran through him.

"Not last time and not this time, you cursed Tzee!" Raising her left hand as a cat might raise its paw to bat something, she muttered a phrase that the Gryphon felt he should recognize. The whispering, which had threatened to increase, vanished abruptly instead.

"Stupid shadow creatures."

Tzee. The name opened new memories for the Gryphon, and none of them were good ones. The woman was wrong if she considered them stupid creatures. He prayed he would not be around when the Tzee proved that to her.

Whatever it was that the faceless not-people were doing was completed swiftly. One of them glanced—at least the front of its head turned—at the Gryphon, and the lionbird suddenly found his body moving without his willing it. As he turned, he saw that Morgis was in like straits; only his eyes were able to show any of the frustration both of them felt.

That frustration melted away when he saw where they were headed. One of the walls was missing an entire section, and that section had been replaced by the Gate. It looked different than before, but the Gryphon remembered that part of its nature was change—for was it not the way into the Dream Lands, where change was the norm and stability more of a freak occurrence?

The doors of the Gate were wide open. Things climbed all over the frame of the artifact, tiny things, but no less deadly because of their size. These were the watchers, the guard dogs of the Gate. There once had been more of them. He was certain of that. Something had happened to them. They had been turned.

Those memories escaped him, not that they mattered at this moment.

Only the Gate and where it led mattered. As his body obediently made its way to the artifact, he could not help thinking how desperately he had wanted to find the Gate and enter the Dream Lands. This had been his home once. No more, apparently. He was returning a prisoner; it was quite possible that all those who had known him were dead and that others now controlled Sirvak Dragoth. It was quite possible that he had traveled across the Eastern Seas and a fair portion of this continent only to die at the hands of those he had been seeking.

For some inexplicable reason, he could not help but picture D'Shay laughing, mocking his adversary for his foolhardiness.

The Gate swallowed him.

THE NOVICE KEEPER knelt before D'Rak. D'Rak frowned briefly, but decided that it must be important if the novice was willing to interrupt his senior. Novices who disturbed their superiors for minor matters never completed their training. They were usually shipped home in a small box.

This one knew better, for he was one of D'Rak's students. The senior keeper pushed aside the notes he was making and leaned back.

"Speak."

"Keeper D'Wendel reports the presence of a foreign ship several days ago near the southwestern coast—approximately due west of Luperion."

D'Rak grew annoyed. "So? This is the news you thought important enough to break my concentration? Probably Xeenian privateers. There are still a few independents left. Another year and we'll have them all. Why bother me with this? Is D'Wendel having some sort of difficulty? You said it was several days ago?"

There was a slight tremor in the novice's voice. "It was not a Xeenian ship, Master. The keeper did not report it earlier because he did not know himself. Pursuit ships were out of range for their associate keepers."

Associate keepers were those who had risen above novice stage. Most of them were assigned minor patrol duties. Despite their youth, they actually outranked anyone captain or lower. It was a symbol of the keepers' power in the Aramite empire.

D'Rak, however, was not concerned with the matter of communication. He had still not been given a reason why his own novice had interrupted him. "I gather there was something significant about the foreign vessel? Something worth saving your miserable hide if you delay any longer?"

The senior keeper's tone was even, but the younger keeper knew how serious he really was. Swallowing heavily, he replied, "After a long hunt in which one pursuit ship perished in flames and another was finally abandoned due to damage, the keepers aboard banded together and succeeded in destroying both ship and crew, save a few scattered survivors."

This did capture D'Rak's attention. "A formidable adversary, indeed. You are forgiven for now. Carry on."

Somewhat relieved, the novice continued. "The pursuit ship that perished in flames was the victim of a dragon, Master. The creature died at the hands of the keepers, who set up a field nullifying its power. The thing fell from the sky and sank like a stone. It was believed at first that the dragon was some sort of rare pet or slave, but some of the survivors fished out of the sea proved to be—to be humanoid, reptilian monsters. Dragon men, Keeper D'Wendel said."

"Dragon men." D'Rak rubbed his chin. "Dragon men."

"He swears it is the truth."

The master keeper smiled vaguely. "Oh, I believe him. I'm just trying to decide what the proper course of action would be."

"Master?"

D'Rak leaned forward. "You've not heard the tales of the new continent west of our domain, have you?"

"No, master. I've been studying here for the past two years. I intend to finish my novice training at least a year early."

The elder man nodded in satisfaction. This novice—D'Rak made it a point to never use or even think of their names in order to prove his impartiality—would be a fine keeper if he survived his years as an associate.

"Be sure to remind me to tell you of them sometime soon. We know of these drakes, but I doubt anyone actually thought they were this bold. I shall have to speak to the Pack Master. Was there anything else?"

"Yes, lord. As I understand it, Keeper D'Wendel believes that they might have set one or more persons on shore. He said traces were found by the keepers present that indicate something of that sort. That was all he knew when he sent the message. He said he would relay any new information the moment it arrived."

"Thank you, novice. You may go."

"Master." The young man stood and backed out, bowing all the way.

D'Rak turned to the Eye of the Wolf. The Pack Master would be interested in this. Why were the drakes seeking to infiltrate the Aramites' empire? Did they know what the wolf raiders planned? The inconsistent war with the Dream Lands was putting too much of a strain on things. The Pack Master was without rival, but it was his responsibility to create results. Until the Dream Lands, no one had been able to stand up to the raiders. As long as that place existed, the empire could not expand. Armies sent east lost their way and began marching every direction but that. Scouts and spies sent out to investigate possibilities beyond those areas under the Dream Lands' protection never returned. Ships sailing around the northern and southern shores of the continent reported storms so fierce and ice so thick that it was impossible for them to proceed any farther, even with the aid of senior keepers and high-level sorcerers.

The Ravager could not possibly be pleased. The last time he had shown his anger, Qualard, the former capital, had vanished in the worst earthquake anyone had ever seen. Some claimed that to have been the work of the lords of the Dream Lands, but D'Rak knew better. The Dream Lands could not possibly have such power, else they would have used it again. But that was the past, more than two centuries ago. No one cared about that now save a few of the near-immortals.

D'Rak ran his hands almost reverently over the Eye. The pride within him swelled, for only a handful had ever truly mastered an artifact as powerful as this. It was one reason why he had grown to be the unofficial third power of the empire—fourth if one counted the Ravager himself.

The question of who was first and second was debatable, as far as he was concerned. The Pack Master was *supposed* to be, but more and more . . .

What is it?

The voice was within his own mind, as he had expected, but it was not the voice of the Pack Master.

"D'Shay!" the keeper snarled. "This is for the Pack Master's attention, not yours!"

He could almost see the confident, aristocratic face. *All things are my concern, Keeper D'Rak. Do you think that the master will not consult me on whatever it is you wish to discuss with him? Has he not said in the past that my ear is his ear?*

The question of who was truly in charge briefly reared its ugly head. D'Rak squashed the thought, for fear that D'Shay might catch it. Though the keeper spoke, it was more his thoughts that were transmitted than his words.

He sighed. Regrettably, his rival was correct. After all, D'Shay was the one who had dealt with the drakes most. He relayed what his novice had told him, pretending that he did not know that D'Shay had scored a victory of sorts over him.

To his surprise, the other wolf raider genuinely thanked him. *At last! I told him that he would come eventually!*

D'Rak realized that he was picking up some of the other's thoughts. He said nothing, though. It was possible that *he* might learn something of importance from D'Shay.

No doubt he thinks I am long dead! Wonderful! The Ravager will have his head and the key to the Gate as well!

The keeper became uneasy. D'Shay always spoke of their god as if he were a personal friend.

Keeper D'Rak! I will inform the Pack Master, but I have a request of you!

"What is it?"

Order the keepers in the region of Luperion to do nothing but observe! They will indeed find at least one stranger, possibly more! If they find someone who seems too different, they should allow him to go unmolested!

"What are you saying? What do you plan?"

It is not for you to know right now.

The keeper stood without realizing it. "Only the Pack Master can decide that!"

He will.

Contact was broken. D'Rak seethed, but he knew there was nothing he could do—for now. D'Shay had the Pack Master's ear, but there were other ways to discover things; he was not a senior keeper for nothing. D'Shay was only a man like any other—wasn't he?

He was not, and D'Rak knew that. Still, the keeper had amassed too much power of his own to allow himself to be ordered around like this. He would do as his rival said—and then some. D'Shay obviously believed that the drakes had dropped off somebody important, perhaps even the one who seemed to prey on the Aramite's mind at all times. What was he called? The Gryphon, that was it. A refugee from the Dream Lands, apparently. It had to be him. No other news would have struck D'Shay so.

Dream Lands. D'Rak smiled. He knew just what was needed to hunt down someone from the Dream Lands. Someone who obviously must be returning there and who might be leaving a trail of sorts.

The Pack Master would not fault him, regardless of what D'Shay might say. The keeper moved his hands slowly across the Eye of the Wolf, observing all until his second sight came upon the kennels. Carefully, for they were an unruly, high-strung lot, he sought out the pack leader and disturbed its slumber.

The Runner woke.

VI

H E HAD BLACKED out.
Eyes still closed, the Gryphon started to raise his head, only to discover that it now weighed at least as much as a full-grown dragon. He gingerly returned it to the soft cushion beneath him and decided to try his eyes.

The light was blinding at first, but his eyes soon became used to it. Unfortunately, his vision refused to clear up, giving everything the appearance of being viewed through muddy water. He blinked several times, and things finally came into focus.

He was in a room of extravagant tastes and proportions. Everything seemed to glitter with gold, silver, and crystal. Tapestries so lifelike that he was tempted to think they watched him hung on every wall. There were sculptures of many fantastic creatures, including his namesake. The room was lit by a single, glowing crystal in the center of the ceiling. He heard tales of such use, but could not recall ever seeing it, though he suspected he had long ago.

With some trepidation, he dared rise from the couch again. This time, he was rewarded with only an incessant pounding in his forehead, a vast improvement over his previous attempt. The Gryphon stumbled to his feet, one hand on the side of his head, and took a deep breath. The pounding lessened.

There were drapes to his left, which meant a window. His strength slowly returning, he made his way to the drapes, which were made of the finest silk, he saw, and pulled them wide open.

He found himself staring at a mirror.

"I am not amused," he muttered, although he knew that it was not necessarily the designer's intention to have played him for a fool.

The Gryphon stared at his reflection. His cloak had been taken from him, and so his true features were revealed. There was something odd about the other him, something not quite right. It was almost as if it were not so much his mirror image, but an independent entity. He could not prove it, but he was certain that its movements did not quite match his own.

One of the faceless creatures stepped into the background of the reflection. The Gryphon released the curtains and whirled. There was no one there.

He turned back to the mirror, only to find that the curtains had completely covered it once more. The lionbird was about to reach out when the door to his room opened. It was one of the faceless ones, clad exactly as the image in the mirror had been—which meant nothing. The Gryphon could not have told one from another even if his life had been at stake.

The garments it wore differed only in color, being a combination of blue and black, with the latter making up the shoulders and hood. The hood was down, fully revealing its frightening lack of any feature. It almost seemed to float as it stepped into the room. The Gryphon thought briefly about assaulting it, then changed his mind when he remembered with what ease the foursome in the alley had captured him.

That thought led to ones concerning the safety of Morgis and the question of just exactly where he was. Not in Luperion. The Dream Lands, he remembered now, but where did one truly exist in a place not quite real?

"Where's my companion?"

The creature gestured at the open doorway behind it. The Gryphon understood that, at least, but was it answering his question or did it have some other destination in mind?

A second of the faceless not-people, as the woman had termed them, entered the room. Evidently, the Gryphon was going to come with them one way or another. There seemed no point in being obstinate; he would have been left lying in the streets of Luperion if it was his death they wanted.

With one creature leading and the other behind the Gryphon, they departed. The lionbird studied the halls, occasionally dredging up some fragment of memory as he spotted various objects. He had been in this place before, but the name escaped him for the moment. This was where he had sought to go.

"Lord Gryphon!"

He turned to see Duke Morgis, also monitored by a pair of the not-people, being led toward him. Apparently, the two of them were on their way to a confrontation with the masters of this place.

"Have you any idea where we are?" The drake was anxious. The Gryphon had not tried his own powers, but he suspected that Morgis had—and had found them wanting.

They were allowed to walk with one another so long as they kept the pace set by their escort. The ex-monarch nodded. The name had come back to him, and he now wondered how he could have ever forgotten. "We've reached Sirvak Dragoth, the citadel of the Dream Lands' guardians."

Morgis turned to study the blank visages of their guards. "Aren't these people supposed to be your friends?"

"Times change. It *has* been well over a hundred years. Maybe much longer."

"Four against two is not bad odds for us," the drake suggested quietly. He was not terribly confident about their chances with whoever was in charge.

"Eight against two," the Gryphon replied. "And I think we've reached our destination."

Four more of the creatures stood watch over a massive, intricately patterned wooden door. Eyeing the new complement, the lionbird came to the sudden realization that these beings were not servants of a sort, but rather a group with a purpose of its own that presently coincided with that of the Master Guardians of the Dream Lands. The Gryphon corrected himself; it was not a realization, but another memory unleashed.

He was irritated. So many memories of things and people around him, but very few useful ones about himself.

The two nearest to the doors opened them wide. The Gryphon and Morgis were ushered through without ceremony into a room as opulent as the one the lionbird had woken in, but obviously designed for holding court . . . for four figures awaited them on a dais. Only one of those figures was recognizable. That was the dark-haired woman who had coordinated their capture. She seemed ready to devour them both.

An identical pair of near-human males in their late years stood to one side in the brightest part of the room, which, the Gryphon thought idly as he glanced up at the skylight, meant that it was daytime. The two moved with such uniformity that one would have thought they were puppets controlled by the same master. When one blinked, the other blinked (even their breathing was in unison). That they were not human was evident by their eyes, which were wide and multifaceted, like those of an insect.

Seated on a chair in the center of the dais was a long, humanoid figure clad in red and white and wearing a veil that completely obscured his or her features. The Gryphon hazarded the guess that it was a man, or at least male. It was this figure that seemed in charge of the situation.

"I trust both of you have rested well," he said by way of an opening remark.

"We rested," Morgis replied angrily, "because we had no choice."

"Ah, that!" The figure shifted somewhat uncomfortably. The two identical men frowned simultaneously, and the woman bared sharp teeth. "Forgive me, but it wasn't supposed to be that way. The not-people had agreed to confront you in your rooms, but you chose to flee and fight the wolf raiders instead."

"Fools," the twins chorused.

"Mrin/Amrin, please." The veiled figure raised a hand in an attempt to regain control. "The Aramite captain had no idea who you were. He was actually heading to one of the buildings near where you happened to be standing. It seems one of the merchants wasn't paying his fair share, so to speak."

The Gryphon and Morgis glanced at each other. The lionbird turned back to the speaker. "Would— Pardon me, first. You seem to know us—at least you haven't asked us our names—but we don't know you."

"Forgive me. I am Haggerth." He rose, being careful to keep his veil in place. "To my right is Mrin/Amrin, and to my left is Troia, whom you have already met." There was a hint of mischief in his voice.

Taking a deep breath, the Gryphon said, "You are, if I recall, Master Guardians, are you not? All four of you?"

He was almost sure that the expression on Haggerth's hidden face included a frown. "You are partially correct. Mrin/Amrin and I are Master Guardians, but Troia is not."

"I am *merely* a Guardian," she purred, her tone implying she was anything but.

"There are only *three* of us, for that matter!" the twins shouted. "There is Haggerth, Troia, and myself!"

Morgis hissed. The Gryphon studied the two identical Master Guardians. They were so much alike that he could not deny that they might be the same man. Was it possible that in the Dream Lands a man could be in two places at the same time?

"Easy, friend," Haggerth was saying to the entity Mrin/Amrin. "You know how the power of the Guardianship affects us in the eyes of others." He turned back to his "guests." "We are all changed by our nature. Mrin/Amrin took pride in his individuality; now people see him as more than one person—not a true individual. Myself, I was a presence that sometimes commanded by sheer appearance alone. My decisions were not always based on deep thought, merely the fact that I knew I could turn people to my point of view. Now, unless I wish to possibly destroy everything I've worked for, I have to rely on ability alone."

Haggerth flicked the bottom of the veil in emphasis.

"We have all given something to protect our land, even if not all things appreciate it," Troia added, smiling invitingly at the Gryphon.

"I see." Beside him, Morgis said nothing.

"Let us now return to the question of these two," Mrin/Amrin chorused. Both bodies had the right arm raised and were pointing at the Gryphon and Morgis. "Let us discover the truth about this hybrid—this misfit."

The Gryphon started at the vehemence behind the words, so much akin to that of D'Shay. "Am I being condemned for my existence? If so, I would like to know the reason why."

Haggerth and even Troia seemed unsettled by Mrin/Amrin's attitude. The veiled guardian shook his head carefully. "You must forgive us at times. We find ourselves in troubling situations of late, and things better left unsaid tend to rear their ugly heads. It was nothing to concern you. Isn't that so, Mrin/Amrin?"

The double man's multifaceted eyes dimmed a little. "My apologies. It was uncalled for."

"Now, then. The crux of this meeting is your existence and its origins." Haggerth reached into a pocket and removed from it a small whistle. The Gryphon's eyes widened, and he frantically searched his own pockets. It was his remaining whistle. His mane stood on end, and the sound that escaped him was more that of the king of beasts than the bird of prey he more resembled.

Troia reacted in kind, becoming more feline as she stepped forward. Oddly, while he became wary of her sharp claws, he also became more and more aware of how desirable she was.

"Cease! Both of you!" Haggerth rose from his chair and, with one smooth movement, tossed the whistle to the Gryphon, who caught it with one clawed hand while holding off the cat-woman with the other.

"I said CEASE!" Haggerth pulled the veil from his face. Mrin/Amrin, as if knowing what to expect, turned away quickly. The Gryphon, Morgis, and Troia, unprepared, all stared at what the Master Guardian hid beneath that veil.

Neither the lionbird nor the drake would ever be able to recall just what the face of Haggerth looked like. They would only remember that it was something that threatened to tear their sanity from their minds. They were fortunate in that the guardian had almost immediately replaced the thin, protective cloth.

The not-people, to no one's surprise, had not been affected.

Haggerth waited while the three stricken beings recovered. He hated the necessity of having had to do that, but he could see no way of avoiding it. It was no less horrible to him than it was to those he unleashed his curse on.

There were times when the guardianship hung heavy.

"Again, our apologies. Knowing what our guardians are like when their own prizes are taken, I should have realized—"

The Gryphon cut him off with a curt wave of his hand. "This is dragging on, and I can't take it anymore. I have a few questions of my own that I'd like to ask, the first of which is do *any* of you know me?"

All three—four, if one counted both bodies of Mrin/Amrin—shook their heads. Haggerth added, "It was our hope that you could clear up the mystery of your existence. You are a guardian of the Dream Lands; that much is obvious. But the question is, who and when?"

"Who and when?"

The Master Guardian sighed. "You know the name of this place—Sirvak Dragoth?"

The Gryphon nodded, his eyes gleaming. "I thought it must be, but to have it verified is like opening another door in my mind."

"You remember very little, I take it. Let me explain more. It is the erroneous belief of the Aramites, or wolf raiders, that we are the lords of the Dream Lands. By that they mean that we control the place."

"And don't you?"

The twin forms of Mrin/Amrin both laughed. "The Aramites and their god find it difficult to fight a land that exists as much in the mind as it does in reality. They should try maintaining some control over it. It is impossible. If anything, the Dream Lands control us."

"A slight exaggeration," Haggerth corrected. "Let us say that we coexist with this place, and in return for what it gives us we aid it against those who would see it destroyed."

"That's what guardians do?" the Gryphon inquired, staring at the trio. Even with their individual skills—and the skills of the double man were still a question mark—he could not see the guardians holding off the concerted efforts of the Ravager's children. He refrained from expressing the thought out loud. Quite obviously, they were doing just that. "I understand that I am—was—one of you. What happened? Why doesn't anyone remember me? Why don't I remember— Wait— I stand corrected. There *was* one who knew me. A wolf raider named D'Shay."

Had he told them that the entire Aramite military was coming through the Gate, along with the Ravager himself, he could not have asked for more startled looks from the trio. Even Haggerth, with his face covered, evinced utter shock and horror.

"I told you!" Mrin/Amrin was shouting madly. "He's one of those!" The double man stared at the Gryphon with wide eyes and clenched both of his right fists.

Something began to churn within the lionbird, and he felt as if he were about to explode. However, an angry shout from Haggerth made the other Master Guardian pause. The sensation, which Mrin/Amrin must have caused, ceased.

"Because he knows of Shaidarol does not make him like that one! Let not your memories cloud your judgment!"

Shaidarol.

Some of it was coming back to him. Not all of it, the Gryphon cursed silently, but some very important pieces fit together now. D'Shay—he could not bring himself to use the other name, for that had been a friend—had betrayed the guardians, had *been* one of the guardians.

It seemed impossible that D'Shay could have been that other. Yet . . . "He was changed the day he took up the mantle of guardianship. I remembered how different he seemed, how much . . . darker his moods became."

"And no one remembers you," muttered Haggerth. "Curious. This must be due to whatever it was you were forced to give up by taking on the burden of the guardianship. The Dream Lands shape all the guardians, sometimes in ways we don't understand until much later."

"You believe this one?" Troia glared at the Gryphon. "You believe what he says when you yourself do not even remember him? There is no record of his existence. You told me."

"No record save Shaidarol himself," added Mrin/Amrin.

"He is certainly not going to tell us anything useful!"

"The Tzee know of me." The Gryphon returned Troia's glare. "You know it. They knew who I was, and they tried to kill me."

She frowned. "That is true. Even I could feel the recognition in whatever passes for their minds—but that's certainly no recommendation!"

"I wish the other Master Guardians were here." Haggerth sighed. "Perhaps they might have a suggestion."

"Others?"

"There are six of us. It is terrible trying to maintain order where none was meant to be. We need all six, plus the other guardians."

The heads of Mrin/Amrin turned toward Morgis. "This one has said nothing for quite some time. Are we to believe that he, too, is a guardian come home?"

"I am not one of your guardians. I am Duke Morgis, son of the Blue Dragon, Lord of Irillian by the Sea, which lies far to the west."

"Across the seas?" asked Haggerth.

"That is correct. It is part of the Dragonrealm, though each Dragon King's region can also be called by that name as well."

"It's your vessels that harass the wolf raiders."

"It is."

The veiled Master Guardian straightened, looking more official than he had since the two had first been ushered into this room. "And why have you traveled with our lost guardian here? Are you a friend?"

Morgis glanced at the Gryphon, who shrugged lightly. If the drake wanted to tell the truth, then that was up to him. If he wanted to lie, the lionbird would not hinder him, but neither would he support the duke.

"At best, Lords of Sirvak Dragoth, I would say we are uneasy allies. Perhaps a little more than a year ago, our lands were threatened by one of my own kind. My sire and the Gryphon made a pact and, with the aid of others, destroyed the mad traitor."

Not exactly the truth, the Gryphon thought, but not far enough from it to be of any concern—so far.

"During that crisis, my sire and the Lord Gryphon, who ruled Penacles at that time, were also confronted by the evil of the one called D'Shay—or Shaidarol, as you called him."

"His evil grows!" Troia hissed, stepping away from the column she had chosen to lean against. "Master Haggerth, you should have let me go after him! I can still hunt him down! The Runners will not find me!"

"Be quiet, young one. You never met Shaidarol before or after he was tempted by the Ravager. You would have found either form more than you could possibly handle."

"But . . ." She trailed off. It was impossible to argue with Haggerth. Not that the young guardian had any desire to truly battle her superior.

The Gryphon frowned and ran the last few bits of conversation through his mind again. There was something wrong.

Morgis continued. "There is no need to worry about D'Shay. He died during a mad attempt to assassinate the Gryphon and my father."

"Died?" Mrin/Amrin looked puzzled. "When did this occur?"

"It happened a month or so prior to our voyage. We were actually planning on leaving immed—"

Haggerth shook his head. "D'Shay is alive, all too well, and has been back here quite some time."

That was what the Gryphon had noticed in the conversation. In a nearly toneless voice, he said, "He's alive after all. I didn't think suicide was his way—but we burned his body."

"There are a few ways to get around that, if need be, and all of them are unspeakable. D'Shay is more than capable of doing something like that. He no longer has any regard for life. His only duty is to the Ravager."

"D'Shay. Alive," the Gryphon muttered as he turned away from the rest of them, ignoring his faceless escorts as well. He stared blindly at some of the tapestries and statues in the chamber. Mrin/Amrin started to speak, but Haggerth waved him quiet. Finally, the lionbird faced the Master Guardians and continued. "Where is D'Shay?"

It was Troia who answered, despite a look from the veiled guardian. "In Canisargos. Everything the wolf raiders do is coordinated out of the capital."

"Canisargos? The capital?" Something about that did not seem accurate.

"It's the center of everything. That's where the Pack Master, their emperor, holds council. D'Shay stands at his right side."

That settled it, then. "How do I get to Canisargos? Do you have a map of the city?"

Mrin/Amrin shook his heads. "I think you presume too much. We have not even settled the problem of whether you are one of us or not."

"Come now." Haggerth turned to his fellow guardian. "I think it safe to assume he is. This is just another of the Dream Lands' tricks. We've seen worse, Mrin/Amrin. Far worse. The Lands do what they have to do to survive."

"Nevertheless, if he is interested in finding out why his 'enemies' remember him but his 'comrades' do not, there is another way."

The Gryphon chose one of the Master Guardian's twin faces and matched gazes with him. It was, nonetheless, slightly unsettling to have the other returning his gaze as well. "I'm going to Canisargos. Whether you believe me or not, there is still a matter to be settled between Shaidarol and myself. A matter put aside for far too long."

He did not notice that he had made mention of D'Shay's original name, but the others did. Mrin/Amrin's faces screwed up as the Master Guardian contemplated something he did not care to think about. Haggerth waited, silently watching the duo. Morgis, who had stood by quietly, was so tense that the Gryphon could literally feel it.

The double man's faces became bland. He scanned each individual in the chamber before returning his attention to the Gryphon. "When . . . D'Shay . . . turned from us, he did not leave us unscathed. We shall never fully know everything he did before he was at last cast out, but I, personally, shall remember one incident in particular."

"Mrin . . . ," Haggerth began.

Mrin/Amrin went on, ignoring his counterpart. "You shall have my full backing in your endeavor to seek out the traitor—and a guide who knows the city—if you agree to furnish the final proof I need in order to believe that you are not yet another ploy on his part."

The Gryphon straightened and studied the guardians. The veiled Haggerth said nothing; he had chosen to withdraw from this discussion until he knew more. Troia appeared oddly anxious for the lionbird, even to the point of giving him a nervous half smile.

It was between the Gryphon and Mrin/Amrin. "What is it? What sort of proof do you want?"

"Go to the Gate. Stand there and tell it you have come for judgment—"

"No!" the cat-woman shouted.

"—and ask it to give you the proof you need to convince others of your loyalty." The Master Guardian looked at Haggerth for confirmation. The veiled figure nodded his head slowly.

"And that's all?"

A peculiar look passed over Mrin/Amrin's face. He almost smiled sadly. "Oh, no, Gryphon. That's not all. I truly hope you succeed, but to do so, you'll have to do more than just stand there. When I say you have to face judgment, I am talking about a judgment that, if you fail to measure up, means you won't be going to Canisargos."

The Gryphon eyed Haggerth for confirmation. The Master Guardian seemed very tired, but he acknowledged the truth of his fellow's statement and added emotionlessly, "Or anywhere else, for that matter. If the Dream Lands find you wanting, there may not even be anything left to burn."

VII

THE SMELL OF death and carnage overwhelmed all else. Here in the dark, one could imagine that all the scavengers of history had gathered, adding to the stench with their rotting meals. Boots kicked at oddly shaped rubble that might have been bones cracked open. There was no light. Those who had a reason for being here knew where they were to kneel. Those who had no right to be here added to the debris scattered on the floor.

It was here that D'Shay had formally sworn his existence to his one true master. It was here that all Pack Leaders, keepers, and even the Pack Master himself came to swear their allegiance.

My prize pup. My hunter. How are you today, Shaidarol?

D'Shay did not look up at the use of his old name. If his master chose to use it for some reason, that would be made clear before long. If not, it was not for D'Shay to know.

"I am well, my lord. The body is stronger than I expected. It will last quite some time."

Something huge stirred in the darkness. *What reason brings you to me?*

"Milord, the Gryphon is in your domain. I am certain of it." D'Shay's mouth was set in a predatory grin, giving him a feral look.

I know. I knew soon after he stepped on this continent.

The wolf raider did not question that, for he would have been surprised if his master had not known.

"D'Rak's people are seeking him now. I ordered him to tell his underlings to do nothing but observe if they find him. I do not want him suspicious."

D'Rak has let loose a Runner pack. They are already nearing the countryside near Luperion.

"What?" D'Shay was standing before it registered on his mind that this was something his master normally forbade. Quickly, he fell back into a kneeling position.

You are forgiven. D'Rak serves his function well. You will not speak to him about this. It is possible that, with the Gryphon searching for a home, he obviously remembers little about how he might accidentally open the Gate. If the Runners gain a pawhold, the Dream Lands are mine.

"And the Gryphon?"

If possible, he shall be saved for your pleasure. If he has forgotten so much, then it must be that he has also forgotten the purpose of his existence. If he did remember, he would be here now.

"Qualard," D'Shay could not help muttering. The old capital of the Aramites' empire had sprung unbidden to his mind.

A savage rage threw him backward. The thing in the darkness shifted angrily, stirring up the ghastly remains about it. Had his wolfhelm not been padded, D'Shay would have cracked his skull on the unseen debris around him. An annoyance for him, yes, but nothing more. What did disturb D'Shay was the anger his master had directed against him. An anger still fresh after more than two centuries.

Qualard is never to be mentioned, the voice howled in his head. *Even you are not indispensable, Shaidarol. The Tzee would gladly take your place.*

"Forgive me, my lord!" D'Shay trembled, and with good reason. Swords and bolts did not bother him much, but the one he truly served had the power to erase him from existence with no more than a breath. It was also true that the Tzee would be more than willing to step in and take his place.

Forgiven. Listen to me, my Shaidarol. The great lizard stirred recently. He has not done that since—since Qualard. It may be that some of his kind are here; it may be that he feels the presence of the Gryphon. Whichever the case, I have no intention of losing my advantage in the game. I am the hunter, not the hunted. I will be the final victor—no one else. If it means forgoing your own pleasure, you will kill the Gryphon the instant he comes too close to the truth.

"I will do so."

Your existence is tied to my existence, Shaidarol. I am the only thing keeping you together. Put your interests ahead of mine . . . The thought did not have to be completed.

"I exist to serve you."

Literally. You would do well to remember that. Go now. It is time for the Pack Master to meet with his council. We would not want them to worry about him.

D'Shay rose and bowed. It may have been that he saw two huge, bloodred eyes staring out at him from the darkness, but he could not be sure. He could never be sure. Even on that night, when he had cast off the laughable guardianship and chosen a new master, he had not been certain. It really did not matter. All that mattered was that his continued existence depended on his value to his master. His only master.

He continued his bow until he was out of the cavern. The cavern beneath Canisargos. A cavern that had once served as a home to gods—and still served as home to one. The only true god, as far as the Aramites were concerned.

The Ravager.

* * *

"WHO IS THIS guide that the Master Guardians have promised me?" the Gryphon asked as he stepped over the fallen tree.

Troia shrugged. "I don't know. The not-people brought him in. He might have been a wolf raider—disgraced probably, if the Runners were after him."

Runners. Shadows of the Ravager's own being. As close as the dark god was said to have true children. No one knew where the Runners had come from, though it was suspected that at one time they had been, like the Tzee, creatures of the Dream Lands. They served their master well, from what Troia had said earlier of them.

She had volunteered to accompany him, and the two Master Guardians had not objected. Haggerth had been reluctant, perhaps fearing that the she-cat might suffer whatever fate befell the Gryphon—not that he claimed to believe that the lionbird was anything but what the guardian said he was. She had insisted. Her initial distrust of the Gryphon had given way to a new, mysterious hope—that, somehow, he would prove of great importance. It was only then that the Gryphon had realized how young she actually was. He was more than two centuries old—maybe more—while she was not even into her third decade, barely an adult.

Or too much of one, the ex-monarch thought wryly as he watched her climb up the side of the hill. She wore little clothing, her soft, tawny fur protecting her from the cold. The only clothing she wore was due to necessity and conventional morals. In Luperion, she had worn clothing that allowed her to look completely human from most distances, but that was not necessary here.

She said little about her kind as they made their way along the winding path that Haggerth had said would definitely lead them to the Gate. They had been dubbed sphinxes by some unknown being far back in history, though the term was not quite correct. In appearance, most looked nearly human—though their features were quite exotic and the fur would, of course, not go unnoticed. In slave markets, their beauty and their strength would have brought them the highest prices. Unfortunately, or perhaps fortunately, they refused to live long in captivity, for they either simply died or fought until they were killed. In battle, their sharp teeth and tearing claws became all too evident and their humanity seemed to vanish.

Perhaps it was due in part to that portion of him that was leonine in nature, that the Gryphon felt a kinship, an understanding with her. He tried to convince himself that it was this reason alone he was attracted to Troia.

Still, she made a much better companion than the drake Morgis had. Despite the growing closeness between the duke and himself, the Gryphon had been relieved when Mrin/Amrin had said in no uncertain terms that the drake was not allowed to go with them. Morgis's first duty was to his father, and so it was still debatable how far he could actually be trusted.

They came at last to a small thicket of woods. The Gryphon grew anxious when Troia rose and looked around, but she only laughed lightly when he warned her that wolf raiders might be on the prowl. She shook her head and smiled at his worries.

"You've forgotten so much, haven't you? We're in the Dream Lands now. This isn't the same land that the Aramites see. They could be standing right next to us and they would see only trees and birds. As long as we exist to give it strength, that is the way of the Dream Lands—or have you forgotten why the first ones dubbed it that?"

"Then what do we fear from the Aramites?"

The smile vanished. "We fear the 'truth' of their Ravager. We fear that his dreams will overwhelm ours. As he grows in strength, the Dream Lands dwindle. Faster and faster his reality overtakes ours." She stretched her arms wide. "Once, the Dream Lands *were* this entire continent. That was before the coming of the Ravager."

"'And the Game began in earnest. . . .'" the Gryphon quoted without thinking.

"What was that?"

He shook his head, trying to gather the memories together. As usual, they sank back into the mire that was his mind. "I don't know. A quote from somewhere . . . but I can't say where." His hands were clenched in frustration. "It's like that all the time! I understand now how Cabe must have felt!"

Troia stepped closer, her worry obvious. "Cabe?"

"A friend. One of the few close ones I have—had. He had a memory problem of sorts as well; perhaps that's why I understood him so well."

"What happened to him?"

The Gryphon glanced around, but the woodlands around seemed to hide no menace greater than a few annoying insects. "Cabe's problem was that he had been born the sickly child to a madman. The Bedlams were the greatest of sorcerers, but Azran was crippled in his mind. He killed his brother, and tried to kill his father. He would have raised Cabe in his image or, more likely, destroyed the poor boy. Cabe's grandfather, Nathan, stole the child and placed it in the care of another. But Nathan saw that the boy would probably not survive and, knowing that he himself was likely to die, gave the lad a part of himself. A part of his soul or essence. In that way, Nathan himself also lived on."

The cat-woman could only shake her head in amazement. "I've never heard anything like that."

"At one point, it was as if two different personalities lived in his head. He grew up not knowing who he was—Azran still lived, you see—and often recalled memories of a life that was not his own. Like my past seems to me."

She gave him a comforting smile. "Perhaps the Gate will take care of that."

"Perhaps the Gate will take care of what?" a soft, but regal voice asked. There was no visible being to accompany the voice.

The Gryphon crouched, ready to use either claw or sorcery, but Troia put a hand on his shoulder and squeezed reassuringly. The lionbird was not convinced; friendly strangers did not leave themselves unseen.

"Relax!" Troia hissed. "It's Lord Petrac, the Will of the Woods!"

While he puzzled over the odd title, a figure that had somehow not been noticeable earlier stepped closer. The Gryphon tilted his head, trying to understand how he could not have noticed a being that his mind now said had been there all the time but had just been ignored.

How one could ignore Lord Petrac—what Will of the Woods meant, the lionbird still could not comprehend—was beyond him as well. Petrac stood as tall as Morgis, with the head of a full-grown stag and a rack of antlers that would have brought any real animal to shame. Most of the remainder of his form was human, though his hands were shaped oddly—more like those of a raccoon—and his feet were cloven. He wore a loincloth, a cape of what appeared to be green leaves, and a belt from which hung several pouches. In his left hand he held a staff, which he utilized at present as a walking stick.

Troia knelt and, with great respect, said, "Hail. Will of the Woods."

Despite—or perhaps because of—having the head of a stag, Petrac's visage was one of power, of purpose. It was a different sort of strength than most leaders revealed, the lionbird thought. Petrac was at peace with his power, a rare, enviable thing in anyone who ruled.

"I do not insist on ceremony, kitten. That I leave to Haggerth and the others."

"If anyone should deserve it, Lord Petrac, it's you."

The mouth of the stag curled up slightly. "That is debatable. But come, your companion and I are strangers, and I would like to know why you and he seek the Gate."

The Gryphon belatedly bowed and introduced himself. Petrac nodded to him, then added, "Mrin/Amrin need not have concerned himself. I can see you are one of us. I daresay that he and Haggerth are becoming much too paranoid of late."

"Haggerth didn't—" Troia began.

The Will of the Woods waved off her objection. "You can be certain that this was as much the veiled one's idea as it was Mrin/Amrin's. He is a good man, but he gives his trust grudgingly. Such is the price of leadership to some."

"I'd still like to go on."

"What need? I will vouch for you."

Shaking his head, the Gryphon explained, "Not for the Master Guardians' sakes, although I would like to make them happy as well, but for my own peace of mind. I'm hoping that a confrontation with the Gate might bring to light some of the essential memories I still lack."

"Sometimes memories are best left forgotten. The Gate is an essential part of the Dream Lands. It is older than any record indicates. You could very well die. I assume they made *that* clear." Petrac shifted his staff, and the look in his eyes indicated that Haggerth and Mrin/Amrin had better have, that otherwise, there was going to be a discussion.

"They did. I still *want* to go there now."

"Then you need not go much farther. It's just over that rise in the woods."

Troia and the Gryphon glanced the way the Master Guardian indicated. The cat-woman frowned. "I was under the impression, Lord Petrac, that it was still much farther."

"I have some advantage being who I am," the Will of the Woods responded in light amusement. "Let us say I know a few shortcuts. Come. I will lead you there so that you make no wrong turns."

As they traveled through the lightly wooded region, the Gryphon began to understand Lord Petrac's unusual title. Animals and birds would come to greet the stag-man. Even creatures normally hostile to one another would forget their instincts in their desire to touch the hand of the Will of the Woods. Yet they did not approach the Master Guardian as one approached a lord or even a deity. They came to him as they would a loved one. Petrac did not rule them; he was one of them. His interests were their interests— which, coincidentally, were the Dream Lands' interests as well, for what was this wooded area but a portion of the magical region itself.

It was a fascinating walk, made only nerve-wracking when two of those who insisted on trundling up and greeting Lord Petrac were full-grown bears. Troia automatically unsheathed her claws, and the Gryphon prepared to cast a spell. The Will of the Woods shook his head at their actions and stepped up to touch the heads of the two beasts. They sniffed his hands and rubbed the sides of their bodies against his. It was a wonder they did not knock him over, but he stood there as if nothing touched him. The Gryphon could only watch in amazement, understanding now why Troia held this particular guardian in so much more awe than the others.

"Be careful where you step over here," the Master Guardian commented, his staff directed at the right side of the path. "The Ravager's reality is pressing forward. You might find yourself in the midst of an unknown woodland with his Runners on your trail."

"I was under the impression that the Aramites were losing ground," the lionbird commented, recalling a remark by the Black Dragon sometime far back. It had been implied that the Aramites' empire had met its match, since D'Shay was cutting off the Dragon King's source of living war material.

"So, too, were we until I noticed that our borders were becoming more indistinct than normal. The Dream Lands are contracting. Somehow, the wolf raiders are winning despite the stalemate."

"They also seek a permanent base of operations in the Dragonrealm," the Gryphon muttered, more to himself. There was a reason for that, too. The wolf raiders did nothing without reason. D'Shay did nothing without reason.

"Here we are. This should do." Petrac indicated an open field ahead of them. There was a strange, almost illusionary feel to it.

"Are you sure it's safe?" The Gryphon eyed the field uneasily. This was the Dream Lands as they once had been. This was a region nearly untouched by the presence of an intelligent race. A region where nature truly ruled.

Would it recognize him as a friend? Would he be, according to its ways, a true friend of the Dream Lands?

"I don't see the Gate."

"You haven't stepped into the field yet."

"Oh." The ex-monarch moved forward. Troia began to follow, but Lord Petrac held her back with his outstretched staff. He shook his head, indicating that this was to be the Gryphon's task alone. She growled quietly but acquiesced.

Each step stirred the field. That was the best way the Gryphon could describe the feeling. He could see the spectrum of lines running this way and that, but they were not as well-organized as in the Dragonrealm. By the rules he had learned, this should not have been possible; it would have made it too difficult to manipulate any of the powers, light or dark. The lionbird had never fully agreed with any of the accepted theories about magic, but this was almost too much even for his radical mind. Nathan Bedlam, Cabe's grandfather, would have had fits if he had been alive.

The waist-high grass whispered as he cautiously made his way through it. Not the mad whisper of the Tzee, but a harmonious whisper of curiosity, as if the Gryphon were as much of a wonder to the field as the field was to him. He noted absently that there was no wind and, therefore, no normal reason for the grass to be swaying to and fro.

When he was in what he reckoned to be approximately the center of the field, he came to a dead stop. If the Gate was going to materialize for him, it would be somewhere about here. At least, this was as far as he planned on going. The rest was up to the Gate.

As if responding to his unspoken challenge, the scene before him ripped open. A gap in reality appeared. First, only an odd, floating line of energy, then a vast hole through which he could see, not the rest of the field, but another land *entirely.* Perhaps the woods that any wolf raider would have noticed if he had come riding over here. Once more, the Gryphon was struck by the truth of what others had said about the Dream Lands. They *were* as much a part of the mind as of the geography.

Standing in the midst of the tear in reality was the Gate itself.

It was changed once more, which only emphasized again its relation to the Dream Lands. It now resembled an arch under which were two huge, wooden doors trimmed to follow the shape of the doorway. The doors had a touch of rot in them, and the metal hinges were covered with rust. The lionbird suspected this was a bad omen. Nevertheless, he had every intention of continuing on.

With time on his side now, he began to notice more. The things he had glimpsed on the Gate were there in greater numbers than before. They crawled all over the stonework, never ceasing for even a second. They had long snouts and great, saucerlike eyes that saw everything. Whether they were reptiles or mammals or even demons was impossible to say. They resembled nothing he was familiar with. Skin color appeared to be black or dark blue; it was difficult to say. Not one of them was exactly like any other, though they all had enough traits in common to prove kinship. It was as if a thousand variations of one creature had been raised just for this purpose— and who was to say that might not have been the case?

He knew that the odd creatures were guardians, and he also knew that they watched him as well as everything else. There was no sense putting it off any longer. The Gryphon raised his hands into the air—the act was not one he had planned, but it seemed the appropriate thing to do—and called out to whatever entity controlled the Gate.

"I have come for judgment. I come as a guardian lost. I come as a friend to the Dream Lands and ask that my claim be proven!" He hesitated, then added, "I also come in the hopes of regaining my own past, good or ill! If I have betrayed a trust in the past, let me work to regain that trust as well!"

The Gate was majestically silent. The minute guardians—actually, some of them were more than two feet in length—continued their hectic pace up, down, and around the artifact and ignored the lionbird save to glance his way as part of their duties.

The Gryphon stood where he was, arms raised, for a good five minutes. He lowered his arms, took a few steps back, and looked back at Troia and the Lord Petrac. The feline woman gave him a quick smile; evidently, she believed that no response was a good response. The Master Guardian's animal visage was almost as hard to read as the lack of reaction on the part of the oh-so-legendary Gate. He merely returned the lionbird's gaze.

The Gryphon turned back to the object of his trek, closed his eyes in exasperation, and then opened them when he realized the Gate was opening.

Troia hissed and Petrac shouted a warning, but the Gryphon was already far more aware of what was now coming through the open Gate than he wanted to be. Not simply one what, either. At least six, maybe seven vicious whats that all fell under one collective name that the Gryphon recalled even as the first of the creatures leaped at him.

Runners.

VIII

M ORGIS DID NOT care for the fact that he had been forced to remain behind while the Gryphon pursued what the drake considered an imbecilic and highly dangerous quest merely to prove himself to the Master Guardians. It should have been the other way around. He knew from his father's talk and the reports of spies what the ex-ruler of Penacles was like. There was much to admire, and their travels together had only emphasized many of those traits that the duke had first noticed. Under other circumstances, Morgis might have called him friend, but drakes were not like that. The Gryphon was a momentary ally, he kept telling himself, and when they returned to the Dragonrealm, the truce between the lionbird and the Blue Dragon would at last come to an end.

He had not told his companion about the small device he carried in one of his pouches. The Gryphon would have surely grown suspicious if he had known that Morgis had been reporting everything back to his sire. It was the drake's duty, after all, but the Gryphon would perhaps see it as a sign of distrust or even a betrayal. All this had been explained by the Blue Dragon, although Morgis had trouble understanding it all. Despite his physical appearance, despite his knowledge and experience, Morgis was still young compared to both his parent and the Gryphon. The violent death of both of his predecessors had shunted him into a position of power he could have done without.

Like most communication artifacts, it was crystal in nature. Morgis did not pretend to understand how it worked; the point was that it did. A thought struck him. Did the use of such items mean that the Crystal Dragon himself might be following everything they said? Was that the secret of the other Dragon King's tremendous power? He shuddered at the thought. With the Ice Dragon dead, his glittering brother in the far southwest was now the eldest and probably the most powerful of the reigning Kings.

He was letting his mind wander again. It was something he had begun doing more and more since first sailing with the Gryphon. The latter called it free thought, an ability that had allowed humanity to rise and spread the way it had. Morgis had reminded him that Toma was a free thinker. That had started a discussion that . . .

He was doing it *again!* With great deliberation, the duke forced his attention to the crystal. The sending would be weak, Morgis knew from past experience, but it had not originally been ensorceled for such a vast distance.

The drake concentrated, willing his mind to seek that of his sire. There was a time difference to consider, but he doubted it would play a major role at the moment. Still, the duke did not want to disturb the Dragon King from his slumber if it was at all possible.

The image refused to come. He had an impression of mist—no, a dense fog—that seemed to shroud the Dream Lands from the outside world. Morgis cursed. Was that why the keepers had left him the crystal? Did they know it would not work?

Abruptly, he made contact with something else. What it was he could not tell, but it was a kindred spirit of sorts. Draconian in nature and so overwhelming that the duke was almost forced to cut the connection himself.

It was a mind and more. The mind of a dragon, but what a dragon!

Then the connection gave way to another image. An image of a gate—the Gate—and the Gryphon standing before it, arms raised. After a brief time, the lionbird lowered his arms and looked behind him, most likely at the female who had accompanied him, Morgis thought sourly. He had a healthy distrust of females, being a drake. If a female drake did not have young to care for, she was often out trying to seduce a male or, worse yet, trying to seduce a human. He could not see what fascination the latter had for the females; it was not just because they could be tasty . . . not that the duke had ever tasted human flesh. The Blue Dragon kept such things to a minimum. It was why his own humans were so honestly loyal.

The Gryphon turned back, a look of consternation on his avian face. Something dark and shadowy was leaping at him—

A pale hand came down and smashed the crystal from his hand. It struck the floor sharply and cracked. A shoe crushed it to fine powder.

Morgis gazed up into the emptiness that was the face of the not-people.

He was not fooled by its soft appearance. The power of the creatures had already made its impression on him. He was not without power of his own, however. Spells had been prepared for just such an occasion, and the first of these the drake unleashed almost automatically. Eyes that saw into the other world where the spectrum of power lay watched as a portion was manipulated and bands of force sought out the ghoulish intruder.

It was impossible to say if the thing could see as humans and drakes did, but the not-person—a tiny part of the duke's mind cursed the Master Guardians for not giving these monstrosities a real name—looked down at its body and seemed to study what the drake was doing. As his control strengthened, Morgis allowed himself a slight smile.

The blank-faced creature stepped through his bands as if they were naught but illusion. The bands closed upon themselves and disintegrated.

Very bad, Morgis thought absently. *Very bad, indeed.*

He let loose with another, more violent spell. Subtlety was a thing of the past; preservation was important at all cost. What he unleashed would tear apart the front half of his room and scatter his adversary in a dozen different directions.

At least, that was what it was supposed to do.

The air around the intruder sparkled brilliantly, blinding the drake. He covered his eyes and stumbled back. The explosion that should have resulted from his spell did not follow.

Morgis was not a subtle being, but he began wracking his mind for some trick with which to take out the not-person. The magical assault had failed miserably. Perhaps, he thought quickly, the physical was called for. Shifting to his dragon form would leave him open far too long to attack. That left his sword—and the duke's prowess with a blade was well known in his region.

The sword was out in his next breath. He had gone beyond defending himself now. Morgis wanted the faceless creature's blood; it seemed likely that nothing short of that would save the drake. He was pleased to see that the robed figure had come to a halt when it became aware of his intentions; that meant that it recognized the blade as a true threat.

He smiled and lunged.

The not-person stretched out a soft, pale hand—and caught hold of the sharp edge of the blade. The specially honed edge, which, combined with the drake's strength, would have nearly cut through a three-foot-thick tree trunk, did not even so much as nick the intruder's palm.

The being pulled the blade toward it. The drake had the forethought to release his grip, at least; otherwise, he would have fallen into its arms. Even so, he was running out of both ideas and space. The faceless creature had slowly and methodically backed him into a corner. Morgis gave into the inevitable and swallowed his pride.

He shouted. At least, he tried. There was nothing wrong with his voice; he was certain of that. Yet, the shout came out as little more than a whisper. He did not have to guess who was responsible for that.

His backside struck against the wall. There was nowhere else to go. Morgis hissed. Very well. If the thing wanted him, it could have him—all of him. He lunged, clawed hands reaching for that blank visage, his form melting and reshaping, calling forth his birth shape. Morgis leered as his jaws widened and he lost all traces of humanity. Now it would be seen whether his assailant had taken on more than it had bargained for.

The hand that reached out and caught him by the face was the same one that had stopped his sharp, deadly blade with so little effort. It expended no more in bringing the drake to an abrupt halt, reversing the change in much the same way the mysterious Tzee had done. The duke's snarl became a cry of pain and he fell to his knees, once more in humanoid form. Fighting the agony, he reached up and tried to tear the other's hand away. He might have been trying to pry the entire Dragonrealm from the earth for all the success he had. Panic set in; Morgis had never come across so helpless a situation.

The not-person appeared to gaze down at its defeated opponent. There was no hint of satisfaction, no hint of anger. If anything, it seemed to be curious about him.

Morgis felt the world slip away.

The faceless being removed its hand and studied the blank-eyed drake. Morgis, oblivious of the world, remained on his knees, staring blindly ahead. The creature reached out with its left hand and drew a pattern on the duke's chest. Then, satisfied, the not-person stepped away, gazed without known sight at the room in general, and then quietly and calmly departed through the doorway.

Less than a minute passed before the drake rose and opened his eyes. He blinked once, then reached into one of his belt pouches.

His crystal was missing. Morgis thought for a moment and then took a step toward the rest of his belongings, his boots at one point stepping on the very spot where the object of his search had been crushed. Now there was no trace. Ignorant of this fact, Morgis searched thoroughly among his few items. At last, he gave up and sat on the edge of one of the chairs in the room. Apparently, he thought, the Master Guardians had recognized the crystal for what it was and decided to confiscate it.

Since there was evidently nothing he could do, Morgis rose from the chair and shifted over to the bed. On his way, he noted the odd placement of his sword on one of the other chairs. For the life of him, he could not recall taking it out. Chiding himself for his carelessness, he retrieved it and placed it where he could reach it on a moment's notice.

The bed was soft. Where a human would have never been able to rest comfortably in full armor, the drake had the advantage in that, since he was only mimicking it, he could adjust it as he needed. Morgis settled back and relaxed.

His last thought before drifting off to sleep was that he hoped the Gryphon would come back soon before boredom drove him crazy.

RUNNERS ARE VERY good at their tasks, and, when presented with a sudden, almost miraculous opportunity, they adapt easily. Thus it was that the first one to discover the open Gate was through it almost a breath later and his fellows were right behind him. It was also this adaptability that allowed the shadowy stalker to size up the situation and attack the nearest target all in the space of a few seconds. It was only the fact that the particular target was the Gryphon that spoiled an otherwise perfect execution of steps.

Where the dark shape assumed its victim would be was not where that would-be victim was in the next instant. The Gryphon had survived a period as a mercenary that had lasted longer than many humans lived. He had not survived through dumb luck. His already well-honed skills, in great part natural to him because of what he was, had reached a peak few could match. The lionbird had not allowed himself to grow soft, despite an equally lengthy period as monarch of a thriving region.

The Runner sailed over his head and landed gracefully some four yards behind him. Its eyes caught sight of the two figures watching from a short distance. A Master Guardian! The Runner, an indistinct, lupine shape, appeared to quiver with anticipation. How the Father would reward it. . . .

Under other circumstances, the Gryphon would have attempted to deal with the creature. His attention, however, was being demanded by several more of the eager, dark shapes, and his acute hearing had already informed him that the first Runner had chosen to attack Troia and Lord Petrac. He assumed that between the two of them they could handle one of the monstrosities. Considering he had at least half a dozen to himself, that was only fair.

The Runners were disconcerting horrors. He caught glimpses of teeth, of glowing, bloodred eyes, and forms akin to lean, swift predators. Yet, they were not ordinary animals. Runners mixed and passed through one another as if they had no substance or as if they were the same creature. If they attacked him, however, the Gryphon knew that they would feel all too real.

They were circling him, some clockwise, some counterclockwise. Four or five. He could really not say how many had come through the Gate before it had decided to close. At least one more must have gone past him to join the first in an attack on the lionbird's two companions. Another, the first to leap at him after the initial attack, was dead—or at least vanquished. The Gryphon had caught it with his claws as it had gone for his throat. Apparently, when solidifying to attack, the Runners were susceptible to retaliation.

He knew it was only a matter of moments before they would attack again. They were trying to cross him up, make him turn the wrong way at the wrong time so that one of them could catch him in a vulnerable spot. The others would close in on him while he fought off the first. It was a simple strategy, but an effective one. One that would have worked against most other adversaries, but not the Gryphon.

He was reaching into the realms of sorcery—a particular spell already in mind—when he noted something astonishing. The Runners awaited him there as well. At least, a portion of each of their minds lay in contact with the very powers he sought. If not for his careful attention, he would have ensnared himself there. He withdrew before the creatures' minds could take notice of him.

An intricate dilemma. The Runners watched on both levels, physical and magical, and knew what to wait for. If he attempted to use sorcery, they would have him. If he used physical force . . .

What? The one that had perished so far had died from a physical assault. Could it be that while the Runners could maintain watch on the two separate planes, they could only attack on the physical? Did that mean that at all other times they were merely harmless phantoms?

The entire thought process had taken place over a span of only a few seconds without taking any of his attention from the danger at hand. It was something he had developed to perfection through countless campaigns; the mercenary who could not think while in a life-and-death situation was one who died early.

There were sounds behind him, sounds of battle, but he knew it was too dangerous to turn for even a moment. Still, if what he had worked out was true, it was quite possible that he could turn the shadowy creatures' wraith-like ability to his advantage. If physically unable to touch him . . .

He let them circle twice more and then left his right side vulnerable. The Runners were intelligent, but they were still animals, not sentient creatures. Instinct took over and the nearest of the lupine forms leaped at his unprotected side.

With a speed impossible for most creatures, the Gryphon took hold of the startled Runner and, before it could phase back into incorporeality, threw it into its fellows. They, of course, still retained their own wraithlike states—which was exactly what he wanted. Even before the airborne Runner regained enough wits to act, the Gryphon had moved with the creature so that when it landed, he was already out of the circle. The Runners bayed, and the one that had been tricked tried to snap at the lionbird, forgetting that it no longer had solid form.

Free of the circle and having roused the anger of the Runners sufficiently, the Gryphon whirled and, snaring what power he could as quickly as possible, unleashed a sloppy, raw burst of energy at the nearest of his pursuers. The lead creature melted in the bright eruption of power, fading to nothing in midlunge. The one closest behind it had only enough time to begin a hasty halt before it, too, vanished like a pebble of ice tossed into a blazing bonfire.

A third of the indistinct, lupine forms succeeded in turning and dodging most of the blast, but the amount that caught him was enough to shear off his back end and both hind legs. The Gryphon was startled to discover that, despite its noncorporeal nature, a Runner bled when wounded badly. At least, something dark and moist poured freely from the rapidly dying monstrosity.

There were still two remaining Runners. They had apparently had enough time to consider their chances, which meant that they had turned tail and would escape momentarily unless he did something. In control of the situation now, he summoned up a spell from his memories and focused on the field in front of the two escaping horrors.

The grass approximately ten yards in front of the Runners bent toward the two with evident purpose. As he had thought, the Runners ignored the physical threat and continued on without ever breaking stride. He watched as the waving field enveloped them. When nothing reappeared, he nodded his satisfaction. As he had not wanted to cause any more damage to the field, he had cast a small gate behind the illusion of a physical attack. The Runners had gone through the gate without a moment's comprehension, and the portal had been designed to close the moment they were through.

Unfortunately for the Runners, there was no exit. The Gryphon had cast them out into the endless, empty Void, a dimension of nothingness that could swallow the entire world and still be no less sated. There was little chance the two creatures would ever find a way out before something else floating in the Void got them, wraithlike or not.

The Gryphon had conceived the trick after he and the Blue Dragon had almost suffered a similar fate at the claws of one of the Dragon King's own sons. The lionbird and the Dragon King had been using a gate much like this one (termed a blink hole for some ancient, obscure reason), and were just onto the path formed through the Void when the Blue Dragon's rebellious offspring had cut off the gate. Only experience and quick thinking had saved them. Morgis now held the title that had once belonged to that particular drake. The dead, after all, had little need for rank.

He recalled suddenly the two that had gone past him to attack Troia and Lord Petrac. The Gryphon paid no attention to the fact that his thoughts were first and foremost for her. If he had indeed noted them, he would have assumed it was because she was not a Master Guardian like the stag-headed Petrac.

To his relief, they seemed none the worse for wear, although the Will of the Woods looked oddly downcast. Troia was trying to soothe him about something. She looked up at the Gryphon's approach.

"He's never been like this before," the cat-woman whispered.

Petrac stirred. He raised his head to look at the lionbird. The deer visage only made his sadness that much more tragic. "Forgive me. As the Dream Lands wane, each violent action I take becomes more repulsive. They were horrors, true, but they lived, they savored life—such as it was. Can they help it if the Ravager made them what they are?"

The Gryphon had not considered it from that point of view, and he determined that he would not try to. War was terrible enough, but to consider the life of one's foe to the point where it threatened your own existence . . . it was a thought too disturbing. He knew that if it came down to his life and his beliefs against his enemy's, he would battle to protect them.

There were no black and white answers, he knew. The Gryphon mumbled something to that effect to Lord Petrac, but it sounded terribly incomplete even to him.

The Master Guardian had calmed. He nodded his thanks and managed to produce a weak smile. "I know we do what we must. The Ravager and his children, the Aramites, will not accept compromise. To give in meekly would be a fool's gamble. The wolf raiders would just trod on our corpses." He shook his head. "I cannot explain what came over me. When I raised my staff and cast them from existence, I was overwhelmed by the loss. I fear the long war is catching up with me."

Relief washed over the Gryphon. Things were bad enough without

having to try to take care of a morality-stricken Master Guardian. Petrac's
role was one he would never wish upon himself. He sighed and turned to
face the Gate once more.

The Gate had not changed appearance during the battle. The dark creatures on the sides continued to swarm up, down, and around. The heavy,
massive doors of the Gate were sealed shut. There was a faint glow surrounding the huge artifact.

Pleased with yourself? the Gryphon mentally raged at it. *Was that my judgment—letting in a pack of those terrors? What kind of games are you playing?*

He was not certain if the Gate was a direct part of the Dream Lands or
if it was merely a device created by someone long ago. Nevertheless, it was
the most solid thing at which he could direct his anger.

Troia took a step toward him. "Gryphon . . . no."

He shrugged off her warning. "Let me be. Lord Petrac has his burdens
to shoulder; I've got a few burdens to dispose of. Just what are we protecting here? Do the Dream Lands really care about us? I want some answers."

The Gryphon stalked toward the Gate. When he was within three yards
of it, it winked out of existence, leaving him to stare at a few wild trees and
more field.

Yet, before it vanished, he had a glimpse of something—as if whatever
it was had chosen that moment to send some sort of message through. He
might have been imagining it, he knew. It had only been for a second, and
the Gryphon could not have described it save to say it gave the impression
of being huge and powerful. Not the Ravager. He would have recognized
the foulness of that creature. No, this was something more.

And it was imprisoned. Bonds of vast skill had been weaved about it; the
Gryphon had felt that, too.

Old memories teased at him from the recesses of his mind. Like so many
of those that hinted at dire need and events of great import, they turned
and buried themselves once more within the mire of his unconsciousness.
He was left standing there, quietly and bitterly cursing himself for returning to a land that threatened to make the Dragonrealm seem peaceful and
understanding.

Now, more than ever, he was determined to go to Canisargos—even if it
meant confronting the Ravager himself.

With his luck, he knew, it probably would.

IX

Dark as the room was, it could not mask the anger of the figure seated in the lone chair.

D'Rak glared down at the young keeper he had ordered to monitor the Runners' moves during his rest. The other Aramite was bowed in cowering obeisance. Senior keeper D'Rak was not known for his kind mercy.

"What do you mean, more than half the pack has vanished?"

The associate keeper, mindful of the fates of some of his predecessors, carefully kept his eyes focused on his own feet. "Master, it is as I said. One minute, they were all there; the next, there were only three."

"And you saw nothing?" D'Rak clenched his fists in impotent fury. Runners lost! The Pack Master would be displeased—*very* displeased. What was worse was that it would only strengthen D'Shay's position. The keeper had hoped that a successful hunt would shake his rival's death-grip hold on his favored position.

"Nothing," his subordinate replied meekly for the third time. He was not concerned with power plays. He was only concerned with getting out with his skin still attached to his living body.

Muttering a number of dark curses concerning his underling's family tree, D'Rak closed his eyes to meditate on the sour turn of events. Nearly a full pack seemingly wiped from existence, the three survivors ignorant of what had occurred—they were animals, after all, despite their intelligence and cunning. Could it have anything to do with the incident in Luperion that had left a small city patrol dead? There had also been reports of increased activity among the not-people, those faceless sorcerers that the Ravager tolerated for some unknown reason. Still, those creatures had always been effectively neutral. Why change now? He knew a little about the Gryphon and his importance, but he suspected that the not-people knew much, much more—as did D'Shay. If they were playing a game, it was one of their own, for even the slightest hint of the Gryphon's true value would have had every guardian of the Dream Lands out looking for him.

The Ravager's spell, then, still held.

There had to be some way of saving face. Offering up the body of the incompetent young keeper was a step in the right direction, but it was far from sufficient. He could have the three remaining Runners scour the area for their brethren; they were already eager to do just that. Trouble was, from past experience he knew that they would find no clues. Still, the very disappearance of the creatures indicated that something was up. The denizens of the Dream Lands never bothered with Runners unless they had to.

He opened his eyes and stared down at the associate keeper who had wisely remained in the same position. "Summon the three surviving Runners back to the Kennels. Alert me when they have returned. I want the keeper in charge to probe their memories, conscious and unconscious. Dismissed."

"Master." The younger Aramite backed out, outwardly unemotional but inwardly jubilant. He did not know that his sacrifice was already ordained. D'Rak planned on cutting his losses as much as possible.

It was nearing that time when he and D'Shay would be at each other's throats, and he knew that for him it was an uphill struggle. He was not concerned over his adversary's special place in the hierarchy of the empire; if D'Shay could not defend himself in the subtleties of Aramite political intrigue, all the favor in the world would gain him little aid from the Ravager. Survival of the fittest.

Still, it would be nice to have something to present to the council that would wipe the perpetual smirk off D'Shay's visage. The senior keeper sighed. It was time to display his own claws, to show the others in the council what a force he truly was to be reckoned with. Most of them knew, but it was always good to give them a reminder.

With no more than a thought, he summoned the Eye of the Wolf from its hidden resting place. The planning for this moment stretched back more than two years—two years since that accidental contact with them. That contact led to the other outsider, the one with the amazing proposition. D'Rak had scoffed at it at the time, believing it a trick, but subsequent months had proven the truth of the offer. In the past few weeks, it had become his top priority, something he had been holding back for the best opportunity available.

D'Rak placed his hands over the top of the crystal and performed the necessary patterns. Another keeper would have noticed intricate differences in each major pattern, and the order of those major patterns would have differed from standard teaching. They had to be; there was no way he could contact his "allies" and still maintain a cloak of secrecy otherwise. There was also the little fact that the minds of the creatures were so different, so alien in their own patterns, that normal procedures would not even have drawn their attention.

He knew he had made contact when the whispering began. D'Rak allowed it to grow, hearing both their name and his own and knowing from past experience that this was necessary for the things. Secretly, the Tzee disgusted him, but they had their uses, the most important of which was their own connection to the one he sought. If the Tzee performed their function, they would be rewarded—and then crushed. An abomination was an abomination, especially when it was no longer of any use.

Tzee . . . Tzee. . . . The whispering built up to such a frenzy that it could hardly be called whispering anymore. D'Rak was thankful he had cast a spell to deaden such noise. He did not want to draw attention to himself. Even the slightest rumor would make its way to D'Shay, who had an amazing knack for drawing out the truth.

A tiny black dot materialized in the middle of the Eye. Slowly, it swelled, like some disease, becoming a black cloud from which countless tiny eyes seemed to stare out in every direction. This was not the true form of the Tzee; they had no true form that he knew of. This was merely how the Eye chose to perceive them—and how the crystal perceived them was based on the mind operating it. He smiled. They looked disgusting, all right. The senior keeper would be happy to be rid of them.

The keeper allowed the Tzee to build to a moderate strength and then quickly imposed his will upon them. It would not be unlike the nebulous colony of creatures to try their hands—or whatever they used—at a little betrayal. He knew they coveted the Eye of the Wolf, among other things. It was what had brought about initial contact. What they wanted it for, he could not discover. That alone, however, was enough reason to maintain a wary vigilance. Any idea the Tzee protected with such secrecy was one that promised dire fates for anyone else. Besides, he thought wryly, it would have been truly ironic to have prepared for his confrontation with D'Shay for so long only to fall prey at the last moment to a living mass of insubstantial paranoia calling themselves the Tzee.

The Tzee were not pleased with his reaction, but they knew better than to struggle. D'Rak eased off his control just a bit. Enough to seem willing to give in a little, but not enough to endanger himself. He had not reached and maintained his position by behaving like a fool.

Over a period of less than a minute, the Tzee related their message to him. The senior keeper's demeanor altered from disgust and disdain to near glee. Where his own aides had failed him at every turn, the Tzee—the damned annoying, insufferable Tzee!—had given him far more information than he could have dreamed!

The Gryphon and one other were indeed here! Foolishly, the Tzee had jumped right in, never planning properly, thinking that their insipid displays would be sufficient, and, of course, failing miserably in the end. He did not relay these thoughts to the Tzee, of course. They had provided him with much of value.

He digested the information over and over in his mind. The Tzee queried whether he still sought contact with the traitor within the Dream Lands. It was odd that the Tzee never saw *themselves* as traitors. Then again, they were merely following their own coarse nature. D'Rak thought for a moment, then broke contact, watching uninterestedly as the image of the whispering mass dissipated. Courtesy was not something the Tzee understood. It was simple enough for them to know that he obviously did not want to include the third party at this time.

D'Rak rose, joyful. He waved one hand over the Eye, returning it to the place that only he knew of. At last, he had his rival. What had seemed a terrible loss of prestige had become his most powerful weapon.

Various creatures he had collected and caged stirred uneasily as he passed out of his private chambers and into his miniature court. The keepership was semireligious, being connected so deeply with the Ravager. As a symbol of the keepership's influence, especially since he had taken office—murdered his way, actually—he held court twice a week. Court consisted of petitions by novices on up for an increase in status. It also consisted of trial for those who had failed, those in the empire found wanting in loyalty, and special cases where only the skills of a keeper could unlock the truth.

Several wolf-visage masks glanced briefly his way and then turned quickly away as the guardsmen snapped to attention. They were handpicked. D'Rak knew that his rival had spies within the keepers' organization, but not among these men. They owed their very lives to him. If he died, they died. It was similar to a Ravager's Tooth, the artifact used by most keepers to monitor soldiers in a particular Pack, only the blood of the individual served a second purpose. Not only did it allow the senior keeper to maintain contact with his own underlings, but it had created a life-bond between them. If that life-bond was severed, they died. D'Rak was careful not to have it a two-way bond. He did not like the thought of suddenly keeling over because one of his guards had fallen victim to a knife in the throat during an off-duty street fight.

"D'Altain."

"Master?" A short, narrow figure materialized at his side. D'Altain had survived for years as one of the senior keeper's top aides solely because of his fanatical desire for efficiency. The underling rubbed a scraggly beard and bowed low. D'Rak was not fooled; he knew that beneath the cowardly exterior was a calculating mind. That suited him fine as long as D'Altain remembered his place.

The guards stirred uneasily at someone being so near their master. There was nothing to worry about, however. With his own prowess with the sword and the nearby protection of so many able men, any physical attack would fail. As an added measure, the senior keeper was covered from head to toe in a complex arrangement of wards that he himself had designed.

"D'Altain, I want you to cancel court tomorrow. I'm going to be much too busy. Do you think there'll be anything you would have trouble rescheduling?" Utilizing the tone of his voice, D'Rak hinted that there had better not be.

"No, master. I shall take care of it immediately." The aide did not depart, sensing, perhaps, that something was still on the senior keeper's mind.

D'Rak turned and made his way to a balcony overlooking the capital proper. The massive city of Canisargos seemed to go on forever—or at least to the horizon. It was a breathtaking sight, the more so because of his own power over so many people. A power that would soon grow.

"Master?" D'Altain had seen his master this happy only twice before, and neither of those two occasions had left pleasant memories. The aide personally thought D'Shay and D'Rak deserved each other. He squashed the thought instantly, knowing that the senior keeper often had others secretly probing the minds of those around him for loose, possibly traitorous thoughts. Not to mention thoughts that he found merely insulting.

D'Rak nodded, more to himself than to his second. "I want two teams of keepers, working in coordination, monitoring an area surrounding the royal district."

"We have such a team already."

"Then we will have another. Besides, I have special instructions for them. One more thing . . ."

"Master?" D'Altain tried to keep the misery from his face. D'Rak was planning something of major proportions. That meant that someone would die at some point. It always did in Aramite politics.

"I want a special team—handpicked sensitives—to go to Qualard and await my instructions."

"Qualard? The ancient capital?"

The senior keeper gave him a rueful but threatening smile. "Careful, D'Altain. Qualard was still the capital when I was born."

Only a handful of the upper rank still lived who recalled the city of Qualard as a flourishing metropolis. Only D'Shay really knew everything that had happened the night it came tumbling down. D'Rak knew some, and what he knew he considered enough for his plans.

An idea struck him. "Have the sensitives marked."

"Marked?" This time, the other Aramite could not keep the surprise from his face. "But that means . . ."

"There will be no further use of their services when this is done."

"Yes, master."

"Dismissed, D'Altain. Do not tarry and, above all else, do not fail me in these tasks."

"I will not." The aide scurried away.

D'Rak watched him depart, the ghost of a smile briefly making an appearance on the senior keeper's face. Then he turned his attention back to the city and its milling crowds. Thousands of people, many of them among the controlling forces of the Ravager's empire. All going about their business as he watched them—and watched over them.

The smile returned, this time lingering for quite some time.

A BRIEF PASSAGE of time, ending with the disruptive clang of metal upon metal as D'Shay closed the cell door behind him. He had gotten nearly all the information he could out of his prisoner. It had been an intricate wolf-and-fox game, with D'Shay's hands tied because he wanted his prisoner in one piece, and his prisoner knew that. Now, though, he suspected the fountain of knowledge had at last run dry. A good thing, too, for D'Shay had begun to notice a graying of his own skin, the first sign that time was catching up to him.

Two armored figures stood by the cell. From far away, they would be taken as Aramite soldiers wearing wolfhelms. Close up? D'Shay smiled, looking much like the images of the wolf god he obeyed. Anyone foolish enough to come down here deserved what they got.

Another armored figure coldly stalked up to him and held out an oval crystal, a crystal that D'Shay's agents had pirated out of D'Rak's citadel, his self-styled empire within an empire. He took the artifact from the servant, who continued to stare in his direction. What the wolfhelm did not obscure revealed only darkness, as if the suit of armor was empty. D'Shay knew better, though.

He waved a hand in dismissal and waited until the servant had departed. Raising the crystal to his face, he stared into it, concentrating. Another visage appeared. D'Altain, his spy, his traitor in the ranks of the fool who would dare be his rival. D'Shay enjoyed turning his rivals' own people against them. It was a tribute, of sorts, to that day when he had turned on the Dream Lands and its inconsistency for the power of the Ravager.

"Speak."

D'Altain relayed everything he had either been told or overheard. D'Shay's mind raced, different ideas raised, pursued, and dropped as his spy continued. When it was over, he broke contact with the treacherous aide without a word, his thoughts deeply ensconced in what his rival was plotting.

He handed the crystal back to the dark, armored servant. It departed as silently as it had arrived.

Qualard. While it was not forbidden to go there, it certainly was not something the Ravager would have approved of had he been asked. Still, if the senior keeper could justify his actions, the savage, lupine god might not only agree, he might reward D'Rak for his vigilance.

It must be the Gryphon, D'Shay thought. No one else would create such an interest in the rubble that was all that remained of the former capital. Add to that the interesting fact that the keepers had lost nearly an entire Runner pack. As much as he distrusted D'Rak as a person, he could not fault the man's abilities. The senior keeper was up to something, perhaps even the major confrontation between the two of them that they both knew would someday come.

D'Shay had been walking while he pondered the new developments, and his travels soon took him to the nearest thing he could call a home. He did not sleep like normal beings. Therein lay his true advantage over his rival and all former rivals. No matter what his power, they still believed him one of them now. Long-lived, yes, but that could just as easily have been a reward for serving the Ravager well. He had sorcery—of a sort—but no one knew the true extent of his abilities or how much he had lost that day he had turned on his former comrades.

The room was decorated sparsely, its occupant having little interest in frivolities. Various trophies of past victories, artifacts gathered—a moderately sized but potentially powerful display.

Two creatures hissed fiercely from cages in the room. D'Shay had had to separate them when it became apparent they would kill one another. Savage creatures made the more savage by his careful mistreatment of them. One of the monsters spread its wings as best it could in the cramped quarters and let loose with a cry that was a mixture of a bird of prey's battle call and the roar of a deadly, huge cat.

They were his special treat for the Gryphon, these creatures. They were the beasts from which the lionbird had taken his title, the true gryphons. Trained for one purpose—to seek out one of their own and tear him to shreds. A poetic piece of work, in D'Shay's opinion. This particular pair represented the tenth generation he had bred, and it pleased him that such perfect killers would be granted the opportunity.

D'Shay leaned toward one of the cages. "What is it you wish to do?"

"Kill! Kill!" the gryphon parroted. The other joined in, recognizing a call that was natural to it, thanks to its owner.

"Kill! Kill!"

The wolf raider let the two monsters squawk several times before calling for quiet. It was an example of his power over them that they grew silent almost instantly. Despite their bravado, the two animals feared him as they feared no other creature—which proved how advanced their powers of reasoning actually were.

Like some birds, they could be trained to repeat dozens of phrases on command, and D'Shay had taught them a variety, all designed to strike at the mind of the Gryphon.

"He is the last of the old guardians, your cousin is," he whispered to the creatures, which stared at him with baleful eyes. "The last of the misfits, the true children of the Dream Lands. The rest . . ." D'Shay waved a hand as if dismissing them. The gryphons cowered, fearing he was about to strike them. He chuckled. ". . . A race of usurpers, also-rans. Not half the power he truly controls—if he could only remember." His eyes lit up with a fiery passion. "The last of the *lizard's* get, the last danger to my existence and that of the lord I serve. With him gone, the bonds are eternal."

The gryphons' feathers and fur were bristling at the tone in his voice. He switched to a tone of soothing that fooled no one and that he expected to fool no one with. It was a mockery, nothing more.

"Do good, children, and I'll reward you as no other has ever been rewarded. Perhaps I'll feed you a nice, plump senior keeper—if he hasn't rotted away by that time."

He did not lie to himself; the Ravager would turn on him if D'Rak proved more efficient, more . . . predatory. The senior keeper was the exact opposite personality of D'Laque, the keeper who had accompanied D'Shay across the seas to the Dragonrealm. Losing D'Laque had been costly in more than one way. The keeper had been powerful; he had also proven accessible and would have made a good ally if he had returned. A mistake that had cost D'Shay much favor with his lord.

No, he thought sourly, *I cannot underestimate you, D'Rak. Despite his words of praise to me, the Lord Ravager has great interest in you as well. Perhaps it is because you and I are so much alike . . . just as the Gryphon and I are so much alike . . . that we are destined to bare our fangs against one another. A pity. Together we might have even toppled a god.*

At the last thought, D'Shay scanned the room guiltily. Gods were notorious for their great ears even when the words were thought and not spoken. He glanced at his slightly grayed flesh once more. Now of all times he dared not annoy his lord. Not until he had passed from this suit of flesh to the next. Not yet, though. To transfer too soon would leave him too weak—and with both D'Rak and the Gryphon meddling in things, that could prove fatal to him.

One of his two prized pets squawked angrily, a garbled "Kill!" escaping from its beak. They were waiting for a chance to stretch their wings, and even their fear of their master could not hold back their eagerness.

As if on cue, two of the armored servants dragged a naked, stinking form in. A convict, most likely. D'Shay generally asked for convicts; they had a survival trait that made them perfect exercise for the gryphons.

D'Shay stalked over to the glaring figure, reached out a gauntleted hand, and harshly pulled the man's head back by the hair. For a second, he imagined the eagle visage of his oldest adversary and former companion.

"We're going to play a little game," he finally began. "A game that *could* offer you freedom . . ."

X

LORD PETRAC INSISTED that they come with him to the grove where he made his home, if only to stay long enough to eat something. The Gryphon was chafing to return to Sirvak Dragoth and be on his way to Canisargos, but Troia quietly implied that what the Will of the Woods offered was an honor few received. Though Lord Petrac was a Master

Guardian and friend to the forest around them, he was still a private soul. Even his fellow Master Guardians had to contact him prior to any desired visitation.

It turned out, however, that Petrac was not the only inhabitant of that particular grove. Much to the surprise of both of his guests, there also existed what passed for a village in the Dream Lands, the first one that the Gryphon could recall seeing. It could only be called a village because of the fact that there were contrived habitats and a population of at least three dozen. The Gryphon was at a loss as to whether the people were elves or some mixture of elf and human. They did not resemble the elves or half-elves he knew, but it was known that the race came in more than one size and was as diverse in society as humans. At least these did not seem to resemble the more annoying, tinier wood elves that their taller brethren referred to as sprites.

They were fair in face and form, as an old saying the Gryphon knew went. Out here, among the wonders of nature, they went more or less un-clothed. What little they did wear—and it was little enough to make Troia appear overdressed—was purely decorative and usually of a color that com-plemented the colors of the grove itself. The Gryphon and Troia received only cursory glances and friendly smiles, but the presence of Lord Petrac was enough to send a few to their knees in what the lionbird could not help thinking was rather imperialistic homage to the stag-headed guardian.

They had barely passed through the village when Petrac stretched out his arms and said, "Here we are. Do you like it?"

From past experience with other dwellers of the forest, the Gryphon had come to expect something combining nature with civilization. Cabe and Gwen Bedlam lived in the Manor, a vast, ancient home that was a comple-ment of stone and the trunk of a massive tree. It was difficult to say where the stone ended and the tree began, so skillfully had the original craftsmen worked. He had expected the Will of the Woods to be housed in something at least as grand.

What the Master Guardian called his home was no more than a tiny, open field in which, from vegetable matter, had been formed an overhang. The wall of plant life was uncomfortably close in design to that constructed by the Tzee, the Gryphon noticed, but here it served a more benevolent pur-pose. Crude chairs of straw and wood created a primitive court of sorts with a large couch obviously serving Petrac's personal needs. There was a bowl of fresh fruit, twigs, leaves, and such on a waist-high, flat rock next to the couch. The Gryphon glanced from the bowl to his host, realizing then that the stag aspect of the guardian was more than just show. He wondered how the human part coped with such a diet.

"Please. Be seated. Have some fruit." Lord Petrac took Troia's arm and led her forward. Like the Gryphon, she was at a loss. From the expression on her face, it was evident that she had expected a more regal residence for one she respected so much. From her side, the lionbird watched as her mouth tightened. He knew that she was assuming there was an unfairness about the situation. Haggerth and Mrin/Amrin lived in the vast, elegant Sirvak Dragoth, while Petrac eked out an existence in a place that could not possibly give him shelter from a moderately strong rain. The Gryphon hardly expected that was the case, but he decided it was best left up to the Will of the Woods to explain such things.

Lord Petrac led the feline woman to one of the chairs and aided her in sitting down, an act that revealed how much she respected him. The Gryphon doubted she would have acted so demurely with anyone else. Oddly, he felt a pang of jealousy, but it was forgotten when he noticed that Troia's chair was *moving*. No, it was *changing*. Unprepared for this, she was clinging on for dear life, as if expecting to be thrown off any minute.

The Will of the Woods laughed, a surprisingly deep laugh at that. "It is only adjusting itself to your contours. I suggest you relax; it will finish sooner if you stop fidgeting."

The Gryphon turned to study the chair beside him. Like the others, it appeared to be a crudely made piece of furniture. He wondered if it had been designed that way, or whether this was merely a sample of the guardian's sense of humor. With some reluctance, he seated himself. The sensation beneath him was astonishingly pleasant. It was warm and soft and, if he remained relaxed, shaped itself perfectly to fit his form. When he found it to his liking, he nodded his approval to his host. Troia, still fidgeting, fumed in his direction.

"Fruit? I apologize for not offering you any meat, but you will, I hope, understand."

Friend that he was to the wildlife of the forest, slaughtering an animal for food probably would have seemed like murder to the Master Guardian. He understood the needs of others, though, and knew that many of the animals he befriended hunted one another when his influence was far away.

Eyeing the piece of fruit, the Gryphon debated over proprieties and finally shifted to the more convenient human form. Lord Petrac watched almost uninterestedly, but Troia stared as if the lionbird had turned into the Tzee. She had never seen him eat and, therefore, did not know of either his ability to shift shape or preference for a human body for certain things.

"You are a versatile being, Gryphon," the Master Guardian commented as he chose a piece of fruit for himself.

"That's the same face you wore when I captured you—only, that was illusion," Troia added.

"Based on fact. I find myself changing without thinking sometimes. This is the only other form I can transform into. Anything else requires great sorcery or intricate illusion. I'm sorry if I disturbed either of you."

"By no means," Petrac replied. He bit into a handful of grass and leaves, a disconcerting sight to both of his guests.

Troia's eyes appraised him. "It takes a little getting used to. Not bad, though."

The Gryphon allowed himself a smile. "Glad you approve."

To his surprise, she looked away, suddenly intent on the piece of fruit she held in her hands. He quickly changed the subject. "Lord Petrac, I do thank you for your hospitality, but I cannot stay. Regardless of the risk, I *must* go to Canisargos. D'Shay is the key to my background and, I believe, the key to much of the present crisis."

"The endless war of attrition, you mean."

"As you say. I grant you, he probably already knows I'm here, and he probably knows that the moment I discovered he was still alive I swore I would track him down."

"Then why bother going? He will have certainly set several novel traps. Shaidarol was always imaginative about such things."

The Gryphon hesitated, then replied, "Because the very fact that he knows I'm coming after him is my ticket for safe passage through the Aramite capital."

"What?" Troia looked up from the contemplation of her piece of fruit. "That's absurd!"

"Is it? D'Shay and I are very much alike in many ways. He wants me for himself, Troia. This is something personal. Forget the wolf raiders. D'Shay has made my life his, and I've begun to do the same with him."

"The deadliest wars are those fought between 'brothers,'" Lord Petrac commented. He shook his head. "The confrontation between you two could possibly prove more of a danger than the Ravager himself."

"Or it could be the end of the wolf raider threat. I want to know why they remember me and no one here does."

There was an uneasy silence after that which was not broken until a bird, a raven, landed suddenly on the left shoulder of the Master Guardian.

Lord Petrac stroked the bird. "I believe Haggerth must be concerned about the results of your 'judgment.'"

The Gryphon frowned. "It was pretty inconclusive, I would say."

"On the contrary, you faced off against a number of the Ravager's children and vanquished them all. You could have just as easily joined them and killed both of us—or tried to, anyway."

"He wouldn't have done that!" Troia spat, her claws out with astonishing speed. She looked down at them and grimaced. "I'm—I'm sorry."

"You believe in him, kitten, as do I." The Will of the Woods took the raven onto his right hand and whispered something to it. The bird squawked several times. Petrac nodded to himself and then whispered again. When he was finished, he held his hand high in the air and let the raven fly off.

"It *was* Haggerth. I think the message I give him will convince him. You have only one more problem, and that concerns your guide, one Jerilon Dane."

"Him!" This time, the feline did not apologize when she unsheathed her claws. "I lost clan to him! He had kittens butchered!"

"He did not. Yes, he is responsible for the deaths of many, but in battle. Jerilon Dane was one of the more civilized Aramite officers. That was his downfall. That was why he was made the fox in a Runner hunt. He failed to make any true headway—at least in the Pack's eyes—and he showed compassion, a trait the wolf raiders have been trying to breed out of their soldiers for centuries."

"I'll leave my judgment of him for when I've spoken to him," the Gryphon said. "Beings can change. Is that the problem? Don't they trust him?"

"Haggerth seems to. Mrin/Amrin . . . I suppose so. The other Master Guardians are not involved with this, and they would likely go along with what we decide. No, the problem is that Dane refuses to go back with you. He says that traveling with you is certain death for him. One miracle is enough. I cannot say I blame him, if you consider his point of view."

The Gryphon *was* considering the former wolf raider's point of view . . . and some of the intriguing possibilities his presence in the Dream Lands meant. "This man was an Aramite commander. High-ranking."

"He was."

He stood. "Then I have to beg your pardon and depart now, Lord

Petrac. Whether or not I can convince this man Dane to come with me to Canisargos, I have to speak to him, if only for my own sanity!"

The Master Guardian frowned as best his features allowed. "I don't follow your logic. . . ."

The Gryphon looked at Troia, but she shook her head, indicating her own lack of understanding. The former monarch of Penacles indicated both of them with his hands and said, "You two—no one in the Dream Lands retains any knowledge of me. It's been said time and time again."

"And it's very, very true," the Will of the Woods interjected. "Despite the fact that few of us are old enough to remember so long ago—the war has done what nature could not—some of us should have remembered."

"And who does remember?"

"Shaidarol, of course, but that's because—"

The Master Guardian broke off as the Gryphon nodded. "—Because he was one of the Ravager's servants. As Jerilon Dane was once." The Gryphon folded his arms and smiled without pleasure. "Jerilon Dane may hold the knowledge of my past, and I'll get it from him even if I have to wring it from him with my claws!"

"I CAN'T HELP you," the former wolf raider stated flatly. "There is nothing I can say to you."

There had been times during his long, colored past that the Gryphon had come close to losing all control. Times when the beast within him had threatened to take permanent control. He prided himself on having never given in completely, although there had been a few occasions where he had teetered on the brink.

He reached such a point now.

They had assembled in the chamber where Haggerth and Mrin/Amrin had questioned him the first time. Aside from the two Master Guardians, there were nearly a dozen others. Many were not-people—or "the Faceless Ones," as Morgis, who disliked the awkwardness of the other title, had started calling them—who waited with their seeming indifference for whatever outcome arose from this meeting. Morgis and Troia were there also. Two other figures of significance to the situation were there as well. One was yet another of the Master Guardians, a thin, balding man who sported a long flute. He sat to one side of his counterparts and said nothing. Neither Haggerth nor Mrin/Amrin made any attempt to introduce him to the others.

The remaining person in the room was, of course, the former wolf raider Jerilon Dane.

Dane was not a cowardly man. While he was younger than the lionbird had expected, he carried the look of a man who had spent years on or near the front, a look the Gryphon saw every time he looked in a mirror. If he was not a coward, then he was holding back because he had no desire to tell what he knew.

The Gryphon had reverted to his normal form, and he made use of his predatory appearance. Reaching out with one clawed hand, he pulled the veteran commander by the front of his shirt and dragged him until the Aramite's nose came within an inch of his very sharp beak. To his credit, Dane did nothing more but swallow very loudly.

"You"—the Gryphon emphasized each word precisely—"will tell me what it is about myself that so concerns your former masters and has been stolen from the memories of my own people, or I will show you exactly why the gryphon of the wild is a beast most others learn to shun—even the largest of the other predators."

Jerilon Dane gave him a dangerous sneer, dangerous to the Aramite for daring to do it at all. The former wolf raider reached up and purposefully removed the hand from his shirt. The Gryphon's mane had risen, and the urge to strike out was becoming difficult to ignore. Yet, Dane still pretended that there was little danger to him.

From behind them, Haggerth said, "There will be no bloodshed in this chamber, Gryphon. Even if it means we strike you down by some other means."

"There won't be any need for *that*," the Aramite snorted. "If the misfit will just *listen* instead of squawking, he would understand what I'm saying."

"I understand quite well, scavenger."

Now it was Dane who bristled, albeit in a different fashion, of course. "You are *not* listening! I can't tell you what you want to know, because I can't remember any of it now!"

The Gryphon stepped back in shock. No one else was making a sound. It was even impossible to detect any breathing.

"What?" was all that the lionbird finally succeeded in blurting out.

Jerilon Dane sneered again. "From the moment I first woke in one of the rooms in this citadel, I knew there were gaps in my memory. Things I had been willing to offer in exchange for asylum—including things dealing specifically with you, as a matter of fact. When I realized what had happened,

I stalled, fearing that the lords of Sirvak Dragoth would return me to the Runners."

"We would never do that," Haggerth assured him.

"None of you has grown up under the rule of the Pack Master or, for that matter, the Lord Ravager. I couldn't be certain. I thought maybe that some of you had retained some piece of knowledge—that's a thought held by many on the council, if I recall *that* correctly."

"There have been many casualties among the elder guardians," Mrin/Amrin commented bitterly. There was a personal conflict inherent in the tones of both his voices, but he did not elaborate and no one wanted to bring it up.

Dane nodded. "Then you are even worse off than we imagined. What I can remember is that there was always the fear that you *people*"—the sarcasm in his voice was unconscious, a throwback to his life as a wolf raider— "would—would—would . . ." He took a deep breath. "I find it hard to formulate the thought even from what has been explained to me and what I can deduce—*that you would search for and find whatever it was that was so important to your cause.*"

The former officer cursed at the exhausting effort of merely making the statement. "I—I'm sorry. That's the best I can do."

"Very strong sorcery," Haggerth muttered.

"Impossibly strong," added Mrin/Amrin.

The other Master Guardian stroked his flute and nodded, nothing more.

Jerilon Dane smiled bitterly. "Can you expect any less from my Lord Ravager?"

"You would do best to remember that he is no longer your lord, Aramite," Troia hissed. It was quite obvious she cared nothing for the man.

"I shall endeavor to do so."

"We can do without futile bickering," the Gryphon interrupted. "What we need is a direction to turn. A course of action. Canisargos."

"I already stated that I will *not* go back there. Luperion is nothing compared to Canisargos. When it became the capital after Qualard's destruction, the keepers were ordered to enshroud the city in such a complex web of sorcery that not even the least of a hearth witch's market wares would escape notice. Can you imagine what your materialization in or near the city would do? More alarms would sound—silent to all save the keepers, of course—than if the Ravager himself had come calling."

"You remember that much, do you?"

"My *former* lord," Dane replied with a glance at Troia, "apparently sees nothing wrong with advertising such precautions."

"I sssshould sssay not," Morgis hissed, so disturbed by events of late that he was allowing his speech patterns to slip. He corrected himself immediately. "Such a defense would be very costly, but certainly effective."

"It *was* costly. I understand most of the keepers involved died under the pressure of binding it."

"More likely they met with 'accidents,'" the drake concluded. "Not an uncommon practice in some places."

The Gryphon eyed his companion closely. In retrospect, it should not have surprised him that such things were practiced by the drakes. The gods knew that more than a few humans had eliminated the possibility of secrets leaking out by eliminating the only other possessors of that knowledge.

Something clicked in his mind. "You mentioned Qualard. The old capital."

Dane shrugged. "What of it?"

More than one of the Faceless Ones—the lionbird found the drake's phrase more comfortable—seemed to stir at talk of the devastated city. They were only slight movements, a flicker of a finger or the twitch of the body, but the Gryphon, a veteran predator, could read the change in the normally ambivalent creatures. He decided to press on.

"What happened to Qualard?"

"Even I can answer that," Troia said, one clawed hand running leisurely along her thigh. The Gryphon forced himself to keep his eyes on her face. "The wolf raider leaders at that time had failed their doggy god miserably. He punished them—and everyone else in the city. Goes to show what a great mind the dog soldiers obey."

The ex-raider whitened, but then remembered where he was. He nodded. "More or less, that's the truth."

The Gryphon was not so sure. "Seems a little extreme, even for what little I recall of what the Ravager is supposed to be like."

"If there's anything else, I can't recall."

"Do you recall how long ago it happened?"

That brought a slight smile. "I'm not an elder like you, bird. Before my time. Still . . . at least a couple of centuries, I think."

"About right," the Gryphon muttered. He reached up a hand and rubbed his neck in thought.

"What is it?" Mrin/Amrin asked Haggerth. "What bird-brained pattern of thought is he following now?"

Haggerth shrugged, but it was possible a smile was hidden beneath his veil. Certainly, he did not seem to share his fellow guardian's worries.

The third Master Guardian, not asked for an opinion, took out a cloth and began to polish the intricate designs on his flute.

"Dane, do you know anything about the layout of Qualard? I know it's unlikely, but—"

"I do, Gryphon."

"You do?"

"Part of military history. In the early days, it saw its share of war. Some of the greatest battles were fought near it. I admit I studied a little more deeply than necessary, but until its fall, Qualard was considered impregnable."

Mrin/Amrin muttered something unintelligible. He did not seem inclined to repeat himself, so no one bothered to ask him.

The Gryphon turned back to the Master Guardians. "With your permission, I've changed my mind. I'd like to go to Qualard."

"Of what use would it be to go to the ruins of a city dead these past two centuries?" Mrin/Amrin asked disdainfully. "It hardly seems that anything of value would remain after so long."

"That may be true. Do I have your permission?"

Haggerth looked at Mrin/Amrin, who shrugged both sets of shoulders in surrender. The veiled guardian turned to the Gryphon. "I don't see why not. I doubt forbidding you to go would keep you from finding a way. Still, Qualard may itself be dead, but you could encounter something that scavenges in the ruins. Even the Aramites tend to steer clear of the place."

There was a glint in the lionbird's eyes that old comrades, such as his former second-in-command Toos (now supposedly King Toos I of Penacles), would have recognized. It was a glint that hinted of what had made the Gryphon successful as a commander and had earned him the respect of any man who served him. "Which is one of the reasons I want to go. Something occurs to me—or maybe it's a memory nagging at me." He held up a hand to forestall what he knew the Master Guardian was going to say. "This would best be done with as few as possible. I've no desire to pull anyone away from their duties. We've not been attacked, besides Runners, since I've been here, but I suspect you've been defending against an assault of sorts all this time."

At that, the guardian with the flute looked up. He did nothing more, merely looked up at the Gryphon.

Haggerth nodded, his veil fluttering slightly. It was weighted in the bottom to prevent breezes from pushing it aside and revealing what no one wanted revealed. "Keepers hound us day and night, though that has lessened a little lately. They cannot touch the Dream Lands itself, but their power strikes at individuals, sapping our strength slowly but surely, as if their soldiers were marching on us. I fear that the stalemate is truly at an end. Senior Keeper D'Rak, who may be D'Shay's only true rival for power, wants this to be a victory for his kind. It is a precursor, I suspect, for a major assault on both the physical and magical planes."

The Gryphon nodded. "I thought as much. If there is no objection, I'd like to take Jerilon Dane and Duke Morgis and leave it at that."

Haggerth looked at the former wolf raider, who closed his eyes in thought and finally, reluctantly, nodded. Apparently, Qualard was a much safer prospect in his mind, and he no doubt knew that, one way or another, he was going to end up traveling with the Gryphon somewhere.

"Very well," the Master Guardian began. Troia cut him off.

"Master Haggerth, Master Mrin/Amrin." She did not mention or even glance at the third member of the august group, who was at that moment back to work on his flute. "If I may, we are sending out two who are unfamiliar—or can't remember—with the way of things in the empire of the Ravager. They are being led by one whose loyalties are recent—which is, of course, not to say I distrust him," she added quickly.

Morgis, who had moved nearer the Gryphon, whispered sarcastically, "Oh, no. By no means is she saying such a thing."

"Hush."

"We need to send one of our own, especially if there is need to return quickly. There is some question as to whether they can summon the Gate if needed. I volunteer to be that one."

"You?" Haggerth asked needlessly. He did not even turn to his counterparts. "Very well. Go. All of you. Go before anything *else* comes up."

"Geas," Mrin/Amrin called out, and the Gryphon realized it was not just a word, but the name of the third Master Guardian. The man looked up indifferently. "Can you bring the Gate here?"

Geas nodded and put the flute to his lips. He began to play a melody. As it developed, those hearing it for the first time felt a stirring, as if a wayward child were being called back by a loving parent—or perhaps a wayward parent being called by a loving child. As the guardian played, his face grew flushed, but it was not due to exertion but some deep emotion.

The not-people took hold of the Gryphon, Jerilon Dane, and Morgis and pulled them aside. The air began to ripple not far from where the three had stood. A tall, wide blotch began to form from the ripple.

"Couldn't we have made a gate of our own?" the Gryphon asked Troia, who had just joined them.

"None of us have been to the city. This is the only sure method. The Gate"—the capital letter was quite evident in her tone—"does not need to have been there."

"Why not use it against Canisargos?"

"There are limits to *our* power. To Geas's ability to persuade it to do this."

"Persuade it?"

"Another time," she said, for the Gate was now fully formed. It was cast completely from iron this time, and the rust was growing. The insane creatures still scurried about, but there was something more anxious in their movements.

The Gryphon shook his head and whispered to Troia, "I'm not so sure about this part. Remember last time we made use of the Gate. . . ."

"That was different."

"Was it?"

Geas suddenly played a questioning note, and the massive doors of the Gate began to slowly swing open. The assembled group seemed to hold its breath—even the Faceless Ones, if they truly breathed.

A scene of ancient but very complete destruction was all they could see no matter what angle they viewed it from. There was no question that this could be anything but poor Qualard. The wind could be seen to be blowing harshly, and the sun was hidden behind a gray haze of clouds.

"Qualard was never a very hospitable place, I understand," Haggerth commented. "You four had best go now. There's no telling how long the Gate will stay open. We rarely ask it to open to such places. It will not stay so for very long."

"What about food and water?" Dane asked, and then grimaced as four of the empty-visaged creatures stepped into the chamber, bearing with them four packs. The Aramite shuddered and whispered to the Gryphon, "Helpful they may be, but they give me shivers the way they seem to anticipate or know things."

The Gryphon nodded and then took the proffered pack from the

Faceless One. He slung it over one shoulder and, when he saw that his companions were ready, started toward the Gate.

"No horses?" questioned Morgis.

"Too rocky a region," Troia responded. "Besides, we won't be traveling too far—I think."

"What do you hope to find when we get there?" Dane asked the Gryphon.

"I'll be depending on your memory and mine to answer that. There's something there—I'm fairly certain of that."

"Oh, fine. Perhaps, I accepted too soon."

Morgis stumbled into them. He had been staring intently at the scene before them. His eyes darted first to the Gryphon and then Jerilon Dane. "He's right. There *is* something there."

"You, too?" the former wolf raider muttered.

"Good hunting!" Haggerth called.

They stepped into the Gate—

—and into the desolation of Qualard—

—and barely had time to recognize the wolfhelmed figures surrounding them, arms raised, before—

—they were sent *elsewhere*—

—where they were surrounded by an even greater number of the wolfhelmed figures and discovered that they could not speak, could not move.

From somewhere beyond the Gryphon's vision, someone chuckled in great satisfaction. The sound of a heavy pair of boots echoed in the dark chamber. A large hand with a powerful grip took hold of the lionbird by the shoulder and spun him around. The face he saw was not a pleasant one.

"Welcome to Canisargos, Gryphon. I am your host. My name is D'Rak, and I am so *very* pleased to finally meet you."

D'Rak smiled. It was a smile frighteningly akin to the one the Gryphon recalled D'Shay had worn during their last encounter. It was the last thing he saw before consciousness vanished abruptly.

It was the smile of a predator about to eat his prey.

XI

THE GRYPHON WOKE.

Anyone glancing his way would have seen no change in his

appearance. His eyes were still closed, and he breathed with the regularity of sleep. He did not even stir. Nonetheless, he was awake . . .

. . . And chained. Beyond him, he could hear one other person nearby. Judging by the consistent hissing each time the other took a breath, he knew it had to be Duke Morgis. The drake was still out. The Gryphon tuned out the pattern of his companion's breathing and sought out other sounds. He heard the distant marching of feet and the mumbled words of male voices, probably guards. The normal sounds of an ancient structure revealing its age, the creaks and groans, were ignored. Occasionally, Morgis moved in his sleep, causing the chains on his wrists, ankles—and, yes, even around the neck—to rattle.

The Gryphon opened one eye and peered around.

Neither Troia nor the Aramite Jerilon Dane were to be seen in the tiny, cramped cell. The lionbird had already known that, but it was always good to have visual evidence as well, especially when dealing with sorcery of one sort or another. He opened his other eye and studied the place in detail.

His surroundings were not what he had grown accustomed to as monarch of Penacles, but neither were they the worst he had ever found himself in. At least it was decently warm in here, if a bit moist. The smell of rot was prevalent, but, to a soldier who had spent most of his life on one battlefield or another, it was little more than an annoyance. Moss grew on most of the walls, and tiny creatures of every shape and form scurried about. The Gryphon shifted uneasily. At least a few of them had decided to check his potential as a host.

Unsheathing his claws, he bent his fingers forward and allowed the tips of the claws to brush against the manacles holding the wrists. Hard and sharp as they were, his claws were also sensitive to the nature of things, something that those who did not have them would never have understood. Claws were more than just weapons to animals; they were tools that aided the senses.

The manacles, as he feared, were enshrouded in a number of binding spells. They had also been cast in an alloy that defied understanding save that it was very strong. The chains were, of course, of the same design. Knowing what sort of work creating such bonds would have entailed, the Gryphon knew that he and his companions—at least Morgis, that is—were not being held in one of the common cells. No, this was a private prison, a dungeon.

He stiffened suddenly, for his mind had finally cleared enough to recall the single whistle he still had. Tiny as it was, it was difficult to tell whether the artifact was still on his person or not. He tried to reach his chest with one hand, but even with his claws he lacked the length needed. It had been bad enough to see it in the hands of Haggerth, but now it might be the prize of one of the highest-ranking wolf raiders—a man supposedly every bit as deadly as D'Shay himself.

D'Rak. The name had come up in conversation at various times. D'Shay's apparent rival. Senior Keeper D'Rak. A man very much like D'Shay.

What could have happened? he wondered. They had arrived in Qualard and there had been wolf raiders. Not ordinary soldiers, but men like D'Laque, bearing tiny artifacts similar to the Ravager's Tooth that keeper had carried before his death. There was a brief moment when it seemed the entire world turned to the side—and they had been teleported here, frozen like statues, unable to defend themselves in any way.

He heard footsteps nearing his cell and realized that they were stopping at the door. There was the rattle of a key in the lock of the heavy wooden door, and then it was shoved open. A hulking, monstrous figure clad in a black apron, trousers, and boots, his face covered by a hood—with no eyeholes!—turned his head in the direction of both prisoners, saw that the chains still held, and stepped back. The jailer moved aside, and a second figure stepped into the cell. The lionbird recognized him immediately, though his only other glimpse had lasted no more than a few seconds.

"Awake. Good. You know who I am? You remember?"

"You're D'Rak."

"I am. But before we begin negotiations, I would like to thank you for your timeliness. My men had barely gotten into position before you and your two companions stepped through the Gate. That was *the* Gate, wasn't it?"

The Gryphon, who had been mulling over the word "negotiations" and then the fact that the keeper's subordinates had captured only *three* people, nodded silently. Had Troia escaped somehow? Was this Mrin/Amrin's way of disposing of three unwanted guests? The Gryphon quietly cursed himself for not using his time with Lord Petrac to ask about the double-bodied Master Guardian. Petrac would have told him everything had he asked. Yet . . .

He *shrieked* in agony as it seemed a million of the tiny vermin crawling about the cell suddenly chose to eat him alive. That was the feeling. Thousands upon thousands of tiny mouths biting—*everywhere*. The very abruptness of it was the worst part. Even as he fought the incredible pain, the Gryphon felt the shame flowing through him. Shame at the weakness he had revealed to an enemy.

D'Rak stood over him, grinning with sadistic pleasure at his torment. No matter what their normal facial structure, the Gryphon could not help noticing that *all* of the Aramites he had studied closely had a definite feral look to them that revealed itself wholeheartedly in moments of anger or dark pleasure.

Children of the Ravager, indeed.

"When I speak to you," D'Rak said sweetly, "I expect the courtesy of a reply." The senior keeper's left hand was on a pendant that hung from his neck. It looked very much like the sharp, wicked tooth of a wolf carved in crystal.

A sharp hiss and a terrible rattling of chains informed both of them that Morgis was awake and furious. He was trying to transform, the Gryphon realized, but, as with the trap of the Tzee, he was being forced back into his humanoid form.

D'Rak turned and gazed at the drake with the look one reserved for a fool. "If you like, I'll give you the ability to shift to your dragon form, but I should warn you that neither the manacles nor the chains will break, and you will be dead from asphyxiation—or possibly decapitation—long before you can do any damage. I made certain to have the collars fairly tight."

Morgis hissed unhappily. "I am growing tired of finding myself in compromising positions. Give me my sword and let me fight to my death! If not a sssword, then at leassst unbind me ssso that I can go down asss a warrior!"

"A true warrior's spirit. Perhaps I'll oblige you later, although, if your companion comes to his senses, there may be no need for your death." The keeper turned his attention back to the Gryphon, who had by now recovered. "I mean what I say."

"You talked about negotiation. . . ."

"I did. We have a mutual enemy, bird. You know who I speak of. I am offering you an alliance of sorts."

The Gryphon tilted his head to one side and gave D'Rak a disparaging look. "An alliance? I agree that it would be nice to be rid of D'Shay once and for all, but an alliance with you? You tell me. What would make me believe that you would honor any bargain we made?"

"Wolf raiders have no honor," Morgis spat. "My sire said so, and I have seen nothing to change that fact."

D'Rak rubbed his chin with one gauntleted hand. "I suppose I could merely promise you a quick, painless death. You, Gryphon, felt a taste of what a slow, painful death could be like. I would like your cooperation, though, for a full effort by both of us is the best way we can rid ourselves of the one you once called Shaidarol."

The lionbird appeared to consider. "What happened at Qualard, D'Rak? You must know; otherwise, you wouldn't have sent men there."

The senior keeper shrugged. "I know enough. That's neither here nor there. We were talking about D'Shay. He fears you, you know."

"What?"

"He fears you. Behind all that anger, that raging confidence, he fears you. I think I may be the only one who knows—other than my lord Ravager, of course."

The Gryphon wanted to reject the idea out of hand, but he was curious as to the Aramite's reasoning. He also hoped that the keeper might say more than he meant. At this point, information was the only thing the Gryphon had any hope of obtaining—and even then it might be of no use should D'Rak decide he didn't need him after all.

"D'Shay has never shown anything remotely resembling fear—and why *should* he fear me?"

D'Rak smiled thinly. "D'Shay fears you because your continued existence lessens him in the eyes of the Ravager. While you were lost for so long, he was given the benefit of the doubt. Now he has a time limit of sorts. The Ravager is not a patient god. Even the most loyal of his followers can fall from favor overnight. D'Shay owes his continued existence—I don't know how—to the Lord Ravager. An existence the Master of the Hunt may cut off at any time."

It was not the answer that the Gryphon had hoped for, and he knew there was another reason, but it at least gave him some information about D'Shay. He *had* hoped for a hint concerning the truth about his own past and his connection with Qualard—which at least had been verified by the senior keeper's trap. D'Rak had *known* that the Gryphon would definitely go to the shattered city.

"You talk about negotiation, but I notice that one of us is missing." The Gryphon prayed that Morgis would not correct him.

"The female is in another cell. I said I wanted your cooperation, but I will take your unwilling aid, if necessary."

The Gryphon turned to Morgis, who returned his gaze but gave no indication of his opinion one way or another. He knew the decision belonged to the lionbird.

Putting on a reluctant appearance, the Gryphon looked up at D'Rak, sighed, and said, "If you can guarantee our lives once this is over, then I'll accept."

D'Rak held out the Ravager's Tooth. "By this token of my lord, I swear that I will bring no harm to you while I live. Any more, I cannot promise."

"I understand." Knowing what D'Shay was like, the Gryphon could not fully accept the ease with which the Aramite had sworn the oath. It *sounded* like an honest oath, but the promises of a hungry wolf . . .

The senior keeper was looking down at them. "Do you two agree to what I have offered? Will you assist me in the downfall of our mutual foe?"

The Gryphon nodded, and Morgis, after some hesitation, did the same. The Aramite held out the crystalline artifact. "I want each of you to touch it. Be careful; it's very sharp on the edge."

"Wait . . ." Morgis clenched his fists and began to protest.

"You want your oaths, and I want mine. You can rot in here—or perhaps I can give you to D'Shay as a peace offering."

Before the drake could reply, the Gryphon reached forward. As he touched the Ravager's Tooth, he felt a slight prick of pain, as if something had cut his— There *was* blood dripping from his finger! He jerked his hand back. The glistening, scarlet liquid dripped onto the crystal—and was absorbed.

D'Rak withdrew the artifact without even offering it to Morgis again. "That will suffice. Now I'm guaranteed of your cooperation, and you of mine."

"What've you done?"

"It was a trick! I knew it!" roared the duke.

The keeper hid the crystal beneath his shirt. "Your destiny is now linked with mine, Gryphon. My goals are now yours. Should anything happen to me, then, through this bond we share, you will die."

If he had expected a look of shock to spread itself over the Gryphon's visage, the wolf raider would have been disappointed. Rather than protest, the lionbird merely looked deep into the Aramite's eyes and said quietly, "Then *both* of us had better be careful, or *both* of us will regret it."

"Indeed." D'Rak seemed a bit taken aback by the lack of what he considered a proper response. "With that done . . ."

He snapped his fingers, and the huge jailer—whom somehow both the

Gryphon and Morgis had forgotten about—lumbered over to the lionbird. It was impossible to tell exactly what the hooded figure did or how he did it, considering he should have been unable to see, but the manacles around both wrists suddenly fell away. There was no click of a lock mechanism, and the jailer had only the key that obviously fit into the cell door.

As the hulking form continued his work, the Gryphon asked something that had been puzzling him. "A question, D'Rak. Don't you see any of what you plan as an attack against your own god?"

"By no means. I serve the Pack Master and, through him, I serve my Lord Ravager. D'Shay serves no one save the Ravager, and he does that reluctantly. Too often, his mind turns to other things and he loses sight of the empire's goals. As for you, I think that the knowledge that you will no longer be a threat to us will be sufficient. The Pack Master will grant you the means to return home—across the seas. There are ways we can assure ourselves of your cooperation, if need be."

The Gryphon stood and stretched, casually checking for the whistle as he pretended to straighten his clothing. It was still there. Something inherent in its nature hid it from the sight of others unless the lionbird chose to reveal it. He had been worried that the ease with which Haggerth had taken it meant that it had lost that masking power. Apparently, though, the Master Guardian had only been able to see it because of what he was. Anyone who was not one of the Dream Lands' guardians still fell prey to its subtle power. That was fortunate, especially now.

D'Rak waited patiently, his eyes seeming to stare *through* the Gryphon rather than at him. When they were ready, he indicated the jailer. "R'Mok will see to your kitten. If you two will follow me . . ."

Outside, they discovered that the corridors of the dungeon were no less unimpressive than the cell. The Gryphon gazed around at the other cells. Some of them were occupied, and he started to look in one. A strong, heavy hand pulled him back. D'Rak's eyes bored into his own. "She's elsewhere. You didn't think I'd put her this close to you? I take no chances."

Behind them, Morgis made a sound. The Keeper ignored it and turned to his left. Without any hesitation, he started off down the corridor, fully confident that his two associates would follow suit. Morgis and the Gryphon looked at each other and then glanced at the monstrous jailer, who watched them silently from behind the eyeless hood.

They started after the Aramite. Morgis leaned toward the Gryphon. "Do you really believe everything he said? His promises, his reasons?"

"Of course not—and he doesn't expect me to believe him."

"He doesn't?"

The lionbird shook his head. He watched D'Rak with one eye as he replied, "He has us for now. He knows it. From what little I understand and remember of the wolf raiders, nothing compares to their political intrigues. They lie to one another's face worse than any human or drake. It's what makes them so deadly—sometimes even they can't tell where the truth ends and the falsehoods begin. D'Rak, because of his pivotal position in the empire, probably thinks they're one and the same now."

Morgis paused. "You remember more."

The Gryphon took hold of his arm and dragged him on. D'Rak was slowing, and it was obvious to him that the senior keeper was about to turn around and check on his new "allies." Hastily, the Gryphon whispered, "Some of it I learned as a monarch. I do remember more, however, especially about the keepers. I remember enough to know we have to keep alert."

"D'Rak may stumble on some steps, slip, and break his neck. What then?"

"You find your way home on your own. Swim, maybe."

"Hmmph. One thing. What happened to our Aramite guide?"

The Gryphon shrugged. "I don't really know."

"Gentlemen?" the keeper called out. The irony was evident in his voice. "If you please."

They hastened their pace.

"Gaze, if you will, upon Canisargos, the greatest city ever raised from the earth!"

D'Rak had led them through the citadel of the keepers, past rooms where men stared at artifacts of all shapes and sizes, others filled with exotic creatures and works of art, all the way to the balcony from which, he said, he watched over his people.

"The Pack Master is a military leader. He does not understand people. Thus it falls to the keepers to oversee the daily functioning of the cities. A keeper travels with each patrol whenever possible, and they may overrule any decision made by that patrol leader if they can justify it."

Justifying actually meant that a keeper generally found some way to coerce the captain, thought the Gryphon as he recalled Captain D'Haaren's patrol. It was not an easy alliance.

Canisargos—politics, madmen, and wolf gods aside—was a spectacle that, for once, daunted the Gryphon completely. The city seemed to go on and on and on all the way to the horizon. Like Luperion, many of the buildings resembled tall, sleek rectangles. Unlike the other city, wicked, jagged spires topped every other tower. What could be seen of the surrounding walls indicated that any would-be conquerer would need to build ladders and siege machines at least three times as high as was the norm.

The Gryphon glanced briefly in the general direction of the sun. A little more than an hour until sunset—of the next day, he knew. What had happened in that time?

There were watch towers everywhere, all manned. He sensed power emanating all around and realized it was not just from the keepers' citadel; it was *everywhere*. There was more use of the fields and lines of power—or the light and dark side of the spectrum, if one chose to believe that theory instead—going on in Canisargos than in most of the Dragonrealm.

"Look there!" Morgis hissed, pointing at the sky.

Men rode on the back of long, muscular, winged creatures that dove hither and yonder. With a shock, the Gryphon understood that he was staring at the beasts from which he had taken his name. There were only a few in the Dragonrealm, and he had never really come across any of them. Here, however, there seemed to be hundreds. He could not see the gryphons' being used for aerial guard duty if they were very rare. No, they would be saved for special, high-priority missions.

He felt a twinge of loneliness. Even the beasts had others of their own kind. He was indeed a misfit.

"Don't we take a chance, being out here?" Morgis was asking the senior keeper.

"Hardly. We are protected from the sight of nonkeepers. They will see nothing but an empty, barred window."

The Gryphon gave Canisargos one last look. From here, the crowds melted into one vast sea of life. He could make out little detail of the lower city. "We still haven't seen our companion. You said your lackey was going to get her."

"And he will." D'Rak snapped his fingers. An unsavory figure seemed to materialize from nowhere. "D'Altain, we would like something to drink, I think. Could you please see to it?"

"Yes, Master." The Aramite vanished into the inner chamber, but not before the Gryphon detected a hint of hatred in the man's eyes.

"You surround yourself with interesting people, Lord D'Rak."

The senior keeper was amused. "D'Altain? He is an efficient aide, if a somewhat unappetizing person."

"Not a servant?"

"I make him double as that on occasion." D'Rak smiled knowingly. "It keeps him in line."

"It breeds rebellion," Duke Morgis snarled. "I would not stand being treated as a menial when my status is much higher."

The Aramite leader gazed back into the chamber. "D'Altain does what I want him to do. Trust me."

"The words of many an assassinated leader," countered the drake wryly.

"My lord!" D'Altain rushed onto the balcony, wringing his hands as he looked at his master.

The amusement vanished from D'Rak's face. "You've forgotten the wine, D'Altain. What is it?"

"The feline. The one that bear R'Mok was supposed to bring!"

Stiffening, the Gryphon pushed heedlessly past the senior keeper and took the underling by the scruff of his collar. "*What about her?*"

"She's gone!"

The lionbird whirled on D'Rak. "Is this more treachery, wolf raider?"

"Gryphon . . . ," Morgis began.

D'Rak shook his head. "Leave it, drake lord. No, my feathered and furred friend, this is not treachery on my account. If you'll let my aide breathe a little, we might get somewhere."

Without realizing it, the Gryphon had pulled D'Altain from the floor. The smaller man bounced a bit as his feet struck the ground, and he wobbled uncertainly for a second. When he had regained his senses, he glared at the former monarch and turned to his master. "R'Mok is dead, master. One of the novices discovered him lying near the cell. His head . . . his head was nowhere to be seen!"

"Damn!" the senior keeper cursed. "All that work! R'Mok was the finest one yet!"

The lionbird got D'Altain's attention again. "The woman—Troia— what about her?"

"No sign. The cell door was locked, and R'Mok's key was still on his belt—unless someone had replaced it."

D'Rak tugged on his mustache as his mind raced. "She must be in the building still, unless . . . Could she have summoned the Gate? Tell me truthfully, my friends."

"As for the truth"—the Gryphon's mane bristled—"how do we know that all of this isn't more of your intrigues, keeper? Aramites are famous on this continent for their games!"

The senior keeper's eyes narrowed, and the lionbird realized that D'Rak now knew that his "ally" remembered much, much more than had been indicated earlier. The Gryphon found he did not care; all that mattered at the moment was finding Troia.

"Master?" A very young man in keeper's robes—obviously a novice—stumbled out onto the balcony, blanched at the sight of first the Gryphon and then Morgis, and then finally remembered why he was here. "Master! There's a messenger here! Asking entrance!"

"Who's here, fool? What messenger?" Having just been handed one piece of disturbing news, D'Rak lashed out far more angrily than necessary at the unfortunate novice.

"Lord D'Shay's man. He seeks an audience." It was astounding that the young keeper could find his voice.

The silence was overwhelming.

"How . . . timely," D'Rak finally muttered. "So soon." He turned to the Gryphon, who had unsheathed his claws at the mere mention of his adversary's name. "I think we have the answer to our questions, Lord Gryphon."

"What do you mean?" *D'Shay. He had to be nearby.* The lionbird forced his breathing to stay regulated. If he allowed himself to lose control . . .

"Isn't it apparent?" The senior keeper seemed surprised that the Gryphon did not agree. "The timing is too perfect. I would say the chances are very good that your friend is now a guest of D'Shay—and that this messenger is his way of extending to us an invitation to meet him in *his* domain."

XII

SHE HAD WOKEN up in a dank prison cell, and her first thoughts, oddly, were not about her own safety but about that of the older, mysterious guardian who called himself the Gryphon. Troia could not say why his safety concerned her so very much; her kind, living as wild as they did, were a people of the moment who did not dwell on long-term matters. Yet her time as one of those working with the Master Guardians of Sirvak Dragoth had changed her, and she did recognize some of her reactions based on what she had seen in that place. Not completely comfortable with what she saw within herself, she turned to other thoughts.

The Aramite called Dane had betrayed them; she was certain about *that*, at the very least. How else could they start out for the desolate region of Qualard only to be waylaid by stalking wolf raiders and transported to . . . to Canisargos? Most likely Canisargos, the feline woman decided, her mind already darting to another track of thought. The Gryphon was the object of a wolf raider hunt, and now he was in their claws. The Gate only knew what they were doing to him even now! She struggled violently against the manacles around her wrists, ankles, and neck, but they refused to give even a little. Troia spat out a childhood epithet that had earned her more than one swat on the behind from her elders. It did nothing to gain her freedom, but it allowed her to vent some hostility. There was too great a possibility that she might lose control, become the wild cat she so closely resembled. Troia refused to allow herself that mental escape; if nothing else, she knew the Gryphon would be counting on her to free herself. She would not let *him* down.

There were no guards outside. If there had been, they would have made an appearance before now, at least to look in and yell at her to settle down. Occasionally, her acute hearing picked up the sounds of people walking down distant corridors. Soldiers, judging from the heavy, trampling sounds of their footfalls. She unsheathed and sheathed her claws automatically at the image of so many wolf raiders close by. If only she could find a way to work herself free of these manacles! She knew how they worked, for more than one dead prisoner had been discovered still wearing them. The chains and manacles were attuned to the strength of the prisoner. They drew their power from the very life of the unfortunate soul. Neither struggling nor remaining still was effective. Death was one possible solution, but a pretty pointless one. The only true key was knowledge of the bonding spell of the manacle itself—and that required a sacrifice on the part of the jailer that Troia understood was even less desirable than death. Something to do with the head . . .

She lost track of the thought when she noticed that someone was walking down the corridor, getting nearer and nearer to her cell.

A hooded head appeared in the tiny window of the cell door. There were no eyeholes, but Troia knew with a chill that ran down her spine and caused her to arch her back a bit that the being beneath the hood could see her quite well—with or without eyes. She hesitated to even think of it as a man.

The jailer stepped back from the cell, and Troia knew he was reaching for the key to the door. Then there was an odd thumping sound from one side of the corridor and the hooded figure was turning to see what was going on. The feline woman watched in shock as the huge guard was pulled bodily from where he stood by something she could not see.

A rough, muffled grunt, that same thumping noise—and then silence again.

When she heard the thump a third time—in her cell yet—Troia renewed her struggles with the manacles. Then the wall beside her opened up and Jerilon Dane, with something large under his left arm, stepped out of a portal. She hissed and spat into his face. He wiped the moisture off his cheek and slapped her once in return before seeming to collect himself.

"I'm here to *free* you, you damn sphinx! Hold still while I deal with those manacles!"

"How—" she began, and then saw that the burden he carried under his arm was the hooded head of the jailer. The head or, if what she had been told was true, something not quite real. Whatever lurked beneath the blank hood, it allowed the Aramite to open her manacles with no difficulty.

Dane rose and started to toss the grisly prize away, but changed his mind before releasing it. He tucked it back under his arm as he waited for Troia to stand. The portal flickered ominously.

The former wolf raider glanced back at it and, with a frown, said, "They've latched on to it sooner than I thought! Go through, before they track it to here!"

She shook her head and backed away, having gained a healthy distrust of portals of late. "I thank you for your aid, but I think I'll make my own way from here! I have to find the Gryphon—"

"From inside a locked cell? Don't be a fool! I'm not risking myself any longer for you! Go through! Your only other choice is to remain here!"

"Just get me the key!"

He scowled. "That's it! I'm leaving! Come now, or wait and see what tender plans Senior Keeper D'Rak has in store for you! Perhaps he'll let you play with the Runners!"

Dane turned his back on her and stepped into the portal. As he vanished, Troia took one last look around and, reluctantly, leaped in after him. It was a good decision; the portal vanished almost immediately afterward.

A SHOUT ERUPTED from the main entrance to the keeper citadel. D'Rak, who was in the midst of herding the Gryphon and Morgis into one of the side chambers, was forced to abandon them to D'Altain. "Take them somewhere safe from probing! I must deal with this messenger!"

"Master." The aide turned to his two charges. "This way. No arguments, please."

Neither of them cared for the brief gleam in his eyes. Morgis's hand strayed to his empty scabbard, while the Gryphon found his mind wandering briefly to the question of where the drake's sword went when he transformed into his dragon shape. He and Morgis were racing to keep pace with D'Rak's second, who moved swiftly for such a small, ungainly figure.

"A strange, very annoying land you've brought me to," whispered the duke as they followed D'Altain down a flight of stairs. "People here have an irritating habit of not being where you expect them to be or showing up when you least expect it—and that includes ourselves! If I could just have a blade, I'd fight this Ravager myself rather than end up in one more place I wasn't expecting to or having one more person show up when they really shouldn't!" The drake sounded somewhat confused by the end of his complaint.

"You may still get the opportunity!" D'Altain hissed. "Quiet now!"

The Gryphon's heart threatened to pound his chest apart. He realized now just what a deadly rivalry he had been thrown into. Until D'Shay's discovery of the lionbird's continued existence, D'Rak must have been his greatest stumbling block. It said something that the keeper could preserve any secrets and grow so powerful despite D'Shay's favored position with the Pack Master and the Ravager.

The senior keeper's aide was leading them deeper and deeper into the citadel, and the Gryphon began to wonder if he intended to march them all the way back to their cell. D'Rak was going to be unpleasantly surprised if he believed they would voluntarily return to that place, Ravager's Tooth oath or not.

"Where *are* we heading?" demanded Morgis, who, like the Gryphon, was beginning to believe that they were returning to the keeper's private dungeons.

"Master D'Rak has standing orders for situations such as this. Lord D'Shay's man would not be here unless his master did not have a good excuse and, most likely, permission from the Pack Master to probe our people. He no doubt suspects you are here and, if he truly has your companion, then he has the proof he needs to gain that permission. You can be certain that D'Shay's servants will be very, very thorough. That's why we have quite some distance to go. What he knows, we cannot help; what he does not know, we can try to keep from him."

A hiss of annoyance. "Why can't we use a portal to reach this place of safety?"

"With Lord D'Shay waiting for just such an occurrence? Do you really think he would not have others secretly probing? We do not expect that all keepers are loyal, either."

"You seem to have this all worked out fairly well," the Gryphon commented quietly. The three of them had come to a long-neglected landing that he estimated must be at least on the same level as the cells, if not lower. Cobwebs decorated the ceilings and walls, and the only true light came from a crystal that D'Altain wore around his neck. The dust was so thick that he wished it were possible not to have to breathe altogether. Morgis, directly behind them, began to cough. Though he preferred dry land to the sea his father reveled in, this was a little extreme for the duke's tastes.

The aide kicked aside a dark form that squealed as it raced down the corridor behind them. "I try my best. Besides, we knew this day might come sometime. Lord D'Shay has probably become very nervous with you running free." He brushed aside a very large cobweb from in front of his face. "Pardon the condition of this area, my lords; its appearance is deceptive. The look of disuse tends to discourage searching parties."

"Won't we leave tracks in the dust?"

"Have we?" D'Altain asked in return.

The two looked down at their boots and, even in the dim light, could see the dust reshaping itself. Footprints vanished after mere seconds. The dust in the air (what they had not swallowed, that is) did not float for very long, but dropped almost like lead the moment the trio was past. A few feet back, it would have been impossible for even the Gryphon to believe that they had actually passed this way.

"You see," was all the Aramite said. He continued on, and, like his master, did not look back to see if his charges were following him.

A few corridors down, they came to a dead end. Judging by the debris lying on the side, the lionbird came to the conclusion that this area had once served as a storage facility of some kind. He was not surprised, however, to see the unsavory D'Altain touch a stone in the far wall and then push the entire wall forward like a massive door. A secret panel in a place like this came as no surprise.

"Through here."

Perhaps it was because the Aramite had been *too* helpful, *too* polite after what the Gryphon had read in his eyes earlier that made the former monarch pause a moment. He could understand D'Rak's almost paranoid caution about D'Shay's resources, but something inside said that this did not ring true.

His patience was rewarded by the impatience of D'Altain. The keeper reached upward to his own chest, no doubt for his talisman. He was unused to the Gryphon's natural speed, however, and before his hand could close on the artifact, the Gryphon had the hand in one of his own. He pulled the hand back, nearly snapping the bone at the wrist. D'Altain shouted something, and immediately the corridor was spilling over with dark armored figures bursting from the passage the Aramite had been trying to convince his two charges to enter.

In the dim light emitted by the crystalline talisman, the Gryphon could make out at least half a dozen figures, probably more, clad in wolf raider armor and wearing full masks such as those worn by the senior keeper's own guards. It occurred to the lionbird as the first one came at him that these might actually be members of that unit.

The Gryphon did the only thing he could do under the circumstances: he threw D'Altain at the foremost man and then shoved the two tangled bodies into the next. In the confusion that reigned, he succeeded in freeing a knife from the keeper and trying to use it against its former owner. D'Altain twisted, however, and the blade found only empty space where the traitorous keeper's side had been. One of the armored figures knocked the blade away with the flat of a sword and closed on the ex-mercenary. The Gryphon unsheathed his claws and met him head-on.

Behind him, he heard the triumphant shout of Duke Morgis as the drake was finally presented with a situation within his powers. The Gryphon hoped Morgis would not enjoy himself too much and become careless. They were still outnumbered in close quarters, with no weapons but their claws and their sorcery still suppressed by the power of the keepership in general. Not that the lionbird had any spells in mind that did not require time. He doubted very much that Morgis had any, either, and the drake would certainly not have tried shifting form in these tight spaces.

The mailed fist that drove into the wall next to him warned that it was he who was becoming careless. He drove his own fist into the midriff of his adversary, the armor giving a little under the force of his blow. The wolf raider was pushed back a step, and, taking advantage of the extra space, the

Gryphon drove his claws into the narrow, unprotected area of the throat between helm and armor, killing the Aramite instantly. Unfortunately, the dead weight was such that he found himself unable to extricate himself from his fallen foe as two more wolf-visage masks closed with him.

The edge of a blade caught his left arm, drawing a long, searing line across it. He finally freed his claws, but by then the Aramites were too close for him to raise his arms properly. With sudden clarity, the Gryphon saw his death coming.

Complete darkness filled the corridor at that point, a sign that D'Altain had either fled or been killed. The sudden lack of light made the two wolf raiders hesitate, if only for a second. The Gryphon, pinned as he was against the wall, found little comfort in the fact that he could now see his oncoming death more clearly than the two about to deliver it.

There was a garbled shout, half astonishment and half sudden fear, and then the wolf raider on his left was flying backward like some mad marionette whose strings had been pulled. The other Aramite could not help but turn in dismay as his fellow seemingly vanished in the darkness—which proved to be his own undoing. Freed, the Gryphon roared and, using the wall as support, threw himself forward, striking his adversary with the full force of his body. Both of them were propelled into the opposing wall. The wolf raider let out a painful grunt as he struck the wall. The lionbird raised his claw for a final strike, but the soldier was already sliding to the floor.

The Gryphon whirled, awaiting a new opponent, but a quick scan with his night vision informed him that only one other form still stood. That form proved to be Morgis, who was relieving one of the corpses of its short sword. The drake's night vision was not as good as his companion's, but he could see well enough to know it was the Gryphon coming toward him. There were at least five bodies near the duke, and the ex-mercenary realized that the drake had taken on the majority of their attackers.

"You should feel fortunate," Morgis began. "I'd say they had orders to take you alive, if possible. Not so with me. When the first one failed to kill me, the rest came charging. Still, only two could fight me at any time. I suppose close quarters has its advantages and disadvantages."

The Gryphon chuckled. It was typical of some drakes—and humans—to start analyzing situations that had been, mere moments before, a matter of life or death. At least, he thought, Morgis would stop wishing for a sword.

Morgis inspected the short sword. "Not much more than a knife, but it will have to do until I can find a *real* weapon. Do you see anything?"

The Gryphon shook his head, afraid that any verbal response would begin a new battle—between the two of them. Some beings were never satisfied.

One thing he had noticed was the absence of one body in particular. D'Altain had vanished, and the lionbird suspected he had fled through the very passage their attackers had entered from. What the keeper's plot had been was still debatable, but it was obvious that D'Rak, paranoid as he was, would have eventually discovered the truth from his subordinate—which meant that D'Altain had been planning on fleeing once the deed was done.

There were only two people in Canisargos with the power to save him, and only one that would even consider it. It was even possible that D'Altain had arranged for the messenger to come at that time. It would explain the assassins; somehow, it seemed unlikely that they had been waiting here on the slim chance that someone would come down here eventually.

"Morgis, we have a way out of here."

Eyeing the darkness of the passage, the drake asked, "What about you? You're still linked to that arrogant warm-blood up there."

"I'll take my chances. I have to find Troia. The longer she's in D'Shay's claws . . ." He trailed off.

Morgis nodded silently. He glanced at his short sword, tested it again in his right hand, and then took it in his left. After a brief mental debate, he returned it to his right. Like many veteran fighters, he was skilled with both hands. It was then a question concerning the balance of the weapon. The wolf raider who had used this sword had used it well, and it was worn in the handle. The difference would have been negligible to many swordsmen, but not one with the skill and experience of either the Gryphon or the drake.

They searched the bodies for any clue concerning Troia and the Aramite capital. The Gryphon found a short sword that suited him and also some of the local coinage. He disliked robbing the dead, but, under the circumstances, there was little choice. They might prove of use. The tiny talismans that were the mark of keeper guardsmen they did not touch; there was too much of a chance that D'Rak could work his sorcery directly through them. There was nothing else of value to the two. Morgis pulled two of the largest cloaks from the bodies and tossed one to his companion.

The passage proved to be fairly straightforward, and the Gryphon could not help but wonder how the senior keeper could not know about it. Evidently, he left more in the hands of his subordinates than he should have. It made the lionbird wonder if there were passages back in his former palace in Penacles that he had never known about. Still, he had placed more faith in his second-in-command, Toos, than D'Rak had in D'Altain—and there was the difference.

Groping, they eventually found the hidden door leading out of the citadel. Pulling the cloaks over their forms as best as they were able, they stood with swords ready while the Gryphon pushed with his free hand. The door gave much more easily than he expected—likely from the fact that D'Altain had preceded them not long before—and the Gryphon almost tumbled forward. Morgis caught him by the shoulder and pulled him back. For several seconds, they stared in the direction of the partially open door. Then, slowly, the lionbird pushed it open enough to allow them access.

The sun was nearing the point when it would soon be no more than a memory. Dark shadows already enveloped this side of the keepers' stronghold. There was no one in sight. The two fugitives stepped outside and scanned the area for danger. Nothing.

Morgis turned and pushed the secret door closed. The hiss that escaped his scaly lips made the Gryphon whirl.

The doorway was gone. There was absolutely no indication that it had ever even existed. Even a careful examination of where they knew the doorway had been revealed nothing but grime. The designer had been a master at his craft.

"What now?"

"We have to find a place to hide you, or at least find something to disguise you with. That cloak is only good for nighttime and long ranges."

"What about you?"

"I'll shift—" The Gryphon halted in midsentence. He had foolishly assumed he still had the ability to transform himself to human form, even though Morgis had been prevented by the power of the keepers. While the drake watched expectantly, he concentrated. There was a brief, tingling feeling that he knew preceded the change, but nothing more. It was as if a block had been put on that part of his mind.

That was not the worst of it; it dawned on the Gryphon that he had quite possibly alerted any number of keepers to the fact that he was there.

There were cries from above, as if his flying namesakes patrolling above the city had suddenly become alert to a danger nearby. He did not doubt that he was that danger and that the beasts would be here, each bearing an armed rider, before long.

Glancing around, the Gryphon knew which direction he needed to go. "Follow me! Quickly!"

"Where are we going?" It was a credit to the drake's trust that he followed instantly.

"Into the center of the city. To the Pack Master's palace."

That almost made the duke halt in midstride. "Madness! We should be going the *opposite* direction!"

"Which . . ." The lionbird took a breath and increased his pace, heading for the protection of an unlit street to the right. He swerved into it and was joined by Morgis a moment later. "Which," he continued, "is the same thing the guards up there will be thinking. *No one* would be crazy enough to go running for the home of the mortal commander of the wolf raiders!"

"I hope you'll remember that statement when they feed us to those Runner pets of theirs."

"I'll expect you to remind me."

They heard the cry of several guard beasts and quieted. Something large flew overhead, but it was heading in the opposite direction, as the Gryphon had hoped. When they were certain that it was gone, they resumed their journey into the heart of Canisargos—and what some called the jaws of the Ravager.

THE MESSENGER FROM D'Shay had been ejected almost as quickly as he had entered. D'Rak took some small satisfaction from that, although he wished that it could have been his rival in form as well as in spirit. In a sense, things had turned out better than he had expected. From the few words he had allowed the man, he knew that D'Shay did not have the female who seemed important to the Gryphon—and that left him with only one other possibility, one he would verify at his own liking.

What pleased him more was that everything had moved as if he had choreographed it himself. D'Altain was a fool to have thought that the senior keeper did not know where the aide's true loyalties lay. He had acted far more swiftly than even D'Rak had estimated, but the end result was the same. Granted, the Gryphon should have been on his way to D'Shay in the custody of several traitorous guards and not loose in the city. However, the Aramite had faith that the lionbird's skill, combined with D'Rak's manipulation, would soon steer the guardian and his reptilian companion to their proper destination. There would be a purging soon, now that the senior keeper was so close to success. No more spies. No more D'Shay. Perhaps, no more Pack Master.

He smiled. Soon, D'Shay and the Gryphon would be face-to-face—and then it would all be over. As for D'Altain . . . he would leave the fate of that one to the aide's new master.

"You, there," D'Rak called out to the young keeper monitoring the watch on the Gryphon. "What was your name?"

The subordinate looked up. He had still not become accustomed to working directly under the senior keeper himself, and so he swallowed several times before his voice returned. "R'Farany, master. Third level."

"Incorrect." D'Rak smiled at the keeper's frightened confusion. "As of now, you are D'Farany, sixth level."

"Milord!" The newly christened D'Farany had the sense not to abandon his post despite the overwhelming promotion in rank and caste he had just received.

"Do your work and I will formally make you tenth level before the year is out. I intend to make you my new second-in-command, providing you know your place." The awed look in D'Farany's face indicated to D'Rak that he had chosen well. He knew that the young man was not only skilled, but a truly dedicated follower of his. Such men were to be cultivated. The older keepers were too long into their power. He could not trust any of them to succeed him. He wanted a pliable successor.

He turned to go, and then recalled one more thing. "Bear in mind, D'Farany, that I am always the one in command. When I say that those under my rule do as I wish, I mean it. *All* keepers and keeper guardsmen perform my desires—whether they know it or not."

Including would-be traitors, he added silently.

XIII

C*AN YOU HEAR me?*
The voice whispered mockingly throughout the conscious portion of his mind. He quickly buried all thought of his intentions, not out of fear, but so that he would not have to begin the tedious process of starting from scratch. Not when the present situation still held promise.

I know you hear me. Cease the pretense of sleep.

He sighed and acknowledged the other. *I hear you. For what reason do you disturb my thoughts? You've chosen not to speak to me since that last incident. Why now? Does something bother you?*

He felt rather than heard the snarl. For some reason, it amused him. *What do you call yourself now? Ravager, is it not? Such a savage name for such a tiny mind.*

A mind great enough to ensnare you while you blindly toyed with your experiments, the Ravager replied triumphantly.

I grant you that. I also granted you a trust you betrayed.

I will win this game, you know.

You still persist in that delusion, do you? The sleeper visualized a great head shaking in sadness, and revealed it to the one called the Ravager. *This is not a game. This is not a competition. The others knew that, and so do you.*

The others have withdrawn. I have only your last, feeble pawns to remove.

I feel sadness for you, Ravager. I was wrong. Your new name is so very appropriate for you. I hope you enjoy it still after you no longer have your delusions to entertain you.

Enough! The psychic shout was enough to give even the imprisoned one a brief headache—or at least the equivalent of one. *I don't know why I bothered to speak with you.*

Perhaps you are realizing your own mortality, the prisoner suggested, but he realized immediately that the Ravager had already withdrawn.

With a sigh, the sleeper returned to his rest, that one conscious portion of his mind already at work on the next step toward freedom.

THOUGH NIGHT HAD come at last, it appeared that Canisargos was not a city that quieted with the darkness. The throngs shrank, but not significantly. Torches, oil lamps, and even crystals lit the city. Shouts and music filled the air. Merchants continued hawking their wares under the lamps. Armed patrols grew larger, a sign that some of the evening festivities occasionally got out of hand.

If this were indeed a sample of life in the capital city of the Aramites, small wonder they were continuously on the move to expand their empire. The little the Gryphon and Morgis had seen indicated that keeping Canisargos supplied with its desires was a full-time project.

"Thisss empire will not fall to enemiesss," Morgis hissed quietly. "Rather, it will burn itssself out."

"A possibility, but I doubt it will happen soon enough for our sakes."

They were lost, and they both knew it. Much to their mutual dismay, the two fugitives had discovered something important about the streets of

Canisargos—their designers would have been masters at creating unbeatable mazes. It was impossible to believe that the citizens of the capital could move around with such assurance. Not even the Gryphon, who prided himself on his skills, could keep track of where they had been and where they should go. Streets that led directly to their chosen goal suddenly veered off to the left or right or, in one case, nearly back the direction they had come. Traveling by rooftops would have been much more straightforward, but airborne patrols still flew overhead every few minutes. It was a miracle that they had not been captured by now. Twice, gryphon riders had flown within a few yards of them, frightening ground dwellers and alerting every foot patrol they came across of two outsiders. Already, wolf raiders were assaulting anyone who looked overly suspicious to them.

Yet another patrol, this one composed of at least twenty men, blocked their only path. The captain, who resembled D'Haaren much too much, was questioning one of the blue-tinted men from the north. Behind the patrol leader, a young keeper, boredom the dominant emotion on his visage, absently stroked the artifact on his chest. It was an image that the Gryphon had noticed more than once tonight. Most of the keepers seemed to be doing as little as possible to aid the search. With so many of them, it should have been near impossible for the two fugitives to evade custody this long. The lionbird suspected that they had been given orders from D'Rak. The senior keeper wanted his two former guests to remain loose in the city—but for what reason?

He wanted them to reach D'Shay; that much was reasonable. But there had to be more. D'Rak was not the type of man to sit back and hope that one of his rival's other enemies might dispose of D'Shay. No, the senior keeper was a man who liked to be certain. The fur and feathers on the Gryphon's back rose in agitation. If he succeeded in defeating D'Shay, would he merely be clearing the way for someone just as evil? While the two fought and the Pack Master apparently was willing to wait for the outcome, the war machine of the wolf raiders moved slowly. With a sense of direction, that would change. The stalemate was almost over; the Dream Lands were losing.

His knowledge of the outermost regions of this continent was sparse, but he hazarded a guess that there were no other enemies strong enough to withstand the Aramites—and then they would turn their claws once more toward the Dragonrealm.

At long last, the captain completed his questioning and, with the look of one who has already had a weary day, ordered the patrol on again. The young keeper's face held a brief smirk, which served only to verify the Gryphon's thoughts. D'Rak *was* up to something.

A horrid sound rose from behind him, and the lionbird whirled, ready to take on what could only be a Runner sent to track them down.

Morgis somehow managed to look sheepish. "There's nothing I can do. We haven't eaten in nearly two days, and a drake's stomach is a demanding thing when he has been active continuously."

At the mention of food, the Gryphon's own stomach began to churn. It *had* been some time. He could recall eating only twice during his stay in the Dream Lands, and both times it had been a few pieces of fruit. While both he and the drake could probably go for days without food, it might be a good idea to grab something while they could. It was impossible to say what might happen if—when—they did reach the Pack Master's stronghold. They might die or they might succeed. Either way, it would not hurt for them to build up their energy reserves—providing they found a safe way to get some food. The Gryphon did not like the thought of being captured because he had been spotted stealing some half-rotted produce from the back of an unsavory inn.

He scanned the street again. The crowd was thinning out, and it appeared that some of the establishments were closing. It made sense; even innkeepers had to sleep occasionally, not to mention clean up from the day's activities.

One annoying problem was that the blue-tinted man was still hanging around. He seemed to have gained an obsessive interest in the area since his conversation with the patrol captain, and the lionbird wondered if he was an informer or some such.

The blue man became a secondary matter, for a familiar form strode into sight. The Gryphon flattened against the wall, with Morgis following suit.

"A Faceless One!" Morgis reached for his sword.

"No! We leave him alone unless he comes for us!"

"I don't trust them! I don't care if they *are* aiding the Dream Lands!"

"I don't trust them, either, but I'm not about to take on something that has free rein in both domains. Whoever or whatever the not-people are, I plan to avoid them—at least until I've taken care of what I originally came for."

They fully expected the blank visage to turn their way, but the Faceless One instead paused before the blue man and stared intently at the startled figure. Within seconds of being under the disturbing perusal of the hooded creature, the blue man ran off wildly. The Faceless One watched (supposedly) calmly until the other was no longer in sight, then continued on its way without so much as a glance in the direction of the two hidden watchers.

"I can't help feeling it knew we were here," Morgis grumbled uneasily.

"Let's hope it didn't." The Gryphon peeked around the corner. The area was deserted for the moment, likely due in part to the brief presence of the blank-faced specter. Across and to their right was a likely spot called the Ravager's Table. The lionbird could not picture a god as savage as the Ravager using a table—or a knife and fork, for that matter—but he guessed that any establishment bearing that particular name had better sell good meals.

Which meant a higher quality of refuse.

It was now or never. "Come on!"

They darted across the street, hoods pulled tight over their heads. Any onlooker less than half drunk would recognize them as outsiders. But they were fortunate; the street remained empty. Only when they were safely across did they dare to breathe again. The Gryphon made his way to the back of the inn. The garbage pile was a disappointment. Scavengers were already at work on the few good pieces, and the rest stunk of rot. After one whiff of the odor floating about the refuse, the Gryphon came to the conclusion that they had been fortunate.

"Well?" The drake came up behind him, sniffed, and shook his head in disgust. "Never mind. I can tell."

Something stirred within the pile of refuse. Something the size of a small dog, but shaped like no dog that the Gryphon had ever seen. It resembled a large rat in some ways, but the face was all pushed in, and no rat had teeth like this creature did.

"If we cleaned it off, it might make good eating," Morgis suggested quietly.

The thing let out a harsh bark. Another rose near it. A name came to the Gryphon. "Verlok."

"Verlok?"

"Some fool's attempt to free the cities of rats. They succeeded, but now they have verloks instead."

A third verlok rose from the back of the rubbish pile. It was bigger than the first two.

"These verloks." Morgis put a hand on the hilt of his sword. "How large a colony do they usually live in?"

The same harsh bark rose from garbage mounds all along the back alley.

"Large enough." The Gryphon pulled out his short sword very carefully. The drake did the same. "Back out of here. We can't fight verloks, not in great numbers."

Morgis gave him no argument, but asked, "Why do the wolf raiders let these vermin thrive? Why not hunt them down? They have the power."

"Why should they? The creatures take care of the garbage situation— probably even a few of the unfortunate souls that the Pack Master would rather ignore."

The creatures nearest to them had grown silent, but they could hear others, much farther away, calling out.

The Gryphon stiffened. "They're alerting others! They're passing along word about us!"

"Gryphon . . ."

At the drake's warning, the lionbird slowly turned. Verloks were slowly converging from the alleys behind them. He could make out at least two or three dozen indistinct shapes, and he knew there had to be more.

Morgis had his sword drawn and used it to ward off a particularly arrogant verlok. The creature let loose with a staccato of harsh barks that they were certain would bring every soldier in Canisargos to them.

The Gryphon glanced around. Not one torch or candle had been lit. The inhabitants of the nearby buildings might have been dead for all the interest they seemed to have in what was going on behind their establishments and homes. Canisargos was evidently a place where people minded their own business. What they did not see they could not be held accountable for—so they thought. For once, he was happy that such an ignorant attitude existed.

That, of course, did not solve their vermin problem.

Slowly, they were edging their way back to the side street from which they had originally entered. The Gryphon's memories would tell him nothing further about the verloks; it seemed that most of his sudden recollections occurred only at the last moment, when they were absolutely needed. He wondered when some memory would return just a bit too late. It probably would not matter; he would not be around to worry about it by then.

The verloks did not follow them down the side street, for which both of them were thankful. It rankled them, especially Morgis, to retreat from such creatures, but both of them were experienced enough to know when they were at too great a disadvantage. There was nothing to be gained from standing and fighting. Better they continue through the maze called Canisargos in the hopes of reaching their destination. . . .

And then . . .

The Gryphon wished he knew what D'Rak planned. Or D'Shay. Both of them wanted a confrontation, but on their own terms. D'Rak wanted to use the lionbird as bait; that much was obvious. Still . . .

A new wave of harsh barking filled the silence of the empty streets, this time with a malevolent touch to it. From behind him, the Gryphon heard Morgis hiss in consternation. He did not have to ask why; one glance told him. For reasons of their own, the verloks had decided to follow them. More than two dozen of the beasts were already in sight, and more were materializing around the corner.

"Do we fight them? I could still use a fresh meal." Despite his words, it was evident that the drake did not really desire to take on the ever-increasing pack.

"No. We move."

"A good plan."

They stepped out into the main street, which was still devoid of any other souls, and scanned the area. Morgis pointed at a path to the right. "That way?"

"We don't have much choice." He pointed to the left. Verloks were coming out of every other possible route in numbers that would have had the local inhabitants fleeing for their lives in complete panic. The lionbird would not have blamed them.

Lest they lose the only path still available to them, they dropped caution and ran for the street that Morgis had chosen. The verloks farthest behind gave silent chase; oddly, those nearest seemed to hesitate.

Morgis led the way down the other street. The creatures followed close enough behind to be a threat but not close enough to actually strike. Something bothersome nudged at the Gryphon's mind.

"There's another intersection ahead! Which way?"

"Try right again."

Morgis whirled around the corner—and then backtracked into the Gryphon as at least a dozen verloks came racing down the direction the two had chosen.

There were more coming from the path that had been on their left. With no other choice remaining, they continued on their original route. The verlok stampede grew as the newcomers joined the main pack. The only benefit

to the entire situation was that so many beasts together in a narrow area
slowed down the group as a whole.

It was the drake that said it first. He was breathing rapidly, more from
frustration than exhaustion, and the words came out in bursts. "We—are—
being—herded."

That was what had been bothering the Gryphon. For scavengers, the
verloks were acting with great precision. The two were being given one route
and one route only. It was also too much of a coincidence that no one—
and in a city such as Canisargos, it was an impossibility—absolutely no one
else had strayed into their path. The city might as well have been deserted.
In the distance, they could hear the sounds of the city's night people. Even
assuming that everything in this section was closed for the night, it was
impossible to believe that not one Aramite patrol had even come within
sight—with two fugitives on the loose yet.

"What can—we do?" Morgis breathed.

"Stand and fight—or see where they want us to go."

"Your choice?"

"We can't fight them all. Let's hope they have other plans than just tiring
us down before dinner."

"If we were only not under the spell of the senior keeper . . ."

"We would've probably brought the full force of the Aramite empire
down on us. This—this is their capital city, remember."

The verloks continued to hound them silently. In their own way, they
were worse than the Runners. At least the shadowy, lupine forms presented
a defeatable opponent. Here, one could cut apart the scavengers all day and
not put much of a dent in their population. It was the futility of the situation that wore at the two the most.

"Gryphon, we're getting—closer to—the palace."

They were, indeed. Ominously close. He had wanted to enter this place,
but under far different circumstances. He had wanted a fighting chance. Run
into the ground like a hapless rabbit was not the way for him. The Gryphon
was tempted to turn and make a stand here and now. Better to die fighting,
even if it was against the stinking, garbage-scavenging verloks. He doubted
a death in the claws of the Ravager's underlings would be an honorable one.

Verloks suddenly came rushing from the path before them. The
Gryphon and Morgis were forced to turn to the left—*away* from the
sanctum of the Pack Master.

"Where—" was all Morgis could say before a portal that had not been there a moment ago materialized directly in their path, swallowing them before they could even react to its presence.

"WELCOME BACK. I'M sorry about that. I had to hurry."

The Gryphon rose angrily from the cold stone floor that the miniature gate had deposited them on from a level two feet aboveground. The unexpected absence of a place to stand had sent both him and the drake tumbling across the room. Their new host apologized again.

"It was a rather desperate maneuver. You wouldn't have liked where the verloks were steering you. Trust me. I know what it is like."

They recognized the voice before the figure itself became distinct in the dim light.

"Jerilon Dane!" Morgis hissed madly and reached down for his borrowed sword, from which he had been separated in the fall. "Warm-blood!"

"Stay your hand!" The Aramite raised both hands high to show that they were empty. "I've no weapons, and the power I used to open the portals is depleted. Are drakes so lacking in honor that they would strike down an unarmed opponent?"

The Gryphon, who remembered well many of the atrocities certain drakes such as Duke Toma could perform, made no move to interfere—yet. He had no love for the former wolf raider, but neither did he kill out of hand. Morgis would have to decide for himself what value he placed on his honor and that of his sire. If the drake made the wrong choice, the lionbird would react then.

Morgis hesitated, the sword point wavering from one side of Dane's chest to the other, and then muttered some incomprehensible drake curse. With great visible effort, he sheathed the blade.

"Better. I mean you no harm."

"You abandoned us to the wolf raiders' senior keeper!" the duke protested bitterly.

"I did nothing of the kind—my departure was hardly by choice. I was rescued myself. By pure chance. It could've been any of us. He only had time enough to focus on one."

The Gryphon glanced around. They were in a dusty, abandoned chamber. The place resembled an old assembly room more than anything else. Much of the back end of the room was hidden under a curtain of darkness. The one visible exit revealed a stone corridor. It was almost as if they were back in the private dungeons of D'Rak. "Where are we?"

"The underworld of Canisargos—what some call one of the three ancient homes of the gods." From the tone in his voice, it was evident that Jerilon Dane believed what he said. That was not comforting, considering what god was supposed to reside in this city now.

"And what about this 'benefactor' of ours? Who is he and what does he want from us?"

"You could ask him all that yourself," a familiar feminine voice added.

"Troia?" Startled by the relief in his own voice, the Gryphon quieted, feeling fortunate at that moment that his avian features prevented others from plumbing the depths of his embarrassment.

Her face *did* seem to light up at his reaction. She stepped into the chamber, a torch in one tawny hand, her every movement seemingly measured for best effect. A true predator, she would have been able to turn the simple act of walking into an offensive or defensive maneuver.

"It's about time you two got here." Closer, she looked a bit strained, as if she had worried far more than her casual airs indicated. "He'll be so pleased!"

"Were you out there all the time?" Jerilon Dane snapped.

"I'm sorry—I wanted—to be nearby in case something other than these two stepped through. You might've needed help."

"Your concern is overwhelming," he snarled. "Unlike your trust!"

"My children, why must you bicker so? We are all allies in this."

The Gryphon stared at the tall, regal figure making his way into the chamber. "Lord Petrac!"

"Gryphon." The Will of the Woods leaned heavily against his staff. He seemed a little haggard, as if the Master Guardian had been through great strain of late. If he had been the mastermind behind the successful escape of all four of them in the midst of the wolf raiders' capital city, then it was more of a surprise than he could stand—even with something to give him support. "Forgive me. I've been overtaxing myself of late, it seems."

Troia went to aid him, but he waved her away.

Morgis, who had never met the Master Guardian before, eyed him critically. "You are the one responsible?"

"I am, Duke Morgis."

"Is it not a little dangerous for you to be here in the stronghold of your enemies?"

The stag's eyes fixed on the drake, and it was Morgis who finally looked away. Lord Petrac was exhausted, yes, but he was by no means weak. "There is a danger, true, but the risk is necessary if I am to salvage any hope for the Dream Lands. Besides, I could not leave you at the mercies of the Aramites."

He included all of them in the statement, but the Gryphon noticed that his gaze had turned to Troia. It was as if the Will of the Woods was speaking for her benefit alone. The lionbird instinctively bristled, then, ashamed at the thoughts running through his mind, he forced the dark emotions down.

"I think," the Master Guardian continued, "that it would be best if you departed Canisargos at once. D'Shay and D'Rak must both be after you by now. My ploy will not fool them long." He did not elaborate on what that particular ploy consisted of.

It was Morgis who surprised everyone then. He stiffened, pointed at Lord Petrac, and, in a voice loud and precise, said, "There is more to this than you have said. *Tell them about your dealings with the Ravager's spawn. Tell them about the betrayal you have concocted with the senior keeper, D'Rak.*"

The Gryphon looked from the drake to the Master Guardian. Instead of the incredulous shock that covered the faces of Jerilon Dane and Troia— not to mention himself—there was only a sadness in the proud visage of the Will of the Woods. He tapped the staff on the dust-covered floor.

"I don't know by what means you discovered this, reptile," he whispered, "but I *am* afraid it is going to cost all of you."

Morgis was looking at everyone in befuddlement. He did not even seem to remember what he had just said. While the drake looked from one person to another for some explanation, Petrac tapped the floor with his staff again.

To the Gryphon's growing horror, a familiar, incessant whisper began to rise throughout the chamber.

"I am *truly* sorry," the Master Guardian repeated softly.

XIV

WHAT AM I to do with you, D'Altain?" D'Shay reached out, took the traitorous keeper by the scruff of his neck, and threw him against the far wall. D'Altain struck with a heavy thud, only his armor and his talisman protecting him from severe damage. In the background, the two gryphons threw themselves at the bars of their cages

582	*Richard A. Knaak*

and cried out again and again. D'Altain wished they would quit screaming about killing. He was not, he knew, in a very comfortable situation. D'Shay might save him from the revenge of D'Rak, but perhaps only so that D'Shay might punish him *himself.*

The master wolf raider reached down and pulled the hapless figure to his feet. "Again. What *am* I to do with you? You failed miserably, you've destroyed what value you had by playing your hand too soon, you've cost me others that I had planted in D'Rak's own guard unit. Can you tell me what I am to do with you?"

"Master." D'Altain was past the point of image. He was pleading now. "Master, I have served you well before this. Always I informed you of where, what, and when. Always you have maintained your favor with the Pack Master. Please, my lord, I know I have failed in this task, but I can still be of service to you! I cannot go back!"

"No, you can't." D'Shay smiled and released the traitor. As he did so, he noticed that his graying skin was now peeling as well. He had held on longer than necessary, hoping to arrange things so that he would not leave himself defenseless during the change. That could no longer be counted on. For a brief moment, he considered using D'Altain, but the Aramite had little enough of a form to work with. He would burn out too soon.

There was still his prisoner. It all depended on the Gryphon—who was nowhere to be found!

"I agree," he continued, noting the slight look of relief on his former spy's features. "You can't go back. You have to remain here."

"Thank you, Master!"

D'Shay looked behind the smaller man to where two of his unliving guards waited. On an unspoken signal, they stepped forward and took hold of the arms of the uncomprehending keeper.

"Lord D'Shay! What are they doing?"

His eyes suddenly turned to the cages holding the master wolf raider's two pet gryphons. Guards similar to the ones holding him prisoner were releasing the savage beasts. They were shrieking in joyous anticipation. The Aramite struggled desperately, but futilely.

"You've served me sufficiently well in the past, D'Altain, but your present failure is unacceptable, so I'm going to serve *you*—as one last treat before my pets receive the main course. The Gryphon." D'Shay reached forward and pulled both talisman and chain from the other wolf raider's neck. "You won't be needing this."

He watched with satisfaction and clinical interest as the unfortunate keeper was tossed into the midst of the two savage beasts. D'Altain proved, he noticed, to be less of a challenge than the last prisoner had. As the two gryphons continued their grisly game, he felt a chill in his hand. He looked down and noticed that the crystal no longer glowed with the power of the keepership. It was no more than a dull stone now. D'Shay dropped it by his feet and crushed it with one heavy heel.

It would have been so much more satisfying if the crystal could have been the senior keeper himself. D'Rak was no longer a constant nuisance; he had become a threat that nearly vied with the Gryphon for priority. Outright assassination was impossible. The Ravager expected more from those who served him. Even a successful assassination would probably lower him in the estimation of his master. No, first the rival had to be humiliated before his counterparts, stripped of his prestige and, consequently, his rank. That would satisfy the true lord of the Aramites.

It would also prevent possible repercussions. He knew that a number of D'Rak's people lived as if their lives depended upon the senior keeper's health; he knew that it was literally true in some cases. While it would rid D'Shay of some annoyances, it would also rid him of some allies that he might find handy in the near future.

Something major was afoot, and he disliked the fact that he knew so little this time. Things seemed to be slipping away from him. Not like the past. Now, he actually worried about his existence and its possible abrupt end. He also worried about the obvious fact that his lord the Ravager was distancing himself of late from his most favored servant. *That* was a warning sign if nothing else was.

Could that mean that the Ravager was looking at D'Rak as his new favorite? D'Shay shuddered at the thought of his master abandoning him. He did not want to end up as the Pack Master had. It was difficult to say whether nonexistence was worse or not.

"I've been a fool!" he muttered to himself. The unliving guards waited patiently for his commands. The gryphons were cleaning up after their meal. They were quick, voracious eaters. Only bits of armor, torn off like the skin of a fruit, left any indication of the late D'Altain's presence.

"A fool," he repeated more softly. He had allowed others to do his work for him, something he had generally shunned in the past. It may have been because of his own failures in the Dragonrealm. Perhaps that was why, he thought, he had started depending too much on others. There was only one being he could trust: himself. He could make others obey, but, in the end, it would have to be his hand that held the blade. That was what had raised him to his present position; that was what was required of him to remain the power he was. He had been a bigger fool than D'Altain not to see that.

As he watched the gryphons being herded back into their cages, their hunger temporarily sated, he wondered where the Gryphon was now. There were other players in this game, the grand game of the Ravager. Not just D'Rak and the Master Guardians of Sirvak Dragoth. He knew, for example, that more than one party was making use of the troublesome Tzee. If he—

D'Shay broke off. The Tzee. Now, *there* was a possibility he had not thought through. . . .

TZEE . . .

They were stronger than the Gryphon could have believed possible.

Tzee . . .

He was on his knees. To the side, Morgis was struggling to maintain a standing position, but his legs were quivering, and only a few seconds more passed before he joined the lionbird on the floor. Jerilon Dane, who the Gryphon was certain had been a part of this, was nonetheless writhing in agony under the savage assault by the nebulous multiple entity. Only Lord Petrac, of course, and Troia were left untouched. The Will of the Woods was speaking softly to her, as if to explain his reasons for what he was doing. Through bleary eyes, the Gryphon watched as she argued with him. The words were smothered under the constant, mind-numbing whisper, and he could only hazard a guess as to what they were actually saying. He could see that Troia was in terrible straits. On the one claw, she worshipped the Master Guardian as someone special, someone above the petty emotions that most beings allowed to control their lives. On the other, she knew that what Lord Petrac was doing went against everything she had been taught at Sirvak Dragoth.

The Gryphon fell beak-first into the floor. Jerilon Dane had ceased moving. Morgis was still struggling feebly, and he would probably last a little longer than the lionbird himself. He took one last look at Troia. The argument was evidently over. With a wave of his staff, the Master Guardian sent her—elsewhere. The Gryphon could take a little comfort in knowing that Lord Petrac cared for her and would not harm her.

The world faded into black.

Oddly, he was not quite unconscious. Either that, or he was dreaming. If it was a dream, it was a lackluster one, for he floated in a place of nothing, much like the Void, but pitch-black. His body would not function, and he worried until he realized that, since this was a dream, it really did not matter.

He suddenly knew he was no longer alone.

Gryphon.

He tried to speak, but no words would come. Nonetheless, he somehow knew that the other understood him.

In a brilliant burst of fire, *he* was there.

More massive than any man the Gryphon had come across. Both wider and taller, with a build that spoke of years of heavy conflict. This was a warrior, not just a man clad in armor—ebony armor trimmed with fur. His face was covered in a full-visage wolfhelm that left only the eyes, searing eyes, open to study. Nothing resembling humanity could be found in those eyes.

Gryphon.

"I—hear you." The sound of his own voice startled the lionbird.

I am the Pack Master.

The Pack Master. As enigmatic a ruler as the Crystal Dragon, the Dragon King who had, in the end, been a telling blow against his own mad brother, the Ice Dragon. Other than that similarity, he could not class the two together. The Crystal Dragon he felt he could trust, but trust was not a word one could associate with the figure floating before him. Not the Pack Master. Not the hand that guided the wolf raiders.

Amusing.

The Pack Master knew what he was thinking. The Gryphon let him see much, much more.

I am tempted to withdraw my offer. Hear me out, misfit.

His dream self bristled at the insult, but could not move otherwise, save to ask, "What offer?"

I will give you the prize that has eluded you so long.

"What prize?" Possibilities ran through his mind.

I can give you . . . D'Shay.

D'Shay! "I'm hardly in the position to take him."

Agree and I will free you. Take D'Shay, do with him as you will, and return across the seas.

"Forever, I suppose."

Yes.

"I won't bother telling you my decision. You know what it is."

He had come here in search of his past and to observe the potential threat of the wolf raiders to the Dragonrealm—especially that one region that had come to mean so much to him. The Gryphon had then discovered that his enemy was not dead, as he had supposed, and that gave him a third purpose. It was not his ultimate purpose, however, and he could no more depart this continent with those tasks undone than he could abandon the inhabitants of the Dream Lands to the dark hordes of the Ravager. D'Shay's death was not the point of it all, though the Gryphon was the first to admit he could become obsessed at times with the thought.

Misfit! Mortal fool! I—I—

The image of the Pack Master seemed to melt. The wolf visage grew, became alive, and burst forth from the rapidly decomposing matter that had been the supreme commander of the Aramites. An enraged lupine face thrust itself high, growing and growing until the jaws were great enough to take the Gryphon whole. A vast, scarlet tongue lolled from the open maw, and saliva dripped in huge buckets.

You had your chance! It cannot be said I did not offer you that! I will win this game, though, and because you could not see sense, you will be crushed like all the rest! You will be mine dead or alive! Then he will never escape his bonds! The game will be mine!

Still howling, the maddening image vanished. The Gryphon, exhausted mentally, gave in to unconsciousness, but not before his mind noted one item of interest. Not the fact that, if what he saw was true, the Pack Master was no more than a vessel for the Ravager, but the simple fact that, from both his words and his tone, the living god of the wolf raiders was frightened.

Frightened of him.

HE WOKE IN a soft field of wild grass. He looked around drowsily for Troia and felt a pang of fear when he did not see her. Then he remembered the pond. It was her favorite place, of course. Unlike the cats she so resembled, Troia loved the water. She was no doubt swimming even now.

Rising from the grass, the Gryphon gazed up at the beautiful morning sky. A few fluffy white clouds dotted the heavens, but other than that it was like staring at a rich pageantry of blue silk. He could not recall ever seeing such a wonderful sight—

—and he could not recall how he had come to be here with Troia—

—which was all that mattered. She would be waiting for him. He yawned. It was a much easier process now that he had shifted to human form. There was something wrong with that, but what it was bothered him only briefly. Once again, it was Troia that made him forget all else. Why not? What else did he need besides her? They had the field, the trees, the pond, and the food that was provided them—what else, indeed?

A brisk swim, the ex-monarch decided, would do him good. Clear the cobwebs from his overrested mind. He removed his tunic and tossed it carelessly aside. No one would take it. There *was* no one else.

Morgis?

He shook his head. No one else. Only Troia.

The pond came into view, a glistening, almost perfectly round pool of clear water. A few trees dotted one side. Someone had built a tiny platform that could be used for diving—who? It did not matter, for at that moment, *she* broke through to the surface of the water. Droplets flew all around as she shook herself. Her lungs filled with fresh air. She had removed the garments the proprieties of Sirvak Dragoth had forced on her, and the perfection of her face and form was enough to make the Gryphon question the unbelievable chance that had brought them together—whatever it had been.

He ran the rest of the way, discarding things along the path, landed on the platform, and, just when it seemed he was about to run straight off into the water, leaped into the air. The dive was not perfect, but it accomplished its secondary goal. Waves of water flew everywhere, but mostly on Troia, drenching her again. She sputtered and slapped at the water playfully.

The Gryphon rose to the surface, his smile matching hers. Then something large bumped against his leg. It was long and sinewy, not at all like the tiny fish that inhabited the pond. He felt it again, and the pleasure of the day gave away again to the uncomfortable feeling that something was amiss.

Coils of scaled flesh wrapped around his legs, tightened, and threw him off balance. As Troia watched, uncomprehending, he fell backward into the pond. His only comfort was that he had had enough warning to take a deep breath.

Claws ready, he tried to make out what the creature was—and especially where its head was located. It was a serpent of some sort. He could not recall ever seeing one here. The Gryphon slashed at it, but the water slowed him enough for it to shift, and the tips of his claws barely grazed it.

"Gryphon!"

A long, reptilian head materialized from behind him, the serpent's body wrapping itself around his forearm as the head twisted forward to better see him.

"Gryphon! Ssstop thissss nonsssensse!"

He had his free hand raised, and this time there would be no mistake. One swipe would shear the serpent's head from its body. One swipe.

"Gryphon, you fool! Look at me! Wake up! I am Morgissss!"

Morgis? The Gryphon shook his head. He knew no Morgis—yes—no! Trapped between conflicting memories, he did not pay heed to the fact that, by rights, he should have drowned by now. The serpent, however, was quick to use his confusion to point that out.

"Thissss isss an illusssion! One of Lord Petrac'sss! You've been under water far too long! Don't you sssee that thisss isss a falssse reality?"

"False?" He heard himself utter the word and then remembered it should have been impossible to do so. He blinked and watched the world flicker. From pond to dank, dusty, long-abandoned chamber to pond again. Then the chamber. Pond. Chamber. With a shriek, he forced the illusion of the pond out of his mind—and with it, the illusion of Troia.

He found he was flat on his back staring up at the ugly, half-hidden features of Morgis. The drake was looking at him with more concern than the lionbird would have thought possible for one of his kind to feel for an outsider.

"He's out of it. You've freed him."

The Gryphon twisted his neck until he could see the second figure. Jerilon Dane, looking more than a little disheveled. There was a hollow look in his eyes, and his skin was pale where it was not covered by a thin coat of black hair.

"What . . . happened? How long was I out?"

"That's two very good questions," the former wolf raider commander commented. "Blame the Tzee for the first. They—it—whatever the Tzee is, our 'good friend' Lord Petrac has given them more power—but he made them use it to ensnare us, not kill us. As for the second question, neither of us have an answer to that just yet."

"More than a day, if the fur growing on this Aramite's face is any indication," Morgis added.

The Gryphon closed his eyes for a moment, seeking the darkness in order to reorganize his thoughts. His conversation with the Ravager returned to him. *That* was no dream. He found himself pushing that incident aside, though, as false memories of the pond and his time with Troia intruded.

"Don't sssink back into it!" A scaled hand slapped the side of his face.

He instinctively brought his claws into play. Strong hands gripped his wrists. The Gryphon forced open his eyes and saw Morgis, long, sharp, predatory teeth clenched, struggling with him.

"The Master Guardian must have given him something truly special," Dane remarked almost clinically.

"The pond . . ." The lionbird shook his head. *It did not exist!* he told himself. *It was a false dream!*

He rejected the memories—this time permanently.

"I'm better. Let me up."

Morgis shifted and, still holding on to the Gryphon's wrists, helped him to his feet. The former monarch gazed at his surroundings. It was the same chamber that they had been brought to by Jerilon Dane. He turned to the Aramite. "How did you escape?"

"I can't take credit for that. It was your scaly companion here who first broke free of the imaginary world the Will of the Woods created for him."

"*Lord Petrac*"—utilized by the drake, the Master Guardian's name became a slur word—"does not understand my people. Once he realized that I had no answers to any of his questions, he tried to set me down in some idyllic world." The duke laughed harshly. "He does not understand what an idyllic world is to a drake. I had to get out before I went crazy. I knew that I would never have consciously chosen a place such as he had created."

"His shouts brought me out of it. I've had keeper training. I understand these sort of traps a little. Once I recognized it, escaping proved simple. I woke just as he was rising to go to your aid."

"You were trapped more deeply in your dream," Morgis continued. "Lord Petrac must have wanted to be very sure of you."

The Gryphon nodded agreement, not wanting to elaborate on just what the Master Guardian had created. He forced his growing anger in check; despite everything else, he was certain that Petrac had been acting in kindness, that he had recognized a growing bond and had brought it to its ultimate conclusion in order to keep the lionbird securely under control.

It did not make the Gryphon any less unforgiving, though. Lord Petrac had much to answer for, especially the pact. . . .

"Morgis." The drake looked expectantly at him. "You don't remember *anything* you said before he turned on us?"

"Nothing."

"I've already asked him that," Dane interjected. "He remembers nothing."

"Interesting." He told them about his encounter with the Ravager. Dane grew even more pale, and began to glance about as if he expected his former master to materialize in his full glory at any moment. Morgis, on the other hand, listened with growing interest.

"What you sssay . . ." He paused, correcting his speech. "What you say makes some sense, though I cannot think of any reason a god should fear a mortal."

"He feared me enough to offer me D'Shay on a platter."

"You should have taken it. I would have liked to see nothing better."

"In return, we would have departed for the Dragonrealm. I can't leave this continent to that bloodthirsty wolf lord and his horde of trained pets."

"The Dream Lands would fall," Jerilon Dane confirmed. "Two years ago, we would not have sworn to that, save to appease the general population and protect our positions. Now, even though my campaign was a farce," the former wolf raider looked bitter, but for which reasons he did not say, "the Dream Lands are slowly losing their reality. In three, maybe four years' time, the only Dream Lands will be those in the memories of the victorious war council."

"You're forgetting one thing," the Gryphon added angrily. "Lord Petrac's alliance."

"With the Tzee?"

"With D'Rak. What do you think he could possibly have offered the senior keeper to seal such a bargain?"

Morgis understood immediately. "The one thing that will secure the Aramite's place among his fellows! Sirvak Dragoth!"

"Sirvak Dragoth and his fellow guardians. I suspect that Petrac's reward for this will be control over whatever remains of the Dream Lands. A tiny preserve of his own where he can sit back and believe that some portion of the domain he was supposed to protect has been saved due to his valiant efforts—forgetting, of course, all those unfortunate enough not to be one of his chosen few survivors."

The Gryphon studied his two companions. They seemed ready for whatever he decided to do. Without their powers, he wondered if the three of them could do anything. The ex-mercenary sighed. What other choice did they have?

He turned to Jerilon Dane, who knew Canisargos better than either of the other two. "We need to find a way out of this city, and fast. Do you have any ideas?"

The look that spread over the former wolf raider's already darkened features told the Gryphon more than he wanted to know.

He closed his eyes in mental exhaustion. "Then I have a suggestion . . ."

XV

Troia savored the last bit of ripe fruit and smiled, revealing sharp, white teeth more suited for tearing the flesh from prey than for biting into an apple or a berry. Nevertheless, she had enjoyed the fruit brought to her by one of Lord Petrac's helpers as she had never enjoyed a meal before. There was something about the things grown within the vicinity of the Master Guardian that made items grown elsewhere taste flat and bland. The cat-woman chalked it down to the inherent goodness in her host, her mentor. No other Master Guardian affected her the way the Will of the Woods did. With Lord Petrac, she felt confident; at peace with the wild beast within, and, best of all, protected from those threats that were beyond her capabilities.

"How are you feeling now, Kitten?" The Master Guardian, looking unusually worn, materialized from the woods surrounding her. He was leaning hard against his staff, and there was a distant look in his eyes. She could feel his concern for her. He cared for her much the way a parent cares for a beloved child.

"I'm well. Why do you ask?"

He frowned momentarily, then said, "I am always concerned with the health of my friends, Troia. Would you want me otherwise?"

"You could never be otherwise." She rose, thinking to depart, but finding instead that her host had, for some reason, moved to block her way.

"You've only just come. I insist you give me more of your time; I so rarely see you."

There was something wrong, something . . . that she had forgotten. Troia tried to make an excuse; she did not feel right being here. "Haggerth will be looking for me."

"Haggerth?" The stag head registered surprise—and possibly consternation. He recovered swiftly. "I doubt that he will be looking for you. When I last spoke to him, not more than an hour before, he indicated that he had no need for you and that you could stay for as long as you wish—or is that it? Have you tired of my company already?"

"Oh, no, my lord!" She felt helpless as he guided her back to where she had been sitting. Her movements were slow, hesitant, not like her at all. Something was not right.

Tzee . . .

She heard it only once, and might have dismissed it if not for the tightening of the Master Guardian's hands upon her. He summoned one of the villagers who aided him and requested drink for her. She did not protest, knowing somehow that he would convince her otherwise. He then rose and gave his apologies, saying he would return in a moment. Not once did he mention exactly what he had to do.

Troia had a great urge to sleep, but she fought against it. Try as she might, she could not accept what was happening to her. That brief whisper stirred something within her, memories that contradicted with the present. Memories that concerned Lord Petrac as well. Unsettling memories of . . . the Gryphon?

"Gryphon." She whispered the name as if by doing so it lent her strength. Memories of capture and escape and . . . treachery began to return to her.

"Lord Petrac." The name that had always meant honor and peace now disgusted her. Troia remembered everything, including the Tzee and Morgis's sudden, shocking declaration concerning a pact between the Will of the Woods and one of the Aramite lords. Her claws extended and retracted in growing anger. An unspoken trust had been betrayed. She wanted blood.

Rising slowly, silently, she moved down the path the Master Guardian had departed by a moment before. One of the villagers, carrying drink, stepped in front of her, openmouthed. She bared her claws, then realized that these people were probably more innocent than she was. The villager, a young male not quite yet into adulthood, dropped what he was carrying and turned. She caught him by the arm, pulled him back to her, and, with an apology that only seemed to confuse the situation further, struck him hard. In appearance, Troia seemed more supple and sleek than strong; in actuality, her strength was such that in hand-to-hand, she more often than not defeated opponents twice her size, veteran fighters all.

She lowered the unconscious boy to the ground, swearing she would make it up to him if she survived this mess. Troia found herself wishing that the Gryphon were here; he always seemed to maintain a presence of mind despite the hopelessness of a situation. She also wished he were here for other reasons, but they had nothing to do with the problem at hand.

Seconds later, she was cursing herself for being such a fool. At the very least, she could have questioned the boy to see if he knew where his master was and what he was doing. Tracking would not be too difficult, but, if there was an easier way, she would have been happy to take it. Only fools overflowing with pride sought the more difficult path.

Minutes passed, and she seriously thought about returning to her place of—captivity, she decided—and seeing if the boy was still there. The one thing she had forgotten was that in this region, Lord Petrac's scent was everywhere. Recent scents mixed with new scents, and it was almost impossible to tell one from the other after a while. She could not give up, though. Not with so much at stake. Not even if the traitor was Lord Petrac, who would very likely push aside her attack like one might push aside a leaf that had landed on the shoulder.

She heard a movement behind her.

"Well, what a delectable little cat we have here."

Without pause, she whirled and leaped at the source of the voice. Two figures clad in armor stepped into her path and, to her dismay and agony, she bounced off them like a pebble, landing in a painful heap three feet back from them. The speaker laughed.

"Such a foolish little cat. Always look before you leap if you want to avoid broken bones and such."

Through tearing eyes, she glanced up in horror at the familiar black, fur-trimmed armor. Wolf raiders in the Dream Lands! It was impossible— unless she had accidentally left the reality of her world and reentered theirs. No . . . she would have noticed that, wouldn't she?

The two figures she had struck gripped her by the arms. She looked into their faces, hidden by wolfhelms, and discovered that nothing peered out from behind the masks. Her struggles increased, though still to no avail. They had a strength more than human.

The third figure stepped closer. It wasn't D'Rak, she knew that already from the sound of the voice. If not the senior keeper, then there was only one other wolf raider who moved with such presence, such confidence and energy.

He cupped her chin in one hand and, in a coldly polite manner, said, "I am D'Shay. We haven't met face-to-face before, but you must be Troia, the Gryphon's female."

Troia found his smile far worse than that of any predator she had ever faced. There was no humanity in it and none of the innocence of a true animal. D'Shay was the worst of both worlds, a true apostle of the Ravager.

"Cat got your tongue?" The smile faded. "You shouldn't have come this way. I have this . . . obsession with things and people related somehow to the Gryphon. I like to take them and mold them to my will or maybe just see that he finds them unrecognizable—if he finds them at all."

She could no longer completely hide the growing fear within her, but she forced herself to reply, "You're pathetic, Shaidarol! Small wonder you and the *scavenger* get along so well!"

He released her chin and slapped her across the face with amazing speed. Blood dripped from her mouth, but she felt some satisfaction.

"There is no more Shaidarol! I am D'Shay, most loyal servant of the Lord Ravager!"

"Unhand her." This voice she recognized, but whether she should be relieved or angered the feline woman no longer knew.

Lord Petrac, a bear on his left side and a very large mountain cat on his right, came striding defiantly down the path. For just the briefest moment, it looked as if the two groups might come to blows, but then D'Shay stepped back and, with that earlier, disconcerting smile back on his face, he ordered the two armored . . . suits to help her to her feet. Once it was obvious that Troia could stand on her own, they released her.

The Will of the Woods held out one hand. "Come to me, child."

"Come to *you?*" she spat in his direction.

D'Shay laughed loud and long. "You seem to be losing the respect and confidence of your people, Master Guardian!"

Petrac looked more annoyed than worried. "Unless you would rather go with Lord D'Shay here, I suggest you come to me, Troia."

Given *that* sort of choice, she reluctantly joined the Master Guardian. Lord Petrac glared at D'Shay with disdain and disgust. "Never touch her. Not even your master will be able to save you from my wrath if you do."

The look on the master wolf raider's visage indicated he was anything but worried about such a threat, but he nodded agreement.

Troia looked up at the being she had once nearly worshipped and, forcing back her anger, whispered, "What is he doing here?"

Shaking his head, the Will of the Woods sadly replied, "He is apparently my new ally, young one."

"*Ally?*" Worse and worse.

Lord Petrac looked pained at the accusations in her eyes. "I will do what

I must to preserve *some* portion of the Dream Lands. If I do not do something, there will be *nothing*. Nothing."

"But the wolf raiders! How can you deal with the spawn of that mad god?"

"I have dealt with them before."

"You will deal with me from now on, Lord Petrac." D'Shay took great pleasure in that statement. The Master Guardian's eyes narrowed, then he agreed.

Troia buried her face in Petrac's chest. "First D'Rak, and now this traitor—and is the Gryphon part of your contract as well? Have you given him to this—this—"

"Hush, child." The Master Guardian glanced warily in D'Shay's direction. "You have my word, Shaidarol, provided you act swiftly and adhere to the same pact I made with D'Rak, though how you know so much . . ."

D'Shay stroked his goatee. "You may thank the Tzee for that. They are the perfect allies; you know they will do what they can to achieve greater power. It's refreshing to have an ally that is so predictable. I contacted them originally in the hopes of using them to locate the Gryphon and to act as my eyes in regards to D'Rak. Imagine my surprise to quickly discover that, in exchange for a measure of power, they were all too willing to tell me about your own deal with my counterpart in the keepership. A good thing, too. The conquering of Sirvak Dragoth would have guaranteed his place as foremost among the Ravager's—that is, the Pack Master's—favorites."

"Something you cannot afford."

Troia listened with growing foreboding. There was no way D'Shay would actually adhere to his agreement with Lord Petrac. As long as one fragment of the Dream Lands remained, the wolf raiders would wonder, wonder if it might ever prove a threat again. The only certain way was to eliminate the problem once and for all. Eliminate the Dream Lands.

She knew Lord Petrac did not see it that way. Though he had already broken his promise to one wolf raider, he still obeyed some sort of code of honor, and he fully expected D'Shay, who was the last one the feline woman would have trusted, to maintain his part of the bargain.

"Something has to be done with her, you know."

At first, it did not dawn on her that D'Shay was speaking about *her*. Only when she felt Petrac start did she realize the danger.

"I have already told you. She will not come to harm!"

D'Shay sneered. "How do you propose to keep her out of the way? She's already proven her willpower. If she was able to escape one of your dream sequences, then she will be able to escape another. Best to give her to the Tzee. They would keep her occupied."

"I will do no such thing—and do not think to threaten me, Shaidarol! You need either myself or Geas to open the Gate long enough for your forces to come through, and I very much doubt you can convince *him* to do it! You also need the Gate to remain open so that the power of the Ravager can maintain your rather fragile personal existence!" The Will of the Woods smiled triumphantly as he watched the master wolf raider step back in momentary panic. "Yes, I know your plight just as I know what your servants are. Anywhere but the Dream Lands, the thread of your existence is safe. You are always in contact with your master. Here his power does not reach, and you must rely on either the Gate being open, allowing him continued access, or the good graces of the Tzee. How would they feel, I wonder, if they knew that you had perverted a portion of their being to create your *loyal* guards? Shall I tell them? It might save me trouble. Then I can go back to dealing with D'Rak."

D'Shay suddenly smiled, and both the Master Guardian and Troia, who had turned to watch the wolf raider's reaction, shivered at the sound.

"Very good, Lord Petrac! Not quite as clear-cut as you think, but close enough! I *will* point out that it would take me a very long time to die, and the first one to suffer will be the little kitten wrapped in your arm. But why should allies argue? This is the time for action, not bickering! D'Rak may, at any time, discover your duplicity. The Gryphon is still loose—"

"He is not. I have him."

"You *have* him?" D'Shay's face lit up with genuine joy. "But this is fantastic!"

"I . . . will turn him over to you, providing you swear to your end of the bargain by the word of your master—the Ravager, not the Pack Master."

"My lord, no!" Troia tried to pull free, but Petrac's arm was as unpliable as the manacles in D'Rak's private cells. The Will of the Woods put a hand over her mouth, holding it closed.

D'Shay ignored her outburst. Incongruously, he looked as if he wanted to hug his ally. "My master and I both thank you for the gift! In his name, I gladly swear to the bargain! Deliver the Gryphon to me and your private domain will forever remain untouched!"

Lord Petrac seemed satisfied with that. "The Gryphon is in a safe place and will keep. He and two companions are . . . resting."

"Then let us begin."

"Agreed." The Master Guardian gazed down at Troia. She tried to bite his hand, but he continued to hold her mouth closed. "I am sorry, young one, but it is time for Sirvak Dragoth to fall so that the Dream Lands may be at peace at last. You will have to sleep this one out. Forgive me."

She hissed a protest. Lord Petrac released her mouth and reached for her forehead. Troia had only time to begin the most vile curse she had heard before the traitorous guardian touched the center of her forehead and consciousness fled. She slumped in his arms, forcing him to allow his staff to fall to the ground. He lowered her down onto the path and retrieved the wooden artifact. Straightening, he stared into the eyes of D'Shay.

"I give you two hours from the moment you depart. In two hours, you must have your forces ready. I will have enough to do to keep the Gate under control, since I expect the other Master Guardians to attempt to close it."

"Two hours will more than suffice. Make it one."

"One?" Petrac blinked. "One hour to gather an army?"

One of D'Shay's unliving guards—it was debatable whether the Tzee or anything derived from them could truly be called life—stepped through a portal. The wolf raider acknowledged the guardian's question. "One hour. *We* have always been ready for this moment; where do you think Senior Keeper D'Rak was going to get his army?"

"I will never understand how such a society could exist."

D'Shay gave him one last smile before he and his remaining guard vanished through the Tzee portal. "I could say the same about yours, Master Guardian."

Lord Petrac watched as the Tzee withdrew. When the portal had dwindled to nothing, he took one last glance at the sleeping form on the path. The Will of the Woods frowned, but he knew that now was not the time to have second thoughts. He would be hated, reviled, but only until the survivors came to understand him. The constant pain of the half-real world called the Dream Lands touched him without respite. He could not let it suffer, and there was only one way to treat old, festering wounds. It was like trimming the trees in his woods so that they might grow better. There would be a new land, forever safe from the outside reality of such as the wolf raiders or the drakes who ruled the continent to the west. The Dream Lands would one day become more magnificent than ever.

Here the day was bright and sunny. He had no idea what it was like in this location in the other reality. Probably dank and miserable, he supposed. It really did not matter. All that mattered was preparing for the beginning of change. Just a little less than an hour before the new glory of the Dream Lands began its birth rites. Born in the ashes of blood and flame to become a stronger, free land.

His mind set at ease, the Master Guardian made his way toward his private place of contemplation. When the time arrived—and he would know exactly when that was—he would be prepared.

SOMEONE WAS *NOT* doing as D'Rak desired.

He knew that, because the Gryphon and his companion were nowhere to be found. There were rumors that they had been seen near the Pack Master's stronghold, rumors that an army of the hideous verloks was on their tails, a rumor that they had even been eaten—which *was* possible, knowing the verloks.

There were also confirmed reports of the hooded, faceless creatures wandering the streets with a sense of purpose no one could recall them ever having. *That* worried the senior keeper. *They* were supposed to be neutral. *They* had never acted for or against the Aramites—at least, to no one's knowledge. Yet . . .

He had dismissed D'Farany so that he could think on these matters in the peace of a barely lit room. In fact, the only true illumination was that which emanated from the Eye of the Wolf. The glow was steady, something he was thankful for. Of late, it had been unreliable, as if . . . as if the power of the Ravager was coming into question. He had not told anyone of this, since it would only weaken his standing. With the capture of the Gryphon, the senior keeper had noticed a return to stability. It had flickered only once the other day, but enough to frighten him.

Still, despite the fact that the Eye appeared to work well, he could find out nothing concerning the Gryphon, his draconian companion, or the female from the Dream Lands. He knew that D'Shay could not possibly have them; his archrival would have made public news of this if he had. The Gryphon's capture would have spelled success for D'Shay and certain doom for the senior keeper.

D'Rak let the power focused by the Eye take him out of the chamber and over the city. He thrilled in becoming such an integral part of the very structure of the world. The hidden design of the world was open to him, and it was a great temptation to become a part of the design forever. He had long ago learned to control such a temptation, but that did not prevent him from basking in the feeling.

A thorough scan of the city proved once more that they were nowhere to be found. That should have been impossible for the Gryphon, at the very least. D'Rak had made certain of that with the smaller talisman around his neck. Like the guards, the Gryphon was marked. Where he went and what he did should have been open to the senior keeper's observations, but they were not. D'Rak doubted very much now that his own death would trigger the death of the lionbird—not that he was going to test that theory. It was just that someone or something seemed to be watching over the misfit, protecting him from powers awarded to the Aramite lord by the Ravager himself. Something on a level with the god—but that was absurd! There had never been and there never would be a force capable of reckoning with the true master of the empire!

D'Rak returned his thoughts to the original capture of the Gryphon. There had been that female who had vanished and the fact that the source of the escape portal could not directly be traced. Continual observation had indicated that it might have happened at least twice, once from within the city walls, but, again, the portals had all but defied study.

"Master!"

The senior keeper looked up in righteous anger, contact with the Eye broken by the interruption. No one, not even his new second-in-command, was permitted to disturb him during his contemplations. He summoned a guard and ordered him to drag the offending keeper to him.

D'Farany allowed himself to be escorted without hesitation. Anxiety was splashed all over his features, but not anxiety for his own precarious situation. D'Rak found that strange. The younger keeper certainly had to know that he had transgressed. Perhaps his news was worth hearing before he sent the boy down to the cells for a few days of . . . tutoring in the rules of the keepership.

"Speak—and you had better make it good!"

"Master!" D'Farany was still trying to catch his breath. He had run for some time, trying to bring the news to his lord in a way that would assure understanding. He no longer trusted his fellows. "Master, those units designated this month for standby duty are being summoned! Everyone! Gryphon riders, keepers, line soldiers, Runner controllers—everyone!"

D'Rak rose, shaking in anger and understanding. Nevertheless, he had to be certain before he did anything. "Are they being activated for maneuvers? What are their orders? Who gave them?"

The young Aramite kneeled, knowing all too well that his own lifespan might be cut short at any moment. "Master, the orders come from D'Shay with the permission of the Pack Master. He . . . he claims he will give them the Dream Lands! Master, is it possible? Could he—"

"Leave me! Return to your post! Your excellent work will be noted!"

Beaming at yet another sudden change in his fortunes, D'Farany saluted and rushed off. The two guards that had brought him in awaited orders of their own. D'Rak gave them one look. They turned and, to their credit, departed in a hasty but military manner.

Frantic, the senior keeper reached out and renewed contact with the Eye. Because of his growing fury, the connection was unstable, but he was able to observe that everything his aide had said was true. The Aramites kept a large force ready at all times purely for the possible invasion of the Dream Lands. The Ravager had so demanded it. Each month, soldiers from different units were assigned standby duty. They would rise, dress for war, and inspect all gear. Items were cycled in, maintained, and then cycled out if they began to grow worn. Rations were checked for spoilage and replaced before they became inedible. This was the preliminary assault unit. Even now, other units were organizing as men returned from wherever they had been. The senior keeper knew that, even now, his own men were preparing for their part. Some would continue to monitor the city's safety, while others would assault the Dream Lands on another scale. As for the senior keeper himself, his duty . . .

His duty was his own survival, and he knew it! Somehow, D'Shay would make certain that he would lose face, that another keeper, more pliant, would take his place.

I have been betrayed!

His supposed ally, the Master Guardian called Lord Petrac, was responsible. Yet, there still might be a chance. Whatever D'Shay offered him, D'Rak would match it and then some. Then the guardian would close the Gate, trapping those who had already gone through. D'Shay would be shamed for falling into a trap, and then the senior keeper would step in and save the day. D'Rak would prove the great hero—and it would cost only a few hundred line soldiers. There were always more of those.

With the aid of the Eye, he sought out the Tzee. He still needed the vermin to maintain contact with anything in the Dream Lands. That would change soon.

Tzee . . .

He was surprised at how readily they revealed themselves. The Tzee had always been a little hesitant, knowing who was the stronger. Even with the power he had granted them, they still knew their place.

Tzee . . .

The Eye shook, and D'Rak could not help but blink. That should have broken contact, but it did not. The Tzee were not only maintaining contact, they were beginning to *manifest.*

Tzee . . .

In his chamber! Why weren't the guards responding? Any unauthorized intrusion into the senior keeper's chambers was an automatic death sentence unless he chose otherwise.

Tzee . . .

A huge, black, nebulous cloud of matter and energy formed above him, pulsating like a living heart. D'Rak could feel a thousand million eyes upon him. Malevolent eyes. The Tzee had been waiting for this moment.

He summoned the power of the Eye of the Wolf and stared in consternation as the glow faded from the great, crystalline artifact. *Not possible!* He reached for the Ravager's Tooth around his neck, but it, too, was dead. Dead.

And still the guards made no move to aid him. They stood as if they heard nothing, as if they saw nothing.

Tzee . . .

There was only one thing left for D'Rak to do. . . .

XVI

WE LEAVE THESE chambers, we leave Lord Petrac's protection. He dared only mask these three chambers from the sight of the wolf raiders. I don't doubt now that he didn't want his *ally*"—Jerilon Dane spat to the side as he said the word—"to know of his own duplicity."

The Gryphon's plan was to find one of the not-people, or Faceless Ones, and convince it to help them. He knew that location was no impediment to the blank-visaged creatures. The Faceless Ones could do what they wanted where they wanted. They were supposedly neutral, but that did not necessarily mean they couldn't interfere. Of all the puzzles crossing his path, the not-people were among those that disturbed him most.

"We can't wait for one of them to come to us," the lionbird replied calmly, ignoring the latter portion of the Aramite's remarks. He had thought it over time and time again. It was their best hope.

"Why not? They seem to have an affinity for showing up when one needs a hand. I should know; the Runners would've had me if they had not."

"I'll not trust my luck to Faceless Ones," Morgis hissed. "I cannot explain it, but I don't trust them."

The Gryphon studied him. Morgis had the same look in his eyes that the lionbird suspected he himself wore when trying desperately to recall a memory. It would not be too surprising to discover that the not-people had plots of their own hatching. Nevertheless . . . "Have you thought of something else?"

"No." The drake's voice was flat, defeated. "Nothing feasible. I've had little experience in trying to escape from the capital city of an enemy empire. Perhaps next time."

From anyone else, it would have been an attempt at humor. From the drake . . . the Gryphon was not quite sure.

"We've no real reason for hesitating, then, do we?" The Aramite had the least reason to be happy with this situation. He had wanted to avoid his former home at all cost. Another chase with the Runners was all that awaited him here if he was captured.

Dane located the dead torch that Troia had been carrying before the discovery of Lord Petrac's betrayal and had apparently left behind when suddenly whisked away by the Master Guardian. While it was not entirely dark—a dim glow emanated from tiny crystals embedded, at regular intervals, in the walls—a torch gave them some security. The Aramite, who had no night vision whatsoever, was especially happy to be able to traverse the halls without falling into something he just could not see. With the torch lit—after some doing—they began their trek through corridors supposedly untouched for generations. *Supposedly* was the key word; the Gryphon recalled the passageway in the citadel of the senior keeper. "Are you certain these halls are unused?"

Dane nodded. "It's not something important enough to need to forget. The corridors date back to the early days of Canisargos, when it was little more than an outpost. As you can see, our ancestors built *very* well, though I don't doubt that this place has been improved on a number of times since then. These passages were more well hidden then. Later, they were used for storage. Many of them are still in use, but many are not." An odd smile flashed across his face. "I find it interesting that such a powerful city could be so indifferent or unknowing about an entire world beneath their feet. We've—*they* have grown too complacent. They think that there is nothing to fear, that they are invincible."

The trio were silent for some time afterward. They checked a few side corridors, but these always ended in some chamber. It was decided that the best thing to do was stay in the main passage and hope it ended at an exit.

They came across yet another side passage, and Morgis decided to give this one a quick look. He leaned in and let his eyes adjust.

"A stairway!" His shout brought the others running—mostly to quiet him in case they were not alone down here. "Leading upward!"

He could not be blamed for his excitement. It was indeed a stairway— what was left of it. Disuse had taken a greater toll on it than the rest of the corridor. It seemed to be an addition, and a late one at that. Dane stepped forward with the torch and, with his eyes, followed the ascent of the stairway up to . . .

The former wolf raider stepped away from the stairs, swearing by the god he claimed he no longer had faith in.

"What isss it?" Morgis asked angrily. He strode over to the steps and peered upward. "It's sealed off! They've covered it over with a wall. There's no door anymore."

Cautiously, the drake climbed the crumbling stairs and vanished into the dark. A minute passed, and then he came back down. "No hidden door— unless it's much more well hidden than any I've encountered, including the one in the keeper's lair. I'd say the work was completed years, perhaps decades, ago."

"There might not be another exit from this part of the corridor," the Aramite added in annoyance. "We might have to backtrack and go down the opposite direction."

The Gryphon considered it. "Would that take us deeper into Canisargos?"

"I couldn't say. I never saw the surface. I'm only assuming we're headed toward the outer walls because our 'savior,' Lord Petrac, gave me some indication that this was the proper way. Things he said, nothing specific and, at the time, I really couldn't be bothered with . . . with— What a forgetful fool I've been! We have to go back to the chambers we started from! He may not have taken it with him!"

"Taken what?" Morgis demanded, but the Aramite was already back-tracking. The other two were plunged into near-darkness as their companion vanished in the distance.

"Follow him!" The Gryphon hoped that whatever Dane wanted was worth a return to their starting point. Every moment they remained trapped in the city, the danger to the Dream Lands increased. With his secret revealed once, Lord Petrac would not be able to help but think that someone *else* might know. Based on his own experience, the lionbird knew that whatever the Master Guardian had planned for his home and his people, it would occur soon. Only then could Lord Petrac rest easy.

THEY FOUND THE former wolf raider searching, not the chamber that the three of them had been trapped in, but a smaller one across from it. He was having difficulty pulling something from a shadowy corner because of the torch he held in one hand. That he had not bothered to do something about the situation pointed out how anxious he was about the object he had uncovered.

In the flickering light, the Gryphon could make out only a cloth-covered object approximately the size of a head—it was a poor choice for comparison, considering their situation—and apparently fragile, for the Aramite treated it like a newborn child.

He held out the torch to the Gryphon. "Hold this while I get a better grip."

"What is that thing?"

"This, Lord Gryphon, is the head of your former jailer, a beast called R'Mok."

"Disgusting!" Morgis hissed. "We would not waste our times with such trophies! We leave our enemy's dead to the carrion creatures or our mounts, should they be hungry."

Jerilon Dane grimaced. "Much more civilized, of course. I have not kept this toy because of some hobby—though I won't deny that some of my former associates might have such keepsakes. Rather, I held on to it because I thought that the head of the keepership's jailer might prove of value to us. Besides, I doubt you really know what's underneath this hood."

The ex-soldier pulled the cloth, so akin to a tiny shroud in appearance, and smiled coldly. "Senior Keeper D'Rak was a master at crystalline structuring."

The head of the late jailer was a parody of a true human head. The entire thing appeared to have been carved from one great gem. A grinning mouth had been carved, but whatever humor it was trying to convey was lost upon the onlookers. There was a ridge that was located approximately where the nose should have been, but, of the eyes, there was no sign. Nor were there any ears or even holes in the sides of the head. In certain ways, the grotesque object was reminiscent of the not-people.

"The man is the foulest of necromancers. He is not even satisfied with merely raising the dead," the drake muttered in great disgust. "He has to mutilate them as well."

The Gryphon noted some markings carved into the side of the false head. "What are these?"

"Part of whatever spells the senior keeper utilized to create this abomination. This is not his first, gentlemen. Only the latest and the best. The others lived only a few months at a time."

"What does he propose to do with these creatures?"

Dane shrugged. "I don't remember. What I've told you is what Lord Petrac told me. He knew I'd need the head to free you. Since he hadn't said to leave it, I took it with me. I still find it hard to reconcile that someone like your Master Guardian could deal with the likes of Lord D'Rak."

The Gryphon was studying the head. There was no discernible place where the neck would connect to D'Rak's terrible toy, but the lionbird knew only a little about magic involving crystal. Most of what he had learned had been derived from what little was known about the most solitary of the Dragon Kings, the self-styled Crystal Dragon. The power of the Crystal Dragon could not be denied. The Gryphon wondered briefly what the mighty drake lord would make of this.

He finally pulled his eyes away from the monstrosity. "Cover that up until we absolutely need it. As for Lord Petrac, I suspect he would deal with the Ravager himself if he could be satisfied that his own little kingdom would remain. In some perverted way, he sees himself as the only hope for any part of the Dream Lands. All he'll end up doing is killing it."

Morgis nodded. "He's mad if he thinks he can keep the survivors under control. Eventually, they'll discover the truth, and that will be the end of it."

The Gryphon blinked. "Listen to us. We're talking as if the Dream Lands are lost already. We may still have time. Lord Petrac may not have even started."

"We can't use this in here." Jerilon Dane made a sloppy attempt at covering up the "face" of D'Rak's creation. "The vestiges of the Master Guardian's masking spell make this thing useless. We have to go out into the corridor."

"Then let's do that. I'm getting tired of catacombs and such. I want to see the sky."

Morgis went first, sword ready just in case something did show up. Dane came next. When he stepped out of the chamber, he yelped in surprise. The Gryphon, behind him, almost stumbled into him. When he finally had a clear view, he could not blame the Aramite for his lack of poise.

The crystalline head was glowing so brightly, it was a wonder that Dane's hands were not burning. The former wolf raider quickly pulled the hood over the gleaming object, but that did little to hide the intense light.

"It's never done this before!"

"What *is* it doing?" Morgis was unconsciously trying to protect himself from the glowing head by waving the tip of his sword in its direction. He realized what he was doing and, chagrined, quickly lowered the blade.

Shaking his head, the Aramite shoved past the Gryphon and dove back into the room. The blinding brilliance dimmed to a more tolerable level but did not die completely.

"I—don't—understand," he puffed.

"I think we've lost much of Lord Petrac's protection," said the Gryphon from the entryway. He pointed at the cloth-covered artifact. "And I think that thing did it. I think it's working against the spell."

"It shouldn't be able to!"

"Tell *it* that! Something's changed that thing! It happened the moment you took it into an unprotected area! If you know how to use that thing— if you still think we can *trust* that thing—then be prepared to do it fast! If the keepers locate us, you can be certain that they'll have soldiers here at any moment!"

That stirred the Aramite. He rose and stared at the glowing, cloth-covered object in his arms. "I think I can still manipulate it. My failure to become a keeper didn't stem from a lack of ability; it stemmed from being unable to bind myself with a talisman of my own. All keepers must bind themselves to talismans blessed by the senior keeper."

Morgis snorted. "Which is also a good way to keep an eye on any troublemakers, I imagine."

"Most likely. Give me a moment." Dane pulled off the hood and stared into the crude face of the artifact. He shivered. "I feel like I'm staring into the face of Lord D'Rak himself. This may prove more difficult than I imagined."

The Gryphon's fur and feathers suddenly stood on end. "You'd best do it quickly. I think our time has just run out."

The corridor abruptly filled with the sounds of many armored men running.

Someone with the voice of youth, who was not quite experienced in giving commands, shouted, "I want them alive, if possible, but *dead*, if necessary!"

Morgis looked from the frantic Jerilon Dane to the corridor and then to the Gryphon. The duke broke into a horrific smile, showing great quantities of sharp teeth. "I'll hold them off! Call me if you get that thing working or can think of a miracle!"

He raced out of the chamber, shouting foul descriptions of wolf raiders that questioned the validity of their bloodlines. Dane could not help looking up at the Gryphon, who shrugged and then unsheathed his own sword. "Do you really think you can get that thing to work?"

"I have to, don't I?"

The lionbird nodded and went to join the drake.

There were Aramite soldiers everywhere. Most looked like members of the keepership guard, but there were two keepers as well, one of whom, much younger than the Gryphon would have expected, was evidently in charge. He, of course, was far from the battle. Still, both he and his companion were clutching their talismans tight while they tried to get a good view of Morgis.

The Gryphon knew then who his targets had to be.

Duke Morgis stood before the three foremost guards, his shortsword carving a wicked path before him. Two wolf raiders were already down, and a third looked to be injured. The corridors were wide enough for three men to move without bumping into one another and that would have meant the end of any foe but a massive, experienced drake warrior. Even with shields, the wolf raiders had actually begun to back away.

Glancing at his shortsword, the Gryphon cursed. There was no way he could get to the keepers, and it would not be long before one or both of them ensnared Morgis. At the very least, they might disrupt him enough for the soldiers to get under his guard. Without his powers, the duke would die as any warrior died. Heroic, yes, but still dead.

One of the dead wolf raiders lay on his back, and the Gryphon spotted one of the dark, curling daggers that seemed to be a favorite with the black-clad figures. He hurried over to the body and relieved the corpse of the weapon. A quick check of the other dead Aramite revealed no such dagger. He would have to make do with the one.

The battle had moved back much farther than the ex-mercenary would have believed. Morgis was a savage, skilled fighter, true, but he was battling members of a people born to war. It was almost as if they were purpose-fully giving way.

It was almost too late before he realized what they were doing. Only when he sought out the keepers and discovered only the commander still in sight did he recognize the trap.

They had passed one or two corridors and even a side chamber. Morgis, caught up in the battle, did not see the one keeper step into the next such chamber to the drake's right. By the time the Gryphon understood what was happening, the duke was already moving past the entryway to that room.

The lionbird flipped the knife, catching it by the flat of the blade. The twisted blade was weighted oddly, but not so much that he was worried.

As the drake, confident of his abilities, moved completely beyond the entranceway, the keeper stepped out from behind, fully intent on bringing Morgis down through the power of his talisman. Like the other keeper, he was young, which explained why he had not bothered to check for a second foe. There was a good reason why most veteran fighters were not fools. Most fools died young.

The Gryphon threw, forgoing some accuracy for the sake of speed.

The keeper must have heard him in that last moment, for he started to turn. Quite possibly, it prevented him from dying immediately when the knife struck, for, had his back been turned as it was, the blade would have sunk itself into his neck. Instead, it caught him along the throat and bounced off his chest plate. The keeper gagged, lost his grip on the crystal-line artifact he wore, and reached upward in a desperate attempt to stem the flow of blood. The Gryphon realized that, despite not striking the neck directly, he had succeeded in cutting the jugular.

Success turned to disaster, for the dying keeper fell to his knees before the lionbird could reach him, stumbling into Morgis's legs and throwing the drake off balance. Wolf raiders swarmed over the duke, and several more came for the Gryphon.

"Gryphon!"

Jerilon Dane's scream was no indication of success. Even as the former monarch was thrown against the wall by sheer numbers, he felt the entire underworld shudder. A brilliant light burst forth from where the hapless Aramite had been working desperately.

The Gryphon felt power wash over him, and immediately understood ⸻east what *that* meant. The only trouble was, there was little he could do ⸻ed against the wall.

⸻ fierce roar added to the pandemonium, and the chamber was almost ⸻tly filled with a rapidly growing dragon.

⸻ much too long, Morgis had been thrust from one situation to ⸻ without his powers and, especially, his inherent magical ability ⸻eshift from his humanoid form to his birth form and back again. ⸻ preferred the dexterity of the humanoid shape, to steal his right ⸻rm from one to the other was like clipping a bird's wings so that ⸻o longer fly.

⸻ like a bird who has realized that his feathers have grown back, ⸻stantly knew his powers had returned.

⸻ramites quickly forgot the Gryphon as they tried to cope with ⸻agon than they had ever seen in their lifetimes. Whatever Dane ⸻ashed, it was tearing at the entire system of spells that the keep- ⸻woven about Canisargos. Morgis thrust his head toward the ceil- ⸻ it was the latter that gave. Heavy stone, including full sections ⸻ing and wall, caved in, crushing more than one wolf raider. Those ⸻ on the same side as the Gryphon foolishly tried to get past the ⸻ding drake. They were either crushed flat against the walls or thrown ⸻assive paws, eventually landing in broken heaps. One mad frustra- ⸻struck at the dragon with his sword, perhaps out of a spotty ⸻. The keeper that Morgis had originally fallen on, the dragon ⸻mory on the floor. w, the lizard

The one great danger at the moment was the now portions of ⸻night inadvertently cause the Gryphon's de the stumbled back had succeeded in avoiding the collapsin rtially, but it was suf- the building above were falling as le chamber. Jerilon Dane toward the blazing light. ad in such a manner that

It took a moment for ⸻ ficient for him to see ⸻ was standing in the ⸻

it appeared he was trying to absorb all the energy flowing out of it. He
seemed not to notice the instability of the walls and ceiling, but a single
step by the Gryphon in his general direction made the Aramite look up.

Their eyes met. The eyes that stared into the lionbird's were *not* the eyes
of Jerilon Dane.

A huge portion of the chamber's ceiling came crashing down with
inches of the former wolf raider. He started to say something but
cided against it. Then, what remained of the ceiling began to fall and
Gryphon was forced back out into the corridor. He was not able to
if Dane survived. A moment later, there was no more entranceway to
room.

"GRYPHON!"

The voice boomed from overhead. Walls and a portion of a ceili
all that remained of whatever structure had been on the surface. Mo
done his best to ensure that his companion was not crushed by the
ing building. The same could not be said of the Aramites who had
them. Perhaps a few had escaped if the other keeper had been able
a portal in time.

Now was not the time to be concerned with that, however. By
entire city was aware of the fact that a full-grown dragon was in the
and the Gryphon doubted that the wolf raiders lacked the means
ling such a problem. The keepers, especially, were a threat.

A massive reptilian head came swooping down toward him.
shouted, "Dane! Is he dead?"

"I can only assume so! The chamber—"

The dragon cut him off. "We have not got the time to look! Climb
m   d!"

was the first time he had seen his companion in this form, an
as th
a th to say that Morgis was as grand, as overwhelming a drago
su ved on had seen, barring the Dragon Kings themselves. If t
the s   Morgis might one day be one of them. He certainly h
If ever e been so simple for the dragon to swallow him whole.
"Once   to have in a situation like this . . .
more secure
Morgis be s building, slide down to my neck. You will be
the corridor an
the Gryphon fe   f the hole that was all that remained of
People were screaming and cursing, and
nd loss of life that must have been

sustained. He knew that, like any other people, not all Aramites were evil. He wondered whether Morgis felt any guilt. Drakes had a more pragmatic view of such matters; in his eyes, he probably viewed the destruction as necessary to the preservation of his own existence. Unlike Duke Toma, however, Morgis did not seem to revel in carnage.

The Gryphon tightened his grip. It would be some time before he completely forgot what had happened here, if he ever did and if he managed to survive this day.

"Where are they? Where are their legions?" At last back in his natural form, the dragon was eager to prove his power. The Gryphon, on the other hand, had no other desire save to leave as soon as possible.

"Their legions will be here soon enough," he shouted at the dragon, although, in his mind, he, too, wondered at the absence of a ready force. There were a few single soldiers trying to make order out of the chaos, and one patrol with a lone keeper who looked as though he would have rather been elsewhere, but nothing vast and organized. That would not be the case for very long, of that the lionbird was certain. Canisargos would never be left completely unprotected, even during a major campaign, and since there was no major campaign on at the present . . .

But there *was*. It was the only explanation. They were already too late.

He leaned close in order to assure that Morgis heard him. The dragon was nearly out onto the surface, his vast body overwhelming and crushing buildings all around them. Most of the people had fled by now, and even the soldiers were starting to retreat. The Gryphon caught sight of the keeper again. The Aramite was staring at his talisman, which evidently was not working as it ought to have. They still had breathing room, then.

"Morgis! Forget the city!"

"No! I want D'Rak! I want this D'Shay! I want this city to know the power of a dragon!"

This was proving more difficult than he had expected. Morgis was building himself up into a frenzied rage. All the frustrations since his arrival on the shores of this continent were coming to a head.

"Morgis! They're attacking the Dream Lands! That's why we haven't been overwhelmed yet!" He did not mention his suspicions concerning D'Rak's toy. Whatever it was and whatever it had done, it was, hopefully, buried forever beneath the rubble, preferably in several thousand little pieces. Sooner or later, the keepers remaining behind during the invasion would regain control, and then that would be all for the two of them.

"Not here?"

"No! Hurry! If we leave now, it might be that we can find a way into the reality of the Dream Lands and stop Lord Petrac!"

"Lord Petrac!"

The Gryphon could see the sudden change in goals. Morgis wanted the Master Guardian as much as he wanted D'Rak, probably more.

"Slide down, Gryphon! We are going to fly!"

Just in time, too. The lionbird suddenly felt a presence, one that he knew could only be the keepers working to regain mastery of the situation. Regaining mastery meant disposing of the main problem, the dragon in their midst.

He slid down to the base of the dragon's neck even as huge, membraned wings spread wide, damaging even more of this section of the wolf raiders' capital. The Gryphon wished the damage could have at least included the citadel of the keepers or the stronghold of the Pack Master.

"Hold tight!" Morgis shouted almost gleefully. He had not flown in too long a time.

The huge, blue-tinted behemoth rose into the air at an astonishing pace. Clinging for dear life, the Gryphon remembered that a dragon's ability to fly depended partly on sorcery, which was why they seemed to pick up altitude and speed at such an alarming rate.

When they were high enough, Morgis leveled out. The Gryphon dared to look down and was astonished to see that, despite the distance they had risen, the city still seemed to go on forever in every direction. They had not been near the outer wall! If anything, he suspected that they had been moving away from it.

"Gryphon! I sense some massive disturbance to the east!"

"It can only be what we're looking for! They have to be moving troops through still! We have a chance!" It seemed impossible that the dragon could hear him, what with the wind, but Morgis nodded.

"How will we enter the Dream Lands?"

"I don't know!"

The great beast *hmmphed.* "Well, at the very least, if we cannot get in, neither will many of the cursed Ravager's dogs!" Morgis twisted his neck and revealed a vast, toothy grin. "We shall see to that, eh?"

As the dragon turned his attention back to the task of flying, the Gryphon, still holding on as tightly as possible, wished he could share his companion's confidence. Somehow, he doubted things would be so easy. After all, they never had been before.

XVII

D'FARANY HAD FAILED and, worse still, had acted without the authority of Senior Keeper D'Rak. Now, with one entire section of the city in ruins and both the dragon and the one called the Gryphon free and out of the range of the Keepers' powers, he had to face his master and explain. D'Rak had not summoned him, but he knew better than to wait for such a summons. His only recourse was to go and explain his story as quickly as possible, before the senior keeper heard other tales. Perhaps he could get off relatively lightly if he could convince his master that he had attempted the capture in an attempt to prove himself worthy.

If he didn't, there was a good chance that he would be joining his predecessor, whom the crystals indicated had gone to his traitor's reward at the hands of D'Shay. *Why did the invasion have to take place at the same time?* he wondered. Because of that, D'Rak would be in the foulest of moods.

The senior keeper was sitting in near darkness, the Eye of the Wolf hovering silently near the right of his chair. The great crystal was ominously dim. D'Farany had heard stories about it. It had always been described as glowing, at the very least. The few times he himself had observed it, it had almost lit the room as well as a dozen of the seeing crystals and several torches combined might have. Was there something *else* amiss?

"Master?"

The figure sat motionless. The head was slumped forward, one hand attempting to keep it at least partially propped up. The younger keeper forgot his own predicament, suddenly fearing that D'Rak might be ill or, worse yet, dying.

"Master?"

The figure stirred. D'Farany breathed a heavy sigh of relief. Lord D'Rak had only been resting.

"What—is—it?" The voice sounded slurred, as if the senior keeper was drunk—an impossibility.

"Master, it's D'Farany. I'm afraid I have disturbing news concerning the one called the Gryphon."

"Gryphon?" The senior keeper looked up. Most of his face was obscured by shadow. D'Farany gazed into the darkness where D'Rak's eyes must have been, but only briefly, finding something unnerving about that area of the other's face. He felt as if the eyes must be watching everything, including what eyes could not normally see.

The senior keeper appeared to be growing impatient, so D'Farany started his tale. D'Rak was motionless during the whole story, as if absorbing the information was all that mattered to him. As he did not give any sign of anger, D'Farany began to relax and his narrative became more clinical. When he had finished, he stood there silently, awaiting the senior keeper's instructions—and possibly his final judgment.

"The Gryphon. He goes to the Dream Lands." D'Rak's voice was raspy. The younger keeper nodded in acknowledgment of the assumption. It made sense. Where else would the outsider go? It was said that he had once been one of the creatures guarding that elusive domain.

"Not this time."

"Master?"

"Nothing." The senior keeper might have been a statue, for all he moved. "D'Shay enters the Dream Lands."

"As you say, my lord." D'Farany was extremely uncomfortable. Perhaps Lord D'Rak was ill after all.

One hand rose, and a finger was pointed at the aide. "You obey me. Understand?"

"Your . . . your will is mine."

"It is. We—I want D'Shay gone. Gryphon gone. Master Guardians gone. The Gate must be closed."

Shock rippled through the other Aramite. "But . . . without the Gate, we cannot invade the Dream Lands!"

"Untrue." For the first time, the shadow-enshrouded figure showed some true confidence. He leaned back. "The power to control the Gate is now in here." D'Rak tapped the side of his head. "We have no need of the others."

"I . . . am overwhelmed, my lord! How did you secure it?"

"A change in thought was all that was needed." The senior keeper's voice was more its old self. D'Farany's fears began to subside.

"There are keepers in the invasion force. Loyal ones."

"Yes."

"Good. I—yes, I—want them to locate D'Shay's ally. A Master Guardian called Lord Petrac. He has the head of a stag."

"Ravager's Teeth! A stag's head?"

"They will kill him or, failing that, turn him against D'Shay. He has a weakness. Love for lessers."

D'Farany understood. A few hostages, utilized in the proper way, would either make the Master Guardian careless or make him furious, which would probably result in his cutting off those soldiers in the Dream Lands from any outside aid. "Those trapped in the Dream Lands will die."

"Possibly, but I will move to save them if timing permits. Go. Now. The instructions are simple enough. I will join you shortly."

"Master." The younger keeper bowed and, his spirits quite the opposite of what they had been when he had entered, departed to organize the betrayal. It did not occur to him that there were many loose ends in the plan outlined to him. As a keeper, he was used to his superiors' taking care of such things. If D'Rak said nothing more, then there was nothing more to be considered.

The shadowy form of the senior keeper rose from his chair. He studied his hands, as if seeing them for the first time. With his right, he guided the Eye to a spot before him. With his left, he summoned forth the power locked within. A few gestures brought him an image of the massive forces of the Ravager moving slowly through the Gate. Thanks to Lord Petrac, the Gate was at least ten times the size it had normally appeared as, but that still did not allow enough men to go through at one time. At least as far as D'Shay was concerned, no doubt. As for the traitorous former guardian himself, he would have been one of the first through. This was to be D'Shay's triumph, and the only way he could assure that was to lead it himself. So much the better. When the Gate closed, it would be the beginning of the end for him. If not through the keepers, then through the simple fact that he was unable to escape from the only place his master's power could not sustain him for very long.

Sirvak Dragoth would fall with the keepership's aid, leaving the Gryphon. But this time, they were prepared—more than they had expected to be. And with the Gryphon dead, the Ravager would reward them with even *greater* power, which was all they lived for.

"No, there is only 'I.'" A smile appeared on the visage of the senior keeper, an involuntary reaction, and one he was not familiar with. It was ignored. "Later, it will be 'we' again. When they are all dead, and only we remain."

Tzee . . .

* * *

A DRAGON FLIES more swiftly than any other creature, portals and demons not included. Thus it was that, when it seemed at first that Canisargos went on forever and ever, the eastern wall came into sight not more than half an hour later. That still said something about the size of the Aramites' mightiest city, the fact that it had taken Morgis even that long. Despite commenting once or twice about possibly leaving a major path of destruction in his wake, Morgis had flown without pause toward the great emanation of power that they could both feel long before they knew for certain what it was.

"The Gate of the Dream Lands! It's grown!"

The Gryphon followed the dragon's gaze. The Gate had indeed grown. It stood nearly as tall as Morgis did now, and the archway where the great doors presently hung open was probably just wide enough for him to squeeze through. Huge, dark shapes flowed over the sides of the Gate, and the lionbird recognized them as the tiny guardians of the artifact, albeit now nearly as large as a pony. He wondered why they did not attack the invaders.

A harsh squawking filled the air. The Gryphon scanned the heavens and spotted several airborne forms moving toward the two of them. "Gryphon riders!"

He counted more than a dozen and hazarded a guess that there were at least twice that many. As the riders neared the dragon, Morgis let loose with a stream of smoking flame.

The gryphon riders separated in precise fashion, the column of fire continuing on harmlessly between what was now two columns. That separated farther into four units and then into eight tiny squads.

"Gnats! They try to beset me with gnats!" Morgis laughed. The Gryphon found the situation much more serious.

"Morgis! They're more dangerous than you think! Don't let them—"

"Worry not! I'll have them swatted aside in no time!"

Three came within range of his paws. He swung at them, claws extended, fully expecting to get at least two. The riders, however, controlled their beasts well and, by the time the dragon's paws reached where the targets had been, the riders were above and below.

Morgis suddenly screamed, and the Gryphon was barely able to hold on as the dragon writhed in pain. "I've been slashed!"

The Gryphon turned. Several riders had taken advantage of the deception in order to strike the unprotected flank of the leviathan. Morgis had twisted away immediately, but there were now several long, bloody gashes in his tail, his lower backside, and, most likely, his stomach region as well. Real gryphons had claws sharper than most any other creature and beaks strong enough to bite apart all but the strongest of metal bars.

As Morgis turned, one massive, leathery wing accidentally struck one of the beasts fully. Both rider and steed plummeted limply toward the ground. The rest of the riders pulled their animals back. Several began flying around the dragon in a circle going from left to right. Others began flying right to left. They were trying to cross Morgis up.

"If they'd stand still . . . What sort of warriors do they call themselves? They should fight in a more seemly manner!"

"They'll *win* if this keeps up, Morgis! You're already bleeding profusely!"

"One lucky strike! I was not prepared!" Nevertheless, the dragon sounded just a bit uncertain.

A rider darted in from the back side. The Gryphon heard the swoop of wings and twisted away just before the claws of the beast could tear him from his place on the dragon. He formed a fist with his left hand and, drawing from the less trustworthy lines of power that crisscrossed the skies, he created a spear of pure power that was his to control. The act of creation took but two seconds, a fortunate thing, because now several riders were daring the powers of the dragon in a deliberate attempt to get the Gryphon. He did not have to ask why. They obviously knew who he was, and both D'Shay and the senior keeper had undoubtedly given orders to capture him if possible—kill him, likely, if it proved necessary.

Those who knew the Gryphon well understood that his eyesight was much like that of an actual bird. The proof of his extraordinary eyesight was the skill with which he found his target. As he did now.

Three riders presented themselves as possibilities, but only one gave him full use of the strength in his arm. He did not hesitate. Sighting on the beast rather than the rider, he threw.

A direct hit. The spear passed through the animal so perfectly that it took several seconds for the creature to understand that it was dead. When it did understand, the eyes glazed over, the paws dropped, and the wings ceased to flap. The Gryphon watched with grim satisfaction as the beast fell like a stone, its rider screaming both in anger and fear. A fear was lifted from his heart; he had wondered if killing one of the creatures would feel like killing a part of himself. It did not. Regardless of resemblance, he felt no kinship with these monsters.

Morgis continued to shout his frustration. Time and time again, the gryphon riders moved in, barely staying out of the reach of his huge claws. Twice he had tried to burn them from the sky, but the beasts were too swift, too tiny. Yet, like a man bitten time after time by countless insects, the dragon was suffering, and it was evident which side would fail in the end. They had to get out of here.

"The Gate! You have to try for the Gate! It's the only way!"

At first, it seemed more likely that Morgis would refuse, that his rage had pushed him past reason, but, at last, he dipped his head in agreement. What happened next almost caught the Gryphon completely off guard. He thanked whoever was controlling his luck that he had gone back to a two-handed grip on the neck of his companion, for Morgis simply stopped flying.

A dragon is a large, massive creature. A large, massive creature that ceases flying can do only one thing.

Drop like a rock.

The gryphon riders watched, stunned. More than a few thought that their adversary had reached his limit and was falling to his death, which was exactly what Morgis wanted them to think. He allowed himself to fall a short distance, just enough to put the attackers out of immediate range, and then spread his wings and flapped with all his might. The inherent magic involved in the process of flying aided in what would have otherwise been suicide, and the dragon was almost immediately in control again.

The lionbird forced himself to look down. "We're going to have to get much, much lower if we want to go through the Gate!"

"Not until the last moment!" Morgis shouted. "I do not want to chance being struck by the power of the keepers! I have had enough of their sorcery! Are you certain there is no other way of entering the Dream Lands?"

"Only the Gate and, apparently, the Faceless Ones have complete control! The Tzee have always had partial control, but I think we can rule them out!"

"I, for one, would like to rule out those blank-faced demons as well!"

"Which leaves us with only one choice! The Gate!"

Morgis nodded determinedly. "The Gate it is, then!"

They heard shrieks of anger from behind them. The gryphon riders had not yet given up. In a long-distance race, the dragon would have left them behind easily. Now, though, Morgis was tired from the endless struggles and had to slow so as not to overshoot the Gate. The longer it took him to enter the Gate, the less chance he had of succeeding, especially when it meant entering in the midst of an invasion. Worse yet, there would literally be troops entering the vast portal at the same moment.

Below, the advance force was already turning to deal with the oncoming leviathan. The Gryphon cursed silently. There would be any number of keepers mixed in that army, and he doubted that even at full strength Morgis would be able to withstand their combined might. The lionbird knew that he himself had no chance whatsoever.

You can manipulate the gate yourself, a calm, commanding voice suggested.

"What was that you said?" the Gryphon shouted, thinking Morgis spoke.

You, Gryphon, have the power to manipulate the gate. You can take it from the grasp of the one called Lord Petrac.

It was frighteningly akin to his confrontation with the Ravager, but there was a calmness here that the mad god had lacked.

No god. Neither am I. You should know that.

It was true; he did know that—now.

Time is short. The mad dog will discover me. You can manipulate the gate, old one. You merely have forgotten that, as you have forgotten so much. Would that I could bring all those memories back—but that must be your doing.

How? How do I manipulate the Gate? the Gryphon asked silently. This reminded him too much of the brief contact he had had with the Dragons Storm and Crystal. Both had sought to use him secretly against the dreaded Ice Dragon. Storm had failed. Crystal had not.

You can—

The voice was gone, contact abruptly cut off—and not by that other. Whoever, whatever it was, the Ravager had evidently discovered it sooner than it had hoped.

There is a thing I must ask of you, old one. This time, the words were not formed by an outsider. Rather, the Gryphon recalled another memory, one far older than any he had remembered before. Old one?

Manipulate the Gate. He had done so without thinking more than once. That had to be why he had seen it as he and Morgis had made their way to Luperion. An unconscious summoning. No. Not a summoning. That was Lord Petrac's way. More like the silent Master Guardian, the one called Geas. He had not really summoned the Gate so much as requested its aid in a matter of import. A matter of import.

"Gryphon!" Morgis's hissing cry freed him from his dreaming. "The Gate! It isss wavering out of control! The scavengers are fleeing from it!"

"I know!" A request for aid. A chance to end this madness, the madness of the Ravager. The madness of D'Shay. The madness of Lord Petrac the Betrayer.

And suddenly, dragon and rider were flying through an immense Gate standing freely in the middle of the air. Huge, black serpents with all-seeing eyes scurried about a massive stone arch with vast wooden doors that were swung back even as it appeared Morgis would crash into them. Though the dark guardians of the Gate hissed at them, it was somehow recognizable as an acknowledgment of an ally, not an enemy.

The Gryphon looked down before they entered, hoping to make out what was going on below. He was not permitted the time. There was only a brief glimpse of the eastern edge of Canisargos and countless ebony figures milling about in confusion—and then he was staring at a sloping hillside upon which other ebony figures were suddenly halting in panic as they realized there would be no reinforcements. Briefly, the shrieking of the pursuing gryphons rose, then the doors of the Gate closed. Not one of the beasts had made it through.

The appearance of a full-grown dragon brought welcome relief, no doubt, to the defenders of Sirvak Dragoth. From above, the Gryphon studied the assault. He was shocked to see, not only so many wolf raiders, but a great number of others that could only be the inhabitants of the Dream Lands. It was amazing to see so many. Not being able to recall memories of his time here, he had judged from what he had seen. In his last visit to the Dream Lands, he had come to think of it as an otherworldly wilderness with a handful of tiny communities and only the stronghold of the Master Guardians as any true defense. He saw then that he had assumed too much. The Gryphon wondered if D'Shay had assumed the same.

He was nearly thrown from Morgis's neck as the dragon ceased flying and, as he had done during the battle with the gryphon riders, began to plummet like so many tons of dead mass.

"Gryphon! I cannot d—"

Some might say that it was fortunate that the dragon had dropped lower to the earth before losing control. Some might have said that it lessened the impact and probably saved both their lives. *They*, as far as the Gryphon would have been concerned, knew nothing about what they were talking about.

The impact set every bone and muscle of the lionbird aquiver. At one point, he truly believed his skull and all of his organs had burst free from his battered body. The soft, numbing touch of unconsciousness offered him respite from the pain. He forced himself to refuse, knowing who and what lurked all about the two of them.

The Gryphon discovered he was lying several yards from the vast, motionless form of his companion. He forced his arms to work, then barely succeeded in smothering a cry when he realized that his right hand was broken. Not just the fingers, though three of those did hang limply. His wrist was, at the very least, fractured. The ex-mercenary leaned on his left side. While painful, at least he knew it would support him. It was still too difficult to raise himself into a sitting position. Standing was impossible for now.

Morgis presented a much, much bigger problem.

At present, the wolf raiders seemed more concerned with Sirvak Dragoth than the two newcomers. The dragon was down and still; that was good enough for them. Undoubtedly, they assumed it was the work of the keepers, although the Gryphon had his doubts. No, the keepers had their hands full just supporting their comrades at the moment, and, unless it had been either a senior keeper of comparable power to D'Rak himself or several keepers of lesser ability pooling their resources, then it had to be someone else. D'Shay or . . .

"It grieved me to do that to you, but you left me no choice."

Lord Petrac, the Will of the Woods (it might have been debatable at this point whether there was any truth to the title), stood over him, seemingly having materialized out of midair. He held his staff with both hands, the lower tip a foot above the injured Gryphon.

"It grieved me, but such is the price that must be paid for the welfare of at least a few of my children."

The hard tip of the staff came crashing down on the lionbird's injured hand.

If his wrist had not been truly broken before, there was no doubt of it now. He forced back the scream of agony, refusing to give the renegade Master Guardian any such satisfaction.

A cloven hoof pressed into his chest, forcing the Gryphon onto his back. He looked up into the dignified, oh-so-misleading features, into the "innocent" eyes of the stag, and discovered that his attacker actually did hate what he was doing. The self-disgust in Lord Petrac's eyes surprised him, but no more than the second blow from the staff. This time, the Master Guardian chose his left shoulder. There was intense pain, and then complete numbness.

"The Gate is mine again. You caught me by surprise; I admit that. But now, I understand about you. It makes sense. All of it. Qualard, Shaidarol, the not-people—all of it makes sense. If only it was not too late."

"Too late—for what?" the Gryphon croaked. Given a few minutes, he might have been able to stand and at least put up a brief struggle. At the moment, he could do neither that, nor concentrate. Spells were beyond him since the moment Lord Petrac had trapped them in the sky.

"It does not matter." The Master Guardian's eyes narrowed as he stared at the lower tip of his staff. The blunt end began to twist and grow. It tapered, thinned, until the Gryphon found himself staring red-eyed at a very sharp point. He did not bother to ask what the Will of the Woods planned to do with it.

Lord Petrac raised his staff high. The Gryphon tried to roll away, but he discovered he was now fastened to the ground. Even with the Gate under his control, Lord Petrac had power to spare.

"Understand, Gryphon, I *am* doing this for my children, so at least some of them will live."

The former monarch could not hold back. He glared in complete disgust at his murderer. "Will they want to after learning the truth?"

Lord Petrac gasped. The staff fell from his hands, clattering against the Gryphon as the Master Guardian reached up to clutch desperately at the river of blood flowing from the back of his neck—or what remained of it. His mouth opened and closed wordlessly, and his dark, round eyes stared without seeing.

The Will of the Woods fell forward, and it was only because his spell no longer held after death that the Gryphon was able to roll away before the lifeless body fell flat across the ground.

The Gryphon, blinded by both pain and splattered blood, wiped his eyes. He heard sobbing from near where the late Master Guardian had stood and knew who it was even before his sight returned.

Troia was on her knees, her right hand covered in the life fluids of one who had been her mentor, almost a father to her. The one she had finally forced herself to kill in order to save, not just the Dream Lands, but perhaps one even more dear to her.

In the middle of a battle, the sounds of her grief were lost to all but the Gryphon.

XVIII

D'SHAY STOOD ATOP a hill and watched as countless ebony-armored soldiers assaulted the Master Guardians' stronghold. The line soldiers were almost a ruse; the real, more successful assault originated from behind him where more than fourscore keepers had combined their might in a battle of wills against the inhabitants of Sirvak Dragoth. They were the best his position in the hierarchy of command could buy. Keepers who believed he would reward them for their loyalty to him rather than to D'Rak.

On this day, he thought to himself, *I rid myself of all my enemies and . . . all my fears.*

And then the Gate had vanished and a dragon had appeared in the south, over the main bulk of the invasion force. D'Shay cried out, but then he realized that it was not the dragon he believed it to be, but only the drake companion of the most hated Gryphon. D'Shay smiled and then watched as the dragon suddenly dropped helplessly from the sky. The Master Guardian had apparently recovered quickly. He could not see where the great beast struck the ground, but he knew that it had done so with enough force to eliminate the dragon as a potential annoyance, possibly permanently.

Only then did he recognize how precarious his position was. D'Shay turned around and stalked quickly to a tent his creatures had constructed for him. Two of the armored beings stood guard at the opening. They saluted him mechanically. D'Shay ignored them and looked inside. The sight of his prisoner still chained relieved him. It meant that his emergency plan was still safe. The danger posed by being cut off from the will of the Ravager was still present, but not so immediate anymore. Still . . .

"My Lord D'Shay!"

He stepped away from the tent and glanced in unmasked disdain at the figure puffing up the slope to join him. Some nameless aide of the military officials coordinating the attack from the field. They did not understand that they could all die for all he cared. The work of his pet keepers was all that mattered. The army merely kept the defenders from concentrating too much on the actual threat.

"What is it?"

"Pack Commander D'Hayn and Pack Leader D'Issial are both requesting knowledge of the temporary disa—"

D'Shay held up a hand to quiet him. He glanced briefly in the direction of the Gate, which was back in place and looking as solid as ever. "Tell your officers that their minds should be on the assault of the enemy stronghold and not on—the—Gate. . . ."

He trailed off, staring in dismay. The aide turned, and his eyes widened, giving his otherwise unremarkable appearance the look of a frog.

The Gate was gone again. Somehow, D'Shay knew it was for good this time. *What had that guardian fool done?* Had he betrayed them? D'Shay closed his eyes. No, Lord Petrac had not betrayed the wolf raiders. Lord Petrac no longer lived. That much he could now discern, but . . .

His eyes opened, and he cursed at the aide for no other reason than that the hapless soldier was standing in front of him. *The Gryphon again!*

The ground rumbled, part of some desperate assault by the defenders, and D'Shay was forced to steady himself. Only years of paranoia made him turn in time to catch two keepers focusing the power of their talismans on *him.* Disbelief almost did him in; these were *his* keepers, their loyalty bought with promises of freedom from the power of D'Rak—and riches as well. Promises, apparently, were not always enough. He was only barely able to deflect their spell.

"Kill them!" he shouted at nobody in particular. The aide drew his sword, then screamed and shriveled to a dry husk. The assassins had turned the spell on him, but that proved their undoing. D'Shay's unliving servants came at them; this sort of spell was useless against something that did not really have a body. One of the keepers died instantly, a blow from a guard smashing his helm and head into one indescribable mess. The other assassin was not so foolish; he turned and ran. The guards began to pursue. During the whole incident, the other keepers, enraptured by their own part in the main battle, had not even noticed.

There was no feeling in D'Shay's right hand, and he quickly held it up. It was gray and shriveled, almost useless. At first he thought that the spell of the two assassins had somehow touched him, but then he realized that the problem was far worse than that. Even a short stay in this realm was too much for him; he was dying and would die within a couple hours unless he made use of his prisoner, his last resort. It would be more difficult here in the damned Dream Lands, but he knew he had the willpower because if he did not then he was dead, something D'Shay could not permit—not without the Gryphon to accompany him.

He turned back to the tent. Time was of the essence. It would mean burning out much sooner than he wanted, but, by then, another suitable "volunteer" would be found. All that mattered now was continued existence.

The prisoner, D'Shay's life, was gone. He had been spirited away, manacles and all, while the two assassins had kept the master wolf raider occupied.

D'Shay felt panic setting in.

I am beyond the terminal stage, he raged. *My mind is in a continuous fog! This should have never happened!*

He had to depart the Dream Lands immediately. Sirvak Dragoth no longer mattered. The Ravager no longer mattered. Even the Gryphon no longer mattered—for the moment.

Tzee . . .

D'Shay stepped away from the tent. The Tzee? Of course!

"I have need of you! Manifest yourself!"

Tzee . . . dying time . . . dying time . . .

The Tzee had yet to manifest themselves, but their harshly whispered words kept echoing in his mind. Dying time? They knew?

Tzee . . . dying time . . . enjoy . . .

"What?" D'Shay raised his fists into the air and shook them uselessly against the invisible presence of the Tzee. "Manifest yourself, or I'll see that you—"

Tzee . . . time to die . . . The last was followed by the quiet, mad laughter of countless entities.

D'Shay realized that the Tzee were departing. He grew desperate. "Come back! I can offer you more power!"

A last, faint reply reached his ears before they departed.

Tzee . . . not enough . . .

He understood then. The Tzee had stolen his prisoner. The Tzee, who had been given power by Lord Petrac, D'Rak, and himself. The Tzee, who everyone had not even bothered to think about, a wild card that had finally been played.

D'Shay stared briefly at his crippled hand. The Tzee were foolish if they believed he was finished. Not yet. Not while the Gryphon still lived.

"Milord!"

He turned, and his first thought was to slay the figure before him, for it was a keeper. This one, however, knelt in obedience and said, "Their defenses are weakening. A few more minutes and Sirvak Dragoth will be open to the advance forces."

D'Shay hid his hand from the sight of the keeper. "I want the Master

Guardians at my feet within the next half hour. Alive. If any of them die, I will kill every man in the squad responsible—even keepers."

"Understood, milord."

As the man departed, D'Shay's servants returned. Blood dripped from their gloves. They came up to him and stopped, awaiting new orders. The master wolf raider felt strength return to him. As long as he remained near them, the process of decay was slowed. A few more hours, precious ones now. A few more hours was all he needed, though. Death had stared him in the face before, and he had laughed at it, mocked it.

As he would again.

"I'M SORRY," TROIA said as she gave him water. "It's the best I can do."

"It will help." The Gryphon held the cup with his one good hand, forcing himself to ignore the needles of pain stabbing his shoulder. His other arm was in fair shape, though, with a broken hand, it was of little practical use. Troia had wrapped up the hand with cloth from his shirt. There was nothing else she could do. Until the Gryphon's strength returned, he was unable to heal himself at all. Fortunately, he could at least walk, though running was definitely out. With the feline woman's aid, he had moved to a more secure place. The lionbird hated to leave Morgis behind, but there was no way he could drag so many tons of unconscious muscle and bone. At least, the Aramites had not come near, for they had assumed the dragon was dead, and that was becoming a distinct likelihood. Morgis was undoubtedly injured badly; the Gryphon had been fortunate in that the huge form had softened his own landing.

"I still don't understand why he had to kill me personally. It was a foolhardy thing to do."

Troia tried to cover the grief she still felt. She did not totally succeed, but the lionbird pretended not to notice. "I knew—thought I knew him, that is. I think your death was something horrible to him, something he decided was necessary, but yet could not leave to another. It had to be him. Alone. I think he wanted the guilt to fall on his shoulders alone."

"If you hadn't come when you had . . ."

He used his good hand to softly touch one of hers. She withdrew it, guilt on her face. "When you called the Gate to you, it disturbed his concentration so much that the spell keeping me asleep faded. Not completely, but enough for me to fight it. I—I followed him; I was there while he broke your hand. Even then, I couldn't believe he'd go any farther. I thought he'd take you prisoner and I could then release you. It wasn't until he raised the staff and I saw what he'd done to the tip that I realized what he had become." She covered her face. "I'm sorry! He could have killed you!"

The Gryphon pulled her hands away, one at a time. "You saved my life in the end. That's what matters. I can understand the way you feel."

"I'll never forget that. . . ." Still, she succeeded in smiling, albeit fleetingly.

He decided it was time to change the subject. "We have to get to Sirvak Dragoth," he told her. "It's vital."

"The citadel is under attack. I'm not injured. I can fight. You should stay here." Her eyes, red from crying, were filled with concern. Troia wanted badly to make up for what she had almost allowed to happen. "I'll bring help."

"You go alone and the wolf raiders will kill you."

"I have some magic—mostly enhancing my fighting. You know as a guardian I have certain inherent abilities. A few soldiers will only whet my appetite." Troia smiled, showing her fangs.

The Gryphon was not so willing to pretend. "Many, many soldiers and more than a few keepers as well. Do you think you could take on a keeper?"

"I wouldn't back down."

"That's not the same thing." He shook his head and tried to rise. "I have to do something about Morgis. I cannot leave him out there. Even now, something could be happening. I've never abandoned a comrade before, and I have no intention of doing so now." The Gryphon tried not to think about Jerilon Dane. Dane had not exactly been a comrade, and it was almost a certainty that he had died, but there was still a little doubt.

She looked at him with an expression normally reserved for madmen. "You can barely walk. What do you think you can do? It has to be me alone. I'll sneak past them, get into the citadel. Haggerth—"

"Has his hands full!" The Gryphon leaned too much on one arm, and pain shot through his entire body. "If only I could concentrate! Maybe bring the Gate to us! Where is it now?"

Troia shrugged. In the distance, the sounds of battle had taken on a new tone. She moved away from the Gryphon, intent on seeing what was happening. She had this dreadful fear that when she looked over the incline, she would see Sirvak Dragoth in ruins and wolf raiders clambering all over its remains like scavengers on a dead deer.

Sirvak Dragoth had not yet fallen, the feline woman saw, but it was obvious that it would hold out for little longer. Even cut off from their home, stranded in another reality, the Aramites fought with the same obsessive determination that they always had. The Dream Lands would soon fall, having no other organized resistance.

And she could watch it all unfold from an unobstructed view.

Unobstructed?

"What is it? What's happened?" From the tone of his voice, she knew that the Gryphon expected the worst. But would he expect what she herself could not believe, even after seeing—or not seeing—it?

Troia ducked back down, confused and afraid. "Gryphon, your friend is gone."

"Friend? Morgis? Gone?" After several seconds, he understood what she meant. "*Gone?* An entire dragon? Unconscious and injured, yet! But why would they . . ." He paused, and then a gleam that she had not seen for some time reappeared in his eyes.

"Why would they what? Why did the Ravager's hounds move him? It would take several keepers or hundreds of soldiers!"

"I doubt they took him. I think someone else took him. Correct that—I *know* someone else took him." His eyes narrowed, and he stared at something beyond her.

Troia turned cautiously around—and then nearly broke down in relief when she found herself matching the sightless gaze of one of three identical, familiar figures.

"The not-people!" she cried happily.

The Gryphon nodded. "Morgis and I have come to call them the Faceless Ones, but, whatever they are, they're very, very welcome at this moment."

He hoped he would not regret saying that at some future date—if there was any future.

The three featureless beings approached them, cowled robes swaying slightly as they seemed to float across the distance. When they were within arm's length, they came to a halt and the one in the center raised its right hand to a point level with its head, palm flat outward. The Gryphon looked at Troia, but the cat-woman had no idea how to reply. The lionbird hesitantly brought his one good hand up in a similar manner. The not-people nodded as one, but, for some reason, they seemed disappointed, as if they had been hoping for something more.

Whatever that might have been, it was evidently not important enough to keep them from their task. As the others—it might have been one or more of this group, but who could tell?—in the alley had done, the Faceless Ones raised their hands.

The Gate materialized, doors wide open.

Two of the odd beings helped the Gryphon to his feet. He already felt much better than he had, and he suspected that the Faceless Ones were doing more than simply assisting him to walk. It was with growing hope that he allowed himself to be escorted through the imposing edifice, Troia and the remaining Faceless One trailing behind.

It was with swiftly fading hope that he entered the central chamber of Sirvak Dragoth.

The room itself was a shambles. Anything loose had fallen to the ground. Marble from the ceiling and walls had broken loose and fallen to the floor. There were faults in the floor itself, and one was a foot wide already. Dust floated everywhere. There were perhaps a dozen figures in the room, not counting the Gryphon and his group. Mrin/Amrin and two women, one incredibly tall, beautiful, and wrapped in something like a long red shroud, and the other average in height with a face like an innocent child's. She was clad in a garment woven from some material that refused to come into focus.

The one called Geas sat in a corner, playing a somber melody on his flute. Haggerth sat in his usual place of authority, speaking to a male and female who resembled the folk from the village in Petrac's former domain. The veiled guardian looked up.

"Gryphon! How glad I am to see you, even if your timing could not be much worse!"

"Then you are losing." The Gryphon almost forgot his wounds as he stumbled away from his companions and toward the Master Guardian.

Haggerth dismissed the two, stood up, and hurried to meet the lionbird halfway. "How badly are you hurt?"

"I can live. You have Morgis?"

"He is resting. Someone saw to him the moment the not-people brought his body here."

"An entire dragon?"

"Dragon? No, they brought him in looking the same way he has always looked, albeit a bit worn. Speaking of damage, if you'll allow me . . ."

The Master Guardian examined the Gryphon's injuries, especially the hand. While his fingers probed, he said quietly, "We know what happened with you and Petrac. Difficult to believe—and yet, not so difficult to believe."

"Troia had to kill him to save my life."

The veil hid whatever emotion was coursing through the mind of Haggerth. "I'll be sure to speak to her later, if we're still around."

"What's happening?"

The guardian sighed. "While their soldiers batter away at our people, the keepers batter away at our walls and our minds. Combined, they are an imposing force. We almost lost control not more than a minute ago. Truthfully, I doubt if we'll last out the hour."

All the while, the Master Guardian had been inspecting the damage done by his former comrade. The pain in the Gryphon's broken hand vanished. He tentatively flexed the fingers. Haggerth had healed the broken hand completely. There was not even any stiffness during movement.

"Thank you, Haggerth. Do you really mean what you say?"

"Yes, but don't tell Troia or the others. Not yet. I've been doing some thinking based on Lord Petrac's betrayal of us."

"And?" The lionbird did not care for the sound of that. What was there to be learned about Petrac's betrayal except that many people were either dead or going to die because of him? That was the real lesson.

"I'll speak to you about it later. If you want to see Morgis, he's in a room down the hall. We have several here that have been brought in by either companions or the not-people."

The Gryphon glanced at one of the featureless beings. "They're on our side completely, I take it."

Haggerth laughed bitterly. "Take nothing at face value. I know. I've heard reports of them aiding enemy wounded as well. I don't think I'll ever figure them out."

The Gryphon thanked Haggerth, promising to return at the first sign of trouble. The veiled figure seemed to only half hear him. The lionbird watched him with growing worry. Haggerth had always seemed the most sensible and understanding of the Master Guardians that he had dealt with. If *he* had lost hope . . . the thought was not one that the Gryphon chose to complete.

Troia came to him. He stared past her at the Faceless Ones, who seemed to be watching him with great interest—though it might have been amusement or disgust and he was merely trying to read his own thoughts into their blank visages.

"Master Haggerth seemed worried," she commented. "I could tell from the way he was standing. I don't think he's rested for quite some time."

"Why bother. He might not wake up if he does." The Gryphon forced a change of subject. "Morgis is nearby. I have to see him before I do anything else."

"I'll help you." She put an arm around him and let him put one over her shoulders. He refrained from mentioning that, thanks to the powers of Haggerth, he could have made it on his own. The sensation of her body next to his was just too pleasant, too distracting, but there were so few things lately that had given him any pleasure at all.

Sirvak Dragoth shook. The Gryphon turned and looked for Haggerth, but the Master Guardian was nowhere to be seen. Troia pulled him to the side as the couple that Haggerth had been speaking to earlier moved past them with towels and water and hurried to where the other Master Guardians, save Geas, were working desperately to save the citadel.

The Gryphon was filled with a sudden sense of urgency. "Take me to Morgis. There's no telling how long this place has left."

They made their way over a rubble-strewn hallway. Part of one wall had fallen and, as they climbed over it, they discovered that someone had been caught under it. It only took one glance, however, to know that the victim was beyond help. Troia swore, and her claws extended, digging into the Gryphon's side. He said nothing.

The room that held the wounded was almost as vast as the central chamber itself. Furniture, unless useful, had been piled in one corner. While the injured filled most of the room, the Gryphon was surprised that there were not many more. He remarked so to Troia.

She corrected his misconception immediately. "Most of those with minor wounds are still out there fighting. There are also a few woodland healers. Those that can't be helped were left where they were."

It sounded like a cold thing to do, even to an ex-mercenary, but he knew that these were a people who lived closer to nature than even he had. He did not doubt that, like some elves and dwarves, they would prefer to die surrounded by nature than linger their last few moments in a crowded room with the smell of death instead of flowers.

"There's Morgis." Troia pointed to their right. The drake lay on a single blanket with a makeshift pillow keeping his head off the floor. It seemed incongruous to see a heavily armored figure lying there, apparently unscathed, surrounded by a variety of beings all looking badly injured. Yet, he knew that Morgis would not be here if the drake could help it. His imposing appearance, the only humanoid form he could create, hid the fact that he had suffered from internal injuries.

Volunteers moved to and fro, giving aid of all sorts. There were maybe two healers in the entire room, trying desperately to keep up with the flow of injured. It was all too frighteningly reminiscent of his own past. His eyes scanned over the various patients as he and Troia made their way to Morgis. Broken limbs, sword and arrow wounds, concussions, shock—

The Gryphon froze.

He believed, though he tended to share it with no one, that, whatever powers did watch over the Dragonrealm and all other regions of the world, someone was going out of their way in the name of coincidence. People appeared suddenly, events changed without warning—all as if some great hand were manipulating everyone and everything. Each time he thought he knew who the manipulators were, he discovered that they, too, were being maneuvered. He could almost believe as had been said that the Ravager believed—that this was all some kind of game.

"What's the matter?"

If it *was* a game, a new piece had been added. He pulled away from her and squatted down by the figure that rocked itself continuously back and forth. A man, a fighter, who, even despite the shaggy growth of beard and the extremely pale skin, was familiar to him. Familiar, yes, but supposedly dead, slain by D'Shay prior to their last meeting in Penacles so long ago. The Captain of the Guard in the Gryphon's palace.

"Freynard? Allyn? Captain Freynard?"

The weathered, cadaverous face became visible as the man stopped rocking and looked up at him. The eyes, which had been staring nowhere, focused on the former monarch. Parched, cracked lips opened, and the ragged figure whispered, "At—at your service, your majesty. Ever—ever at your service."

For a brief moment, the Gryphon would have sworn that he heard D'Shay laughing.

XIX

Physical form was still something new to the Tzee and, at the time, it proved annoying. It was necessary, however, for the mortal creatures who called themselves the wolf raiders would never take orders from such as them—at least, not knowingly. The Tzee could change that later, when they were more secure in their reign and the Ravager had given them the power they needed to be truly free of the constraints of the Dream Lands. It was the goal of the Tzee for countless centuries to escape from the bonds that kept them a part of the reality of that misty region and prevented them from extending their presence throughout the rest of the world, the Dragonrealm, for instance.

"*Tzee . . .*" They made the body whisper without thinking. The Ravager would change that, they were certain. When the true lord of the Aramites understood what they had done, he could not help but grant their request.

The body stumbled momentarily through the dark while they searched beyond human perceptions for the proper path. It was dark down here, even for the Tzee, yet, there was still a light of sorts. The Tzee could not comprehend this and were briefly awed. Yes, the Ravager would have the power.

They would offer him the Dream Lands and the Gryphon. They had wanted the Gryphon, but not more than they wanted their freedom. The Gryphon had broken their power once, long ago, just prior to the near-calamity he had caused the Ravager in the human city of Qual—

The name is never to be thought of or spoken! The angry declaration was followed by a savage snarl, as if some great beast were lurking just beyond the darkness.

D'Rak's body stumbled over what the Tzee knew to be human remains. They made the head turn toward the presence they now felt. There was the impression of something large moving closer, and the eyes of D'Rak briefly caught sight of another pair of eyes, savage eyes. The Tzee themselves could see nothing, but could definitely not deny the other.

Tzee, little Tzee, you come to beg favors of a god?

In deference to the great power before them, the Tzee utilized the human's mouth and voice. It was their way of showing what an effort they were making.

"Great one." The voice was slurred. For a time, they had found their control of the body to be almost perfect. Now, though, it did not always function with its normal efficiency.

Your new form needs rest, little Tzee. Humans need sleep, and yours is a human body.

So that was it. "Great one," the Tzee continued, "we have striven—Tzee—to prove ourselves to you. We have shown our cunning. We have shown our power. We have shown that you need—Tzee—only us to achieve your goals. We can offer you—"

The Dream Lands and the Gryphon. I know, little Tzee. Am I not the Ravager? Am I not a god? I will win this game, little Tzee.

"We know of no game, great one, but—Tzee—if our skills—Tzee . . ." The Tzee found themselves growing uncomfortably nervous. ". . . Can be of service to you, then that is what we—Tzee—wish. We seek only one thing in return—"

Power. I know you well. You desire power, little Tzee.

They became excited at such understanding. D'Rak's body quivered as the Tzee lost control of some of the motor functions for a brief spell. Then, realizing how they must look, the Tzee forced themselves calm. "Yes—Tzee—power."

I shall reveal power to you.

Something stumbled through the darkness and, at first, the Tzee had the terrible notion that the Ravager himself was coming toward them. They were partially correct. Though it was a human form that finally revealed itself in the odd light, there was no mind, not even any life. The Tzee knew of this. The Ravager had a fascination with dead forms, using them as its hands at times. The Tzee disliked the dead; they did not have such wondrous abilities as the wolf lord had. They could only overwhelm the living and force their minds down into some remote void the Tzee themselves did not understand. They just did it.

This one was only recently dead. The face it knew from somewhere, but that did not matter. What mattered was the object the corpse held before it the way flesh-and-blood creatures often held their young. A large, possibly oval object covered by cloth. It radiated power, enough so that the Tzee actually hungered for it. The unliving slave seemed to offer them the object. The Tzee looked away to that spot where, maybe, the Ravager waited.

It is yours to unveil. It is almost as if it was designed for you all along, little Tzee.

They could not hold off any longer. Anticipation got the best of them, and the Tzee raised the right arm and tore the cloth from their prize.

Power! Too much—Tzee!—power! In their panic, they no longer thought to speak through the mouth of their purloined body.

It is only power returning to its rightful place, little Tzee! A place you usurped! Do you think I would deal with anything spawned in the Dream Lands? Anything I planned to eliminate once its usefulness was at an end?

Power continued to overwhelm the Tzee. They could no longer maintain control of the body and the level of power, especially when the power itself seemed to be fighting them.

The Tzee reached their limit. Their essence, their . . . presence, for lack of a better word, began to break apart. The colony mind splintered, becoming

vast numbers of weaker, less coherent thoughts. In a last effort, the largest remaining colony of the nebulous multiple entity withdrew completely
from the body and abandoned the smaller, fractionating bits to their fates.

Tricked . . . Tzee . . . tricked . . . tricked . . . it whispered madly as it departed
from the lair of the Ravager.

The body of the senior keeper swayed back and forth, and a hand went
upward to tentatively touch the face. The voice was no more than a whisper.
"They're gone! The cursed things are gone!"

You have rightful control of yourself once more. Remember who saved you.

D'Rak fell to his knees, his face pale, his tone one of incredible relief.
"Master, I thank you!"

Thank me by serving me well.

The senior keeper glanced over toward the object that had been a part
of his salvation. The crystalline head he had created—and held by one he
knew, the failure R'Dane—but, R'Dane—

*R'Dane was saved by those in the Dream Lands, but foolishly returned with the
Gryphon! He perished during the escape of the misfit, trying to work your precious toy!*

"Then that was what—" D'Rak stopped short, understanding now that
he might have just betrayed himself.

Yes . . . say it. Say what you wanted to do with this toy!

"I wanted to . . . live forever. Just as D'Shay does. I wanted to be immortal!" He said the last defiantly. At this point, there was nothing left to lose.
"The crystal was to hold my essence—but on death!"

You wanted to be immortal . . . like D'Shay.

"Yes." Was the Lord Ravager playing with him? Had he rid D'Rak of
the Tzee just to pass judgment over the keeper? Despite the fact that he
had been born while Qualard was still the capital, D'Rak knew that time
was catching up to him. His position as senior keeper had given him access
to the power he needed to extend his life, but not make him immortal, as
D'Shay was. He would do whatever it took. He did not want to die, especially now that he had had a taste of something akin to it!

A mocking laugh echoed through the chamber. The wolf raider cringed.

You know your place now! You know you will obey! The Ravager seemed amused
by his reactions. *You will do!*

"Do, Master? Do for what?"

Do you question me? There was a brief, angry snarl and, once more, the impression of two great eyes in the dark.

"No, my lord!"

Better! You would be immortal like D'Shay, my favorite hound.

"I—"

A silly notion, keeper. Silly because it is not true. D'Shay is not immortal; he is no longer even my favorite!

This time, D'Rak said nothing, but his heart beat faster. Did he understand correctly what his master had just told him?

You understand. The time has come, my faithful Runner. The Dream Lands, though they have cut me off from my children, will still fall! Sirvak Dragoth is the only obstacle and, before the Gate vanished, it was understood that its defenses were crumbling!

D'Rak took this on faith. Much of that time he had been . . . elsewhere. "What of D'Shay, milord?"

If he is not dead, cut off from my will—which is what truly keeps him alive—then he will perish soon. His fate does not matter. He has served the purpose I originally planned for him. I have you now.

The senior keeper's chest swelled with pride. "What is it you wish of me?"

The Dream Lands will fall before the might of my children, but there is one danger that remains. . . .

"The Gryphon."

He will be forced to go to Qualard, believing it is the only way he may be able to save his friends, save the foul Dream Lands. He will go very soon, I think.

"I'll assemble an armed force. Hitai is the closest outpost to Qual—to that place. I'll—"

D'Rak rose and stumbled backward as a blood-chilling growl rose from the darkness. He could feel hot, fetid breath on his face, though nothing was there.

Fool! Pup! This is not why I saved you! An armed force? He will know of their existence long before you know of his! This is a creature with far more knowledge of war than you! Do you think he will come with an army of his own?

"A—a small group, then. Two keepers to form a triangle and half a dozen handpicked guards. No more."

Better, pup. This game will not be won with numbers but with craft. The Gryphon will be there, and he will, of course, bring his constant companion, that—that reptilian mongrel. Possibly his female as well.

"And a guardian, or perhaps . . . even one of the blank-faced creatures." Yes, D'Rak saw that. If there was indeed a guardian—a Master Guardian— then he might be "persuaded" to reopen the Gate for the wolf raiders.

Better, my loyal hound! Better!

He bowed, confidence restored. "I must depart now, if what you say is true, milord."

Go! This audience is at an end.

The senior keeper turned and started to make his way back to the stairway, when a voice called out to him. He froze, for the last thing he had expected to hear was the voice of R'Dane, the dead traitor.

"One last thing, my hound." Though the voice was R'Dane's, the eyes, when D'Rak turned to face him, were the fierce, red orbs of the Aramite's lord and master. "Fail me not, or else you will come to envy this ungainly puppet of mine!" The battered face of R'Dane smiled, revealing in the light that was not light its broken mouth and dried blood caked everywhere.

The body collapsed, falling upon the crystal it still clutched in its arms and shattering it against the mound of bones. *Fail . . . and I shall give you immortality of a sort. You have my promise.*

D'Rak stared at the latest addition to the Ravager's collection and swallowed hard. He turned and stumbled to the steps, which were to prove to be the longest flight of stairs he had ever climbed.

When he at last reached the top, the senior keeper ran as if his life depended upon it—which it did.

"FREYNARD! GODS ABOVE, Freynard! How did you come to be here?"

Captain Allyn Freynard had been a tough, young soldier. He would have taken the place of General Toos as commander of the armies of Penacles had he lived—or rather, had he not been spirited away, apparently by D'Shay.

Freynard's eyes darted back and forth, as if he expected to be reclaimed by his captors even now. The time he had spent as a prisoner of D'Shay could hardly have been a pleasant one. Beneath the beard, still partly visible, were old bruises and scars. Something that resembled a jagged pentagram had been carved into the upper portion of his right cheek. Other, less elaborate marks had been cut into his hands and neck. When he spoke, it was not to answer his lord's question, but to recall a terrible memory. "I held out for as long as I could, Majesty. After seeing what he'd done to the other man, I knew that the moment I was of no more value to him as a source of information, the ghoul would take me when next he needed a victim! I didn't mean to betray you, milord! It—it was just that it had been so long! Months, I think!"

It had been, in fact, longer, and the Gryphon felt a terrible shame grow within him. He had not bothered, not even considered that the captain might be alive. D'Shay had spoken of disposing of Freynard and one other guard, but the lionbird and General Toos had simply assumed that it meant they had been murdered, two more victims of the foul wolf raiders. There had been proper mourning, and then plans had been made by the Gryphon to journey across the Eastern Seas. Freynard had become a memory.

"This is really one of your men?" Troia whispered. She, knowing the Aramites better, thought it might be a trick.

The Gryphon nodded, self-disgust swelling within him as he spoke. "This is Captain Allyn Freynard. Like a fool, I took what D'Shay said at face value, forgetting at that moment that D'Shay had more than one face. Because of that, two men suffered and one of them died. I cannot say which was the luckier."

"He took him that night," Freynard was saying. The captain was making a visible effort to increase his newly discovered hold on sanity. "Transported us through one of those big portals you spoke of, Majesty. You called them . . . called them—"

"Blink holes. Not important, Freynard. Forget them."

"Yes, sir. Blink hole. I can't remember the other man's name, Majesty. I don't even remember if I ever knew it. I only knew that, when the horror came to him, I swore I would remember him!" The captain grabbed the Gryphon by the shoulders. "I swore it, and I can't remember! To watch a man lose his self and have no one able to remember even his name! It was . . . it was . . ."

A short female figure akin to Troia in appearance but with gray, mottled fur came over and said anxiously, "If you excite him too much, I will have to ask you to go away. There are many here who need rest and, the Lands know, there's more than enough noise outside."

Outside. The battle. *How much time has passed since I came in here?* the Gryphon wondered frantically. He took hold of Freynard and made the captain look him in the eyes. "Allyn, I've got to go. There's danger, a battle. I still have one chance to possibly save the situation."

"A battle?" This seemed to excite the ragged man. "A weapon, milord! Give me a weapon and I'll fight at your side!"

"Don't be ridiculous, Freynard. You're not well, and I can't ask you to go out there, not after what you've been through!"

"Your Majesty"—the captain's eyes burned—"it is because of what happened to me that I ask to go with you. You might have need of my arm. I've fought in worse physical condition than this, and I can assure, milord, that fighting at your side would only strengthen, not lessen, my mind—especially if my sword gets a taste of wolf raider blood."

He had never abandoned a comrade . . . did this count? The Gryphon closed his eyes and reluctantly nodded. When he opened them, the young man was smiling. "Understand, Freynard, that if you are not ready when we depart in a few minutes, I will leave you here."

"I will be waiting—thank you, Your Majesty!"

The Gryphon could not help a short chuckle. "That's another thing, Allyn. I'm no longer 'Your Majesty.' I gave that up when I sailed across the Eastern Seas. Call me as everyone who knows me does—Gryphon."

Freynard shook his head. "I shall call you 'milord' and 'Your Majesty,' sir. I'm sure that General Toos considers himself to be merely holding Penacles for you while you are away."

It was too soon to talk about going back—especially when the lionbird was uncertain as to whether he wanted or would be able to return. Beside him, he had felt Troia stiffen at such talk. There was something he wanted to talk of, as well, when they were alone. For now . . .

He rose and patted the captain on the shoulder. "You should be able to borrow a sword from someone; there are always more weapons late in a battle than there are children to use them. Also, see if you can locate some supplies. Enough for a day or two, no more. Wait in the corridor when you are done. Ten minutes, no more."

"Yes, Your Majesty!" Freynard rose with a speed and dexterity that was surprising in a man who looked as worn as he did. Serving his old master had rekindled a spark within him. The Gryphon knew that much of it was momentary; Freynard would weaken—hopefully to the point where the former monarch could keep him from going with them. He did not want to cause a useless death. It was at times like this that he regretted the loyalty those men who had served under him always seemed to have. He did not like people dying for his sake.

While Freynard sought out a sword or some other weapon, the Gryphon and Troia finally made their way over to Morgis. The drake had not moved. He still looked like a warrior whose body had been readied for some death ritual. Only a faint hiss and the slow rise and fall of his chest proved that he was still alive.

Troia, who had never really paid attention to the appearance of the duke, tightened her grip on the Gryphon's arm. Even asleep and seemingly helpless, Morgis was an imposing figure that could easily unnerve more than one brave soul. The caretakers and healers had had to make extra room for him, what with an overall height of at least seven feet, but it was not his size that so fascinated her. Rather, it was the crude, partly human face that the drake kept half hidden within the dragonhelm that, so the Gryphon had explained, was as much a part of the duke as his hand or foot was. A blue-tinted, scaled skin covered the face, just as it did the entire body, but it was the incompleteness of the drake's visage that disturbed the onlooker. There was practically no nose, merely two slits that acted as nostrils, and the mouth was a long gash that, when opened, would reveal teeth far more predatory than hers. The eyes were narrow, and she knew that when they opened, they would be all one color. Troia wondered briefly if Morgis had ears—he heard somehow.

The Gryphon had made some mention about the Dragonrealm while she had bound his wounds. According to him, the drakes were slowly moving to a permanent, almost human form.

He had told her other things about the Dragonrealm, and she had secretly wondered what it would be like to go there. Now was not the time for such a subject, however.

Even as the Gryphon's hand reached out to wake Morgis, the drake's eyes opened, burning with life. Troia gasped. She was able to tolerate him, but now, seeing him up close, she could not fathom an entire race like the duke. There was nothing like the drakes in the Dream Lands.

She would have been surprised if she knew that Morgis had the same opinion of the Dream Lands. He had seen creatures and things here that he would not have ever believed existed.

"You are well. Good." The drake spoke matter-of-factly, but there was still a hint of strain in the tone of his voice.

"How are you?" The Gryphon gave Morgis a visual inspection, knowing, however, that most of the injuries were inside.

"I am well. The healers did what they could. Once they steered my body toward recovery, I took over. Sirvak Dragoth still stands, I take it?"

The lionbird nodded, more pleased than he had expected that his companion was better. He had come to think of Morgis as a friend. It was a shock, but true. "They're living on borrowed time. Each minute it looks like the wolf raiders will break through—there are a great number of keepers out there, not on a level with D'Rak, but they are working in concert, much like they did when we tried to go to Qualard. Where we need to go now, I think."

"What *is* in Qualard? It is an ancient, ruined city. The place of the Ravager's wrath at his own people."

"It holds the key, though. They tried to stop us once and almost succeeded. We have no real choice. I think Qualard is the place we have to go if we want to save the Sirvak Dragoth and the Dream Lands—not to mention ourselves."

Morgis raised himself up to a sitting position, which made more than one head turn to look at him. He smiled, revealing those teeth that made even Troia shiver. "Then go we must. Things have been a little boring of late. This little quest sounds of interest—and perhaps I will yet get to run my blade through the senior keeper!"

"We can only hope—" The citadel shook, as it had often before, but this time, there was a difference. It failed to stop shaking and, in fact, the quake—it could no longer simply be called shaking—was threatening to tear Sirvak Dragoth apart. A small crack in the floor suddenly yawned open, forcing those administering to the wounded to bunch them together even tighter for fear of some of the unconscious ones tumbling into the new crevice.

Haggerth came stumbling into the room. "Get everyone into the underground chambers and out of Sirvak Dragoth!"

Someone nearby asked a question. The Master Guardian's veiled face turned in the general direction of the speaker. "What do you think?" he snapped irritably. Despite his generally calm demeanor, there was a point where even Haggerth could stand no more. "The citadel is falling! The Master Guardians will remain here in order to delay the wolf raiders as long as possible, but the first of them will be over the outer walls in little more than a quarter hour! That's all! Hurry, but, by the Lands' sake, do not rush out in a panic or no one will survive!"

It was to Haggerth's credit that the inhabitants acted more or less in some uniform fashion. Those who had the strength to walk helped carry those who either could not or were completely unconscious. The Master Guardian, meanwhile, moved through the crowds—which was difficult with the building still continuing to shake and a fissure large enough for a man to fall into now cutting through the center of the room—until he had reached the trio.

"You still plan to go to Qualard, don't you." It was not a question, but a statement. Haggerth had something in mind.

Morgis, who had just risen, nodded. The Gryphon did also, and then added, "Right now, I think it's the only way to save the Dream Lands—even if Sirvak Dragoth is lost."

Tiny bits of the ceiling began raining upon them. Haggerth looked up. "It has stood so long. I was beginning to think it would be here until the end of time—or at least longer than my lifetime."

"What was it you wanted, Master Guardian?"

The veiled man pulled himself together. "You will need help in Qualard."

"You want to go with me."

"I do not, Gryphon. The choice was made by my fellows. My . . . abilities"—Haggerth touched the veil—"are more useful up close. The others felt that one of us should accompany you; after all, you will need a Gate. Evidently, they felt I was the most useless here." The Master Guardian's voice had a touch of bitterness in it.

Troia shook her head at that. "Not useless, Master Haggerth. Not you."

A great block of marble fell from the ceiling. They could not see where it landed, but the screams that followed spoke of the terrible damage it had done. The rest of the ceiling was covered with ominous cracks.

"I would say," Morgis shouted over the din, "that there is no time to discuss this! Master Haggerth will come, yes? I think it's time someone called the Gate!"

"I'll do it," the Gryphon replied.

Both Troia and Haggerth looked at him, and the feline woman, growing awe on her face, asked, "You can summon the Gate? Only Master Guardians, not-people, and a few creatures like the Tzee, who are actually extensions of the Dream Lands themselves, can summon the Gate! When I saved you from the Tzee, I was only able to do it because one of the not-people agreed to help me!"

"I do not summon it; I ask it to help." He raised his arms and closed his eyes, not so much as part of the act of contacting the Gate, but more to silence the two guardians' questions.

Would it come this time? He had the brief inward fear that it would not respond to him, would not respond to anyone now that the guardians, himself included, had seemingly failed in their duties. The fear proved to be without substance, for he felt then the presence of the portal, a living presence, he knew now. The Gate *was* the Dream Lands, and it was an entity as well. Why it should have answered the summons of Lord Petrac that final time, the Gryphon could not say. He could only guess, from what he sensed, that the mind—or whatever it was—of the Gate was so different, so incomprehensible, that it must have ideas of its own concerning what was right and what was wrong. Perhaps, somehow, it had answered the Master Guardian's summons because doing so fit into some plan of its own.

The lionbird opened his eyes as the Gate materialized before them. It was taller than the chamber, yet it did not break through the ceiling. The same black creatures swarmed about it, but they seemed slower, possibly ill. The portal itself was open, but one of the massive doors hung slightly loose, as if the hinges were starting to come off.

Beyond lay a scene of desolation that the Gryphon had already seen before. It had, of course, not changed. Nothing had changed in Qualard for two centuries.

Troia put a hand on his shoulder. "Remember last time."

"I've scanned the area as far as I was able. I found no one."

They were alone in the room. The quake had subsided without the Gryphon realizing it, but now it began anew. Haggerth uttered a curse.

"That can only mean the others are failing to hold the keepers. We haven't much time at all."

"Then what are we tarrying for?" Morgis asked, and then, without bothering to wait for a reply, leaped into the portal.

Troia looked at the Gryphon. He took a deep breath and, with a last glance toward her, followed after the drake.

The ceiling began to collapse.

XX

DURING THE FIRST tremors of what would soon become a quake to those inside, D'Shay waited silently, his mind brooding as he watched the results of the keepers' work. A watch tower had already fallen. Soldiers trying to overrun the walls of the citadel cheered at this, but the master wolf raider found little to be pleased about. Already, the predicted "victory in minutes" was dragging out longer than it should have. The gray had already spread up most of his arm, and now one of his legs was showing the first signs. Signs of decay. Signs that this body would not last too much longer.

He needed one of the Master Guardians. They knew how to control the Gate. They or the not-people. Forcing the latter to do something they did not desire to do was next to impossible. For some reason, they were willing to assist the Gryphon far beyond their normally neutral ways. In fact, since the Gryphon's arrival on this continent, the faceless beings had almost become allies to the Dream Lands in their efforts to aid D'Shay's enemy.

They must know more than I, he thought. *They know more than just the surface facts about Qualard. They know something about the Gryphon's origins and what makes him such a threat to the Lord Ravager.*

But what?

For now, the two servants he had brought with him supported him. Best to conserve strength. He had contemplated releasing these portions of the Tzee, turning them back into the colony creatures once more, but it was more likely that they would turn on him and, in his present condition, that might prove fatal. Yet, if they remained his slaves, it meant losing their ability to traverse from the Dream Lands to the outside world.

Cracks and fissures danced about the structure of Sirvak Dragoth. Some of the ground below the citadel had given way. At this rate, D'Shay supposed sourly, the great keep would tumble on top of his men before they were able to breach the defenses and overwhelm the inhabitants. If Sirvak Dragoth fell, odds were that the Master Guardians would die—which meant that *he* would die.

Not yet!

If nothing else, he would have the Gryphon. If it meant crawling into the struggle, then so be it.

The former prisoner, Freynard, had to be in the citadel. Either that, or he had been transported to the outside world by the Tzee. Whichever the case, D'Shay could not locate him. Matters were not helped by the fact that, without a direct link to the Ravager, his own abilities were greatly lessened.

He thought he heard someone speak, but, when he turned, there was no one near enough. Irritated at his own jumpiness, he ordered the two servants to assist him back to his tent. There was nothing he could do now, nothing at all until Sirvak Dragoth fell "in another few minutes."

Tzee . . .

"Hold," he ordered. The three of them came to a dead stop.

Tzee . . .

It *was* them! Faint, yes, but the Tzee had returned. Why? "What do you want from me now?"

Tzee . . . aid . . . will aid . . .

D'Shay hid his growing excitement. If the Tzee were willing to aid him, it was because they needed something in return. There was something wrong with them. They were very faint, almost impossible to hear at times.

Tzee . . . help . . . power . . .

It was hard to understand at first, but D'Shay finally comprehended. They needed power again. Something had broken the Tzee, literally fragmented it so that this was likely the largest coherent colony remaining. In return, they would aid him.

"If you wish to trade with me, I want you where I can see you. Manifest yourself!" He ordered the two servants away. For now, he would have to draw from his own strength. He could not show any more weakness than necessary.

Tzee . . . strain . . .

"Do it, or you will be left to dissipate here!" It was a gamble, to be sure. If the Tzee did not obey, then D'Shay would eventually "dissipate" himself. He had to know the extent of his power over the Tzee.

Slowly, a churning mass, dark as night, grew before his eyes. From a tiny point before him, it expanded and expanded until, at long last, it was a living cloud of energy and matter—but not as great in size as the wolf raider remembered it.

"So, the mighty Tzee have been humbled by someone. Was it D'Rak?"

Tzee . . . was all the cloud would say, but somehow D'Shay felt that his rival was involved.

"Where is he now?" The senior keeper could not be in the Dream Lands. Lord Petrac was dead, the Tzee were not aiding him, and the not-people—well, that went without saying.

Tzee . . . Qualard . . . Even fragmented, the Tzee were one. What the tinier colonies, abandoned, heard and saw, the larger entity that had fled knew as well.

"*Qualard?*" The surprise and realization in D'Shay's voice was enough to send the cloud scurrying back a few feet.

Qualard! It was all coming together now! A desperate attempt to save the Dream Lands by fulfilling his mission after all this time—but, then, what did time have to do with this? What the Gryphon sought was still there, still waiting.

"Come back here!" he snapped at the Tzee. The cloud moved slowly forward, all those eyes seemingly downcast like those of children about to be punished. It paused at eye level no more than an arm's width from him. "Where is the prisoner you stole from me? Where is Freynard?"

Tzee . . . not Dragoth . . . not . . . here . . .

"You turned him over to the Gryphon's allies?"

646 Richard A. Knaak

Tzee . . .

"But he's not there anymore?"

Tzee . . . not . . .

"Then he's with the Gryphon. In Qualard."

Tzee . . . do not—

"I wasn't asking you." While the chastised Tzee floated impatiently, D'Shay's mind raced. He did not have time to go back to Canisargos, and he doubted that would be a good idea at the moment. With him supposedly trapped in the Dream Lands, it was not unlikely that the senior keeper's position had grown. D'Shay knew that he might return to discover that his private chambers had been ransacked by keepership guards.

His eyes narrowed on the Tzee. As if feeling this, the nebulous form tried to shrink inward. "You must transport me to Qualard. I will picture the exact location."

Tzee . . . need . . . power. . . .

D'Shay shook his head. He did not really have the power to give, but that was not for the Tzee to know. "*After* you deliver me to my destination."

Tzee . . .

"You have no one else who will deal with you—and in your present state, you're hardly a threat to anyone. Well?"

Tzee . . . yesss. . . .

As the wolf raider watched, the Tzee seemed to compact themselves into a tighter, thicker mass, as if preparing to sacrifice a portion of the colony itself. They were not summoning the Gate but creating a portal of their own, something the Dream Lands allowed only them to do. That was the only true power the Tzee really had. Yet, being a part of the Dream Lands, they no doubt drew their ability from whatever had created the Gate in the first place. D'Shay dismissed the theory from his mind. Now was not the time to be concerned with something that did not concern his own survival. He felt the Tzee touch his thoughts briefly, but only to draw forth the needed destination. He had only to wait a few seconds now.

D'Shay glanced around. The keepers were still at work, breaking down the last desperate defenses of the Master Guardians. Given time, they might be able to bring one to him—and the key word was *might*. Given the choice between a possible solution and a probable one, D'Shay would always choose the latter.

Tzee . . . Gate . . . hurry . . .

A portal that shimmered ominously materialized next to one of the unliving guards. D'Shay glanced up at the Tzee. It was struggling to maintain both the portal and its own existence, and he doubted it could do both for very long. He ordered the two servants through. While they passed through the portal, he took a quick look around. Victory was assured here, and no one would notice for now that the commanding officer was missing, not when that officer was D'Shay, known for his eccentric ways. All that mattered right now to the Aramites was victory over this, their only major stumbling block. They did not even realize what they were really fighting for.

He laughed, albeit a little bitterly, turned, and stepped through the portal.

THE LAST PERSON through the portal was a bit of a surprise. He came flying through, rolled forward once, and came up standing, somewhat wobbly, a short sword in his hands.

Morgis had his own blade ready and would have made short work of the newcomer if the Gryphon had not caught his wrist. "No! Captain Freynard is one of my men!"

The drake looked at him doubtfully. "One of your men? Here across the Eastern Seas?"

"I haven't got time to explain it. Suffice it to say that he's been a prisoner of D'Shay."

"Was he?" Morgis was still not convinced. "Then how did you escape? This D'Shay does not mark me as a careless sort."

Freynard opened his mouth to speak and then hesitated. After a few seconds, his shoulders slumped. He shook his head and said slowly, "I don't know how I escaped, Your Majesty. I only recall a sudden dark fog—and then I was wandering in the wilderness, my bonds hanging loose, near the place you call Sirvak Dragoth. Two of those—those faceless things took hold of me. . . ."

"And you ended up inside the citadel," the Gryphon finished. "It sounds to me as if someone wanted you away from D'Shay, but not dead. The dark fog sounds like the Tzee, but I do not recall them being quite so strong."

"Nor I," added Haggerth.

"I still don't trust this one."

The Gryphon finally snapped at him. "Then you question my judgment and you question the loyalty of a man who has always been willing to lay down his life for me—not that I have ever wanted such a thing to happen."

"I would do it anyway," Freynard added quietly.

"Let us hope you never have to. Well, Duke Morgis? I would like to continue with this mission."

The drake hissed, but he nodded. "So, where do we start?"

They took their first long look at what awaited them.

Qualard had been a vast metropolis with high towers and massive walls. What remained now spoke more about how much had been lost rather than how great the city had been. Even after two centuries of being worn down by the forces of nature—and that did not even include the initial quake that had destroyed the city (and may or may not have been the work of the Ravager; the Gryphon was skeptical)—the ruins of Qualard were still impressive. Many structures were now no more than great piles of unidentifiable debris. Most of the wood had long rotted, but marble floors and columns—what had not been crushed to pieces—were everywhere. Some walls, amazingly enough, still stood. A few streets were passable to at least some extent, though one or two dropped off into chasms. One portion of the city had been raised up at least twenty feet; a few buildings, minus roots, stood. To their right, a deep ravine was all that remained of one building, save a cornerstone.

No one said anything at first. Troia was the one to break the silence, finally whispering, "What it must have been like that day!"

"It was terrible," the Gryphon muttered quietly—and then jolted to awareness when he realized what he had just said.

"You *were* here when it happened."

He looked at her. Nothing, besides that admission, would come to him. No memory of that day, merely that it was terrible.

The place they stood in must have been a square, for it was clear some distance around. The Gryphon turned in a full circle, trying to get his bearings with the phantoms of lost memories. "If I guess correctly, we're somewhere near the center of the city."

With a return to the task at hand came notice of the bitter wind that blew hither through the ruins of the former Aramite capital. Haggerth took hold of the bottom of his veil and held it in place with one hand while he used the other to secure one of the corners, which had a tiny loop, to a hook in his robe. When both corners were thus secured, he shook his head and made a comment about some of the more unsavory regions of the afterlife as he believed it.

Troia's fur was on end. Her reply to the Master Guardian's remark was unrepeatable, but she got her point across.

The cold would take its toll on all of them the longer they stood around. The Gryphon satisfied himself that they were near where he had wanted to be. He had no real memories of Qualard, but he had had a suspicion it would resemble the design of Canisargos—and it had. That alone confirmed what he had assumed prior to his first attempt to come here—that he would find what he was looking for in approximately the same region as the Pack Master's stronghold was in the present capital.

"Considering the time we have," he began, "we're going to have to split up."

"That's a bit unwise, wouldn't you think?" Morgis hissed.

"Any other time, yes. This time, we have no choice. We have to hurry. There are three probable areas. Troia, Master Haggerth, if you have no objections, I would like you to search over there." The Gryphon pointed to a fairly stable expanse far to his left.

Troia protested. "I . . . don't want to leave you—not here."

"There's nothing here but ruins. No life, no danger except from crumbling masonry." He shook his head briefly, as if unconcerned himself, though he felt the opposite. "Morgis, I'd like you and Captain Freynard to search toward the north where it starts to sink down. There might be passages underneath. If anyone finds anything, return here. At worst, we meet . . ." He looked up. Sunlight was not something common to this region. Clouds obscured the entire sky. "Try to estimate a half hour."

Freynard cleared his throat. "With all due respect, Majesty, I would be remiss in my duty if I did not stay with you."

"I'm no longer your liegelord. You have no duty toward me."

"Then"—Freynard managed a grin through the birds'-nest beard—"you can't order me *not* to accompany you."

Morgis put a heavy hand on the man's shoulder. "And if *you* think I'm going to leave you alone with him, you are a fool."

Before anything could happen, the Gryphon separated them. "If both of you cannot follow directions—and I'm only asking this because of time, which is drastically running short even as we continue to speak—then stay here. I need people willing to work, not argue."

After a pause, both warriors gave in. He breathed a sigh of relief.

"Where will you go, Gryphon?" Haggerth asked.

"South. Now. No more talk."

They separated reluctantly, Haggerth having to encourage Troia to leave, and Morgis and Freynard watching one another as they walked. The lion-bird refused to look at any of them, instead turning his back and moving resolutely southward. He made his way over jutting bits of street and long narrow chasms and did not stop until he was more than a hundred long paces from where he had started. He jumped down to a spot where the ground had sunk partially and turned back to check on the others.

Morgis and Freynard were out of sight. Once they became accustomed to the situation, they would start concentrating on the search. Both men were veteran warriors and pragmatic when all was said and done.

He could just barely see Troia and Haggerth. Not certain as to how old or how agile the Master Guardian was, he had chosen the easiest path for them. Even as the Gryphon watched, first Troia and then the veiled guardian disappeared over a rise that might have once been the first floor of a building.

The lionbird waited for several seconds until he was certain that no one was going to backtrack in an attempt to return to him. Then he climbed up from his hiding place, caught his breath, and began working his way—*east*.

He knew where he had to go, just as he knew that someone might already be waiting for him there. To kill him or be killed. The Gryphon knew these things, had known these things, the moment he had started to separate the group. He also knew a little more about what secret was hidden here.

It was not a thing he sought, but rather a prisoner. Some . . . entity . . . that had been ensnared by the Ravager long before the existence of the wolf raiders. An entity that had waited patiently, biding its time, knowing freedom could be its if it was careful . . . And now the time had come, but the Ravager's agents were here as well. That is, at least one was.

A short climb over some unidentifiable piece of architecture brought him to a relatively clear area. This had been the floor of the palace of the Pack Master, mortal ruler—in name—of the wolf raiders. The Gryphon wondered if the Pack Master of that time had been a shell, a puppet of the horror that called itself the Ravager, as the present one was. Probably. It would fit into the pattern of things.

At least four chambers were identifiable by the remnants of wall, and, of the four of these, only one was large enough to be what he sought. There was rubble strewn over various parts of it, but the placement of the fragments was just a bit too precise. As he suspected, the largest pile was located near one of the far corners. Moving over there, the lionbird began the tedious process of removing the rubble.

He worked for what he estimated to be ten minutes before the fruit of his labors became apparent. The wind had picked up, but the former mercenary scarcely noticed it as he stared at what he had uncovered. A trapdoor. To most eyes, it would have been invisible, but, by careful inspection, he located the edges. The door was puzzling; it had no handle that he could see, and it was such a perfect fit that his claws could not even get a hold on the sides.

"Not now," the Gryphon muttered. "Not when I'm so close to it at last!" In a sense, the freeing of whatever being lay chained within was secondary to at last discovering his true past. Given the choice, however, he would have traded the latter for the former. A few memories were not worth the lives of even one person.

A miniature rock slide from somewhere behind him warned of the fact that he was no longer alone.

Carefully, as if he had not noticed, the Gryphon rose from his examination of the stone door, crossing his arms as he straightened. His back was toward whoever had joined him, so it was impossible for the newcomer to notice that one of the lionbird's hands now rested on the hilt of his sword.

The intruder moved again, creating another tiny avalanche. This time he could not ignore the noise. His grip tightened on the hilt.

"Kill! Kill!"

The shrill, birdlike voice startled him so much that he almost failed to draw the sword. The Gryphon whirled around even before the second shout began. Surprise was no longer an element in this venture. Not now that he knew what he was up against. The call of the creature had decided it for him. He recognized it, though not because of the words. Rather, the lionbird recalled the cries of its kin as he and Morgis had battled to escape Canisargos.

Surprise proved it had yet one more card to play, for the gryphon that stood overlooking him was possibly the largest he had ever encountered. The ones ridden by the sentries could not have been more than half the size of this great beast. Had he not known how savage it truly was, it would have almost looked majestic. *Almost* majestic, for the blood on its beak and foreclaws eliminated any sort of illusion in that respect.

The blood was still fairly fresh.

It had a terrible rent in one wing, which explained why it had not simply swooped down and finished him before he even had time to react to its presence. There were other wounds, mostly minor ones, but he did notice that the beast was breathing harshly, as if it had been damaged within as well. Knowing this did not raise his confidence. If there was one thing deadlier than a gryphon, barring dragons, it was a wounded gryphon. *That* was one thing he had in common with the creature.

The monster tried to circle around him, but the footing was too precarious, and it started to slide downward. The wings, or rather one wing, spread in a feeble attempt to fly, the failure of which only made the gryphon angrier. It continued to cry out the word that someone had obviously worked hard to make it say.

He tried to reach out with his power and end this quickly, but, to his astonishment, the animal had some sort of protection that was by no means natural in origin.

"There were two of them originally, you know."

The ex-mercenary backed up so that he could keep the animal in sight and yet still confront the newcomer as well.

"What did you need them for?" The Gryphon turned, trying to get both in his range of sight. "You're far more of a mad beast than a dozen of these, D'Shay."

D'Shay, still out of sight, chuckled and, to the lionbird's aggravation, started moving so that animal and master were always one hundred and eighty degrees apart from one another. The Gryphon continued to turn, but he found that, even with his unique eyesight, he would have needed eyes in the back of his head to keep track of both of them simultaneously.

"I'll take that as a compliment. You know, this really shows how fortunes can change at times."

"In what way?" the Gryphon asked, wishing his would change for the better as soon as possible.

"When we met again, after so long, in the cavern of the Black Dragon— Lochivar, wasn't it—I was ending a commitment to the drake lord because we could no longer afford to trade him slaves for an emergency port. We thought we might actually need them. We'd conquered as much of this continent as necessary and had decided it was time to deal with the Master Guardians of Sirvak Dragoth. Imagine our surprise when, even with my aid, they not only held us but they actually pushed us back."

The beast chose that moment to shout, "Kill! Kill!"

D'Shay shouted something at it, a sound more than a word, and the animal quieted. The wolf raider apologized. "They tend to be impatient creatures."

"I can see why. You certainly are long-winded."

He could almost imagine the smile on D'Shay's wolfish visage. "Just a little bit longer. I want to savor this. Until a few minutes ago, I thought I was going to die. Now I am safe. I was trapped in the Dream Lands; did I mention that? The Tzee, who I admit were more cunning than I imagined, had some plan of their own backfire, so they came to the one person who might still be willing to bargain with them."

The Gryphon stumbled momentarily, but quickly regained his balance. "You should never bargain with the Tzee."

D'Shay continued to move. "Yes, I learned that. No time to worry now, though. They only had enough power to create a portal and get me here. I was no sooner here than they were dissipated from lack of power—exactly as I hoped. So much for betrayal."

"Would that they had left you floating in the Void by accident."

"You would have liked that. As I said, fortunes change. The stalemate continued, and I searched for new ports, supposedly to appease unrest in the council, but actually because I knew you still lived. You know the rest. The stalemate finally ended, with us on the side that was winning. As I see it now, we have changed places, you and I. You had a country behind you, and I was forced to slink around; now, I have the power of an empire, and you, you are the lone hope. The predator has become the prey."

D'Shay ceased moving. As if by some unseen signal, the Gryphon halted as well. It pawed at the unstable footing, beak open, rage and hunger in its mad eyes.

"I'd like to say," the wolf raider added, "that the blood is from your companions. But I won't. That will come with time."

"D'Rak?" The Gryphon silently cursed himself. He had hoped that he had sent them *away* from the danger.

"Not his, but surely some of his fools'. He is here somewhere, but he lacks complete knowledge. A pity. I think he would've enjoyed the poetry of this moment."

The beast roared, reacting to a new signal, and leaped for the Gryphon.

XXI

MORGIS AND FREYNARD, while not yet prepared to consider each other in terms such as "comrade" or "friend," had at least come to the point where they respected one another's skills. Now and then, to keep the boredom of their task from overwhelming them, they would discuss the ways of the warrior and how it was the little things that always seemed to be the deciding factor in the greatest battles.

They had just begun to discuss the Turning War, the war that was still causing changes in drake and human society today—due mainly to Cabe Bedlam and the Gryphon—when Freynard spotted something and called out quietly but urgently. Morgis, regaining his balance for what he considered the "thousandth damned time," rushed as quickly as was possible.

"What is it?" he hissed softly. There seemed to be no one around, but if the warm-blood thought it best to talk quietly, Morgis would not argue.

Freynard pointed at a congealed, dark liquid splattered across some of the rubble. He stuck a finger into it and held it up for the drake to see.

"Blood."

"An animal, perhaps." The drake doubted his own suggestion. It would have been the first one they had seen since arriving here. There were not even any birds.

Freynard's eyes met the duke's. "Follow it, milord?"

Morgis knew that, as things stood, the captain did not have to acknowledge his rank. Nonetheless, the act of respect did please him, and he unconsciously returned courtesy with courtesy. "As you think, Captain Freynard."

"It heads toward Troia and the Master Guardian. We should take a look."

"Haggerth is his name. Yes. Who knows, we may find what we seek on the way."

"Whatever that may be." Freynard smiled briefly.

The trail went haphazardly for several hundred yards, but was always clear enough for them to follow. Knowing the time limit that they had, they dared increase their pace even more. Thus it was that they were nearly over the bodies before they saw them.

There were four bodies. Three mangled forms that could be identified as Aramites and one that Morgis recognized and that gave him pause because of the incredible size. He shivered briefly, but convinced himself it was only the wind.

Most of the blood, it seemed, was from the hapless wolf raiders. The thing that had killed them, the gryphon, had several slashes across its flanks, but something else had finished it off. The drake stepped over to the beast and studied it from head to tip of tail. There was something wrong with its inner structure—as if the bones and organs were not quite in the right places.

Keepers.

"Freynard!" he spat quietly. The captain looked up from his clinical examination of one raider who was missing most of his midsection. "Check for a keeper!"

While Freynard searched his man, Morgis moved to one that lay broken over the jagged edge of an upturned piece of street. The man's arm was gone, and his face was a pulp—the wolfhelm had been torn from his head, apparently—but his uniform was more reminiscent of those worn by the keepership guards. Better kept. A bit flashier, including a tiny symbol on the chest that, when the blood was wiped away, was revealed to be a tiny crystal.

A hand fell on his shoulder. He was standing straight, sword over his head, before he recognized the human. "You could find yourself without a head if you make a habit of that!"

"You said you wanted me to find a keeper. The last body is one, I think. The only keeper I remember was one named D'Laque, but he had something like this." Allyn Freynard opened his hand to reveal a small, toothlike crystal. Unlike those Morgis had seen, it was dull and cold-looking. He suspected that was one way of knowing that the keeper was dead—the other was to look at what remained of him.

"There were trails of blood," the captain continued. His eyes were not on his companion, but on the area around them. "The one we followed here, and another one moving on the way we were going."

"Toward the Master Guardian and the Gryphon's female."

"Is she?"

"I know it, even if they do not."

"Then"—Freynard rose—"it is my duty to protect her as well. Let's go."

The trail of blood, unfortunately, went only a little farther before dwindling to nothing. Someone had obviously finally had the good sense to either heal the wound or, lacking that power, bind it. That did not deter them. They were more concerned with finding the other two than with finding whatever survivors of the Aramite party still remained. That was a problem best dealt with afterward, when they knew everyone was safe.

After several more minutes of clambering over the ancient wreckage of Qualard, Morgis called a halt by raising his hand. To Freynard, it seemed that the duke was listening to something that he himself could not hear.

That was indeed the case. "There are voices coming from that direction—and I think one of them belongs to someone whose acquaintance I have been hoping to renew."

He did not expand on the last comment, but instead signaled the captain forward again. With the practiced stealth of two survivors, they moved closer.

The voices, especially one, became audible, if not necessarily understandable.

Morgis was about to continue forward when Freynard grabbed hold of him and pointed to their left.

A single Aramite, definitely a keepership guard as far as the drake was able to tell, kept an eye out for any intruders. He seemed nervous, a totally reasonable emotion if he had recently survived a gryphon attack. Morgis looked for another path that would lead them closer. It was not that he feared a lone sentry or even D'Rak himself; it was just that charging in would not save Troia and the Master Guardian Haggerth if they were prisoners, which seemed likely. Shifting to dragon form would not help, either; he would be too susceptible to attack by the senior keeper while he was transforming. After all, it was hardly something he could keep secret.

He found a likely route, a place where two large buildings had apparently fallen together. Time and erosion had more or less fused them into one mass, but there was still a tunnel—actually, more of a gap—down between the foundations. It would require crawling, but that was not what bothered him. The tunnel was barely large enough for him to fit in, and any wolf raider who discovered them before they were through would be able to kill them at his leisure. There was no way they could defend themselves properly while inside.

Still, it was the most likely choice. Morgis pointed at the tunnel and whispered, "There."

Freynard nodded and followed as the drake worked his way to the opening. Morgis wasted no time; holding his sword before him, he went down on his knees and began crawling.

Just inside, the duke discovered that the tunnel extended much longer and would bring them even closer to the Aramites than he had first expected. Inside, the voices came stronger, though with an echoing effect, and the words were more or less understandable.

". . . Dragoth! It would go . . . you told me where the Gryphon is now!"

Morgis hissed in barely restrained anger. "D'Rak!"

"You seem to be growing more . . . worried with each passing. . . . There something wrong?" The other voice was unmistakably that of Haggerth. Was Troia there as well?

"We have to move," Freynard reminded him. Morgis grunted quietly and continued on.

"There is nothing wrong," D'Rak was saying, but there was tension in his voice. "How could there be with Sirvak Dragoth falling even as we speak, you two my prisoners, and the Gryphon to follow? Even D'Shay is no longer a problem."

"What is it about Qualard, D'Rak? What is here that you and your god fear so much that you tried to remove all knowledge of it from us?"

The two reached the other end of the tunnel and hesitated. Someone in a heavy pair of boots walked nearby and then moved away again. Another guard. Morgis waited until the sentry's footfalls had faded into the distance and then slowly crawled from the passage. A wall that had stood the test of time stretched in both directions. Morgis realized that D'Rak and the others were on the other side. Freynard joined him, seeming to grasp the situation immediately.

The senior keeper's voice rose slightly. "It's not something that you need to know where you will be going—unless, Master Guardian, you would be willing to trade access to the Dream Lands for that secret and your own miserable life."

"You don't know. He doesn't know, Master Haggerth!"

Morgis nodded to the captain. Troia *was* there, after all—and still fighting, he was pleased to see. Too many creatures gave up when faced with death. Even drakes.

There was a heavy *crack* and a gasp of pain. "I will know all soon enough, misfit. I know many things even now. For instance, it is not a thing your friend seeks, but a being, a being ensnared here long ago by the lord Ravager himself—your god, guardians."

"What you say could not possibly be true!" Haggerth was apparently growing upset. The drake frowned; he had thought the man stronger, steadier. This was not the Haggerth who seemed always to find reason when others, like Mrin/Amrin, could not.

"He's going to kill them at this rate!" Freynard practically mouthed the words so as not to alert the others to their presence.

"You should be glad that my veil obscures my face, wolf raider, else my anger would probably strike you dead!"

Drake and man stared wide-eyed at each other. Haggerth knew he was going to die, but like Troia, he was still fighting—and, at the moment, he had only one weapon remaining.

Morgis pointed at himself and then behind him. He then pointed at the captain and indicated the opposite direction. Freynard nodded. They would come from both sides. The drake held up three fingers and then created a zero, indicating a count of thirty once both of them were in position. In case the keeper did not fall into the trap, they would still commit themselves. Before they separated, Morgis mouthed one last word—*D'Rak.*

Freynard nodded once. No matter what else, one of them had to kill the senior keeper.

Silent as a cat, the drake moved swiftly toward his end of the wall.

D'Rak had been laughing, but when he calmed enough to speak, there was poison in his words. "Small wonder they call it the Dream Lands! You've been hiding behind your kerchief much too long to be so arrogant at a time like this. Do you think that you invoke mystery or power with your little piece of cloth?"

So intent was the drake on the Aramite's words that he did not hear the clink of rock upon metal. He was only halfway to the end of the wall when the sentry came around the corner. Both froze, the guard because he had come this way more than a dozen times before and Morgis because everything had seemed to time itself so right.

The sentry opened his mouth to give the alarm. Morgis jumped at him, knocking the other's sword away.

"Let me show you what your power is worth!" D'Rak snarled from the other side of the wall.

The guard slipped from the drake's grasp. "Alert!"

Morgis ran him through as he tried to recover his weapon. The duke rushed to the end of the wall, glanced briefly behind himself, and saw Freynard vanishing around the corner even as D'Rak's shocked "Ravager's Blood!" cut through all other noise. The shout was followed by a scream of denial. Troia's scream.

Morgis cursed, shielded his eyes, and charged around the edge of the wall wondering which would get him first, a sword point or an accidental glance at one of the two people he was trying to save. He hoped it was the sword point; at least *that* could be explained to his sire—if someone remained alive to explain it.

"That's it, old friend, delay it! Delay it as long as possible!" D'Shay's laugh was more of a cackle, a mad one at that.

Blood seeped from the Gryphon's right side where one of the beast's claws had caught him during that initial leap. D'Shay's pet was used to slower prey, not something with a swiftness to match its own. Unfortunately, despite that swiftness, it was impossible to escape from the monster. If the Gryphon turned away for even a second, he knew that the beast would get him.

It was not all one-sided. He still had his short sword, though now he wished he had traded it for something with a little more reach. D'Shay's creature had already received a slash across its chest, and it did not seem too eager to try for a second. Instead, the two of them circled about the area with the master wolf raider the only audience—a partial one at that.

Moving about had at least allowed the Gryphon a chance to study D'Shay. What he had seen had shocked him: D'Shay was dying. Almost half of his visible skin was gray, and some of it was peeling. One of his arms hung loosely at his side and, when D'Shay did move, it was with some hesitation, as if he was uncertain of his own ability to function.

"Why don't you try another spell? The last one might have only misfired!"

Misfired? Not likely, the lionbird knew. D'Shay's pet had been specially bred, but it was also magically enhanced, shielded, and capable of dampening his powers to a level that had proved useless so far. A special treat that D'Shay had raised for several generations just on the off chance that his adversary would return.

There had been *two* of these. The Gryphon gave a brief mental thanks to whatever patron was watching over him that D'Rak had been unfortunate enough to arrive so near the creatures and thus relieved the lionbird of some of the trouble. Two such beasts would have been fighting over his remains long ago.

"It will be nice to rest without wondering when you might reappear. I still think of the last time we were here."

"I'm sorry," the Gryphon interrupted, his eyes remaining on the animal before him, "but my memory is a little hazy about that last time."

"Suffice to say that I would have died because of you. Died, if not for the Lord Ravager."

"Why, what happened?" An idle thought had occurred to the lionbird, an idle thought concerning a similar situation to this. He had to keep D'Shay distracted while he concentrated.

"That, I am afraid, is something I would like you to go to your death guessing about."

"I already know a little about who you have imprisoned down there." D'Shay's pet took another swipe at him; the Gryphon held off the blow with his sword, but his arm was growing heavy and the loss of blood from his wound was slowing him. He could not afford to lose speed, not now.

"Do you?"

"Enough to know that it was not the Ravager that devastated this city."

D'Shay did not laugh. As he came into view once more, the Gryphon saw that he was growing a bit anxious and not merely because of whatever was killing him. "It seems I arrived here just in time, then. I thought you had almost no memory, but now I think you might even know what you did wrong last time and how you could change that."

The lionbird was almost ready to admit his true ignorance on that point, but then found that he suddenly *did* possess the knowledge. The discovery nearly cost him his life, because the gryphon lunged toward him and he barely managed to dodge its paws. It was to prove an unfortunate choice, for he landed on his injured side, and the sharp pain wreaked havoc with his motor functions. The sword dropped from his clawing fingers. The beast shrieked and moved toward him. Tears in his eyes, he rolled away and succeeded in stumbling to his feet.

The sword lay beneath the hind legs of D'Shay's pet.

"I think a conclusion is imminent now," D'Shay said with a growing smile. "The last of the misfits, the special ones. My only regret is never really being certain of where you came from. I don't suppose you remember *that?*"

The Gryphon shook his head, as much to clear it as to answer his foe's question.

"Pity." D'Shay shouted out a command. The beast stood poised, knowing now that its prey was more or less helpless. Even with his claws, the Gryphon had no chance against this mad version of himself. He had a knife, as well, but it seemed unlikely that it would do any better than his claws.

It was now or never. He prayed it would listen to him.

"Kill!" shouted the wolf raider.

"Kill! Kill!" The huge creature leaped at him, aiming for his uninjured side. It knew by instinct that its prey would then be forced to depend on the weaker side, and even a moment of hesitation due to pain was all the skilled hunter needed.

The Gryphon, however, did not move in either direction. Rather, he fell to the ground, an act that, under normal circumstances, would have meant his death. The beast would have landed, turned, and caught him while he was still struggling to his feet. That is, if it had landed where it expected to.

Behind where he had stood, the Gate, doors open, materialized and accepted the unsuspecting gryphon. The animal roared its confusion, a roar that was cut off as the gryphon disappeared and the portal returned to wherever it had come from. It was over before the lionbird could draw another breath.

He could not believe that it had actually worked.

Neither could D'Shay. His uncomprehending face was gray, but it was hard to tell if it was from whatever was killing him or from what he had just seen. "What—did—you do?"

His question went unanswered, for the Gryphon was taking full advantage of the situation. He had rolled to a position that left him facing his adversary, and then his knife was out, ready for throwing. D'Shay finally woke from his madness and began shouting. Two heavily armored figures joined him on the rise, figures that were probably not human, the Gryphon supposed.

D'Shay turned, his body shifting slowly, uncertainly. The Gryphon released the knife, aiming, not for his back, which the two guards were moving to block, but for his leg. One of the servants made a late attempt to put his own leg in the way, but he was too slow.

Had his condition not slowed him, the knife would have flown uselessly over his shoulder. Instead, the blade caught D'Shay in the unprotected back side of his leg near his knee. The wolf raider let out a cry, made a feeble grab at the handle of the knife, and finally fell from sight. The Gryphon, meanwhile, retrieved his sword and prepared to face off against the two armored figures, only to discover that they had stopped moving. He waited, expecting some trick, but the two continued to stand where they were, frozen in the midst of whatever movement they had been making when D'Shay fell. Evidently, D'Shay's will was their will, period. That they were unmoving meant that he was now unconscious—or dead.

Taking a chance, the Gryphon sheathed his sword and climbed to the top. Carefully, for past experience with his adversary had taught him never to take anything at face value, he looked over.

The master wolf raider lay in a very crumpled, very dead heap. In addition to his knife wound, which apparently had resulted in a broken leg on the way down, his head was bent back at an awkward angle. If it was a ploy, it was a very good one—yet, he had seen D'Shay die before. Best not to take a chance, he decided. Hoping he would not regret his decision, he worked his way down to the body.

Had he not seen it happen and been responsible for it, the Gryphon would have supposed that someone had killed D'Shay more than a week before. His skin was nearly completely gray now, and even partially mummified. He remembered some of the things Freynard had mentioned, but they

only served to confuse him further. The former mercenary rose. Whatever
Shaidarol had become during all those years in service to the mad wolf god,
this body would give him no more service. He pulled out the sword, raised
it over his head, and brought it down on the neck with all his strength.

The resistance was negligible; his sword dug deep in the ground, and
the rapidly decaying head rolled away. The Gryphon dragged the body a
hundred yards away and, just for good measure, buried it under some heavy
rubble. He then did the same for the head.

Rest in pieces, he could not help thinking, and then added as an after-
thought, *and stay there.*

The Gryphon finally examined his side. It had stopped bleeding, and,
if he held his hand on it, it did not hurt as much. With neither D'Shay
nor his pet to interfere, he could use his powers to heal himself. It would
be a slow process; he had still not completely recovered from his previous
wounds, though he had tried not to show that to anyone. Now was not the
time to worry about them. Now was the time to worry about finding a way
into—what?

He climbed once more over the rise, stopping briefly to inspect the two
armored servants. Empty though the suits appeared, he knew better. These
were portions of the Tzee that D'Shay had secretly ensnared. They had no
consciousness of their own and did not respond to his commands. In the
end, the Gryphon decided to leave them to the elements.

His eyes focused on the approximate location of the trapdoor, an action
that almost proved fatal, for his foot was just coming down when it hit him
that he was staring at, not the well-disguised entrance, but a square hole cut
deep into the foundation of the ancient building. The Gryphon slipped and
slid halfway down the slope (fortunately, on his good side) before he was
able to stop himself. He completed the downward climb in a more standard
manner, though it was difficult not to keep staring at the uncovered entrance to Qualard's underworld.

Once down, he raced over to the hole. Someone, somehow, had removed
the slab. The prisoner, perhaps? It was doubtful, but there was no way to be
certain. At the moment, he could not sense the other. It was almost as if a
wall was preventing contact.

A row of steps led into darkness. The Gryphon cursed himself for not
bringing a torch or something. He would have to rely on his night vision,
which, while excellent, was by no means a substitute for light.

Sword ready, the lionbird slowly descended, feeling much like a bird walking blindly into the mouth of a cat . . . or in this case, a wolf. He moved slowly, allowing his eyes to become accustomed to the dark. The air was dry but breathable and fairly dust free. No small creatures had made their home here, not ever. It was like walking into a tomb only recently sealed—only, the occupant was still alive.

There was light after all. As in Canisargos, small crystals dotted the walls. They seemed to come alive slowly, as if those closer to him were waking those farther away. He thought for a moment that the dim light from above had started some sort of reaction, but then he noticed that those behind him gradually darkened once more. They were responding to *him*.

The city sleeps above us, a memory told him.

"The wolf raiders never sleep," he replied before realizing he was merely repeating something he had said long, long ago.

Can you do it? another memory, seemingly female, asked pensively.

He wondered about that. Could he do what? Free the one entombed here?

Can you die without screaming out your fear?

This was not a memory! The crystals ahead of the Gryphon died abruptly, followed by those near and behind him. He was plunged into total darkness, which his eyes attempted to compensate, albeit inadequately, for.

The clean, dry air gave way to a pungent scent like a thousand years of rotting meat. He heard the sounds of bones rattling as something huge crushed them beneath its massive paws. Hot breath seemed to wash over his face.

Two burning, bloodred eyes glared death at him from the corridor. He was forced to look upward, for the thing, its form indistinguishable from the darkness save for those eyes, towered over him. It snarled.

This is no dream this time. I am so very real, as you can see.

Behind him, the light from above vanished and the Gryphon heard the sound of stone scraping against stone. The entrance was sealed once more.

He was trapped—and alone with the Ravager himself.

XXII

MORGIS HAD CHARGED out into the open, fully expecting to take on any number of opponents single-handedly. That everyone had fallen victim to Haggerth's trap was too much to hope for. If D'Rak alone had suffered the consequences, that would be sufficient.

He stood there for several seconds, his right side virtually blind because he feared to remove his hand. There was no one to fight. One wolf raider, lying facedown, was visible, but he looked to have been dead for some time, perhaps at the claws of Troia, more likely from the gryphon. Another, a keeper, was on his knees and staring blindly into space, mouth open in a pitiful expression of incomprehension—perhaps at the cause of his own collapse. The drake paid no more heed to the unfortunate save to register him as one less threat. He had, of course, no idea how many other, actual threats *did* remain.

D'Rak was here somewhere, and that was what truly mattered. Hand still shielding his eyes, he moved nearer to where he guessed Troia and Haggerth were, hoping one of them would alert him to any nearby danger.

He bumped into something clad in metal. It pulled away from him as quickly as he pulled away from it.

"Rep-reptile!" The voice was slurred, as if the speaker were talking in slow motion, but it was unequivocally D'Rak.

The drake cursed. He'd walked right into the one person who could kill him with little more than a glance! Half blind was no way to fight a battle—and where was Freynard? Had he accidentally caught sight of what-ever horror the Master Guardian hid behind his veil? "Haggerth! Turn away from me!"

"He—he cannot—he cannot hear you—you!" D'Rak muttered. "His—his ears—his whole head—are no longer on speaking—on speaking terms!"

"Dead?" Morgis pulled his hand away. Whether or not the Master Guardian's visage would affect him after death was now unimportant; what was important was that someone else had suffered at the senior keeper's hands—and this time was dead. He could not even guess about Troia; was the scream for herself or the elder human? And *why* had D'Rak not laid him low with some spell?

Morgis was not greeted by the sight of his worst nightmares come to life, which was what he had half expected, but then he saw the form slumped against the wall, head turned from him, and knew why. Next to the unmoving body, Troia was struggling, slowly loosening her bonds. It occurred to him that she could use some assistance. Morgis started toward her, calling out. Troia looked up, and the expression on her face was one of sudden fear. He puzzled over it for perhaps a second or two . . . and knew with growing horror that he had fallen under the spell of D'Rak after all.

Without hesitation, he cried out in the name of his father and swung the sword in a vicious arc, not really caring if he struck anything, but hoping he would disrupt the senior keeper's concentration. When his blade suddenly sank deep into something other than stone, something that let out one gasp and then became dead weight, he thanked the Blue Dragon for guiding his aim and quickly pulled the sword back out. Morgis stepped back and turned even as an ebony-clad form fell lifelessly at his feet.

It was not D'Rak. He knew that instantly, for while the senior keeper was indeed in front of him, he was also several yards away. In one hand he held a crystalline talisman; with the other hand, he kept himself from falling over. The body before the drake was yet another guard. D'Rak himself looked only half alive. The lower right portion of his face was slack, lifeless, and he constantly blinked, as if even the dark, cloud-covered day was too bright for his eyes. His skin was as pale as death. What was most important, however, was that he was now alone.

"You—" Morgis's observation was confirmed. The right side of D'Rak's mouth did not move when he spoke. "You—you are as difficult to kill—to kill as the bird!"

Morgis still had no idea what had happened to Freynard, but that became secondary as he faced what was left of Lord D'Rak. Either through willpower or the protection of his crystal, D'Rak had succeeded in resisting the trap—at least partially, that is. His mind had suffered a strain that the drake, who had caught only a glimpse of Haggerth's face that one time in Sirvak Dragoth, could not begin to comprehend sufficiently. Small wonder that he had not killed Morgis outright. It was hard enough for the Aramite to stand, let alone concentrate. The senior keeper had obviously hoped that his one remaining follower would be able to walk right up to the ensorceled drake and finish him from behind, but either D'Rak's will was too weak now or he had sadly underestimated Morgis. Whatever the case, it was doubtful the senior keeper could summon up sufficient will to do it again.

He smiled slowly at D'Rak, every sharp, predatory tooth revealed in all its glory. "It's my turn now."

D'Rak held up his talisman, as if the crystal alone would be enough to stop the duke. "Not—not yet. Not while—not while I—I control the Eye of the Wolf!"

The keeper smiled defiantly at Morgis—and then the smile faded, first incomprehension and then panic setting in. "I—cannot feel it! The Eye is—Eye is hidden from me!"

"A pity." Morgis raised his sword. He had no compunction about killing D'Rak outright. The Aramite was one of the lords of the wolf raiders. Morgis did not doubt that the path to that position of power was even bloodier than he imagined.

"Fool!" Spittle ran down the senior keeper's chin and onto his breastplate. His eyes spoke volumes; why had his lord abandoned him now? "Kill me and you kill your—"

After D'Rak had fallen, Morgis bent down and opened wide the Aramite's hand, removing the talisman from his limp grip. He stood up and examined it. Like the last one he had seen, it was dull and cold.

Just for good measure, the duke dropped it at his own feet—and crushed it beneath his boot. As a further safety precaution, and one that seemed to come to him out of the blue, he severed the wolf raider's body from his head. Then he went to Troia, who had finally freed herself of her bonds and was leaning over Haggerth. His head was covered by the hood of his cloak.

"How is he?"

"Dead." She was worn. A trail of blood, still fresh, went from her mouth to her chin, the result of D'Rak's anger. "It was a reflex action. I—rolled away when he pulled the veil off, but I saw him hold out his—his crystal in order to save himself. There's not much left. D'Rak *was* senior keeper."

"It was not enough to save him. He was half mad and half crippled, which by no means meant he wasn't dangerous." Morgis scanned the area. "Is this it? Are there any more?"

She touched Haggerth's head lightly and whispered something. Then the feline woman rose. "There was one more, I'm sure of it. D'Rak used his crystal to capture us, but then he had his men bind us. Naturally, I counted their strength, in case I was able to break free. I think there was another guard. That way."

Morgis frowned. That was where Freynard had been. He pulled Troia closer. "You must do something for me."

"What?"

"Cut off the heads of the other wolf raiders. I—I do not understand it myself, but I feel it is important. Meanwhile, I have to find Captain Freynard. Will you do it?"

To his surprise, she actually seemed to draw strength from the suggestion. "Of course I'll do it. It's the right thing to do."

"The right thing?"

Troia shook her head. "I can't explain it. I just know. Like you."

"Curious." Sword in hand, he left her to the grisly task and headed cautiously to the other end of the wall, where he had last seen the Gryphon's man. Freynard, he knew, had not been in the best condition for this trek, but he had not weakened, either. Morgis was no longer concerned with his loyalty; now he was concerned for a soldier whom he had come to respect.

He saw nothing at first. It might have seemed that Freynard had never been there. Then the drake caught sight of something stirring in the rubble nearby. He stepped over what might possibly have been the remains of a stone bench or table and pulled a piece of masonry away.

It was Freynard, pale as if he had just died. His eyes were open, but he seemed not to recognize the drake at first, for he pulled away as if he expected to be killed. Morgis caught him by the shoulders and shook him. "Freynard! Curse you, it's me! Duke Morgis!"

"Morgis?" The captain looked at him oddly, then seemed to collect himself. He put a hand to his head. "I'm sorry. I wasn't myself."

"What happened here? Were you attacked?"

The man gazed around him, as if seeing things for the first time. Slowly, he explained everything. "Guard saw me. We struggled—lost my sword after wounding him. Was chased up there, then everything collapsed."

"Where's the wolf raider?"

"Underneath that." Freynard pointed at a new mound of marble and rock to his left. A boot and part of a leg were barely visible in the middle of the pile. There was no question about whether or not the Aramite was dead.

Morgis helped the human to his feet. "Haggerth is dead."

"Haggerth? Dead?"

"But D'Rak is as well."

That brought a broad smile to the captain's features. "D'Rak dead! The keepership is without a leader now!"

The drake thought about it. "Yes, I suppose that is an important consideration. What's more important right now is to get Troia and find the Gryphon. Suddenly, Qualard is becoming the most popular place on this continent!"

Coming around the wall, they spotted Troia. Freynard began to tremble. "What is she *doing*?"

The cat woman had taken care of the other bodies as Morgis had requested, and now she stood before the one survivor, the keeper who had lost his mind. Before Morgis could explain, she had slit the wolf raider's throat.

Freynard started to struggle. He was proving stronger than the duke had imagined. "Stop her!"

Morgis held on to him. Troia turned at the noise, her borrowed sword raised to strike the head off the Aramite. Clutching the captain tightly, the drake spat, "Cut it off! Now!"

With a precision that spoke of skills he had not imagined of her, she took the head off with one smooth strike.

"Release me!" Freynard nearly pulled free. Morgis turned him so that they faced one another and then quickly said, "It had to be done, Captain! I don't know if I can explain it, and I doubt that Troia could, either! We just know it has to be done!"

The man in his hands shivered uncontrollably, then slumped. "As you wish, then. If you think it was necessary, my lord, I will take your word."

Troia threw the sword down by the decapitated keeper and walked toward them. She seemed more at ease than earlier.

"You might need that," the drake suggested carefully.

She shook her head defiantly and extended her claws. "I'll settle for what my ancestors gave me."

Freynard gazed down at his empty hands. "I need one. I forgot to retrieve mine."

"Take your pick."

His eyes focused on what remained of the senior keeper. "Did he have a sword?"

Morgis squinted. "Possibly, though he did not make use of it. I do not think he had the physical strength or the coordination to lift it."

The captain pulled away from the drake and wandered over to D'Rak's corpse. Morgis took advantage of the time to speak with Troia. "I've been doing some thinking. I'm beginning to believe that the Gryphon decided it might be too dangerous for us wherever he was going. Notice he made certain he remained alone. A hunch, I admit, but I've learned from him, you could say."

"You really think he sent us on false trails?"

"Exactly. . . . And judging from what happened here, he may be in great trouble. I think there is a real gryphon tracking him and, the Dragon of the Depths knows, D'Shay might—scratch that—*will* be there."

"D'Shay?" Freynard had succeeded in returning without either of them hearing him. Held in place by his belt was a long, narrow blade. It was almost too long, more of a zweihander than a longsword.

Morgis looked at it and then at the captain. "Where did you get *that*? I am certain I would have remembered it."

Freynard shrugged. "I pulled back his cloak and it was there. I didn't question my luck. I like it better than the short sword I had."

"Do you even have the strength for that?"

"Like to test me?" A cunning smile briefly lit the man's face.

"Not from the way you are looking at me, no."

Thunder cracked. They had grown used to the wind, even the chill, but this was something new. It did not even sound like normal thunder, for it continued on and on for what seemed like an eternity, before finally fading away slowly.

"Gryphon!" Troia whispered.

The drake nodded sharply. "I think you may be right—and I think we may already be too late to help him!"

"No! I won't believe that!"

"It does not matter whether you or I or the captain here believes it, because we are going after him regardless. Any objections?"

There were none. There were only fears, but those they kept to themselves.

THE THUNDER, RATHER than being muted by the thick ceiling above him, seemed to reverberate through the passages. The Gryphon went down on one knee, his hands over his ears. Before him, the Ravager laughed mockingly, his laughter blending into the thunder so well that it was hard to say where one ended and the other began. Finally, though, only the laughter remained, eventually dying away.

The Ravager's eyes burned through him. *I shall call the elements and have you broken by each . . . Yet you will never be allowed to die. I shall worry your body and cast it upon my hoard, where I will let you spend eternity, never moving, among the bones of those who have fallen to me. You will beg for release, but I, not being merciful, will never grant it.*

His head pounded, and he felt dry, almost mummified. The Gryphon refused to yield, however. For all his bluster, all his savage threats, the Ravager had not yet touched him. Why? He was trapped with no way out. It was doubtful that the wolf god was merely toying with him.

Plead for mercy—I won't grant it, but it might be humorous to see. Go on. Maybe you will touch some tender part of my . . . soul. The mad god laughed again, but was it forced?

The Gryphon forced himself to his feet. He had dropped his sword, but it was foolish to think that it would have any effect on the Ravager. What choice did that leave him, then?

None, misfit.

He felt a sharp, stabbing pain in his chest, and his first thought was that at last the Ravager was striking. It was too small a pain, though, and, when it did not increase, he realized what was causing it.

Are your fears killing you, old one? Give in to them; you'll die that much easier!

Do you remember what it was like? an old memory asked curiously. *Are you still the same?*

The same what? the Ravager snarled, confusion evident. *What are you thinking?*

Memories. Bits of memories. He reached into his shirt and pulled out a single tiny whistle. Once, he had owned three. His only heritage. Each represented, to a guardian, portions of his heritage. The lionbird had never made use of this one, fearing what he would discover. One had summoned birds from all about, an incredible flock that had destroyed an assault by the clans of the Black Dragon. Another had called Troia, a cat by nature, as he, too, was. But what was his third and final piece of heritage?

Your only heritage is death, Gryphon! Bow to me! Bow to my will or I will tear you to blood-soaked bits of meat, which I shall dine on at my leisure!

Perhaps that was meant to frighten him further, but it had the opposite effect. The Ravager threatened too much, but he still held back—and the wolf god's fear, the fear that the Gryphon had felt that last time, was evident more than ever.

He put the whistle up to his beak. It did not matter that this was not as efficient for blowing the whistle as a human mouth. As before, it was only important that he actually force some air through.

Stop!

A brief note, a curious one. It was a questioning note, as if he were an enigma, a being without a distinct personality to call his own.

The darkness within the darkness, that which was the Ravager, seemed to pull away. The eyes still burned with anger, but uncertainty and fear continued to manifest themselves.

The Ravager snarled and then yelped like a hurt pup as the tunnel was bathed in brilliance. A portal—the Gate itself—materialized in one of the walls. As before, the Gate seemed much taller than the corridor allowed. It also had changed. Not just in its basic physical appearance. The rust was gone; the hinges held once more. The creatures that scurried along its sides moved with new life, with a vibrance they had lacked the last time.

As one, the two great doors swung open—and out stepped the first of at least half a dozen of the Faceless Ones, the not-people.

The Gryphon's people.

He received no blinding understanding of his past. Some memories fell in place, but it seemed others still desired to remain buried. Yet, there was no denying now that he had been one of them, had moved along through the centuries adjusting things here, instigating things there, assisting in other places—but never truly taking sides.

Until the Ravager dared the unspeakable.

He looked at the shadowy form. It cringed, but still put on a false face of power. *I do what I desire to do! The game is mine; it is too late to change that! I've won! Do you hear? I've won! The rules are mine to change as I see fit!*

"*You* made me!" The Gryphon stepped forward in wonder. As he moved closer, the darkness of the Ravager retreated deeper into the tunnel. The Faceless Ones stood by silently. Though they did nothing, their very presence aided. It gave the lionbird the understanding he needed, such as why they had turned from their own ways to help him more than they had ever helped another. Regardless of the change, he was still one of them.

But he was more, as well. The Ravager was apparently not the final arbiter. Whatever he had done to take one of the blank-visaged beings and turn it into a parody of the actual animal had disturbed some power. If there was one rule that could not be broken, it was *there were those who could not be touched.* They lacked a true name, but those who needed to know did. The wolf god knew the penalty but had ignored it in his obsession with "the game."

The Gryphon reached out a hand toward the shadows. He heard a gasp, and then the Ravager was again retreating.

"You have no power over me. Not after that first time. That's why you fear me more than the other guardians. You cannot touch me directly; you have to work through agents, which was why you originally seduced Shaidarol. You knew what I was even though the Master Guardians did not."

Lies! I permit you to live because I have won and can be magnanimous! Look! See! I give you your freedom!

The lionbird glanced back, not worried in the least that the Ravager might try to destroy him. He could not. The wolf god's powers were limited, probably had been limited since the day he had succeeded in trapping one of his own kind down here.

"You have a rival down here, don't you? One who watched over the Dream Lands. That's why they stood so long." He advanced again.

The darkness, the shadows, all that was the Ravager vanished in the midst of one long howl. Even the stench of rotting meat was gone, if it had ever been there. Illusion could be very real—and not all of the Ravager's power was illusion. He did have limited control over the dead, but that was not his chief weapon. First and foremost, he was the master of fear. That fear had created an empire in his name.

Turning, he faced his brethren. Despite their lack of features, he could feel the sadness. His existence was not the purpose they had either chosen or been created for. The Gryphon doubted he would ever learn completely what had happened.

I know a bit—if you will free me, old one.

As if that were a cue, the Faceless Ones began to return through the Gate. They did not look back, and he understood that they considered him lost forever. By listening, he had decided to continue to choose sides. They had broken their own rules to aid him, feeling he deserved that much, but the rest was up to him.

That is about right. Even I cannot say for certain what they believe.

"Who are you?" he called out, his eyes fixed on the vanishing Gate. "What are you? Another god?"

By your terms—almost. Let us say . . . one of a superior group, though he who calls himself the Ravager does not paint us as such.

"Where are you?"

You have not decided whether you are going to release me. What can I do to prove myself? I aided you in Canisargos. I would have done more, but I could not without arousing his suspicions. I am more susceptible to his powers than you little ones are. A fine jest that. It serves me right for underestimating him, but he had been so quiet since regaining his freedom. At the very least, you owe me for saving your life a few moments ago.

"When? The Ravager did nothing but try to scare me."

Not him, but one of his lapdogs, the one called D'Rak—or have you forgotten when he touched your hand? He truly meant for you to die if he did.

It was true; he had forgotten about that. Now, though, it did not seem to matter. The Gryphon, for lack of someone to look at, eyed the ceiling. "You seem to display more power than the Ravager, yet you still cannot escape?"

The bonds that hold me were designed for one of our kind. Once, they held that one called the Ravager. When we saw what he had become, we worried that the same would happen to us, so we turned the—let us call it the key—to the only ones all could trust.

"And—as one of them—I had the key."

You do.

"Then tell me what to do. I'll release you."

He could almost feel the hesitation. *There, we have a problem.*

The Gryphon knew what was coming. From what he remembered and what he could piece together, it made sense. Unfortunately. "You can't. You don't know."

All knowledge of the key was given to your kind. That way, those who would misuse it could not.

"What happened last time? What destroyed Qualard?" The lionbird knew, but he wanted confirmation.

You are wrong.

"Wrong?" It all added up, or so he had thought.

Misinformation and misdirection—the Ravager's forte. Qualard was the birthplace of the wolf raiders. Why do you suppose that was?

This was ridiculous. He was passing the time talking history with an unseen being, while the Aramites must be now seeking out the refugees of Sirvak Dragoth and his own companions might be dead.

We are wasting no time. In here, time goes very slowly. A part of the punishment—the worst part, you can believe me. Besides, it has been so long since I could speak to another.

Qualard the birthplace of the wolf raiders? It made some sense, but why was that . . . "This was the Ravager's prison."

It was. The Aramites were his way to pass the time, but, when we finally asked for his release, his obsession with them continued. I wanted to know why, because it began to disrupt the pattern of life in what you now call the Dream Lands—and then I discovered that his pets, his children, were doing what he could not physically do.

The keepers, the Ravager's sorcerers, had captured, on his command, one of the blank-faced observers. The wolf god wanted his own key—and not merely to the prison he had endured. The not-people were allowed to do many things he could not. As they were, he could not control them.

His faithful followers *could*—but something went amiss.

Yes, they chose, as the mortal link, possibly the worst beast to control. A gryphon. Even I cannot say why. I discovered all and so I came to your plane, to Qualard—and found he was waiting for me. He had the key to the prison, and he used it. I . . . struggled . . . and the city perished. But I had gained control over his key. Over you. You know most of the rest.

"The false memories?"

Partly the spell that he—or rather, his children—cast upon the Dream Lands, and partly one the Master Guardians cast for me, though it cost them protection from the Ravager's spell.

All this subterfuge; for what? "What does he truly fear about the Dream Lands? Is it simply because he cannot control it?"

To those who thrive on power, a thing they cannot control is a thing to fear . . . and thus they seek to destroy it to prove their mastery.

"I think I know how to release you—wherever you are. Some of the fog has lifted."

He felt the pleasure and relief that the other could not hide, despite its seemingly calm demeanor. *Then I have one request that you, as one of them as any could be, may grant or not.*

The Gryphon saw what he wanted and nodded. Taking a deep breath, he steadied himself. "Are you ready?"

I have been ready from the day I was bound. I am tired of sleeping.

The Gryphon summoned the Gate.

XXIII

HE MET THEM a hundred or so paces east of where they had agreed to rendezvous. His sword he clutched in his left hand. In his right, he held something so small that his closed fist hid it. That did not matter at the moment; all that mattered then were the words he spoke when they were near enough to hear him.

"It's over."

Freynard was the first to speak. "Over? You've done it, Gryphon?"

He nodded slowly. "The . . . prisoner has been freed, and D'Shay . . . he's dead."

"At last," Morgis hissed. "We can leave this inhospitable place and return to the peace of the Dragonrealm."

The Gryphon could not help cheering a little at the drake's words. Peaceful? He suspected—*hoped*, actually—that Morgis was jesting.

Troia, on the other hand, did not seem so happy. "Is that what you plan to do? Return there?"

He looked at her, trying to tell her some of the things he was too uncomfortable with to say out loud. "Not yet. Not until I'm sure that the wolf raiders are on the run, that their empire is going to collapse . . ." For the first time, his exhausted mind registered the fact that Haggerth was missing. The dark expression on Troia's face deepened. "What happened to him?"

"D'Rak killed him—but he was able to strike a blow of his own, which Duke Morgis completed." She looked up at him. "We gave him a burial of sorts, Gryphon, but I want to go back—"

"We will. Now that the wolf raiders have been removed from the Dream Lands, we can afford to do that."

They all looked at him. Freynard, most disbelieving of all, asked, "How could that be? They should have overrun Sirvak Dragoth by now! There was no way to stop them!"

He thought back to the underworld prison. Releasing the other had proved anticlimactic. After being freed, the joyous presence spoke into his mind once more. *I have already broken many rules, old one, chief of which was compounding the situation by trying to hide your continued existence. That failed. One or two more cannot harm me, and I think they would understand.*

"'They'?" the Gryphon had coaxed.

The other had not fallen to the bait. *The wolf raiders should have never been able to invade the Dream Lands. Those lands are the last legacy of one I owe a great deal to. A free, untouched land, nothing more, but special because of that. I will remove the blight of the Aramites from it . . . and then I will tell you one last thing of importance. It concerns the one once called Shaidarol. . . .*

That was a memory now. He sighed, a bit bitterly, and, looking at all three of them, replied, "Let us say that the prisoner was grateful."

Morgis and Troia looked confused. Freynard looked pale. They waited for more, but the lionbird was finished with the subject for the present. One thing did occur to him, and he felt the drake had, at least, a right to know.

"It's a pity you weren't there, Morgis. I'm sure there was so much you would have wanted to ask him."

"Why? What was he?" The drake shivered. They were all shivering now that they had been standing in one place. "Could we not return to the Dream Lands and discuss this?"

"As you wish." It was easy now, contacting that which was the Gate. The Gate—the Dream Lands themselves—were a presence of a sort akin to the prisoner and the Ravager, and, as such, he could feel the joy and gratitude—and still a bit of apprehension, which he quickly relieved.

This time, it shone more brilliantly than even the last time. The doors were wide open, and they could see Sirvak Dragoth, untouched and whole, standing in the distance. There was no sign that there had ever been a battle.

It was an imposing sight, a miracle. Behind him, he heard someone mutter something. "What was that, Allyn?"

"Nothing, Gryphon. Astonishment, though I should be used to that where you're concerned."

"How true," Morgis added.

The Gryphon stood to one side and indicated the duke. "You first, Morgis."

"If you think I'll protest, you are dead wrong." The drake stalked up to the portal and was about to step through when the lionbird caught his arm. "The prisoner, Morgis. Some mortal creatures once called him the Dragon of the Depths, he said."

"The Dragon—" The duke's mouth was wide open, an almost religious awe spreading itself across his face. To the drake race, the Dragon of the Depths was the closest thing they had to a god, a wondrous being whom some claimed had prodded the drakes on the road to power. From the being's tone, the Gryphon thought that such flagrant interference was doubtful, but he was not about to tell his companion that.

Morgis still stood frozen, trying to accept the idea. The Gryphon chuckled loudly, though, within, he felt nothing approaching happiness. "We'll talk about it where it's warmer, remember?"

He pushed the drake through the Gate.

Troia was next, though she wanted to wait. The Gryphon had to insist. He pulled her close and whispered, "Lord Petrac put me under a dream to keep me occupied, but I came to realize that he was merely pulling my own desires from my subconscious. If I get back, I want to tell you about them and see if you might share some of them."

Her eyes said she did—and then she caught the one menacing word. "What do you mean, 'if'?"

He pushed her through and, as he had silently requested of the Gate, the massive doors swung shut. The Gate itself remained fixed in place.

Freynard stepped back, startled. He looked around as if expecting foes to come leaping out of the ruins of the city. The wind whipped his hair about. He looked narrower in the face, more like a fox or some such animal. "Is there something wrong?"

The Gryphon shook his head. "No, I just wanted to speak to you alone. I still haven't forgiven myself for what you went through at D'Shay's hands."

"I survived."

"And I'm glad about that." The former monarch held out his right hand. "It was good to see you again."

Freynard took the proffered hand in his own, a smile growing.

He screamed and tried to pull away, but the Gryphon held his hand tightly. The captain went to his knees, his body shivering uncontrollably, as if he were experiencing a tremendous shock.

The Gryphon glared down at him like a bird of death. "And it was so terrible to lose you so quickly. I should have known better from last time. You always had one last trick."

He finally released the other's hand. The face that looked up to his, even through the beard, was not Allyn Freynard's. It had fast become another, familiar visage.

D'Shay.

"I held it back!" the master wolf raider gasped. "I held back the transformation, figuring that somehow . . . somehow I would be the last. My powers were still weak. You couldn't—couldn't have known!"

He held up his right hand for D'Shay to see. On it was a mark similar to that he had seen earlier on Freynard's cheek, but inverted. It had not been visible until the two of them had touched each other.

"A little gift from the senior keeper to both of us. It was supposed to burn your new body out, giving you no time to prepare yet another, and burn me out as well. The Dragon of the Depths informed me and altered it slightly—his last gift. He has gone away, Shaidarol, to atone for all the interference he himself has caused."

A gleam came into D'Shay's eyes. The Gryphon shook his head, more sad now than angry.

"You'll receive no help from your lord and master. He was going to abandon you anyway. Reach out. See if his power still supports you."

He watched as his adversary did, the arrogant face slowly draining of the last vestiges of color as D'Shay realized that he had now become very, very mortal. It was as if the Ravager no longer existed. There was nothing.

Reaching down, the Gryphon pulled him up by the front of his shirt. D'Shay's face was no more than a hair's width from the tip of the lionbird's sharp, predatory beak.

"You're looking a little gray. It's all over. You can claim you were seduced and then forced to be what you are, but I know better. You merely hid what you really were—in mind, anyway—from the other guardians. I remember that much. It was *you* who first contacted the Ravager."

He knew when D'Shay started reaching for his long sword and caught the wolf raider's wrist with his free hand. He almost did not see that this was a ploy until he realized that, even as desperate as he was, D'Shay would know how useless it was to try to draw such a lengthy weapon when so close to his opponent.

The dagger had been hidden behind D'Shay's back. He brought it around while the Gryphon's eyes were still on the sword. There was nothing the ex-mercenary could do but try to push away. Now, however, it was D'Shay who was holding tight.

"You will join me!" D'Shay spat. "You *have* to!"

The knife caught the Gryphon low, but he twisted enough so that it cut only flesh, not an organ. Instinctively, he struck out, and his claws tore through the master wolf raider's unprotected chest as if it were water. D'Shay released him and fell back, gasping as the blood of his new body spilled forth.

His eyes tried to focus on the Gryphon, but instead looked off into empty space. "No. I cannot—"

D'Shay might have escaped then, for all the attention his enemy was able to give him. The Gryphon pulled the knife free, cursing himself for being overdramatic and acquiring yet another healthy wound to tax his healing abilities on. Emotion still had the upper hand, no matter how hard he strove.

"Gryphon!" D'Shay forced out. Their eyes met ever so briefly, the hatred still in full flame, until D'Shay finally fell forward, striking the ground just inches from the staggering lionbird.

D'Shay shuddered, then lay limp.

With one hand on his wound, the lionbird pushed the body onto its back. Death would not make it look like Freynard once more; that he knew from the last two times. What was different now, however, was the fact that he knew, under no uncertain terms, that D'Shay was truly dead. The inverted mark on his palm was D'Rak's way of assuring that. In the end, the senior keeper had finally outwitted his rival—and the Gryphon was only too happy to give him the credit. He wanted nothing out of all this save a little peace.

How many times had D'Shay cheated death? he wondered suddenly. Even one had been too many. For this alone, it had been worth it. He only wished he had realized the truth sooner. Staring at the hated face, he could not help saying, "You've stolen your last life, you bastard."

Out of respect for the unfortunate Allyn Freynard, who deserved some memorial, he dragged the body to the Gate. The portal did not open, would not open until he desired it—and, at the moment, the lionbird just wanted to catch his breath. The wound pained him, but he knew that, once through the Gate, he would have no time for himself.

He could not return to the Dragonrealm until the wolf raiders were at least on the defensive. Even with the great loss, the Aramites would not bend easily. They had been born to war and conquest, and to ask them to simply lay down their arms and surrender was madness. He also hoped to still learn more about himself and this land in general. Somehow, he felt that there was a bond between this continent and the Dragonrealm. It went beyond what little the Dragon of the Depths had told him. He doubted if even that incredible being knew everything.

The Gryphon *would* go back, however. He had been here long enough to know that his home lay across the Eastern Seas—and if Troia chose to come with him, so much the better. The lionbird hoped Morgis would stay until they could all sail together, but that was up to the duke. It would be nice to have one familiar face, even if it had to be a scaly, pointy-toothed drake lord.

He looked up at the Gate. The dark creatures seemed to be watching him, but there was no malice in their alien eyes. On an unspoken request, the huge doors slowly began to open.

When they were open wide, he lifted his burden—ignoring the agonizing pain—and stepped through to the arms of anxious, curious friends. Instead of an end, he knew it was only a beginning.

The Gate closed behind him, and the ancient structure faded away, leaving the wind to run alone through the battered remains of Qualard.

XXIV

THE BONDS HELD tight this time. Not in the physical sense, but they served the same purpose in the long run. He could not communicate with the outside, could not touch those who would come to his aid.

The Ravager stirred, tried to shake the bonds loose so that his mind could reach beyond his prison—the prison *they* had forced him back into. With the Gryphon's aid, for he had the key, of course.

It's not fair! he had cried. *The game was won!*

They did not understand. They had never understood.

Despite his latest attempt, he was still fettered to this place. The bonds held, as they always had and always would, and he felt the fear grow uncontrollable, for, this time, they had said they did not know if they could ever ask for his release.

But I won!

The emptiness was his only companion. He could not even hear the wind above. The wind that blew constantly through Qualard, a place *no one* ever came to if they could help it.

Didn't I?

ABOUT THE AUTHOR

RICHARD A. KNAAK is a *New York Times* bestselling author of forty novels, more than a dozen short stories, and several manga. He has been a regular contributor to the Dragonlance series since his first short story in *The Magic of Krynn* and is best known for the worldwide bestseller *The Legend of Huma* and the epic *Minotaur Wars* trilogy. He has also contributed heavily to other series as well, including the Age of Conan for Ace/Penguin Books and, most of all, Warcraft and Diablo for Simon & Schuster, based on the wildly successful game franchises from Blizzard Entertainment. Readers of those series will know him for his popular *War of the Ancients* saga for Warcraft and, for Diablo, *The Sin War* trilogy. Richard has also written several novels of his own, from the contemporary fantasy *Frostwing* to his *Dragonrealm* series, consisting thus far of ten books and half a dozen shorter stories.

In addition to his novel work for Warcraft, he also penned the first manga trilogy based on the game and is in the process of writing the second, *Dragons of Outland*. Richard has also contributed to background stories for other games.

Currently he has several projects in the works. In addition to finishing *The Gargoyle King*—the final volume of *Ogre Titans*—Richard is at work on *Stormrage* for Warcraft and a new project of his own. Pocket Books recently released *Night of the Dragon*, a sequel to his first Warcraft story and the first Warcraft novel to be originally published in trade paperback. Richard also has several other manga stories on tap, including a serial featuring the tauren, Trag, in the Legends anthologies from Tokyopop. He will also be returning to the Blizzard worlds for future tales.

Richard currently divides his time between northwest Arkansas and Chicago. While he cannot promise to respond, he reads all his email and may be contacted at www.richardaknaak.com.